*The* FIRST *and* LAST *of*
CONRAD

D1264602

# *The*
# FIRST *and* LAST *of*
# CONRAD

---

Almayer's Folly
An Outcast of the Islands
The Arrow of Gold
*&*
The Rover
*by Joseph Conrad*

London
ERNEST BENN LIMITED
1929

PRINTED IN GREAT BRITAIN
BY RICHARD CLAY & SONS
BUNGAY, SUFFOLK

# CONTENTS

|  | PAGE |
|---|---|
| ALMAYER'S FOLLY (1895) | 7 |
| AN OUTCAST OF THE ISLANDS (1896) | 183 |
| THE ARROW OF GOLD (1919) | 485 |
| THE ROVER (1923) | 783 |

# ALMAYER'S FOLLY

# CHAPTER I

" KASPAR ! Makan ! "

The well-known shrill voice startled Almayer from his dream of splendid future into the unpleasant realities of the present hour. An unpleasant voice too. He had heard it for many years, and with every year he liked it less. No matter; there would be an end to all this soon.

He shuffled uneasily, but took no further notice of the call. Leaning with both his elbows on the balustrade of the verandah, he went on looking fixedly at the great river that flowed—indifferent and hurried—before his eyes. He liked to look at it about the time of sunset; perhaps because at that time the sinking sun would spread a glowing gold tinge on the waters of the Pantai, and Almayer's thoughts were often busy with gold; gold he had failed to secure; gold the others had secured—dishonestly, of course—or gold he meant to secure yet, through his own honest exertions, for himself and Nina. He absorbed himself in his dream of wealth and power away from this coast where he had dwelt for so many years, forgetting the bitterness of toil and strife in the vision of a great and splendid reward. They would live in Europe, he and his daughter. They would be rich and respected. Nobody would think of her mixed blood in the presence of her great beauty and of his immense wealth. Witnessing her triumphs he would grow young again, he would forget the twenty-five years of heart-breaking struggle on this coast where he felt like a prisoner. All this was nearly within his reach. Let only Dain return ! And return soon he must—in his own interest, for his own share. He was now more than a week late ! Perhaps he would return to-night.

Such were Almayer's thoughts as, standing on the verandah

of his new but already decaying house—that last failure of his life—he looked on the broad river. There was no tinge of gold on it this evening, for it had been swollen by the rains, and rolled an angry and muddy flood under his inattentive eyes, carrying small drift-wood and big dead logs, and whole uprooted trees with branches and foliage, amongst which the water swirled and roared angrily.

One of those drifting trees grounded on the shelving shore, just by the house, and Almayer, neglecting his dream, watched it with languid interest. The tree swung slowly round, amid the hiss and foam of the water, and soon getting free of the obstruction began to move down stream again, rolling slowly over, raising upwards a long, denuded branch, like a hand lifted in mute appeal to heaven against the river's brutal and unnecessary violence. Almayer's interest in the fate of that tree increased rapidly. He leaned over to see if it would clear the low point below. It did; then he drew back, thinking that now its course was free down to the sea, and he envied the lot of that inanimate thing now growing small and indistinct in the deepening darkness. As he lost sight of it altogether he began to wonder how far out to sea it would drift. Would the current carry it north or south? South, probably, till it drifted in sight of Celebes, as far as Macassar, perhaps!

Macassar! Almayer's quickened fancy distanced the tree on its imaginary voyage, but his memory lagging behind some twenty years or more in point of time saw a young and slim Almayer, clad all in white and modest-looking, landing from the Dutch mail-boat on the dusty jetty of Macassar, coming to woo fortune in the godowns of old Hudig. It was an important epoch in his life, the beginning of a new existence for him. His father, a subordinate official employed in the Botanical Gardens of Buitenzorg, was no doubt delighted to place his son in such a firm. The young man himself too was nothing loth to leave the poisonous shores of Java, and the meagre comforts of the parental bungalow, where the father grumbled all day at the stupidity of native gardeners, and the mother from the depths of her long easy-chair bewailed the lost glories of Amsterdam, where she had been brought up, and of her position as the daughter of a cigar dealer there.

Almayer had left his home with a light heart and a lighter pocket, speaking English well, and strong in arithmetic; ready to conquer the world, never doubting that he would.

After those twenty years, standing in the close and stifling heat of a Bornean evening, he recalled with pleasurable regret the image of Hudig's lofty and cool warehouses with their long and straight avenues of gin cases and bales of Manchester goods; the big door swinging noiselessly; the dim light of the place, so delightful after the glare of the streets; the little railed-off spaces amongst piles of merchandise where the Chinese clerks, neat, cool, and sad-eyed, wrote rapidly and in silence amidst the din of the working gangs rolling casks or shifting cases to a muttered song, ending with a desperate yell. At the upper end, facing the great door, there was a larger space railed off, well lighted; there the noise was subdued by distance, and above it rose the soft and continuous clink of silver guilders which other discreet Chinamen were counting and piling up under the supervision of Mr. Vinck, the cashier, the genius presiding in the place—the right hand of the Master.

In that clear space Almayer worked at his table not far from a little green painted door, by which always stood a Malay in a red sash and turban, and whose hand, holding a small string dangling from above, moved up and down with the regularity of a machine. The string worked a punkah on the other side of the green door, where the so-called private office was, and where old Hudig—the Master—sat enthroned, holding noisy receptions. Sometimes the little door would fly open disclosing to the outer world, through the bluish haze of tobacco smoke, a long table loaded with bottles of various shapes and tall water-pitchers, rattan easy-chairs occupied by noisy men in sprawling attitudes, while the Master would put his head through and, holding by the handle, would grunt confidentially to Vinck; perhaps send an order thundering down the warehouse, or spy a hesitating stranger and greet him with a friendly roar, "Welgome, Gapitan! ver' you gome vrom? Bali, eh?

Got bonies? I vant bonies! Vant all you got; ha! ha! ha! Gome in!" Then the stranger was dragged in, in a tempest of yells the door was shut, and the usual noises refilled the place; the song of the workmen, the rumble of barrels, the scratch of rapid pens; while above all rose the musical chink of broad silver pieces streaming ceaselessly through the yellow fingers of the attentive Chinamen.

At that time Macassar was teeming with life and commerce. It was the point in the islands where tended all those bold spirits who, fitting out schooners on the Australian coast, invaded the Malay Archipelago in search of money and adventure. Bold, reckless, keen in business, not disinclined for a brush with the pirates that were to be found on many a coast as yet, making money fast, they used to have a general "rendezvous" in the bay for purposes of trade and dissipation. The Dutch merchants called those men English pedlars; some of them were undoubtedly gentlemen for whom that kind of life had a charm; most were seamen; the acknowledged king of them all was Tom Lingard, he whom the Malays, honest or dishonest, quiet fishermen or desperate cut-throats, recognised as "the Rajah-Laut"—the King of the Sea.

Almayer had heard of him before he had been three days in Macassar, had heard the stories of his smart business transactions, his loves, and also of his desperate fights with the Sulu pirates, together with the romantic tale of some child—a girl—found in a piratical prau by the victorious Lingard, when, after a long contest, he boarded the craft, driving the crew overboard. This girl, it was generally known, Lingard had adopted, was having her educated in some convent in Java, and spoke of her as "my daughter." He had sworn a mighty oath to marry her to a white man before he went home and to leave her all his money. "And Captain Lingard has lots of money," would say Mr. Vinck solemnly, with his head on one side, "lots of money; more than Hudig!" And after a pause—just to let his hearers recover from their astonishment at such an incredible assertion—he would add in an explanatory whisper, "You know, he has discovered a river."

That was it! He had discovered a river! That was the fact placing old Lingard so much above the common crowd of sea-going adventurers who traded with Hudig in the daytime and drank champagne, gambled, sang noisy songs, and made love to half-cast girls under the broad verandah of the Sunda Hotel at night. Into that river, whose entrances himself only knew, Lingard used to take his assorted cargo of Manchester goods, brass gongs, rifles and gunpowder. His brig *Flash*, which he commanded himself, would on those occasions disappear quietly during the night from the road-stead while his companions were sleeping off the effects of the midnight carouse, Lingard seeing them drunk under the table before going on board, himself unaffected by any amount of liquor. Many tried to follow him and find that land of plenty for gutta-percha and rattans, pearl shells and birds' nests, wax and gum-dammar, but the little *Flash* could outsail every craft in those seas. A few of them came to grief on hidden sandbanks and coral reefs, losing their all and barely escaping with life from the cruel grip of this sunny and smiling sea; others got discouraged; and for many years the green and peaceful-looking islands guarding the entrances to the promised land kept their secret with all the merciless serenity of tropical nature. And so Lingard came and went on his secret or open expeditions, becoming a hero in Almayer's eyes by the boldness and enormous profits of his ventures, seeming to Almayer a very great man indeed as he saw him marching up the warehouse, grunting a " how are you ? " to Vinck, or greeting Hudig, the Master, with a boisterous " Hallo, old pirate ! Alive yet ? " as a pre-liminary to transacting business behind the little green door. Often of an evening, in the silence of the then deserted ware-house, Almayer putting away his papers before driving home with Mr. Vinck, in whose household he lived, would pause listening to the noise of a hot discussion in the private office, would hear the deep and monotonous growl of the Master, and the roared-out interruptions of Lingard—two mastiffs fighting over a marrowy bone. But to Almayer's ears it sounded like a quarrel of Titans—a battle of the gods.

After a year or so Lingard, having been brought often in contact with Almayer in the course of business, took a sudden and, to the onlookers, a rather inexplicable fancy to the young man. He sang his praises, late at night, over a convivial glass to his cronies in the Sunda Hotel, and one fine morning electrified Vinck by declaring that he must have "that young fellow for a supercargo. Kind of captain's clerk. Do all my quill-driving for me." Hudig consented. Almayer, with youth's natural craving for change, was nothing loth, and packing his few belongings, started in the *Flash* on one of those long cruises when the old seaman was wont to visit almost every island in the archipelago. Months slipped by, and Lingard's friendship seemed to increase. Often pacing the deck with Almayer, when the faint night breeze, heavy with aromatic exhalations of the islands, shoved the brig gently along under the peaceful and sparkling sky, did the old seaman open his heart to his entranced listener. He spoke of his past life, of escaped dangers, of big profits in his trade, of new combinations that were in the future to bring profits bigger still. Often he had mentioned his daughter, the girl found in the pirate prau, speaking of her with a strange assumption of fatherly tenderness. "She must be a big girl now," he used to say. "It's nigh unto four years since I have seen her! Damme, Almayer, if I don't think we will run into Sourabaya this trip." And after such a declaration he always dived into his cabin muttering to himself, "Something must be done—must be done." More than once he would astonish Almayer by walking up to him rapidly, clearing his throat with a powerful "Hem!" as if he was going to say something, and then turning abruptly away to lean over the bulwarks in silence, and watch, motionless, for hours, the gleam and sparkle of the phosphorescent sea along the ship's side. It was the night before arriving in Sourabaya when one of those attempts at confidential communication succeeded. After clearing his throat he spoke. He spoke to some purpose. He wanted Almayer to marry his adopted daughter. "And don't you kick because you're white!" he shouted, suddenly, not giving the surprised young man the time to say a word. "None of that with me! Nobody will see the colour of your wife's skin. The dollars are too thick for that, I tell you! And mind you, they will be thicker yet before I die. There will be millions, Kaspar! Millions I say! And all for her—and for you, if you do what you are told."

Startled by the unexpected proposal, Almayer hesitated, and remained silent for a minute. He was gifted with a strong and active imagination, and in that short space of time he saw, as in a flash of dazzling light, great piles of shining guilders, and realised all the possibilities of an opulent existence. The consideration, the indolent ease of life—for which he felt himself so well fitted—his ships, his warehouses, his merchandise (old Lingard would not live for ever), and, crowning all, in the far future gleamed like a fairy palace the big mansion in Amsterdam, that earthly paradise of his dreams, where, made king amongst men by old Lingard's money, he would pass the evening of his days in inexpressible splendour. As to the other side of the picture—the companionship for life of a Malay girl, that legacy of a boatful of pirates—there was only within him a confused consciousness of shame that he a white man—— Still, a convent education of four years!—and then she may mercifully die. He was always lucky, and money is powerful! Go through it. Why not? He had a vague idea of shutting her up somewhere, anywhere, out of his gorgeous future. Easy enough to dispose of a Malay woman, a slave, after all, to his Eastern mind, convent or no convent, ceremony or no ceremony.

He lifted his head and confronted the anxious yet irate seaman.

"I—of course—anything you wish, Captain Lingard."

"Call me father, my boy. She does," said the mollified old adventurer. "Damme, though, if I didn't think you were going to refuse. Mind you, Kaspar, I always get my way, so it would have been no use. But you are no fool."

He remembered well that time—the look, the accent, the words, the effect they produced on him, his very surroundings. He remembered the narrow slanting deck of the brig, the silent sleeping coast, the smooth black surface of the sea with a great bar of gold laid on it by the rising moon. He remembered it all, and he remembered his feelings of mad exultation at the thought of that fortune thrown into his hands. He was no fool then, and he was no fool now. Circumstances had been against him; the fortune was gone, but hope remained.

He shivered in the night air, and suddenly became aware of the intense darkness which, on the sun's departure, had closed in upon the river, blotting out the outlines of the opposite shore. Only the fire of dry branches lit outside the stockade of the Rajah's compound called fitfully into view the ragged trunks of the surrounding trees, putting a stain of glowing red half-way across the river where the drifting logs were hurrying towards the sea through the impenetrable gloom. He had a hazy recollection of having been called some time during the evening by his wife. To his dinner probably. But a man busy contemplating the wreckage of his past in the dawn of new hopes cannot be hungry whenever his rice is ready. Time he went home, though; it was getting late.

He stepped cautiously on the loose planks towards the ladder. A lizard, disturbed by the noise, emitted a plaintive note and scurried through the long grass growing on the bank. Almayer descended the ladder carefully, now thoroughly recalled to the realities of life by the care necessary to prevent a fall on the uneven ground where the stones, decaying planks, and half-sawn beams were piled up in inextricable confusion. As he turned towards the house where he lived—" my old house " he called it—his ear detected the splash of paddles away in the darkness of the river. He stood still in the path, attentive and surprised at anybody being on the river at this late hour during such a heavy freshet. Now he could hear the paddles distinctly, and even a rapidly exchanged word in low tones, the heavy breathing of men fighting with the current, and hugging the bank on which he stood. Quite close, too, but it was too dark to distinguish anything under the overhanging bushes.

"Arabs, no doubt," muttered Almayer to himself, peering into the solid blackness. "What are they up to now? Some of Abdulla's business; curse him!"

The boat was very close now.

"Oh, ya! Man!" hailed Almayer.

The sound of voices ceased, but the paddles worked as furiously as before. Then the bush in front of Almayer shook, and the sharp sound of the paddles falling into the canoe rang in the quiet night. They were holding on to the bush now; but Almayer could hardly make out an indistinct dark shape of a man's head and shoulders above the bank.

"You, Abdulla?" said Almayer doubtfully.

A grave voice answered—

"Tuan Almayer is speaking to a friend. There is no Arab here."

Almayer's heart gave a great leap.

"Dain!" he exclaimed. "At last! at last! I have been waiting for you every day and every night. I had nearly given you up."

"Nothing could have stopped me from coming back here," said the other, almost violently. "Not even death," he whispered to himself.

"This is a friend's talk, and is very good," said Almayer, heartily. "But you are too far here. Drop down to the jetty and let your men cook their rice in my campong while we talk in the house."

There was no answer to that invitation.

"What is it?" asked Almayer, uneasily. "There is nothing wrong with the brig, I hope?"

"The brig is where no Orang Blanda can lay his hands on her," said Dain, with a gloomy tone in his voice, which Almayer, in his elation, failed to notice.

"Right," he said. "But where are all your men? There are only two with you."

"Listen, Tuan Almayer," said Dain. "To-morrow's sun shall see me in your house, and then we will talk. Now I must go to the Rajah."

"To the Rajah! Why? What do you want with Lakamba?"

"Tuan, to-morrow we talk like friends. I must see Lakamba to-night."

"Dain, you are not going to abandon me now, when all is ready?" asked Almayer, in a pleading voice.

"Have I not returned? But I must see Lakamba first for your good and mine."

The shadowy head disappeared abruptly. The bush, released from the grasp of the bowman, sprung back with a swish, scattering a shower of muddy water over Almayer, as he bent forward, trying to see.

In a little while the canoe shot into the streak of light that streamed on the river from the big fire on the opposite shore, disclosing the outline of two men bending to their work, and a third figure in the stern flourishing the steering paddle, his head covered with an enormous round hat, like a fantastically exaggerated mushroom.

Almayer watched the canoe till it passed out of the line of light. Shortly after the murmur of many voices reached him across the water. He could see the torches being snatched out of the burning pile, and rendering visible for a moment the gate in the stockade round which they crowded. Then they went in apparently. The torches disappeared, and the scattered fire sent out only a dim and fitful glare.

Almayer stepped homewards with long strides and mind uneasy. Surely Dain was not thinking of playing him false. It was absurd. Dain and Lakamba were both too much interested in the success of his scheme. Trusting to Malays was poor work; but then even Malays have some sense and understand their own interest. All would be well—must be well. At this point in his meditation he found himself at the foot of the steps leading to the verandah of his home. From the low point of land where he stood he could see both branches of the river. The main branch of the Pantai was lost in complete darkness, for the fire at the Rajah's had gone out altogether; but up the Sambir reach his eye could follow the long line of Malay houses crowding the bank, with here and there a dim light twinkling through bamboo walls, or a smoky torch burning on the platforms built out over the river. Further away, where the island ended in a low cliff, rose a dark mass of buildings towering above the Malay structures. Founded solidly on a firm ground with plenty of space, starred by many lights burning strong and white, with a suggestion of paraffin and lamp-glasses, stood the house and the godowns of Abdulla bin Selim, the great trader of Sambir. To Almayer the sight was very distasteful, and he shook his fist towards the buildings that in their evident prosperity looked to him cold and insolent, and contemptuous of his own fallen fortunes.

He mounted the steps of his house slowly.

In the middle of the verandah there was a round table. On it a paraffin lamp without a globe shed a hard glare on the three inner sides. The fourth side was open, and faced the river. Between the rough supports of the high-pitched roof hung torn rattan screens. There was no ceiling, and the harsh brilliance of the lamp was toned above into a soft half-light that lost itself in the obscurity amongst the rafters. The front wall was cut in two by the doorway of a central passage closed by a red curtain. The women's room opened into that passage, which led to the back courtyard and to the cooking shed. In one of the side walls there was a doorway. Half obliterated words —" Office : Lingard and Co." —were still legible on the dusty door, which looked as if it had not been opened for a very long time. Close to the other side wall stood a bent-wood rocking-chair, and by the table and about the verandah four wooden armchairs straggled forlornly, as if ashamed of their shabby surroundings. A heap of common mats lay in one corner, with an old hammock slung diagonally above. In the other corner, his head wrapped in a piece of red calico, huddled into a shapeless heap, slept a Malay, one of Almayer's domestic slaves—" my own people," he used to call them. A numerous and representative assembly of moths were holding high revels round the lamp to the spirited music of swarming mosquitoes. Under the palm-leaf thatch lizards raced on the beams calling softly. A monkey, chained to one of the verandah supports—retired for the night under the eaves—peered and grinned at Almayer, as it swung to one of the bamboo roof sticks and caused a shower of dust and bits of dried leaves to

settle on the shabby table. The floor was uneven, with
many withered plants and dried earth scattered about. A
general air of squalid neglect pervaded the place. Great
red stains on the floor and walls testified to frequent and
indiscriminate betel-nut chewing. The light breeze from
the river swayed gently the tattered blinds, sending from
the woods opposite a faint and sickly perfume as of decaying
flowers.

Under Almayer's heavy tread the boards of the verandah
creaked loudly. The sleeper in the corner moved uneasily,
muttering indistinct words. There was a slight rustle
behind the curtained doorway, and a soft voice asked in
Malay, " Is it you, father ? "

" Yes, Nina. I am hungry. Is everybody asleep in this
house ? "

Almayer spoke jovially and dropped with a contented sigh
into the armchair nearest to the table. Nina Almayer came
through the curtained doorway followed by an old Malay
woman, who busied herself in setting upon the table a plateful
of rice and fish, a jar of water, and a bottle half full of
genever. After carefully placing before her master a cracked
glass tumbler and a tin spoon she went away noiselessly.
Nina stood by the table, one hand lightly resting on its
edge, the other hanging listlessly by her side. Her face
turned towards the outer darkness, through which her
dreamy eyes seemed to see some entrancing picture, wore a
look of impatient expectancy. She was tall for a half-caste,
with the correct profile of the father, modified and strengthened by the squareness of the lower part of the face
inherited from her maternal ancestors—the Sulu pirates.
Her firm mouth, with the lips slightly parted and disclosing
a gleam of white teeth, put a vague suggestion of ferocity
into the impatient expression of her features. And yet her
dark and perfect eyes had all the tender softness of expression
common to Malay women, but with a gleam of superior
intelligence ; they looked gravely, wide open and steady, as
if facing something invisible to all other eyes, while she
stood there all in white, straight, flexible, graceful, unconscious of herself, her low but broad forehead crowned with a

shining mass of long black hair that fell in heavy tresses over her shoulders, and made her pale olive complexion look paler still by the contrast of its coal-black hue.

Almayer attacked his rice greedily, but after a few mouthfuls he paused, spoon in hand, and looked at his daughter curiously.

" Did you hear a boat pass about half an hour ago, Nina ? " he asked.

The girl gave him a quick glance, and moving away from the light stood with her back to the table.

" No," she said, slowly.

" There was a boat. At last ! Dain himself ; and he went on to Lakamba. I know it, for he told me so. I spoke to him, but he would not come here to-night. Will come to-morrow, he said."

He swallowed another spoonful, then said—

" I am almost happy to-night, Nina. I can see the end of a long road, and it leads us away from this miserable swamp. We shall soon get away from here, I and you, my dear little girl, and then——"

He rose from the table and stood looking fixedly before him as if contemplating some enchanting vision.

" And then," he went on, " we shall be happy, you and I. Live rich and respected far from here, and forget this life, and all this struggle, and all this misery ! "

He approached his daughter and passed his hand caressingly over her hair.

" It is bad to have to trust a Malay," he said, " but I must own that this Dain is a perfect gentleman—a perfect gentleman," he repeated.

" Did you ask him to come here, father ? " inquired Nina, not looking at him.

" Well, of course. We shall start on the day after to-morrow," said Almayer, joyously. " We must not lose any time. Are you glad, little girl ? "

She was nearly as tall as himself, but he liked to recall the time when she was little and they were all in all to each other.

" I am glad," she said, very low.

"Of course," said Almayer, vivaciously, "you cannot imagine what is before you. I myself have not been to Europe, but I have heard my mother talk so often that I seem to know all about it. We shall live a—a glorious life. You shall see."

Again he stood silent by his daughter's side looking at that enchanting vision. After a while he shook his clenched hand towards the sleeping settlement.

"Ah! my friend Abdulla," he cried, "we shall see who will have the best of it after all these years!"

He looked up the river and remarked calmly:

"Another thunderstorm. Well! No thunder will keep me awake to-night, I know! Good-night, little girl," he whispered, tenderly kissing her cheek. "You do not seem to be very happy to-night, but to-morrow you will show a brighter face. Eh?"

Nina had listened to her father with her face unmoved, with her half-closed eyes still gazing into the night now made more intense by a heavy thunder-cloud that had crept down from the hills blotting out the stars, merging sky, forest, and river into one mass of almost palpable blackness. The faint breeze had died out, but the distant rumble of thunder and pale flashes of lightning gave warning of the approaching storm. With a sigh the girl turned towards the table.

Almayer was in his hammock now, already half asleep.

"Take the lamp, Nina," he muttered, drowsily. "This place is full of mosquitoes. Go to sleep, daughter."

But Nina put the lamp out and turned back again towards the balustrade of the verandah, standing with her arm round the wooden support and looking eagerly towards the Pantai reach. And motionless there in the oppressive calm of the tropical night she could see at each flash of lightning the forest lining both banks up the river, bending before the furious blast of the coming tempest, the upper reach of the river whipped into white foam by the wind, and the black clouds torn into fantastic shapes trailing low over the swaying trees. Round her all was as yet stillness and peace, but she could hear afar off the roar of the wind, the hiss of heavy rain, the wash of the waves on the tormented river. It came nearer and nearer, with loud thunder-claps and long flashes of vivid lightning, followed by short periods of appalling blackness. When the storm reached the low point dividing the river, the house shook in the wind, and the rain pattered loudly on the palm-leaf roof, the thunder spoke in one prolonged roll, and the incessant lightning disclosed a turmoil of leaping waters, driving logs, and the big trees bending before a brutal and merciless force.

Undisturbed by the nightly event of the rainy monsoon, the father slept quietly, oblivious alike of his hopes, his misfortunes, his friends, and his enemies; and the daughter stood motionless, at each flash of lightning eagerly scanning the broad river with a steady and anxious gaze.

## CHAPTER II

WHEN, in compliance with Lingard's abrupt demand, Almayer consented to wed the Malay girl, no one knew that on the day when the interesting young convert had lost all her natural relations and found a white father, she had been fighting desperately like the rest of them on board the prau, and was only prevented from leaping overboard, like the few other survivors, by a severe wound in the leg. There, on the fore-deck of the prau, old Lingard found her under a heap of dead and dying pirates, and had her carried on the poop of the *Flash* before the Malay craft was set on fire and sent adrift. She was conscious, and in the great peace and stillness of the tropical evening succeeding the turmoil of the battle, she watched all she held dear on earth after her own savage manner drift away into the gloom in a great roar of flame and smoke. She lay there unheeding the careful hands attending to her wound, silent and absorbed in gazing at the funeral pile of those brave men she had so much admired and so well helped in their contest with the redoubtable " Rajah-Laut."

The light night breeze fanned the brig gently to the south-ward, and the great blaze of light got smaller and smaller till it twinkled only on the horizon like a setting star. It set : the heavy canopy of smoke reflected the glare of hidden flames for a short time and then disappeared also.

She realised that with this vanishing gleam her old life departed too. Thenceforth there was slavery in the far countries, amongst strangers, in unknown and perhaps terrible surroundings. Being fourteen years old, she realised her position and came to that conclusion, the only one possible to a Malay girl, soon ripened under a tropical sun, and not unaware of her personal charms, of which she heard many a young brave warrior of her father's crew express an appreciative admiration. There was in her the dread of the unknown ; otherwise she accepted her position calmly, after the manner of her people, and even considered it quite natural ; for was she not a daughter of warriors, conquered in battle, and did she not belong rightfully to the victorious Rajah ? Even the evident kindness of the terrible old man must spring, she thought, from admiration for his captive, and the flattered vanity eased for her the pangs of sorrow after such an awful calamity. Perhaps had she known of the high walls, the quiet gardens, and the silent nuns of the Samarang convent, where her destiny was leading her, she would have sought death in her dread and hate of such a restraint. But in imagination she pictured to herself the usual life of a Malay girl—the usual succession of heavy work and fierce love, of intrigues, gold ornaments, of domestic drudgery, and of that great but occult influence which is one of the few rights of half-savage womankind. But her destiny in the rough hands of the old sea-dog, acting under unreasoning impulses of the heart, took a strange and to her a terrible shape. She bore it all—the restraint and the teaching and the new faith—with calm submission, concealing her hate and contempt for all that new life. She learned the language very easily, yet understood but little of the new faith the good sisters taught her, assimilating quickly only the superstitious elements of the religion. She called Lingard father, gently and caressingly, at each of his short and noisy visits, under the clear impression that he was a great and dangerous power it was good to propitiate. Was he not now her master? And during those long four years she nourished a hope of finding favour in his eyes and ultimately becoming his wife, counsellor, and guide.

Those dreams of the future were dispelled by the Rajah Laut's "fiat," which made Almayer's fortune, as that young man fondly hoped. And dressed in the hateful finery of Europe, the centre of an interested circle of Batavian society, the young convert stood before the altar with an unknown and sulky-looking white man. For Almayer was uneasy, a little disgusted, and greatly inclined to run away. A judicious fear of the adopted father-in-law and a just regard for his own material welfare prevented him from making a scandal; yet, while swearing fidelity, he was concocting plans for getting rid of the pretty Malay girl in a more or less distant future. She, however, had retained enough of conventual teaching to understand well that according to white men's laws she was going to be Almayer's companion and not his slave, and promised to herself to act accordingly.

So when the *Flash* freighted with materials for building a new house left the harbour of Batavia, taking away the young couple into the unknown Borneo, she did not carry on her deck so much love and happiness as old Lingard was wont to boast of before his casual friends in the verandahs of various hotels. The old seaman himself was perfectly happy. Now he had done his duty by the girl. "You know I made her an orphan," he often concluded solemnly, when talking about his own affairs to a scratch audience of shore loafers—as it was his habit to do. And the approbative shouts of his half-intoxicated auditors filled his simple soul with delight and pride. "I carry everything right through," was another of his sayings, and in pursuance of that principle he pushed the building of house and godowns on the Pantai River with feverish haste. The house for the young couple; the godowns for the big trade Almayer was going to develop while he (Lingard) would be able to give himself up to some mysterious work which was only spoken of in hints, but was understood to relate to gold and diamonds in the interior of

the island.  Almayer was impatient too.  Had he known
what was before him he might not have been so eager and
full of hope as he stood watching the last canoe of the Lingard
expedition disappear in the bend up the river.  When,
turning round, he beheld the pretty little house, the big
godowns built neatly by an army of Chinese carpenters, the
new jetty round which were clustered the trading canoes,
he felt a sudden elation in the thought that the world was his.

But the world had to be conquered first, and its conquest
was not so easy as he thought.  He was very soon made to
understand that he was not wanted in that corner of it where
old Lingard and his own weak will placed him, in the midst
of unscrupulous intrigues and of a fierce trade competition.
The Arabs had found out the river, had established a trading
post in Sambir, and where they traded they would be
masters and suffer no rival.  Lingard returned unsuccessful
from his first expedition, and departed again, spending all the
profits of the legitimate trade on his mysterious journeys.
Almayer struggled with the difficulties of his position,
friendless and unaided, save for the protection given to him
for Lingard's sake by the old Rajah, the predecessor of
Lakamba.  Lakamba himself, then living as a private individual on a rice clearing, seven miles down the river, exercised
all his influence towards the help of the white man's enemies,
plotting against the old Rajah and Almayer with a certainty
of combination, pointing clearly to a profound knowledge of
their most secret affairs.  Outwardly friendly, his portly form
was often to be seen on Almayer's verandah; his green
turban and gold-embroidered jacket shone in the front rank
of the decorous throng of Malays coming to greet Lingard
on his returns from the interior; his salaams were of the
lowest, and his hand-shakings of the heartiest, when welcoming the old trader.  But his small eyes took in the signs
of the times, and he departed from those interviews with a
satisfied and furtive smile to hold long consultations with his
friend and ally, Syed Abdulla, the chief of the Arab trading
post, a man of great wealth and of great influence in the
islands.

It was currently believed at that time in the settlement that

Lakamba's visits to Almayer's house were not limited to those official interviews. Often on moonlight nights the belated fishermen of Sambir saw a small canoe shooting out from the narrow creek at the back of the white man's house, and the solitary occupant paddle cautiously down the river in the deep shadows of the bank; and those events, duly reported, were discussed round the evening fires far into the night with the cynicism of expression common to aristocratic Malays, and with a malicious pleasure in the domestic misfortunes of the Orang Blando—the hated Dutchman. Almayer went on struggling desperately, but with a feebleness of purpose depriving him of all chance of success against men so unscrupulous and resolute as his rivals the Arabs. The trade fell away from the large godowns, and the godowns themselves rotted piecemeal. The old man's banker, Hudig of Macassar, failed, and with this went the whole available capital. The profits of past years had been swallowed up in Lingard's exploring craze. Lingard was in the interior— perhaps dead—at all events giving no sign of life. Almayer stood alone in the midst of those adverse circumstances, deriving only a little comfort from the companionship of his little daughter, born two years after the marriage, and at the time some six years old. His wife had soon commenced to treat him with a savage contempt expressed by sulky silence, only occasionally varied by a flood of savage invective. He felt she hated him, and saw her jealous eyes watching himself and the child with almost an expression of hate. She was jealous of the little girl's evident preference for the father, and Almayer felt he was not safe with that woman in the house. While she was burning the furniture, and tearing down the pretty curtains in her unreasoning hate of those signs of civilisation, Almayer, cowed by these outbursts of savage nature, meditated in silence on the best way of getting rid of her. He thought of everything; even planned murder in an undecided and feeble sort of way, but dared do nothing—expecting every day the return of Lingard with news of some immense good fortune. He returned indeed, but aged, ill, a ghost of his former self, with the fire of fever burning in his sunken eyes, almost the only survivor of the

numerous expedition. But he was successful at last ! Untold riches were in his grasp ; he wanted more money—only
a little more to realise a dream of fabulous fortune. And
Hudig had failed ! Almayer scraped all he could together,
but the old man wanted more. If Almayer could not get it
he would go to Singapore—to Europe even, but before all
to Singapore ; and he would take the little Nina with him.
The child must be brought up decently. He had good
friends in Singapore who would take care of her and have
her taught properly. All would be well, and that girl, upon
whom the old seaman seemed to have transferred all his
former affection for the mother, would be the richest woman
in the East—in the world even. So old Lingard shouted,
pacing the verandah with his heavy quarter-deck step, gesticulating with a smouldering cheroot ; ragged, dishevelled,
enthusiastic ; and Almayer, sitting huddled up on a pile of
mats, thought with dread of the separation with the only
human being he loved—with greater dread still, perhaps, of
the scene with his wife, the savage tigress deprived of her
young. She will poison me, thought the poor wretch, well
aware of that easy and final manner of solving the social,
political, or family problems in Malay life.

To his great surprise she took the news very quietly,
giving only him and Lingard a furtive glance, and saying
not a word. This, however, did not prevent her the next
day from jumping into the river and swimming after the boat
in which Lingard was carrying away the nurse with the
screaming child. Almayer had to give chase with his whale-
boat and drag her in by the hair in the midst of cries and
curses enough to make heaven fall. Yet after two days
spent in wailing, she returned to her former mode of life,
chewing betel-nut, and sitting all day amongst her women
in stupefied idleness. She aged very rapidly after that, and
only roused herself from her apathy to acknowledge by a
scathing remark or an insulting exclamation the accidental
presence of her husband. He had built for her a riverside
hut in the compound where she dwelt in perfect seclusion.
Lakamba's visits had ceased when, by a convenient decree of
Providence and the help of a little scientific manipulation,

the old ruler of Sambir departed this life. Lakamba reigned in his stead now, having been well served by his Arab friends with the Dutch authorities. Syed Abdulla was the great man and trader of the Pantai. Almayer lay ruined and helpless under the close-meshed net of their intrigues, owing his life only to his supposed knowledge of Lingard's valuable secret. Lingard had disappeared. He wrote once from Singapore saying the child was well, and under the care of a Mrs. Vinck, and that he himself was going to Europe to raise money for the great enterprise. "He was coming back soon. There would be no difficulties," he wrote; "people would rush in with their money." Evidently they did not, for there was only one letter more from him saying he was ill, had found no relation living, but little else besides. Then came a complete silence. Europe had swallowed up the Rajah Laut apparently, and Almayer looked vainly westward for a ray of light out of the gloom of his shattered hopes. Years passed, and the rare letters from Mrs. Vinck, later on from the girl herself, were the only things to be looked to to make life bearable amongst the triumphant savagery of the river. Almayer lived now alone, having even ceased to visit his debtors who would not pay, sure of Lakamba's protection. The faithful Sumatrese Ali cooked his rice and made his coffee, for he dared not trust anyone else, and least of all his wife. He killed time wandering sadly in the overgrown paths round the house, visiting the ruined godowns where a few brass guns covered with verdigris and only a few broken cases of mouldering Manchester goods reminded him of the good early times when all this was full of life and merchandise, and he overlooked a busy scene on the river bank, his little daughter by his side. Now the up-country canoes glided past the little rotten wharf of Lingard and Co., to paddle up the Pantai branch, and cluster round the new jetty belonging to Abdulla. Not that they loved Abdulla, but they dared not trade with the man whose star had set. Had they done so they knew there was no mercy to be expected from Arab or Rajah; no rice to be got on credit in the times of scarcity from either; and Almayer could not help them, having at times hardly enough for himself.

Almayer, in his isolation and despair, often envied his near neighbour the Chinaman, Jim-Eng, whom he could see stretched on a pile of cool mats, a wooden pillow under his head, an opium pipe in his nerveless fingers. He did not seek, however, consolation in opium—perhaps it was too expensive—perhaps his white man's pride saved him from that degradation; but most likely it was the thought of his little daughter in the far-off Straits Settlements. He heard from her oftener since Abdulla bought a steamer, which ran now between Singapore and the Pantai settlement every three months or so. Almayer felt himself nearer his daughter. He longed to see her, and planned a voyage to Singapore, but put off his departure from year to year, always expecting some favourable turn of fortune. He did not want to meet her with empty hands and with no words of hope on his lips. He could not take her back into that savage life to which he was condemned himself. He was also a little afraid of her. What would she think of him? He reckoned the years. A grown woman. A civilised woman, young and hopeful; while he felt old and hopeless, and very much like those savages round him. He asked himself what was going to be her future. He could not answer that question yet, and he dared not face her. And yet he longed after her. He hesitated for years.

His hesitation was put an end to by Nina's unexpected appearance in Sambir. She arrived in the steamer under the captain's care. Almayer beheld her with surprise not unmixed with wonder. During those ten years the child had changed into a woman, black-haired, olive-skinned, tall, and beautiful, with great sad eyes, where the startled expression common to Malay womankind was modified by a thoughtful tinge inherited from her European ancestry. Almayer thought with dismay of the meeting of his wife and daughter, of what this grave girl in European clothes would think of her betel-nut chewing mother, squatting in a dark hut, disorderly, half naked, and sulky. He also feared an outbreak of temper on the part of that pest of a woman he had hitherto managed to keep tolerably quiet, thereby saving the remnants of his dilapidated furniture. And he stood there before the closed

door of the hut in the blazing sunshine listening to the
murmur of voices, wondering what went on inside, wherefrom all the servant-maids had been expelled at the beginning
of the interview, and now stood clustered by the palings with
half-covered faces in a chatter of curious speculation.  He
forgot himself there trying to catch a stray word through
the bamboo walls, till the captain of the steamer, who had
walked up with the girl, fearing a sunstroke, took him under
the arm and led him into the shade of his own verandah
where Nina's trunk stood already, having been landed by
the steamer's men.  As soon as Captain Ford had his glass
before him and his cheroot lighted, Almayer asked for the
explanation of his daughter's unexpected arrival.  Ford said
little beyond generalising in vague but violent terms upon
the foolishness of women in general, and of Mrs. Vinck in
particular.

"You know, Kaspar," said he, in conclusion, to the
excited Almayer, "it is deucedly awkward to have a half-
caste girl in the house.  There's such a lot of fools about.
There was that young fellow from the bank who used to ride
to the Vinck bungalow early and late.  That old woman
thought it was for that Emma of hers.  When she found out
what he wanted exactly, there was a row, I can tell you.
She would not have Nina—not an hour longer—in the
house.  Fact is, I heard of this affair and took the girl to my
wife.  My wife is a pretty good woman—as women go—and
upon my word we would have kept the girl for you, only she
would not stay.  Now, then!  Don't flare up, Kaspar.  Sit
still.  What can you do?  It is better so.  Let her stay with
you.  She was never happy over there.  Those two Vinck
girls are no better than dressed-up monkeys.  They slighted
her.  You can't make her white.  It's no use you swearing
at me.  You can't.  She is a good girl for all that, but she
would not tell my wife anything.  If you want to know, ask
her yourself; but if I was you I would leave her alone.
You are welcome to her passage money, old fellow, if you
are short now."  And the skipper, throwing away his cigar,
walked off to "wake them up on board," as he expressed it.

Almayer vainly expected to hear of the cause of his

daughter's return from his daughter's lips. Not that day,
not on any other day did she ever allude to her Singapore
life. He did not care to ask, awed by the calm impassiveness
of her face, by those solemn eyes looking past him on the
great, still forests sleeping in majestic repose to the murmur
of the broad river. He accepted the situation, happy in
the gentle and protecting affection the girl showed him,
fitfully enough, for she had, as she called it, her bad days
when she used to visit her mother and remain long hours
in the riverside hut, coming out as inscrutable as ever, but
with a contemptuous look and a short word ready to answer
any of his speeches. He got used even to that, and on those
days kept quiet, although greatly alarmed by his wife's
influence upon the girl. Otherwise Nina adapted herself
wonderfully to the circumstances of a half-savage and miserable life. She accepted without question or apparent disgust
the neglect, the decay, the poverty of the household, the
absence of furniture, and the preponderance of rice diet on
the family table. She lived with Almayer in the little
house (now sadly decaying) built originally by Lingard for
the young couple. The Malays eagerly discussed her arrival.
There were at the beginning crowded levées of Malay women
with their children, seeking eagerly after "Ubat" for all
the ills of the flesh from the young Mem Putih. In the cool
of the evening grave Arabs in long white shirts and yellow
sleeveless jackets walked slowly on the dusty path by the
riverside towards Almayer's gate, and made solemn calls
upon that Unbeliever under shallow pretences of business,
only to get a glimpse of the young girl in a highly decorous
manner. Even Lakamba came out of his stockade in a great
pomp of war canoes and red umbrellas, and landed on the
rotten little jetty of Lingard and Co. He came, he said, to
buy a couple of brass guns as a present to his friend the chief
of Sambir Dyaks; and while Almayer, suspicious but polite,
busied himself in unearthing the old popguns in the godowns,
the Rajah sat on an armchair in the verandah, surrounded by
his respectful retinue waiting in vain for Nina's appearance.
She was in one of her bad days, and remained in her mother's
hut watching with her the ceremonious proceedings on the

verandah. The Rajah departed, baffled but courteous, and soon Almayer began to reap the benefit of improved relations with the ruler in the shape of the recovery of some debts, paid to him with many apologies and many a low salaam by debtors till then considered hopelessly insolvent. Under these improving circumstances Almayer brightened up a little. All was not lost perhaps. Those Arabs and Malays saw at last that he was a man of some ability, he thought. And he began, after his manner, to plan great things, to dream of great fortunes for himself and Nina. Especially for Nina! Under these vivifying impulses he asked Captain Ford to write to his friends in England making inquiries after Lingard. Was he alive or dead? If dead, had he left any papers, documents; any indications or hints as to his great enterprise? Meantime he had found amongst the rubbish in one of the empty rooms a notebook belonging to the old adventurer. He studied the crabbed handwriting of its pages and often grew meditative over it. Other things also woke him up from his apathy. The stir made in the whole of the island by the establishment of the British Borneo Company affected even the sluggish flow of the Pantai life. Great changes were expected; annexation was talked of; the Arabs grew civil. Almayer began building his new house for the use of the future engineers, agents, or settlers of the new Company. He spent every available guilder on it with a confiding heart. One thing only disturbed his happiness : his wife came out of her seclusion, importing her green jacket, scant sarongs, shrill voice, and witch-like appearance, into his quiet life in the small bungalow. And his daughter seemed to accept that savage intrusion into their daily existence with wonderful equanimity. He did not like it, but dared say nothing.

## CHAPTER III

THE deliberations conducted in London have a far-reaching importance, and so the decision issued from the fog-veiled offices of the Borneo Company darkened for Almayer the

B

brilliant sunshine of the Tropics, and added another drop
of bitterness to the cup of his disenchantments.   The claim
to that part of the East Coast was abandoned, leaving the
Pantai river under the nominal power of Holland.   In
Sambir there was joy and excitement.   The slaves were
hurried out of sight into the forest and jungle, and the flags
were run up to tall poles in the Rajah's compound in
expectation of a visit from Dutch man-of-war boats.

The frigate remained anchored outside the mouth of the
river, and the boats came up in tow of the steam launch,
threading their way cautiously amongst a crowd of canoes
filled with gaily dressed Malays.   The officer in command
listened gravely to the loyal speeches of Lakamba, returned
the salaams of Abdulla, and assured those gentlemen in
choice Malay of the great Rajah's—down in Batavia—friendship and goodwill towards the ruler and inhabitants of this
model state of Sambir.

Almayer from his verandah watched across the river the
festive proceedings, heard the report of brass guns saluting
the new flag presented to Lakamba, and the deep murmur of
the crowd of spectators surging round the stockade.   The
smoke of the firing rose in white clouds on the green background of the forests, and he could not help comparing his
own fleeting hopes to the rapidly disappearing vapour.   He
was by no means patriotically elated by the event, yet he
had to force himself into a gracious behaviour when, the
official reception being over, the naval officers of the Commission crossed the river to pay a visit to the solitary white
man of whom they had heard, no doubt wishing also to catch
a glimpse of his daughter.   In that they were disappointed,
Nina refusing to show herself ; but they seemed easily consoled by the gin and cheroots set before them by the hospitable Almayer ;   and sprawling comfortably on the lame
armchairs under the shade of the verandah, while the blazing
sunshine outside seemed to set the great river simmering
in the heat, they filled the little bungalow with the unusual
sounds of European languages, with noise and laughter produced by naval witticisms at the expense of the fat Lakamba
whom they had been complimenting so much that very

morning. The younger men in an access of good fellowship made their host talk, and Almayer, excited by the sight of European faces, by the sound of European voices, opened his heart before the sympathising strangers, unaware of the amusement the recital of his many misfortunes caused to those future admirals. They drank his health, wished him many big diamonds and a mountain of gold, expressed even an envy of the high destinies awaiting him yet. Encouraged by so much friendliness, the grey-headed and foolish dreamer invited his guests to visit his new house. They went there through the long grass in a straggling procession while their boats were got ready for the return down the river in the cool of the evening. And in the great empty rooms where the tepid wind entering through the sashless windows whirled gently the dried leaves and the dust of many days of neglect, Almayer in his white jacket and flowered sarong, surrounded by a circle of glittering uniforms, stamped his foot to show the solidity of the neatly-fitting floors and expatiated upon the beauties and convenience of the building. They listened and assented, amazed by the wonderful simplicity and the foolish hopefulness of the man, till Almayer, carried away by his excitement, disclosed his regret at the non-arrival of the English, " who knew how to develop a rich country," as he expressed it. There was a general laugh amongst the Dutch officers at that unsophisticated statement, and a move was made towards the boats; but when Almayer, stepping cautiously on the rotten boards of the Lingard jetty, tried to approach the chief of the Commission with some timid hints anent the protection required by the Dutch subject against the wily Arabs, that salt water diplomat told him significantly that the Arabs were better subjects than Hollanders who dealt illegally in gunpowder with the Malays. The innocent Almayer recognised there at once the oily tongue of Abdulla and the solemn persuasiveness of Lakamba, but ere he had time to frame an indignant protest the steam launch and the string of boats moved rapidly down the river, leaving him on the jetty, standing open-mouthed in his surprise and anger. There are thirty miles of river from Sambir to the gem-like islands of the estuary where the frigate was awaiting the return of the boats. The moon rose long before the boats had traversed half that distance, and the black forest sleeping peacefully under her cold rays woke up that night to the ringing laughter in the small flotilla provoked by some reminiscence of Almayer's lamentable narrative. Salt-water jests at the poor man's expense were passed from boat to boat, the non-appearance of his daughter was commented upon with severe displeasure, and the half-finished house built for the reception of Englishmen received on that joyous night the name of " Almayer's Folly " by the unanimous vote of the lighthearted seamen.

For many weeks after this visit life in Sambir resumed its even and uneventful flow. Each day's sun shooting its morning rays above the tree-tops lit up the usual scene of daily activity. Nina walking on the path that formed the only street in the settlement saw the accustomed sight of men lolling on the shady side of the houses, on the high platforms; of women busily engaged in husking the daily rice; of naked brown children racing along the shady and narrow paths leading to the clearings. Jim-Eng, strolling before his house, greeted her with a friendly nod before climbing up indoors to seek his beloved opium pipe. The elder children clustered round her, daring from long acquaintance, pulling the skirts of her white robe with their dark fingers, and showing their brilliant teeth in expectation of a shower of glass beads. She greeted them with a quiet smile, but always had a few friendly words for a Siamese girl, a slave owned by Bulangi, whose numerous wives were said to be of a violent temper. Well-founded rumour said also that the domestic squabbles of that industrious cultivator ended generally in a combined assault of all his wives upon the Siamese slave. The girl herself never complained—perhaps from dictates of prudence, but more likely through the strange, resigned apathy of half-savage womankind. From early morning she was to be seen on the paths amongst the houses—by the riverside or on the jetties, the tray of pastry, it was her mission to sell, skilfully balanced on her head. During the great heat of the day she usually sought refuge in Almayer's campong, often finding shelter in a shady corner of the verandah, where she squatted with her tray before her, when invited by Nina. For " Mem Putih " she had always a smile, but the presence of Mrs. Almayer, the very sound of her shrill voice, was the signal for a hurried departure.

To this girl **Nina** often spoke; the other inhabitants of Sambir seldom or never heard the sound of her voice. They got used to the silent figure moving in their midst calm and white-robed, a being from another world and incomprehensible to them. Yet Nina's life, for all her outward composure, for all the seeming detachment from the things and people surrounding her, was far from quiet, in consequence of Mrs. Almayer being much too active for the happiness and even safety of the household. She had resumed some intercourse with Lakamba, not personally, it is true (for the dignity of that potentate kept him inside his stockade), but through the agency of that potentate's prime minister, harbour master, financial adviser, and general factotum. That gentleman—of Sulu origin—was certainly endowed with statesmanlike qualities, although he was totally devoid of personal charms. In truth he was perfectly repulsive, possessing only one eye and a pock-marked face, with nose and lips horribly disfigured by the small-pox. This unengaging individual often strolled into Almayer's garden in unofficial costume, composed of a piece of pink calico round his waist. There at the back of the house, squatting on his heels on scattered embers, in close proximity to the great iron boiler, where the family daily rice was being cooked by the women under Mrs. Almayer's superintendence, did that astute negotiator carry on long conversations in Sulu language with Almayer's wife. What the subject of their discourses was might have been guessed from the subsequent domestic scenes by Almayer's hearthstone.

Of late Almayer had taken to excursions up the river. In a small canoe with two paddlers and the faithful Ali for a steersman he would disappear for a few days at a time. All his movements were no doubt closely watched by Lakamba

and Abdulla, for the man once in the confidence of Rajah
Laut was supposed to be in possession of valuable secrets.
The coast population of Borneo believes implicitly in
diamonds of fabulous value, in gold mines of enormous
richness in the interior.   And all those imaginings are heightened by the difficulty of penetrating far inland, especially
on the north-east coast, where the Malays and the river
tribes of Dyaks or Head-hunters are eternally quarrelling.
It is true enough that some gold reaches the coast in the
hands of those Dyaks when, during short periods of truce
in the desultory warfare, they visit the coast settlements of
Malays.   And so the wildest exaggerations are built up and
added to on the slight basis of that fact.

Almayer in his quality of white man—as Lingard before
him—had somewhat better relations with the up-river
tribes.   Yet even his excursions were not without danger,
and his returns were eagerly looked for by the impatient
Lakamba.   But every time the Rajah was disappointed.
Vain were the conferences by the rice-pot of his factotum
Babalatchi with the white man's wife.   The white man
himself was impenetrable—impenetrable to persuasion,
coaxing, abuse; to soft words and shrill revilings; to desperate beseechings or murderous threats; for Mrs. Almayer, in
her extreme desire to persuade her husband into an alliance
with Lakamba, played upon the whole gamut of passion.
With her soiled robe wound tightly under the armpits
across her lean bosom, her scant grayish hair tumbled in
disorder over her projecting cheek-bones, in suppliant
attitude, she depicted with shrill volubility the advantages
of close union with a man so good and so fair dealing.

"Why don't you go to the Rajah?" she screamed.
"Why do you go back to those Dyaks in the great forest?
They should be killed.   You cannot kill them, you cannot;
but our Rajah's men are brave!   You tell the Rajah where
the old white man's treasure is.   Our Rajah is good!   He
is our very grandfather, Datu Besar!   He will kill those
wretched Dyaks, and you shall have half the treasure.   Oh,
Kaspar, tell where the treasure is!   Tell me!   Tell me

out of the old man's surat where you read so often at
night."

On those occasions Almayer sat with rounded shoulders
bending to the blast of this domestic tempest, accentuating
only each pause in the torrent of his wife's eloquence by an
angry growl, "There is no treasure! Go away, woman!"
Exasperated by the sight of his patiently bent back, she
would at last walk round so as to face him across the table,
and clasping her robe with one hand she stretched the other
lean arm and claw-like hand to emphasise, in a passion of
anger and contempt, the rapid rush of scathing remarks
and bitter cursings heaped on the head of the man unworthy
to associate with brave Malay chiefs. It ended generally
by Almayer rising slowly, his long pipe in hand, his face set
into a look of inward pain, and walking away in silence. He
descended the steps and plunged into the long grass on his
way to the solitude of his new house, dragging his feet in a
state of physical collapse from disgust and fear before that
fury. She followed to the head of the steps, and sent the
shafts of indiscriminate abuse after the retreating form.
And each of those scenes was concluded by a piercing shriek,
reaching him far away. "You know, Kaspar, I am your
wife! your own Christian wife after your own Blanda law!"
For she knew that this was the bitterest thing of all; the
greatest regret of that man's life.

All these scenes Nina witnessed unmoved. She might
have been deaf, dumb, without any feeling as far as any
expression of opinion went. Yet oft when her father had
sought the refuge of the great dusty rooms of "Almayer's
Folly," and her mother, exhausted by rhetorical efforts,
squatted wearily on her heels with her back against the leg
of the table, Nina would approach her curiously, guarding
her skirts from betel juice besprinkling the floor, and gaze
down upon her as one might look into the quiescent crater of
a volcano after a destructive eruption. Mrs. Almayer's
thoughts, after these scenes, were usually turned into a
channel of childhood reminiscences, and she gave them utterance in a kind of monotonous recitative—slightly discon-

nected, but generally describing the glories of the Sultan of
Sulu, his great splendour, his power, his great prowess; the
fear which benumbed the hearts of white men at the sight
of his swift piratical praus. And these muttered statements
of her grandfather's might were mixed up with bits of later
recollections, where the great fight with the "White
Devil's" brig and the convent life in Samarang occupied
the principal place. At that point she usually dropped the
thread of her narrative, and pulling out the little brass cross,
always suspended round her neck, she contemplated it with
superstitious awe. That superstitious feeling connected
with some vague talismanic properties of the little bit of
metal, and the still more hazy but terrible notion of some
bad Djinns and horrible torments invented, as she thought,
for her especial punishment by the good Mother Superior
in case of the loss of the above charm, were Mrs. Almayer's
only theological luggage for the stormy road of life. Mrs.
Almayer had at least something tangible to cling to, but
Nina, brought up under the Protestant wing of the proper
Mrs. Vinck, had not even a little piece of brass to remind
her of past teaching. And listening to the recital of those
savage glories, those barbarous fights and savage feasting, to
the story of deeds valorous, albeit somewhat bloodthirsty,
where men of her mother's race shone far above the Orang
Blanda, she felt herself irresistibly fascinated, and saw with
vague surprise the narrow mantle of civilised morality, in
which good-meaning people had wrapped her young soul,
fall away and leave her shivering and helpless as if on the
edge of some deep and unknown abyss. Strangest of all,
this abyss did not frighten her when she was under the
influence of the witch-like being she called her mother.
She seemed to have forgotten in civilised surroundings her
life before the time when Lingard had, so to speak, kidnapped
her from Brow. Since then she had had Christian teaching,
social education, and a good glimpse of civilised life. Unfortunately her teachers did not understand her nature, and
the education ended in a scene of humiliation, in an outburst
of contempt from white people for her mixed blood. She

had tasted the whole bitterness of it and remembered distinctly that the virtuous Mrs. Vinck's indignation was not so much directed against the young man from the bank as against the innocent cause of that young man's infatuation. And there was also no doubt in her mind that the principal cause of Mrs. Vinck's indignation was the thought that such a thing should happen in a white nest, where her snow-white doves, the two Misses Vinck, had just returned from Europe, to find shelter under the maternal wing, and there await the coming of irreproachable men of their destiny. Not even the thought of the money so painfully scraped together by Almayer, and so punctually sent for Nina's expenses, could dissuade Mrs. Vinck from her virtuous resolve. Nina was sent away, and in truth the girl herself wanted to go, although a little frightened by the impending change. And now she had lived on the river for three years with a savage mother and a father walking about amongst pitfalls, with his head in the clouds, weak, irresolute, and unhappy. She had lived a life devoid of all the decencies of civilisation, in miserable domestic conditions; she had breathed in the atmosphere of sordid plottings for gain, of the no less disgusting intrigues and crimes for lust or money; and those things, together with the domestic quarrels, were the only events of her three years' existence. She did not die from despair and disgust the first month, as she expected and almost hoped for. On the contrary, at the end of half a year it had seemed to her that she had known no other life. Her young mind having been unskilfully permitted to glance at better things, and then thrown back again into the hopeless quagmire of barbarism, full of strong and uncontrolled passions, had lost the power to discriminate. It seemed to Nina that there was no change and no difference. Whether they traded in brick godowns or on the muddy river bank; whether they reached after much or little; whether they made love under the shadows of the great trees or in the shadow of the cathedral on the Singapore promenade; whether they plotted for their own ends under the protection of laws and according to the rules of Christian conduct, or whether they sought the

B 2

gratification of their desires with the savage cunning and
the unrestrained fierceness of natures as innocent of culture
as their own immense and gloomy forests, Nina saw only the
same manifestations of love and hate and of sordid greed
chasing the uncertain dollar in all its multifarious and vanishing shapes. To her resolute nature, however, after all these
years, the savage and uncompromising sincerity of purpose
shown by her Malay kinsmen seemed at last preferable to the
sleek hypocrisy, to the polite disguises, to the virtuous pretences of such white people as she had had the misfortune to
come in contact with. After all it was her life; it was
going to be her life, and so thinking she fell more and more
under the influence of her mother. Seeking, in her ignorance, a better side to that life, she listened with avidity to
the old woman's tales of the departed glories of the Rajahs,
from whose race she had sprung, and she became gradually
more indifferent, more contemptuous of the white side of
her descent represented by a feeble and traditionless father.

Almayer's difficulties were by no means diminished by
the girl's presence in Sambir. The stir caused by her arrival
had died out, it is true, and Lakamba had not renewed his
visits; but about a year after the departure of the man-of-
war boats the nephew of Abdulla, Syed Reshid, returned
from his pilgrimage to Mecca, rejoicing in a green jacket
and the proud title of Hadji. There was a great letting off
of rockets on board the steamer which brought him in, and
a great beating of drums all night in Abdulla's compound,
while the feast of welcome was prolonged far into the small
hours of the morning. Reshid was the favourite nephew
and heir of Abdulla, and that loving uncle, meeting Almayer
one day by the riverside, stopped politely to exchange
civilities and to ask solemnly for an interview. Almayer
suspected some attempt at a swindle, or at any rate something unpleasant, but of course consented with a great show
of rejoicing. Accordingly the next evening, after sunset,
Abdulla came, accompanied by several other greybeards
and by his nephew. That young man—of a very rakish
and dissipated appearance—affected the greatest indifference

as to the whole of the proceedings. When the torch-bearers
had grouped themselves below the steps, and the visitors had
seated themselves on various lame chairs, Reshid stood apart
in the shadow, examining his aristocratically small hands with
great attention. Almayer, surprised by the great solemnity
of his visitors, perched himself on the corner of the table
with a characteristic want of dignity quickly noted by the
Arabs with grave disapproval. But Abdulla spoke now,
looking straight past Almayer at the red curtain hanging in
the doorway, where a slight tremor disclosed the presence
of women on the other side. He began by neatly complimenting Almayer upon the long years they had dwelt
together in cordial neighbourhood, and called upon Allah
to give him many more years to gladden the eyes of his
friends by his welcome presence. He made a polite allusion
to the great consideration shown him (Almayer) by the
Dutch " Commissie," and drew thence the flattering infer-
ence of Almayer's great importance amongst his own people.
He—Abdulla—was also important amongst all the Arabs,
and his nephew Reshid would be heir of that social position
and of great riches. Now Reshid was a Hadji. He was
possessor of several Malay women, went on Abdulla, but it
was time he had a favourite wife, the first of the four
allowed by the Prophet. And, speaking with well-bred
politeness, he explained further to the dumbfounded Almayer
that, if he would consent to the alliance of his offspring
with that true believer and virtuous man Reshid, she would
be the mistress of all the splendours of Reshid's house, and
first wife of the first Arab in the Islands, when he—Abdulla
—was called to the joys of Paradise by Allah the All-merciful.
" You know, Tuan," he said, in conclusion, " the other
women would be her slaves, and Reshid's house is great.
From Bombay he has brought great divans, and costly
carpets, and European furniture. There is also a great
looking-glass in a frame shining like gold. What could a
girl want more ? " And while Almayer looked upon him
in silent dismay Abdulla spoke in a more confidential tone,
waving his attendants away, and finished his speech by

pointing out the material advantages of such an alliance, and offering to settle upon Almayer three thousand dollars as a sign of his sincere friendship and the price of the girl.

Poor Almayer was nearly having a fit. Burning with the desire of taking Abdulla by the throat, he had but to think of his helpless position in the midst of lawless men to comprehend the necessity of diplomatic conciliation. He mastered his impulses, and spoke politely and coldly, saying the girl was young and was the apple of his eye. Tuan Reshid, a Faithful and a Hadji, would not want an infidel woman in his harem; and, seeing Abdulla smile sceptically at that last objection, he remained silent, not trusting himself to speak more, not daring to refuse point-blank, nor yet to say anything compromising. Abdulla understood the meaning of that silence, and rose to take leave with a grave salaam. He wished his friend Almayer " a thousand years," and moved down the steps, helped dutifully by Reshid. The torch-bearers shook their torches, scattering a shower of sparks into the river, and the cortège moved off, leaving Almayer agitated but greatly relieved by their departure. He dropped into a chair and watched the glimmer of the lights amongst the tree trunks till they disappeared and complete silence succeeded the tramp of feet and the murmur of voices. He did not move till the curtain rustled and Nina came out on the verandah and sat in the rocking-chair, where she used to spend many hours every day. She gave a slight rocking motion to her seat, leaning back with half-closed eyes, her long hair shading her face from the smoky light of the lamp on the table. Almayer looked at her furtively, but the face was as impassible as ever. She turned her head slightly towards her father, and, speaking, to his great surprise, in English, asked—

" Was that Abdulla here ? "

" Yes," said Almayer—" just gone."

" And what did he want, father ? "

" He wanted to buy you for Reshid," answered Almayer, brutally, his anger getting the better of him, and looking at the girl as if in expectation of some outbreak of feeling. But

Nina remained apparently unmoved, gazing dreamily into the black night outside.

"Be careful, Nina," said Almayer, after a short silence and rising from his chair, "when you go paddling alone into the creeks in your canoe. That Reshid is a violent scoundrel, and there is no saying what he may do. Do you hear me?"

She was standing now, ready to go in, one hand grasping the curtain in the doorway. She turned round, throwing her heavy tresses back by a sudden gesture.

"Do you think he would dare?" she asked, quickly, and then turned again to go in, adding in a lower tone, "He would not dare. Arabs are all cowards."

Almayer looked after her, astonished. He did not seek the repose of his hammock. He walked the floor absently, sometimes stopping by the balustrade to think. The lamp went out. The first streak of dawn broke over the forest; Almayer shivered in the damp air. "I give it up," he muttered to himself, lying down wearily. "Damn those women! Well! If the girl did not look as if she wanted to be kidnapped!"

And he felt a nameless fear creep into his heart, making him shiver again.

## CHAPTER IV

That year, towards the breaking up of the south-west monsoon, disquieting rumours reached Sambir. Captain Ford, coming up to Almayer's house for an evening's chat, brought late numbers of the *Straits Times* giving the news of Acheen war and of the unsuccessful Dutch expedition. The Nakhodas of the rare trading praus ascending the river paid visits to Lakamba, discussing with that potentate the unsettled state of affairs, and wagged their heads gravely over the recital of Orang Blanda exaction, severity, and general tyranny, as exemplified in the total stoppage of gunpowder trade and the rigorous visiting of all suspicious craft trading in the straits of Macassar. Even the loyal soul of Lakamba was stirred into a state of inward discontent by the withdrawal of his licence for powder and by the abrupt confiscation of one hundred and fifty barrels of that commodity by the gunboat *Princess Amelia*, when, after a hazardous voyage, it had almost reached the mouth of the river. The unpleasant news was given him by Reshid, who, after the unsuccessful issue of his matrimonial projects, had made a long voyage amongst the islands for trading purposes; had bought the powder for his friend, and was overhauled and deprived of it on his return when actually congratulating himself on his acuteness in avoiding detection. Reshid's wrath was principally directed against Almayer, whom he suspected of having notified the Dutch authorities of the desultory warfare carried on by the Arabs and the Rajah with the up-river Dyak tribes.

To Reshid's great surprise the Rajah received his complaints very coldly, and showed no signs of vengeful disposition towards the white man. In truth, Lakamba knew very well that Almayer was perfectly innocent of any meddling in state affairs; and besides, his attitude towards that much persecuted individual was wholly changed in consequence of a reconciliation effected between him and his old enemy by Almayer's newly-found friend, Dain Maroola.

Almayer had now a friend. Shortly after Reshid's departure on his commercial journey, Nina, drifting slowly with the tide in the canoe on her return home after one of her solitary excursions, heard in one of the small creeks a splashing, as if of heavy ropes dropping in the water, and the prolonged song of Malay seamen when some heavy pulling is to be done. Through the thick fringe of bushes hiding the mouth of the creek she saw the tall spars of some European-rigged sailing vessel overtopping the summits of the Nipa palms. A brig was being hauled out of the small creek into the main stream. The sun had set, and during the short moments of twilight Nina saw the brig, aided by the evening breeze and

the flowing tide, head towards Sambir under her set foresail.
The girl turned her canoe out of the main river into one
of the many narrow channels amongst the wooded islets,
and paddled vigorously over the black and sleepy backwaters
towards Sambir. Her canoe brushed the water-palms, skirted
the short spaces of muddy bank where sedate alligators looked
at her with lazy unconcern, and, just as darkness was setting
in, shot out into the broad junction of the two main branches
of the river, where the brig was already at anchor with sails
furled, yards squared, and decks seemingly untenanted by
any human being. Nina had to cross the river and pass
pretty close to the brig in order to reach home on the low
promontory between the two branches of the Pantai. Up
both branches, in the houses built on the banks and over
the water, the lights twinkled already, reflected in the still
waters below. The hum of voices, the occasional cry of a
child, the rapid and abruptly interrupted roll of a wooden
drum, together with some distant hailing in the darkness
by the returning fishermen, reached her over the broad
expanse of the river. She hesitated a little before crossing,
the sight of such an unusual object as an European-rigged
vessel causing her some uneasiness, but the river in its wide
expansion was dark enough to render a small canoe invisible.
She urged her small craft with swift strokes of her paddle,
kneeling in the bottom and bending forward to catch any
suspicious sound while she steered towards the little jetty
of Lingard and Co., to which the strong light of the paraffin
lamp shining on the whitewashed verandah of Almayer's
bungalow served as a convenient guide. The jetty itself,
under the shadow of the bank overgrown by drooping bushes,
was hidden in darkness. Before even she could see it she
heard the hollow bumping of a large boat against its rotten
posts, and heard also the murmur of whispered conversation
in that boat whose white paint and great dimensions, faintly
visible on nearer approach, made her rightly guess that it
belonged to the brig just anchored. Stopping her course
by a rapid motion of her paddle, with another swift stroke
she sent it whirling away from the wharf and steered for a

little rivulet which gave access to the back courtyard of the house. She landed at the muddy head of the creek and made her way towards the house over the trodden grass of the courtyard. To the left, from the cooking shed, shone a red glare through the banana plantation she skirted, and the noise of feminine laughter reached her from there in the silent evening. She rightly judged her mother was not near, laughter and Mrs. Almayer not being close neighbours. She must be in the house, thought Nina, as she ran lightly up the inclined plane of shaky planks leading to the back door of the narrow passage dividing the house in two. Outside the doorway, in the black shadow, stood the faithful Ali.

"Who is there?" asked Nina.

"A great Malay man has come," answered Ali, in a tone of suppressed excitement. "He is a rich man. There are six men with lances. Real Soldat, you understand. And his dress is very brave. I have seen his dress. It shines! What jewels! Don't go there, Mem Nina. Tuan said not; but the old Mem is gone. Tuan will be angry. Merciful Allah! what jewels that man has got!"

Nina slipped past the outstretched hand of the slave into the dark passage where, in the crimson glow of the hanging curtain, close by its other end, she could see a small dark form crouching near the wall. Her mother was feasting her eyes and ears with what was taking place on the front verandah, and Nina approached to take her share in the rare pleasure of some novelty. She was met by her mother's extended arm and by a low murmured warning not to make a noise.

"Have you seen them, mother?" asked Nina, in a breathless whisper.

Mrs. Almayer turned her face towards the girl, and her sunken eyes shone strangely in the red half-light of the passage.

"I saw him," she said, in an almost inaudible tone, pressing her daughter's hand with her bony fingers. "A great Rajah has come to Sambir—a Son of Heaven," muttered the old woman to herself. "Go away, girl!"

The two women stood close to the curtain, Nina wishing to approach the rent in the stuff, and her mother defending the position with angry obstinacy. On the other side there was a lull in the conversation, but the breathing of several men, the occasional light tinkling of some ornaments, the clink of metal scabbards, or of brass siri-vessels passed from hand to hand, was audible during the short pause. The women struggled silently, when there was a shuffling noise and the shadow of Almayer's burly form fell on the curtain.

The women ceased struggling and remained motionless. Almayer had stood up to answer his guest, turning his back to the doorway, unaware of what was going on on the other side. He spoke in a tone of regretful irritation.

"You have come to the wrong house, Tuan Maroola, if you want to trade as you say. I was a trader once, not now, whatever you may have heard about me in Macassar. And if you want anything, you will not find it here; I have nothing to give, and want nothing myself. You should go to the Rajah here; you can see in the daytime his houses across the river, there, where those fires are burning on the shore. He will help you and trade with you. Or, better still, go to the Arabs over there," he went on bitterly, pointing with his hand towards the houses of Sambir. "Abdulla is the man you want. There is nothing he would not buy, and there is nothing he would not sell; believe me, I know him well."

He waited for an answer a short time, then added—

"All that I have said is true, and there is nothing more."

Nina, held back by her mother, heard a soft voice reply with a calm evenness of intonation peculiar to the better class Malays—

"Who would doubt a white Tuan's words? A man seeks his friends where his heart tells him. Is this not true also? I have come, although so late, for I have something to say which you may be glad to hear. To-morrow I will go to the Sultan; a trader wants the friendship of great men. Then I shall return here to speak serious words, if Tuan permits. I shall not go to the Arabs; their lies are very great! What are they? Chelakka!"

Almayer's voice sounded a little more pleasantly in reply.

"Well, as you like. I can hear you to-morrow at any time if you have anything to say. Bah! After you have seen the Sultan Lakamba you will not want to return here, Inchi Dain. You will see. Only mind, I will have nothing to do with Lakamba. You may tell him so. What is your business with me, after all?"

"To-morrow we talk, Tuan, now I know you," answered the Malay. "I speak English a little, so we can talk and nobody will understand, and then——"

He interrupted himself suddenly, asking surprised, "What's that noise, Tuan?"

Almayer had also heard the increasing noise of the scuffle recommenced on the women's side of the curtain. Evidently Nina's strong curiosity was on the point of overcoming Mrs. Almayer's exalted sense of social proprieties. Hard breathing was distinctly audible, and the curtain shook during the contest, which was mainly physical, although Mrs. Almayer's voice was heard in angry remonstrance with its usual want of strictly logical reasoning, but with the well-known richness of invective.

"You shameless woman! Are you a slave?" shouted shrilly the irate matron. "Veil your face, abandoned wretch! You white snake, I will not let you!"

Almayer's face expressed annoyance and also doubt as to the advisability of interfering between mother and daughter. He glanced at his Malay visitor, who was waiting silently for the end of the uproar in an attitude of amused expectation, and waving his hand contemptuously he murmured—

"It is nothing. Some women."

The Malay nodded his head gravely, and his face assumed an expression of serene indifference, as etiquette demanded after such an explanation. The contest was ended behind the curtain, and evidently the younger will had its way, for the rapid shuffle and click of Mrs. Almayer's high-heeled sandals died away in the distance. The tranquillised master of the house was going to resume the conversation when, struck by an unexpected change in the expression of his guest's countenance, he turned his head and saw Nina standing in the doorway.

After Mrs. Almayer's retreat from the field of battle, Nina, with a contemptuous exclamation, " It's only a trader," had lifted the conquered curtain and now stood in full light, framed in the dark background on the passage, her lips slightly parted, her hair in disorder after the exertion, the angry gleam not yet faded out of her glorious and sparkling eyes. She took in at a glance the group of white-clad lance-men standing motionless in the shadow of the far-off end of the verandah, and her gaze rested curiously on the chief of that imposing cortège. He stood, almost facing her, a little on one side, and struck by the beauty of the unexpected apparition had bent low, elevating his joint hands above his head in a sign of respect accorded by Malays only to the great of this earth. The crude light of the lamp shone on the gold embroidery of his black silk jacket, broke in a thousand sparkling rays on the jewelled hilt of his kriss pro-truding from under the many folds of the red sarong gathered into a sash round his waist, and played on the precious stones of the many rings on his dark fingers. He straightened him-self up quickly after the low bow, putting his hand with a graceful ease on the hilt of his heavy short sword ornamented with brilliantly dyed fringes of horsehair. Nina, hesitating on the threshold, saw an erect lithe figure of medium height with a breadth of shoulder suggesting great power. Under the folds of a blue turban, whose fringed ends hung gracefully over the left shoulder, was a face full of determination and expressing a reckless good-humour, not devoid, however, of some dignity. The squareness of lower jaw, the full red lips, the mobile nostrils, and the proud carriage of the head gave the impression of a being half-savage, untamed, perhaps cruel, and corrected the liquid softness of the almost feminine eye, that general characteristic of the race. Now, the first surprise over, Nina saw those eyes fixed upon her with such an uncontrolled expression of admiration and desire that she felt a hitherto unknown feeling of shyness, mixed with alarm and some delight, enter and penetrate her whole being. Confused by those unusual sensations she stopped in the doorway and instinctively drew the lower part of the curtain across her face, leaving only half a rounded cheek, a stray tress, and one eye exposed, wherewith to contemplate the gorgeous and bold being so unlike in appearance to the rare specimens of traders she had seen before on that same verandah.

Dain Maroola, dazzled by the unexpected vision, forgot the confused Almayer, forgot his brig, his escort staring in open-mouthed admiration, the object of his visit and all things else, in his overpowering desire to prolong the contemplation of so much loveliness met so suddenly in such an unlikely place—as he thought.

"It is my daughter," said Almayer, in an embarrassed manner. "It is of no consequence. White women have their customs, as you know Tuan, having travelled much, as you say. However, it is late; we will finish our talk to-morrow."

Dain bent low trying to convey in a last glance towards the girl the bold expression of his overwhelming admiration. The next minute he was shaking Almayer's hand with grave courtesy, his face wearing a look of stolid unconcern as to any feminine presence. His men filed off, and he followed them quickly, closely attended by a thick-set, savage-looking Sumatrese he had introduced before as the commander of his brig. Nina walked to the balustrade of the verandah and saw the sheen of moonlight on the steel spear-heads and heard the rhythmic jingle of brass anklets as the men moved in single file towards the jetty. The boat shoved off after a little while, looming large in the full light of the moon, a black shapeless mass in the slight haze hanging over the water. Nina fancied she could distinguish the graceful figure of the trader standing erect in the stern sheets, but in a little while all the outlines got blurred, confused, and soon disappeared in the folds of white vapour shrouding the middle of the river.

Almayer had approached his daughter, and leaning with both arms over the rail, was looking moodily down on the heap of rubbish and broken bottles at the foot of the verandah.

"What was all that noise just now?" he growled peevishly, without looking up. "Confound you and your mother! What did she want? What did you come out for?"

"She did not want to let me come out," said Nina. "She is angry. She says the man just gone is some Rajah. I think she is right now."

"I believe all you women are crazy," snarled Almayer. "What's that to you, to her, to anybody? The man wants to collect trepang and birds' nests on the islands. He told me so, that Rajah of yours. He will come to-morrow. I want you both to keep away from the house, and let me attend to my business in peace."

Dain Maroola came the next day and had a long conversation with Almayer. This was the beginning of a close and friendly intercourse which, at first, was much remarked in Sambir, till the population got used to the frequent sight of many fires burning in Almayer's campong, where Maroola's men were warming themselves during the cold nights of the north-east monsoon, while their master had long conferences with the Tuan Putih—as they styled Almayer amongst themselves. Great was the curiosity in Sambir on the subject of the new trader. Had he seen the Sultan? What did the Sultan say? Had he given any presents? What would he sell? What would he buy? Those were the questions broached eagerly by the inhabitants of bamboo houses built over the river. Even in more substantial buildings, in Abdulla's house, in the residences of principal traders, Arab, Chinese, and Bugis, the excitement ran high, and lasted many days. With inborn suspicion they would not believe the simple account of himself the young trader was always ready to give. Yet it had all the appearance of truth. He said he was a trader, and sold rice. He did not want to buy gutta-percha or beeswax, because he intended to employ his numerous crew in collecting trepang on the coral reefs

outside the river, and also in seeking for bird's nests on the
mainland. Those two articles he professed himself ready to
buy if there were any to be obtained in that way. He said
he was from Bali, and a Brahmin, which last statement he
made good by refusing all food during his often repeated
visits to Lakamba's and Almayer's houses. To Lakamba he
went generally at night and had long audiences. Babalatchi,
who was always a third party at those meetings of potentate
and trader, knew how to resist all attempts on the part of
the curious to ascertain the subject of so many long talks.
When questioned with languid courtesy by the grave Abdulla
he sought refuge in a vacant stare of his one eye, and in the
affectation of extreme simplicity.

"I am only my master's slave," murmured Babalatchi, in
a hesitating manner. Then as if making up his mind suddenly for a reckless confidence he would inform Abdulla of
some transaction in rice, repeating the words, "A hundred
big bags the Sultan bought; a hundred, Tuan!" in a tone
of mysterious solemnity. Abdulla, firmly persuaded of the
existence of some more important dealings, received, however, the information with all the signs of respectful astonishment. And the two would separate, the Arab cursing
inwardly the wily dog, while Babalatchi went on his way
walking on the dusty path, his body swaying, his chin with
its few grey hairs pushed forward, resembling an inquisitive
goat bent on some unlawful expedition. Attentive eyes
watched his movements. Jim-Eng, descrying Babalatchi
far away, would shake off the stupor of an habitual opium
smoker and, tottering on to the middle of the road, would
await the approach of that important person, ready with
hospitable invitation. But Babalatchi's discretion was proof
even against the combined assaults of good fellowship and
of strong gin generously administered by the open-hearted
Chinaman. Jim-Eng, owning himself beaten, was left
uninformed with the empty bottle, and gazed sadly after
the departing form of the statesman of Sambir pursuing his
devious and unsteady way, which, as usual, led him to
Almayer's compound. Ever since a reconciliation had been

effected by Dain Maroola between his white friend and the
Rajah, the one-eyed diplomatist had again become a frequent guest in the Dutchman's house. To Almayer's great
disgust he was to be seen there at all times, strolling about in
an abstracted kind of way on the verandah, skulking in the
passages, or else popping round unexpected corners, always
willing to engage Mrs. Almayer in confidential conversation.
He was very shy of the master himself, as if suspicious that
the pent-up feelings of the white man towards his person
might find vent in a sudden kick. But the cooking shed was
his favourite place, and he became an habitual guest there,
squatting for hours amongst the busy women, with his chin
resting on his knees, his lean arms clasped round his legs, and
his one eye roving uneasily—the very picture of watchful
ugliness. Almayer wanted more than once to complain to
Lakamba of his Prime Minister's intrusion, but Dain dis-
suaded him. "We cannot say a word here that he does not
hear," growled Almayer.

"Then come and talk on board the brig," retorted Dain,
with a quiet smile. "It is good to let the man come here.
Lakamba thinks he knows much. Perhaps the Sultan thinks
I want to run away. Better let the one-eyed crocodile sun
himself in your campong, Tuan."

And Almayer assented unwillingly, muttering vague threats
of personal violence, while he eyed malevolently the aged
statesman sitting with quiet obstinacy by his domestic
rice-pot.

## CHAPTER V

AT last the excitement had died out in Sambir. The
inhabitants got used to the sight of comings and goings
between Almayer's house and the vessel, now moored to the
opposite bank, and speculation as to the feverish activity
displayed by Almayer's boatmen in repairing old canoes ceased
to interfere with the due discharge of domestic duties by the

women of the Settlement. Even the baffled Jim-Eng left
off troubling his muddled brain with secrets of trade, and
relapsed by the aid of his opium pipe into a state of stupefied
bliss, letting Babalatchi pursue his way past his house unin-
vited and seemingly unnoticed.

So on that warm afternoon, when the deserted river
sparkled under the vertical sun, the statesman of Sambir
could, without any hindrance from friendly inquirers, shove
off his little canoe from under the bushes, where it was
usually hidden during his visits to Almayer's compound.
Slowly and languidly Babalatchi paddled, crouching low in
the boat, making himself small under his enormous sun hat
to escape the scorching heat reflected from the water. He
was not in a hurry; his master, Lakamba, was surely
reposing at this time of the day. He would have ample time
to cross over and greet him on his waking with important
news. Will he be displeased? Will he strike his ebony wood
staff angrily on the floor, frightening him by the incoherent
violence of his exclamations; or will he squat down with a
good-humoured smile, and, rubbing his hands gently over
his stomach with a familiar gesture, expectorate copiously
into the brass siri-vessel, giving vent to a low, approbative
murmur? Such were Babalatchi's thoughts as he skilfully
handled his paddle, crossing the river on his way to the
Rajah's campong, whose stockades showed from behind the
dense foliage of the bank just opposite to Almayer's bungalow.

Indeed, he had a report to make. Something certain at
last to confirm the daily tale of suspicions, the daily hints of
familiarity, of stolen glances he had seen, of short and
burning words he had overheard exchanged between Dain
Maroola and Almayer's daughter. Lakamba had, till then,
listened to it all, calmly and with evident distrust; now he
was going to be convinced, for Babalatchi had the proof;
had it this very morning, when fishing at break of day in
the creek over which stood Bulangi's house. There from his
skiff he saw Nina's long canoe drift past, the girl sitting in
the stern bending over Dain, who was stretched in the bottom
with his head resting on the girl's knees. He saw it. He

followed them, but in a short time they took to the paddles and got away from under his observant eye. A few minutes afterwards he saw Bulangi's slave-girl paddling in a small dug-out to the town with her cakes for sale. She also had seen them in the grey dawn. And Babalatchi grinned confidentially to himself at the recollection of the slave-girl's discomposed face, of the hard look in her eyes, of the tremble in her voice, when answering his questions. That little Taminah evidently admired Dain Maroola. That was good! And Babalatchi laughed aloud at the notion; then becoming suddenly serious, he began by some strange association of ideas to speculate upon the price for which Bulangi would, possibly, sell the girl. He shook his head sadly at the thought that Bulangi was a hard man, and had refused one hundred dollars for that same Taminah only a few weeks ago; then he became suddenly aware that the canoe had drifted too far down during his meditation. He shook off the despondency caused by the certitude of Bulangi's mercenary disposition, and, taking up his paddle, in a few strokes sheered alongside the water-gate of the Rajah's house.

That afternoon Almayer, as was his wont lately, moved about on the water-side, overlooking the repairs to his boats. He had decided at last. Guided by the scraps of information contained in old Lingard's pocket-book, he was going to seek for the rich gold-mine, for that place where he had only to stoop to gather up an immense fortune and realise the dream of his young days. To obtain the necessary help he had shared his knowledge with Dain Maroola, he had consented to be reconciled with Lakamba, who gave his support to the enterprise on condition of sharing the profits; he had sacrificed his pride, his honour, and his loyalty in the face of the enormous risk of his undertaking, dazzled by the greatness of the results to be achieved by this alliance so distasteful yet so necessary. The dangers were great, but Maroola was brave; his men seemed as reckless as their chief, and with Lakamba's aid success seemed assured.

For the last fortnight Almayer was absorbed in the pre-

parations, walking amongst his workmen and slaves in a kind
of waking trance, where practical details as to the fitting
out of the boats were mixed up with vivid dreams of untold
wealth, where the present misery of burning sun, of the
muddy and malodorous river bank disappeared in a gorgeous
vision of a splendid future existence for himself and Nina.
He hardly saw Nina during these last days, although the
beloved daughter was ever present in his thoughts. He
hardly took notice of Dain, whose constant presence in his
house had become a matter of course to him now they were
connected by a community of interests. When meeting the
young chief he gave him an absent greeting and passed on,
seemingly wishing to avoid him, bent upon forgetting the
hated reality of the present by absorbing himself in his
work, or else by letting his imagination soar far above the
tree-tops into the great white clouds away to the westward,
where the paradise of Europe was awaiting the future Eastern
millionaire. And Maroola, now the bargain was struck and
there was no more business to be talked over, evidently did
not care for the white man's company. Yet Dain was
always about the house, but he seldom stayed long by the
riverside. On his daily visits to the white man the Malay
chief preferred to make his way quietly through the central
passage of the house, and would come out into the garden
at the back, where the fire was burning in the cooking shed,
with the rice kettle swinging over it, under the watchful
supervision of Mrs. Almayer. Avoiding that shed, with its
black smoke and the warbling of soft, feminine voices, Dain
would turn to the left. There, on the edge of a banana
plantation, a clump of palms and mango trees formed a
shady spot, a few scattered bushes giving it a certain seclusion
into which only the serving women's chatter or an occasional
burst of laughter could penetrate. Once in, he was invisible;
and hidden there, leaning against the smooth trunk of a tall
palm, he waited with gleaming eyes and an assured smile to
hear the faint rustle of dried grass under the light footsteps
of Nina.

From the very first moment when his eyes beheld this—

to him—perfection of loveliness he felt in his inmost heart
the conviction that she would be his; he felt the subtle
breath of mutual understanding passing between their two
savage natures, and he did not want Mrs. Almayer's encouraging smiles to take every opportunity of approaching the girl;
and every time he spoke to her, every time he looked into
her eyes, Nina, although averting her face, felt as if this
bold-looking being who spoke burning words into her willing
ear was the embodiment of her fate, the creature of her
dreams—reckless, ferocious, ready with flashing kriss for his
enemies, and with passionate embrace for his beloved—the
ideal Malay chief of her mother's tradition.

She recognised with a thrill of delicious fear the mysterious
consciousness of her identity with that being. Listening to
his words, it seemed to her she was born only then to a
knowledge of a new existence, that her life was complete
only when near him, and she abandoned herself to a feeling
of dreamy happiness, while with half-veiled face and in
silence—as became a Malay girl—she listened to Dain's
words giving up to her the whole treasure of love and passion
his nature was capable of with all the unrestrained enthusiasm
of a man totally untrammelled by any influence of civilised
self-discipline.

And they used to pass many a delicious and fast-fleeting
hour under the mango trees behind the friendly curtain of
bushes till Mrs. Almayer's shrill voice gave the signal of
unwilling separation. Mrs. Almayer had undertaken the
easy task of watching her husband lest he should interrupt
the smooth course of her daughter's love affair, in which she
took a great and benignant interest. She was happy and
proud to see Dain's infatuation, believing him to be a great
and powerful chief, and she found also a gratification of her
mercenary instincts in Dain's open-handed generosity.

On the eve of the day when Babalatchi's suspicions were
confirmed by ocular demonstration, Dain and Nina had
remained longer than usual in their shady retreat. Only
Almayer's heavy step on the verandah and his querulous
clamour for food decided Mrs. Almayer to lift a warning

cry. Maroola leaped lightly over the low bamboo fence,
and made his way stealthily through the banana plantation
down to the muddy shore of the back creek, while Nina
walked slowly towards the house to minister to her father's
wants, as was her wont every evening. Almayer felt happy
enough that evening; the preparations were nearly completed; to-morrow he would launch his boats. In his
mind's eye he saw the rich prize in his grasp; and, with
tin spoon in his hand, he was forgetting the plateful of rice
before him in the fanciful arrangement of some splendid
banquet to take place on his arrival in Amsterdam. Nina,
reclining in the long chair, listened absently to the few
disconnected words escaping from her father's lips. Expedition! Gold! What did she care for all that? But at
the name of Maroola mentioned by her father she was all
attention. Dain was going down the river with his brig
to-morrow to remain away for a few days, said Almayer.
It was very annoying, this delay. As soon as Dain returned
they would have to start without loss of time, for the river
was rising. He would not be surprised if a great flood was
coming. And he pushed away his plate with an impatient
gesture on rising from the table. But now Nina heard him
not. Dain going away! That's why he had ordered her,
with that quiet masterfulness it was her delight to obey, to
meet him at break of day in Bulangi's creek. Was there a
paddle in her canoe? she thought. Was it ready? She
would have to start early—at four in the morning, in a very
few hours.

She rose from her chair, thinking she would require rest
before the long pull in the early morning. The lamp was
burning dimly, and her father, tired with the day's labour,
was already in his hammock. Nina put the lamp out and
passed into a large room she shared with her mother on
the left of the central passage. Entering, she saw that
Mrs. Almayer had deserted the pile of mats serving her as
bed in one corner of the room, and was now bending over
the opened lid of her large wooden chest. Half a shell of
cocoanut filled with oil, where a cotton rag floated for a

wick, stood on the floor, surrounding her with a ruddy
halo of light shining through the black and odorous smoke.
Mrs. Almayer's back was bent, and her head and shoulders
hidden in the deep box. Her hands rummaged in the
interior, where a soft clink as of silver money could be heard.
She did not notice at first her daughter's approach, and
Nina, standing silently by her, looked down on many little
canvas bags ranged in the bottom of the chest, wherefrom
her mother extracted handfuls of shining guilders and
Mexican dollars, letting them stream slowly back again
through her claw-like fingers. The music of tinkling silver
seemed to delight her, and her eyes sparkled with the
reflected gleam of freshly-minted coins. She was muttering
to herself : " And this, and this, and yet this ! Soon he will
give more—as much more as I ask. He is a great Rajah—a
Son of Heaven ! And she will be a Ranee—he gave all this
for her ! Who ever gave anything for me ? I am a slave !
Am I ? I am the mother of a great Ranee ! " She became
aware suddenly of her daughter's presence, and ceased her
droning, shutting the lid down violently ; then, without
rising from her crouching position, she looked up at the girl
standing by with a vague smile on her dreamy face.

"You have seen. Have you ? " she shouted, shrilly.
" That is all mine, and for you. It is not enough ! He
will have to give more before he takes you away to the
southern island where his father is king. You hear me ?
You are worth more, granddaughter of Rajahs ! More !
More ! "

The sleepy voice of Almayer was heard on the verandah
recommending silence. Mrs. Almayer extinguished the light
and crept into her corner of the room. Nina laid down on
her back on a pile of soft mats, her hands entwined under
her head, gazing through the shutterless hole, serving as a
window, at the stars twinkling in the black sky ; she was
awaiting the time of start for her appointed meeting-place.
With quiet happiness she thought of that meeting in the
great forest, far from all human eyes and sounds. Her soul,
lapsing again into the savage mood, which the genius of

civilisation working by the hand of Mrs. Vinck could never destroy, experienced a feeling of pride and of some slight trouble at the high value her worldly-wise mother had put upon her person; but she remembered the expressive glances and words of Dain, and, tranquillised, she closed her eyes in a shiver of pleasant anticipation.

There are some situations where the barbarian and the, so-called, civilised man meet upon the same ground. It may be supposed that Dain Maroola was not exceptionally delighted with his prospective mother-in-law, nor that he actually approved of that worthy woman's appetite for shining dollars. Yet on that foggy morning when Baba-latchi, laying aside the cares of state, went to visit his fish-baskets in the Bulangi creek, Maroola had no misgivings, experienced no feelings but those of impatience and longing, when paddling to the east side of the island forming the backwater in question. He hid his canoe in the bushes and strode rapidly across the islet, pushing with impatience through the twigs of heavy undergrowth intercrossed over his path. From motives of prudence he would not take his canoe to the meeting-place, as Nina had done. He had left it in the main stream till his return from the other side of the island. The heavy warm fog was closing rapidly round him, but he managed to catch a fleeting glimpse of a light away to the left, proceeding from Bulangi's house. Then he could see nothing in the thickening vapour, and kept to the path only by a sort of instinct, which also led him to the very point on the opposite shore he wished to reach. A great log had stranded there, at right angles to the bank, forming a kind of jetty against which the swiftly flowing stream broke with a loud ripple. He stepped on it with a quick but steady motion, and in two strides found himself at the outer end, with the rush and swirl of the foaming water at his feet.

Standing there alone, as if separated from the world; the heavens, earth; the very water roaring under him swallowed up in the thick veil of the morning fog, he breathed out the name of Nina before him into the apparently limitless space, sure of being heard, instinctively sure of the nearness of the delightful creature; certain of her being aware of his near presence as he was aware of hers.

The bow of Nina's canoe loomed up close to the log, canted high out of the water by the weight of the sitter in the stern. Maroola laid his hand on the stem and leaped lightly in, giving it a vigorous shove off. The light craft, obeying the new impulse, cleared the log by a hair's breadth, and the river, with obedient complicity, swung it broadside to the current, and bore it off silently and rapidly between the invisible banks. And once more Dain, at the feet of Nina, forgot the world, felt himself carried away helpless by a great wave of supreme emotion, by a rush of joy, pride, and desire; understood once more with overpowering certitude that there was no life possible without that being he held clasped in his arms with passionate strength in a prolonged embrace.

Nina disengaged herself gently with a low laugh.

"You will overturn the boat, Dain," she whispered.

He looked into her eyes eagerly for a minute and let her go with a sigh, then lying down in the canoe he put his head on her knees, gazing upwards and stretching his arms backwards till his hands met round the girl's waist. She bent over him, and, shaking her head, framed both their faces in the falling locks of her long black hair.

And so they drifted on, he speaking with all the rude eloquence of a savage nature giving itself up without restraint to an overmastering passion, she bending low to catch the murmur of words sweeter to her than life itself. To those two nothing existed then outside the gunwales of the narrow and fragile craft. It was their world, filled with their intense and all-absorbing love. They took no heed of thickening mist, or of the breeze dying away before sunrise; they forgot the existence of the great forests surrounding them, of all the tropical nature awaiting the advent of the sun in a solemn and impressive silence.

Over the low river-mist hiding the boat with its freight of young passionate life and all-forgetful happiness, the stars paled, and a silvery-grey tint crept over the sky from the eastward. There was not a breath of wind, not a rustle of stirring leaf, not a splash of leaping fish to disturb the serene repose of all living things on the banks of the great river. Earth, river, and sky were wrapped up in a deep sleep, from which it seemed there would be no waking. All the seething life and movement of tropical nature seemed concentrated in the ardent eyes, in the tumultuously beating hearts of the two beings drifting in the canoe, under the white canopy of mist, over the smooth surface of the river.

Suddenly a great sheaf of yellow rays shot upwards from behind the black curtain of trees lining the banks of the Pantai. The stars went out; the little black clouds at the zenith glowed for a moment with crimson tints, and the thick mist, stirred by the gentle breeze, the sigh of waking nature, whirled round and broke into fantastically torn pieces, disclosing the wrinkled surface of the river sparkling in the broad light of day. Great flocks of white birds wheeled screaming above the swaying tree-tops. The sun had risen on the east coast.

Dain was the first to return to the cares of everyday life. He rose and glanced rapidly up and down the river. His eye detected Babalatchi's boat astern, and another small black speck on the glittering water, which was Taminah's canoe. He moved cautiously forward, and, kneeling, took up a paddle; Nina at the stern took hers. They bent their bodies to the work, throwing up the water at every stroke, and the small craft went swiftly ahead, leaving a narrow wake fringed with a lace-like border of white and gleaming foam. Without turning his head, Dain spoke.

"Somebody behind us, Nina. We must not let him gain. I think he is too far to recognise us."

"Somebody before us also," panted out Nina, without ceasing to paddle.

"I think I know," rejoined Dain. "The sun shines over there, but I fancy it is the girl Taminah. She comes down every morning to my brig to sell cakes—stays often all day. It does not matter; steer more into the bank; we must get under the bushes. My canoe is hidden not far from here."

As he spoke his eyes watched the broad-leaved nipas which they were brushing in their swift and silent course.

"Look out, Nina," he said at last; "there, where the water palms end and the twigs hang down under the leaning tree. Steer for the big green branch."

He stood up attentive, and the boat drifted slowly in shore, Nina guiding it by a gentle and skilful movement of her paddle. When near enough Dain laid hold of the big branch, and leaning back shot the canoe under a low green archway of thickly matted creepers giving access to a miniature bay formed by the caving in of the bank during the last great flood. His own boat was there anchored by a stone, and he stepped into it, keeping his hand on the gunwale of Nina's canoe. In a moment the two little nutshells with their occupants floated quietly side by side, reflected by the black water in the dim light struggling through a high canopy of dense foliage; while above, away up in the broad day, flamed immense red blossoms sending down on their heads a shower of great dew-sparkling petals that descended rotating slowly in a continuous and perfumed stream; and over them, under them, in the sleeping water; all around them in a ring of luxuriant vegetation bathed in the warm air charged with strong and harsh perfumes, the intense work of tropical nature went on : plants shooting upward, entwined, interlaced in inextricable confusion, climbing madly and brutally over each other in the terrible silence of a desperate struggle towards the life-giving sunshine above—as if struck with sudden horror at the seething mass of corruption below, at the death and decay from which they sprang.

"We must part now," said Dain, after a long silence. "You must return at once, Nina. I will wait till the brig drifts down here, and shall get on board then."

"And will you be long away, Dain?" asked Nina, in a low voice.

"Long!" exclaimed Dain. "Would a man willingly

c

remain long in a dark place? When I am not near you, Nina, I am like a man that is blind. What is life to me without light?"

Nina leaned over, and with a proud and happy smile took Dain's face between her hands, looking into his eyes with a fond yet questioning gaze. Apparently she found there the confirmation of the words just said, for a feeling of grateful security lightened for her the weight of sorrow at the hour of parting. She believed that he, the descendant of many great Rajahs, the son of a great chief, the master of life and death, knew the sunshine of life only in her presence. An immense wave of gratitude and love welled forth out of her heart towards him. How could she make an outward and visible sign of all she felt for the man who had filled her heart with so much joy and so much pride? And in the great tumult of passion, like a flash of lightning came to her the reminiscence of that despised and almost forgotten civilisation she had only glanced at in her days of restraint, of sorrow, and of anger. In the cold ashes of that hateful and miserable past she would find the sign of love, the fitting expression of the boundless felicity of the present, the pledge of a bright and splendid future. She threw her arms around Dain's neck and pressed her lips to his in a long and burning kiss. He closed his eyes, surprised and frightened at the storm raised in his breast by the strange and to him hitherto unknown contact, and long after Nina had pushed her canoe into the river he remained motionless, without daring to open his eyes, afraid to lose the sensation of intoxicating delight he had tasted for the first time.

Now he wanted but immortality, he thought, to be the equal of gods, and the creature that could open so the gates of paradise must be his—soon would be his for ever!

He opened his eyes in time to see through the archway of creepers the bows of his brig come slowly into view, as the vessel drifted past on its way down the river. He must go on board now, he thought; yet he was loth to leave the place where he had learned to know what happiness meant. "Time yet. Let them go," he muttered to himself; and he closed his eyes again under the red shower of scented petals, trying to recall the scene with all its delight and all its fear.

He must have been able to join his brig in time, after all, and found much occupation outside, for it was in vain that Almayer looked for his friend's speedy return. The lower reach of the river where he so often and so impatiently directed his eyes remained deserted, save for the rapid flitting of some fishing canoe; but down the upper reaches came black clouds and heavy showers heralding the final setting in of the rainy season with its thunderstorms and great floods making the river almost impossible of ascent for native canoes.

Almayer, strolling along the muddy beach between his houses, watched uneasily the river rising inch by inch, creeping slowly nearer to the boats, now ready and hauled up in a row under the cover of dripping Kajang-mats. Fortune seemed to elude his grasp, and in his weary tramp backwards and forwards under the steady rain falling from the lowering sky, a sort of despairing indifference took possession of him. What did it matter? It was just his luck! Those two infernal savages, Lakamba and Dain, induced him, with their promises of help, to spend his last dollar in the fitting out of boats, and now one of them was gone somewhere, and the other shut up in his stockade would give no sign of life. No, not even the scoundrelly Babalatchi, thought Almayer, would show his face near him, now they had sold him all the rice, brass gongs, and cloth necessary for his expedition. They had his very last coin, and did not care whether he went or stayed. And with a gesture of abandoned discouragement Almayer would climb up slowly to the verandah of his new house to get out of the rain, and leaning on the front rail with his head sunk between his shoulders he would abandon himself to the current of bitter thoughts, oblivious of the flight of time and the pangs of hunger, deaf to the shrill cries of his wife calling him to the evening meal. When, roused from his sad meditations by the first roll of the evening thunderstorm, he

stumbled slowly towards the glimmering light of his old
house, his half-dead hope made his ears preternaturally
acute to any sound on the river.   Several nights in succession
he had heard the splash of paddles and had seen the indistinct form of a boat, but when hailing the shadowy apparition, his heart bounding with sudden hope of hearing Dain's
voice, he was disappointed each time by the sulky answer
conveying to him the intelligence that the Arabs were on
the river, bound on a visit to the home-staying Lakamba.
This caused him many sleepless nights, spent in speculating
upon the kind of villainy those estimable personages were
hatching now.   At last, when all hope seemed dead, he was
overjoyed on hearing Dain's voice; but Dain also appeared
very anxious to see Lakamba, and Almayer felt uneasy owing
to a deep and ineradicable distrust as to that ruler's disposition towards himself.   Still, Dain had returned at last.
Evidently he meant to keep to his bargain.   Hope revived,
while Nina watched the angry river under the lash of the
thunderstorm sweeping onward towards the sea.

## CHAPTER VI

Dain was not long in crossing the river after leaving Almayer.
He landed at the water-gate of the stockade enclosing the
group of houses which composed the residence of the Rajah
of Sambir.   Evidently somebody was expected there, for the
gate was open, and men with torches were ready to precede
the visitor up the inclined plane of planks leading to the
largest house where Lakamba actually resided, and where all
the business of state was invariably transacted.   The other
buildings within the enclosure served only to accommodate
the numerous household and the wives of the ruler.

Lakamba's own house was a strong structure of solid
planks, raised on high piles, with a verandah of split bamboos

surrounding it on all sides; the whole was covered in by an immensely high-pitched roof of palm-leaves, resting on beams blackened by the smoke of many torches.

The building stood parallel to the river, one of its long sides facing the water-gate of the stockade. There was a door in the short side looking up the river, and the inclined plank-way led straight from the gate to that door. By the uncertain light of smoky torches, Dain noticed the vague outlines of a group of armed men in the dark shadows to his right. From that group Babalatchi stepped forward to open the door, and Dain entered the audience chamber of the Rajah's residence. About one-third of the house was curtained off, by heavy stuff of European manufacture, for that purpose; close to the curtain there was a big arm-chair of some black wood, much carved, and before it a rough deal table. Otherwise the room was only furnished with mats in great profusion. To the left of the entrance stood a rude arm-rack, with three rifles with fixed bayonets in it. By the wall, in the shadow, the body-guard of Lakamba—all friends or relations—slept in a confused heap of brown arms, legs, and multi-coloured garments, from whence issued an occasional snore or a subdued groan of some uneasy sleeper. An European lamp with a green shade standing on the table made all this indistinctly visible to Dain.

"You are welcome to your rest here," said Babalatchi, looking at Dain interrogatively.

"I must speak to the Rajah at once," answered Dain.

Babalatchi made a gesture of assent, and, turning to the brass gong suspended under the arm-rack, struck two sharp blows.

The ear-splitting din woke up the guard. The snores ceased; outstretched legs were drawn in; the whole heap moved, and slowly resolved itself into individual forms, with much yawning and rubbing of sleepy eyes; behind the curtains there was a burst of feminine chatter; then the bass voice of Lakamba was heard.

"Is that the Arab trader?"

"No, Tuan," answered Babalatchi; "Dain has returned

at last. He is here for an important talk, bitcharra—if you mercifully consent."

Evidently Lakamba's mercy went so far—for in a short while he came out from behind the curtain—but it did not go to the length of inducing him to make an extensive toilet. A short red sarong tightened hastily round his hips was his only garment. The merciful ruler of Sambir looked sleepy and rather sulky. He sat in the arm-chair, his knees well apart, his elbows on the arm-rests, his chin on his breast, breathing heavily and waiting malevolently for Dain to open the important talk.

But Dain did not seem anxious to begin. He directed his gaze towards Babalatchi, squatting comfortably at the feet of his master, and remained silent with a slightly bent head as if in attentive expectation of coming words of wisdom.

Babalatchi coughed discreetly, and, leaning forward, pushed over a few mats for Dain to sit upon, then lifting up his squeaky voice he assured him with eager volubility of everybody's delight at this long-looked-for return. His heart had hungered for the sight of Dain's face, and his ears were withering for the want of the refreshing sound of his voice. Everybody's hearts and ears were in the same sad predicament, according to Babalatchi, as he indicated with a sweeping gesture the other bank of the river where the settlement slumbered peacefully, unconscious of the great joy awaiting it on the morrow when Dain's presence amongst them would be disclosed. " For "—went on Babalatchi— " what is the joy of a poor man if not the open hand of a generous trader or of a great——"

Here he checked himself abruptly with a calculated embarrassment of manner, and his roving eye sought the floor, while an apologetic smile dwelt for a moment on his misshapen lips. Once or twice during this opening speech an amused expression flitted across Dain's face, soon to give way, however, to an appearance of grave concern. On Lakamba's brow a heavy frown had settled, and his lips moved angrily as he listened to his Prime Minister's oratory.

In the silence that fell upon the room when Babalatchi ceased speaking arose a chorus of varied snores from the corner where the body-guard had resumed their interrupted slumbers, but the distant rumble of thunder filling then Nina's heart with apprehension for the safety of her lover passed unheeded by those three men intent each on their own purposes, for life or death.

After a short silence, Babalatchi, discarding now the flowers of polite eloquence, spoke again, but in short and hurried sentences and in a low voice. They had been very uneasy. Why did Dain remain so long absent? The men dwelling on the lower reaches of the river heard the reports of big guns and saw a fire-ship of the Dutch amongst the islands of the estuary. So they were anxious. Rumours of a disaster had reached Abdulla a few days ago, and since then they had been waiting for Dain's return under the apprehension of some misfortune. For days they had closed their eyes in fear, and woke up alarmed, and walked abroad trembling, like men before an enemy. And all on account of Dain. Would he not allay their fears for his safety, not for themselves? They were quiet and faithful, and devoted to the great Rajah in Batavia—may his fate lead him ever to victory for the joy and profit of his servants! "And here," went on Babalatchi, "Lakamba my master was getting thin in his anxiety for the trader he had taken under his protection; and so was Abdulla, for what would wicked men not say if perchance——"

"Be silent, fool!" growled Lakamba, angrily.

Babalatchi subsided into silence with a satisfied smile, while Dain, who had been watching him as if fascinated, turned with a sigh of relief towards the ruler of Sambir. Lakamba did not move, and, without raising his head, looked at Dain from under his eyebrows, breathing audibly, with pouted lips, in an air of general discontent.

"Speak! O Dain!" he said at last. "We have heard many rumours. Many nights in succession has my friend Reshid come here with bad tidings. News travels fast along the coast. But they may be untrue; there are more lies in men's mouths in these days than when I was young, but I am not easier to deceive now."

"All my words are true," said Dain, carelessly. "If you want to know what befell my brig, then learn that it is in the hands of the Dutch. Believe me, Rajah," he went on, with sudden energy, "the Orang Blanda have good friends in Sambir, or else how did they know I was coming thence?"

Lakamba gave Dain a short and hostile glance. Babalatchi rose quietly, and, going to the arm-rack, struck the gong violently.

Outside the door there was a shuffle of bare feet; inside, the guard woke up and sat staring in sleepy surprise.

"Yes, you faithful friend of the white Rajah," went on Dain, scornfully, turning to Babalatchi, who had returned to his place, "I have escaped, and I am here to gladden your heart. When I saw the Dutch ship I ran the brig inside the reefs and put her ashore. They did not dare to follow with the ship, so they sent the boats. We took to ours and tried to get away, but the ship dropped fireballs at us, and killed many of my men. But I am left, O Babalatchi! The Dutch are coming here. They are seeking for me. They are coming to ask their faithful friend Lakamba and his slave Babalatchi. Rejoice!"

But neither of his hearers appeared to be in a joyful mood. Lakamba had put one leg over his knee, and went on gently scratching it with a meditative air, while Babalatchi, sitting cross-legged, seemed suddenly to become smaller and very limp, staring straight before him vacantly. The guard evinced some interest in the proceedings, stretching themselves full length on the mats to be nearer the speaker. One of them got up and now stood leaning against the arm-rack, playing absently with the fringes of his sword-hilt.

Dain waited till the crash of thunder had died away in distant mutterings before he spoke again.

"Are you dumb, O ruler of Sambir, or is the son of a great Rajah unworthy of your notice? I am come here to

seek refuge and to warn you, and want to know what you
intend doing."

"You came here because of the white man's daughter,"
retorted Lakamba, quickly. "Your refuge was with your
father, the Rajah of Bali, the Son of Heaven, the 'Anak
Agong' himself. What am I to protect great princes?
Only yesterday I planted rice in a burnt clearing; to-day
you say I hold your life in my hand."

Babalatchi glanced at his master. "No man can escape
his fate," he murmured piously. "When love enters a
man's heart he is like a child—without any understanding.
Be merciful, Lakamba," he added, twitching the corner of
the Rajah's sarong warningly.

Lakamba snatched away the skirt of the sarong angrily.
Under the dawning comprehension of intolerable embar-
rassments caused by Dain's return to Sambir he began to
lose such composure as he had been, till then, able to main-
tain; and now he raised his voice loudly above the whistling
of the wind and the patter of rain on the roof in the hard
squall passing over the house.

"You came here first as a trader with sweet words and
great promises, asking me to look the other way while you
worked your will on the white man there. And I did. What
do you want now? When I was young I fought. Now I
am old, and want peace. It is easier for me to have you
killed than to fight the Dutch. It is better for me."

The squall had now passed, and, in the short stillness of
the lull in the storm, Lakamba repeated softly, as if to himself, "Much easier. Much better."

Dain did not seem greatly discomposed by the Rajah's
threatening words. While Lakamba was speaking he had
glanced once rapidly over his shoulder, just to make sure
that there was nobody behind him, and, tranquillised in that
respect, he had extracted a siri-box out of the folds of his
waist-cloth, and was wrapping carefully the little bit of
betel-nut and a small pinch of lime in the green leaf tendered
him politely by the watchful Babalatchi. He accepted this
as a peace-offering from the silent statesman—a kind of

C 2

mute protest against his master's undiplomatic violence, and as an omen of a possible understanding to be arrived at yet. Otherwise Dain was not uneasy. Although recognising the justice of Lakamba's surmise that he had come back to Sambir only for the sake of the white man's daughter, yet he was not conscious of any childish lack of understanding, as suggested by Babalatchi. In fact, Dain knew very well that Lakamba was too deeply implicated in the gun-powder smuggling to care for an investigation by the Dutch authorities into that matter. When sent off by his father, the independent Rajah of Bali, at the time when the hostilities between Dutch and Malay threatened to spread from Sumatra over the whole archipelago, Dain had found all the big traders deaf to his guarded proposals, and above the temptation of the great prices he was ready to give for gun-powder. He went to Sambir as a last and almost hopeless resort, having heard in Macassar of the white man there, and of the regular steamer trading from Singapore—allured also by the fact that there was no Dutch resident on the river, which would make things easier, no doubt. His hopes got nearly wrecked against the stubborn loyalty of Lakamba arising from well-understood self-interest; but at last the young man's generosity, his persuasive enthusiasm, the prestige of his father's great name, overpowered the prudent hesitation of the ruler of Sambir. Lakamba would have nothing to do himself with any illegal traffic. He also objected to the Arabs being made use of in that matter; but he suggested Almayer, saying that he was a weak man easily persuaded, and that his friend, the English captain of the steamer, could be made very useful—very likely even would join in the business, smuggling the powder in the steamer without Abdulla's knowledge. There again Dain met in Almayer with unexpected resistance; Lakamba had to send Babalatchi over with the solemn promise that his eyes would be shut in friendship for the white man, Dain paying for the promise and the friendship in good silver guilders of the hated Orang Blanda. Almayer, at last consenting, said the powder would be obtained, but Dain must trust him with dollars to send to Singapore in payment for it. He would induce Ford to buy and smuggle it in the steamer on board the brig. He did not want any money for himself out of the transaction, but Dain must help him in his great enterprise after sending off the brig. Almayer had explained to Dain that he could not trust Lakamba alone in that matter; he would be afraid of losing his treasure and his life through the cupidity of the Rajah; yet the Rajah had to be told, and insisted on taking a share in that operation, or else his eyes would remain shut no longer. To this Almayer had to submit. Had Dain not seen Nina he would have probably refused to engage himself and his men in the projected expedition to Gunong Mas—the mountain of gold. As it was he intended to return with half of his men as soon as the brig was clear of the reefs, but the persistent chase given him by the Dutch frigate had forced him to run south and ultimately to wreck and destroy his vessel in order to preserve his liberty or perhaps even his life. Yes, he had come back to Sambir for Nina, although aware that the Dutch would look for him there, but he had also calculated his chances of safety in Lakamba's hands. For all his ferocious talk, the merciful ruler would not kill him, for he had long ago been impressed with the notion that Dain possessed the secret of the white man's treasure; neither would he give him up to the Dutch, for fear of some fatal disclosure of complicity in the treasonable trade. So Dain felt tolerably secure as he sat meditating quietly his answer to the Rajah's bloodthirsty speech. Yes, he would point out to him the aspect of his position should he—Dain—fall into the hands of the Dutch and should he speak the truth. He would have nothing more to lose then, and he would speak the truth. And if he did return to Sambir, disturbing thereby Lakamba's peace of mind, what then? He came to look after his property. Did he not pour a stream of silver into Mrs. Almayer's greedy lap? He had paid, for the girl, a price worthy of a great prince, although unworthy of that delightfully maddening creature for whom his untamed soul longed in an intensity of desire far more tormenting than the sharpest pain. He wanted his happiness. He had the right to be in Sambir.

He rose, and, approaching the table, leaned both his elbows on it; Lakamba responsively edged his seat a little closer, while Babalatchi scrambled to his feet and thrust his inquisitive head between his master's and Dain's. They interchanged their ideas rapidly, speaking in whispers into each other's faces, very close now, Dain suggesting, Lakamba contradicting, Babalatchi conciliating and anxious in his vivid apprehension of coming difficulties. He spoke most, whispering earnestly, turning his head slowly from side to side so as to bring his solitary eye to bear upon each of his interlocutors in turn. Why should there be strife? said he. Let Tuan Dain, whom he loved only less than his master, go trustfully into hiding. There were many places for that. Bulangi's house away in the clearing was best. Bulangi was a safe man. In the network of crooked channels no white man could find his way. White men were strong, but very foolish. It was undesirable to fight them, but deception was easy. They were like silly women—they did not know the use of reason, and he was a match for any of them— went on Babalatchi, with all the confidence of deficient experience. Probably the Dutch would seek Almayer. Maybe they would take away their countryman if they were suspicious of him. That would be good. After the Dutch went away Lakamba and Dain would get the treasure without any trouble, and there would be one person less to share it. Did he not speak wisdom? Will Tuan Dain go to Bulangi's house till the danger is over, go at once?

Dain accepted this suggestion of going into hiding with a certain sense of conferring a favour upon Lakamba and the anxious statesman, but he met the proposal of going at once with a decided no, looking Babalatchi meaningly in the eye. The statesman sighed as a man accepting the inevitable would do, and pointed silently towards the other bank of the river. Dain bent his head slowly.

"Yes, I am going there," he said.

"Before the day comes?" asked Babalatchi.

"I am going there now," answered Dain, decisively. "The Orang Blanda will not be here before to-morrow night, perhaps, and I must tell Almayer of our arrangements."

"No, Tuan. No; say nothing," protested Babalatchi. "I will go over myself at sunrise and let him know."

"I will see," said Dain, preparing to go.

The thunderstorm was recommencing outside, the heavy clouds hanging low overhead now. There was a constant rumble of distant thunder punctuated by the nearer sharp crashes, and in the continuous play of blue lightning the woods and the river showed fitfully, with all the elusive distinctness of detail characteristic of such a scene. Outside the door of the Rajah's house Dain and Babalatchi stood on the shaking verandah as if dazed and stunned by the violence of the storm. They stood there amongst the cowering forms of the Rajah's slaves and retainers seeking shelter from the rain, and Dain called aloud to his boatmen, who responded with an unanimous "Ada! Tuan!" while they looked uneasily at the river.

"This is a great flood!" shouted Babalatchi into Dain's ear. "The river is very angry. Look! Look at the drifting logs! Can you go?"

Dain glanced doubtfully on the livid expanse of seething water bounded far away on the other side by the narrow black line of the forests. Suddenly, in a vivid white flash, the low point of land with the bending trees on it and Almayer's house leaped into view, flickered and disappeared. Dain pushed Babalatchi aside and ran down to the water-gate followed by his shivering boatmen.

Babalatchi backed slowly in and closed the door, then turned round and looked silently upon Lakamba. The Rajah sat still, glaring stonily upon the table, and Babalatchi gazed curiously at the perplexed mood of the man he had served so many years through good and evil fortune. No doubt the one-eyed statesman felt within his savage and much sophisticated breast the unwonted feelings of sympathy with, and perhaps even pity for, the man he called his master. From the safe position of a confidential adviser, he

could, in the dim vista of past years, see himself—a casual
cut-throat—finding shelter under that man's roof in the
modest rice-clearing of early beginnings.  Then came a long
period of unbroken success, of wise counsels, and deep plottings resolutely carried out by the fearless Lakamba, till the
whole east coast from Poulo Laut to Tanjong Batu listened
to Babalatchi's wisdom speaking through the mouth of the
ruler of Sambir.  In those long years how many dangers
escaped, how many enemies bravely faced, how many white
men successfully circumvented!  And now he looked upon
the result of so many years of patient toil : the fearless
Lakamba cowed by the shadow of an impending trouble.
The ruler was growing old, and Babalatchi, aware of an
uneasy feeling at the pit of his stomach, put both his hands
there with a suddenly vivid and sad perception of the fact
that he himself was growing old too ; that the time of
reckless daring was past for both of them, and that they
had to seek refuge in prudent cunning.  They wanted peace ;
they were disposed to reform ;  they were ready even to
retrench, so as to have the wherewithal to bribe the evil
days away, if bribed away they could be.  Babalatchi sighed
for the second time that night as he squatted again at his
master's feet and tendered him his betel-nut box in mute
sympathy.  And they sat there in close yet silent communion
of betel-nut chewers, moving their jaws slowly, expectorating
decorously into the wide-mouthed brass vessel they passed
to one another, and listening to the awful din of the battling
elements outside.

"There is a very great flood," remarked Babalatchi,
sadly.

"Yes," said Lakamba.  "Did Dain go ? "

"He went, Tuan.  He ran down to the river like a man
possessed of the Sheitan himself."

There was another long pause.

"He may get drowned," suggested Lakamba at last, with
some show of interest.

"The floating logs are many," answered Babalatchi,
"but he is a good swimmer," he added languidly.

" He ought to live," said Lakamba; " he knows where the treasure is."

Babalatchi assented with an ill-humoured grunt. His want of success in penetrating the white man's secret as to the locality where the gold was to be found was a sore point with the statesman of Sambir, as the only conspicuous failure in an otherwise brilliant career.

A great peace had now succeeded the turmoil of the storm. Only the little belated clouds, which hurried past overhead to catch up the main body flashing silently in the distance, sent down short showers that pattered softly with a soothing hiss over the palm-leaf roof.

Lakamba roused himself from his apathy with an appearance of having grasped the situation at last.

" Babalatchi," he called briskly, giving him a slight kick.

" Ada Tuan!  I am listening."

" If the Orang Blanda come here, Babalatchi, and take Almayer to Batavia to punish him for smuggling gunpowder, what will he do, you think? "

" I do not know, Tuan."

" You are a fool," commented Lakamba, exultingly.  " He will tell them where the treasure is, so as to find mercy. He will."

Babalatchi looked up at his master and nodded his head with by no means a joyful surprise.  He had not thought of this; there was a new complication.

" Almayer must die," said Lakamba, decisively, " to make our secret safe.  He must die quietly, Babalatchi.  You must do it."

Babalatchi assented, and rose wearily to his feet.  " To-morrow? " he asked.

" Yes; before the Dutch come.  He drinks much coffee," answered Lakamba, with seeming irrelevancy.

Babalatchi stretched himself yawning, but Lakamba, in the flattering consciousness of a knotty problem solved by his own unaided intellectual efforts, grew suddenly very wakeful.

" Babalatchi," he said to the exhausted statesman, " fetch

the box of music the white captain gave me. I cannot sleep."

At this order a deep shade of melancholy settled upon Babalatchi's features. He went reluctantly behind the curtain and soon reappeared carrying in his arms a small hand-organ, which he put down on the table with an air of deep dejection. Lakamba settled himself comfortably in his arm-chair.

" Turn, Babalatchi, turn," he murmured, with closed eyes.

Babalatchi's hand grasped the handle with the energy of despair, and as he turned, the deep gloom on his countenance changed into an expression of hopeless resignation. Through the open shutter the notes of Verdi's music floated out on the great silence over the river and forest. Lakamba listened with closed eyes and a delighted smile ; Babalatchi turned, at times dozing off and swaying over, then catching himself up in a great fright with a few quick turns of the handle. Nature slept in an exhausted repose after the fierce turmoil, while under the unsteady hand of the statesman of Sambir the Trovatore fitfully wept, wailed, and bade good-bye to his Leonore again and again in a mournful round of tearful and endless iteration.

## CHAPTER VII

THE bright sunshine of the clear mistless morning, after the stormy night, flooded the main path of the settlement leading from the low shore of the Pantai branch of the river to the gate of Abdulla's compound. The path was deserted this morning ; it stretched its dark yellow surface, hard beaten by the tramp of many bare feet, between the clusters of palm trees, whose tall trunks barred it with strong black lines at irregular intervals, while the newly risen sun threw the shadows of their leafy heads far away over the roofs of the buildings lining the river, even over the river itself as it flowed swiftly and silently past the deserted houses. For the houses were deserted too. On the narrow strip of trodden grass intervening between their open doors and the road, the morning fire smouldered untended, sending thin fluted columns of smoke into the cool air, and spreading the thinnest veil of mysterious blue haze over the sunlit solitude of the settlement. Almayer, just out of his hammock, gazed sleepily at the unwonted appearance of Sambir, wondering vaguely at the absence of life. His own house was very quiet; he could not hear his wife's voice, nor the sound of Nina's footsteps in the big room, opening on the verandah, which he called his sitting-room, whenever, in the company of white men, he wished to assert his claims to the common-place decencies of civilisation. Nobody ever sat there; there was nothing there to sit upon, for Mrs. Almayer in her savage moods, when excited by the reminiscences of the piratical period of her life, had torn off the curtains to make sarongs for the slave girls, and had burnt the showy furniture piecemeal to cook the family rice. But Almayer was not thinking of his furniture now. He was thinking of Dain's return, of Dain's nocturnal interview with Lakamba, of its possible influence on his long-matured plans, now nearing the period of their execution. He was also uneasy at the non-appearance of Dain who had promised him an early visit. "The fellow had plenty of time to cross the river," he mused, "and there was so much to be done to-day. The settling of details for the early start on the morrow; the launching of the boats; the thousand and one finishing touches. For the expedition must start complete, nothing should be forgotten, nothing should——"

The sense of the unwonted solitude grew upon him suddenly, and in the unusual silence he caught himself long-ing even for the usually unwelcome sound of his wife's voice to break the oppressive stillness which seemed, to his fright-ened fancy, to portend the advent of some new misfortune. "What has happened?" he muttered half aloud, as he shuffled in his imperfectly adjusted slippers towards the balustrade of the verandah. " Is everybody asleep or dead ? "

The settlement was alive and very much awake. It was awake ever since the early break of day, when Mahmat Banjer, in a fit of unheard-of energy, arose and, taking up his hatchet, stepped over the sleeping forms of his two wives and walked shivering to the water's edge to make sure that the new house he was building had not floated away during the night.

The house was being built by the enterprising Mahmat on a large raft, and he had securely moored it just inside the muddy point of land at the junction of the two branches of the Pantai so as to be out of the way of drifting logs that would no doubt strand on the point during the freshet. Mahmat walked through the wet grass saying bourrouh, and cursing softly to himself the hard necessities of active life that drove him from his warm couch into the cold of the morning. A glance showed him that his house was still there, and he congratulated himself on his foresight in haul-ing it out of harm's way, for the increasing light showed him a confused wrack of drift-logs, half-stranded on the muddy flat, interlocked into a shapeless raft by their branches, tossing to and fro and grinding together in the eddy caused by the meeting currents of the two branches of the river. Mahmat walked down to the water's edge to examine the rattan moorings of his house just as the sun cleared the trees of the forest on the opposite shore. As he bent over the fastenings he glanced again carelessly at the unquiet jumble of logs and saw there something that caused him to drop his hatchet and stand up, shading his eyes with his hand from the rays of the rising sun. It was something red, and the logs rolled over it, at times closing round it, sometimes hiding it. It looked to him at first like a strip of red cloth. The next moment Mahmat had made it out and raised a great shout.

" Ah ya ! There ! " yelled Mahmat. " There's a man amongst the logs." He put the palms of his hand to his lips and shouted, enunciating distinctly, his face turned

towards the settlement : " There's a body of a man in the
river ! Come and see ! A dead—stranger ! "

The women of the nearest house were already outside
kindling the fires and husking the morning rice. They took
up the cry shrilly, and it travelled so from house to house,
dying away in the distance. The men rushed out excited
but silent, and ran towards the muddy point where the
unconscious logs tossed and ground and bumped and rolled
over the dead stranger with the stupid persistency of inanimate things. The women followed, neglecting their
domestic duties and disregarding the possibilities of domestic
discontent, while groups of children brought up the rear,
warbling joyously, in the delight of unexpected excitement.

Almayer called aloud for his wife and daughter, but
receiving no response, stood listening intently. The murmur
of the crowd reached him faintly, bringing with it the
assurance of some unusual event. He glanced at the river
just as he was going to leave the verandah and checked
himself at the sight of a small canoe crossing over from the
Rajah's landing-place. The solitary occupant (in whom
Almayer soon recognised Babalatchi) effected the crossing a
little below the house and paddled up to the Lingard jetty
in the dead water under the bank. Babalatchi clambered
out slowly and went on fastening his canoe with fastidious
care, as if not in a hurry to meet Almayer, whom he saw
looking at him from the verandah. This delay gave Almayer
time to notice and greatly wonder at Babalatchi's official
get-up. The statesman of Sambir was clad in a costume
befitting his high rank. A loudly checkered sarong encircled
his waist, and from its many folds peeped out the silver hilt
of the kriss that saw the light only on great festivals or during
official receptions. Over the left shoulder and across the
otherwise unclad breast of the aged diplomatist glistened a
patent leather belt bearing a brass plate with the arms of
Netherlands under the inscription, " Sultan of Sambir."
Babalatchi's head was covered by a red turban, whose fringed
ends falling over the left cheek and shoulder gave to his
aged face a ludicrous expression of joyous recklessness.

When the canoe was at last fastened to his satisfaction he
straightened himself up, shaking down the folds of his sarong,
and moved with long strides towards Almayer's house,
swinging regularly his long ebony staff, whose gold head
ornamented with precious stones flashed in the morning
sun. Almayer waved his hand to the right towards the
point of land, to him invisible, but in full view from the
jetty.

"Oh, Babalatchi! oh!" he called out; "what is the
matter there? can you see?"

Babalatchi stopped and gazed intently at the crowd on
the river bank, and after a little while the astonished Almayer
saw him leave the path, gather up his sarong in one hand,
and break into a trot through the grass towards the muddy
point. Almayer, now greatly interested, ran down the
steps of the verandah. The murmur of men's voices and
the shrill cries of women reached him quite distinctly now,
and as soon as he turned the corner of his house he could
see the crowd on the low promontory swaying and pushing
round some object of interest. He could indistinctly hear
Babalatchi's voice, then the crowd opened before the aged
statesman and closed after him with an excited hum, ending
in a loud shout.

As Almayer approached the throng a man ran out and
rushed past him towards the settlement, unheeding his call
to stop and explain the cause of this excitement. On the
very outskirts of the crowd Almayer found himself arrested
by an unyielding mass of humanity, regardless of his entreaties
for a passage, insensible to his gentle pushes as he tried to
work his way through it towards the riverside.

In the midst of his gentle and slow progress he fancied
suddenly he had heard his wife's voice in the thickest of the
throng. He could not mistake very well Mrs. Almayer's
high-pitched tones, yet the words were too indistinct for
him to understand their purport. He paused in his
endeavours to make a passage for himself, intending to get
some intelligence from those around him, when a long and
piercing shriek rent the air, silencing the murmurs of the

crowd and the voices of his informants. For a moment Almayer remained as if turned into stone with astonishment and horror, for he was certain now that he had heard his wife wailing for the dead. He remembered Nina's unusual absence, and maddened by his apprehensions as to her safety, he pushed blindly and violently forward, the crowd falling back with cries of surprise and pain before his frantic advance.

On the point of land in a little clear space lay the body of the stranger just hauled out from amongst the logs. On one side stood Babalatchi, his chin resting on the head of his staff and his one eye gazing steadily at the shapeless mass of broken limbs, torn flesh, and bloodstained rags. As Almayer burst through the ring of horrified spectators, Mrs. Almayer threw her own head-veil over the upturned face of the drowned man, and, squatting by it, with another mournful howl, sent a shiver through the now silent crowd. Mahmat, dripping wet, turned to Almayer, eager to tell his tale.

In the first moment of reaction from the anguish of his fear the sunshine seemed to waver before Almayer's eyes, and he listened to words spoken around him without comprehending their meaning. When, by a strong effort of will, he regained the possession of his senses, Mahmat was saying—

"That is the way, Tuan. His sarong was caught in the broken branch, and he hung with his head under water. When I saw what it was I did not want it here. I wanted it to get clear and drift away. Why should we bury a stranger in the midst of our houses for his ghost to frighten our women and children? Have we not enough ghosts about this place?"

A murmur of approval interrupted him here. Mahmat looked reproachfully at Babalatchi.

"But the Tuan Babalatchi ordered me to drag the body ashore"—he went on looking round at his audience, but addressing himself only to Almayer—"and I dragged him by the feet; in through the mud I have dragged him,

although my heart longed to see him float down the river
to strand perchance on Bulangi's clearing—may his father's
grave be defiled ! "

There was subdued laughter at this, for the enmity of
Mahmat and Bulangi was a matter of common notoriety and
of undying interest to the inhabitants of Sambir. In
the midst of that mirth Mrs. Almayer wailed suddenly
again.

"Allah ! What ails the woman ! " exclaimed Mahmat,
angrily. "Here, I have touched this carcass which came
from nobody knows where, and have most likely defiled
myself before eating rice. By orders of Tuan Babalatchi I
did this thing to please the white man. Are you pleased,
O Tuan Almayer ? And what will be my recompense ?
Tuan Babalatchi said a recompense there will be, and from
you. Now consider. I have been defiled, and if not
defiled I may be under the spell. Look at his anklets !
Who ever heard of a corpse appearing during the night
amongst the logs with gold anklets on its legs ? There is
witchcraft there. However," added Mahmat, after a
reflective pause, "I will have the anklet if there is permission, for I have a charm against the ghosts and am not
afraid. God is great ! "

A fresh outburst of noisy grief from Mrs. Almayer checked
the flow of Mahmat's eloquence. Almayer, bewildered,
looked in turn at his wife, at Mahmat, at Babalatchi, and
at last arrested his fascinated gaze on the body lying on the
mud with covered face in a grotesquely unnatural contortion
of mangled and broken limbs, one twisted and lacerated
arm, with white bones protruding in many places through
the torn flesh, stretched out ; the hand with outspread fingers
nearly touching his foot.

"Do you know who this is ? " he asked of Babalatchi, in a
low voice.

Babalatchi, staring straight before him, hardly moved his
lips, while Mrs. Almayer's persistent lamentations drowned
the whisper of his murmured reply intended only for
Almayer's ear.

"It was fate. Look at your feet, white man. I can see a ring on those torn fingers which I know well."

Saying this, Babalatchi stepped carelessly forward, putting his foot as if accidentally on the hand of the corpse and pressing it into the soft mud. He swung his staff menacingly towards the crowd, which fell back a little.

"Go away," he said sternly, "and send your women to their cooking fires, which they ought not to have left to run after a dead stranger. This is men's work here. I take him now in the name of the Rajah. Let no man remain here but Tuan Almayer's slaves. Now go!"

The crowd reluctantly began to disperse. The women went first, dragging away the children that hung back with all their weight on the maternal hand. The men strolled slowly after them in ever forming and changing groups that gradually dissolved as they neared the settlement and every man regained his own house with steps quickened by the hungry anticipation of the morning rice. Only on the slight elevation where the land sloped down towards the muddy point a few men, either friends or enemies of Mahmat, remained gazing curiously for some time longer at the small group standing around the body on the river bank.

"I do not understand what you mean, Babalatchi," said Almayer. "What is the ring you are talking about? Whoever he is, you have trodden the poor fellow's hand right into the mud. Uncover his face," he went on, addressing Mrs. Almayer, who, squatting by the head of the corpse, rocked herself to and fro, shaking from time to time her dishevelled grey locks, and muttering mournfully.

"Hai!" exclaimed Mahmat, who had lingered close by. "Look, Tuan; the logs came together so," and here he pressed the palms of his hands together, "and his head must have been between them, and now there is no face for you to look at. There are his flesh and his bones, the nose, and the lips, and maybe his eyes, but nobody could tell the one from the other. It was written the day he was born that no man could look at him in death and be able to say, ' This is my friend's face.' "

" Silence, Mahmat; enough ! " said Babalatchi, " and take thy eyes off his anklet, thou eater of pigs' flesh. Tuan Almayer," he went on, lowering his voice, " have you seen Dain this morning ? "

Almayer opened his eyes wide and looked alarmed. " No," he said quickly ; " haven't you seen him ? Is he not with the Rajah ? I am waiting ; why does he not come ? "

Babalatchi nodded his head sadly.

" He is come, Tuan. He left last night when the storm was great and the river spoke angrily. The night was very black, but he had within him a light that showed the way to your house as smooth as a narrow backwater, and the many logs no bigger than wisps of dried grass. Therefore he went ; and now he lies here." And Babalatchi nodded his head towards the body.

" How can you tell ? " said Almayer, excitedly, pushing his wife aside. He snatched the cover off and looked at the formless mass of flesh, hair, and drying mud, where the face of the drowned man should have been. " Nobody can tell," he added, turning away with a shudder.

Babalatchi was on his knees wiping the mud from the stiffened fingers of the outstretched hand. He rose to his feet and flashed before Almayer's eyes a gold ring set with a large green stone.

" You know this well," he said. " This never left Dain's hand. I had to tear the flesh now to get it off. Do you believe now ? "

Almayer raised his hands to his head and let them fall listlessly by his side in the utter abandonment of despair. Babalatchi, looking at him curiously, was astonished to see him smile. A strange fancy had taken possession of Almayer's brain, distracted by this new misfortune. It seemed to him that for many years he had been falling into a deep precipice. Day after day, month after month, year after year, he had been falling, falling, falling ; it was a smooth, round, black thing, and the black walls had been rushing upwards with wearisome rapidity. A great rush, the noise of which he fancied he could hear yet; and now, with an awful shock, he had reached the bottom, and behold! he was alive and whole, and Dain was dead with all his bones broken. It struck him as funny. A dead Malay; he had seen many dead Malays without any emotion; and now he felt inclined to weep, but it was over the fate of a white man he knew; a man that fell over a deep precipice and did not die. He seemed somehow to himself to be standing on one side, a little way off, looking at a certain Almayer who was in great trouble. Poor, poor fellow! Why doesn't he cut his throat? He wished to encourage him; he was very anxious to see him lying dead over that other corpse. Why does he not die and end this suffering? He groaned aloud unconsciously and started with affright at the sound of his own voice. Was he going mad? Terrified by the thought he turned away and ran towards his house repeating to himself, " I am not going mad; of course not, no, no, no ! " He tried to keep a firm hold of the idea. Not mad, not mad. He stumbled as he ran blindly up the steps repeating fast and ever faster those words wherein seemed to lie his salvation. He saw Nina standing there, and wished to say something to her, but could not remember what, in his extreme anxiety not to forget that he was not going mad, which he still kept repeating mentally as he ran round the table, till he stumbled against one of the arm-chairs and dropped into it exhausted. He sat staring wildly at Nina, still assuring himself mentally of his own sanity and wondering why the girl shrank from him in open-eyed alarm. What was the matter with her? This was foolish. He struck the table violently with his clenched fist and shouted hoarsely, " Give me some gin ! Run ! " Then, while Nina ran off, he remained in the chair, very still and quiet, astonished at the noise he had made.

Nina returned with a tumbler half filled with gin, and found her father staring absently before him. Almayer felt very tired now, as if he had come from a long journey. He felt as if he had walked miles and miles that morning and now wanted to rest very much. He took the tumbler with a shaking hand, and as he drank his teeth chattered against the glass which he drained and set down heavily on the table. He turned his eyes slowly towards Nina standing beside him, and said steadily—

"Now all is over, Nina. He is dead, and I may as well burn all my boats."

He felt very proud of being able to speak so calmly. Decidedly he was not going mad. This certitude was very comforting, and he went on talking about the finding of the body, listening to his own voice complacently. Nina stood quietly, her hand resting lightly on her father's shoulder, her face unmoved, but every line of her features, the attitude of her whole body expressing the most keen and anxious attention.

"And so Dain is dead," she said coldly, when her father ceased speaking.

Almayer's elaborately calm demeanour gave way in a moment to an outburst of violent indignation.

"You stand there as if you were only half alive, and talk to me," he exclaimed angrily, "as if it was a matter of no importance. Yes, he is dead! Do you understand? Dead! What do you care? You never cared; you saw me struggle, and work, and strive, unmoved; and my suffering you could never see. No, never. You have no heart, and you have no mind, or you would have understood that it was for you, for your happiness I was working. I wanted to be rich; I wanted to get away from here. I wanted to see white men bowing low before the power of your beauty and your wealth. Old as I am I wished to seek a strange land, a civilisation to which I am a stranger, so as to find a new life in the contemplation of your high fortunes, of your triumphs, of your happiness. For that I bore patiently the burden of work, of disappointment, of humiliation amongst these savages here, and I had it all nearly in my grasp."

He looked at his daughter's attentive face and jumped to his feet upsetting the chair.

"Do you hear? I had it all there; so; within reach of my hand."

He paused, trying to keep down his rising anger, and failed.

"Have you no feeling?" he went on. "Have you lived without hope?" Nina's silence exasperated him; his voice rose, although he tried to master his feelings.

"Are you content to live in this misery and die in this wretched hole? Say something, Nina; have you no sympathy? Have you no word of comfort for me? I that loved you so."

He waited for a while for an answer, and receiving none shook his fist in his daughter's face.

"I believe you are an idiot!" he yelled.

He looked round for the chair, picked it up and sat down stiffly. His anger was dead within him, and he felt ashamed of his outburst, yet relieved to think that now he had laid clear before his daughter the inner meaning of his life. He thought so in perfect good faith, deceived by the emotional estimate of his motives, unable to see the crookedness of his ways, the unreality of his aims, the futility of his regrets. And now his heart was filled only with a great tenderness and love for his daughter. He wanted to see her miserable, and to share with her his despair; but he wanted it only as all weak natures long for a companionship in misfortune with beings innocent of its cause. If she suffered herself she would understand and pity him; but now she would not, or could not, find one word of comfort or love for him in his dire extremity. The sense of his absolute loneliness came home to his heart with a force that made him shudder. He swayed and fell forward with his face on the table, his arms stretched straight out, extended and rigid. Nina made a quick movement towards her father and stood looking at the grey head, on the broad shoulders shaken convulsively by the violence of feelings that found relief at last in sobs and tears.

Nina sighed deeply and moved away from the table. Her features lost the appearance of stony indifference that had exasperated her father into his outburst of anger and sorrow. The expression of her face, now unseen by her father, underwent a rapid change. She had listened to Almayer's appeal for sympathy, for one word of comfort, apparently indifferent, yet with her breast torn by conflicting impulses raised unexpectedly by events she had not foreseen, or at least did not expect to happen so soon. With her heart deeply moved by the sight of Almayer's misery, knowing it in her power to end it with a word, longing to bring peace to that troubled heart, she heard with terror the voice of her overpowering love commanding her to be silent. And she submitted after a short and fierce struggle of her old self against the new principle of her life. She wrapped herself up in absolute silence, the only safeguard against some fatal admission. She could not trust herself to make a sign, to murmur a word for fear of saying too much; and the very violence of the feelings that stirred the innermost recesses of her soul seemed to turn her person into a stone. The dilated nostrils and the flashing eyes were the only signs of the storm raging within, and those signs of his daughter's emotion Almayer did not see, for his sight was dimmed by self-pity, by anger, and by despair.

Had Almayer looked at his daughter as she leant over the front rail of the verandah he could have seen the expression of indifference give way to a look of pain, and that again pass away, leaving the glorious beauty of her face marred by deep-drawn lines of watchful anxiety. The long grass in the neglected courtyard stood very straight before her eyes in the noonday heat. From the river-bank there were voices and a shuffle of bare feet approaching the house; Babalatchi could be heard giving directions to Almayer's men, and Mrs. Almayer's subdued wailing became audible as the small procession bearing the body of the drowned man and headed by that sorrowful matron turned the corner of the house. Babalatchi had taken the broken anklet off the man's leg, and now held it in his hand as he moved by the side of the bearers, while Mahmat lingered behind timidly, in the hopes of the promised reward.

"Lay him there," said Babalatchi to Almayer's men, pointing to a pile of drying planks in front of the verandah. "Lay him there. He was a Kaffir and the son of a dog, and he was the white man's friend. He drank the white man's strong water," he added, with affected horror. "That I have seen myself."

The men stretched out the broken limbs on two planks they had laid level, while Mrs. Almayer covered the body with a piece of white cotton cloth, and after whispering for some time with Babalatchi departed to her domestic duties. Almayer's men, after laying down their burden, dispersed themselves in quest of shady spots wherein to idle the day away. Babalatchi was left alone by the corpse that laid rigid under the white cloth in the bright sunshine.

Nina came down the steps and joined Babalatchi, who put his hand to his forehead, and squatted down with great deference.

"You have a bangle there," said Nina, looking down on Babalatchi's upturned face and into his solitary eye.

"I have, Mem Putih," returned the polite statesman. Then turning towards Mahmat he beckoned him closer, calling out, "Come here!"

Mahmat approached with some hesitation. He avoided looking at Nina, but fixed his eyes on Babalatchi.

"Now, listen," said Babalatchi, sharply. "The ring and the anklet you have seen, and you know they belonged to Dain the trader, and to no other. Dain returned last night in a canoe. He spoke with the Rajah, and in the middle of the night left to cross over to the white man's house. There was a great flood, and this morning you found him in the river."

"By his feet I dragged him out," muttered Mahmat under his breath. "Tuan Babalatchi, there will be a recompense!" he exclaimed aloud.

Babalatchi held up the gold bangle before Mahmat's eyes. "What I have told you, Mahmat, is for all ears. What I give you now is for your eyes only. Take."

Mahmat took the bangle eagerly and hid it in the folds of

his waist-cloth. "Am I a fool to show this thing in a house with three women in it?" he growled. "But I shall tell them about Dain the trader, and there will be talk enough."

He turned and went away, increasing his pace as soon as he was outside Almayer's compound.

Babalatchi looked after him till he disappeared behind the bushes. "Have I done well, Mem Putih?" he asked, humbly addressing Nina.

"You have," answered Nina. "The ring you may keep yourself."

Babalatchi touched his lips and forehead, and scrambled to his feet. He looked at Nina, as if expecting her to say something more, but Nina turned towards the house and went up the steps, motioning him away with her hand.

Babalatchi picked up his staff and prepared to go. It was very warm, and he did not care for the long pull to the Rajah's house. Yet he must go and tell the Rajah—tell of the event; of the change in his plans; of all his suspicions. He walked to the jetty and began casting off the rattan painter of his canoe.

The broad expanse of the lower reach, with its shimmering surface dotted by the black specks of the fishing canoes, lay before his eyes. The fishermen seemed to be racing. Babalatchi paused in his work, and looked on with sudden interest. The man in the foremost canoe, now within hail of the first houses of Sambir, laid in his paddle and stood up shouting—

"The boats! the boats! The man-of-war's boats are coming! They are here!"

In a moment the settlement was again alive with people rushing to the riverside. The men began to unfasten their boats, the women stood in groups looking towards the bend down the river. Above the trees lining the reach a slight puff of smoke appeared like a black stain on the brilliant blue of the cloudless sky.

Babalatchi stood perplexed, the painter in his hand. He looked down the reach, then up towards Almayer's house, and back again at the river as if undecided what to do. At

last he made the canoe fast again hastily, and ran towards
the house and up the steps of the verandah.

"Tuan! Tuan!" he called, eagerly. "The boats are
coming. The man-of-war's boats. You had better get
ready. The officers will come here, I know."

Almayer lifted his head slowly from the table, and looked
at him stupidly.

"Mem Putih!" exclaimed Babalatchi to Nina, "look at
him. He does not hear. You must take care," he added
meaningly.

Nina nodded to him with an uncertain smile, and was going
to speak, when a sharp report from the gun mounted in the
bow of the steam launch that was just then coming into
view arrested the words on her parted lips. The smile died
out, and was replaced by the old look of anxious attention.
From the hills far away the echo came back like a long-drawn
and mournful sigh, as if the land had sent it in answer to
the voice of its masters.

## CHAPTER VIII

THE news as to the identity of the body lying now in
Almayer's compound spread rapidly over the settlement.
During the forenoon most of the inhabitants remained in
the long street discussing the mysterious return and the
unexpected death of the man who had become known to
them as the trader. His arrival during the north-east
monsoon, his long sojourn in their midst, his sudden departure with his brig, and, above all, the mysterious appearance
of the body, said to be his, amongst the logs, were subjects
to wonder at and to talk over and over again with undimin-
ished interest. Mahmat moved from house to house and
from group to group, always ready to repeat his tale: how
he saw the body caught by the sarong in a forked log; how
Mrs. Almayer coming, one of the first, at his cries, recognised it, even before he had it hauled on shore; how Baba-

latchi ordered him to bring it out of the water. "By the feet I dragged him in, and there was no head," exclaimed Mahmat, "and how could the white man's wife know who it was? She was a witch, it was well known. And did you see how the white man himself ran away at the sight of the body? Like a deer he ran!" And here Mahmat imitated Almayer's long strides, to the great joy of the beholders. And for all his trouble he had nothing. The ring with the green stone Tuan Babalatchi kept. "Nothing! Nothing!" He spat down at his feet in sign of disgust, and left that group to seek further on a fresh audience.

The news spreading to the furthermost parts of the settlement found out Abdulla in the cool recess of his godown, where he sat overlooking his Arab clerks and the men loading and unloading the up-country canoes. Reshid, who was busy on the jetty, was summoned into his uncle's presence and found him, as usual, very calm and even cheerful, but very much surprised. The rumour of the capture or destruction of Dain's brig had reached the Arab's ears three days before from the sea-fishermen and through the dwellers on the lower reaches of the river. It had been passed up-stream from neighbour to neighbour till Bulangi, whose clearing was nearest to the settlement, had brought that news himself to Abdulla whose favour he courted. But rumour also spoke of a fight and of Dain's death on board his own vessel. And now all the settlement talked of Dain's visit to the Rajah and of his death when crossing the river in the dark to see Almayer. They could not understand this. Reshid thought that it was very strange. He felt uneasy and doubtful. But Abdulla, after the first shock of surprise, with the old age's dislike for solving riddles, showed a becoming resignation. He remarked that the man was dead now at all events, and consequently no more dangerous. Where was the use to wonder at the decrees of Fate, especially if they were propitious to the True Believers? And with a pious ejaculation to Allah the Merciful, the Compassionate, Abdulla seemed to regard the incident as closed for the present.

Not so Reshid. He lingered by his uncle, pulling thoughtfully his neatly trimmed beard.

"There are many lies," he murmured. "He has been dead once before, and came to life to die again now. The Dutch will be here before many days and clamour for the man. Shall I not believe my eyes sooner than the tongues of women and idle men?"

"They say that the body is being taken to Almayer's compound," said Abdulla. "If you want to go there you must go before the Dutch arrive here. Go late. It should not be said that we have been seen inside that man's enclosure lately."

Reshid assented to the truth of this last remark and left his uncle's side. He leaned against the lintel of the big doorway and looked idly across the courtyard through the open gate on to the main road of the settlement. It lay empty, straight, and yellow under the flood of light. In the hot noontide the smooth trunks of palm trees, the outlines of the houses, and away there at the other end of the road the roof of Almayer's house visible over the bushes on the dark background of forest, seemed to quiver in the heat radiating from the steaming earth. Swarms of yellow butterflies rose, and settled to rise again in short flights before Reshid's half-closed eyes. From under his feet arose the dull hum of insects in the long grass of the courtyard. He looked on sleepily.

From one side of the side paths amongst the houses a woman stepped out on the road, a slight girlish figure walking under the shade of a large tray balanced on its head. The consciousness of something moving stirred Reshid's half-sleeping senses into a comparative wakefulness. He recognised Taminah, Bulangi's slave-girl, with her tray of cakes for sale—an apparition of daily recurrence and of no importance whatever. She was going towards Almayer's house. She could be made useful. He roused himself up and ran towards the gate calling out, "Taminah O!" The girl stopped, hesitated, and came back slowly. Reshid waited, signing to her impatiently to come nearer.

D

When near Reshid Taminah stood with downcast eyes. Reshid looked at her a while before he asked—

"Are you going to Almayer's house? They say in the settlement that Dain the trader, he that was found drowned this morning, is lying in the white man's campong."

"I have heard this talk," whispered Taminah; "and this morning by the riverside I saw the body. Where it is now I do not know."

"So you have seen it?" asked Reshid, eagerly. "Is it Dain? You have seen him many times. You would know him."

The girl's lips quivered and she remained silent for a while, breathing quickly.

"I have seen him, not a long time ago," she said at last. "The talk is true; he is dead. What do you want from me, Tuan? I must go."

Just then the report of the gun fired on board the steam launch was heard, interrupting Reshid's reply. Leaving the girl he ran to the house, and met in the courtyard Abdulla coming towards the gate.

"The Orang Blanda are come," said Reshid, "and now we shall have our reward."

Abdulla shook his head doubtfully. "The white men's rewards are long in coming," he said. "White men are quick in anger and slow in gratitude. We shall see."

He stood at the gate stroking his grey beard and listening to the distant cries of greeting at the other end of the settlement. As Taminah was turning to go he called her back.

"Listen, girl," he said: "there will be many white men in Almayer's house. You shall be there selling your cakes to the men of the sea. What you see and what you hear you may tell me. Come here before the sun sets and I will give you a blue handkerchief with red spots. Now go, and forget not to return."

He gave her a push with the end of his long staff as she was going away and made her stumble.

"This slave is very slow," he remarked to his nephew, looking after the girl with great disfavour.

Taminah walked on, her tray on the head, her eyes fixed on the ground. From the open doors of the houses were heard, as she passed, friendly calls inviting her within for business purposes, but she never heeded them, neglecting her sales in the preoccupation of intense thinking. Since the very early morning she had heard much, she had also seen much that filled her heart with a joy mingled with great suffering and fear. Before the dawn, before she left Bulangi's house to paddle up to Sambir she had heard voices outside the house when all in it but herself were asleep. And now, with her knowledge of the words spoken in the darkness, she held in her hand a life and carried in her breast a great sorrow. Yet from her springy step, erect figure, and face veiled over by the everyday look of apathetic indifference, nobody could have guessed of the double load she carried under the visible burden of the tray piled up high with cakes manufactured by the thrifty hands of Bulangi's wives. In that supple figure straight as an arrow, so graceful and free in its walk, behind those soft eyes that spoke of nothing but of unconscious resignation, there slept all feelings and all passions, all hopes and all fears, the curse of life and the consolation of death. And she knew nothing of it all. She lived like the tall palms amongst whom she was passing now, seeking the light, desiring the sunshine, fearing the storm, unconscious of either. The slave had no hope, and knew of no change. She knew of no other sky, no other water, no other frost, no other world, no other life. She had no wish, no hope, no love, no fear except of a blow, and no vivid feeling but that of occasional hunger, which was seldom, for Bulangi was rich and rice was plentiful in the solitary house in his clearing. The absence of pain and hunger was her happiness, and when she felt unhappy she was simply tired, more than usual, after the day's labour. Then in the hot nights of the south-west monsoon she slept dreamlessly under the bright stars on the platform built outside the house and over the river. Inside they slept too: Bulangi by the door; his wives further in; the children with their mothers. She could hear their breathing; Bulangi's sleepy voice; the

sharp cry of a child soon hushed with tender words. And
she closed her eyes to the murmur of the water below her,
to the whisper of the warm wind above, ignorant of the
never-ceasing life of that tropical nature that spoke to her in
vain with the thousand faint voices of the near forest, with the
breath of tepid wind ; in the heavy scents that lingered around
her head ; in the white wraiths of morning mist that hung
over her in the solemn hush of all creation before the dawn.

Such had been her existence before the coming of the brig
with the strangers. She remembered well that time ; the
uproar in the settlement, the never-ending wonder, the days
and nights of talk and excitement. She remembered her
own timidity with the strange men, till the brig moored to
the bank became in a manner part of the settlement, and the
fear wore off in the familiarity of constant intercourse. The
call on board then became part of her daily round. She
walked hesitatingly up the slanting planks of the gangway
amidst the encouraging shouts and more or less decent jokes
of the men idling over the bulwarks. There she sold her
wares to those men that spoke so loud and carried themselves
so free. There was a throng, a constant coming and going ;
calls interchanged, orders given and executed with shouts ;
the rattle of blocks, the flinging about of coils of rope. She
sat out of the way under the shade of the awning, with her
tray before her, the veil drawn well over her face, feeling
shy amongst so many men. She smiled at all buyers, but
spoke to none, letting their jests pass with stolid unconcern.
She heard many tales told around her of far-off countries,
of strange customs, of events stranger still. Those men
were brave ; but the most fearless of them spoke of their
chief with fear. Often the man they called their master
passed before her, walking erect and indifferent, in the pride
of youth, in the flash of rich dress, with a tinkle of gold
ornaments, while everybody stood aside watching anxiously
for a movement of his lips, ready to do his bidding. Then
all her life seemed to rush into her eyes, and from under her
veil she gazed at him, charmed, yet fearful to attract attention. One day he noticed her and asked, " Who is that

girl?" "A slave, Tuan! A girl that sells cakes," a dozen
voices replied together. She rose in terror to run on shore,
when he called her back; and as she stood trembling with
head hung down before him, he spoke kind words, lifting her
chin with his hands and looking into her eyes with a smile.
"Do not be afraid," he said. He never spoke to her any
more. Somebody called out from the river bank; he turned
away and forgot her existence. Taminah saw Almayer
standing on the shore with Nina on his arm. She heard
Nina's voice calling out gaily, and saw Dain's face brighten
with joy as he leaped on shore. She hated the sound of
that voice ever since.

After that day she left off visiting Almayer's compound,
and passed the noon hours under the shade of the brig
awning. She watched for his coming with heart beating
quicker and quicker, as he approached, into a wild tumult
of newly-aroused feelings of joy and hope and fear that
died away with Dain's retreating figure, leaving her tired
out, as if after a struggle, sitting still for a long time in
dreamy languor. Then she paddled home slowly in the
afternoon, often letting her canoe float with the lazy stream
in the quiet backwater of the river. The paddle hung idle
in the water as she sat in the stern, one hand supporting her
chin, her eyes wide open, listening intently to the whispering
of her heart that seemed to swell at last into a song of extreme
sweetness. Listening to that song she husked the rice at
home; it dulled her ears to the shrill bickerings of Bulangi's
wives, to the sound of angry reproaches addressed to herself.
And when the sun was near its setting she walked to the
bathing-place and heard it as she stood on the tender grass
of the low bank, her robe at her feet, and looked at the
reflection of her figure on the glass-like surface of the creek.
Listening to it she walked slowly back, her wet hair hanging
over her shoulders; laying down to rest under the bright
stars, she closed her eyes to the murmur of the water below,
of the warm wind above; to the voice of nature speaking
through the faint noises of the great forest, and to the song
of her own heart.

She heard, but did not understand, and drank in the dreamy joy of her new existence without troubling about its meaning or its end, till the full consciousness of life came to her through pain and anger. And she suffered horribly the first time she saw Nina's long canoe drift silently past the sleeping house of Bulangi, bearing the two lovers into the white mist of the great river. Her jealousy and rage culminated into a paroxysm of physical pain that left her lying panting on the river bank, in the dumb agony of a wounded animal. But she went on moving patiently in the enchanted circle of slavery, going through her task day after day with all the pathos of the grief she could not express, even to herself, locked within her breast. She shrank from Nina as she would have shrunk from the sharp blade of a knife cutting into her flesh, but she kept on visiting the brig to feed her dumb, ignorant soul on her own despair. She saw Dain many times. He never spoke, he never looked. Could his eyes see only one woman's image? Could his ears hear only one woman's voice? He never noticed her; not once.

And then he went away. She saw him and Nina for the last time on that morning when Babalatchi, while visiting his fish baskets, had his suspicions of the white man's daughter's love affair with Dain confirmed beyond the shadow of doubt. Dain disappeared, and Taminah's heart, where lay useless and barren the seeds of all love and of all hate, the possibilities of all passions and of all sacrifices, forgot its joys and its sufferings when deprived of the help of the senses. Her half-formed, savage mind, the slave of her body—as her body was the slave of another's will—forgot the faint and vague image of the ideal that had found its beginning in the physical promptings of her savage nature. She dropped back into the torpor of her former life and found consolation—even a certain kind of happiness—in the thought that now Nina and Dain were separated, probably for ever. He would forget. This thought soothed the last pangs of dying jealousy that had nothing now to feed upon, and Taminah found peace. It was like the dreary tranquillity of a desert, where there is peace only because there is no life.

And now he had returned. She had recognised his voice calling aloud in the night for Bulangi. She had crept out after her master to listen closer to the intoxicating sound. Dain was there, in a boat, talking to Bulangi. Taminah, listening with arrested breath, heard another voice. The maddening joy, that only a second before she thought herself incapable of containing within her fast-beating heart, died out, and left her shivering in the old anguish of physical pain that she had suffered once before at the sight of Dain and Nina. Nina spoke now, ordering and entreating in turns, and Bulangi was refusing, expostulating, at last consenting. He went in to take a paddle from the heap lying behind the door. Outside the murmur of two voices went on, and she caught a word here and there. She understood that he was fleeing from white men, that he was seeking a hiding-place, that he was in some danger. But she heard also words which woke the rage of jealousy that had been asleep for so many days in her bosom. Crouching low on the mud in the black darkness amongst the piles, she heard the whisper in the boat that made light of toil, of privation, of danger, of life itself, if in exchange there could be but a short moment of close embrace, a look from the eyes, the feel of light breath, the touch of soft lips. So spoke Dain as he sat in the canoe holding Nina's hands while waiting for Bulangi's return; and Taminah, supporting herself by the slimy pile, felt as if a heavy weight was crushing her down, down into the black oily water at her feet. She wanted to cry out; to rush at them and tear their vague shadows apart; to throw Nina into the smooth water, cling to her close, hold her to the bottom where that man could not find her. She could not cry, she could not move. Then footsteps were heard on the bamboo platform above her head; she saw Bulangi get into his smallest canoe and take the lead, the other boat following, paddled by Dain and Nina. With a slight splash of the paddles dipped stealthily into the water, their indistinct forms passed before her aching eyes and vanished in the darkness of the creek.

She remained there in the cold and wet, powerless to move, breathing painfully under the crushing weight that the mysterious hand of Fate had laid so suddenly upon her slender shoulders, and shivering, she felt within a burning fire, that seemed to feed upon her very life. When the breaking day had spread a pale golden ribbon over the black outline of the forests, she took up her tray and departed towards the settlement, going about her task purely from the force of habit. As she approached Sambir she could see the excitement and she heard with momentary surprise of the finding of Dain's body. It was not true, of course. She knew it well. She regretted that he was not dead. She should have liked Dain to be dead, so as to be parted from that woman—from all women. She felt a strong desire to see Nina, but without any clear object. She hated her, and feared her, and she felt an irresistible impulse pushing her towards Almayer's house to see the white woman's face, to look close at those eyes, to hear again that voice, for the sound of which Dain was ready to risk his liberty, his life even. She had seen her many times; she had heard her voice daily for many months past. What was there in her? What was there in that being to make a man speak as Dain had spoken, to make him blind to all other faces, deaf to all other voices?

She left the crowd by the riverside, and wandered aimlessly among the empty houses, resisting the impulse that pushed her towards Almayer's campong to seek there in Nina's eyes the secret of her own misery. The sun mounting higher, shortened the shadows and poured down upon her a flood of light and of stifling heat as she passed on from shadow to light, from light to shadow, amongst the houses, the bushes, the tall trees, in her unconscious flight from the pain in her own heart. In the extremity of her distress she could find no words to pray for relief, she knew of no heaven to send her prayer to, and she wandered on with tired feet in the dumb surprise and terror at the injustice of the suffering inflicted upon her without cause and without redress.

The short talk with Reshid, the proposal of Abdulla steadied her a little and turned her thoughts into another channel. Dain was in some danger. He was hiding from white men. So much she had overheard last night. They all thought him dead. She knew he was alive, and she knew of his hiding-place. What did the Arabs want to know about the white men? The white men want with Dain? Did they wish to kill him? She could tell them all—no, she would say nothing, and in the night she would go to him and sell him his life for a word, for a smile, for a gesture even, and be his slave in far-off countries, away from Nina. But there were dangers. The one-eyed Babalatchi who knew everything; the white man's wife—she was a witch. Perhaps they would tell. And then there was Nina. She must hurry on and see.

In her impatience she left the path and ran towards Almayer's dwelling through the undergrowth between the palm trees. She came out at the back of the house, where a narrow ditch, full of stagnant water that overflowed from the river, separated Almayer's campong from the rest of the settlement. The thick bushes growing on the bank were hiding from her sight the large courtyard with its cooking shed. Above them rose several thin columns of smoke, and from behind the sound of strange voices informed Taminah that the Men of the Sea belonging to the warship had already landed and were camped between the ditch and the house. To the left one of Almayer's slave-girls came down to the ditch and bent over the shiny water, washing a kettle. To the right the tops of the banana plantation, visible above the bushes, swayed and shook under the touch of invisible hands gathering the fruit. On the calm water several canoes moored to a heavy stake were crowded together, nearly bridging the ditch just at the place where Taminah stood. The voices in the courtyard rose at times into an outburst of calls, replies, and laughter, and then died away into a silence that soon was broken again by a fresh clamour. Now and again the thin blue smoke rushed out thicker and blacker, and drove in odorous masses over the creek, wrapping her for a moment in a suffocating veil; then, as the fresh wood caught well alight, the smoke vanished in the bright sunlight, and only the scent of aromatic wood drifted afar, to leeward of the crackling fires.

Taminah rested her tray on a stump of a tree, and remained standing with her eyes turned towards Almayer's house, whose roof and part of a whitewashed wall were visible over the bushes. The slave-girl finished her work, and after looking for a while curiously at Taminah, pushed her way through the dense thicket back to the courtyard. Round Taminah there was now a complete solitude. She threw herself down on the ground, and hid her face in her hands. Now when so close she had no courage to see Nina. At every burst of louder voices from the courtyard she shivered in the fear of hearing Nina's voice. She came to the resolution of waiting where she was till dark, and then going straight to Dain's hiding-place. From where she was she could watch the movements of white men, of Nina, of all Dain's friends, and of all his enemies. Both were hateful alike to her, for both would take him away beyond her reach. She hid herself in the long grass to wait anxiously for the sunset that seemed so slow to come.

On the other side of the ditch, behind the bush, by the clear fires, the seamen of the frigate had encamped on the hospitable invitation of Almayer. Almayer, roused out of his apathy by the prayers and importunity of Nina, had managed to get down in time to the jetty so as to receive the officers at their landing. The lieutenant in command accepted his invitation to his house with the remark that in any case their business was with Almayer—and perhaps not very pleasant, he added. Almayer hardly heard him. He shook hands with them absently and led the way towards the house. He was scarcely conscious of the polite words of welcome he greeted the strangers with, and afterwards repeated several times over again in his efforts to appear at ease. The agitation of their host did not escape the officer's eyes, and the chief confided to his subordinate, in a low voice, his doubts as to Almayer's sobriety. The young sub-lieutenant laughed and expressed in a whisper the hope that the white man was not intoxicated enough to neglect the offer of some refreshments. " He does not seem very dangerous," he added, as they followed Almayer up the steps of the verandah.

" No, he seems more of a fool than a knave ; I have heard of him," returned the senior.

They sat around the table. Almayer with shaking hands made gin cocktails, offered them all round, and drank himself, with every gulp feeling stronger, steadier, and better able to face all the difficulties of his position. Ignorant of the fate of the brig, he did not suspect the real object of the officer's visit. He had a general notion that something must have leaked out about the gunpowder trade, but apprehended nothing beyond some temporary inconvenience. After emptying his glass he began to chat easily, lying back in his chair with one of his legs thrown negligently over the arm. The lieutenant astride on his chair, a glowing cheroot in the corner of his mouth, listened with a sly smile from behind the thick volumes of smoke that escaped from his compressed lips. The young sub-lieutenant, leaning with both elbows on the table, his head between his hands, looked on sleepily in the torpor induced by fatigue and the gin. Almayer talked on—

" It is a great pleasure to see white faces here. I have lived here many years in great solitude. The Malays, you understand, are not company for a white man ; moreover they are not friendly ; they do not understand our ways. Great rascals they are. I believe I am the only white man on the east coast that is a settled resident. We get visitors from Macassar or Singapore sometimes—traders, agents, or explorers, but they are rare. There was a scientific explorer here a year or more ago. He lived in my house : drank from morning to night. He lived joyously for a few months, and when the liquor he brought with him was gone he returned to Batavia with a report on the mineral wealth of the interior. Ha, ha, ha! Good, is it not?"

He ceased abruptly and looked at his guests with a meaningless stare. While they laughed he was reciting to himself the old story: "Dain dead, all my plans destroyed. This is the end of all hope and of all things." His heart sank within him. He felt a kind of deadly sickness.

"Very good. Capital!" exclaimed both officers.

Almayer came out of his despondency with another burst of talk.

"Eh! what about the dinner? You have got a cook with you. That's all right. There is a cooking shed in the other courtyard. I can give you a goose. Look at my geese—the only geese on the east coast—perhaps on the whole island. Is that your cook? Very good. Here, Ali, show this Chinaman the cooking place and tell Mem Almayer to let him have room there. My wife, gentlemen, does not come out; my daughter may. Meantime have some more drink. It is a hot day."

The lieutenant took the cigar out of his mouth, looked at the ash critically, shook it off and turned towards Almayer.

"We have a rather unpleasant business with you," he said.

"I am sorry," returned Almayer. "It can be nothing very serious, surely."

"If you think an attempt to blow up forty men at least, not a serious matter you will not find many people of your opinion," retorted the officer sharply.

"Blow up! What? I know nothing about it," exclaimed Almayer. "Who did that, or tried to do it?"

"A man with whom you had some dealings," answered the lieutenant. "He passed here under the name of Dain Maroola. You sold him the gunpowder he had in that brig we captured?"

"How did you hear about the brig?" asked Almayer. "I know nothing about the powder he may have had."

"An Arab trader of this place has sent the information about your goings on here to Batavia, a couple of months ago," said the officer. "We were waiting for the brig out-side, but he slipped past us at the mouth of the river, and we had to chase the fellow to the southward. When he sighted us he ran inside the reefs and put the brig ashore. The crew escaped in boats before we could take possession. As our boats neared the craft it blew up with a tremendous explosion; one of the boats being too near got swamped. Two men drowned—that is the result of your speculation, Mr. Almayer. Now we want this Dain. We have good grounds to suppose he is hiding in Sambir. Do you know where he is? You had better put yourself right with the authorities as much as possible by being perfectly frank with me. Where is this Dain?"

Almayer got up and walked towards the balustrade of the verandah. He seemed not to be thinking of the officer's question. He looked at the body lying straight and rigid under its white cover on which the sun, declining amongst the clouds to the westward, threw a pale tinge of red. The lieutenant waited for the answer, taking quick pulls at his half-extinguished cigar. Behind them Ali moved noiselessly laying the table, ranging solemnly the ill-assorted and shabby crockery, the tin spoons, the forks with broken prongs, and the knives with saw-like blades and loose handles. He had almost forgotten how to prepare the table for white men. He felt aggrieved; Mem Nina would not help him. He stepped back to look at his work admiringly, feeling very proud. This must be right; and if the master afterwards is angry and swears, then so much the worse for Mem Nina. Why did she not help? He left the verandah to fetch the dinner.

"Well, Mr. Almayer, will you answer my question as frankly as it is put to you?" asked the lieutenant, after a long silence.

Almayer turned round and looked at his interlocutor steadily. "If you catch this Dain what will you do with him?" he asked.

The officer's face flushed. "This is not an answer," he said, annoyed.

"And what will you do with me?" went on Almayer, not heeding the interruption.

"Are you inclined to bargain?" growled the other. "It would be bad policy, I assure you. At present I have no orders about your person, but we expected your assistance in catching this Malay."

"Ah!" interrupted Almayer, "just so: you can do nothing without me, and I, knowing the man well, am to help you in finding him."

"This is exactly what we expect," assented the officer. "You have broken the law, Mr. Almayer, and you ought to make amends."

"And save yourself?"

"Well, in a sense yes. Your head is not in any danger," said the lieutenant, with a short laugh.

"Very well," said Almayer, with decision, "I shall deliver the man up to you."

Both officers rose to their feet quickly, and looked for their side-arms which they had unbuckled. Almayer laughed harshly.

"Steady, gentlemen!" he exclaimed. "In my own time and in my own way. After dinner, gentlemen, you shall have him."

"This is preposterous," urged the lieutenant. "Mr. Almayer, this is no joking matter. The man is a criminal. He deserves to hang. While we dine he may escape; the rumour of our arrival——"

Almayer walked towards the table. "I give you my word of honour, gentlemen, that he shall not escape; I have him safe enough."

"The arrest should be effected before dark," remarked the young sub.

"I shall hold you responsible for any failure. We are ready, but can do nothing just now without you," added the senior, with evident annoyance.

Almayer made a gesture of assent. "On my word of honour," he repeated vaguely. "And now let us dine," he added briskly.

Nina came through the doorway and stood for a moment holding the curtain aside for Ali and the old Malay woman bearing the dishes; then she moved towards the three men by the table.

"Allow me," said Almayer, pompously. "This is my daughter. Nina, these gentlemen, officers of the frigate outside, have done me the honour to accept my hospitality."

Nina answered the low bows of the two officers by a slow inclination of the head and took her place at the table opposite her father. All sat down. The coxswain of the steam launch came up carrying some bottles of wine.

"You will allow me to have this put upon the table?" said the lieutenant to Almayer.

"What! Wine! You are very kind. Certainly. I have none myself. Times are very hard."

The last words of his reply were spoken by Almayer in a faltering voice. The thought that Dain was dead recurred to him vividly again, and he felt as if an invisible hand was gripping his throat. He reached for the gin bottle while they were uncorking the wine and swallowed a big gulp. The lieutenant, who was speaking to Nina, gave him a quick glance. The young sub began to recover from the astonishment and confusion caused by Nina's unexpected appearance and great beauty. "She was very beautiful and imposing," he reflected, "but after all a half-caste girl." This thought caused him to pluck up heart and look at Nina sideways. Nina, with composed face, was answering in a low, even voice the elder officer's polite questions as to the country and her mode of life. Almayer pushed his plate away and drank his guest's wine in gloomy silence.

## CHAPTER IX

"Can I believe what you tell me? It is like a tale for men that listen only half awake by the camp fire, and it seems to have run off a woman's tongue."

"Who is there here for me to deceive, O Rajah?" answered Babalatchi. "Without you I am nothing. All I have told you I believe to be true. I have been safe for many years in the hollow of your hand. This is no time to harbour suspicions. The danger is very great. We should advise and act at once, before the sun sets."

"Right. Right," muttered Lakamba, pensively.

They had been sitting for the last hour together in the audience chamber of the Rajah's house, for Babalatchi, as soon as he had witnessed the landing of the Dutch officers, had crossed the river to report to his master the events of the morning, and to confer with him upon the line of conduct to pursue in the face of altered circumstances. They were both puzzled and frightened by the unexpected turn the events had taken. The Rajah, sitting crosslegged on his chair, looked fixedly at the floor; Babalatchi was squatting close by in an attitude of deep dejection.

"And where did you say he is hiding now?" asked Lakamba, breaking at last the silence full of gloomy forebodings in which they both had been lost for a long while.

"In Bulangi's clearing—the furthest one, away from the house. They went there that very night. The white man's daughter took him there. She told me so herself, speaking to me openly, for she is half white and has no decency. She said she was waiting for him while he was here; then, after a long time, he came out of the darkness and fell at her feet exhausted. He lay like one dead, but she brought him back to life in her arms, and made him breathe again with her own breath. That is what she said, speaking to my face, as I am speaking now to you, Rajah. She is like a white woman and knows no shame."

He paused, deeply shocked. Lakamba nodded his head. " Well, and then ? " he asked.

" They called the old woman," went on Babalatchi, " and he told them all—about the brig, and how he tried to kill many men. He knew the Orang Blanda were very near, although he had said nothing to us about that ; he knew his great danger. He thought he had killed many, but there were only two dead, as I have heard from the men of the sea that came in the warship's boats."

" And the other man, he that was found in the river ? " interrupted Lakamba.

" That was one of his boatmen. When his canoe was overturned by the logs those two swam together, but the other man must have been hurt. Dain swam, holding him up. He left him in the bushes when he went up to the house. When they all came down his heart had ceased to beat ; then the old woman spoke ; Dain thought it was good. He took off his anklet and broke it, twisting it round the man's foot. His ring he put on that slave's hand. He took off his sarong and clothed that thing that wanted no clothes, the two women holding it up meanwhile, their intent being to deceive all eyes and to mislead the minds in the settlement, so that they could swear to the thing that was not, and that there could be no treachery when the white men came. Then Dain and the white woman departed to call up Bulangi and find a hiding-place. The old woman remained by the body." ·

" Hai ! " exclaimed Lakamba. " She has wisdom."

" Yes, she has a Devil of her own to whisper counsel in her ear," assented Babalatchi. " She dragged the body with great toil to the point where many logs were stranded. All these things were one in the darkness after the storm had passed away. Then she waited. At the first sign of daylight she battered the face of the dead with a heavy stone, and she pushed him amongst the logs. She remained near, watching. At sunrise Mahmat Banjer came and found him.

They all believed; I myself was deceived, but not for long.
The white man believed, and, grieving, fled to his house.
When we were alone I, having doubts, spoke to the woman,
and she, fearing my anger and your might, told me all, asking
for help in saving Dain."

"He must not fall into the hands of the Orang Blanda,"
said Lakamba; "but let him die, if the thing can be done
quietly."

"It cannot, Tuan! Remember there is that woman
who, being half white, is ungovernable, and would raise a
great outcry. Also the officers are here. They are angry
enough already. Dain must escape; he must go. We must
help him now for our own safety."

"Are the officers very angry?" inquired Lakamba, with
interest.

"They are. The principal chief used strong words when
speaking to me—to me when I salaamed in your name. I
do not think," added Babalatchi, after a short pause and
looking very worried—"I do not think I saw a white chief so
angry before. He said we were careless or even worse. He
told me he would speak to the Rajah, and that I was of no
account."

"Speak to the Rajah!" repeated Lakamba, thoughtfully.
"Listen, Babalatchi: I am sick, and shall withdraw; you
cross over and tell the white men."

"Yes," said Babalatchi, "I am going over at once; and
as to Dain?"

"You get him away as you can best. This is a great
trouble in my heart," sighed Lakamba.

Babalatchi got up, and, going close to his master, spoke
earnestly.

"There is one of our praus at the southern mouth of the
river. The Dutch warship is to the northward watching
the main entrance. I shall send Dain off to-night in a canoe,
by the hidden channels, on board the prau. His father is a
great prince, and shall hear of our generosity. Let the prau
take him to Ampanam. Your glory shall be great, and your
reward in powerful friendship. Almayer will no doubt

deliver the dead body as Dain's to the officers, and the foolish white men shall say, 'This is very good; let there be peace.' And the trouble shall be removed from your heart, Rajah."

"True! true!" said Lakamba.

"And, this being accomplished by me who am your slave, you shall reward with a generous hand. That I know! The white man is grieving for the lost treasure, in the manner of white men who thirst after dollars. Now, when all other things are in order, we shall perhaps obtain the treasure from the white man. Dain must escape, and Almayer must live."

"Now go, Babalatchi, go!" said Lakamba, getting off his chair. "I am very sick, and want medicine. Tell the white chief so."

But Babalatchi was not to be got rid of in this summary manner. He knew that his master, after the manner of the great, liked to shift the burden of toil and danger on to his servants' shoulders, but in the difficult straits in which they were now the Rajah must play his part. He may be very sick for the white men, for all the world if he liked, as long as he would take upon himself the execution of part at least of Babalatchi's carefully thought-of plan. Babalatchi wanted a big canoe manned by twelve men to be sent out after dark towards Bulangi's clearing. Dain may have to be over-powered. A man in love cannot be expected to see clearly the path of safety if it leads him away from the object of his affections, argued Babalatchi, and in that case they would have to use force in order to make him go. Would the Rajah see that trusty men manned the canoe? The thing must be done secretly. Perhaps the Rajah would come himself, so as to bring all the weight of his authority to bear upon Dain if he should prove obstinate and refuse to leave his hiding-place. The Rajah would not commit himself to a definite promise, and anxiously pressed Babalatchi to go, being afraid of the white men paying him an unexpected visit. The aged statesman reluctantly took his leave and went into the courtyard.

Before going down to his boat Babalatchi stopped for a while in the big open space where the thick-leaved trees put black patches of shadow which seemed to float on a flood of smooth, intense light that rolled up to the houses and down to the stockade and over the river, where it broke and sparkled in thousands of glittering wavelets, like a band woven of azure and gold edged with the brilliant green of the forests guarding both banks of the Pantai. In the perfect calm before the coming of the afternoon breeze the irregularly jagged line of tree-tops stood unchanging, as if traced by an unsteady hand on the clear blue of the hot sky. In the space sheltered by the high palisades there lingered the smell of decaying blossoms from the surrounding forest, a taint of drying fish; with now and then a whiff of acrid smoke from the cooking fires when it eddied down from under the leafy boughs and clung lazily about the burnt-up grass.

As Babalatchi looked up at the flagstaff overtopping a group of low trees in the middle of the courtyard, the tri-colour flag of the Netherlands stirred slightly for the first time since it had been hoisted that morning on the arrival of the man-of-war boats. With a faint rustle of trees came down in light puffs, playing capriciously for a time with this emblem of Lakamba's power, that was also the mark of his servitude; then the breeze freshened in a sharp gust of wind, and the flag flew out straight and steady above the trees. A dark shadow ran along the river, rolling over and covering up the sparkle of declining sunlight. A big white cloud sailed slowly across the darkening sky, and hung to the westward as if waiting for the sun to join it there. Men and things shook off the torpor of the hot afternoon and stirred into life under the first breath of the sea breeze.

Babalatchi hurried down to the water-gate; yet before he passed through it he paused to look round the courtyard, with its light and shade, with its cheery fires, with the groups of Lakamba's soldiers and retainers scattered about. His own house stood amongst the other buildings in that enclosure and the statesman of Sambir asked himself with a sinking heart when and how would it be given him to return to that house.  He had to deal with a man more dangerous than any wild beast of his experience : a proud man, a man wilful after the manner of princes, a man in love.  And he was going forth to speak to that man words of cold and worldly wisdom. Could anything be more appalling ?  What if that man should take umbrage at some fancied slight to his honour or disregard of his affections and suddenly " amok " ?  The wise adviser would be the first victim, no doubt, and death would be his reward.  And underlying the horror of this situation there was the danger of those meddlesome fools, the white men.  A vision of comfortless exile in far-off Madura rose up before Babalatchi.  Wouldn't that be worse than death itself ?  And there was that half-white woman with threatening eyes.  How could he tell what an incomprehensible creature of that sort would or would not do ?  She knew so much that she made the killing of Dain an impossibility. That much was certain.  And yet the sharp, rough-edged kriss is a good and discreet friend, thought Babalatchi, as he examined his own lovingly, and put it back in the sheath, with a sigh of regret, before unfastening his canoe.  As he cast off the painter, pushed out into the stream, and took up his paddle, he realised vividly how unsatisfactory it was to have women mixed up in state affairs.  Young women, of course.  For Mrs. Almayer's mature wisdom, and for the easy aptitude in intrigue that comes with years to the feminine mind, he felt the most sincere respect.

He paddled leisurely, letting the canoe drift down as he crossed towards the point.  The sun was high yet, and nothing pressed.  His work would commence only with the coming of darkness.  Avoiding the Lingard jetty, he rounded the point, and paddled up the creek at the back of Almayer's house.  There were many canoes lying there, their noses all drawn together, fastened all to the same stake.  Babalatchi pushed his little craft in amongst them and stepped on shore. On the other side of the ditch something moved in the grass.

"Who's that hiding ? " hailed Babalatchi.  " Come out and speak to me."

Nobody answered. Babalatchi crossed over, passing from boat to boat, and poked his staff viciously in the suspicious place. Taminah jumped up with a cry.

"What are you doing here?" he asked, surprised. "I have nearly stepped on your tray. Am I a Dyak that you should hide at my sight?"

"I was weary, and—I slept," whispered Taminah, confusedly.

"You slept! You have not sold anything to-day, and you will be beaten when you return home," said Babalatchi.

Taminah stood before him abashed and silent. Babalatchi looked her over carefully with great satisfaction. Decidedly he would offer fifty dollars more to that thief Bulangi. The girl pleased him.

"Now you go home. It is late," he said sharply. "Tell Bulangi that I shall be near his house before the night is half over, and that I want him to make all things ready for a long journey. You understand? A long journey to the southward. Tell him that before sunset, and do not forget my words."

Taminah made a gesture of assent, and watched Babalatchi recross the ditch and disappear through the bushes bordering Almayer's compound. She moved a little further off the creek and sank in the grass again, lying down on her face, shivering in dry-eyed misery.

Babalatchi walked straight towards the cooking-shed looking for Mrs. Almayer. The courtyard was in a great uproar. A strange Chinaman had possession of the kitchen fire and was noisily demanding another saucepan. He hurled objurgations, in the Canton dialect and bad Malay, against the group of slave-girls standing a little way off, half frightened, half amused, at his violence. From the camping fires round which the seamen of the frigate were sitting came words of encouragement, mingled with laughter and jeering. In the midst of this noise and confusion Babalatchi met Ali, an empty dish in his hand.

"Where are the white men?" asked Babalatchi.

"They are eating in the front verandah," answered Ali. "Do not stop me, Tuan. I am giving the white men their food and am busy."

"Where's Mem Almayer?"

"Inside in the passage. She is listening to the talk."

Ali grinned and passed on; Babalatchi ascended the plankway to the rear verandah, and beckoning out Mrs. Almayer, engaged her in earnest conversation. Through the long passage, closed at the further end by the red curtain, they could hear from time to time Almayer's voice mingling in conversation with an abrupt loudness that made Mrs. Almayer look significantly at Babalatchi.

"Listen," she said. "He has drunk much."

"He has," whispered Babalatchi. "He will sleep heavily to-night."

Mrs. Almayer looked doubtful.

"Sometimes the devil of strong gin makes him keep awake, and he walks up and down the verandah all night, cursing; then we stand afar off," explained Mrs. Almayer, with the fuller knowledge born of twenty odd years of married life.

"But then he does not hear, nor understand, and his hand, of course, has no strength. We do not want him to hear to-night."

"No," assented Mrs. Almayer, energetically, but in a cautiously subdued voice. "If he hears he will kill."

Babalatchi looked incredulous.

"Hai Tuan, you may believe me. Have I not lived many years with that man? Have I not seen death in that man's eyes more than once when I was younger and he guessed at many things. Had he been a man of my own people I would not have seen such a look twice; but he——"

With a contemptuous gesture she seemed to fling unutterable scorn on Almayer's weak-minded aversion to sudden bloodshed.

"If he has the wish but not the strength, then what do we fear?" asked Babalatchi, after a short silence during which they both listened to Almayer's loud talk till it subsided into the murmur of general conversation. "What do we fear?" repeated Babalatchi again.

"To keep the daughter whom he loves he would strike into your heart and mine without hesitation," said Mrs. Almayer. "When the girl is gone he will be like the devil unchained. Then you and I had better beware."

"I am an old man and fear not death," answered Babalatchi, with a mendacious assumption of indifference. "But what will you do?"

"I am an old woman, and wish to live," retorted Mrs. Almayer. "She is my daughter also. I shall seek safety at the feet of our Rajah, speaking in the name of the past when we both were young, and he——"

Babalatchi raised his hand.

"Enough. You shall be protected," he said soothingly.

Again the sound of Almayer's voice was heard, and again interrupting their talk, they listened to the confused but loud utterance coming in bursts of unequal strength, with unexpected pauses and noisy repetitions that made some words and sentences fall clear and distinct on their ears out of the meaningless jumble of excited shoutings emphasised by the thumping of Almayer's fist upon the table. On the short intervals of silence, the high complaining note of tumblers, standing close together and vibrating to the shock, lingered, growing fainter, till it leapt up again into tumultuous ringing, when a new idea started a new rush of words and brought down the heavy hand again. At last the quarrelsome shouting ceased, and the thin plaint of disturbed glass died away into reluctant quietude.

Babalatchi and Mrs. Almayer had listened curiously, their bodies bent and their ears turned towards the passage. At every louder shout they nodded at each other with a ridiculous affectation of scandalised propriety, and they remained in the same attitude for some time after the noise had ceased.

"This is the devil of gin," whispered Mrs. Almayer. "Yes; he talks like that sometimes when there is nobody to hear him."

"What does he say?" inquired Babalatchi, eagerly. "You ought to understand."

"I have forgotten their talk. A little I understood. He spoke without any respect of the white ruler in Batavia, and of protection, and said he had been wronged; he said that several times. More I did not understand. Listen! Again he speaks!"

"Tse! tse! tse!" clicked Babalatchi, trying to appear shocked, but with a joyous twinkle in his solitary eye. "There will be great trouble between those white men. I will go round now and see. You tell your daughter that there is a sudden and a long journey before her, with much glory and splendour at the end. And tell her that Dain must go, or he must die, and that he will not go alone."

"No, he will not go alone," slowly repeated Mrs. Almayer, with a thoughtful air, as she crept into the passage after seeing Babalatchi disappear round the corner of the house.

The statesman of Sambir, under the impulse of vivid curiosity, made his way quickly to the front of the house, but once there he moved slowly and cautiously as he crept step by step up the stairs of the verandah. On the highest step he sat down quietly, his feet on the steps below, ready for flight should his presence prove unwelcome. He felt pretty safe so. The table stood nearly endways to him, and he saw Almayer's back; at Nina he looked full face, and had a side view of both officers; but of the four persons sitting at the table only Nina and the younger officer noticed his noiseless arrival. The momentary dropping of Nina's eyelids acknowledged Babalatchi's presence; she then spoke at once to the young sub, who turned towards her with attentive alacrity, but her gaze was fastened steadily on her father's face while Almayer was speaking uproariously.

". . . disloyalty and unscrupulousness! What have you ever done to make me loyal? You have no grip on this country. I had to take care of myself, and when I asked for protection I was met with threats and contempt, and had Arab slander thrown in my face. I! a white man!"

"Don't be violent, Almayer," remonstrated the lieutenant, "I have heard all this already."

"Then why do you talk to me about scruples? I wanted money, and I gave powder in exchange. How could I know that some of your wretched men were going to be blown up? Scruples! Pah!"

He groped unsteadily amongst the bottles, trying one after another, grumbling to himself the while. "No more wine," he muttered discontentedly.

"You have had enough, Almayer," said the lieutenant, as he lighted a cigar. "Is it not time to deliver to us your prisoner? I take it you have that Dain Maroola stowed away safely somewhere. Still we had better get that business over, and then we shall have more drink. Come! don't look at me like this."

Almayer was staring with stony eyes, his trembling fingers fumbling about his throat.

"Gold," he said with difficulty. "Hem! A hand on the windpipe, you know. Sure you will excuse. I wanted to say—a little gold for a little powder. What's that?"

"I know, I know," said the lieutenant soothingly.

"No! You don't know. Not one of you knows!" shouted Almayer. "The government is a fool, I tell you. Heaps of gold. I am the man that knows; I and another one. But he won't speak. He is——"

He checked himself with a feeble smile, and, making an unsuccessful attempt to pat the officer on the shoulder, knocked over a couple of empty bottles.

"Personally you are a fine fellow," he said very distinctly, in a patronising manner. His head nodded drowsily as he sat muttering to himself.

The two officers looked at each other helplessly.

"This won't do," said the lieutenant, addressing his junior. "Have the men mustered in the compound here. I must get some sense out of him. Hi! Almayer! Wake up, man. Redeem your word. You gave your word of honour, you know."

Almayer shook off the officer's hand with impatience, but

his ill-humour vanished at once, and he looked up, putting his forefinger to the side of his nose.

"You are very young; there is time for all things," he said, with an air of great sagacity.

The lieutenant turned towards Nina, who, leaning back in her chair, watched her father steadily.

"Really I am very much distressed by all this for your sake," he exclaimed. "I do not know," he went on, speaking with some embarrassment, "whether I have any right to ask you anything, unless, perhaps, to withdraw from this painful scene, but I feel that I must—for your father's good— suggest that you should—— I mean if you have any influence over him you ought to exert it now to make him keep the promise he gave me before he—before he got into this state."

He observed with discouragement that she seemed not to take any notice of what he said sitting still with half-closed eyes.

"I trust——" he began again.

"What is the promise you speak of?" abruptly asked Nina, leaving her seat and moving towards her father.

"Nothing that is not just and proper. He promised to deliver to us a man who in time of profound peace took the lives of innocent men to escape the punishment he deserved for breaking the law. He planned his mischief on a large scale. It is not his fault if it failed, partially. Of course you have heard of Dain Maroola. Your father secured him, I understand. We know he escaped up this river. Perhaps you——"

"And he killed white men!" interrupted Nina.

"I regret to say they were white. Yes, two white men lost their lives through that scoundrel's freak."

"Two only!" exclaimed Nina.

The officer looked at her in amazement.

"Why! why! You——" he stammered, confused.

"There might have been more," interrupted Nina. "And when you get this—this scoundrel, will you go?"

The lieutenant, still speechless, bowed his assent.

"Then I would get him for you if I had to seek him in a burning fire," she burst out with intense energy. "I hate the sight of your white faces. I hate the sound of your gentle voices. That is the way you speak to women, dropping sweet words before any pretty face. I have heard your voices before. I hoped to live here without seeing any other white face but this," she added in a gentler tone, touching lightly her father's cheek.

Almayer ceased his mumbling and opened his eyes. He caught hold of his daughter's hand and pressed it to his face, while Nina with the other hand smoothed his rumpled grey hair, looking defiantly over her father's head at the officer, who had now regained his composure and returned her look with a cool, steady stare. Below, in front of the verandah, they could hear the tramp of seamen mustering there according to orders. The sub-lieutenant came up the steps, while Babalatchi stood up uneasily and, with finger on lip, tried to catch Nina's eye.

"You are a good girl," whispered Almayer, absently, dropping his daughter's hand.

"Father! father!" she cried, bending over him with passionate entreaty. "See those two men looking at us. Send them away. I cannot bear it any more. Send them away. Do what they want and let them go."

She caught sight of Babalatchi and ceased speaking suddenly, but her foot tapped the floor with rapid beats in a paroxysm of nervous restlessness. The two officers stood close together looking on curiously.

"What has happened? What is the matter?" whispered the younger man.

"Don't know," answered the other, under his breath. "One is furious, and the other is drunk. Not so drunk, either. Queer, this. Look!"

Almayer had risen, holding on to his daughter's arm. He hesitated a moment, then he let go his hold and lurched half-way across the verandah. There he pulled himself together, and stood very straight, breathing hard and glaring round angrily.

"Are the men ready?" asked the lieutenant.

"All ready, sir."

"Now, Mr. Almayer, lead the way," said the lieutenant.

Almayer rested his eyes on him as if he saw him for the first time.

"Two men," he said thickly. The effort of speaking seemed to interfere with his equilibrium. He took a quick step to save himself from a fall, and remained swaying backwards and forwards. "Two men," he began again, speaking with difficulty. "Two white men—men in uniform—honourable men. I want to say—men of honour. Are you?"

"Come! None of that," said the officer impatiently. "Let us have that friend of yours."

"What do you think I am?" asked Almayer, fiercely.

"You are drunk, but not so drunk as not to know what you are doing. Enough of this tomfoolery," said the officer sternly, "or I will have you put under arrest in your own house."

"Arrest!" laughed Almayer, discordantly. "Ha! ha! ha! Arrest! Why, I have been trying to get out of this infernal place for twenty years, and I can't. You hear, man! I can't, and never shall! Never!"

He ended his words with a sob, and walked unsteadily down the stairs. When in the courtyard the lieutenant approached him, and took him by the arm. The sub-lieutenant and Babalatchi followed close.

"That's better, Almayer," said the officer encouragingly. "Where are you going to? There are only planks there. Here," he went on, shaking him slightly, "do we want the boats?"

"No," answered Almayer, viciously. "You want a grave."

"What? Wild again! Try to talk sense."

"Grave!" roared Almayer, struggling to get himself free. "A hole in the ground. Don't you understand? You must be drunk. Let me go! Let go, I tell you!"

He tore away from the officer's grasp, and reeled towards

the planks where the body lay under its white cover; then he turned round quickly, and faced the semicircle of interested faces. The sun was sinking rapidly, throwing long shadows of house and trees over the courtyard, but the light lingered yet on the river, where the logs went drifting past in mid-stream, looking very distinct and black in the pale red glow. The trunks of the trees in the forest on the east bank were lost in gloom while their highest branches swayed gently in the departing sunlight. The air felt heavy and cold in the breeze, expiring in slight puffs that came over the water.

Almayer shivered as he made an effort to speak, and again with an uncertain gesture he seemed to free his throat from the grip of an invisible hand. His bloodshot eyes wandered aimlessly from face to face.

"There!" he said at last. "Are you all there? He is a dangerous man."

He dragged at the cover with hasty violence, and the body rolled stiffly off the planks and fell at his feet in rigid helplessness.

"Cold, perfectly cold," said Almayer, looking round with a mirthless smile. "Sorry can do no better. And you can't hang him, either. As you observe, gentlemen," he added gravely, "there is no head, and hardly any neck."

The last ray of light was snatched away from the tree-tops, the river grew suddenly dark, and in the great stillness the murmur of the flowing water seemed to fill the vast expanse of grey shadow that descended upon the land.

"This is Dain," went on Almayer to the silent group that surrounded him. "And I have kept my word. First one hope, then another, and this is my last. Nothing is left now. You think there is one dead man here? Mistake, I'sure you. I am much more dead. Why don't you hang me?" he suggested suddenly, in a friendly tone, addressing the lieutenant. "I assure, assure you it would be a mat—matter of form altog—altogether."

These last words he muttered to himself, and walked zig-zagging towards his house. "Get out!" he thundered at Ali, who was approaching timidly with offers of assistance.

From afar, scared groups of men and women watched his devious progress. He dragged himself up the stairs by the banister, and managed to reach a chair into which he fell heavily. He sat for awhile panting with exertion and anger, and looking round vaguely for Nina ; then making a threatening gesture towards the compound, where he had heard Babalatchi's voice, he overturned the table with his foot in a great crash of smashed crockery. He muttered yet menacingly to himself, then his head fell on his breast, his eyes closed, and with a deep sigh he fell asleep.

That night—for the first time in its history—the peaceful and flourishing settlement of Sambir saw the lights shining about "Almayer's Folly." These were the lanterns of the boats hung up by the seamen under the verandah where the two officers were holding a court of inquiry into the truth of the story related to them by Babalatchi. Babalatchi had regained all his importance. He was eloquent and persuasive, calling Heaven and Earth to witness the truth of his statements. There were also other witnesses. Mahmat Banjer and a good many others underwent a close examination that dragged its weary length far into the evening. A messenger was sent for Abdulla, who excused himself from coming on the score of his venerable age, but sent Reshid. Mahmat had to produce the bangle, and saw with rage and mortification the lieutenant put it in his pocket, as one of the proofs of Dain's death, to be sent in with the official report of the mission. Babalatchi's ring was also impounded for the same purpose, but the experienced statesman was resigned to that loss from the very beginning. He did not mind as long as he was sure that the white men believed. He put that question to himself earnestly as he left, one of the last, when the proceedings came to a close. He was not certain. Still, if they believed only for a night, he would put Dain beyond their reach and feel safe himself. He walked away fast, looking from time to time over his shoulder in the fear of being followed, but he saw and heard nothing.

" Ten o'clock," said the lieutenant, looking at his watch and yawning. " I shall hear some of the captain's complimentary remarks when we get back.  Miserable business, this."

"Do you think all this is true?" asked the younger man.

"True!  It is just possible.  But if it isn't true what can we do?  If we had a dozen boats we could patrol the creeks; and that wouldn't be much good.  That drunken madman was right; we haven't enough hold on this coast.  They do what they like.  Are our hammocks slung?"

"Yes, I told the coxswain.  Strange couple over there," said the sub, with a wave of his hand towards Almayer's house.

"Hem!  Queer, certainly.  What have you been telling her?  I was attending to the father most of the time."

"I assure you I have been perfectly civil," protested the other warmly.

"All right.  Don't get excited.  She objects to civility, then, from what I understand.  I thought you might have been tender.  You know we are on service."

"Well, of course.  Never forget that.  Coldly civil. That's all."

They both laughed a little, and not feeling sleepy began to pace the verandah side by side.  The moon rose stealthily above the trees, and suddenly changed the river into a stream of scintillating silver.  The forest came out of the black void and stood sombre and pensive over the sparkling water.  The breeze died away into a breathless calm.

Seamanlike, the two officers tramped measuredly up and down without exchanging a word.  The loose planks rattled rhythmically under their steps with obtrusive dry sound in the perfect silence of the night.  As they were wheeling round again the younger man stood attentive.

"Did you hear that?" he asked.

"No!" said the other.  "Hear what?"

"I thought I heard a cry.  Ever so faint.  Seemed a woman's voice.  In that other house.  Ah!  Again!  Hear it?"

"No," said the lieutenant, after listening awhile.  "You young fellows always hear women's voices.  If you are going to dream you had better get into your hammock. Good-night."

The moon mounted higher, and the warm shadows grew smaller and crept away as if hiding before the cold and cruel light.

## CHAPTER X

"It has set at last," said Nina to her mother, pointing towards the hills behind which the sun had sunk. " Listen, mother, I am going now to Bulangi's creek, and if I should never return——"

She interrupted herself, and something like doubt dimmed for a moment the fire of suppressed exaltation that had glowed in her eyes and had illuminated the serene impassiveness of her features with a ray of eager life during all that long day of excitement—the day of joy and anxiety, of hope and terror, of vague grief and indistinct delight. While the sun shone with that dazzling light in which her love was born and grew till it possessed her whole being, she was kept firm in her unwavering resolve by the mysterious whisperings of desire which filled her heart with impatient longing for the darkness that would mean the end of danger and strife, the beginning of happiness, the fulfilling of love, the complete-ness of life. It had set at last ! The short tropical twilight went out before she could draw the long breath of relief ; and now the sudden darkness seemed to be full of menacing voices calling upon her to rush headlong into the unknown ; to be true to her own impulses, to give herself up to the passion she had evoked and shared. He was waiting ! In the solitude of the secluded clearing, in the vast silence of the forest he was waiting alone, a fugitive in fear of his life. Indifferent to his danger he was waiting for her. It was for her only that he had come ; and now as the time approached when he should have his reward, she asked herself with dis-

E

may what meant that chilling doubt of her own will and of her
own desire? With an effort she shook off the fear of the
passing weakness. He should have his reward. Her woman's
love and her woman's honour overcame the faltering distrust
of that unknown future waiting for her in the darkness of
the river.

"No, you will not return," muttered Mrs. Almayer,
prophetically. "Without you he will not go, and if he
remains here——" She waved her hand towards the lights
of "Almayer's Folly," and the unfinished sentence died out
in a threatening murmur.

The two women had met behind the house, and now were
walking slowly together towards the creek where all the
canoes were moored. Arrived at the fringe of bushes they
stopped by a common impulse, and Mrs. Almayer, laying her
hand on her daughter's arm, tried in vain to look close into
the girl's averted face. When she attempted to speak her
first words were lost in a stifled sob that sounded strangely
coming from that woman who, of all human passions, seemed
to know only those of anger and hate.

"You are going away to be a great Ranee," she said at last,
in a voice that was steady enough now, "and if you be wise
you shall have much power that will endure many days, and
even last into your old age. What have I been? A slave
all my life, and I have cooked rice for a man who had no
courage and no wisdom. Hai! I! even I, was given in gift
by a chief and a warrior to a man that was neither. Hai!
Hai!"

She wailed to herself softly, lamenting the lost possibilities
of murder and mischief that could have fallen to her lot had
she been mated with a congenial spirit. Nina bent down
over Mrs. Almayer's slight form and scanned attentively,
under the stars that had rushed out on the black sky and now
hung breathless over that strange parting, her mother's
shrivelled features, and looked close into the sunken eyes that
could see into her own dark future by the light of a long and a
painful experience. Again she felt herself fascinated, as of
old, by her mother's exalted mood and by the oracular

certainty of expression which, together with her fits of violence, had contributed not a little to the reputation for witchcraft she enjoyed in the settlement.

"I was a slave, and you shall be a queen," went on Mrs. Almayer, looking straight before her; "but remember men's strength and their weakness. Tremble before his anger, so that he may see your fear in the light of day; but in your heart you may laugh, for after sunset he is your slave."

"A slave! He! The master of life! You do not know him, mother."

Mrs. Almayer condescended to laugh contemptuously.

"You speak like a fool of a white woman," she exclaimed. "What do you know of men's anger and of men's love? Have you watched the sleep of men weary of dealing death? Have you felt about you the strong arm that could drive a kriss deep into a beating heart? Yah! you are a white woman, and ought to pray to a woman-god!"

"Why do you say this? I have listened to your words so long that I have forgotten my old life. If I was white would I stand here, ready to go? Mother, I shall return to the house and look once more at my father's face."

"No!" said Mrs. Almayer, violently. "No, he sleeps now the sleep of gin; and if you went back he might awake and see you. No, he shall never see you. When the terrible old man took you away from me you were little, you remember——"

"It was such a long time ago," murmured Nina.

"I remember," went on Mrs. Almayer, fiercely. "I wanted to look at your face again. He said no! I heard you cry and jumped into the river. You were his daughter then; you are my daughter now. Never shall you go back to that house; you shall never cross this courtyard again. No! no!"

Her voice rose almost to a shout. On the other side of the creek there was a rustle in the long grass. The two women heard it, and listened for a while in startled silence.

" I shall go," said Nina, in a cautious but intense whisper.
" What is your hate or your revenge to me ? "

She moved towards the house, Mrs. Almayer clinging to
her and trying to pull her back.

" Stop, you shall not go ! " she gasped.

Nina pushed away her mother impatiently and gathered up
her skirts for a quick run, but Mrs. Almayer ran forward and
turned round, facing her daughter with outstretched arms.

" If you move another step," she exclaimed, breathing
quickly, " I shall cry out. Do you see those lights in the big
house ? There sit two white men, angry because they
cannot have the blood of the man you love. And in those
dark houses," she continued, more calmly as she pointed
towards the settlement, " my voice could wake up men that
would lead the Orang Blanda soldiers to him who is waiting—
for you."

She could not see her daughter's face, but the white figure
before her stood silent and irresolute in the darkness. Mrs.
Almayer pursued her advantage.

" Give up your old life ! Forget ! " she said in entreating
tones. " Forget that you ever looked at a white face ;
forget their words ; forget their thoughts. They speak lies.
And they think lies because they despise us that are better
than they are, but not so strong. Forget their friendship
and their contempt ; forget their many gods. Girl, why
do you want to remember the past when there is a warrior
and a chief ready to give many lives—his own life—for one
of your smiles ? "

While she spoke she pushed gently her daughter towards
the canoes, hiding her own fear, anxiety, and doubt under
the flood of passionate words that left Nina no time to think
and no opportunity to protest, even if she had wished it.
But she did not wish it now. At the bottom of that passing
desire to look again at her father's face there was no strong
affection. She felt no scruples and no remorse at leaving
suddenly that man whose sentiment towards herself she
could not understand, she could not even see. There was
only an instinctive clinging to old life, to old habits, to old

faces; that fear of finality which lurks in every human breast and prevents so many heroisms and so many crimes. For years she had stood between her mother and her father, the one so strong in her weakness, the other so weak where he could have been strong. Between those two beings so dissimilar, so antagonistic, she stood with mute heart wondering and angry at the fact of her own existence. It seemed so unreasonable, so humiliating to be flung there in that settlement and to see the days rush by into the past, without a hope, a desire, or an aim that would justify the life she had to endure in ever-growing weariness. She had little belief and no sympathy for her father's dreams; but the savage ravings of her mother chanced to strike a responsive chord, deep down somewhere in her despairing heart; and she dreamed dreams of her own with the persistent absorption of a captive thinking of liberty within the walls of his prison cell. With the coming of Dain she found the road to freedom by obeying the voice of the new-born impulses, and with surprised joy she thought she could read in his eyes the answer to all the questionings of her heart. She understood now the reason and the aim of life; and in the triumphant unveiling of that mystery she threw away disdainfully her past with its sad thoughts, its bitter feelings, and its faint affections, now withered and dead in contact with her fierce passion.

Mrs. Almayer unmoored Nina's own canoe and, straightening herself painfully, stood, painter in hand, looking at her daughter.

"Quick," she said; "get away before the moon rises, while the river is dark. I am afraid of Abdulla's slaves. The wretches prowl in the night often, and might see and follow you. There are two paddles in the canoe."

Nina approached her mother and hesitatingly touched lightly with her lips the wrinkled forehead. Mrs. Almayer snorted contemptuously in protest against that tenderness which she, nevertheless, feared could be contagious.

"Shall I ever see you again, mother?" murmured Nina.

"No," said Mrs. Almayer, after a short silence. "Why

should you return here where it is my fate to die ? You will live far away in splendour and might. When I hear of white men driven from the islands, then I shall know that you are alive, and that you remember my words."

"I shall always remember," returned Nina, earnestly; "but where is my power, and what can I do ?"

"Do not let him look too long in your eyes, nor lay his head on your knees without reminding him that men should fight before they rest. And if he lingers, give him his kriss yourself and bid him go, as the wife of a mighty prince should do when the enemies are near. Let him slay the white men that come to us to trade, with prayers on their lips and loaded guns in their hands. Ah "—she ended with a sigh— "they are on every sea, and on every shore; and they are very many !"

She swung the bow of the canoe towards the river, but did not let go the gunwale, keeping her hand on it in irresolute thoughtfulness. Nina put the point of the paddle against the bank, ready to shove off into the stream.

"What is it, mother ?" she asked, in a low voice. "Do you hear anything ?"

"No," said Mrs. Almayer, absently. "Listen, Nina," she continued, abruptly, after a slight pause, "in after years there will be other women——"

A stifled cry in the boat interrupted her, and the paddle rattled in the canoe as it slipped from Nina's hands, which she put out in a protesting gesture. Mrs. Almayer fell on her knees on the bank and leaned over the gunwale so as to bring her own face close to her daughter's.

"There will be other women," she repeated firmly; "I tell you that, because you are half white, and may forget that he is a great chief, and that such things must be. Hide your anger, and do not let him see on your face the pain that will eat your heart. Meet him with joy in your eyes and wisdom on your lips, for to you he will turn in sadness or in doubt. As long as he looks upon many women your power will last, but should there be one, one only with whom he seems to forget you, then——"

"I could not live," exclaimed Nina, covering her face with both her hands. "Do not speak so, mother; it could not be."

"Then," went on Mrs. Almayer, steadily, "to that woman, Nina, show no mercy."

She moved the canoe down towards the stream by the gunwale, and gripped it with both her hands, the bow pointing into the river.

"Are you crying?" she asked sternly of her daughter, who sat still with covered face. "Arise, and take your paddle, for he has waited long enough. And remember, Nina, no mercy; and if you must strike, strike with a steady hand."

She put out all her strength, and swinging her body over the water, shot the light craft far into the stream. When she recovered herself from the effort she tried vainly to catch a glimpse of the canoe that seemed to have dissolved suddenly into the white mist trailing over the heated waters of the Pantai. After listening for a while intently on her knees, Mrs. Almayer rose with a deep sigh, while two tears wandered slowly down her withered cheeks. She wiped them off quickly with a wisp of her grey hair as if ashamed of herself, but could not stifle another loud sigh, for her heart was heavy and she suffered much, being unused to tender emotions. This time she fancied she had heard a faint noise, like the echo of her own sigh, and she stopped, straining her ears to catch the slightest sound, and peering apprehensively towards the bushes near her.

"Who is there?" she asked, in an unsteady voice, while her imagination peopled the solitude of the riverside with ghost-like forms. "Who is there?" she repeated faintly.

There was no answer: only the voice of the river murmuring in sad monotone behind the white veil seemed to swell louder for a moment, to die away again in a soft whisper of eddies washing against the bank.

Mrs. Almayer shook her head as if in answer to her own thoughts, and walked quickly away from the bushes, looking to the right and left watchfully. She went straight towards the cooking-shed, observing that the embers of the fire there glowed more brightly than usual, as if somebody had been adding fresh fuel to the fires during the evening. As she approached, Babalatchi, who had been squatting in the warm glow, rose and met her in the shadow outside.

" Is she gone ? " asked the anxious statesman, hastily.

" Yes," answered Mrs. Almayer. " What are the white men doing ? When did you leave them ? "

" They are sleeping now, I think. May they never wake ! " exclaimed Babalatchi, fervently. " Oh ! but they are devils, and made much talk and trouble over that carcass. The chief threatened me twice with his hand, and said he would have me tied up to a tree. Tie me up to a tree ! Me ! " he repeated, striking his breast violently.

Mrs. Almayer laughed tauntingly.

" And you salaamed and asked for mercy. Men with arms by their side acted otherwise when I was young."

" And where are they, the men of your youth ? You mad woman ! " retorted Babalatchi, angrily. " Killed by the Dutch. Aha ! But I shall live to deceive them. A man knows when to fight and when to tell peaceful lies. You would know that if you were not a woman."

But Mrs. Almayer did not seem to hear him. With bent body and outstretched arm she appeared to be listening to some noise behind the shed.

" There are strange sounds," she whispered, with evident alarm. " I have heard in the air the sounds of grief, as of a sigh and weeping. That was by the riverside. And now again I heard—— "

" Where ? " asked Babalatchi, in an altered voice. " What did you hear ? "

" Close here. It was like a breath long drawn. I wish I had burnt the paper over the body before it was buried."

" Yes," assented Babalatchi. " But the white men had him thrown into a hole at once. You know he found his death on the river," he added cheerfully, " and his ghost may hail the canoes, but would leave the land alone."

Mrs. Almayer, who had been craning her neck to look round the corner of the shed, drew back her head.

"There is nobody there," she said, reassured. "Is it not time for the Rajah war-canoe to go to the clearing?"

"I have been waiting for it here, for I myself must go," explained Babalatchi. "I think I will go over and see what makes them late. When will you come? The Rajah gives you refuge."

"I shall paddle over before the break of day. I cannot leave my dollars behind," muttered Mrs. Almayer.

They separated. Babalatchi crossed the courtyard towards the creek to get his canoe, and Mrs. Almayer walked slowly to the house, ascended the plankway, and passing through the back verandah entered the passage leading to the front of the house; but before going in she turned in the doorway and looked back at the empty and silent courtyard, now lit up by the rays of the rising moon. No sooner had she disappeared, however, than a vague shape flitted out from amongst the stalks of the banana plantation, darted over the moonlit space, and fell in the darkness at the foot of the verandah. It might have been the shadow of a driving cloud, so noiseless and rapid was its passage, but for the trail of disturbed grass, whose feathery heads trembled and swayed for a long time in the moonlight before they rested motionless and gleaming, like a design of silver sprays embroidered on a sombre background.

Mrs. Almayer lighted the cocoanut lamp, and lifting cautiously the red curtain, gazed upon her husband, shading the light with her hand. Almayer, huddled up in the chair, one of his arms hanging down, the other thrown across the lower part of his face as if to ward off an invisible enemy, his legs stretched straight out, slept heavily, unconscious of the unfriendly eyes that looked upon him in disparaging criticism. At his feet lay the overturned table, amongst a wreck of crockery and broken bottles. The appearance as of traces left by a desperate struggle was accentuated by the chairs, which seemed to have been scattered violently all over the place, and now lay about the verandah with a

E 2

lamentable aspect of inebriety in their helpless attitudes. Only Nina's big rocking-chair, standing black and motionless on its high runners, towered above the chaos of demoralised furniture, unflinchingly dignified and patient, waiting for its burden.

With a last scornful look towards the sleeper, Mrs. Almayer passed behind the curtain into her own room. A couple of bats, encouraged by the darkness and the peaceful state of affairs, resumed their silent and oblique gambols above Almayer's head, and for a long time the profound quiet of the house was unbroken, save for the deep breathing of the sleeping man and the faint tinkle of silver in the hands of the woman preparing for flight. In the increasing light of the moon that had risen now above the night mist, the objects on the verandah came out strongly outlined in black splashes of shadow with all the uncompromising ugliness of their disorder, and a caricature of the sleeping Almayer appeared on the dirty whitewash of the wall behind him in a grotesquely exaggerated detail of attitude and feature enlarged to a heroic size. The discontented bats departed in quest of darker places, and a lizard came out in short, nervous rushes, and, pleased with the white table-cloth, stopped on it in breathless immobility that would have suggested sudden death had it not been for the melodious call he exchanged with a less adventurous friend hiding amongst the lumber in the courtyard. Then the boards in the passage creaked, the lizard vanished, and Almayer stirred uneasily with a sigh : slowly, out of the senseless annihilation of drunken sleep, he was returning, through the land of dreams, to waking consciousness. Almayer's head rolled from shoulder to shoulder in the oppression of his dream ; the heavens had descended upon him like a heavy mantle, and trailed in starred folds far under him. Stars above, stars all round him ; and from the stars under his feet rose a whisper full of entreaties and tears, and sorrowful faces flitted amongst the clusters of light filling the infinite space below. How escape from the importunity of lamentable cries and from the look of staring, sad eyes in the faces which pressed round him till he gasped for breath under the crushing weight of worlds that hung over his aching shoulders? Get away! But how? If he attempted to move he would step off into nothing, and perish in the crashing fall of that universe of which he was the only support. And what were the voices saying? Urging him to move! Why? Move to destruction! Not likely! The absurdity of the thing filled him with indignation. He got a firmer foothold and stiffened his muscles in heroic resolve to carry his burden to all eternity. And ages passed in the superhuman labour, amidst the rush of circling worlds; in the plaintive murmur of sorrowful voices urging him to desist before it was too late—till the mysterious power that had laid upon him the giant task seemed at last to seek his destruction. With terror he felt an irresistible hand shaking him by the shoulder, while the chorus of voices swelled louder into an agonised prayer to go, go before it is too late. He felt himself slipping, losing his balance, as something dragged at his legs, and he fell. With a faint cry he glided out of the anguish of perishing creation into an imperfect waking that seemed to be still under the spell of his dream.

"What? What?" he murmured sleepily, without moving or opening his eyes. His head still felt heavy, and he had not the courage to raise his eyelids. In his ears there still lingered the sound of entreating whisper.—"Am I awake?—Why do I hear the voices?" he argued to himself, hazily.—"I cannot get rid of the horrible nightmare yet.—I have been very drunk.—What is that shaking me? I am dreaming yet.—I must open my eyes and be done with it. I am only half awake, it is evident."

He made an effort to shake off his stupor and saw a face close to his, glaring at him with staring eyeballs. He closed his eyes again in amazed horror and sat up straight in the chair, trembling in every limb. What was this apparition?—His own fancy, no doubt.—His nerves had been much tried the day before—and then the drink! He would not see it again if he had the courage to look.—He would look directly. —Get a little steadier first.—So.—Now.

He looked. The figure of a woman standing in the steely light, her hands stretched forth in a suppliant gesture, confronted him from the far-off end of the verandah ; and in the space between him and the obstinate phantom floated the murmur of words that fell on his ears in a jumble of torturing sentences, the meaning of which escaped the utmost efforts of his brain. Who spoke the Malay words ? Who ran away ? Why too late—and too late for what ? What meant those words of hate and love mixed so strangely together, the ever-recurring names falling on his ears again and again—Nina, Dain ; Dain, Nina ? Dain was dead, and Nina was sleeping, unaware of the terrible experience through which he was now passing. Was he going to be tormented for ever, sleeping or waking, and have no peace either night or day ? What was the meaning of this ?

He shouted the last words aloud. The shadowy woman seemed to shrink and recede a little from him towards the doorway, and there was a shriek. Exasperated by the incomprehensible nature of his torment, Almayer made a rush upon the apparition, which eluded his grasp, and he brought up heavily against the wall. Quick as lightning he turned round and pursued fiercely the mysterious figure fleeing from him with piercing shrieks that were like fuel to the flames of his anger. Over the furniture, round the overturned table, and now he had it cornered behind Nina's chair. To the left, to the right they dodged, the chair rocking madly between them, she sending out shriek after shriek at every feint, and he growling meaningless curses through his hard set teeth. " Oh ! the fiendish noise that split his head and seemed to choke his breath.—It would kill him.—It must be stopped ! " An insane desire to crush that yelling thing induced him to cast himself recklessly over the chair with a desperate grab, and they came down together in a cloud of dust amongst the splintered wood. The last shriek died out under him in a faint gurgle, and he had secured the relief of absolute silence.

He looked at the woman's face under him. A real woman ! He knew her. By all that is wonderful ! Taminah ! He jumped up ashamed of his fury and stood perplexed, wiping his forehead. The girl struggled to a kneeling posture and embraced his legs in a frenzied prayer for mercy.

"Don't be afraid," he said, raising her. "I shall not hurt you. Why do you come to my house in the night? And if you had to come, why not go behind the curtain where the women sleep?"

"The place behind the curtain is empty," gasped Taminah, catching her breath between the words . "There are no women in your house any more, Tuan. I saw the old Mem go away before I tried to wake you. I did not want your women, I wanted you."

"Old Mem!" repeated Almayer. "Do you mean my wife?"

She nodded her head.

"But of my daughter you are not afraid?" said Almayer.

"Have you not heard me?" she exclaimed. "Have I not spoken for a long time when you lay there with eyes half open? She is gone too."

"I was asleep. Can you not tell when a man is sleeping and when awake?"

"Sometimes," answered Taminah in a low voice; "some- times the spirit lingers close to a sleeping body and may hear. I spoke a long time before I touched you, and I spoke softly for fear it would depart at a sudden noise and leave you sleeping for ever. I took you by the shoulder only when you began to mutter words I could not understand. Have you not heard, then, and do you know nothing?"

"Nothing of what you said. What is it? Tell again if you want me to know."

He took her by the shoulder and led her unresisting to the front of the verandah into a stronger light. She wrung her hands with such an appearance of grief that he began to be alarmed.

"Speak," he said. "You made noise enough to wake even dead men. And yet nobody living came," he added to himself in an uneasy whisper. "Are you mute? Speak!" he repeated.

In a rush of words which broke out after a short struggle

from her trembling lips she told him the tale of Nina's love
and her own jealousy. Several times he looked angrily into
her face and told her to be silent; but he could not stop the
sounds that seemed to him to run out in a hot stream, swirl
about his feet, and rise in scalding waves about him, higher,
higher, drowning his heart, touching his lips with a feel of
molten lead, blotting out his sight in scorching vapour,
closing over his head, merciless and deadly. When she spoke
of the deception as to Dain's death of which he had been
the victim only that day, he glanced again at her with terrible
eyes, and made her falter for a second, but he turned away
directly, and his face suddenly lost all expression in a stony
stare far away over the river. Ah! the river! His old
friend and his old enemy, speaking always with the same voice
as he runs from year to year bringing fortune or disappointment, happiness or pain, upon the same varying but unchanged
surface of glancing currents and swirling eddies. For many
years he had listened to the passionless and soothing murmur
that sometimes was the song of hope, at times the song of
triumph, of encouragement; more often the whisper of
consolation that spoke of better days to come. For so many
years! So many years! And now to the accompaniment
of that murmur he listened to the slow and painful beating
of his heart. He listened attentively, wondering at the
regularity of its beats. He began to count mechanically.
One, two. Why count? At the next beat it must stop.
No heart could suffer so and beat so steadily for long. Those
regular strokes as of a muffled hammer that rang in his ears
must stop soon. Still beating unceasing and cruel. No
man can bear this; and is this the last, or will the next one
be the last?—How much longer? O God! how much
longer? His hand weighed heavier unconsciously on the
girl's shoulder, and she spoke the last words of her story
crouching at his feet with tears of pain and shame and anger.
Was her revenge to fail her? This white man was like a
senseless stone. Too late! Too late!

"And you saw her go?" Almayer's voice sounded harshly
above her head.

"Did I not tell you?" she sobbed, trying to wriggle gently out from under his grip. "Did I not tell you that I saw the witchwoman push the canoe? I lay hidden in the grass and heard all the words. She that we used to call the white Mem wanted to return to look at your face, but the witchwoman forbade her, and——"

She sank lower yet on her elbow, turning half round under the downward push of the heavy hand, her face lifted up to him with spiteful eyes.

"And she obeyed," she shouted out in a half-laugh, half-cry of pain. "Let me go, Tuan. Why are you angry with me? Hasten, or you shall be too late to show your anger to the deceitful woman."

Almayer dragged her up to her feet and looked close into her face while she struggled, turning her head away from his wild stare.

"Who sent you here to torment me?" he asked, violently. "I do not believe you. You lie."

He straightened his arm suddenly and flung her across the verandah towards the doorway, where she lay immobile and silent, as if she had left her life in his grasp, a dark heap, without a sound or a stir.

"Oh! Nina!" whispered Almayer, in a voice in which reproach and love spoke together in pained tenderness. "Oh! Nina! I do not believe."

A light draught from the river ran over the courtyard in a wave of bowing grass and, entering the verandah, touched Almayer's forehead with its cool breath, in a caress of infinite pity. The curtain in the women's doorway blew out and instantly collapsed with startling helplessness. He stared at the fluttering stuff.

"Nina!" cried Almayer. "Where are you, Nina?"

The wind passed out of the empty house in a tremulous sigh, and all was still.

Almayer hid his face in his hands as if to shut out a loathsome sight. When, hearing a slight rustle, he uncovered his eyes, the dark heap by the door was gone.

## CHAPTER XI

In the middle of a shadowless square of moonlight, shining on a smooth and level expanse of young rice-shoots, a little shelter-hut perched on high posts, the pile of brushwood near by and the glowing embers of a fire with a man stretched before it, seemed very small and as if lost in the pale green iridescence reflected from the ground. On three sides of the clearing, appearing very far away in the deceptive light, the big trees of the forest, lashed together with manifold bonds by a mass of tangled creepers, looked down at the growing young life at their feet with the sombre resignation of giants that had lost faith in their strength. And in the midst of them the merciless creepers clung to the big trunks in cable-like coils, leaped from tree to tree, hung in thorny festoons from the lower boughs, and, sending slender tendrils on high to seek out the smallest branches, carried death to their victims in an exulting riot of silent destruction.

On the fourth side, following the curve of the bank of that branch of the Pantai that formed the only access to the clearing, ran a black line of young trees, bushes, and thick second growth, unbroken save for a small gap chopped out in one place. At that gap began the narrow footpath leading from the water's edge to the grass-built shelter used by the night watchers when the ripening crop had to be protected from the wild pigs. The pathway ended at the foot of the piles on which the hut was built, in a circular space covered with ashes and bits of burnt wood. In the middle of that space, by the dim fire, lay Dain.

He turned over on his side with an impatient sigh, and, pillowing his head on his bent arm, lay quietly with his face to the dying fire. The glowing embers shone redly in a small circle, throwing a gleam into his wide-open eyes, and at every deep breath the fine white ash of bygone fires rose in a light

cloud before his parted lips, and danced away from the
warm glow into the moonbeams pouring down upon Bulangi's
clearing.  His body was weary with the exertion of the past
few days, his mind more weary still with the strain of solitary
waiting for his fate.  Never before had he felt so helpless.
He had heard the report of the gun fired on board the
launch, and he knew that his life was in untrustworthy hands,
and that his enemies were very near.  During the slow hours
of the afternoon he roamed about on the edge of the forest,
or, hiding in the bushes, watched the creek with unquiet
eyes for some sign of danger.  He feared not death, yet he
desired ardently to live, for life to him was Nina.  She had
promised to come, to follow him, to share his danger and his
splendour.  But with her by his side he cared not for danger,
and without her there could be no splendour and no joy
in existence.  Crouching in his shady hiding-place, he closed
his eyes, trying to evoke the gracious and charming image of
the white figure that for him was the beginning and the end
of life.  With eyes shut tight, his teeth hard set, he tried in a
great effort of passionate will to keep his hold on that vision
of supreme delight.  In vain !  His heart grew heavy as the
figure of Nina faded away to be replaced by another vision
this time—a vision of armed men, of angry faces, of glittering
arms—and he seemed to hear the hum of excited and triumphant voices as they discovered him in his hiding-place.
Startled by the vividness of his fancy, he would open his
eyes, and, leaping out into the sunlight, resume his aimless
wanderings around the clearing.  As he skirted in his weary
march the edge of the forest he glanced now and then into
its dark shade, so enticing in its deceptive appearance of
coolness, so repellent with its unrelieved gloom, where lay,
entombed and rotting, countless generations of trees, and
where their successors stood as if mourning, in dark green
foliage, immense and helpless, awaiting their turn.  Only
the parasites seemed to live there in a sinuous rush upwards
into the air and sunshine, feeding on the dead and the dying
alike, and crowning their victims with pink and blue flowers
that gleamed amongst the boughs, incongruous and cruel,

like a strident and mocking note in the solemn harmony of the doomed trees.

A man could hide there, thought Dain, as he approached a place where the creepers had been torn and hacked into an archway that might have been the beginning of a path. As he bent down to look through he heard angry grunting, and a sounder of wild pig crashed away in the undergrowth. An acrid smell of damp earth and of decaying leaves took him by the throat, and he drew back with a scared face, as if he had been touched by the breath of Death itself. The very air seemed dead in there—heavy and stagnating, poisoned with the corruption of countless ages. He went on, staggering on his way, urged by the nervous restlessness that made him feel tired yet caused him to loathe the very idea of immobility and repose. Was he a wild man to hide in the woods and perhaps be killed there—in the darkness—where there was no room to breathe? He would wait for his enemies in the sunlight, where he could see the sky and feel the breeze. He knew how a Malay chief should die. The sombre and desperate fury, that peculiar inheritance of his race, took possession of him, and he glared savagely across the clearing towards the gap in the bushes by the riverside. They would come from there. In imagination he saw them now. He saw the bearded faces and the white jackets of the officers, the light on the levelled barrels of the rifles. What is the bravery of the greatest warrior before the firearms in the hand of a slave? He would walk towards them with a smiling face, with his hands held out in a sign of submission till he was very near them. He would speak friendly words— come nearer yet—yet nearer—so near that they could touch him with their hands and stretch them out to make him a captive. That would be the time : with a shout and a leap he would be in the midst of them, kriss in hand, killing, killing, killing, and would die with the shouts of his enemies in his ears, their warm blood spurting before his eyes.

Carried away by his excitement, he snatched the kriss hidden in his sarong, and, drawing a long breath, rushed forward, struck at the empty air, and fell on his face. He lay

as if stunned in the sudden reaction from his exaltation,
thinking that, even if he died thus gloriously, it would have
to be before he saw Nina. Better so. If he saw her again
he felt that death would be too terrible. With horror he, the
descendant of Rajahs and of conquerors, had to face the doubt
of his own bravery. His desire of life tormented him in a
paroxysm of agonising remorse. He had not the courage
to stir a limb. He had lost faith in himself, and there was
nothing else in him of what makes a man. The suffering
remained, for it is ordered that it should abide in the human
body even to the last breath, and fear remained. Dimly he
could look into the depths of his passionate love, see its
strength and its weakness, and felt afraid.

The sun went down slowly. The shadow of the western
forest marched over the clearing, covered the man's scorched
shoulders with its cool mantle, and went on hurriedly to
mingle with the shadows of other forests on the eastern side.
The sun lingered for a while amongst the light tracery of
the higher branches, as if in friendly reluctance to abandon
the body stretched in the green paddy-field. Then Dain,
revived by the cool of the evening breeze, sat up and stared
round him. As he did so the sun dipped sharply, as if
ashamed of being detected in a sympathising attitude, and
the clearing, which during the day was all light, became
suddenly all darkness, where the fire gleamed like an eye.
Dain walked slowly towards the creek, and, divesting himself
of his torn sarong, his only garment, entered the water
cautiously. He had had nothing to eat that day, and had
not dared show himself in daylight by the water-side to
drink. Now, as he swam silently, he swallowed a few
mouthfuls of water that lapped about his lips. This did him
good, and he walked with greater confidence in himself and
others as he returned towards the fire. Had he been betrayed
by Lakamba all would have been over by this. He made up
a big blaze, and while it lasted dried himself, and then lay
down by the embers. He could not sleep, but he felt a great
numbness in all his limbs. His restlessness was gone, and he
was content to lay still, measuring the time by watching the

stars that rose in endless succession above the forests, while the slight puffs of wind under the cloudless sky seemed to fan their twinkle into a greater brightness. Dreamily he assured himself over and over again that she would come, till the certitude crept into his heart and filled him with a great peace. Yes, when the next day broke, they would be together on the great blue sea that was like life—away from the forests that were like death. He murmured the name of Nina into the silent space with a tender smile : this seemed to break the spell of stillness, and far away by the creek a frog croaked loudly as if in answer. A chorus of loud roars and plaintive calls rose from the mud along the line of bushes. He laughed heartily ; doubtless it was their love-song. He felt affectionate towards the frogs and listened, pleased with the noisy life near him.

When the moon peeped above the trees he felt the old impatience and the old restlessness steal over him. Why was she so late ? True, it was a long way to come with a single paddle. With what skill and what endurance could those small hands manage a heavy paddle ! It was very wonderful —such small hands, such soft little palms that knew how to touch his cheek with a feel lighter than the fanning of a butterfly's wing. Wonderful ! He lost himself lovingly in the contemplation of this tremendous mystery, and when he looked at the moon again it had risen a hand's breadth above the trees. Would she come ? He forced himself to lay still, overcoming the impulse to rise and rush round the clearing again. He turned this way and that ; at last, quivering with the effort, he lay on his back, and saw her face among the stars looking down on him.

The croaking of frogs suddenly ceased. With the watchfulness of a hunted man Dain sat up, listening anxiously, and heard several splashes in the water as the frogs took rapid headers into the creek. He knew that they had been alarmed by something, and stood up suspicious and attentive. A slight grating noise, then the dry sound as of two pieces of wood struck against each other. Somebody was about to land ! He took up an armful of brushwood, and, without

taking his eyes from the path, held it over the embers of his
fire. He waited, undecided, and saw something gleam
amongst the bushes; then a white figure came out of the
shadows and seemed to float towards him in the pale light.
His heart gave a great leap and stood still, then went on
shaking his frame in furious beats. He dropped the brushwood upon the glowing coals, and had an impression of
shouting her name—of rushing to meet her; yet he emitted
no sound, he stirred not an inch, but he stood silent and
motionless like chiselled bronze under the moonlight that
streamed over his naked shoulders. As he stood still, fighting
with his breath, as if bereft of his senses by the intensity of
his delight, she walked up to him with quick, resolute steps,
and, with the appearance of one about to leap from a dangerous height, threw both her arms round his neck with a
sudden gesture. A small blue gleam crept amongst the dry
branches, and the crackling of reviving fire was the only
sound as they faced each other in the speechless emotion of
that meeting; then the dry fuel caught at once, and a bright
hot flame shot upwards in a blaze as high as their heads, and
in its light they saw each other's eyes.

Neither of them spoke. He was regaining his senses in a
slight tremor that ran upwards along his rigid body and hung
about his trembling lips. She drew back her head and
fastened her eyes on his in one of those long looks that are a
woman's most terrible weapon; a look that is more stirring
than the closest touch, and more dangerous than the thrust
of a dagger, because it also whips the soul out of the body,
but leaves the body alive and helpless, to be swayed here and
there by the capricious tempests of passion and desire; a
look that enwraps the whole body, and that penetrates into
the innermost recesses of the being, bringing terrible defeat
in the delirious uplifting of accomplished conquest. It has
the same meaning for the man of the forests and the sea as for
the man threading the paths of the more dangerous wilderness
of houses and streets. Men that had felt in their breasts the
awful exultation such a look awakens become mere things of
to-day—which is paradise; forget yesterday—which was

suffering; care not for to-morrow—which may be perdition. They wish to live under that look for ever. It is the look of woman's surrender.

He understood, and, as if suddenly released from his invisible bonds, fell at her feet with a shout of joy, and, embracing her knees, hid his head in the folds of her dress, murmuring disjointed words of gratitude and love. Never before had he felt so proud as now, when at the feet of that woman that half belonged to his enemies. Her fingers played with his hair in an absent-minded caress as she stood absorbed in thought. The thing was done. Her mother was right. The man was her slave. As she glanced down at his kneeling form she felt a great pitying tenderness for that man she was used to call—even in her thoughts—the master of life. She lifted her eyes and looked sadly at the southern heavens under which lay the path of their lives—her own, and that man's at her feet. Did he not say himself that she was the light of his life? She would be his light and his wisdom; she would be his greatness and his strength; yet hidden from the eyes of all men she would be, above all, his only and lasting weakness. A very woman! In the sublime vanity of her kind she was thinking already of moulding a god from the clay at her feet. A god for others to worship. She was content to see him as he was now, and to feel him quiver at the slightest touch of her light fingers. And while her eyes looked sadly at the southern stars a faint smile seemed to be playing about her firm lips. Who can tell in the fitful light of a camp fire? It might have been a smile of triumph, or of conscious power, or of tender pity, or, perhaps, of love.

She spoke softly to him, and he rose to his feet, putting his arm round her in quiet consciousness of his ownership; she laid her head on his shoulder with a sense of defiance to all the world in the encircling protection of that arm. He was hers with all his qualities and all his faults. His strength and his courage, his recklessness and his daring, his simple wisdom and his savage cunning—all were hers. As they passed together out of the red light of the fire into the silver shower of rays that fell upon the clearing he bent his head over her face, and she saw in his eyes the dreamy intoxication of boundless felicity from the close touch of her slight figure clasped to his side.   With a rhythmical swing of their bodies they walked through the light towards the outlying shadows of the forests that seemed to guard their happiness in solemn immobility.    Their forms melted in the play of light and shadow at the foot of the big trees, but the murmur of tender words lingered over the empty clearing, grew faint, and died out.    A sigh as of immense sorrow passed over the land in the last effort of the dying breeze, and in the deep silence which succeeded, the earth and the heavens were suddenly hushed up in the mournful contemplation of human love and human blindness.

They walked slowly back to the fire.   He made for her a seat out of the dry branches, and, throwing himself down at her feet, lay his head in her lap and gave himself up to the dreamy delight of the passing hour.   Their voices rose and fell, tender or animated as they spoke of their love and of their future.   She, with a few skilful words spoken from time to time, guided his thoughts, and he let his happiness flow in a stream of talk passionate and tender, grave or menacing, according to the mood which she evoked.   He spoke to her of his own island, where the gloomy forests and the muddy rivers were unknown.   He spoke of its terraced fields, of the murmuring clear rills of sparkling water that flowed down the sides of great mountains, bringing life to the land and joy to its tillers.   And he spoke also of the mountain peak that rising lonely above the belt of trees knew the secrets of the passing clouds, and was the dwelling-place of the mysterious spirit of his race, of the guardian genius of his house.   He spoke of vast horizons swept by fierce winds that whistled high above the summits of burning mountains.   He spoke of his forefathers that conquered ages ago the island of which he was to be the future ruler.   And then as, in her interest, she brought her face nearer to his, he, touching lightly the thick tresses of her long hair, felt a sudden impulse to speak to her of the sea he loved so well ; and he told her of its never-ceasing voice, to which he had listened as a child, wondering at its hidden meaning that no living man has penetrated yet; of its enchanting glitter; of its senseless and capricious fury; how its surface was for ever changing, and yet always enticing, while its depths were for ever the same, cold and cruel, and full of the wisdom of destroyed life. He told her how it held men slaves of its charm for a lifetime, and then, regardless of their devotion, swallowed them up, angry at their fear of its mystery, which it would never disclose, not even to those that loved it most. While he talked, Nina's head had been gradually sinking lower, and her face almost touched his now. Her hair was over his eyes, her breath was on his forehead, her arms were about his body. No two beings could be closer to each other, yet she guessed rather than understood the meaning of his last words that came out after a slight hesitation in a faint murmur, dying out imperceptibly into a profound and significant silence : " The sea, O Nina, is like a woman's heart."

She closed his lips with a sudden kiss, and answered in a steady voice—

" But to the men that have no fear, O master of my life, the sea is ever true."

Over their heads a film of dark, thread-like clouds, looking like immense cobwebs drifting under the stars, darkened the sky with the presage of the coming thunderstorm. From the invisible hills the first distant rumble of thunder came in a prolonged roll which, after tossing about from hill to hill, lost itself in the forests of the Pantai. Dain and Nina stood up, and the former looked at the sky uneasily.

" It is time for Babalatchi to be here," he said. " The night is more than half gone. Our road is long, and a bullet travels quicker than the best canoe."

" He will be here before the moon is hidden behind the clouds," said Nina. " I heard a splash in the water," she added. " Did you hear it too ? "

" Alligator," answered Dain shortly, with a careless glance towards the creek. " The darker the night," he continued, " the shorter will be our road, for then we could keep in the current of the main stream, but if it is light—even no more than now—we must follow the small channels of sleeping water, with nothing to help our paddles."

"Dain," interposed Nina, earnestly, "it was no alligator. I heard the bushes rustling near the landing-place."

"Yes," said Dain, after listening awhile. "It cannot be Babalatchi, who would come in a big war canoe, and openly. Those that are coming, whoever they are, do not wish to make much noise. But you have heard, and now I can see," he went on quickly. "It is but one man. Stand behind me, Nina. If he is a friend he is welcome; if he is an enemy you shall see him die."

He laid his hand on his kriss, and awaited the approach of his unexpected visitor. The fire was burning very low, and small clouds—precursors of the storm—crossed the face of the moon in rapid succession, and their flying shadows darkened the clearing. He could not make out who the man might be, but he felt uneasy at the steady advance of the tall figure walking on the path with a heavy tread, and hailed it with a command to stop. The man stopped at some little distance, and Dain expected him to speak, but all he could hear was his deep breathing. Through a break in the flying clouds a sudden and fleeting brightness descended upon the clearing. Before the darkness closed in again, Dain saw a hand holding some glittering object extended towards him, heard Nina's cry of "Father!" and in an instant the girl was between him and Almayer's revolver. Nina's loud cry woke up the echoes of the sleeping woods, and the three stood still as if waiting for the return of silence before they would give expression to their various feelings. At the appearance of Nina, Almayer's arm fell by his side, and he made a step forward. Dain pushed the girl gently aside.

"Am I a wild beast that you should try to kill me suddenly and in the dark, Tuan Almayer?" said Dain, breaking the strained silence. "Throw some brushwood on the fire," he went on, speaking to Nina, "while I watch my white friend, lest harm should come to you or to me, O delight of my heart!"

Almayer ground his teeth and raised his arm again. With a quick bound Dain was at his side : there was a short scuffle, during which one chamber of the revolver went off harmlessly, then the weapon, wrenched out of Almayer's hand, whirled through the air and fell in the bushes. The two men stood close together, breathing hard. The replenished fire threw out an unsteady circle of light and shone on the terrified face of Nina, who looked at them with outstretched hands.

" Dain ! " she cried out warningly, " Dain ! "

He waved his hand towards her in a reassuring gesture, and, turning to Almayer, said with great courtesy—

" Now we may talk, Tuan. It is easy to send out death, but can your wisdon recall the life ? She might have been harmed," he continued, indicating Nina. " Your hand shook much ; for myself I was not afraid."

" Nina ! " exclaimed Almayer, " come to me at once. What is this sudden madness ? What bewitched you ? Come to your father, and together we shall try to forget this horrible nightmare ! "

He opened his arms with the certitude of clasping her to his breast in another second. She did not move. As it dawned upon him that she did not mean to obey he felt a deadly cold creep into his heart, and, pressing the palms of his hands to his temples, he looked down on the ground in mute despair. Dain took Nina by the arm and led her towards her father.

" Speak to him in the language of his people," he said. " He is grieving—as who would not grieve at losing thee, my pearl ! Speak to him the last words he shall hear spoken by that voice, which must be very sweet to him, but is all my life to me."

He released her, and, stepping back a few paces out of the circle of light, stood in the darkness looking at them with calm interest. The reflection of a distant flash of lightning lit up the clouds over their heads, and was followed after a short interval by the faint rumble of thunder, which mingled with Almayer's voice as he began to speak.

"Do you know what you are doing? Do you know what is waiting for you if you follow that man? Have you no pity for yourself? Do you know that you shall be at first his plaything and then a scorned slave, a drudge, and a servant of some new fancy of that man?"

She raised her hand to stop him, and turning her head slightly, asked—

"You hear this Dain! Is it true?"

"By all the gods!" came the impassioned answer from the darkness—"by heaven and earth, by my head and thine I swear: this is a white man's lie. I have delivered my soul into your hands for ever; I breathe with your breath, I see with your eyes, I think with your mind, and I take you into my heart for ever."

"You thief!" shouted the exasperated Almayer.

A deep silence succeeded this outburst, then the voice of Dain was heard again.

"Nay, Tuan," he said in a gentle tone, "that is not true also. The girl came of her own will. I have done no more but to show her my love like a man; she heard the cry of my heart, and she came, and the dowry I have given to the woman you call your wife."

Almayer groaned in his extremity of rage and shame. Nina laid her hand lightly on his shoulder, and the contact, light as the touch of a falling leaf, seemed to calm him. He spoke quickly, and in English this time.

"Tell me," he said—"tell me, what have they done to you, your mother and that man? What made you give yourself up to that savage? For he is a savage. Between him and you there is a barrier that nothing can remove. I can see in your eyes the look of those who commit suicide when they are mad. You are mad. Don't smile. It breaks my heart. If I were to see you drowning before my eyes, and I without the power to help you, I could not suffer a greater torment. Have you forgotten the teaching of so many years?"

"No," she interrupted, "I remember it well. I remember how it ended also. Scorn for scorn, contempt for contempt, hate for hate. I am not of your race. Between your people and me there is also a barrier that nothing can remove. You ask why I want to go, and I ask you why I should stay."

He staggered as if struck in the face, but with a quick, unhesitating grasp she caught him by the arm and steadied him.

" Why you should stay ! " he repeated slowly, in a dazed manner, and stopped short, astounded at the completeness of his misfortune.

"You told me yesterday," she went on again, "that I could not understand or see your love for me : it is so. How can I ? No two human beings understand each other. They can understand but their own voices. You wanted me to dream your dreams, to see your own visions—the visions of life amongst the white faces of those who cast me out from their midst in angry contempt. But while you spoke I listened to the voice of my own self ; then this man came, and all was still ; there was only the murmur of his love. You call him a savage ! What do you call my mother, your wife ? "

" Nina ! " cried Almayer, " take your eyes off my face."

She looked down directly, but continued speaking only a little above a whisper.

" In time," she went on, " both our voices, that man's and mine, spoke together in a sweetness that was intelligible to our ears only. You were speaking of gold then, but our ears were filled with the song of our love, and we did not hear you. Then I found that we could see through each other's eyes ; that he saw things that nobody but myself and he could see. We entered a land where no one could follow us, and least of all you. Then I began to live."

She paused. Almayer sighed deeply. With her eyes still fixed on the ground she began speaking again.

" And I mean to live. I mean to follow him. I have been rejected with scorn by the white people, and now I am a Malay ! He took me in his arms, he laid his life at my feet. He is brave ; he will be powerful, and I hold his bravery and his strength in my hand, and I shall make him great. His name shall be remembered long after both our bodies are laid in the dust. I love you no less than I did before, but I shall never leave him, for without him I cannot live."

"If he understood what you have said," answered Almayer, scornfully, "he must be highly flattered. You want him as a tool for some incomprehensible ambition of yours. Enough, Nina. If you do not go down at once to the creek, where Ali is waiting with my canoe, I shall tell him to return to the settlement and bring the Dutch officers here. You cannot escape from this clearing, for I have cast adrift your canoe. If the Dutch catch this hero of yours they will hang him as sure as I stand here. Now go."

He made a step towards his daughter and laid hold of her by the shoulder, his other hand pointing down the path to the landing-place.

"Beware!" exclaimed Dain; "this woman belongs to me!"

Nina wrenched herself free and looked straight at Almayer's angry face.

"No, I will not go," she said with desperate energy. "If he dies I shall die too!"

"You die!" said Almayer, contemptuously. "Oh, no! You shall live a life of lies and deception till some other vagabond comes along to sing; how did you say that? The song of love to you! Make up your mind quickly."

He waited for a while, and then added meaningly—

"Shall I call out to Ali?"

"Call out," she answered in Malay, "you that cannot be true to your own countrymen. Only a few days ago you were selling the powder for their destruction; now you want to give up to them the man that yesterday you called your friend. Oh, Dain," she said, turning towards the motionless but attentive figure in the darkness, "instead of bringing you life I bring you death, for he will betray unless I leave you for ever!"

Dain came into the circle of light, and, throwing his arm around Nina's neck, whispered in her ear—

"I can kill him where he stands, before a sound can pass

his lips. For you it is to say yes or no. Babalatchi cannot be far now."

He straightened himself up, taking his arm off her shoulder, and confronted Almayer, who looked at them both with an expression of concentrated fury.

" No ! " she cried, clinging to Dain in wild alarm. " No ! Kill me ! Then perhaps he will let you go. You do not know the mind of a white man. He would rather see me dead than standing where I am. Forgive me, your slave, but you must not." She fell at his feet sobbing violently and repeating, " Kill me ! Kill me ! "

" I want you alive," said Almayer, speaking also in Malay, with sombre calmness. " You go, or he hangs. Will you obey ? "

Dain shook Nina off, and, making a sudden lunge, struck Almayer full in the chest with the handle of his kriss, keeping the point towards himself.

" Hai, look ! It was easy for me to turn the point the other way," he said in his even voice. " Go, Tuan Putih," he added with dignity. " I give you your life, my life, and her life. I am the slave of this woman's desire, and she wills it so."

There was not a glimmer of light in the sky now, and the tops of the trees were as invisible as their trunks, being lost in the mass of clouds that hung low over the woods, the clearing, and the river. Every outline had disappeared in the intense blackness that seemed to have destroyed everything but space. Only the fire glimmered like a star forgotten in this annihilation of all visible things, and nothing was heard after Dain ceased speaking but the sobs of Nina, whom he held in his arms, kneeling beside the fire. Almayer stood looking down at them in gloomy thoughtfulness. As he was opening his lips to speak they were startled by a cry of warning by the riverside, followed by the splash of many paddles and the sound of voices.

" Babalatchi ! " shouted Dain, lifting up Nina as he got upon his feet quickly.

" Ada ! Ada ! " came the answer from the panting

statesman who ran up the path and stood amongst them.
"Run to my canoe," he said to Dain excitedly, without
taking any notice of Almayer.   "Run! we must go.   That
woman has told them all!"

"What woman?" asked Dain, looking at Nina.  Just
then there was only one woman in the whole world for him.

"The she-dog with white teeth; the seven times accursed
slave of Bulangi.   She yelled at Abdulla's gate till she woke
up all Sambir.   Now the white officers are coming, guided
by her and Reshid.   If you want to live, do not look at me,
but go!"

"How do you know this?" asked Almayer.

"Oh, Tuan! what matters how I know!   I have only one
eye, but I saw lights in Abdulla's house and in his campong
as we were paddling past.   I have ears, and while we lay
under the bank I have heard the messengers sent out to the
white men's house."

"Will you depart without that woman who is my
daughter?" said Almayer, addressing Dain, while Babalatchi
stamped with impatience, muttering, "Run! Run at
once!"

"No," answered Dain, steadily, "I will not go; to no man
will I abandon this woman."

"Then kill me and escape yourself," sobbed out Nina.

He clasped her close, looking at her tenderly, and whispered,
"We will never part, O Nina!"

"I shall not stay here any longer," broke in Babalatchi,
angrily.   "This is great foolishness.   No woman is worth
a man's life.   I am an old man, and I know."

He picked up his staff, and, turning to go, looked at Dain
as if offering him his last chance of escape.   But Dain's face
was hidden amongst Nina's black tresses, and he did not see
this last appealing glance.

Babalatchi vanished in the darkness.   Shortly after his
disappearance they heard the war canoe leave the landing-
place in the swish of the numerous paddles dipped in the
water together.   Almost at the same time Ali came up from
the riverside, two paddles on his shoulder.

"Our canoe is hidden up the creek, Tuan Almayer," he said, "in the dense bush where the forest comes down to the water. I took it there because I heard from Babalatchi's paddlers that the white men are coming here."

"Wait for me there," said Almayer, "but keep the canoe hidden."

He remained silent, listening to Ali's footsteps, then turned to Nina.

"Nina," he said sadly, "will you have no pity for me?"

There was no answer. She did not even turn her head, which was pressed close to Dain's breast.

He made a movement as if to leave them and stopped. By the dim glow of the burning-out fire he saw their two motionless figures. The woman's back turned to him with the long black hair streaming down over the white dress, and Dain's calm face looking at him above her head.

"I cannot," he muttered to himself. After a long pause he spoke again a little lower, but in an unsteady voice, "It would be too great a disgrace. I am a white man." He broke down completely there, and went on tearfully, "I am a white man, and of good family. Very good family," he repeated, weeping bitterly. "It would be a disgrace . . . all over the islands, . . . the only white man on the east coast. No, it cannot be . . . white men finding my daughter with this Malay. My daughter!" he cried aloud, with a ring of despair in his voice.

He recovered his composure after a while, and said distinctly—

"I will never forgive you, Nina—never! If you were to come back to me now, the memory of this night would poison all my life. I shall try to forget. I have no daughter. There used to be a half-caste woman in my house, but she is going even now. You, Dain, or whatever your name may be, I shall take you and that woman to the island at the mouth of the river myself. Come with me."

He led the way, following the bank as far as the forest. Ali answered to this call, and, pushing their way through the dense bush, they stepped into the canoe hidden under the

overhanging branches. Dain laid Nina in the bottom, and
sat holding her head on his knees. Almayer and Ali each
took up a paddle. As they were going to push out Ali
hissed warningly. All listened.

In the great stillness before the bursting out of the
thunderstorm they could hear the sound of oars working
regularly in their row-locks. The sound approached
steadily, and Dain, looking through the branches, could see
the faint shape of a big white boat. A woman's voice said
in a cautious tone—

"There is the place where you may land, white men; a
little higher—there!"

The boat was passing them so close in the narrow creek
that the blades of the long oars nearly touched the canoe.

"Way enough! Stand by to jump on shore! He is
alone and unarmed," was the quiet order in a man's voice,
and in Dutch.

Somebody else whispered: "I think I can see a glimmer
of a fire through the bush." And then the boat floated past
them, disappearing instantly in the darkness.

"Now," whispered Ali, eagerly, "let us push out and
paddle away."

The little canoe swung into the stream, and as it sprang
forward in response to the vigorous dig of the paddles they
could hear an angry shout.

"He is not by the fire. Spread out, men, and search for
him!"

Blue lights blazed out in different parts of the clearing,
and the shrill voice of a woman cried in accents of rage and
pain—

"Too late! O senseless white men! He has escaped!"

## CHAPTER XII

"That is the place," said Dain, indicating with the blade of his paddle a small islet about a mile ahead of the canoe— "that is the place where Babalatchi promised that a boat from the prau would come for me when the sun is overhead. We will wait for that boat there."

Almayer, who was steering, nodded without speaking, and by a slight sweep of his paddle laid the head of the canoe in the required direction.

They were just leaving the southern outlet of the Pantai, which lay behind them in a straight and long vista of water shining between two walls of thick verdure that ran down-wards and towards each other, till at last they joined and sank together in the far-away distance. The sun, rising above the calm waters of the Straits, marked its own path by a streak of light that glided upon the sea and darted up the wide reach of the river, a hurried messenger of light and life to the gloomy forests of the coast ; and in this radiance of the sun's pathway floated the black canoe heading for the islet which lay bathed in sunshine, the yellow sands of its encircling beach shining like an inlaid golden disc on the polished steel of the unwrinkled sea. To the north and south of it rose other islets, joyous in their brilliant colouring of green and yellow, and on the main coast the sombre line of mangrove bushes ended to the southward in the reddish cliffs of Tanjong Mirrah, advancing into the sea, steep and shadowless under the clear light of the early morning.

The bottom of the canoe grated upon the sand as the little craft ran upon the beach. Ali leaped on shore and held on while Dain stepped out carrying Nina in his arms, exhausted by the events and the long travelling during the night. Almayer was the last to leave the boat, and together with Ali ran it higher up on the beach. Then Ali, tired out by the long paddling, laid down in the shade of the canoe, and

incontinently fell asleep.    Almayer sat sideways on the gunwale, and with his arms crossed on his breast, looked to the
southward upon the sea.

After carefully laying Nina down in the shade of the
bushes growing in the middle of the islet, Dain threw himself
beside her and watched in silent concern the tears that ran
down from under her closed eyelids, and lost themselves in
that fine sand upon which they both were lying face to face.
These tears and this sorrow were for him a profound and
disquieting mystery.    Now, when the danger was past, why
should she grieve?    He doubted her love no more than he
would have doubted the fact of his own existence, but as he
lay looking ardently in her face, watching her tears, her parted
lips, her very breath, he was uneasily conscious of something
in her he could not understand.    Doubtless she had the
wisdom of perfect beings.    He sighed.    He felt something
invisible that stood between them, something that would let
him approach her so far, but no farther.    No desire, no
longing, no effort of will or length of life could destroy this
vague feeling of their difference.    With awe but also with
great pride he concluded that it was her own incomparable
perfection.    She was his, and yet she was like a woman from
another world.    His!    His!    He exulted in the glorious
thought; nevertheless her tears pained him.

With a wisp of her own hair which he took in his hand
with timid reverence he tried in an access of clumsy tenderness
to dry the tears that trembled on her eyelashes.    He had his
reward in a fleeting smile that brightened her face for the
short fraction of a second, but soon the tears fell faster than
ever, and he could bear it no more.    He rose and walked
towards Almayer, who still sat absorbed in his contemplation
of the sea.    It was a very, very long time since he had seen
the sea—that sea that leads everywhere, brings everything,
and takes away so much.    He had almost forgotten why he
was there, and dreamily he could see all his past life on the
smooth and boundless surface that glittered before his eyes.

Dain's hand laid on Almayer's shoulder recalled him with
a start from some country very far away indeed.    He turned

round, but his eyes seemed to look rather at the place where Dain stood than at the man himself. Dain felt uneasy under the unconscious gaze.

" What ? " said Almayer.

" She is crying," murmured Dain, softly.

" She is crying ! Why ? " asked Almayer, indifferently.

" I came to ask you. My Ranee smiles when looking at the man she loves. It is the white woman that is crying now. You would know."

Almayer shrugged his shoulders and turned away again towards the sea.

" Go, Tuan Putih," urged Dain. " Go to her ; her tears are more terrible to me than the anger of gods."

" Are they ? You will see them more than once. She told me she could not live without you," answered Almayer, speaking without the faintest spark of expression in his face, " so it behoves you to go to her quick, for fear you may find her dead."

He burst into a loud and unpleasant laugh which made Dain stare at him with some apprehension, but got off the gunwale of the boat and moved slowly towards Nina, glancing up at the sun as he walked.

" And you go when the sun is overhead ? " he said.

" Yes, Tuan. Then we go," answered Dain.

" I have not long to wait," muttered Almayer. " It is most important for me to see you go. Both of you. Most important," he repeated, stopping short and looking at Dain fixedly.

He went on again towards Nina, and Dain remained behind. Almayer approached his daughter and stood for a time looking down on her. She did not open her eyes, but hearing footsteps near her, murmured in a low sob, " Dain."

Almayer hesitated for a minute and then sank on the sand by her side. She, not hearing a responsive word, not feeling a touch, opened her eyes—saw her father, and sat up suddenly with a movement of terror.

" Oh, father ! " she murmured faintly, and in that word there was expressed regret and fear and dawning hope.

"I shall never forgive you, Nina," said Almayer, in a dispassionate voice. "You have torn my heart from me while I dreamt of your happiness. You have deceived me. Your eyes that for me were like truth itself lied to me in every glance—for how long? You know that best. When you were caressing my cheek you were counting the minutes to the sunset that was the signal for your meeting with that man—there!"

He ceased, and they both sat silent side by side, not looking at each other, but gazing at the vast expanse of the sea. Almayer's words had dried Nina's tears, and her look grew hard as she stared before her into the limitless sheet of blue that shone limpid, unwaving, and steady like heaven itself. He looked at it also, but his features had lost all expression, and life in his eyes seemed to have gone out. The face was a blank, without a sign of emotion, feeling, reason, or even knowledge of itself. All passion, regret, grief, hope, or anger—all were gone, erased by the hand of fate, as if after this last stroke everything was over and there was no need for any record. Those few who saw Almayer during the short period of his remaining days were always impressed by the sight of that face that seemed to know nothing of what went on within: like the blank wall of a prison enclosing sin, regrets, and pain, and wasted life, in the cold indifference of mortar and stones.

"What is there to forgive?" asked Nina, not addressing Almayer directly, but more as if arguing with herself. "Can I not live my own life as you have lived yours? The path you would have wished me to follow has been closed to me by no fault of mine."

"You never told me," muttered Almayer.

"You never asked me," she answered, "and I thought you were like the others and did not care. I bore the memory of my humiliation alone, and why should I tell you that it came to me because I am your daughter? I knew you could not avenge me."

"And yet I was thinking of that only," interrupted Almayer, "and I wanted to give you years of happiness for the short day of your suffering. I only knew of one way."

"Ah! but it was not my way!" she replied. "Could you give me happiness without life? Life!" she repeated with sudden energy that sent the word ringing over the sea. "Life that means power and love," she added in a low voice.

"That!" said Almayer, pointing his finger at Dain standing close by and looking at them in curious wonder.

"Yes, that!" she replied, looking her father full in the face and noticing for the first time with a slight gasp of fear the unnatural rigidity of his features.

"I would have rather strangled you with my own hands," said Almayer, in an expressionless voice which was such a contrast to the desperate bitterness of his feelings that it surprised even himself. He asked himself who spoke, and, after looking slowly round as if expecting to see somebody, turned again his eyes towards the sea.

"You say that because you do not understand the meaning of my words," she said sadly. "Between you and my mother there never was any love. When I returned to Sambir I found the place which I thought would be a peaceful refuge for my heart filled with weariness and hatred—and mutual contempt. I have listened to your voice and to her voice. Then I saw that you could not understand me; for was I not part of that woman? Of her who was the regret and shame of your life? I had to choose—I hesitated. Why were you so blind? Did you not see me struggling before your eyes? But, when he came, all doubt disappeared, and I saw only the light of the blue and cloudless heaven——"

"I will tell you the rest," interrupted Almayer: "when that man came I also saw the blue and the sunshine of the sky. A thunderbolt has fallen from that sky, and suddenly all is still and dark around me for ever. I will never forgive you, Nina; and to-morrow I shall forget you! I shall never forgive you," he repeated with mechanical obstinacy while she sat, her head bowed down as if afraid to look at her father.

To him it seemed of the utmost importance that he should assure her of his intention of never forgiving. He was convinced that his faith in her had been the foundation of his hopes, the motive of his courage, of his determination to live and struggle, and to be victorious for her sake. And now his faith was gone, destroyed by her own hands; destroyed cruelly, treacherously, in the dark; in the very moment of success. In the utter wreck of his affections and of all his feelings, in the chaotic disorder of his thoughts, above the confused sensation of physical pain that wrapped him up in a sting as of a whiplash curling round him from his shoulders down to his feet, only one idea remained clear and definite—not to forgive her; only one vivid desire—to forget her. And this must be made clear to her—and to himself—by frequent repetition. That was his idea of his duty to himself—to his race—to his respectable connections; to the whole universe unsettled and shaken by this frightful catastrophe of his life. He saw it clearly and believed he was a strong man. He had always prided himself upon his unflinching firmness. And yet he was afraid. She had been all in all to him. What if he should let the memory of his love for her weaken the sense of his dignity? She was a remarkable woman; he could see that; all the latent greatness of his nature—in which he honestly believed —had been transfused into that slight, girlish figure. Great things could be done! What if he should suddenly take her to his heart, forget his shame, and pain, and anger, and— follow her! What if he changed his heart if not his skin and made her life easier between the two loves that would guard her from any mischance! His heart yearned for her. What if he should say that his love for her was greater than . . .

"I will never forgive you, Nina!" he shouted, leaping up madly in the sudden fear of his dream.

This was the last time in his life that he was heard to raise his voice. Henceforth he spoke always in a monotonous whisper like an instrument of which all the strings but one are broken in a last ringing clamour under a heavy blow.

She rose to her feet and looked at him. The very violence of his cry soothed her in an intuitive conviction of his love, and she hugged to her breast the lamentable remnants of that affection with the unscrupulous greediness of women who cling desperately to the very scraps and rags of love, any kind of love, as a thing that of right belongs to them and is the very breath of their life. She put both her hands on Almayer's shoulders, and looking at him half tenderly, half playfully, she said—

"You speak so because you love me."

Almayer shook his head.

"Yes, you do," she insisted softly; then after a short pause she added, "and you will never forget me."

Almayer shivered slightly. She could not have said a more cruel thing.

"Here is the boat coming now," said Dain, his arm outstretched towards a black speck on the water between the coast and the islet.

They all looked at it and remained standing in silence till the little canoe came gently on the beach and a man landed and walked towards them. He stopped some distance off and hesitated.

"What news?" asked Dain.

"We have had orders secretly and in the night to take off from this islet a man and a woman. I see the woman. Which of you is the man?"

"Come, delight of my eyes," said Dain to Nina. "Now we go, and your voice shall be for my ears only. You have spoken your last words to the Tuan Putih, your father. Come."

She hesitated for a while, looking at Almayer, who kept his eyes steadily on the sea, then she touched his forehead in a lingering kiss, and a tear—one of her tears—fell on his cheek and ran down his immovable face.

"Goodbye," she whispered, and remained irresolute till he pushed her suddenly into Dain's arms.

"If you have any pity for me," murmured Almayer, as if repeating some sentence learned by heart, "take that woman away."

He stood very straight, his shoulders thrown back, his head held high, and looked at them as they went down the beach to the canoe, walking enlaced in each other's arms. He looked at the line of their footsteps marked in the sand. He followed their figures moving in the crude blaze of the vertical sun, in that light violent and vibrating, like a triumphal flourish of brazen trumpets. He looked at the man's brown shoulders, at the red sarong round his waist; at the tall, slender, dazzling white figure he supported. He looked at the white dress, at the falling masses of the long black hair. He looked at them embarking, and at the canoe growing smaller in the distance, with rage, despair, and regret in his heart, and on his face a peace as that of a carved image of oblivion. Inwardly he felt himself torn to pieces, but Ali—who now aroused—stood close to his master, saw on his features the blank expression of those who live in that hopeless calm which sightless eyes only can give.

The canoe disappeared, and Almayer stood motionless with his eyes fixed on its wake. Ali from under the shade of his hand examined the coast curiously. As the sun declined, the sea-breeze sprang up from the northward and shivered with its breath the glassy surface of the water.

"Dapat!" exclaimed Ali, joyously. "Got him, master! Got prau! Not there! Look more Tanah Mirrah side. Aha! That way! Master, see? Now plain. See?"

Almayer followed Ali's forefinger with his eyes for a long time in vain. At last he sighted a triangular patch of yellow light on the red background of the cliffs of Tanjong Mirrah. It was the sail of the prau that had caught the sunlight and stood out, distinct with its gay tint, on the dark red of the cape. The yellow triangle crept slowly from cliff to cliff, till it cleared the last point of land and shone brilliantly for a fleeting minute on the blue of the open sea. Then the prau bore up to the southward: the light went out of the sail, and all at once the vessel itself disappeared, vanishing in the shadow of the steep headland that looked on, patient and lonely, watching over the empty sea.

Almayer never moved. Round the little islet the air was full of the talk of the rippling water. The crested wavelet ran up the beach audaciously, joyously, with the lightness of young life, and died quickly, unresistingly, and graciously, in the wide curves of transparent foam on the yellow sand. Above, the white clouds sailed rapidly southwards as if intent upon overtaking something. Ali seemed anxious.

"Master," he said timidly, "time to get house now. Long way off to pull. All ready, sir."

"Wait," whispered Almayer.

Now she was gone his business was to forget, and he had a strange notion that it should be done systematically and in order. To Ali's great dismay he fell on his hands and knees, and, creeping along the sand, erased carefully with his hand all traces of Nina's footsteps. He piled up small heaps of sand, leaving behind him a line of miniature graves right down to the water. After burying the last slight imprint of Nina's slipper he stood up, and, turning his face towards the headland where he had last seen the prau, he made an effort to shout out loud again his firm resolve to never forgive. Ali watching him uneasily saw only his lips move, but heard no sound. He brought his foot down with a stamp. He was a firm man—firm as a rock. Let her go. He never had a daughter. He would forget. He was forgetting already.

Ali approached him again, insisting on immediate departure, and this time he consented, and they went together towards their canoe, Almayer leading. For all his firmness he looked very dejected and feeble as he dragged his feet slowly through the sand on the beach; and by his side—invisible to Ali—stalked that particular fiend whose mission it is to jog the memories of men, lest they should forget the meaning of life. He whispered in Almayer's ear a childish prattle of many years ago. Almayer, his head bent on one side, seemed to listen to his invisible companion, but his face was like the face of a man that has died struck from behind—a face from which all feelings and all expression are suddenly wiped off by the hand of unexpected death.

They slept on the river that night, mooring their canoe under the bushes and lying down in the bottom side by side, in the absolute exhaustion that kills hunger, thirst, all feeling and all thought in the overpowering desire for that deep sleep which is like the temporary annihilation of the tired body. Next day they started again and fought doggedly with the current all the morning, till about mid-day they reached the settlement and made fast their little craft to the jetty of Lingard and Co. Almayer walked straight to the house, and Ali followed, paddles on shoulder, thinking that he would like to eat something. As they crossed the front courtyard they noticed the abandoned look of the place. Ali looked in at the different servants' houses : all were empty. In the back courtyard there was the same absence of sound and life. In the cooking-shed the fire was out and the black embers were cold. A tall, lean man came stealthily out of the banana plantation and went away rapidly across the open space looking at them with big, frightened eyes over his shoulder. Some vagabond without a master; there were many such in the settlement, and they looked upon Almayer as their patron. They prowled about his premises and picked their living there, sure that nothing worse could befall them than a shower of curses when they got in the way of the white man, whom they trusted and liked, and called a fool amongst themselves. In the house, which Almayer entered through the back verandah, the only living thing that met his eyes was his small monkey which, hungry and unnoticed for the last two days, began to cry and complain in monkey language as soon as it caught sight of the familiar face. Almayer soothed it with a few words and ordered Ali to bring in some bananas, then while Ali was gone to get them he stood in the doorway of the front verandah looking at the

chaos of overturned furniture. Finally he picked up the
table and sat on it while the monkey let itself down from
the roof-stick by its chain and perched on his shoulder.
When the bananas came they had their breakfast together ;
both hungry, both eating greedily and showering the skins
round them recklessly, in the trusting silence of perfect
friendship. Ali went away, grumbling, to cook some rice
himself, for all the women about the house had disappeared ;
he did not know where. Almayer did not seem to
care, and, after he finished eating, he sat on the table
swinging his legs and staring at the river as if lost in
thought.

After some time he got up and went to the door of a
room on the right of the verandah. That was the office.
The office of Lingard and Co. He very seldom went in
there. There was no business now, and he did not want
an office. The door was locked, and he stood biting his
lower lip, trying to think of the place where the key could
be. Suddenly he remembered : in the women's room
hung upon a nail. He went over to the doorway where the
red curtain hung down in motionless folds, and hesitated
for a moment before pushing it aside with his shoulder as
if breaking down some solid obstacle. A great square of
sunshine entering through the window lay on the floor. On
the left he saw Mrs. Almayer's big wooden chest, the lid
thrown back, empty ; near it the brass nails of Nina's
European trunk shone in the large initials N. A. on the
cover. A few of Nina's dresses hung on wooden pegs,
stiffened in a look of offended dignity at their abandonment.
He remembered making the pegs himself and noticed that
they were very good pegs. Where was the key ? He looked
round and saw it near the door where he stood. It was red
with rust. He felt very much annoyed at that, and directly
afterwards wondered at his own feeling. What did it
matter ? There soon would be no key—no door—nothing !
He paused, key in hand, and asked himself whether he knew
well what he was about. He went out again on the verandah
and stood by the table thinking. The monkey jumped

down, and, snatching a banana skin, absorbed itself in
picking it to shreds industriously.

"Forget!" muttered Almayer, and that word started
before him a sequence of events, a detailed programme of
things to do. He knew perfectly well what was to be done
now. First this, then that, and then forgetfulness would
come easy. Very easy. He had a fixed idea that if he
should not forget before he died he would have to remember
to all eternity. Certain things had to be taken out of his
life, stamped out of sight, destroyed, forgotten. For a
long time he stood in deep thought, lost in the alarming
possibilities of unconquerable memory, with the fear of
death and eternity before him. "Eternity!" he said
aloud, and the sound of that word recalled him out of his
reverie. The monkey started, dropped the skin, and
grinned up at him amicably.

He went towards the office door and with some difficulty
managed to open it. He entered in a cloud of dust that
rose under his feet. Books open with torn pages bestrewed
the floor; other books lay about grimy and black, looking
as if they had never been opened. Account books. In
those books he had intended to keep day by day a record
of his rising fortunes. Long time ago. A very long time.
For many years there had been no record to keep on the
blue and red ruled pages! In the middle of the room the
big office desk, with one of its legs broken, careened over
like the hull of a stranded ship; most of the drawers had
fallen out, disclosing heaps of paper yellow with age and
dirt. The revolving office chair stood in its place, but he
found the pivot set fast when he tried to turn it. No
matter. He desisted, and his eyes wandered slowly from
object to object. All those things had cost a lot of money
at the time. The desk, the paper, the torn books, and the
broken shelves, all under a thick coat of dust. The very
dust and bones of a dead and gone business. He looked at
all these things, all that was left after so many years of
work, of strife, of weariness, of discouragement, conquered
so many times. And all for what? He stood thinking

mournfully of his past life till he heard distinctly the clear voice of a child speaking amongst all this wreck, ruin, and waste. He started with a great fear in his heart, and fever-ishly began to rake in the papers scattered on the floor, broke the chair into bits, splintered the drawers by banging them against the desk, and made a big heap of all that rubbish in one corner of the room.

He came out quickly, slammed the door after him, turned the key, and, taking it out, ran to the front rail of the veran-dah, and, with a great swing of his arm, sent the key whizzing into the river. This done he went back slowly to the table, called the monkey down, unhooked its chain, and induced it to remain quiet in the breast of his jacket. Then he sat again on the table and looked fixedly at the door of the room he had just left. He listened also intently. He heard a dry sound of rustling; sharp cracks as of dry wood snap-ping; a whirr like of a bird's wings when it rises suddenly, and then he saw a thin stream of smoke come through the keyhole. The monkey struggled under his coat. Ali appeared with his eyes starting out of his head.

"Master! House burn!" he shouted.

Almayer stood up holding by the table. He could hear the yells of alarm and surprise in the settlement. Ali wrung his hands, lamenting aloud.

"Stop this noise, fool!" said Almayer, quietly. "Pick up my hammock and blankets and take them to the other house. Quick, now!"

The smoke burst through the crevices of the door, and Ali, with the hammock in his arms, cleared in one bound the steps of the verandah.

"It has caught well," muttered Almayer to himself. "Be quiet, Jack," he added, as the monkey made a frantic effort to escape from its confinement.

The door split from top to bottom, and a rush of flame and smoke drove Almayer away from the table to the front rail of the verandah. He held on there till a great roar overhead assured him that the roof was ablaze. Then he ran down the steps of the verandah, coughing, half choked with the smoke that pursued him in bluish wreaths curling about his head.

On the other side of the ditch, separating Almayer's courtyard from the settlement, a crowd of the inhabitants of Sambir looked at the burning house of the white man. In the calm air the flames rushed up on high, coloured pale brick-red, with violet gleams in the strong sunshine. The thin column of smoke ascended straight and unwavering till it lost itself in the clean blue of the sky, and in the great empty space between the two houses the interested spectators could see the tall figure of the Tuan Putih, with bowed head and dragging feet, walking slowly away from the fire towards the shelter of " Almayer's Folly."

In that manner did Almayer move into his new house. He took possession of the new ruin, and in the undying folly of his heart set himself to wait in anxiety and pain for that forgetfulness which was so slow to come. He had done all he could. Every vestige of Nina's existence had been destroyed ; and now with every sunrise he asked himself whether the longed-for oblivion would come before sunset, whether it would come before he died ? He wanted to live only long enough to be able to forget, and the tenacity of his memory filled him with dread and horror of death ; for should it come before he could accomplish the purpose of his life he would have to remember for ever ! He also longed for loneliness. He wanted to be alone. But he was not. In the dim light of the rooms with their closed shutters, in the bright sunshine of the verandah, wherever he went, whichever way he turned, he saw the small figure of a little maiden with pretty olive face, with long black hair, her little pink robe slipping off her shoulders, her big eyes looking up at him in the tender trustfulness of a petted child. Ali did not see anything, but he also was aware of the presence of a child in the house. In his long talks by the evening fires of the settlement he used to tell of his intimate friends of Almayer's strange doings. His master had turned sorcerer in his old age. Ali said that often when Tuan Putih had retired for the night he could hear him talking

to something in his room. Ali thought that it was a spirit
in the shape of a child. He knew his master spoke to a
child from certain expressions and words his master used.
His master spoke in Malay a little, but mostly in English,
which he, Ali, could understand. Master spoke to the child
at times tenderly, then he would weep over it, laugh at it,
scold it, beg of it to go away; curse it. It was a bad and
stubborn spirit. Ali thought his master had imprudently
called it up, and now could not get rid of it. His master
was very brave; he was not afraid to curse this spirit in the
very Presence; and once he fought with it. Ali had heard
a great noise as of running about inside the room and groans.
His master groaned. Spirits do not groan. His master
was brave, but foolish. You cannot hurt a spirit. Ali
expected to find his master dead next morning, but he
came out very early, looking much older than the day
before, and had no food all day.

So far Ali to the settlement. To Captain Ford he was
much more communicative, for the good reason that Captain
Ford had the purse and gave orders. On each of Ford's
monthly visits to Sambir Ali had to go on board with a
report about the inhabitant of "Almayer's Folly." On
his first visit to Sambir, after Nina's departure, Ford had
taken charge of Almayer's affairs. They were not cumbersome. The shed for the storage of goods was empty, the
boats had disappeared, appropriated—generally in night-
time—by various citizens of Sambir in need of means of
transport. During a great flood the jetty of Lingard and
Co. left the bank and floated down the river, probably in
search of more cheerful surroundings; even the flock of
geese—" the only geese on the east coast "—departed somewhere, preferring the unknown dangers of the bush to the
desolation of their old home. As time went on the grass
grew over the black patch of ground where the old house
used to stand, and nothing remained to mark the place of
the dwelling that had sheltered Almayer's young hopes, his
foolish dream of splendid future, his awakening, and his
despair.

Ford did not often visit Almayer, for visiting Almayer was not a pleasant task. At first he used to respond listlessly to the old seaman's boisterous inquiries about his health; he even made efforts to talk, asking for news in a voice that made it perfectly clear that no news from this world had any interest for him. Then gradually he became more silent—not sulkily—but as if he was forgetting how to speak. He used also to hide in the darkest rooms of the house, where Ford had to seek him out guided by the patter of the monkey galloping before him. The monkey was always there to receive and introduce Ford. The little animal seemed to have taken complete charge of its master, and whenever it wished for his presence on the verandah it would tug perseveringly at his jacket, till Almayer obediently came out into the sunshine, which he seemed to dislike so much.

One morning Ford found him sitting on the floor of the verandah, his back against the wall, his legs stretched stiffly out, his arms hanging by his side. His expressionless face, his eyes open wide with immobile pupils, and the rigidity of his pose, made him look like an immense man-doll broken and flung there out of the way. As Ford came up the steps he turned his head slowly.

"Ford," he murmured from the floor, "I cannot forget."

"Can't you?" said Ford, innocently, with an attempt at joviality: "I wish I was like you. I am losing my memory —age, I suppose; only the other day my mate——"

He stopped, for Almayer had got up, stumbled, and steadied himself on his friend's arm.

"Hallo! You are better to-day. Soon be all right," said Ford, cheerfully, but feeling rather scared.

Almayer let go his arm and stood very straight with his head up and shoulders thrown back, looking stonily at the multitude of suns shining in ripples of the river. His jacket and his loose trousers flapped in the breeze on his thin limbs.

"Let her go!" he whispered in a grating voice. "Let

her go.  To-morrow I shall forget.  I am a firm man, . . .
firm as a . . . rock, . . . firm . . ."

Ford looked at his face—and fled.  The skipper was a
tolerably firm man himself—as those who had sailed with
him could testify—but Almayer's firmness was altogether
too much for his fortitude.

Next time the steamer called in Sambir Ali came on
board early with a grievance.  He complained to Ford
that Jim-Eng the Chinaman had invaded Almayer's house,
and actually had lived there for the last month.

"And they both smoke," added Ali.

"Phew!  Opium, you mean?"

Ali nodded, and Ford remained thoughtful; then he
muttered to himself, "Poor devil!  The sooner the better
now."  In the afternoon he walked up to the house.

"What are you doing here?"  he asked of Jim-Eng,
whom he found strolling about on the verandah.

Jim-Eng explained in bad Malay, and speaking in that
monotonous, uninterested voice of an opium smoker pretty
far gone, that his house was old, the roof leaked, and the
floor was rotten.  So, being an old friend for many, many
years, he took his money, his opium, and two pipes, and
came to live in this big house.

"There is plenty of room.  He smokes, and I live here.
He will not smoke long," he concluded.

"Where is he now?" asked Ford.

"Inside.  He sleeps," answered Jim-Eng, wearily.

Ford glanced in through the doorway.  In the dim light
of the room he could see Almayer lying on his back on the
floor, his head on a wooden pillow, the long white beard
scattered over his breast, the yellow skin of the face, the
half-closed eyelids showing the whites of the eye only. . . .

He shuddered and turned away.  As he was leaving he
noticed a long strip of faded red silk, with some Chinese
letters on it, which Jim-Eng had just fastened to one of
the pillars.

"What's that?" he asked.

"That," said Jim-Eng, in his colourless voice, "that is

the name of the house. All the same like my house. Very good name."

Ford looked at him for awhile and went away. He did not know what the crazy-looking maze of the Chinese inscription on the red silk meant. Had he asked Jim-Eng, that patient Chinaman would have informed him with proper pride that its meaning was : " House of heavenly delight."

In the evening of the same day Babalatchi called on Captain Ford. The captain's cabin opened on deck, and Babalatchi sat astride on the high step, while Ford smoked his pipe on the settee inside. The steamer was leaving next morning, and the old statesman came as usual for a last chat.

" We had news from Bali last moon," remarked Babalatchi. " A grandson is born to the old Rajah, and there is great rejoicing."

Ford sat up interested.

" Yes," went on Babalatchi, in answer to Ford's look. " I told him. That was before he began to smoke."

" Well, and what ? " asked Ford.

" I escaped with my life," said Babalatchi, with perfect gravity, " because the white man is very weak and fell as he rushed upon me." Then, after a pause, he added, " She is mad with joy."

" Mrs. Almayer, you mean ? "

" Yes, she lives in our Rajah's house. She will not die soon. Such women live a long time," said Babalatchi, with a slight tinge of regret in his voice. " She has dollars, and she has buried them, but we know where. We had much trouble with those people. We had to pay a fine and listen to threats from the white men, and now we have to be careful." He sighed and remained silent for a long while. Then with energy :

" There will be fighting. There is a breath of war on the islands. Shall I live long enough to see ? . . . Ah, Tuan ! " he went on, more quietly, " the old times were best. Even I have sailed with Lanun men, and boarded in the night silent ships with white sails. That was before an English Rajah ruled in Kuching. Then we fought amongst ourselves and were happy. Now when we fight with you we can only die ! "

He rose to go. "Tuan," he said, "you remember the girl that man Bulangi had ? Her that caused all the trouble ? "

"Yes," said Ford. "What of her ? "

"She grew thin and could not work. Then Bulangi, who is a thief and a pig-eater, gave her to me for fifty dollars. I sent her amongst my women to grow fat. I wanted to hear the sound of her laughter, but she must have been bewitched, and . . . she died two days ago. Nay, Tuan. Why do you speak bad words ? I am old—that is true— but why should I not like the sight of a young face and the sound of a young voice in my house ? " He paused, and then added with a little mournful laugh, " I am like a white man talking too much of what is not men's talk when they speak to one another."

And he went off looking very sad.

\*    \*    \*    \*    \*    \*

The crowd massed in a semicircle before the steps of "Almayer's Folly," swayed silently backwards and for- wards, and opened out before the group of white-robed and turbaned men advancing through the grass towards the house. Abdulla walked first, supported by Reshid and followed by all the Arabs in Sambir. As they entered the lane made by the respectful throng there was a subdued murmur of voices, where the word "Mati" was the only one distinctly audible. Abdulla stopped and looked round slowly.

"Is he dead ? " he asked.

"May you live ! " answered the crowd in one shout, and then there succeeded a breathless silence.

Abdulla made a few paces forward and found himself for the last time face to face with his old enemy. Whatever he might have been once he was not dangerous now, lying stiff and lifeless in the tender light of the early day. The only white man on the east coast was dead, and his soul, delivered from the trammels of his earthly folly, stood now in the presence of Infinite Wisdom. On the upturned face there was that serene look which follows the sudden relief from anguish and pain, and it testified silently before the cloudless heaven that the man lying there under the gaze of indifferent eyes had been permitted to forget before he died.

Abdulla looked down sadly at this Infidel he had fought so long and had bested so many times. Such was the reward of the Faithful! Yet in the Arab's old heart there was a feeling of regret for that thing gone out of his life. He was leaving fast behind him friendships, and enmities, successes, and disappointments—all that makes up a life; and before him was only the end. Prayer would fill up the remainder of the days allotted to the True Believer! He took in his hand the beads that hung at his waist.

"I found him here, like this, in the morning," said Ali, in a low and awed voice.

Abdulla glanced coldly once more at the serene face.

"Let us go," he said, addressing Reshid.

And as they passed through the crowd that fell back before them, the beads in Abdulla's hand clicked, while in a solemn whisper he breathed out piously the name of Allah! The Merciful! The Compassionate!

# AN OUTCAST OF THE ISLANDS

# PART I

## I

WHEN he stepped off the straight and narrow path of his
peculiar honesty, it was with an inward assertion of unflinching resolve to fall back again into the monotonous but safe
stride of virtue as soon as his little excursion into the wayside
quagmires had produced the desired effect.  It was going to
be a short episode—a sentence in brackets, so to speak—in the
flowing tale of his life : a thing of no moment, to be done
unwillingly, yet neatly, and to be quickly forgotten.  He
imagined that he could go on afterwards looking at the sunshine, enjoying the shade, breathing in the perfume of flowers
in the small garden before his house.  He fancied that nothing
would be changed, that he would be able as heretofore to
tyrannise good-humouredly over his half-caste wife, to notice
with tender contempt his pale yellow child, to patronise loftily
his dark-skinned brother-in-law, who loved pink neckties and
wore patent-leather boots on his little feet, and was so humble
before the white husband of the lucky sister.  Those were the
delights of his life, and he was unable to conceive that the
moral significance of any act of his could interfere with the
very nature of things, could dim the light of the sun, could
destroy the perfume of the flowers, the submission of his wife,
the smile of his child, the awestruck respect of Leonard da
Souza and of all the Da Souza family.  That family's admiration was the great luxury of his life.  It rounded and completed his existence in a perpetual assurance of unquestionable
superiority.  He loved to breathe the coarse incense they
offered before the shrine of the successful white man ; the
man that had done them the honour to marry their daughter,
sister, cousin ; the rising man sure to climb very high ; the

confidential clerk of Hudig & Co. They were a numerous and
an unclean crowd, living in ruined bamboo houses, surrounded
by neglected compounds, on the outskirts of Macassar. He
kept them at arm's length and even further off, perhaps,
having no illusions as to their worth. They were a half-
caste, lazy lot, and he saw them as they were—ragged, lean,
unwashed, undersized men of various ages, shuffling about
aimlessly in slippers; motionless old women who looked like
monstrous bags of pink calico stuffed with shapeless lumps of
fat, and deposited askew upon decaying rattan chairs in shady
corners of dusty verandahs; young women, slim and yellow,
big-eyed, long-haired, moving languidly amongst the dirt and
rubbish of their dwellings as if every step they took was going
to be their very last. He heard their shrill quarrellings, the
squalling of their children, the grunting of their pigs; he
smelt the odours of the heaps of garbage in their courtyards :
and he was greatly disgusted. But he fed and clothed that
shabby multitude; those degenerate descendants of Portuguese conquerors; he was their providence; he kept them
singing his praises in the midst of their laziness, of their dirt,
of their immense and hopeless squalor : and he was greatly
delighted. They wanted much, but he could give them all
they wanted without ruining himself. In exchange he had
their silent fear, their loquacious love, their noisy veneration.
It is a fine thing to be a providence, and to be told so on every
day of one's life. It gives one a feeling of enormously remote
superiority, and Willems revelled in it. He did not analyse
the state of his mind, but probably his greatest delight lay
in the unexpressed but intimate conviction that, should he
close his hand, all those admiring human beings would starve.
His munificence had demoralised them. An easy task.
Since he descended amongst them and married Joanna they
had lost the little aptitude and strength for work they might
have had to put forth under the stress of extreme necessity.
They lived now by the grace of his will. This was power.
Willems loved it.

In another, and perhaps a lower plane, his days did not
want for their less complex but more obvious pleasures. He

liked the simple games of skill—billiards; also games not so simple, and calling for quite another kind of skill—poker. He had been the aptest pupil of a steady-eyed, sententious American, who had drifted mysteriously into Macassar from the wastes of the Pacific, and, after knocking about for a time in the eddies of town life, had drifted out enigmatically into the sunny solitudes of the Indian Ocean. The memory of the Californian stranger was perpetuated in the game of poker— which became popular in the capital of Celebes from that time —and in a powerful cocktail, the recipe for which is transmitted—in the Kwang-tung dialect—from head boy to head boy of the Chinese servants in the Sunda Hotel even to this day. Willems was a connoisseur in the drink and an adept at the game. Of those accomplishments he was moderately proud. Of the confidence reposed in him by Hudig—the master—he was boastfully and obtrusively proud. This arose from his great benevolence, and from an exalted sense of his duty to himself and the world at large. He experienced that irresistible impulse to impart information which is inseparable from gross ignorance. There is always some one thing which the ignorant man knows, and that thing is the only thing worth knowing; it fills the ignorant man's universe. Willems knew all about himself. On the day when, with many misgivings, he ran away from a Dutch East-Indiaman in Samarang roads, he had commenced that study of himself, of his own ways, of his own abilities, of those fate-compelling qualities of his which led him towards that lucrative position which he now filled. Being of a modest and diffident nature, his success amazed, almost frightened him, and ended—as he got over the succeeding shocks of surprise—by making him ferociously conceited. He believed in his genius and in his knowledge of the world. Others should know of it also; for their own good and for his greater glory. All those friendly men who slapped him on the back and greeted him noisily should have the benefit of his example. For that he must talk. He talked to them conscientiously. In the afternoon he expounded his theory of success over the little tables, dipping now and then his moustache in the crushed ice of the

cocktails; in the evening he would often hold forth, cue in
hand, to a young listener across the billiard table. The
billiard balls stood still as if listening also, under the vivid
brilliance of the shaded oil lamps hung low over the cloth;
while away in the shadows of the big room the Chinaman
marker would lean wearily against the wall, the blank mask of
his face looking pale under the mahogany marking-board; his
eyelids dropped in the drowsy fatigue of late hours and in the
buzzing monotony of the unintelligible stream of words
poured out by the white man. In a sudden pause of the
talk the game would recommence with a sharp click and go
on for a time in the flowing soft whir and the subdued thuds
as the balls rolled zig-zagging towards the inevitably successful
cannon. Through the big windows and the open doors the
salt dampness of the sea, the vague smell of mould and flowers
from the garden of the hotel drifted in and mingled with the
odour of lamp oil, growing heavier as the night advanced.
The players' heads dived into the light as they bent down for
the stroke, springing back again smartly into the greenish
gloom of broad lamp-shades; the clock ticked methodically;
the unmoved Chinaman continuously repeated the score in a
lifeless voice, like a big talking doll—and Willems would win
the game. With a remark that it was getting late, and that
he was a married man, he would say a patronising good-night
and step out into the long, empty street. At that hour its
white dust was like a dazzling streak of moonlight where the
eye sought repose in the dimmer gleam of rare oil lamps.
Willems walked homewards, following the line of walls over-
topped by the luxuriant vegetation of the front gardens. The
houses right and left were hidden behind the black masses of
flowering shrubs. Willems had the street to himself. He
would walk in the middle, his shadow gliding obsequiously
before him. He looked down on it complacently. The
shadow of a successful man! He would be slightly dizzy
with the cocktails and with the intoxication of his own glory.
As he often told people, he came east fourteen years ago—
a cabin boy. A small boy. His shadow must have been very
small at that time; he thought with a smile that he was not

aware then he had anything—even a shadow—which he dared call his own. And now he was looking at the shadow of the confidential clerk of Hudig & Co. going home. How glorious ! How good was life for those that were on the winning side ! He had won the game of life ; also the game of billiards. He walked faster, jingling his winnings, and thinking of the white stone days that had marked the path of his existence. He thought of the trip to Lombok for ponies—that first important transaction confided to him by Hudig ; then he reviewed the more important affairs : the quiet deal in opium ; the illegal traffic in gunpowder ; the great affair of smuggled firearms, the difficult business of the Rajah of Goak. He carried that last through by sheer pluck ; he had bearded the savage old ruler in his council room ; he had bribed him with a gilt glass coach, which, rumour said, was used as a hen-coop now ; he had overpersuaded him ; he had bested him in every way. That was the way to get on. He disapproved of the elementary dishonesty that dips the hand in the cash-box, but one could evade the laws and push the principles of trade to their furthest consequences. Some call that cheating. Those are the fools, the weak, the contemptible. The wise, the strong, the respected have no scruples. Where there are scruples there can be no power. On that text he preached often to the young men. It was his doctrine, and he, himself, was a shining example of its truth.

Night after night he went home thus, after a day of toil and pleasure, drunk with the sound of his own voice celebrating his own prosperity. On his thirtieth birthday he went home thus. He had spent in good company a nice, noisy evening, and, as he walked along the empty street, the feeling of his own greatness grew upon him, lifted him above the white dust of Macassar road, and filled him with exultation and regrets. He had not done himself justice over there in the hotel, he had not talked enough about himself, he had not impressed his hearers enough. Never mind. Some other time. Now he would go home and make his wife get up and listen to him. Why should she not get up ?—and mix a cocktail for him—and listen patiently. Just so. She shall.

If he wanted he could make all the Da Souza family get up.
He had only to say a word and they would all come and sit
silently in their night vestments on the hard, cold ground of
his compound and listen, as long as he wished to go on explaining to them from the top of the stairs, how great and good he
was. They would. However, his wife would do—for
to-night.

His wife! He winced inwardly. A dismal woman with
startled eyes and dolorously drooping mouth, that would
listen to him in pained wonder and mute stillness. She was
used to those night-discourses now. She had rebelled once
—at the beginning. Only once. Now, while he sprawled
in the long chair and drank and talked, she would stand at the
further end of the table, her hands resting on the edge, her
frightened eyes watching his lips, without a sound, without a
stir, hardly breathing, till he dismissed her with a contemptuous: "Go to bed, dummy." She would draw a long breath
then and trail out of the room, relieved but unmoved.
Nothing could startle her, make her scold or make her cry.
She did not complain, she did not rebel. That first difference
of theirs was decisive. Too decisive, thought Willems,
discontentedly. It had frightened the soul out of her body
apparently. A dismal woman! A damn'd business altogether! What the devil did he want to go and saddle
himself. . . . Ah! Well! he wanted a home, and the match
seemed to please Hudig, and Hudig gave him the bungalow,
that flower-bowered house to which he was wending his way
in the cool moonlight. And he had the worship of the Da
Souza tribe. A man of his stamp could carry off anything,
do anything, aspire to anything. In another five years those
white people who attended the Sunday card-parties of the
Governor would accept him—half-caste wife and all! Hooray!
He saw his shadow dart forward and wave a hat, as big as a rum
barrel, at the end of an arm several yards long. . . . Who
shouted hooray? . . . He smiled shamefacedly to himself,
and, pushing his hands deep into his pockets, walked faster
with a suddenly grave face.

Behind him—to the left—a cigar end glowed in the gateway of Mr. Vinck's front yard. Leaning against one of the brick pillars, Mr. Vinck, the cashier of Hudig & Co., smoked the last cheroot of the evening. Amongst the shadows of the trimmed bushes Mrs. Vinck crunched slowly, with measured steps, the gravel of the circular path before the house.

"There's Willems going home on foot—and drunk, I fancy," said Mr. Vinck over his shoulder. "I saw him jump and wave his hat."

The crunching of the gravel stopped.

"Horrid man," said Mrs. Vinck, calmly. "I have heard he beats his wife."

"Oh no, my dear, no," muttered absently Mr. Vinck, with a vague gesture. The aspect of Willems as a wife-beater presented to him no interest. How women do misjudge! If Willems wanted to torture his wife he would have recourse to less primitive methods. Mr. Vinck knew Willems well, and believed him to be very able, very smart—objectionably so. As he took the last quick draws at the stump of his cheroot, Mr. Vinck reflected that the confidence accorded by Hudig to Willems was open, under the circumstances, to loyal criticism from Hudig's cashier.

"He is becoming dangerous; he knows too much. He will have to be got rid of," said Mr. Vinck aloud. But Mrs. Vinck had gone already, and after shaking his head he threw away his cheroot and followed her slowly.

Willems walked on homeward weaving the splendid web of his future. The road to greatness lay plainly before his eyes, straight and shining, without any obstacle that he could see. He had stepped off the path of honesty, as he understood it, but he would soon regain it, never to leave it any more! It was a very small matter. He would soon put it right again. Meantime his duty was not to be found out, and he trusted in his skill, in his luck, in his well-established reputation that would disarm suspicion if anybody dared to suspect. But nobody would dare! True, he was conscious of a slight deterioration. He had appropriated temporarily some of Hudig's money. A deplorable necessity. But he judged himself with the indulgence that should be extended to the weaknesses of genius. He would make reparation and all would be as before; nobody would be the loser for it, and he would go on unchecked towards the brilliant goal of his ambition.

Hudig's partner!

Before going up the steps of his house he stood for awhile, his feet well apart, chin in hand, contemplating mentally Hudig's future partner. A glorious occupation. He saw him quite safe; solid as the hills; deep—deep as an abyss; discreet as the grave.

## II

THE sea, perhaps because of its saltness, roughens the outside but keeps sweet the kernel of its servants' soul. The old sea; the sea of many years ago, whose servants were devoted slaves and went from youth to age or to a sudden grave without needing to open the book of life, because they could look at eternity reflected on the element that gave the life and dealt the death. Like a beautiful and unscrupulous woman, the sea of the past was glorious in its smiles, irresistible in its anger, capricious, enticing, illogical, irresponsible; a thing to love, a thing to fear. It cast a spell, it gave joy, it lulled gently into boundless faith; then with quick and causeless anger it killed. But its cruelty was redeemed by the charm of its inscrutable mystery, by the immensity of its promise, by the supreme witchery of its possible favour. Strong men with childlike hearts were faithful to it, were content to live by its grace—to die by its will. That was the sea before the time when the French mind set the Egyptian muscle in motion and produced a dismal but profitable ditch. Then a great pall of smoke sent out by countless steamboats was spread over the restless mirror of the Infinite. The hand of the engineer tore down the veil of the terrible beauty in order that greedy and faithless landlubbers might pocket dividends. The mystery was destroyed. Like all mysteries, it lived only in the hearts of its worshippers. The hearts changed; the men changed. The once loving and devoted servants went out armed with fire and iron, and conquering the fear of their own hearts became a calculating crowd of cold and exacting masters. The sea of the past was an incomparably beautiful mistress, with inscrutable face, with cruel and promising eyes. The sea of to-day is a used-up drudge, wrinkled and defaced by the churned-up wakes of brutal propellers, robbed of the enslaving charm of its vastness, stripped of its beauty, of its mystery and of its promise.

Tom Lingard was a master, a lover, a servant of the sea. The sea took him young, fashioned him body and soul; gave him his fierce aspect, his loud voice, his fearless eyes, his stupidly guileless heart. Generously it gave him his absurd faith in himself, his universal love of creation, his wide indulgence, his contemptuous severity, his straightforward simplicity of motive and honesty of aim. Having made him what he was, womanlike, the sea served him humbly and let him bask unharmed in the sunshine of its terribly uncertain favour. Tom Lingard grew rich on the sea and by the sea. He loved it with the ardent affection of a lover, he made light of it with the assurance of perfect mastery, he feared it with the wise fear of a brave man, and he took liberties with it as a spoiled child might do with a paternal and good-natured ogre. He was grateful to it, with the gratitude of an honest heart. His greatest pride lay in his profound conviction of its faithfulness—in the deep sense of his unerring knowledge of its treachery.

The little brig *Flash* was the instrument of Lingard's fortune. They came north together—both young—out of an Australian port, and after a very few years there was not a white man in the islands, from Palembang to Ternate, from Ombawa to Palawan, that did not know Captain Tom and his lucky craft. He was liked for his reckless generosity, for his unswerving honesty, and at first was a little feared on account of his violent temper. Very soon, however, they found him out, and the word went round that Captain Tom's fury was less dangerous than many a man's smile. He prospered

G

greatly. After his first—and successful—fight with the sea robbers, when he rescued, as rumour had it, the yacht of some big wig from home, somewhere down Carimata way, his great popularity began. As years went on it grew apace. Always visiting out-of-the-way places of that part of the world, always in search of new markets for his cargoes—not so much for profit as for the pleasure of finding them—he soon became known to the Malays, and by his successful recklessness in several encounters with pirates established the terror of his name. Those white men with whom he had business, and who naturally were on the look-out for his weaknesses, could easily see that it was enough to give him his Malay title to flatter him greatly. So when there was anything to be gained by it, and sometimes out of pure and unprofitable good nature, they would drop the ceremonious " Captain Lingard " and address him half seriously as Rajah Laut—the King of the Sea.

He carried the name bravely on his broad shoulders. He had carried it many years already when the boy Willems ran barefooted on the deck of the ship *Kosmopoliet IV.* in Samarang roads, looking with innocent eyes on the strange shore and objurgating his immediate surroundings with blasphemous lips, while his childish brain worked upon the heroic idea of running away. From the poop of the *Flash* Lingard saw in the early morning the Dutch ship get lumberingly under weigh, bound for the eastern ports. Very late in the evening of the same day he stood on the quay of the landing canal, ready to go on board of his brig. The night was starry and clear; the little custom-house building was shut up, and as the gharry that brought him down disappeared up the long avenue of dusty trees leading to the town, Lingard thought himself alone on the quay. He roused up his sleeping boat-crew and stood waiting for them to get ready, when he felt a tug at his coat and a thin voice said, very distinctly—

" English Captain."

Lingard turned round quickly, and what seemed to be a very lean boy jumped back with commendable activity.

"Who are you? Where do you spring from?" asked Lingard, in startled surprise.

From a safe distance the boy pointed towards a cargo lighter moored to the quay.

"Been hiding there, have you?" said Lingard. "Well, what do you want? Speak out, confound you. You did not come here to scare me to death, for fun, did you?"

The boy tried to explain in imperfect English, but very soon Lingard interrupted him.

"I see," he exclaimed, "you ran away from the big ship that sailed this morning. Well, why don't you go to your countrymen here?"

"Ship gone only a little way—to Sourabaya. Make me go back to the ship," explained the boy.

"Best thing for you," affirmed Lingard with conviction.

"No," retorted the boy; "me want stop here; not want go home. Get money here; home no good."

"This beats all my going a-fishing," commented the astonished Lingard. "It's money you want? Well! well! And you were not afraid to run away, you bag of bones, you!"

The boy intimated that he was frightened of nothing but of being sent back to the ship. Lingard looked at him in meditative silence.

"Come closer," he said at last. He took the boy by the chin, and turning up his face gave him a searching look. "How old are you?"

"Seventeen."

"There's not much of you for seventeen. Are you hungry?"

"A little."

"Will you come with me, in that brig there?"

The boy moved without a word towards the boat and scrambled into the bows.

"Knows his place," muttered Lingard to himself as he stepped heavily into the stern sheets and took up the yoke lines. "Give way there."

The Malay boat-crew lay back together, and the gig sprang

away from the quay, heading towards the brig's riding light.

Such was the beginning of Willems' career.

Lingard learned in half an hour all that there was of Willems' commonplace story. Father outdoor clerk of some ship-broker in Rotterdam; mother dead. The boy quick in learning, but idle in school. The straitened circumstances in the house filled with small brothers and sisters, sufficiently clothed and fed but otherwise running wild, while the disconsolate widower tramped about all day in a shabby overcoat and imperfect boots on the muddy quays, and in the evening piloted wearily the half-intoxicated foreign skippers amongst the places of cheap delights, returning home late, sick with too much smoking and drinking—for company's sake—with these men, who expected such attentions in the way of business. Then the offer of the good-natured captain of *Kosmopoliet IV.*, who was pleased to do something for the patient and obliging fellow; young Willems' great joy, his still greater disappointment with the sea that looked so charming from afar, but proved so hard and exacting on closer acquaintance—and then this running away by a sudden impulse. The boy was hopelessly at variance with the spirit of the sea. He had an instinctive contempt for the honest simplicity of that work which led to nothing he cared for. Lingard soon found this out. He offered to send him home in an English ship, but the boy begged hard to be permitted to remain. He wrote a beautiful hand, became soon perfect in English, was quick at figures; and Lingard made him useful in that way. As he grew older his trading instincts developed themselves astonishingly, and Lingard left him often to trade in one island or another while he, himself, made an intermediate trip to some out-of-the-way place. On Willems expressing a wish to that effect, Lingard let him enter Hudig's service. He felt a little sore at that abandonment because he had attached himself, in a way, to his protégé. Still he was proud of him, and spoke up for him loyally. At first it was, "Smart boy that—never make a seaman, though." Then when Willems was helping in the trading he referred to him as " that clever young fellow." Later on, when Willems became the confidential agent of Hudig, employed in many a delicate affair, the simple-hearted old seaman would point an admiring finger at his back and whisper to whoever stood near at the moment, " Long-headed chap that ; deuced long-headed chap. Look at him. Confidential man of old Hudig. I picked him up in a ditch, you may say, like a starved cat. Skin and bone. 'Pon my word I did. And now he knows more than I do about island trading. Fact. I am not joking. More than I do," he would repeat, seriously, with innocent pride in his honest eyes.

From the safe elevation of his commercial successes Willems patronised Lingard. He had a liking for his benefactor, not unmixed with some disdain for the crude directness of the old fellow's methods of conduct. There were, however, certain sides of Lingard's character for which Willems felt a qualified respect. The talkative seaman knew how to be silent on certain matters that to Willems were very interesting. Besides, Lingard was rich, and that in itself was enough to compel Willems' unwilling admiration. In his confidential chats with Hudig, Willems generally alluded to the benevolent Englishman as the " lucky old fool " in a very distinct tone of vexation ; Hudig would grunt an unqualified assent, and then the two would look at each other in a sudden immobility of pupils fixed by a stare of unexpressed thought.

" You can't find out where he gets all that indiarubber, hey, Willems ? " Hudig would ask at last, turning away and bending over the papers on his desk.

" No, Mr. Hudig. Not yet. But I am trying," was Willems' invariable reply, delivered with a ring of regretful deprecation.

" Try ! Always try ! You may try ! You think yourself clever perhaps," rumbled on Hudig, without looking up. " I have been trading with him twenty—thirty years now. The old fox. And I have tried. Bah ! "

He stretched out a short, podgy leg and contemplated the bare instep and the grass slipper hanging by the toes. " You can't make him drunk?" he would add, after a pause of stertorous breathing.

"No, Mr. Hudig, I can't really," protested Willems, earnestly.

"Well, don't try. I know him. Don't try," advised the master, and, bending again over his desk, his staring bloodshot eyes close to the paper, he would go on tracing laboriously with his thick fingers the slim unsteady letters of his correspondence, while Willems waited respectfully for his further good pleasure before asking, with great deference—

"Any orders, Mr. Hudig?"

"Hm! yes. Go to Bun-Hin yourself and see the dollars of that payment counted and packed, and have them put on board the mail-boat for Ternate. She's due here this afternoon."

"Yes, Mr. Hudig."

"And, look here. If the boat is late, leave the case in Bun-Hin's godown till to-morrow. Seal it up. Eight seals as usual. Don't take it away till the boat is here."

"No, Mr. Hudig."

"And don't forget about these opium cases. It's for to-night. Use my own boatmen. Tranship them from the *Caroline* to the Arab barque," went on the master in his hoarse undertone. "And don't you come to me with another story of a case dropped overboard like last time," he added, with sudden ferocity, looking up at his confidential clerk.

"No, Mr. Hudig. I will take care."

"That's all. Tell that pig as you go out that if he doesn't make the punkah go a little better I will break every bone in his body," finished up Hudig, wiping his purple face with a red silk handkerchief nearly as big as a counterpane.

Noiselessly Willems went out, shutting carefully behind him the little green door through which he passed to the warehouse. Hudig, pen in hand, listened to him bullying the punkah boy with profane violence, born of unbounded zeal for the master's comfort, before he returned to his writing amid the rustling of papers fluttering in the wind sent down by the punkah that waved in wide sweeps above his head.

Willems would nod familiarly to Mr. Vinck, who had his
desk close to the little door of the private office, and march
down the warehouse with an important air. Mr. Vinck—
extreme dislike lurking in every wrinkle of his gentlemanly
countenance—would follow with his eyes the white figure
flitting in the gloom amongst the piles of bales and cases till it
passed out through the big archway into the glare of the
street.

## III

THE opportunity and the temptation were too much for
Willems, and under the pressure of sudden necessity he abused
that trust which was his pride, the perpetual sign of his
cleverness and a load too heavy for him to carry. A run of
bad luck at cards, the failure of a small speculation undertaken
on his own account, an unexpected demand for money from
one or another member of the Da Souza family—and almost
before he was well aware of it he was off the path of his
peculiar honesty. It was such a faint and ill-defined track
that it took him some time to find out how far he had strayed
amongst the brambles of the dangerous wilderness he had been
skirting for so many years, without any other guide than his
own convenience and that doctrine of success which he had
found for himself in the book of life—in those interesting
chapters that the Devil has been permitted to write in it, to
test the sharpness of men's eyesight and the steadfastness of
their hearts. For one short, dark and solitary moment he
was dismayed, but he had that courage that will not scale
heights, yet will wade bravely through the mud—if there be
no other road. He applied himself to the task of restitution,
and devoted himself to the duty of not being found out.
On his thirtieth birthday he had almost accomplished the
task—and the duty had been faithfully and cleverly performed.
He saw himself safe. Again he could look hopefully toward
the goal of his legitimate ambition. Nobody would dare to

suspect him, and in a few days there would be nothing to suspect. He was elated. He did not know that his prosperity had touched then its high-water mark, and that the tide was already on the turn.

Two days afterwards he knew. Mr. Vinck, hearing the rattle of the door-handle, jumped up from his desk—where he had been tremulously listening to the loud voices in the private office—and buried his face in the big safe with nervous haste. For the last time Willems passed through the little green door leading to Hudig's sanctum, which, during the past half-hour, might have been taken—from the fiendish noise within—for the cavern of some wild beast. Willems' troubled eyes took in the quick impression of men and things as he came out from the place of his humiliation. He saw the scared expression of the punkah boy; the Chinamen tellers sitting on their heels with unmovable faces turned up blankly towards him, while their arrested hands hovered over the little piles of bright guilders ranged on the floor; Mr. Vinck's shoulder-blades with the fleshy rims of two red ears above. He saw the long avenue of gin cases stretching from where he stood to the arched doorway beyond which he would be able to breathe perhaps. A thin rope's end lay across his path and he saw it distinctly, yet stumbled heavily over it as if it had been a bar of iron. Then he found himself in the street at last, but could not find air enough to fill his lungs. He walked towards his home, gasping.

As the sound of Hudig's insults that lingered in his ears grew fainter by the lapse of time, the feeling of shame was replaced slowly by a passion of anger against himself and still more against the stupid concourse of circumstances that had driven him into his idiotic indiscretion. Idiotic indiscretion; that is how he defined his guilt to himself. Could there be anything worse from the point of view of his undeniable cleverness? What a fatal aberration of an acute mind! He did not recognise himself there. He must have been mad. That's it. A sudden gust of madness. And now the work of long years was destroyed utterly. What would become of him?

Before he could answer that question he found himself in the garden before his house, Hudig's wedding gift. He looked at it with a vague surprise to find it there. His past was so utterly gone from him that the dwelling which belonged to it appeared to him incongruous standing there intact, neat, and cheerful in the sunshine of the hot afternoon. The house was a pretty little structure all doors and windows, surrounded on all sides by the deep verandah supported on slender columns clothed in the green foliage of creepers, which also fringed the overhanging eaves of the high-pitched roof. Slowly, Willems mounted the dozen steps that led to the verandah. He paused at every step. He must tell his wife. He felt frightened at the prospect, and his alarm dismayed him. Frightened to face her! Nothing could give him a better measure of the greatness of the change around him, and in him. Another man and another life with the faith in himself gone. He could not be worth much if he was afraid to face that woman.

He dared not enter the house through the open door of the dining-room, but stood irresolute by the little work-table where trailed a white piece of calico, with a needle stuck in it, as if the work had been left hurriedly. The pink-crested cockatoo started, on his appearance, into clumsy activity and began to climb laboriously up and down his perch, calling "Joanna" with indistinct loudness and a persistent screech that prolonged the last syllable of the name as if in a peal of insane laughter. The screen in the doorway moved gently once or twice in the breeze, and each time Willems started slightly, expecting his wife, but he never lifted his eyes, although straining his ears for the sound of her footsteps. Gradually he lost himself in his thoughts, in the endless speculation as to the manner in which she would receive his news—and his orders. In this pre-occupation he almost forgot the fear of her presence. No doubt she will cry, she will lament, she will be helpless and frightened and passive as ever. And he would have to drag that limp weight on and on through the darkness of a spoiled life. Horrible! Of course he could not abandon her and the child to certain misery or possible starvation. The wife and the child of Willems. Willems the successful, the smart ; Willems the conf . . . . Pah ! And what was Willems now ? Willems the . . . . He strangled the half-born thought, and cleared his throat to stifle a groan. Ah ! Won't they talk to-night in the billiard-room—his world, where he had been first—all those men to whom he had been so superciliously condescending. Won't they talk with surprise, and affected regret, and grave faces, and wise nods. Some of them owed him money, but he never pressed anybody. Not he. Willems, the prince of good fellows, they called him. And now they will rejoice, no doubt, at his downfall. A crowd of imbeciles. In his abasement he was yet aware of his superiority over those fellows, who were merely honest or simply not found out yet. A crowd of imbeciles ! He shook his fist at the evoked image of his friends, and the startled parrot fluttered its wings and shrieked in desperate fright.

In a short glance upwards Willems saw his wife come round the corner of the house. He lowered his eyelids quickly, and waited silently till she came near and stood on the other side of the little table. He would not look at her face, but he could see the red dressing-gown he knew so well. She trailed through life in that red dressing-gown, with its row of dirty blue bows down the front, stained, and hooked on awry ; a torn flounce at the bottom following her like a snake as she moved languidly about, with her hair negligently caught up, and a tangled wisp straggling untidily down her back. His gaze travelled upwards from bow to bow, noticing those that hung only by a thread, but it did not go beyond her chin. He looked at her lean throat, at the obtrusive collar-bone visible in the disarray of the upper part of her attire. He saw the thin arm and the bony hand clasping the child she carried, and he felt an immense distaste for those encumbrances of his life. He waited for her to say something, but as he felt her eyes rest on him in unbroken silence he sighed and began to speak.

It was a hard task. He spoke slowly, lingering amongst the

memories of this early life in his reluctance to confess that this was the end of it and the beginning of a less splendid existence. In his conviction of having made her happiness in the full satisfaction of all material wants he never doubted for a moment that she was ready to keep him company on no matter how hard and stony a road. He was not elated by this certitude. He had married her to please Hudig, and the greatness of his sacrifice ought to have made her happy without any further exertion on his part. She had years of glory as Willems' wife, and years of comfort, of loyal care, and of such tenderness as she deserved. He had guarded her carefully from any bodily hurt; and of any other suffering he had no conception. The assertion of his superiority was only another benefit conferred on her. All this was a matter of course, but he told her all this so as to bring vividly before her the greatness of her loss. She was so dull of understanding that she would not grasp it else. And now it was at an end. They would have to go. Leave this house, leave this island, go far away where he was unknown. To the English Straits Settlements perhaps. He would find an opening there for his abilities—and juster men to deal with than old Hudig. He laughed bitterly.

"You have the money I left at home this morning, Joanna?" he asked. "We will want it all now."

As he spoke those words he thought he was a fine fellow. Nothing new that. Still, he surpassed there his own expectations. Hang it all, there are sacred things in life, after all. The marriage tie was one of them, and he was not the man to break it. The solidity of his principles caused him great satisfaction, but he did not care to look at his wife, for all that. He waited for her to speak. Then he shall have to console her; tell her not to be a crying fool; to get ready to go. Go where? How? When? He shook his head. They must leave at once; that was the principal thing. He felt a sudden need to hurry up his departure.

"Well, Joanna," he said, a little impatiently—"don't stand there in a trance. Do you hear? We must . . ."

He looked up at his wife, and whatever he was going to add

remained unspoken. She was staring at him with her big, slanting eyes, that seemed to him twice their natural size. The child, its dirty little face pressed to its mother's shoulder, was sleeping peacefully. The deep silence of the house was not broken, but rather accentuated, by the low mutter of the cockatoo, now very still on its perch. As Willems was looking at Joanna her upper lip was drawn up on one side, giving to her melancholy face a vicious expression altogether new to his experience. He stepped back in his surprise.

"Oh! You great man!" she said distinctly, but in a voice that was hardly above a whisper.

Those words, and still more her tone, stunned him as if somebody had fired a gun close to his ear. He stared back at her stupidly.

"Oh! You great man!" she repeated slowly, glancing right and left as if meditating a sudden escape. "And you think that I am going to starve with you. You are nobody now. You think my mamma and Leonard would let me go away? And with you! With you," she repeated scornfully, raising her voice, which woke up the child and caused it to whimper feebly.

"Joanna!" exclaimed Willems.

"Do not speak to me. I have heard what I have waited for all these years. You are less than dirt, you that have wiped your feet on me. I have waited for this. I am not afraid now. I do not want you; do not come near me. Ah—h!" she screamed shrilly, as he held out his hand in an entreating gesture—"Ah! Keep off me! Keep off me! Keep off!"

She backed away, looking at him with eyes both angry and frightened. Willems stared motionless, in dumb amazement at the mystery of anger and revolt in the head of his wife. Why? What had he ever done to her? This was the day of injustice indeed. First Hudig—and now his wife. He felt a terror at this hate that had lived stealthily so near him for years. He tried to speak, but she shrieked again, and it was like a needle through his heart. Again he raised his hand.

"Help!" called Mrs. Willems, in a piercing voice.
"Help!"

"Be quiet! You fool!" shouted Willems, trying to
drown the noise of his wife and child in his own angry
accents and rattling violently the little zinc table in his
exasperation.

From under the house, where there were bath-rooms and a
tool chest, appeared Leonard, a rusty iron bar in his hand.
He called threateningly from the bottom of the stairs.

"Do not hurt her, Mr. Willems. You are a savage. Not
at all like we whites."

"You too!" said the bewildered Willems. "I haven't
touched her. Is this a madhouse?" He moved towards
the stairs, and Leonard dropped the bar with a clang and
made for the gate of the compound. Willems turned back
to his wife.

"So you expected this," he said. "It is a conspiracy.
Who's that sobbing and groaning in the room? Some more
of your precious family. Hey?"

She was more calm now, and putting hastily the crying
child in the big chair walked towards him with sudden
fearlessless.

"My mother," she said, "my mother who came to defend
me from you—man from nowhere; a vagabond!"

"You did not call me a vagabond when you hung round
my neck—before we were married," said Willems, contemptuously.

"You took good care that I should not hang round your
neck after we were," she answered, clenching her hands, and
putting her face close to his. "You boasted while I suffered
and said nothing. What has become of your greatness;
of our greatness—you were always speaking about? Now I
am going to live on the charity of your master. Yes. That
is true. He sent Leonard to tell me so. And you will go
and boast somewhere else, and starve. So! Ah! I can
breathe now! This house is mine."

"Enough!" said Willems, slowly, with an arresting
gesture.

She leaped back, the fright again in her eyes, snatched up the child, pressed it to her breast, and, falling into a chair, drummed insanely with her heels on the resounding floor of the verandah.

"I shall go," said Willems, steadily. "I thank you. For the first time in your life you make me happy. You were a stone round my neck; you understand. I did not mean to tell you that as long as you lived, but you made me—now. Before I pass this gate you shall be gone from my mind. You made it very easy. I thank you."

He turned and went down the steps without giving her a glance, while she sat upright and quiet, with wide-open eyes, the child crying querulously in her arms. At the gate he came suddenly upon Leonard, who had been dodging about there and failed to get out of the way in time.

"Do not be brutal, Mr. Willems," said Leonard, hurriedly. "It is unbecoming between white men with all those natives looking on." Leonard's legs trembled very much, and his voice wavered between high and low tones without any attempt at control on his part. "Restrain your improper violence," he went on mumbling rapidly. "I am a respectable man of very good family, while you . . . it is regrettable . . . they all say so . . ."

"What?" thundered Willems. He felt a sudden impulse of mad anger, and before he knew what had happened he was looking at Leonard da Souza rolling in the dust at his feet. He stepped over his prostrate brother-in-law and tore blindly down the street, everybody making way for the frantic white man.

When he came to himself he was beyond the outskirts of the town, stumbling on the hard and cracked earth of reaped rice fields. How did he get there? It was dark. He must get back. As he walked towards the town slowly, his mind reviewed the events of the day and he felt a sense of bitter loneliness. His wife had turned him out of his own house. He had assaulted brutally his brother-in-law, a member of the Da Souza family—of that band of his worshippers. He did. Well, no! It was some other man.

Another man was coming back. A man without a past, without a future, yet full of pain and shame and anger. He stopped and looked round. A dog or two glided across the empty street and rushed past him with a frightened snarl. He was now in the midst of the Malay quarter whose bamboo houses, hidden in the verdure of their little gardens, were dark and silent. Men, women and children slept in there. Human beings. Would he ever sleep, and where? He felt as if he was the outcast of all mankind, and as he looked hopelessly round, before resuming his weary march, it seemed to him that the world was bigger, the night more vast and more black; but he went on doggedly with his head down as if pushing his way through some thick brambles. Then suddenly he felt planks under his feet and, looking up, saw the red light at the end of the jetty. He walked quite to the end and stood leaning against the post, under the lamp, looking at the roadstead where two vessels at anchor swayed their slender rigging amongst the stars. The end of the jetty; and here in one step more the end of life; the end of everything. Better so. What else could he do? Nothing ever comes back. He saw it clearly. The respect and admiration of them all, the old habits and old affections finished abruptly in the clear perception of the cause of his disgrace. He saw all this; and for a time he came out of himself, out of his selfishness—out of the constant pre-occupation of his interests and his desires—out of the temple of self and the concentration of personal thought.

His thoughts now wandered home. Standing in the tepid stillness of a starry tropical night he felt the breath of the bitter east wind, he saw the high and narrow fronts of tall houses under the gloom of a clouded sky; and on muddy quays he saw the shabby, high-shouldered figure—the patient, faded face of the weary man earning bread for the children that waited for him in a dingy home. It was miserable, miserable. But it would never come back. What was there in common between those things and Willems the clever, Willems the successful? He had cut himself adrift from that home many years ago. Better for

him then. Better for them now. All this was gone, never
to come back again; and suddenly he shivered, seeing himself alone in the presence of unknown and terrible dangers.

For the first time in his life he felt afraid of the future,
because he had lost his faith, the faith in his own success.
And he had destroyed it foolishly with his own hands!


## IV

HIS meditation, which resembled slow drifting into suicide,
was interrupted by Lingard, who, with a loud " I've got you
at last !" dropped his hand heavily on Willems' shoulder.
This time it was the old seaman himself going out of his way
to pick up the uninteresting waif—all that there was left of
that sudden and sordid shipwreck. To Willems, the rough,
friendly voice was a quick and fleeting relief followed by a
sharper pang of anger and unavailing regret. That voice
carried him back to the beginning of his promising career, the
end of which was very visible now from the jetty where they
both stood. He shook himself free from the friendly grasp,
saying with ready bitterness—

" It's all your fault. Give me a push now, do, and send
me over. I have been standing here waiting for help. You
are the man—of all men. You helped at the beginning;
you ought to have a hand in the end."

" I have better use for you than to throw you to the
fishes," said Lingard, seriously, taking Willems by the arm
and forcing him gently to walk up the jetty. " I have been
buzzing over this town like a bluebottle fly, looking for you
high and low. I have heard a lot. I will tell you what,
Willems; you are no saint, that's a fact. And you have not
been overwise either. I am not throwing stones," he added,
hastily, as Willems made an effort to get away, " but I am
not going to mince matters. Never could ! You keep quiet
while I talk. Can't you ? "

With a gesture of resignation and a half-stifled groan

Willems submitted to the stronger will, and the two men paced slowly up and down the resounding planks, while Lingard disclosed to Willems the exact manner of his undoing. After the first shock Willems lost the faculty of surprise in the overpowering feeling of indignation. So it was Vinck and Leonard who had served him so. They had watched him, tracked his misdeeds, reported them to Hudig. They had bribed obscure Chinamen, wormed out confidences from tipsy skippers, got at various boatmen, and had pieced out in that way the story of his irregularities. The blackness of this dark intrigue filled him with horror. He could understand Vinck. There was no love lost between them. But Leonard! Leonard!

"Why, Captain Lingard," he burst out, " the fellow licked my boots."

"Yes, yes, yes," said Lingard, testily, " we know that, and you did your best to cram your boot down his throat. No man likes that, my boy."

"I was always giving money to all that hungry lot," went on Willems, passionately. " Always my hand in my pocket. They never had to ask twice."

"Just so. Your generosity frightened them. They asked themselves where all that came from, and concluded that it was safer to throw you overboard. After all, Hudig is a much greater man than you, my friend, and they have a claim on him also."

"What do you mean, Captain Lingard?"

"What do I mean?" repeated Lingard, slowly. "Why, you are not going to make me believe you did not know your wife was Hudig's daughter. Come now!"

Willems stopped suddenly and swayed about.

"Ah! I understand," he gasped. " I never heard . . . Lately I thought there was . . . But no, I never guessed."

"Oh, you simpleton!" said Lingard, pityingly. " 'Pon my word," he muttered to himself, " I don't believe the fellow knew. Well! well! Steady now. Pull yourself together. What's wrong there? She is a good wife to you."

"Excellent wife," said Willems, in a dreary voice, looking far over the black and scintillating water.

"Very well, then," went on Lingard, with increasing friendliness. "Nothing wrong there. But did you really think that Hudig was marrying you off and giving you a house and I don't know what out of love for you?"

"I had served him well," answered Willems. "How well, you know yourself—through thick and thin. No matter what work and what risk, I was always there; always ready."

How well he saw the greatness of his work and the immensity of that injustice which was his reward. She was that man's daughter! In the light of this disclosure the facts of the last five years of his life stood clearly revealed in their full meaning. He had spoken first to Joanna at the gate of their dwelling as he went to his work in the brilliant flush of the early morning, when women and flowers are charming even to the dullest eyes. A most respectable family—two women and a young man—were his next-door neighbours. Nobody ever came to their little house but the priest, a native from the Spanish islands, now and then. The young man Leonard he had met in town, and was flattered by the little fellow's immense respect for the great Willems. He let him bring chairs, call the waiters, chalk his cues when playing billiards, express his admiration in choice words. He even condescended to listen patiently to Leonard's allusions to "our beloved father," a man of official position, a Government agent in Koti, where he died of cholera, alas! a victim to duty, like a good Catholic and a good man. It sounded very respectable, and Willems approved of those feeling references. Moreover, he prided himself upon having no colour-prejudices and no racial antipathies. He consented to drink curaçoa one afternoon on the verandah of Mrs. da Souza's house. He remembered Joanna that day, swinging in a hammock. She was untidy even then, he remembered, and that was the only impression he carried away from that visit. He had no time for love in those glorious days, no time even for a passing fancy, but gradually he fell into the habit of calling almost every day at that little house where he was greeted by Mrs. da Souza's shrill voice screaming for Joanna to come and entertain the gentleman from Hudig & Co. And then the sudden and unexpected visit of the priest. He remembered the man's flat, yellow face, his thin legs, his propitiatory smile, his beaming black eyes, his conciliating manner, his veiled hints which he did not understand at the time. How he wondered what the man wanted, and how unceremoniously he got rid of him. And then came vividly into his recollection the morning when he met again that fellow coming out of Hudig's office, and how he was amused at the incongruous visit. And that morning with Hudig! Would he ever forget it? Would he ever forget his surprise as the master, instead of plunging at once into business, looked at him thoughtfully before turning, with a furtive smile, to the papers on the desk? He could hear him now, his nose in the paper before him, dropping astonishing words in the intervals of wheezy breathing.

"Heard said . . . called there often . . . most respectable ladies . . . knew the father very well . . . estimable . . . best thing for a young man . . . settle down. . . . Personally, very glad to hear . . . thing arranged . . . Suitable recognition of valuable services. . . . Best thing—best thing to do."

And he believed! What credulity! What an ass! Hudig knew the father! Rather. And so did everybody else probably; all except himself. How proud he had been of Hudig's benevolent interest in his fate! How proud he was when invited by Hudig to stay with him at his little house in the country—where he could meet men, men of official position—as a friend. Vinck had been green with envy. Oh, yes! He had believed in the best thing, and took the girl like a gift of fortune. How he boasted to Hudig of being free from prejudices. The old scoundrel must have been laughing in his sleeve at his fool of a confidential clerk. He took the girl, guessing nothing. How could he? There had been a father of some kind to the common knowledge. Men knew him; spoke about him. A lank man of hopelessly

mixed descent, but otherwise—apparently—unobjectionable.
The shady relations came out afterwards, but—with his
freedom from prejudices—he did not mind them, because,
with their humble dependence, they completed his triumphant life. Taken in! taken in! Hudig had found an easy
way to provide for the begging crowd. He had shifted the
burden of his youthful vagaries on to the shoulders of his
confidential clerk; and while he worked for the master, the
master had cheated him; had stolen his very self from him.
He was married. He belonged to that woman, no matter
what she might do! . . . Had sworn . . . for all life! . . .
Thrown himself away. . . . And that man dared this very
morning call him a thief! Damnation!

"Let go, Lingard!" he shouted, trying to get away by
a sudden jerk from the watchful old seaman. "Let me go
and kill that . . ."

"No, you don't!" panted Lingard, hanging on manfully.
"You want to kill, do you? You lunatic. Ah!—I've got
you now! Be quiet, I say!"

They struggled violently, Lingard forcing Willems slowly
towards the guard-rail. Under their feet the jetty sounded
like a drum in the quiet night. On the shore end the native
caretaker of the wharf watched the combat, squatting
behind the safe shelter of some big cases. The next day he
informed his friends, with calm satisfaction, that two drunken
white men had fought on the jetty. It had been a great
fight. They fought without arms, like wild beasts, after the
manner of white men. No! nobody was killed, or there
would have been trouble and a report to make. How could
he know why they fought? White men have no reason
when they are like that.

Just as Lingard was beginning to fear that he would be
unable to restrain much longer the violence of the younger
man, he felt Willems' muscles relaxing, and took advantage
of this opportunity to pin him, by a last effort, to the rail.
They both panted heavily, speechless, their faces very close.

"All right," muttered Willems at last. "Don't break
my back over this infernal rail. I will be quiet."

"Now you are reasonable," said Lingard, much relieved. "What made you fly into that passion?" he asked, leading him back to the end of the jetty, and, still holding him prudently with one hand, he fumbled with the other for his whistle and blew a shrill and prolonged blast. Over the smooth water of the roadstead came in answer a faint cry from one of the ships at anchor.

"My boat will be here directly," said Lingard. "Think of what you are going to do. I sail to-night."

"What is there for me to do, except one thing?" said Willems, gloomily.

"Look here," said Lingard; "I picked you up as a boy, and consider myself responsible for you in a way. You took your life into your own hands many years ago—but still . . ."

He paused, listening, till he heard the regular grind of the oars in the rowlocks of the approaching boat, then went on again.

"I have made it all right with Hudig. You owe him nothing now. Go back to your wife. She is a good woman. Go back to her."

"Why, Captain Lingard," exclaimed Willems, "she . . ."

"It was most affecting," went on Lingard, without heeding him. "I went to your house to look for you and there I saw her in despair. It was heart-breaking. She called for you; she entreated me to find you. She spoke wildly, poor woman, as if all this was her fault."

Willems listened amazed. The blind old idiot! How queerly he misunderstood! But if it was true, if it was even true, the very idea of seeing her filled his soul with intense loathing. He did not break his oath, but he would not go back to her. Let hers be the sin of that separation; of the sacred bond broken. He revelled in the extreme purity of his heart, and he would not go back to her. Let her come back to him. He had the comfortable conviction that he would never see her again, and that through her own fault only. In this conviction he told himself solemnly that if she would come to him he would receive her with generous forgiveness, because such was the praiseworthy solidity of his principles. But he hesitated whether he would or would not disclose to Lingard the revolting completeness of his humiliation. Turned out of his house—and by his wife; that woman who hardly dared to breathe in his presence, yesterday. He remained perplexed and silent. No. He lacked the courage to tell the ignoble story.

As the boat of the brig appeared suddenly on the black water close to the jetty, Lingard broke the painful silence.

"I always thought," he said, sadly, "I always thought you were somewhat heartless, Willems, and apt to cast adrift those that thought most of you. I appeal to what is best in you; do not abandon that woman."

"I have not abandoned her," answered Willems, quickly, with conscious truthfulness. "Why should I? As you so justly observed, she had been a good wife to me. A very good, quiet, obedient, loving wife, and I love her as much as she loves me. Every bit. But as to going back now, to that place where I . . . To walk again amongst those men who yesterday were ready to crawl before me, and then feel on my back the sting of their pitying or satisfied smiles—no! I can't. I would rather hide from them at the bottom of the sea," he went on, with resolute energy. "I don't think, Captain Lingard," he added, more quietly, "I don't think that you realise what my position was there."

In a wide sweep of his hand he took in the sleeping shore from north to south, as if wishing it a proud and threatening good-bye. For a short moment he forgot his downfall in the recollection of his brilliant triumphs. Amongst the men of his class and occupation who slept in those dark houses he had been indeed the first.

"It is hard," muttered Lingard, pensively. "But whose the fault? Whose the fault?"

"Captain Lingard!" cried Willems, under the sudden impulse of a felicitous inspiration, "if you leave me here on this jetty—it's murder. I shall never return to that place alive, wife or no wife. You may just as well cut my throat at once."

The old seaman started.

"Don't try to frighten me, Willems," he said, with great severity, and paused.

Above the accents of Willems' brazen despair he heard, with considerable uneasiness, the whisper of his own absurd conscience. He meditated for awhile with an irresolute air.

"I could tell you to go and drown yourself, and be damned to you," he said, with an unsuccessful assumption of brutality in his manner, "but I won't. We are responsible for one another—worse luck. I am almost ashamed of myself, but I can understand your dirty pride. I can! By . . ."

He broke off with a loud sigh and walked briskly to the steps, at the bottom of which lay his boat, rising and falling gently on the slight and invisible swell.

"Below there! Got a lamp in the boat? Well, light it and bring it up, one of you. Hurry now!"

He tore out a page of his pocket-book, moistened his pencil with great energy and waited, stamping his feet impatiently.

"I will see this thing through," he muttered to himself. "And I will have it all square and shipshape; see if I don't! Are you going to bring that lamp, you son of a crippled mud-turtle? I am waiting."

The gleam of the light on the paper placated his professional anger, and he wrote rapidly, the final dash of his signature curling the paper up in a triangular tear.

"Take that to this white Tuan's house. I will send the boat back for you in half an hour."

The coxswain raised his lamp deliberately to Willems' face.

"This Tuan? Tau! I know."

"Quick then!" said Lingard, taking the lamp from him —and the man went off at a run.

"Kassi mem! To the lady herself," called Lingard after him.

Then, when the man disappeared, he turned to Willems.

"I have written to your wife," he said. "If you do not return for good, you do not go back to that house only for another parting. You must come as you stand. I won't have that poor woman tormented. I will see to it that you are not separated for long. Trust me!"

Willems shivered, then smiled in the darkness.

"No fear of that," he muttered, enigmatically. "I trust you implicitly, Captain Lingard," he added, in a louder tone.

Lingard led the way down the steps, swinging the lamp and speaking over his shoulder.

"It is the second time, Willems, I take you in hand. Mind it is the last. The second time; and the only difference between then and now is that you were barefooted then and have boots now. In fourteen years. With all your smartness! A poor result that. A very poor result."

He stood for awhile on the lowest platform of the steps, the light of the lamp falling on the upturned face of the stroke oar, who held the gunwale of the boat close alongside, ready for the captain to step in.

"You see," he went on, argumentatively, fumbling about the top of the lamp, "you got yourself so crooked amongst those 'longshore quill-drivers that you could not run clear in any way. That's what comes of such talk as yours, and of such a life. A man sees so much falsehood that he begins to lie to himself. Pah!" he said, in disgust, "there's only one place for an honest man. The sea, my boy, the sea! But you never would; didn't think there was enough money in it; and now—look!"

He blew the light out, and, stepping into the boat, stretched quickly his hand towards Willems, with friendly care. Willems sat by him in silence, and the boat shoved off, sweeping in a wide circle towards the brig.

"Your compassion is all for my wife, Captain Lingard," said Willems, moodily. "Do you think I am so very happy?"

"No! no!" said Lingard, heartily. "Not a word more shall pass my lips. I had to speak my mind once, seeing that I knew you from a child, so to speak. And now I shall forget; but you are young yet. Life is very long," he went on, with unconscious sadness; "let this be a lesson to you."

He laid his hand affectionately on Willems' shoulder, and they both sat silent till the boat came alongside the ship's ladder.

When on board Lingard gave orders to his mate, and leading Willems on the poop, sat on the breech of one of the brass six-pounders with which his vessel was armed. The boat went off again to bring back the messenger. As soon as it was seen returning dark forms appeared on the brig's spars; then the sails fell in festoons with a swish of their heavy folds, and hung motionless under the yards in the dead calm of the clean and dewy night. From the forward end came the clink of the windlass, and soon afterwards the hail of the chief mate informing Lingard that the cable was hove short.

"Hold on everything," hailed back Lingard; "we must wait for the land-breeze before we let go our hold of the ground."

He approached Willems, who sat on the skylight, his body bent down, his head low, and his hands hanging listlessly between his knees.

"I am going to take you to Sambir," he said. "You've never heard of the place, have you? Well, it's up that river of mine about which people talk so much and know so little. I've found out the entrance for a ship of *Flash's* size. It isn't easy. You'll see. I will show you. You have been at sea long enough to take an interest. . . . Pity you didn't stick to it. Well, I am going there. I have my own trading post in the place. Almayer is my partner. You knew him when he was at Hudig's. Oh, he lives there as happy as a king. D'ye see, I have them all in my pocket. The rajah is an old friend of mine. My word is law—and I am the only trader. No other white man but Almayer had ever been in that settlement. You will live quietly there till I come back from my next cruise to the westward. We shall see then what can be done for you. Never fear. I have no doubt my secret will be safe with you. Keep mum about my river when you get amongst the traders again. There's many would give their ears for the knowledge of it. I'll tell

you something : that's where I get all my guttah and rattans.
Simply inexhaustible, my boy."

While Lingard spoke Willems looked up quickly, but soon
his head fell on his breast in the discouraging certitude that
the knowledge he and Hudig had wished for so much had
come to him too late.   He sat in a listless attitude.

" You will help Almayer in his trading if you have a heart
for it," continued Lingard, " just to kill time till I come
back for you.   Only six weeks or so."

Over their heads the damp sails fluttered noisily in the first
faint puff of the breeze ; then, as the airs freshened, the brig
tended to the wind, and the silenced canvas lay quietly aback.
The mate spoke with low distinctness from the shadows of
the quarter-deck.

" There's the breeze.   Which way do you want to cast her
head, Captain Lingard ? "

Lingard's eyes, that had been fixed aloft, glanced down at
the dejected figure of the man sitting on the skylight.   He
seemed to hesitate for a minute.

" To the northward, to the northward," he answered,
testily, as if annoyed at his own fleeting thought, " and bear
a hand there.   Every puff of wind is worth money in these
seas."

He remained motionless, listening to the rattle of blocks
and the creaking of trusses as the head-yards were hauled
round.   Sail was made on the ship and the windlass manned
again while he stood still, lost in thought.   He only roused
himself when a barefooted seacannie glided past him silently
on his way to the wheel.

" Put the helm aport !   Hard over ! " he said, in his harsh
sea-voice, to the man whose face appeared suddenly out of
the darkness in the circle of light thrown upwards from the
binnacle lamps.

The anchor was secured, the yards trimmed, and the brig
began to move out of the roadstead.   The sea woke up under
the push of the sharp cutwater, and whispered softly to the
gliding craft in that tender and rippling murmur in which it
speaks sometimes to those it nurses and loves.   Lingard stood

by the taffrail listening, with a pleased smile till the *Flash* began to draw close to the only other vessel in the anchorage.

"Here, Willems," he said, calling him to his side, "d'ye see that barque here? That's an Arab vessel. White men have mostly given up the game, but this fellow drops in my wake often, and lives in hopes of cutting me out in that settlement. Not while I live, I trust. You see, Willems, I brought prosperity to that place. I composed their quarrels, and saw them grow under my eyes. There's peace and happiness there. I am more master there than his Dutch Excellency down in Batavia ever will be when some day a lazy man-of-war blunders at last against the river. I mean to keep the Arabs out of it, with their lies and their intrigues. I shall keep the venomous breed out, if it costs me my fortune."

The *Flash* drew quietly abreast of the barque, and was beginning to drop it astern when a white figure started up on the poop of the Arab vessel, and a voice called out—

"Greeting to the Rajah Laut!"

"To you greeting!" answered Lingard, after a moment of hesitating surprise. Then he turned to Willems with a grim smile. "That's Abdullah's voice," he said. "Mighty civil all of a sudden, isn't he? I wonder what it means. Just like his impudence! No matter! His civility or his impudence are all one to me. I know that this fellow will be under way and after me like a shot. I don't care! I have the heels of anything that floats in these seas," he added, while his proud and loving glance ran over and rested fondly amongst the brig's lofty and graceful spars.

## V

"It was the writing on his forehead," said Babalatchi, adding a couple of small sticks to the little fire by which he was squatting, and without looking at Lakamba, who lay down supported on his elbow on the other side of the embers. "It was written when he was born that he should end his life in darkness, and now he is like a man walking in a black night—with his eyes open, yet seeing not. I knew him well when he had slaves, and many wives, and much merchandise, and trading praus, and praus for fighting. Hay—ya! He was a great fighter in the days before the breath of the Merciful put out the light in his eyes. He was a pilgrim, and had many virtues : he was brave, his hand was open, and he was a great robber. For many years he led the men that drank blood on the sea : first in prayer and first in fight. Have I not stood behind him when his face was turned to the West? Have I not watched by his side ships with high masts burning in a straight flame on the calm water? Have I not followed him on dark nights amongst sleeping men that woke up only to die? His sword was swifter than the fire from Heaven, and struck before it flashed. Haï! Tuan! Those were the days and that was a leader, and I myself was younger; and in those days there were not so many fireships with guns that deal fiery death from afar. Over the hill and over the forest—O! Tuan Lakamba! they dropped whistling fireballs into the creek where our praus took refuge, and where they dared not follow men who had arms in their hands."

He shook his head with mournful regret and threw another handful of fuel on the fire. The burst of clear flame lit up his broad, dark, and pock-marked face, where the big lips, stained with betel-juice, looked like a deep and bleeding gash of a fresh wound. The reflection of the firelight gleamed brightly in his solitary eye, lending it for a moment a fierce animation that died out together with the short-lived flame. With quick touches of his bare hands he raked the embers into a heap, then, wiping the warm ash on his waistcoat—his only garment—he clasped his thin legs with his entwined fingers, and rested his chin on his drawn-up knees. Lakamba stirred slightly without changing his position or taking his eyes off the glowing coals, on which they had been fixed in dreamy immobility.

"Yes," went on Babalatchi, in a low monotone, as if pursuing aloud a train of thought that had its beginning in the silent contemplation of the unstable nature of earthly greatness—"yes. He has been rich and strong, and now he lives on alms: old, feeble, blind and without companions, but for his daughter. The Rajah Patalolo gives him rice, and the pale woman—his daughter—cooks it for him, for he has no slave."

"I saw her from afar," muttered Lakamba, disparagingly. "A she-dog with white teeth, like a woman of the Orang-Putih."

"Right, right," assented Babalatchi; "but you have not seen her near. Her mother was a woman from the west; a Baghdadi woman with veiled face. Now she goes uncovered, like our women do, for she is poor and he is blind, and nobody ever comes near them unless to ask for a charm or a blessing and depart quickly for fear of his anger and of the Rajah's hand. You have not been on that side of the river?"

"Not for a long time. If I go . . ."

"True! true!" interrupted Babalatchi, soothingly! "but I go often alone—for your good—and look—and listen. When the time comes; when we both go together towards the Rajah's campong, it will be to enter—and to remain."

Lakamba sat up and looked at Babalatchi gloomily.

"This is good talk, once, twice; when it is heard too often it becomes foolish, like the prattle of children."

"Many, many times have I seen the cloudy sky and have heard the wind of the rainy seasons," said Babalatchi, impressively.

"And where is your wisdom? It must be with the wind and the clouds of seasons past, for I do not hear it in your talk."

"Those are the words of the ungrateful!" shouted Babalatchi, with sudden exasperation. "Verily, our only refuge is with the One, the Mighty, the Redresser of . . ."

"Peace! peace!" growled the startled Lakamba. "It is but a friend's talk."

Babalatchi subsided into his former attitude, muttering to himself. After awhile he went on again in a louder voice—

"Since the Rajah Laut left another white man here in Sambir, the daughter of the blind Omar el Badavi has spoken to other ears than mine."

"Would a white man listen to a beggar's daughter?" said Lakamba, doubtingly.

"Haï! I have seen . . ."

"And what did you see? O one-eyed one!" exclaimed Lakamba, contemptuously.

"I have seen the strange white man walking on the narrow path before the sun could dry the drops of dew on the bushes, and I have heard the whisper of his voice when he spoke through the smoke of the morning fire to that woman with big eyes and a pale skin. Woman in body, but in heart a man! She knows no fear and no shame. I have heard her voice too."

He nodded twice at Lakamba sagaciously and gave himself up to silent musing, his solitary eye fixed immovably upon the straight wall of forest on the opposite bank. Lakamba lay silent, staring vacantly. Under them Lingard's own river rippled softly amongst the piles supporting the bamboo platform of the little watch-house before which they were lying. Behind the house the ground rose in a gentle swell of a low hill cleared of the big timber, but thickly overgrown with the grass and bushes, now withered and burnt up in the long drought of the dry season. This old rice clearing, which had been several years lying fallow, was framed on three sides by the impenetrable and tangled growth of the untouched forest, and on the fourth came down to the muddy river bank. There was not a breath of wind on the land or river, but high above, in the transparent sky, little clouds rushed past the moon, now appearing in her diffused rays with the brilliance of silver, now obscuring her face with the blackness of ebony. Far away, in the middle of the river, a fish would leap now and then with a short splash, the very loudness of which measured the profundity of the overpowering silence that swallowed up the sharp sound suddenly.

Lakamba dozed uneasily off, but the wakeful Babalatchi sat thinking deeply, sighing from time to time, and slapping himself over his naked torso incessantly in a vain endeavour to keep off an occasional and wandering mosquito that, rising as high as the platform above the swarms of the riverside, would settle with a ping of triumph on the unexpected victim. The moon, pursuing her silent and toilsome path, attained her highest elevation, and chasing the shadow of the roof-eaves from Lakamba's face, seemed to hang arrested over their heads. Babalatchi revived the fire and woke up his companion, who sat up yawning and shivering discontentedly.

Babalatchi spoke again in a voice which was like the murmur of a brook that runs over the stones : low, monotonous, persistent ; irresistible in its power to wear out and to destroy the hardest obstacles. Lakamba listened, silent but interested. They were Malay adventurers ; ambitious men of that place and time ; the Bohemians of their race. In the early days of the settlement, before the ruler Patalolo had shaken off his allegiance to the Sultan of Koti, Lakamba appeared in the river with two small trading vessels. He was disappointed to find already some semblance of organisation amongst the settlers of various races who recognised the unobtrusive sway of old Patalolo, and he was not politic enough to conceal his disappointment. He declared himself to be a man from the east, from those parts where no white man ruled, and to be of an oppressed race, but of a princely family. And truly enough he had all the gifts of an exiled prince. He was discontented, ungrateful, turbulent ; a man full of envy and ready for intrigue, with brave words and empty promises for ever on his lips. He was obstinate, but his will was made up of short impulses that never lasted long enough to carry him to the goal of his ambition. Received coldly by the suspicious Patalolo, he persisted—permission or no permission—in clearing the ground on a good spot some fourteen miles down the river from Sambir, and built himself a house there, which he fortified by a high palisade. As he had many followers and seemed very reckless, the old Rajah did not think it prudent at the time to interfere with him by force. Once settled, he began to intrigue. The quarrel of Patalolo with the Sultan of Koti was of his fomenting, but failed to produce the result he expected because the Sultan could not back him up effectively at such a great distance. Disappointed in that scheme, he promptly organised an outbreak of the Bugis settlers, and besieged the old Rajah in his stockade with much noisy valour and a fair chance of success; but Lingard then appeared on the scene with the armed brig, and the old seaman's hairy forefinger, shaken menacingly in his face, quelled his martial ardour. No man cared to encounter the Rajah Laut, and Lakamba, with momentary resignation, subsided into a half-cultivator, half-trader, and nursed in his fortified house his wrath and his ambition, keeping it for use on a more propitious occasion. Still faithful to his character of a prince-pretender, he would not recognise the constituted authorities, answering sulkily the Rajah's messenger, who claimed the tribute for the cultivated fields, that the Rajah had better come and take it himself. By Lingard's advice he was left alone, notwithstanding his rebellious mood; and for many days he lived undisturbed amongst his wives and retainers, cherishing that persistent and causeless hope of better times, the possession of which seems to be the universal privilege of exiled greatness.

But the passing days brought no change. The hope grew faint and the hot ambition burnt itself out, leaving only a feeble and expiring spark amongst a heap of dull and tepid ashes of indolent acquiescence with the decrees of Fate, till

Babalatchi fanned it again into a bright flame. Babalatchi had blundered upon the river while in search of a safe refuge for his disreputable head. He was a vagabond of the seas, a true Orang-Laut, living by rapine and plunder of coasts and ships in his prosperous days; earning his living by honest and irksome toil when the days of adversity were upon him. So, although at times leading the Sulu rovers, he had also served as Serang of country ships, and in that wise had visited the distant seas, beheld the glories of Bombay, the might of the Mascati Sultan; had even struggled in a pious throng for the privilege of touching with his lips the Sacred Stone of the Holy City. He gathered experience and wisdom in many lands, and after attaching himself to Omar el Badavi, he affected great piety (as became a pilgrim), although unable to read the inspired words of the Prophet. He was brave and bloodthirsty without any affectation, and he hated the white men who interfered with the manly pursuits of throat-cutting, kidnapping, slave-dealing, and fire-raising that were the only possible occupation for a true man of the sea. He found favour in the eyes of his chief, the fearless Omar el Badavi, the leader of Brunei rovers, whom he followed with unquestioning loyalty through the long years of successful depredation. And when that long career of murder, robbery and violence received its first serious check at the hands of white men, he stood faithfully by his chief, looked steadily at the bursting shells, was undismayed by the flames of the burning stronghold, by the death of his companions, by the shrieks of their women, the wailing of their children; by the sudden ruin and destruction of all that he deemed indispensable to a happy and glorious existence. The beaten ground between the houses was slippery with blood, and the dark mangroves of the muddy creeks were full of sighs of the dying men who were stricken down before they could see their enemy. They died helplessly, for into the tangled forest there was no escape, and their swift praus, in which they had so often scoured the coast and the seas, now wedged together in the narrow creek, were burning fiercely. Babalatchi, with the clear perception of the coming

H

end, devoted all his energies to saving if it was but only one
of them. He succeeded in time. When the end came in the
explosion of the stored powder-barrels, he was ready to look
for his chief. He found him half dead and totally blinded,
with nobody near him but his daughter Aïssa :—the sons
had fallen earlier in the day, as became men of their courage.
Helped by the girl with the steadfast heart, Babalatchi carried
Omar on board the light prau and succeeded in escaping, but
with very few companions only. As they hauled their craft
into the network of dark and silent creeks, they could hear
the cheering of the crews of the man-of-war's boats dashing
to the attack of the rover's village. Aïssa, sitting on the
high after-deck, her father's blackened and bleeding head in
her lap, looked up with fearless eyes at Babalatchi. "They
shall find only smoke, blood and dead men, and women mad
with fear there, but nothing else living," she said, mournfully. Babalatchi, pressing with his right hand the deep
gash on his shoulder, answered sadly : "They are very
strong. When we fight with them we can only die. Yet,"
he added, menacingly—"some of us still live! Some of us
still live!"

For a short time he dreamed of vengeance, but his dream
was dispelled by the cold reception of the Sultan of Sulu, with
whom they sought refuge at first and who gave them only
a contemptuous and grudging hospitality. While Omar,
nursed by Aïssa, was recovering from his wounds, Babalatchi
attended industriously before the exalted Presence that had
extended to them the hand of protection. For all that, when
Babalatchi spoke into the Sultan's ear certain proposals of a
great and profitable raid, that was to sweep the islands from
Ternate to Acheen, the Sultan was very angry. "I know
you, you men from the west," he exclaimed, angrily. "Your
words are poison in a Ruler's ears. Your talk is of fire and
murder and booty—but on our heads falls the vengeance of
the blood you drink. Begone!"

There was nothing to be done. Times were changed.
So changed that, when a Spanish frigate appeared before the
island and a demand was sent to the Sultan to deliver Omar

and his companions, Babalatchi was not surprised to hear that they were going to be made the victims of political expediency. But from that sane appreciation of danger to tame submission was a very long step. And then began Omar's second flight. It began arms in hand, for the little band had to fight in the night on the beach for the possession of the small canoes in which those that survived got away at last. The story of that escape lives in the hearts of brave men even to this day. They talk of Babalatchi and of the strong woman who carried her blind father through the surf under the fire of the warship from the north. The companions of that piratical and son-less Æneas are dead now, but their ghosts wander over the waters and the islands at night—after the manner of ghosts—and haunt the fires by which sit armed men, as is meet for the spirits of fearless warriors who died in battle. There they may hear the story of their own deeds, of their own courage, suffering and death, on the lips of living men. That story is told in many places. On the cool mats in breezy verandahs of Rajahs' houses it is alluded to disdainfully by impassible statesmen, but amongst armed men that throng the courtyards it is a tale which stills the murmur of voices and the tinkle of anklets; arrests the passage of the siri-vessel, and fixes the eyes in absorbed gaze. They talk of the fight, of the fearless woman, of the wise man; of long suffering on the thirsty sea in leaky canoes; of those who died. . . . Many died. A few survived. The chief, the woman, and another one who became great.

There was no hint of incipient greatness in Babalatchi's unostentatious arrival in Sambir. He came with Omar and Aïssa in a small prau loaded with green cocoanuts, and claimed the ownership of both vessel and cargo. How it came to pass that Babalatchi, fleeing for his life in a small canoe, managed to end his hazardous journey in a vessel full of a valuable commodity, is one of those secrets of the sea that baffle the most searching inquiry. In truth nobody inquired much. There were rumours of a missing trading prau belonging to Menado, but they were vague and remained

mysterious. Babalatchi told a story which—it must be said
in justice to Patalolo's knowledge of the world—was not
believed. When the Rajah ventured to state his doubts,
Babalatchi asked him in tones of calm remonstrance whether
he could reasonably suppose that two oldish men—who had
only one eye amongst them—and a young woman were likely
to gain possession of anything whatever by violence? Charity
was a virtue recommended by the Prophet. There were
charitable people, and their hand was open to the deserving.
Patalolo wagged his aged head doubtingly, and Babalatchi
withdrew with a shocked mien and put himself forthwith
under Lakamba's protection. The two men who completed
the prau's crew followed him into that magnate's campong.
The blind Omar, with Aïssa, remained under the care of the
Rajah, and the Rajah confiscated the cargo. The prau
hauled up on the mud-bank, at the junction of the two
branches of the Pantai, rotted in the rain, warped in the sun,
fell to pieces and gradually vanished into the smoke of household fires of the settlement. Only a forgotten plank and a
rib or two, sticking neglected in the shiny ooze for a long time,
served to remind Babalatchi during many months that he
was a stranger in the land.

Otherwise, he felt perfectly at home in Lakamba's establishment, where his peculiar position and influence were
quickly recognised and soon submitted to even by the women.
He had all a true vagabond's pliability to circumstances and
adaptiveness to momentary surroundings. In his readiness
to learn from experience that contempt for early principles
so necessary to a true statesman, he equalled the most
successful politicians of any age; and he had enough persuasiveness and firmness of purpose to acquire a complete
mastery over Lakamba's vacillating mind—where there was
nothing stable but an all-pervading discontent. He kept
the discontent alive, he rekindled the expiring ambition, he
moderated the poor exile's not unnatural impatience to
attain a high and lucrative position. He—the man of
violence—deprecated the use of force, for he had a clear comprehension of the difficult situation. From the same cause,

he—the hater of white men—would to some extent admit the eventual expediency of Dutch protection. But nothing should be done in a hurry. Whatever his master Lakamba might think, there was no use in poisoning old Patalolo, he maintained. It could be done, of course ; but what then ? As long as Lingard's influence was paramount—as long as Almayer, Lingard's representative, was the only great trader of the settlement, it was not worth Lakamba's while—even if it had been possible—to grasp the rule of the young state. Killing Almayer and Lingard was so difficult and so risky that it might be dismissed as impracticable. What was wanted was an alliance ; somebody to set up against the white man's influence—and somebody who, while favourable to Lakamba, would at the same time be a person of a good standing with the Dutch authorities. A rich and considered trader was wanted. Such a person once firmly established in Sambir would help them to oust the old Rajah, to remove him from power or from life if there was no other way. Then it would be time to apply to the Orang Blanda for a flag ; for a recognition of their meritorious services ; for that protection which would make them safe for ever ! The word of a rich and loyal trader would mean something with the Ruler down in Batavia. The first thing to do was to find such an ally and to induce him to settle in Sambir. A white trader would not do. A white man would not fall in with their ideas— would not be trustworthy. The man they wanted should be rich, unscrupulous, have many followers, and be a well-known personality in the islands. Such a man might be found amongst the Arab traders. Lingard's jealousy, said Baba- latchi, kept all the traders out of the river. Some were afraid, and some did not know how to get there ; others ignored the very existence of Sambir ; a good many did not think it worth their while to run the risk of Lingard's enmity for the doubtful advantage of trade with a com- paratively unknown settlement. The great majority were undesirable or untrustworthy. And Babalatchi mentioned regretfully the men he had known in his young days : wealthy, resolute, courageous, reckless, ready for any enterprise !

But why lament the past and speak about the dead ? There is one man—living—great—not far off. . . .

Such was Babalatchi's line of policy laid before his ambitious protector. Lakamba assented, his only objection being that it was very slow work. In his extreme desire to grasp dollars and power, the unintellectual exile was ready to throw himself into the arms of any wandering cut-throat whose help could be secured, and Babalatchi experienced great difficulty in restraining him from unconsidered violence. It would not do to let it be seen that they had any hand in introducing a new element into the social and political life of Sambir. There was always a possibility of failure, and in that case Lingard's vengeance would be swift and certain. No risk should be run. They must wait.

Meantime he pervaded the settlement, squatting in the course of each day by many household fires, testing the public temper and public opinion—and always talking about his impending departure. At night he would often take Lakamba's smallest canoe and depart silently to pay mysterious visits to his old chief on the other side of the river. Omar lived in the odour of sanctity under the wing of Patalolo. Between the bamboo fence, enclosing the houses of the Rajah, and the wild forest, there was a banana plantation, and on its further edge stood two little houses built on low piles under a few precious fruit trees that grew on the banks of a clear brook, which, bubbling up behind the house, ran in its short and rapid course down to the big river. Along the brook a narrow path led through the dense second growth of a neglected clearing to the banana plantation and to the houses in it which the Rajah had given for residence to Omar. The Rajah was greatly impressed by Omar's ostentatious piety, by his oracular wisdom, by his many misfortunes, by the solemn fortitude with which he bore his affliction. Often the old ruler of Sambir would visit informally the blind Arab and listen gravely to his talk during the hot hours of an afternoon. In the night, Babalatchi would call and interrupt Omar's repose, unrebuked. Aïssa, standing silently at the door of one of the huts, could see the two old friends

as they sat very still by the fire in the middle of the beaten
ground between the two houses, talking in an indistinct
murmur far into the night. She could not hear their words,
but she watched the two formless shadows curiously. Finally
Babalatchi would rise and, taking her father by the wrist,
would lead him back to the house, arrange his mats for him,
and go out quietly. Instead of going away, Babalatchi,
unconscious of Aïssa's eyes, often sat again by the fire, in a
long and deep meditation. Aïssa looked with respect on
that wise and brave man—she was accustomed to see at her
father's side as long as she could remember—sitting alone and
thoughtful in the silent night by the dying fire, his body
motionless and his mind wandering in the land of memories,
or—who knows?—perhaps groping for a road in the waste
spaces of the uncertain future.

Babalatchi noted the arrival of Willems with alarm at this
new accession to the white men's strength. Afterwards he
changed his opinion. He met Willems one night on the
path leading to Omar's house, and noticed later on, with only
a moderate surprise, that the blind Arab did not seem to be
aware of the new white man's visits to the neighbourhood
of his dwelling. Once, coming unexpectedly in the daytime,
Babalatchi fancied he could see the gleam of a white jacket in
the bushes on the other side of the brook. That day he
watched Aïssa pensively as she moved about preparing the
evening rice ; but after awhile he went hurriedly away before
sunset, refusing Omar's hospitable invitation, in the name of
Allah, to share their meal. That same evening he startled
Lakamba by announcing that the time had come at last to
make the first move in their long-deferred game. Lakamba
asked excitedly for explanation. Babalatchi shook his head
and pointed to the flitting shadows of moving women and
to the vague forms of men sitting by the evening fires in the
courtyard. Not a word would he speak here, he declared.
But when the whole household was reposing, Babalatchi and
Lakamba passed silently amongst sleeping groups to the
riverside, and, taking a canoe, paddled off stealthily on their
way to the dilapidated guard-hut in the old rice-clearing.

There they were safe from all eyes and ears, and could account, if need be, for their excursion by the wish to kill a deer, the spot being well known as the drinking-place of all kinds of game. In the seclusion of its quiet solitude Babalatchi explained his plan to the attentive Lakamba. His idea was to make use of Willems for the destruction of Lingard's influence.

" I know the white men, Tuan," he said, in conclusion. " In many lands have I seen them; always the slaves of their desires, always ready to give up their strength and their reason into the hands of some woman. The fate of the Believers is written by the hand of the Mighty One, but they who worship many gods are thrown into the world with smooth foreheads, for any woman's hand to mark their destruction there. Let one white man destroy another. The will of the Most High is that they should be fools. They know how to keep faith with their enemies, but towards each other they know only deception. Haï! I have seen! I have seen ! "

He stretched himself full length before the fire, and closed his eye in real or simulated sleep. Lakamba, not quite convinced, sat for a long time with his gaze riveted on the dull embers. As the night advanced, a slight white mist rose from the river, and the declining moon, bowed over the tops of the forest, seemed to seek the repose of the earth, like a wayward and wandering lover who returns at last to lay his tired and silent head on his beloved's breast.

## VI

" LEND me your gun, Almayer," said Willems, across the table on which a smoky lamp shone redly above the disorder of a finished meal. " I have a mind to go and look for a deer when the moon rises to-night."

Almayer, sitting sidewise to the table, his elbow pushed amongst the dirty plates, his chin on his breast and his legs stretched stiffly out, kept his eyes steadily on the toes of his grass slippers and laughed abruptly.

"You might say yes or no instead of making that unpleasant noise," remarked Willems, with calm irritation.

"If I believed one word of what you say, I would," answered Almayer without changing his attitude and speaking slowly, with pauses, as if dropping his words on the floor. "As it is—what's the use? You know where the gun is; you may take it or leave it. Gun. Deer. Bosh! Hunt deer! Pah! It's a . . . gazelle you are after, my honoured guest. You want gold anklets and silk sarongs for that game —my mighty hunter. And you won't get those for the asking, I promise you. All day amongst the natives. A fine help you are to me."

"You shouldn't drink so much, Almayer," said Willems, disguising his fury under an affected drawl. "You have no head. Never had, as far as I can remember, in the old days in Macassar. You drink too much."

"I drink my own," retorted Almayer, lifting his head quickly and darting an angry glance at Willems.

Those two specimens of the superior race glared at each other savagely for a minute, then turned away their heads at the same moment as if by previous arrangement, and both got up. Almayer kicked off his slippers and scrambled into his hammock, which hung between two wooden columns of the verandah so as to catch every rare breeze of the dry season, and Willems, after standing irresolutely by the table for a short time, walked without a word down the steps of the house and over the courtyard towards the little wooden jetty, where several small canoes and a couple of big white whale-boats were made fast, tugging at their short painters and bumping together in the swift current of the river. He jumped into the smallest canoe, balancing himself clumsily, slipped the rattan painter, and gave an unnecessary and violent shove, which nearly sent him headlong overboard. By the time he regained his balance the canoe had drifted some fifty yards down the river. He knelt in the bottom of his little craft and fought the current with long sweeps of the

H 2

paddle. Almayer sat up in his hammock, grasping his feet and peering over the river with parted lips till he made out the shadowy form of man and canoe as they struggled past the jetty again.

"I thought you would go," he shouted. "Won't you take the gun? Hey?" he yelled, straining his voice. Then he fell back in his hammock and laughed to himself feebly till he fell asleep. On the river, Willems, his eyes fixed intently ahead, swept his paddle right and left, unheeding the words that reached him faintly.

It was now three months since Lingard had landed Willems in Sambir and had departed hurriedly, leaving him in Almayer's care. The two white men did not get on well together. Almayer, remembering the time when they both served Hudig, and when the superior Willems treated him with offensive condescension, felt a great dislike towards his guest. He was also jealous of Lingard's favour. Almayer had married a Malay girl whom the old seaman had adopted in one of his accesses of unreasoning benevolence, and as the marriage was not a happy one from a domestic point of view, he looked to Lingard's fortune for compensation in his matrimonial unhappiness. The appearance of that man, who seemed to have a claim of some sort upon Lingard, filled him with considerable uneasiness, the more so because the old seaman did not choose to acquaint the husband of his adopted daughter with Willems' history, or to confide to him his intentions as to that individual's future fate. Suspicious from the first, Almayer discouraged Willems' attempts to help him in his trading, and then when Willems drew back, he made, with characteristic perverseness, a grievance of his unconcern. From cold civility in their relations, the two men drifted into silent hostility, then into outspoken enmity, and both wished ardently for Lingard's return and the end of a situation that grew more intolerable from day to day. The time dragged slowly. Willems watched the succeeding sunrises wondering dismally whether before the evening some change would occur in the deadly dulness of his life. He missed the commercial activity of that existence which seemed to him far off, irreparably lost, buried out of sight under the ruins of his past success—now gone from him beyond the possibility of redemption. He mooned disconsolately about Almayer's courtyard, watching from afar, with uninterested eyes, the upcountry canoes discharging guttah or rattans, and loading rice or European goods on the little wharf of Lingard & Co. Big as was the extent of ground owned by Almayer, Willems felt that there was not enough room for him inside those neat fences. The man who, during long years, became accustomed to think of himself as indispensable to others felt a bitter and savage rage at the cruel consciousness of his superfluity, of his uselessness; at the cold hostility visible in every look of the only white man in this barbarous corner of the world. He gnashed his teeth when he thought of the wasted days, of the life thrown away in the unwilling company of that peevish and suspicious fool. He heard the reproach of his idleness in the murmurs of the river, in the unceasing whisper of the great forests. Round him everything stirred, moved, swept by in a rush; the earth under his feet and the heavens above his head. The very savages around him strove, struggled, fought, worked—if only to prolong a miserable existence; but they lived, they lived! And it was only himself that seemed to be left outside the scheme of creation in a hopeless immobility filled with tormenting anger and with everstinging regret.

He took to wandering about the settlement. The afterwards flourishing Sambir was born in a swamp and passed its youth in malodorous mud. The houses crowded the bank, and, as if to get away from the unhealthy shore, stepped boldly into the river, shooting over it in a close row of bamboo platforms elevated on high piles, amongst which the current below spoke in a soft and unceasing plaint of murmuring eddies. There was only one path in the whole town and it ran at the back of the houses along the succession of blackened circular patches that marked the place of the household fires. On the other side the virgin forest bordered the path, coming close to it, as if to provoke impudently any passer-by to the solution of the gloomy problem of its depths. Nobody would accept the deceptive challenge. There were only a few feeble attempts at a clearing here and there, but the ground was low and the river, retiring after its yearly floods, left on each a gradually diminishing mud-hole, where the imported buffaloes of the Bugis settlers wallowed happily during the heat of the day. When Willems walked on the path, the indolent men stretched on the shady side of the houses looked at him with calm curiosity, the women busy round the cooking fires would send after him wondering and timid glances, while the children would only look once, and then run away yelling with fright at the horrible appearance of the man with a red and white face. These manifestations of childish disgust and fear stung Willems with a sense of absurd humiliation; he sought in his walks the comparative solitude of the rudimentary clearings, but the very buffaloes snorted with alarm at his sight, scrambled lumberingly out of the cool mud and stared wildly in a compact herd at him as he tried to slink unperceived along the edge of the forest. One day, at some unguarded and sudden movement of his, the whole herd stampeded down the path, scattered the fires, sent the women flying with shrill cries, and left behind a track of smashed pots, trampled rice, overturned children, and a crowd of angry men brandishing sticks in loud-voiced pursuit. The innocent cause of that disturbance ran shame-facedly the gauntlet of black looks and unfriendly remarks, and hastily sought refuge in Almayer's campong. After that he left the settlement alone.

Later on, when the enforced confinement grew irksome, Willems took one of Almayer's many canoes and crossed the main branch of the Pantai in search of some solitary spot where he could hide his discouragement and his weariness. He skirted in his little craft the wall of tangled verdure, keeping in the dead water close to the bank where the spreading nipa palms nodded their broad leaves over his head as if in contemptuous pity of the wandering outcast. Here and there he could see the beginnings of chopped-out path-ways, and, with the fixed idea of getting out of sight of the busy river, he would land and follow the narrow and winding path, only to find that it led nowhere, ending abruptly in the discouragement of thorny thickets. He would go back slowly, with a bitter sense of unreasonable disappointment and sadness; oppressed by the hot smell of earth, dampness, and decay in that forest which seemed to push him mercilessly back into the glittering sunshine of the river. And he would recommence paddling with tired arms to seek another opening, to find another deception.

As he paddled up to the point where the Rajah's stockade came down to the river, the nipas were left behind rattling their leaves over the brown water, and the big trees would appear on the bank, tall, strong, indifferent in the immense solidity of their life, which endures for ages, to that short and fleeting life in the heart of the man who crept painfully amongst their shadows in search of a refuge from the unceasing reproach of his thoughts. Amongst their smooth trunks a clear brook meandered for a time in twining lacets before it made up its mind to take a leap into the hurrying river, over the edge of the steep bank. There was also a pathway there and it seemed frequented. Willems landed, and following the capricious promise of the track soon found himself in a comparatively clear space, where the confused tracery of sunlight fell through the branches and the foliage overhead, and lay on the stream that shone in an easy curve like a bright swordblade dropped amongst the long and feathery grass. Further on, the path continued narrowed again in the thick undergrowth. At the end of the first turning Willems saw a flash of white and colour, a gleam of gold like a sun-ray lost in shadow, and a vision of blackness darker than the deepest shade of the forest. He stopped, surprised, and fancied he had heard light footsteps—growing lighter—ceasing. He looked around. The grass on the bank of the stream trembled and a tremulous path of its shivering, silver-grey tops ran from the water to the beginning of the thicket. And yet there was not a breath of wind. Somebody had passed there. He looked pensive while the tremor died out in a quick tremble under his eyes; and the grass stood high, unstirring, with drooping heads in the warm and motionless air.

He hurried on, driven by a suddenly awakened curiosity, and entered the narrow way between the bushes. At the next turn of the path he caught again the glimpse of coloured stuff and of a woman's black hair before him. He hastened his pace and came in full view of the object of his pursuit. The woman, who was carrying two bamboo vessels full of water, heard his footsteps, stopped, and putting the bamboos down half turned to look back. Willems also stood still for a minute, then walked steadily on with a firm tread, while the woman moved aside to let him pass. He kept his eyes fixed straight before him, yet almost unconsciously he took in every detail of the tall and graceful figure. As he approached her the woman tossed her head slightly back, and with a free gesture of her strong, round arm, caught up the mass of loose black hair and brought it over her shoulder and across the lower part of her face. The next moment he was passing her close, walking rigidly, like a man in a trance. He heard her rapid breathing and he felt the touch of a look darted at him from half-open eyes. It touched his brain and his heart together. It seemed to him to be something loud and stirring like a shout, silent and penetrating like an inspiration. The momentum of his motion carried him past her, but an invisible force made up of surprise and curiosity and desire spun him round as soon as he had passed.

She had taken up her burden already, with the intention of pursuing her path. His sudden movement arrested her at the first step, and again she stood straight, slim, expectant, with a readiness to dart away suggested in the light immobility of her pose. High above, the branches of the trees met in a transparent shimmer or waving green mist, through which the rain of yellow rays descended upon her head, streamed in glints down her black tresses, shone with the changing glow of liquid metal on her face, and lost itself in vanishing sparks in the sombre depths of her eyes that, wide open now, with enlarged pupils, looked steadily at the man in her path. And Willems stared at her, charmed with a charm that carries with it a sense of irreparable loss, tingling with that feeling which begins like a caress and ends in a blow, in that sudden hurt of a new emotion making its way into a human heart, with the brusque stirring of sleeping sensations awakening suddenly to the rush of new hopes, new fears, new desires—and to the flight of one's old self.

She moved a step forward and again halted. A breath of wind that came through the trees, but in Willems' fancy seemed to be driven by her moving figure, rippled in a hot wave round his body and scorched his face in a burning touch. He drew it in with a long breath, the last long breath of a soldier before the rush of battle, of a lover before he takes in his arms the adored woman; the breath that gives courage to confront the menace of death of the storm of passion.

Who was she? Where did she come from? Wonderingly he took his eyes off her face to look round at the serried trees of the forest that stood big and still and straight, as if watching him and her breathlessly. He had been baffled, repelled, almost frightened by the intensity of that tropical life which wants the sunshine but works in gloom; which seems to be all grace of colour and form, all brilliance, all smiles, but is only the blossoming of the dead; whose mystery holds the promise of joy and beauty, yet contains nothing but poison and decay. He had been frightened by the vague perception of danger before, but now, as he looked at that life again, his eyes seemed able to pierce the fantastic veil of creepers and leaves, to look past the solid trunks, to see through the forbidding gloom—and the mystery was disclosed—enchanting, subduing, beautiful. He looked at the woman. Through the checkered light between them she appeared to him with the impalpable distinctness of a dream. She seemed to him at once enticing and brilliant—sombre and repelling: the very spirit of that land of mysterious forests, standing before him, with the vague beauty of wavering outline; like an apparition behind a transparent veil—a veil woven of sunbeams and shadows.

She had approached him still nearer. He felt a strange impatience within him at her advance. Confused thoughts rushed through his head, disordered, shapeless, stunning. Then he heard his own voice asking—

" Who are you ? "

" I am the daughter of the blind Omar," she answered, in a low but steady tone. " And you," she went on, a little louder, " you are the white trader—the great man of this place."

" Yes," said Willems, holding her eyes with his in a sense of extreme effort, " Yes, I am white." Then he added, feeling as if he spoke about some other man, " But I am the outcast of my people."

She listened to him gravely. Through the mesh of scattered hair her face looked like the face of a golden statue with living eyes. The heavy eyelids dropped slightly, and from between the long eyelashes she sent out a sidelong look : hard, keen, and narrow, like the gleam of sharp steel. Her lips were firm and composed in a graceful curve, but the distended nostrils, the upward poise of the half-averted head, gave to her whole person the expression of a wild and resentful defiance.

A shadow passed over Willems' face. He put his hand over his lips as if to keep back the words that wanted to come out in a surge of impulsive necessity, the outcome of dominant thought that rushes from the heart to the brain and must be spoken in the face of doubt, of danger, of fear of destruction itself.

" You are beautiful," he whispered.

She looked at him again with a glance that, running in one quick flash of her eyes over his sunburnt features, his broad shoulders, his straight, tall, motionless figure, rested at last on the ground at his feet. Then she smiled. In the sombre beauty of her face that smile was like a gleam of dawn on a stormy morning ; like the first ray of eastern light that darts evanescent and pale through the gloomy clouds : the forerunner of sunrise and of thunder.

## VII

THERE are in our lives short periods which hold no place in memory but only as the recollection of a feeling. There is no remembrance of gesture, of action, of any outward manifestation of life; those are lost in the unearthly brilliance or in the unearthly gloom of such moments. We are absorbed in the contemplation of that something, within our bodies, which rejoices or suffers while the body goes on breathing, instinctively runs away or, not less instinctively, fights—perhaps dies. But death in such a moment is the privilege of the fortunate, it is a high and rare favour, a supreme grace.

Willems never remembered how and when he parted from Aïssa. He caught himself drinking the muddy water out of the hollow of his hand, while his canoe was drifting in mid-stream past the last houses of Sambir. With his returning wits came the fear of something unknown that had taken possession of his heart, of something inarticulate and masterful which could not speak and would be obeyed. His first impulse was that of revolt. He would never go back there. Never! He looked round slowly at the brilliance of things in the deadly sunshine and took up his paddle! How changed everything seemed! The river was broader, the sky was higher. How fast the canoe flew under the strokes of his paddle! Since when had he acquired the strength of two men or more? He looked up and down the reach at the forests of the bank with a confused notion that with one sweep of his hand he could tumble all these trees into the stream. His face felt burning. He drank again, and shuddered with a depraved sense of pleasure at the after-time of slime in the water.

It was late when he reached Almayer's house, but he crossed the dark and uneven courtyard without stumbling, unhesitatingly, walking lightly in the radiance of some light of his own that was invisible to other eyes. His host's sulky

greeting jarred him like a sudden fall down a great height.
He took his place at the table opposite Almayer and tried to
speak cheerfully to his gloomy companion, but when the
meal was ended and they sat smoking in silence he felt an
abrupt discouragement, a lassitude in all his limbs, a sense of
immense sadness as after some great and irreparable loss.
The light died out and the darkness of the night entered his
heart, bringing with it doubt and hesitation and dull anger
with himself and all the world. He had an impulse to shout
horrible curses, to quarrel with Almayer, to do something
violent. Quite without any immediate provocation he
thought he would like to assault the wretched, sulky beast.
He glanced at him ferociously from under his eyebrows. The
unconscious Almayer smoked thoughtfully, planning to-
morrow's work probably. The man's composure seemed to
Willems an unpardonable insult. Why didn't that idiot
talk to-night when he wanted him to ? . . . on other nights
he was ready enough to chatter. And such dull nonsense
too ! And Willems, trying hard to repress his own senseless
rage, looked fixedly through the thick tobacco-smoke at the
stained tablecloth.

They retired early, as usual, but in the middle of the night
Willems leaped out of his hammock with a stifled execration
and ran down the steps into the courtyard. The two night
watchmen, who sat by a little fire talking together in a
monotonous undertone, lifted their heads to look wonderingly at the discomposed features of the white man as he
crossed the circle of light thrown out by the fire. He disappeared in the darkness and then came back again, passing
them close, but with no sign of consciousness of their presence
on his face. Backwards and forwards he paced, muttering
to himself, and the two Malays, after a short consultation in
whispers, left the fire quietly, not thinking it safe to remain
in the vicinity of a white man who behaved in such a strange
manner. They retired round the corner of the godown and
watched Willems curiously through the night, till the short
daybreak was followed by the sudden blaze of the rising sun,
and Almayer's establishment woke up to life and work.

As soon as he could get away unnoticed in the bustle of the busy riverside, Willems crossed the river on his way to the place where he had met Aïssa. He threw himself down in the grass by the side of the brook and listened for the sound of her footsteps. The brilliant light of day fell through the irregular opening in the high branches of the trees and streamed down, softened, amongst the shadows of big trunks. Here and there a narrow sunbeam touched the rugged bark of a tree with a golden splash, sparkled on the leaping water of the brook, or rested on a leaf that stood out, shimmering and distinct, on the monotonous background of sombre green tints. The clear gap of blue above his head was crossed by the quick flight of white rice-birds whose wings flashed in the sunlight, while through it the heat poured down from the sky, clung about the steaming earth, rolled among the trees, and wrapped up Willems in the soft and odorous folds of air heavy with the faint scent of blossoms and with the acrid smell of decaying life. And in that atmosphere of Nature's workshop Willems felt soothed and lulled into forgetfulness of his past, into indifference as to his future. The recollections of his triumphs, of his wrongs and of his ambition vanished in that warmth, which seemed to melt all regrets, all hope, all anger, all strength out of his heart. And he lay there, dreamily contented, in the tepid and perfumed shelter, thinking of Aïssa's eyes; recalling the sound of her voice, the quiver of her lips—her frowns and her smile.

She came, of course. To her he was something new, unknown and strange. He was bigger, stronger than any man she had seen before, and altogether different from all those she knew. He was of the victorious race. With a vivid remembrance of the great catastrophe of her life he appeared to her with all the fascination of a great and dangerous thing; of a terror vanquished, surmounted, made a plaything of. They spoke with just such a deep voice—those victorious men; they looked with just such hard blue eyes at their enemies. And she made that voice speak softly to her, those eyes look tenderly at her face! He was indeed a man. She could not understand all he told her of his life, but the fragments she understood she made up for herself into a story of a man great amongst his own people, valorous and unfortunate; an undaunted fugitive dreaming of vengeance against his enemies. He had all the attractiveness of the vague and other unknown—of the unforeseen and of the sudden; of a being strong, dangerous, alive, and human, ready to be enslaved.

She felt that he was ready. She felt it with the unerring intuition of a primitive woman confronted by a simple impulse. Day after day, when they met and she stood a little way off, listening to his words, holding him with her look, the undefined terror of the new conquest became faint and blurred like the memory of a dream, and the certitude grew distinct, and convincing, and visible to the eyes like some material thing in full sunlight. It was a deep joy, a great pride, a tangible sweetness that seemed to leave the taste of honey on her lips. He lay stretched at her feet without moving, for he knew from experience how a slight movement of his could frighten her away in those first days of their intercourse. He lay very quiet, with all the ardour of his desire ringing in his voice and shining in his eyes, whilst his body was still, like death itself. And he looked at her, standing above him, her head lost in the shadow of broad and graceful leaves that touched her cheek; while the slender spikes of pale green orchids streamed down from amongst the boughs and mingled with the black hair that framed her face, as if all those plants claimed her for their own—the animated and brilliant flower of all that exuberant life which, born in gloom, struggles for ever towards the sunshine.

Every day she came a little nearer. He watched her slow progress—the gradual taming of that woman by the words of his love. It was the monotonous song of praise and desire that, commencing at creation, wraps up the world like an atmosphere and shall end only in the end of all things— when there are no lips to sing and no ears to hear. He told her that she was beautiful and desirable, and he repeated it again and again; for when he told her that, he had said all there was within him—he had expressed his only thought, his only feeling. And he watched the startled look of wonder and mistrust vanish from her face with the passing days, her eyes soften, the smile dwell longer and longer on her lips; a smile as of one charmed by a delightful dream, with the slight exaltation of intoxicating triumph lurking in its dawning tenderness.

And while she was near there was nothing in the whole world—for that idle man—but her look and her smile. Nothing in the past, nothing in the future; and in the present only the luminous fact of her existence. But in the sudden darkness of her going he would be left weak and helpless, as though despoiled violently of all that was himself. He who had lived all his life with no preoccupation but that of his own career, contemptuously indifferent to all feminine influence, full of scorn for men that would submit to it, if ever so little; he, so strong, so superior even in his errors, realised at last that his very individuality was snatched from within himself by the hand of a woman. Where were the assurance and pride of his cleverness; the belief in success, the anger of failure, the wish to retrieve his fortune, the certitude of his ability to accomplish it yet? Gone. All gone. All that had been a man within him was gone, and there remained only the trouble of his heart—that heart which had become a contemptible thing; which could be fluttered by a look or a smile, tormented by a word, soothed by a promise.

When the longed-for day came at last, when she sank on the grass by his side and with a quick gesture took his hand in hers, he sat up suddenly with the movement and look of a man awakened by the crash of his own falling house. All his blood, all his sensation, all his life seemed to rush into that hand, leaving him without strength, in a cold shiver, in the sudden clamminess and collapse as of a deadly gun-shot wound. He flung her hand away brutally, like something burning, and sat motionless, his head fallen forward, staring on the ground and catching his breath in painful gasps. His impulse of fear and apparent horror did not dismay her in the least. Her face was grave and her eyes looked seriously at him. Her fingers touched the hair of his temple, ran in a light caress down his cheek, twisted gently the end of his long moustache; and while he sat in the tremor of that contact she ran off with startling fleetness and disappeared in a peal of clear laughter, in the stir of grass, in the nod of young twigs growing over the path; leaving behind only a vanishing trail of motion and sound.

He scrambled to his feet slowly and painfully, like a man with a burden on his shoulders, and walked towards the riverside. He hugged to his breast the recollection of his fear and of his delight, but told himself seriously over and over again that this must be the end of that adventure. After shoving off his canoe into the stream he lifted his eyes to the bank and gazed at it long and steadily, as if taking his last look at a place of charming memories. He marched up to Almayer's house with the concentrated expression and the determined step of a man who had just taken a momentous resolution. His face was set and rigid, his gestures and movements were guarded and slow. He was keeping a tight hand on himself. A very tight hand. He had a vivid illusion—as vivid as reality almost—of being in charge of a slippery prisoner. He sat opposite Almayer during that dinner—which was their last meal together—with a perfectly calm face and within him a growing terror of escape from his own self. Now and then he would grasp the edge of the table and set his teeth hard in a sudden wave of acute despair, like one who, falling down a smooth and rapid declivity that ends in a precipice, digs his finger-nails into the yielding surface and feels himself slipping helplessly to inevitable destruction.

Then, abruptly, came a relaxation of his muscles, the giving way of his will. Something seemed to snap in his head, and that wish, that idea kept back during all those hours, darted into his brain with the heat and noise of a conflagration. He must see her! See her at once! Go now! To-night! He had the raging regret of the lost hour, of every passing moment. There was no thought of resistance now. Yet with the instinctive fear of the irrevocable, with the innate

falseness of the human heart, he wanted to keep open the
way of retreat. He had never absented himself during the
night. What did Almayer know? What would Almayer
think? Better ask him for the gun. A moonlight night.
. . . Look for deer. . . . A colourable pretext. He would
lie to Almayer. What did it matter! He lied to himself
every minute of his life. And for what? For a woman.
And such. . . .

Almayer's answer showed him that deception was useless.
Everything gets to be known, even in this place. Well, he
did not care. Cared for nothing but for the lost seconds.
What if he should suddenly die. Die before her saw her.
Before he could . . .

As, with the sound of Almayer's laughter in his ears, he
urged his canoe in a slanting course across the rapid current,
he tried to tell himself that he could return at any moment.
He would just go and look at the place where they used to
meet, at the tree under which he lay when she took his hand,
at the spot where she sat by his side. Just go there and then
return—nothing more; but when his little skiff touched the
bank he leaped out, forgetting the painter, and the canoe
hung for a moment amongst the bushes and then swung out
of sight before he had time to dash into the water and secure
it. He was thunderstruck at first. Now he could not go
back unless he called up the Rajah's people to get a boat and
rowers—and the way to Patalolo's campong led past Aïssa's
house!

He went up the path with the eager eyes and reluctant
steps of a man pursuing a phantom, and when he found
himself at a place where a narrow track branched off to the
left towards Omar's clearing he stood still, with a look of
strained attention on his face as if listening to a far-off voice—
the voice of his fate. It was a sound inarticulate but full of
meaning; and following it there came a rending and tearing
within his breast. He twisted his fingers together, and the
joints of his hands and arms cracked. On his forehead the
perspiration stood out in small pearly drops. He looked
round wildly. Above the shapeless darkness of the forest

undergrowth rose the tree-tops with their high boughs and leaves standing out black on the pale sky—like fragments of night floating on moonbeams. Under his feet warm steam rose from the heated earth. Round him there was a great silence.

He was looking round for help. This silence, this immobility of his surroundings seemed to him a cold rebuke, a stern refusal, a cruel unconcern. There was no safety outside of himself—and in himself there was no refuge; there was only the image of that woman. He had a sudden moment of lucidity—of that cruel lucidity that comes once in life to the most benighted. A strange disclosure of weakness, of want of logic, of the usual blindness of our impulses. He seemed to see what went on within him, and was horrified at the strange sight. He, a white man! A man of practical ambitions, whose worst fault till then had been a little want of judgment and too much confidence in the rectitude of his kind. That woman was a pretty savage, and . . . He tried to tell himself that the thing was of no consequence. No consequence. It was a vain effort. Hudig's partner was gone already, and now the feeling that the clever Willems was going too forced itself upon him mercilessly. The novelty of the sensations he had never experienced before in the slightest degree, yet had despised on hearsay from his safe position of a civilised man, destroyed his courage. He was disappointed with himself. He seemed to be surrendering to a wild creature the unstained purity of his life, of his race, of his civilisation. He did not tell himself all this, but he had a notion of being lost amongst shapeless things that were dangerous and ghastly. He struggled with the sense of certain defeat—lost his footing—fell back into the darkness. With a faint cry and an upward throw of his arms he gave up as a tired swimmer gives up : because the swamped craft is gone from under his feet ; because the night is dark and the shore is far ;—because death is better than strife.

# PART II

## I

THE light and heat fell upon the settlement, the clearings, and the river as if flung down by an angry hand. The land lay silent, still, and brilliant under the avalanche of burning rays that had destroyed all sound and all motion, had buried all shadows, had choked every breath. No living thing dared to affront the serenity of this cloudless sky, dared to revolt against the oppression of this glorious and cruel sunshine. Strength and resolution, body and mind alike were helpless, and tried to hide before the rush of the fire from heaven. Only the frail butterflies, the fearless children of the sun, the capricious tyrants of the flowers, fluttered audaciously in the open, and their minute shadows hovered in swarms over the drooping blossoms, ran lightly on the withering grass, or glided on the dry and cracked earth. No voice was heard in this hot noontide but the faint murmur of the river that hurried on in swirls and eddies, its sparkling wavelets chasing each other in their joyous course to the sheltering depths, to the cool refuge of the sea.

Almayer had dismissed his workmen for the midday rest, and, his little daughter on his shoulder, ran quickly across the courtyard, making for the shade of the verandah of his house. He laid the sleepy child on the seat of the big rocking-chair, on a pillow which he took out of his own hammock, and stood for a while looking down at her with tender and pensive eyes. The child, tired and hot, moved uneasily, sighed, and looked up at him with the veiled look of sleepy fatigue. He picked up from the floor a broken palm-leaf fan, and began fanning gently the flushed little face. Her eyelids fluttered and Almayer smiled. A responsive smile brightened for a second her heavy eyes, broke with a dimple the soft outline of her cheek; then the eyelids dropped suddenly, she drew a long breath through the parted lips—and was in a deep sleep before the fleeting smile could vanish from her face.

Almayer moved lightly off, took one of the wooden arm-chairs, and placing it close to the balustrade of the verandah sat down with a sigh of relief. He spread his elbows on the top rail and resting his chin on his clasped hands looked absently at the river, at the dance of sunlight on the flowing water. Gradually the forest of the further bank became smaller, as if sinking below the level of the river. The outlines wavered, grew thin, dissolved in the air. Before his eyes there was now only a space of undulating blue—one big, empty sky growing dark at times. . . . Where was the sunshine? . . . He felt soothed and happy, as if some gentle and invisible hand had removed from his soul the burden of his body. In another second he seemed to float out into a cool brightness where there was no such thing as memory or pain. Delicious. His eyes closed—opened—closed again.

" Almayer ! "

With a sudden jerk of his whole body he sat up, grasping the front rail with both his hands, and blinked stupidly.

" What? What's that? " he muttered, looking round vaguely.

" Here ! Down here, Almayer."

Half rising in his chair, Almayer looked over the rail at the foot of the verandah, and fell back with a low whistle of astonishment.

" A ghost, by heavens ! " he exclaimed softly to himself.

" Will you listen to me ? " went on the husky voice from the courtyard. " May I come up, Almayer ? "

Almayer stood up and leaned over the rail.

" Don't you dare," he said, in a voice subdued but distinct. " Don't you dare ! The child sleeps here. And I don't want to hear you—or speak to you either."

" You must listen to me ! It's something important."

" Not to me, surely."

" Yes ! To you. Very important."

" You were always a humbug," said Almayer, after a short silence, in an indulgent tone. " Always ! I remember the old days. Some fellows used to say there was no one like you for smartness—but you never took me in. Not quite. I never quite believed in you, Mr. Willems."

" I admit your superior intelligence," retorted Willems, with scornful impatience, from below. " Listening to me would be a further proof of it. You will be sorry if you don't."

" Oh, you funny fellow ! " said Almayer, banteringly. " Well, come up. Don't make a noise, but come up. You'll catch a sunstroke down there and die on my doorstep perhaps. I don't want any tragedy here. Come on ! "

Before he finished speaking Willems' head appeared above the level of the floor, then his shoulders rose gradually and he stood at last before Almayer—a masquerading spectre of the once so very confidential clerk of the richest merchant in the islands. His jacket was soiled and torn ; below the waist he was clothed in a worn-out and faded sarong. He flung off his hat, uncovering his long, tangled hair that stuck in wisps on his perspiring forehead and straggled over his eyes, which glittered deep down in the sockets like the last sparks amongst the black embers of a burnt-out fire. An unclean beard grew out of the caverns of his sunburnt cheeks. The hand he put out towards Almayer was very unsteady. The once firm mouth had the tell-tale droop of mental suffering and physical exhaustion. He was bare-footed. Almayer surveyed him with leisurely composure.

" Well ! " he said at last, without taking the extended hand which dropped slowly along Willems' body.

" I am come," began Willems.

" So I see," interrupted Almayer. " You might have spared me this treat without making me unhappy. You have been away five weeks, if I am not mistaken. I got on very well without you—and now you are here you are not pretty to look at."

"Let me speak, will you!" exclaimed Willems.

"Don't shout like this. Do you think yourself in the forest with your . . . your friends? This is a civilised man's house. A white man's. Understand?"

"I am come," began Willems again; "I am come for your good and mine."

"You look as if you had come for a good feed," chimed in the irrepressible Almayer, while Willems waved his hand in a discouraged gesture. "Don't they give you enough to eat," went on Almayer, in a tone of easy banter, "those —what am I to call them—those new relations of yours? That old blind scoundrel must be delighted with your company. You know, he was the greatest thief and murderer of those seas. Say! do you exchange confidences? Tell me, Willems, did you kill somebody in Macassar, or did you only steal something?"

"It is not true!" exclaimed Willems, hotly. "I only borrowed. . . . They all lied! I . . ."

"Sh-sh!" hissed Almayer, warningly, with a look at the sleeping child. "So you did steal," he went on, with repressed exultation. "I thought there was something of the kind. And now, here, you steal again."

For the first time Willems raised his eyes to Almayer's face.

"Oh, I don't mean from me. I haven't missed anything," said Almayer, with mocking haste. "But that girl. Hey! You stole her. You did not pay the old fellow. She is no good to him now, is she?"

"Stop that, Almayer!"

Something in Willems' tone caused Almayer to pause. He looked narrowly at the man before him, and could not help being shocked at his appearance.

"Almayer," went on Willems, "listen to me. If you are a human being you will. I suffer horribly—and for your sake."

Almayer lifted his eyebrows. "Indeed! How? But you are raving," he added, negligently.

"Ah! You don't know," whispered Willems. "She

is gone. Gone," he repeated, with tears in his voice, " gone two days ago."

" No ! " exclaimed the surprised Almayer. " Gone ! I haven't heard that news yet." He burst into a subdued laugh. " How funny. Had enough of you already ? You know it's not flattering for you, my superior countryman."

Willems—as if not hearing him—leaned against one of the columns of the roof and looked over the river. " At first," he whispered, dreamily, " my life was like a vision of heaven—or hell; I didn't know which. Since she went I know what perdition means ; what darkness is. I know what it is to be torn to pieces alive. That's how I feel."

" You may come and live with me again," said Almayer, coldly. " After all, Lingard—whom I call my father and respect as such—left you under my care. You pleased yourself by going away. Very good. Now you want to come back. Be it so. I am no friend of yours. I act for Captain Lingard."

" Come back," repeated Willems, passionately. " Come back to you and abandon her ? Do you think I am mad ? Without her ! Man ! what are you made of ? To think that she moves, lives, breathes out of my sight. I am jealous of the wind that fans her, of the air she breathes, of the earth that receives the caress of her foot, of the sun that looks at her now, while I . . . I haven't seen her for two days—two days."

The intensity of Willems' feeling moved Almayer somewhat, but he affected to yawn elaborately.

" You do bore me," he muttered. " Why don't you go after her instead of coming here ? "

" Why indeed ? "

" Don't you know where she is ? She can't be very far. No native craft has left this river for the last fortnight."

" No ! not very far—and I will tell you where she is. She is in Lakamba's campong." And Willems fixed his eyes steadily on Almayer's face.

" Phew ! Patalolo never sent to let me know. Strange,"

said Almayer, thoughtfully. "Are you afraid of that lot?" he added, after a short pause.

"I—afraid!"

"Then is it the care of your dignity which prevents you from following her there, my high-minded friend?" asked Almayer, with mock solicitude. "How noble of you!"

There was a short silence; then Willems said, quietly, "You are a fool. I should like to kick you."

"No fear," answered Almayer, carelessly; "you are too weak for that. You look starved."

"I don't think I have eaten anything for the last two days; perhaps more—I don't remember. It does not matter. I am full of live embers," said Willems, gloomily. "Look!" and he bared an arm covered with fresh scars. "I have been biting myself to forget in that pain the fire that hurts me there!" He struck his breast violently with his fist, reeled under his own blow, fell into a chair that stood near and closed his eyes slowly.

"Disgusting exhibition," said Almayer, loftily. "What could father ever see in you? You are as estimable as a heap of garbage."

"You talk like that! You, who sold your soul for a few guilders," muttered Willems, wearily, without opening his eyes.

"Not so few," said Almayer, with instinctive readiness, and stopped confused for a moment. He recovered himself quickly, however, and went on: "But you—you have thrown yours away for nothing; flung it under the feet of a damned savage woman who has made you already the thing you are, and will kill you very soon, one way or another, with her love or with her hate. You spoke just now about guilders. You meant Lingard's money, I suppose. Well, whatever I have sold, and for whatever price, I never meant you—you of all people—to spoil my bargain. I feel pretty safe, though. Even father, even Captain Lingard, would not touch you now with a pair of tongs; not with a ten-foot pole." . . .

He spoke excitedly, all in one breath, and, ceasing suddenly, glared at Willems and breathed hard through his nose in an access of sulky resentment. Willems looked at him steadily for a moment, then got up.

"Almayer," he said resolutely, "I want to become a trader in this place."

Almayer shrugged his shoulders.

"Yes. And you shall set me up. I want a house and trade goods—perhaps a little money. I ask you for it."

"Anything else you want? Perhaps this coat?" and here Almayer unbuttoned his jacket—"or my house—or my boots?"

"After all it's natural," went on Willems, without paying any attention to Almayer—"it's natural that she should expect the advantages which . . . and then I could shut up that old wretch and then . . ."

He paused, his face brightened with the soft light of dreamy enthusiasm, and he turned his eyes upwards. With his gaunt figure and dilapidated appearance he looked like some ascetic dweller in a wilderness, finding the reward of a self-denying life in a vision of dazzling glory. He went on in an impassioned murmur—

"And then I would have her all to myself away from her people—all to myself—under my own influence—to fashion —to mould—to adore—to soften—to . . . Oh! Delight! And then—then go away to some distant place where, far from all she knew, I would be all the world to her! All the world to her!"

His face suddenly changed. His eyes wandered for awhile and then became steady all at once.

"I would repay every cent, of course," he said, in a business-like tone, with something of his old assurance, of his old belief in himself, in it. "Every cent. I need not interfere with your business. I shall cut out the small native traders. I have ideas—but never mind that now. And Captain Lingard would approve, I feel sure. After all it's a loan, and I shall be at hand. Safe thing for you."

"Ah! Captain Lingard would approve! He would app . . ." Almayer choked. The notion of Lingard doing something for Willems enraged him. His face was purple. He spluttered insulting words. Willems looked at him coolly.

"I assure you, Almayer," he said, gently, "that I have good grounds for my demand."

"Your cursed impudence!"

"Believe me, Almayer, your position here is not so safe as you may think. An unscrupulous rival here would destroy your trade in a year. It would be ruin. Now Lingard's long absence gives courage to certain individuals. You know?—I have heard much lately. They made proposals to me . . . You are very much alone here. Even Patalolo . . ."

"Damn Patalolo! I am master in this place."

"But Almayer, don't you see . . ."

"Yes, I see. I see a mysterious ass," interrupted Almayer, violently. "What is the meaning of your veiled threats? Don't you think I know something also? They have been intriguing for years—and nothing has happened. The Arabs have been hanging about outside this river for years—and I am still the only trader here; the master here. Do you bring me a declaration of war? Then it's from yourself only. I know all my other enemies. I ought to knock you on the head. You are not worth powder and shot, though. You ought to be destroyed with a stick—like a snake."

Almayer's voice woke up the little girl, who sat up on the pillow with a sharp cry. He rushed over to the chair, caught up the child in his arms, walked back blindly, stumbled against Willems' hat which lay on the floor, and kicked it furiously down the steps.

"Clear out of this! Clear out!" he shouted.

Willems made an attempt to speak, but Almayer howled him down.

"Get out! Get out! Get out! Don't you see you frighten the child—you scarecrow! No! no! dear," he went on to his little daughter, soothingly, while Willems walked down the steps slowly. "No. Don't cry. See!

Bad man going away. Look! He is afraid of your papa. Nasty, bad man. Never come back again. He shall live in the woods and never come near my little girl. If he comes papa will kill him—so!" He struck his fist on the rail of the balustrade to show how he would kill Willems, and, perching the consoled child on his shoulder held her with one hand, while he pointed towards the retreating figure of his visitor.

"Look how he runs away, dearest," he said, coaxingly. "Isn't he funny? Call 'pig' after him, dearest. Call after him."

The seriousness of her face vanished into dimples. Under the long eyelashes, glistening with recent tears, her big eyes sparkled and danced with fun. She took firm hold of Almayer's hair with one hand, while she waved the other joyously and called out with all her might, in a clear note, soft and distinct like the twitter of a bird :—

"Pig! Pig! Pig!"

## II

A SIGH under the flaming blue, a shiver of the sleeping sea, a cool breath as if a door had been swung upon the frozen spaces of the universe, and with a stir of leaves, with the nod of boughs, with the tremble of slender branches the sea breeze struck the coast, rushed up the river, swept round the broad reaches, and travelled on in a soft ripple of darkening water, in the whisper of branches, in the rustle of leaves of the awakened forests. It fanned in Lakamba's campong the dull red of expiring embers into a pale brilliance; and, under its touch, the slender, upright spirals of smoke that rose from every glowing heap swayed, wavered, and eddying down filled the twilight of clustered shade trees with the aromatic scent of the burning wood. The men who had been dozing in the shade during the hot hours of

I

the afternoon woke up, and the silence of the big courtyard was broken by the hesitating murmur of yet sleepy voices, by coughs and yawns, with now and then a burst of laughter, a loud hail, a name or a joke sent out in a soft drawl. Small groups squatted round the little fires, and the monotonous undertone of talk filled the enclosure; the talk of barbarians, persistent, steady, repeating itself in the soft syllables, in musical tones of the never-ending discourses of those men of the forests and the sea, who can talk most of the day and all the night; who never exhaust a subject, never seem able to thresh a matter out; to whom that talk is poetry and painting and music, all art, all history; their only accomplishment, their only superiority, their only amusement. The talk of camp fires, which speaks of bravery and cunning, of strange events and of far countries, of the news of yesterday and the news of to-morrow. They talk about the dead and the living—about those who fought and those who loved.

Lakamba came out on the platform before his own house and sat down—perspiring, half asleep, and sulky—in a wooden armchair under the shade of the overhanging eaves. Through the darkness of the doorway he could hear the soft warbling of his womenkind, busy round the looms where they were weaving the checkered pattern of his gala sarongs. Right and left of him on the flexible bamboo floor those of his followers to whom their distinguished birth, long devotion, or faithful service had given the privilege of using the chief's house, were sleeping on mats or just sat up rubbing their eyes: while the more wakeful had mustered enough energy to draw a chessboard with red clay on a fine mat and were now meditating silently over their moves. Above the prostrate forms of the players, who lay face downward supported on elbow, the soles of their feet waving irresolutely about, in the absorbed meditation of the game, there towered here and there the straight figure of an attentive spectator looking down with dispassionate but profound interest. On the edge of the platform a row of high-heeled leather sandals stood ranged carefully in a

level line, and against the rough wooden rail leaned the
slender shafts of the spears belonging to these gentlemen,
the broad blades of dulled steel looking very black in the
reddening light of approaching sunset.

A boy of about twelve—the personal attendant of Lakamba
—squatted at his master's feet and held up towards him a
silver siri box. Slowly Lakamba took the box, opened it,
and tearing off a piece of green leaf deposited in it a pinch
of lime, a morsel of gambier, a small bit of areca nut, and
wrapped up the whole with a dexterous twist. He paused,
morsel in hand, seemed to miss something, turned his head
from side to side, slowly, like a man with a stiff neck, and
ejaculated in an ill-humoured bass—

"Babalatchi!"

The players glanced up quickly, and looked down again
directly. Those men who were standing stirred uneasily
as if prodded by the sound of the chief's voice. The one
nearest to Lakamba repeated the call, after a while, over the
rail into the courtyard. There was a movement of upturned faces below by the fires, and the cry trailed over
the enclosure in sing-song tones. The thumping of wooden
pestles husking the evening rice stopped for a moment and
Babalatchi's name rang afresh shrilly on women's lips in
various keys. A voice far off shouted something—another,
nearer, repeated it; there was a short hubbub which died
out with extreme suddenness. The first crier turned to
Lakamba, saying indolently—

"He is with the blind Omar."

Lakamba's lips moved inaudibly. The man who had
just spoken was again deeply absorbed in the game going on
at his feet; and the chief—as if he had forgotten all about
it already—sat with a stolid face amongst his silent followers,
leaning back squarely in his chair, his hands on the arms of
his seat, his knees apart, his big blood-shot eyes blinking
solemnly, as if dazzled by the noble vacuity of his thoughts.

Babalatchi had gone to see old Omar late in the afternoon. The delicate manipulation of the ancient pirate's
susceptibilities, the skilful management of Aïssa's violent

impulses engrossed him to the exclusion of every other business—interfered with his regular attendance upon his chief and protector—even disturbed his sleep for the last three nights, as his wife—the gift of Lakamba—had remarked, with piercing and reproachful volubility, more than once. That day when he left his own bamboo hut—which stood amongst others in Lakamba's campong—his heart was heavy with anxiety and with doubt as to the success of his intrigue. He walked slowly, with his usual air of detachment from his surroundings, as if unaware that many sleepy eyes watched from all parts of the courtyard his progress towards a small gate at its upper end. That gate gave access to a separate enclosure in which a rather large house, built of planks, had been prepared by Lakamba's orders for the reception of Omar and Aïssa. It was a superior kind of habitation which Lakamba intended for the dwelling of his chief adviser—whose abilities were worth that honour, he thought. But after the consultation in the deserted clearing —when Babalatchi had disclosed his plan—they both had agreed that the new house should be used at first to shelter Omar and Aïssa after they had been persuaded to leave the Rajah's place, or had been kidnapped from there—as the case might be. Babalatchi did not mind in the least the putting off of his own occupation of the house of honour, because it had many advantages for the quiet working out of his plans. It had a certain seclusion, having an enclosure of its own, and that enclosure communicated also with Lakamba's private courtyard at the back of his residence— a place set apart for the female household of the chief. The only communication with the river was through the great front courtyard always full of armed men and watchful eyes. Behind the whole group of buildings there stretched the level ground of rice-clearings, which in their turn were closed in by the wall of untouched forests with under-growth so thick and tangled that nothing but a bullet—and that fired at pretty close range—could penetrate any distance there.

Babalatchi slipped quietly through the little gate and,

closing it, tied up carefully the rattan fastenings. Before the house there was a square space of ground, beaten hard into the level smoothness of asphalte. A big buttressed tree, a giant left there on purpose during the process of clearing the land, roofed in the clear space with a high canopy of gnarled boughs and thick, sombre leaves. To the right—and some small distance away from the large house—a little hut of reeds, covered with mats, had been put up for the special convenience of Omar, who, being blind and infirm, had some difficulty in ascending the steep plankway that led to the more substantial dwelling, which was built on low posts and had an uncovered verandah. Close by the trunk of the tree, and facing the doorway of the hut, the household fire glowed in a small handful of embers in the midst of a large circle of white ashes. An old woman—some humble relation of one of Lakamba's wives, who had been ordered to attend on Aïssa—was squatting over the fire and lifted up her bleared eyes to gaze at Babalatchi in an uninterested manner, as he advanced rapidly across the courtyard.

Babalatchi took in the courtyard with a keen glance of his solitary eyes, and without looking down at the old woman muttered a question. Silently, the woman stretched a tremulous and emaciated arm towards the hut. Babalatchi made a few steps toward the doorway, but stopped outside in the sunlight.

"O! Tuan Omar, Omar besar! It is I—Babalatchi!"

Within the hut there was a feeble groan, a fit of coughing and an indistinct murmur in the broken tones of a vague plaint. Encouraged evidently by those signs of dismal life within, Babalatchi entered the hut, and after some time came out leading with rigid carefulness the blind Omar, who followed with both his hands on his guide's shoulders. There was a rude seat under the tree, and there Babalatchi led his old chief, who sat down with a sigh of relief and leaned wearily against the rugged trunk. The rays of the setting sun, darting under the spreading branches, rested on the white-robed figure sitting with head thrown back in stiff dignity, on the thin hands moving uneasily, and on the stolid face with its eyelids dropped over the destroyed eyeballs; a face set into the immobility of a plaster cast yellowed by age.

"Is the sun near its setting?" asked Omar, in a dull voice.

"Very near," answered Babalatchi.

"Where am I? Why have I been taken away from the place which I knew—where I, blind, could move without fear. It is like black night to those who see. And the sun is near its setting—and I have not heard the sound of her footsteps since the morning! Twice a strange hand has given me my food to-day. Why? Why? Where is she?"

"She is near," said Babalatchi.

"And he?" went on Omar, with sudden eagerness, and a drop in his voice. "Where is he? Not here. Not here!" he repeated, turning his head from side to side as if in deliberate attempt to see.

"No! He is not here now," said Babalatchi, soothingly. Then, after a pause, he added very low, "But he shall soon return."

"Return! O crafty one! Will he return? I have cursed him three times," exclaimed Omar, with weak violence.

"He is—no doubt—accursed," assented Babalatchi, in a conciliating manner—"and yet he will be here before very long—I know!"

"You are crafty and faithless. I have made you great. You were dirt under my feet—less than dirt," said Omar, with tremulous energy.

"I have fought by your side many times," said Babalatchi, calmly.

"Why did he come?" went on Omar. "Did you send him? Why did he come to defile the air I breathe—to mock at my fate—to poison her mind and steal her body. She has grown hard of heart to me. Hard and merciless and stealthy like rocks that tear a ship's life out under the smooth sea." He drew a long breath, struggled with his anger, then broke down suddenly. " I have been hungry," he continued, in a whimpering tone—" often I have been very hungry—and cold—and neglected—and nobody near me. She has often forgotten me—and my sons are dead, and that man is an infidel and a dog. Why did he come? Did you show him the way? "

" He found the way himself, O Leader of the brave," said Babalatchi, sadly. " I only saw a way for their destruction and our own greatness. And if I saw aright, then you shall never suffer from hunger any more. There shall be peace for us, and glory and riches."

" And I shall die to-morrow," murmured Omar, bitterly.

" Who knows? Those things have been written since the beginning of the world," whispered Babalatchi, thoughtfully.

" Do not let him come back," exclaimed Omar.

" Neither can he escape his fate," went on Babalatchi. " He shall come back, and the power of men we always hated, you and I, shall crumble into dust in our hand." Then he added with enthusiasm, " They shall fight amongst themselves and perish both."

" And you shall see all this, while I . . ."

" True! " murmured Babalatchi, regretfully. " To you life is darkness."

" No! Flame! " exclaimed the old Arab, half rising, then falling back in his seat. " The flame of that last day! I see it yet—the last thing I saw! And I hear the noise of the rent earth—when they all died. And I live to be the plaything of a crafty one," he added, with inconsequential peevishness.

" You are my master still," said Babalatchi, humbly. " You are very wise—and in your wisdom you shall speak to Syed Abdulla when he comes here—you shall speak to him as I advised, I, your servant, the man who fought at your right hand for many years. I have heard by a messenger that the Syed Abdulla is coming to-night, perhaps late; for those things must be done secretly, lest the white man,

the trader up the river, should know of them. But he will
be here. There has been a surat delivered to Lakamba.
In it, Syed Abdulla says he will leave his ship, which is
anchored outside the river, at the hour of noon to-day.
He will be here before daylight if Allah wills."

He spoke with his eye fixed on the ground, and did not
become aware of Aïssa's presence till he lifted his head when
he ceased speaking. She had approached so quietly that
even Omar did not hear her footsteps, and she stood now
looking at them with troubled eyes and parted lips, as if
she was going to speak; but at Babalatchi's entreating gesture
she remained silent. Omar sat absorbed in thought.

"Ay wa! Even so!" he said at last, in a weak voice.
"I am to speak your wisdom, O Babalatchi! Tell him to
trust the white man! I do not understand. I am old and
blind and weak. I do not understand. I am very cold,"
he continued, in a lower tone, moving his shoulders uneasily.
He ceased, then went on rambling in a faint whisper. "They
are the sons of witches, and their father is Satan the stoned.
Sons of witches. Sons of witches." After a short silence
he asked suddenly, in a firmer voice—"How many white
men are there here, O crafty one?"

"There are two here. Two white men to fight one
another," answered Babalatchi, with alacrity.

"And how many will be left then? How many? Tell
me, you who are wise."

"The downfall of an enemy is the consolation of the
unfortunate," said Babalatchi, sententiously. "They are
on every sea; only the wisdom of the Most High knows their
number—but you shall know that some of them suffer."

"Tell me, Babalatchi, will they die? Will they both
die?" asked Omar, in sudden agitation.

Aïssa made a movement. Babalatchi held up a warning
hand.

"They shall, surely, die," he said steadily, looking at the
girl with unflinching eye.

"Ay wa! But die soon! So that I can pass my hand
over their faces when Allah has made them stiff."

"If such is their fate and yours," answered Babalatchi, without hesitation. "God is great!"

A violent fit of coughing doubled Omar up, and he rocked himself to and fro, wheezing and moaning in turns, while Babalatchi and the girl looked at him in silence. Then he leaned back against the tree, exhausted.

"I am alone, I am alone," he wailed feebly, groping vaguely about with his trembling hands. "Is there anybody near me? Is there anybody? I am afraid of this strange place."

"I am by your side, O Leader of the brave," said Babalatchi, touching his shoulder lightly. "Always by your side as in the days when we both were young: as in the time when we both went with arms in our hands."

"Has there been such a time, Babalatchi?" said Omar, wildly; "I have forgotten. And now when I die there will be no man, no fearless man to speak of his father's bravery. There was a woman! A woman! And she has forsaken me for an infidel dog. The hand of the Compassionate is heavy on my head! Oh, my calamity! Oh, my shame!"

He calmed down after a while, and asked quietly—"Is the sun set, Babalatchi?"

"It is now as low as the highest tree I can see from here," answered Babalatchi.

"It is the time of prayer," said Omar, attempting to get up.

Dutifully Babalatchi helped his old chief to rise, and they walked slowly towards the hut. Omar waited outside, while Babalatchi went in and came out directly, dragging after him the old Arab's praying carpet. Out of a brass vessel he poured the water of absolution on Omar's outstretched hands, and eased him carefully down into a kneeling posture, for the venerable robber was far too infirm to be able to stand. Then as Omar droned out the first words and made his first bow towards the Holy City, Babalatchi stepped noiselessly towards Aïssa, who did not move all that time.

I 2

Aïssa looked steadily at the one-eyed sage, who was approaching her slowly and with a great show of deference. For a moment they stood facing each other in silence. Babalatchi appeared embarrassed. With a sudden and quick gesture she caught hold of his arm, and with the other hand pointed towards the sinking red disc that glowed, rayless, through the floating mists of evening.

"The third sunset! The last! And he is not here," she whispered; "what have you done, man without faith? What have you done?"

"Indeed I have kept my word," murmured Babalatchi, earnestly. "This morning Bulangi went with a canoe to look for him. He is a strange man, but our friend, and shall keep close to him and watch him without ostentation. And at the third hour of the day I have sent another canoe with four rowers. Indeed, the man you long for, O daughter of Omar! may come when he likes."

"But he is not here! I waited for him yesterday. To-day! To-morrow I shall go."

"Not alive!" muttered Babalatchi to himself. "And do you doubt your power," he went on in a louder tone—"you that to him are more beautiful than a houri of the seventh heaven. He is your slave."

"A slave does run away sometimes," she said, gloomily, "and then the master must go and seek him out."

"And do you want to live and die a beggar?" asked Babalatchi, impatiently.

"I care not," she exclaimed, wringing her hands; and the black pupils of her wide-open eyes darted wildly here and there like petrels before the storm.

"Sh! Sh!" hissed Babalatchi, with a glance towards Omar. "Do you think, O girl! that he himself would live like a beggar, even with you?"

"He is great," she said, ardently. "He despises you all! He despises you all! He is indeed a man!"

"You know that best," muttered Babalatchi, with a fugitive smile—"but remember, woman with the strong heart, that to hold him now you must be to him like the great sea to thirsty men—a never-ceasing torment, and a madness."

He ceased and they stood in silence, both looking on the ground, and for a time nothing was heard above the crackling of the fire but the intoning of Omar glorifying the God —his God, and the Faith—his faith. Then Babalatchi cocked his head on one side and appeared to listen intently to the hum of voices in the big courtyard. The dull noise swelled into distinct shouts, then into a great tumult of voices, dying away, recommencing, growing louder, to cease again abruptly; and in those short pauses the shrill vociferations of women rushed up, as if released, towards the quiet heaven. Aïssa and Babalatchi started, but the latter gripped in his turn the girl's arm and restrained her with a strong grasp.

"Wait," he whispered.

The little door in the heavy stockade which separated Lakamba's private ground from Omar's enclosure swung back quickly, and the noble exile appeared with disturbed mien and a naked short sword in his hand. His turban was half unrolled, and the end trailed on the ground behind him. His jacket was open. He breathed thickly for a moment before he spoke.

"He came in Bulangi's boat," he said, "and walked quietly till he was in my presence, when the senseless fury of white men caused him to rush upon me I have been in great danger," went on the ambitious nobleman in an aggrieved tone. "Do you hear that, Babalatchi? That eater of swine aimed a blow at my face with his unclean fist. He tried to rush amongst my household. Six men are holding him now."

A fresh outburst of yells stopped Lakamba's discourse. Angry voices shouted: "Hold him. Beat him down. Strike at his head." Then the clamour ceased with sudden completeness, as if strangled by a mighty hand, and after a second of surprising silence the voice of Willems was heard alone, howling maledictions in Malay, in Dutch, and in English.

"Listen," said Lakamba, speaking with unsteady lips, "he blasphemes his God. His speech is like the raving of a mad dog. Can we hold him for ever? He must be killed!"

"Fool!" muttered Babalatchi, looking up at Aïssa, who stood with set teeth, with gleaming eyes and distended nostrils, yet obedient to the touch of his restraining hand. "It is the third day, and I have kept my promise," he said to her, speaking very low. "Remember," he added warningly—"like the sea to the thirsty! And now," he said aloud, releasing her and stepping back, "go, fearless daughter, go!"

Like an arrow, rapid and silent she flew down the enclosure, and disappeared through the gate of the courtyard. Lakamba and Babalatchi looked after her. They heard the renewed tumult, the girl's clear voice calling out, "Let him go!" Then after a pause in the din no longer than half the human breath the name of Aïssa rang in a shout loud, discordant, and piercing, which sent through them an involuntary shudder. Old Omar collapsed on his carpet and moaned feebly; Lakamba stared with gloomy contempt in the direction of the inhuman sound; but Babalatchi, forcing a smile, pushed his distinguished protector through the narrow gate in the stockade, followed him, and closed it quickly.

The old woman, who had been most of the time kneeling by the fire, now rose, glanced round fearfully and crouched hiding behind the tree. The gate of the great courtyard flew open with a great clatter before a frantic kick, and Willems darted in carrying Aïssa in his arms. He rushed up the enclosure like a tornado, pressing the girl to his breast, her arms round his neck, her head hanging back over his arm, her eyes closed and her long hair nearly touching the ground. They appeared for a second in the glare of the fire, then, with immense strides, he dashed up the planks and disappeared with his burden in the doorway of the big house.

Inside and outside the enclosure there was silence. Omar

lay supporting himself on his elbow, his terrified face with its closed eyes giving him the appearance of a man tormented by a nightmare.

"What is it? Help! Help me to rise!" he called out faintly.

The old hag, still crouching in the shadow, stared with bleared eyes at the doorway of the big house, and took no notice of his call. He listened for a while, then his arm gave way, and, with a deep sigh of discouragement, he let himself fall on the carpet.

The boughs of the tree nodded and trembled in the unsteady currents of the light wind. A leaf fluttered down slowly from some high branch and rested on the ground, immobile, as if resting for ever, in the glow of the fire; but soon it stirred, then soared suddenly, and flew, spinning and turning before the breath of the perfumed breeze, driven helplessly into the dark night that had closed over the land.

## III

For upwards of forty years Abdulla had walked in the way of his Lord. Son of the rich Syed Selim bin Sali, the great Mohammedan trader of the Straits, he went forth at the age of seventeen on his first commercial expedition, as his father's representative on board a pilgrim ship chartered by the wealthy Arab to convey a crowd of pious Malays to the Holy Shrine. That was in the days when steam was not in those seas—or, at least, not so much as now. The voyage was long, and the young man's eyes were opened to the wonders of many lands. Allah had made it his fate to become a pilgrim very early in life. This was a great favour of Heaven, and it could not have been bestowed upon a man who prized it more, or who made himself more worthy of it by the unswerving piety of his heart and by the religious solemnity of his demeanour. Later on it became clear that the book of his destiny contained the programme of a wandering life. He visited Bombay and Calcutta, looked in at the Persian Gulf, beheld in due course the high and barren coasts of the Gulf of Suez, and this was the limit of his wanderings westward. He was then twenty-seven, and the writing on his forehead decreed that the time had come for him to return to the Straits and take from his dying father's hands the many threads of a business that was spread over all the Archipelago : from Sumatra to New Guinea, from Batavia to Palawan. Very soon his ability, his will—strong to obstinacy—his wisdom beyond his years, caused him to be recognised as the head of a family whose members and connections were found in every part of those seas. An uncle here—a brother there ; a father-in-law in Batavia, another in Palembang ; husbands of numerous sisters ; cousins innumerable scattered north, south, east, and west—in every place where there was trade : the great family lay like a network over the islands. They lent money to princes, influenced the council-rooms, faced —if need be—with peaceful intrepidity the white rulers who held the land and the sea under the edge of sharp swords ; and they all paid a great deference to Abdulla, listened to his advice, entered into his plans—because he was wise, pious, and fortunate.

He bore himself with the humility becoming a Believer, who never forgets, even for one moment of his waking life, that he is the servant of the Most High. He was largely charitable because the charitable man is the friend of Allah, and when he walked out of his house—built of stone, just outside the town of Penang—on his way to his godowns in the port, he had often to snatch his hand away sharply from under the lips of men of his race and creed ; and often he had to murmur deprecating words, or even to rebuke with severity those who attempted to touch his knees with their finger-tips in gratitude or supplication. He was very handsome, and carried his small head high with meek gravity. His lofty brow, straight nose, narrow, dark face with its chiselled delicacy of feature, gave him an aristocratic appearance which proclaimed his pure descent. His beard was trimmed close and to a rounded point. His large brown eyes looked out steadily with a sweetness that was belied by the expression of his thin-lipped mouth. His aspect was serene. He had a belief in his own prosperity which nothing could shake.

Restless, like all his people, he very seldom dwelt for many days together in his splendid house in Penang. Owner of ships, he was often on board one or another of them, traversing in all directions the field of his operations. In every port he had a household—his own or that of a relation —to hail his advent with demonstrative joy. In every port there were rich and influential men eager to see him, there was business to talk over, there were important letters to read : an immense correspondence, enclosed in silk envelopes —a correspondence which had nothing to do with the infidels of colonial post-offices, but came into his hands by devious, yet safe, ways. It was left for him by taciturn nakhodas of native trading craft, or was delivered with profound salaams by travel-stained and weary men who would withdraw from his presence calling upon Allah to bless the generous giver of splendid rewards. And the news was always good, and all his attempts always succeeded, and in his ears there rang always a chorus of admiration, of gratitude, of humble entreaties.

A fortunate man. And his felicity was so complete that the good genii, who ordered the stars at his birth, had not neglected—by a refinement of benevolence strange in such primitive beings—to provide him with a desire difficult to attain, and with an enemy hard to overcome. The envy of Lingard's political and commercial successes, and the wish to get the best of him in every way, became Abdulla's mania, the paramount interest of his life, the salt of his existence.

For the last few months he had been receiving mysterious messages from Sambir urging him to decisive action. He had found the river a couple of years ago, and had been anchored more than once off that estuary where the, till then, rapid Pantai, spreading slowly over the lowlands, seems to hesitate, before it flows gently through twenty outlets; over a maze of mudflats, sandbanks and reefs, into the expectant sea. He had never attempted the entrance, however, because men of his race, although brave and adventurous travellers, lack the true seamanlike instincts, and he was afraid of getting wrecked. He could not bear the idea of the Rajah Laut being able to boast that Abdulla bin Selim, like other and lesser men, had also come to grief when trying to wrest his secret from him. Meantime he returned encouraging answers to his unknown friends in Sambir, and waited for his opportunity in the calm certitude of ultimate triumph.

Such was the man whom Lakamba and Babalatchi expected to see for the first time on the night of Willems' return to Aïssa. Babalatchi, who had been tormented for three days by the fear of having overreached himself in his little plot, now, feeling sure of his white man, felt lighthearted and happy as he superintended the preparations in the courtyard for Abdulla's reception. Half-way between Lakamba's house and the river a pile of dry wood was made ready for the torch that would set fire to it at the moment of Abdulla's landing. Between this and the house again there was, ranged in a semicircle, a set of low bamboo frames, and on those were piled all the carpets and cushions of Lakamba's household. It had been decided that the reception was to take place in the open air, and that it should be made impressive by the great number of Lakamba's retainers, who, clad in clean white, with their red sarongs gathered round their waists, chopper at side and lance in hand, were moving about the compound or, gathering into small knots, discussed eagerly the coming ceremony.

Two little fires burned brightly on the water's edge on each side of the landing place. A small heap of damar-gum torches lay by each, and between them Babalatchi strolled backwards and forwards, stopping often with his face to the river and his head on one side, listening to the sounds that came from the darkness over the water. There was no moon and the night was very clear overhead, but, after the afternoon breeze had expired in fitful puffs, the vapours hung thickening over the glancing surface of the Pantai and clung to the shore, hiding from view the middle of the stream.

A cry in the mist—then another—and, before Babalatchi could answer, two little canoes dashed up to the landing-place, and two of the principal citizens of Sambir, Daoud Sahamin and Hamet Bahassoen, who had been confidentially invited to meet Abdulla, landed quickly, and after greeting Babalatchi walked up the dark courtyard towards the house. The little stir caused by their arrival soon subsided, and another silent hour dragged its slow length while Babalatchi tramped up and down between the fires, his face growing more anxious with every passing moment.

At last there was heard a loud hail from down the river. At a call from Babalatchi men ran down to the riverside and, snatching the torches, thrust them into the fires, then waved them above their heads till they burst into a flame. The smoke ascended in thick, wispy streams, and hung in a ruddy cloud above the glare that lit up the courtyard and flashed over the water, showing three long canoes manned by many paddlers lying a little off ; the men in them lifting their paddles on high and dipping them down together, in an easy stroke that kept the small flotilla motionless in the strong current, exactly abreast of the landing-place. A man stood up in the largest craft and called out—

" Syed Abdulla bin Selim is here ! "

Babalatchi answered aloud in a formal tone—

" Allah gladdens our hearts !  Come to the land ! "

Abdulla landed first, steadying himself by the help of Babalatchi's extended hand.  In the short moment of his passing from the boat to the shore they exchanged sharp glances and a few rapid words.

" Who are you ? "

" Babalatchi.  The friend of Omar.  The protected of Lakamba."

" You wrote ? "

" My words were written, O Giver of alms ! "

And then Abdulla walked with composed face between the two lines of men holding torches, and met Lakamba in front of the big fire that was crackling itself up into a great blaze. For a moment they stood with clasped hands invoking peace upon each other's head, then Lakamba, still holding his honoured guest by the hand, led him round the fire to the prepared seats. Babalatchi followed close behind his protector. Abdulla was accompanied by two Arabs. He, like his companions, was dressed in a white robe of starched muslin, which fell in stiff folds straight from the neck. It was buttoned from the throat halfway down with a close row of very small gold buttons; round the tight sleeves there was a narrow braid of gold lace. On his shaven head he wore a small skull-cap of plaited grass. He was shod in patent leather slippers over his naked feet. A rosary of heavy wooden beads hung by a round turn from his right wrist. He sat down slowly in the place of honour, and, dropping his slippers, tucked up his legs under him decorously.

The improvised divan was arranged in a wide semicircle, of which the point most distant from the fire—some ten yards—was also the nearest to Lakamba's dwelling. As soon as the principal personages were seated, the verandah of the house was filled silently by the muffled-up forms of Lakamba's female belongings. They crowded close to the rail and looked down, whispering faintly. Below, the formal exchange of compliments went on for some time between Lakamba and Abdulla, who sat side by side. Babalatchi squatted humbly at his protector's feet, with nothing but a thin mat between himself and the hard ground.

Then there was a pause. Abdulla glanced round in an expectant manner, and after a while Babalatchi, who had been sitting very still in a pensive attitude, seemed to rouse himself with an effort, and began to speak in gentle and persuasive tones. He described in flowing sentences the first beginnings of Sambir, the dispute of the present ruler, Patalolo, with the Sultan of Koti, the consequent troubles ending with the rising of Bugis settlers under the leader-

ship of Lakamba. At different points of the narrative he
would turn for confirmation to Sahamin and Bahassoen,
who sat listening eagerly and assented together with a
Betul! Betul! Right! Right! ejaculated in a fervent
undertone.

Warming up with his subject as the narrative proceeded,
Babalatchi went on to relate the facts connected with
Lingard's action at the critical period of those internal dis-
sensions. He spoke in a restrained voice still, but with a
growing energy of indignation. What was he, that man of
fierce aspect, to keep all the world away from them? Was
he a government? Who made him ruler? He took possession of Patalolo's mind and made his heart hard; he put
severe words into his mouth and caused his hand to strike
right and left. That unbeliever kept the Faithful panting
under the weight of his senseless oppression. They had to
trade with him—accept such goods as he would give—such
credit as he would accord. And he exacted payment every
year . . .

"Very true!" exclaimed Sahamin and Bahassoen together.

Babalatchi glanced at them approvingly and turned to
Abdulla.

"Listen to those men, O Protector of the oppressed!"
he exclaimed. "What could we do? A man must trade.
There was nobody else."

Sahamin got up, staff in hand, and spoke to Abdulla with
ponderous courtesy, emphasising his words by the solemn
flourishes of his right arm.

"It is so. We are weary of paying our debts to that
white man here, who is the son of the Rajah Laut. That
white man—may the grave of his mother be defiled!—is
not content to hold us all in his hand with a cruel grasp.
He seeks to cause our very death. He trades with the
Dyaks of the forest, who are no better than monkeys. He
buys from them guttah and rattans—while we starve. Only
two days ago I went to him and said, 'Tuan Almayer'—
even so; we must speak politely to that friend of Satan—
'Tuan Almayer, I have such and such goods to sell. Will

you buy ? ' And he spoke thus—because those white men have no understanding of any courtesy—he spoke to me as if I was a slave : ' Daoud, you are a lucky man '—remark, O First amongst the Believers ! that by those words he could have brought misfortune on my head—' you are a lucky man to have anything in these hard times. Bring your goods quickly, and I shall receive them in payment of what you owe me from last year.' And he laughed, and struck me on the shoulder with his open hand. May Jehannum be his lot ! "

"We will fight him," said young Bahassoen, crisply. "We shall fight if there is help and a leader. Tuan Abdulla, will you come among us ? "

Abdulla did not answer at once. His lips moved in an inaudible whisper and the beads passed through his fingers with a dry click. All waited in respectful silence. " I shall come if my ship can enter this river," said Abdulla at last, in a solemn tone.

"It can, Tuan," exclaimed Babalatchi. "There is a white man here who . . ."

"I want to see Omar el Badavi and that white man you wrote about," interrupted Abdulla.

Babalatchi got on his feet quickly, and there was a general move. The women on the verandah hurried indoors, and from the crowd that had kept discreetly in distant parts of the courtyard a couple of men ran with armfuls of dry fuel, which they cast upon the fire. One of them, at a sign from Babalatchi, approached and, after getting his orders, went towards the little gate and entered Omar's enclosure. While waiting for his return, Lakamba, Abdulla, and Babalatchi talked together in low tones. Sahamin sat by himself chewing betel-nut sleepily with a slight and indolent motion of his heavy jaw. Bahassoen, his hand on the hilt of his short sword, strutted backwards and forwards in the full light of the fire, looking very warlike and reckless ; the envy and admiration of Lakamba's retainers, who stood in groups or flitted about noiselessly in the shadows of the courtyard.

The messenger who had been sent to Omar came back

and stood at a distance, waiting till somebody noticed him. Babalatchi beckoned him close.

" What are his words ? " asked Babalatchi.

" He says that Syed Abdulla is welcome now," answered the man.

Lakamba was speaking low to Abdulla, who listened to him with deep interest.

" . . . We could have eighty men if there was need," he was saying—" eighty men in fourteen canoes. The only thing we want is gunpowder . . ."

" Haï ! there will be no fighting," broke in Babalatchi. " The fear of your name will be enough and the terror of your coming."

" There may be powder too," muttered Abdulla with great nonchalance, " if only the ship enters the river safely."

" If the heart is stout the ship will be safe," said Babalatchi. " We will go now and see Omar el Badavi and the white man I have here."

Lakamba's dull eyes became animated suddenly.

" Take care, Tuan Abdulla," he said, " take care. The behaviour of that unclean white madman is furious in the extreme. He offered to strike . . ."

" On my head, you are safe, O Giver of alms ! " interrupted Babalatchi.

Abdulla looked from one to the other, and the faintest flicker of a passing smile disturbed for a moment his grave composure. He turned to Babalatchi, and said with decision—

" Let us go."

" This way, O Uplifter of our hearts ! " rattled on Babalatchi, with fussy deference. " Only a very few paces and you shall behold Omar the brave, and a white man of great strength and cunning. This way."

He made a sign for Lakamba to remain behind, and with respectful touches on the elbow steered Abdulla towards the gate at the upper end of the courtyard. As they walked on slowly, followed by the two Arabs, he kept on talking in a rapid undertone to the great man, who never looked at him once, although appearing to listen with flattering attention. When near the gate Babalatchi moved forward and stopped, facing Abdulla, with his hand on the fastenings.

"You shall see them both," he said. "All my words about them are true. When I saw him enslaved by the one of whom I spoke, I knew he would be soft in my hand like the mud of the river. At first he answered my talk with bad words of his own language, after the manner of white men. Afterwards, when listening to the voice he loved, he hesitated. He hesitated for many days—too many. I, knowing him well, made Omar withdraw here with his . . . household. Then this red-faced man raged for three days like a black panther that is hungry. And this evening, this very evening, he came. I have him here. He is in the grasp of one with a merciless heart. I have him here," ended Babalatchi, exultingly tapping the upright of the gate with his hand.

"This is good," murmured Abdulla.

"And he shall guide your ship and lead in the fight—if fight there be," went on Babalatchi. "If there is any killing—let him be the slayer. You should give him arms —a short gun that fires many times."

"Yes, by Allah!" assented Abdulla, with slow thoughtfulness.

"And you will have to open your hand, O First amongst the generous!" continued Babalatchi. "You will have to satisfy the rapacity of a white man, and also of one who is not a man, and therefore greedy of ornaments."

"They shall be satisfied," said Abdulla; "but . . ." He hesitated, looking down on the ground and stroking his beard, while Babalatchi waited, anxious, with parted lips. After a short time he spoke again jerkily in an indistinct whisper, so that Babalatchi had to turn his head to catch the words. "Yes. But Omar is the son of my father's uncle . . . and all belonging to him are of the Faith . . . while that man is an unbeliever. It is most unseemly . . . very unseemly. He cannot live under my shadow. Not that dog. Penitence! I take refuge with my God," he

mumbled rapidly. "How can he live under my eyes with
that woman, who is of the Faith? Scandal! O abomination!"

He finished with a rush and drew a long breath, then
added dubiously—

"And when that man has done all we want, what is to
be done with him?"

They stood close together, meditative and silent, their
eyes roaming idly over the courtyard. The big bonfire
burned brightly, and a wavering splash of light lay on the
dark earth at their feet, while the lazy smoke wreathed itself
slowly in gleaming coils amongst the black boughs of the
trees. They could see Lakamba, who had returned to his
place, sitting hunched up spiritlessly on the cushions, and
Sahamin, who had got on his feet again and appeared to be
talking to him with dignified animation. Men in twos or
threes came out of the shadows into the light, strolling
slowly, and passed again into the shadows, their faces turned
to each other, their arms moving in restrained gestures.
Bahassoen, his head proudly thrown back, his ornaments,
embroideries, and sword-hilt flashing in the light, circled
steadily round the fire like a planet round the sun. A cool
whiff of damp air came from the darkness of the riverside;
it made Abdulla and Babalatchi shiver, and woke them up
from their abstraction.

"Open the gate and go first," said Abdulla; "there is
no danger?"

"On my life, no!" answered Babalatchi, lifting the
rattan ring. "He is all peace and content, like a thirsty
man who has drunk water after many days."

He swung the gate wide, made a few paces into the gloom
of the enclosure, and retraced his steps suddenly.

"He may be made useful in many ways," he whispered
to Abdulla, who had stopped short, seeing him come back.

"O Sin! O Temptation!" sighed out Abdulla, faintly.
"Our refuge is with the Most High. Can I feed this
infidel for ever and ever?" he added, impatiently.

"No," breathed out Babalatchi. "No! Not for ever.

Only while he serves your designs, O Dispenser of Allah's gifts! When the time comes—and your order . . ."

He sidled close to Abdulla, and brushed with a delicate touch the hand that hung down listlessly, holding the prayer-beads.

"I am your slave and your offering," he murmured, in a distinct and polite tone, into Abdulla's ear. "When your wisdom speaks, there may be found a little poison that will not lie. Who knows!"


## IV

BABALATCHI saw Abdulla pass through the low and narrow entrance into the darkness of Omar's hut; heard them exchange the usual greetings and the distinguished visitor's grave voice asking: "There is no misfortune—please God —but the sight?" and then, becoming aware of the disapproving looks of the two Arabs who had accompanied Abdulla, he followed their example and fell back out of earshot. He did it unwillingly, although he did not ignore that what was going to happen in there was now absolutely beyond his control. He roamed irresolutely about for awhile, and at last wandered with careless steps towards the fire, which had been moved, from under the tree, close to the hut and a little to windward of its entrance. He squatted on his heels and began playing pensively with live embers, as was his habit when engrossed in thought, withdrawing his hand sharply and shaking it above his head when he burnt his fingers in a fit of deeper abstraction. Sitting there he could hear the murmur of the talk inside the hut, and he could distinguish the voices but not the words. Abdulla spoke in deep tones, and now and then this flowing monotone was interrupted by a querulous exclamation, a weak moan or a plaintive quaver of the old man. Yes. It was annoying not to be able to make out what they were saying, thought Babalatchi, as he sat gazing fixedly at the unsteady glow of the fire. But it will be right. All will be right. Abdulla inspired him with confidence. He came up fully to his expectation. From the very first moment when he set his eye on him he felt sure that this man—whom he had known by reputation only—was very resolute. Perhaps too resolute. Perhaps he would want to grasp too much later on. A shadow flitted over Babalatchi's face. On the eve of the accomplishment of his desires he felt the bitter taste of that drop of doubt which is mixed with the sweetness of every success.

When, hearing footsteps on the verandah of the big house, he lifted his head, the shadow had passed away and on his face there was an expression of watchful alertness. Willems was coming down the plankway, into the courtyard. The light within trickled through the cracks of the badly joined walls of the house, and in the illuminated doorway appeared the moving form of Aïssa. She also passed into the night outside and disappeared from view. Babalatchi wondered where she had got to, and for the moment forgot the approach of Willems. The voice of the white man speaking roughly above his head made him jump to his feet as if impelled upwards by a powerful spring.

"Where's Abdulla?"

Babalatchi waved his hand towards the hut and stood listening intently. The voices within had ceased, then recommenced again. He shot an oblique glance at Willems, whose indistinct form towered above the glow of dying embers.

"Make up this fire," said Willems, abruptly. "I want to see your face."

With obliging alacrity Babalatchi put some dry brushwood on the coals from a handy pile, keeping all the time a watchful eye on Willems. When he straightened himself up his hand wandered almost involuntarily towards his left side to feel the handle of a kriss amongst the folds of his sarong, but he tried to look unconcerned under the angry stare.

"You are in good health, please God?" he murmured.

" Yes ! " answered Willems, with an unexpected loudness that caused Babalatchi to start nervously. "Yes! . . . Health ! . . . You . . ."

He made a long stride and dropped both his hands on the Malay's shoulders. In the powerful grip Babalatchi swayed to and fro limpy, but his face was as peaceful as when he sat—a little while ago—dreaming by the fire. With a final vicious jerk Willems let go suddenly, and turning away on his heel stretched his hands over the fire. Babalatchi stumbled backwards, recovered himself, and wriggled his shoulders laboriously.

" Tse ! Tse ! Tse ! " he clicked, deprecatingly. After a short silence he went on with accentuated admiration : " What a man it is ! What a strong man ! A man like that "—he concluded, in a tone of meditative wonder— " a man like that could upset mountains—mountains ! "

He gazed hopefully for a while at Willems' broad shoulders, and continued, addressing the inimical back, in a low and persuasive voice—

" But why be angry with me ? With me who think only of your good ? Did I not give her refuge, in my own house ? Yes, Tuan ! This is my own house. I will let you have it without any recompense, because she must have a shelter. Therefore you and she shall live here. Who can know a woman's mind ? And such a woman ! If she wanted to go away from that other place, who am I—to say no ! I am Omar's servant. I said : ' Gladden my heart by taking my house.' Did I say right ? "

" I'll tell you something," said Willems, without changing his position ; " if she takes a fancy to go away from this place it is you who shall suffer. I will wring your neck."

" When the heart is full of love there is no room in it for justice," recommenced Babalatchi, with unmoved and persistent softness. " Why slay me ? You know, Tuan, what she wants. A splendid destiny is her desire—as of all women. You have been wronged and cast out by your people. She knows that. But you are brave, you are strong—you are a man; and, Tuan—I am older than you —you are in her hand. Such is the fate of strong men. And she is of noble birth and cannot live like a slave. You know her—and you are in her hand. You are like a snared bird, because of your strength. And—remember I am a man that has seen much—submit, Tuan! Submit! . . . Or else . . ."

He drawled out the last words in a hesitating manner and broke off his sentence. Still stretching his hands in turns towards the blaze and without moving his head, Willems gave a short, lugubrious laugh, and asked—

"Or else—what?"

"She may go away again. Who knows?" finished Babalatchi, in a gentle and insinuating tone.

This time Willems spun round sharply. Babalatchi stepped back.

"If she does it will be the worse for you," said Willems, in a menacing voice. "It will be your doing, and I . . ."

Babalatchi spoke, from beyond the circle of light, with calm disdain.

"Haï—ya! I have heard before. If she goes—then I die. Good! Will that bring her back, do you think— Tuan? If it is my doing it shall be well done, O white man! and—who knows—you will have to live without her."

Willems gasped and started back like a confident wayfarer who, pursuing a path he thinks safe, should see just in time a bottomless chasm under his feet. Babalatchi came into the light and approached Willems sideways, with his head thrown back and a little on one side so as to bring his only eye to bear full on the countenance of the tall white man.

"You threaten me," said Willems, indistinctly.

"I, Tuan!" exclaimed Babalatchi, with a slight suspicion of irony in the affected surprise of his tone. "I, Tuan? Who spoke of death? Was it I? No! I spoke of life only. Only of life. Of a long life for a lonely man!"

They stood with the fire between them, both silent,

both aware, each in his own way, of the importance of the passing minutes. Babalatchi's fatalism gave him only an insignificant relief in his suspense, because no fatalism can kill the thought of the future, the desire of success, the pain of waiting for the disclosure of the immutable decrees of Heaven. Fatalism is born of the fear of failure, for we all believe that we carry success in our own hands, and we suspect that our hands are weak. Babalatchi looked at Willems and congratulated himself upon his ability to manage that white man. There was a pilot for Abdulla—a victim to appease Lingard's anger in case of any mishap. He would take good care to put him forward in everything. In any case let the white men fight it out amongst themselves. They were fools. He hated them—the strong fools—and knew that for his righteous wisdom was reserved the safe triumph.

Willems measured dismally the depth of his degradation. He—a white man, the admired of white men, was held by those miserable savages whose tool he was about to become. He felt for them all the hate of his race, of his morality, of his intelligence. He looked upon himself with dismay and pity. She had him. He had heard of such things. He had heard of women who . . . He would never believe such stories. . . . Yet they were true. But his own captivity seemed more complete, terrible and final—without the hope of any redemption. He wondered at the wickedness of Providence that had made him what he was; that, worse still, permitted such a creature as Almayer to live. He had done his duty by going to him. Why did he not understand? All men were fools. He gave him his chance. The fellow did not see. It was hard, very hard on himself —Willems. He wanted to take her from amongst her own people. That's why he had condescended to go to Almayer. He examined himself. With a sinking heart he thought that really he could not—somehow—live without her. It was terrible and sweet. He remembered the first days. Her appearance, her face, her smile, her eyes, her words. A savage woman! Yet he perceived that he could think of nothing else but of the three days of their separation, of the few hours since their reunion. Very well. If he could not take her away, then he would go to her. . . . He had, for a moment, a wicked pleasure in the thought that what he had done could not be undone. He had given himself up. He felt proud of it. He was ready to face anything, do anything. He cared for nothing, for nobody. He thought himself very fearless, but as a matter of fact he was only drunk; drunk with the poison of passionate memories.

He stretched his hands over the fire, looked round, and called out—

"Aïssa !"

She must have been near, for she appeared at once within the light of the fire. The upper part of her body was wrapped up in the thick folds of a head covering which was pulled down over her brow, and one end of it thrown across from shoulder to shoulder hid the lower part of her face. Only her eyes were visible—sombre and gleaming like a starry night.

Willems, looking at this strange, muffled figure, felt exasperated, amazed and helpless. The ex-confidential clerk of the rich Hudig would hug to his breast settled conceptions of respectable conduct. He sought refuge within his ideas of propriety from the dismal mangroves, from the darkness of the forests and of the heathen souls of the savages that were his masters. She looked like an animated package of cheap cotton goods ! It made him furious. She had disguised herself so because a man of her race was near ! He told her not to do it, and she did not obey. Would his ideas ever change so as to agree with her own notions of what was becoming, proper and respectable ? He was really afraid they would, in time. It seemed to him awful. She would never change ! This manifestation of her sense of proprieties was another sign of their hopeless diversity; something like another step downwards for him. She was too different from him. He was so civilised ! It struck him suddenly that they had nothing in common— not a thought, not a feeling; he could not make clear to her the simplest motive of any act of his . . . and he could not live without her.

The courageous man who stood facing Babalatchi gasped unexpectedly with a gasp that was half a groan. This little matter of her veiling herself against his wish acted upon him like a disclosure of some great disaster. It increased his contempt for himself as the slave of a passion he had always derided, as the man unable to assert his will. This will, all his sensations, his personality—all this seemed to be lost in the abominable desire, in the priceless promise of that woman. He was not, of course, able to discern clearly the causes of his misery; but there are none so ignorant as not to know suffering, none so simple as not to feel and suffer from the shock of warring impulses. The ignorant must feel and suffer from their complexity as well as the wisest; but to them the pain of struggle and defeat appears strange, mysterious, remediable and unjust. He stood watching her, watching himself. He tingled with rage from head to foot, as if he had been struck in the face. Suddenly he laughed; but his laugh was like a distorted echo of some insincere mirth very far away.

From the other side of the fire Babalatchi spoke hurriedly—
"Here is Tuan Abdulla."

## V

Directly on stepping outside Omar's hut Abdulla caught sight of Willems. He expected, of course, to see a white man, but not that white man, whom he knew so well. Everybody who traded in the islands, and who had any dealings with Hudig, knew Willems. For the last two years of his stay in Macassar the confidential clerk had been managing all the local trade of the house under a very slight supervision only on the part of the master. So everybody knew Willems, Abdulla amongst others—but he was ignorant of Willems' disgrace. As a matter of fact the thing had been kept very quiet—so quiet that a good many people in Macassar were expecting Willems' return there, supposing him to be absent on some confidential mission. Abdulla, in his surprise, hesitated on the threshold. He had prepared himself to see some seaman—some old officer of Lingard; a common man—perhaps difficult to deal with, but still no match for him. Instead, he saw himself confronted by an individual whose reputation for sagacity in business was well known to him. How did he get here, and why? Abdulla, recovering from his surprise, advanced in a dignified manner towards the fire, keeping his eyes fixed steadily on Willems. When within two paces from Willems he stopped and lifted his right hand in grave salutation. Willems nodded slightly and spoke after a while.

"We know each other, Tuan Abdulla," he said, with an assumption of easy indifference.

"We have traded together," answered Abdulla, solemnly, "but it was far from here."

"And we may trade here also," said Willems.

"The place does not matter. It is the open mind and the true heart that are required in business."

"Very true. My heart is as open as my mind. I will tell you why I am here."

"What need is there? In leaving home one learns life. You travel. Travelling is victory! You shall return with much wisdom."

"I shall never return," interrupted Willems. "I have done with my people. I am a man without brothers. Injustice destroys fidelity."

Abdulla expressed his surprise by elevating his eyebrows. At the same time he made a vague gesture with his arm that could be taken as an equivalent of an approving and conciliating "just so!"

Till then the Arab had not taken any notice of Aïssa, who stood by the fire, but now she spoke in the interval of silence following Willems' declaration. In a voice that was much deadened by her wrappings she addressed Abdulla in a few words of greeting, calling him a kinsman. Abdulla

glanced at her swiftly for a second, and then, with perfect
good breeding, fixed his eyes on the ground. She put out
towards him her hand, covered with a corner of her face-
veil, and he took it, pressed it twice, and dropping it turned
towards Willems. She looked at the two men searchingly,
then backed away and seemed to melt suddenly into the
night.

" I know what you came for, Tuan Abdulla," said Willems ;
" I have been told by that man there." He nodded towards
Babalatchi, then went on slowly, " It will be a difficult
thing."

" Allah makes everything easy," interjected Babalatchi,
piously, from a distance.

The two men turned quickly and stood looking at him
thoughtfully, as if in deep consideration of the truth of that
proposition. Under their sustained gaze Babalatchi experienced an unwonted feeling of shyness, and dared not approach
nearer. At last Willems moved slightly, Abdulla followed
readily, and they both walked down the courtyard, their
voices dying away in the darkness. Soon they were heard
returning, and the voices grew distinct as their forms came
out of the gloom. By the fire they wheeled again, and
Babalatchi caught a few words. Willems was saying——

" I have been at sea with him many years when young.
I have used my knowledge to observe the way into the river
when coming in, this time."

Abdulla assented in general terms.

" In the variety of knowledge there is safety," he said ;
and then they passed out of earshot.

Babalatchi ran to the tree and took up his position in the
solid blackness under its branches, leaning against the trunk.
There he was about midway between the fire and the other
limit of the two men's walk. They passed him close. Abdulla slim, very straight, his head high, and his hands hanging
before him and twisting mechanically the string of beads ;
Willems tall, broad, looking bigger and stronger in contrast to
the slight white figure by the side of which he strolled carelessly,
taking one step to the other's two ; his big arms in constan

motion as he gesticulated vehemently, bending forward to look Abdulla in the face.

They passed and repassed close to Babalatchi some half a dozen times, and, whenever they were between him and the fire, he could see them plain enough. Sometimes they would stop short, Willems speaking emphatically, Abdulla listening with rigid attention, then, when the other had ceased, bending his head slightly as if consenting to some demand, or admitting some statement. Now and then Babalatchi caught a word here and there, a fragment of a sentence, a loud exclamation. Impelled by curiosity he crept to the very edge of the black shadow under the tree. They were nearing him, and he heard Willems say—

"You will pay that money as soon as I come on board. That I must have."

He could not catch Abdulla's reply. When they went past again, Willems was saying——

"My life is in your hand anyway. The boat that brings me on board your ship shall take the money to Omar. You must have it ready in a sealed bag."

Again they were out of hearing, but instead of coming back they stopped by the fire facing each other. Willems moved his arm, shook his hand on high, talking all the time, then brought it down jerkily—stamped his foot. A short period of immobility ensued. Babalatchi, gazing intently, saw Abdulla's lips move almost imperceptibly. Suddenly Willems seized the Arab's passive hand and shook it. Babalatchi drew the long breath of relieved suspense. The conference was over. All well, apparently.

He ventured now to approach the two men, who saw him and waited in silence. Willems had retired within himself already, and wore a look of grim indifference. Abdulla moved away a step or two. Babalatchi looked at him inquisitively.

"I go now," said Abdulla, "and shall wait for you outside the river, Tuan Willems, till the second sunset. You have only one word, I know."

"Only one word," repeated Willems.

K

Abdulla and Babalatchi walked together down the enclosure, leaving the white man alone by the fire. The two
Arabs who had come with Abdulla preceded them and passed
at once through the little gate into the light and the murmur
of voices of the principal courtyard, but Babalatchi and
Abdulla stopped on this side of it. Abdulla said——

"It is well. We have spoken of many things. He
consents."

"When?" asked Babalatchi, eagerly.

"On the second day from this. I have promised everything. I mean to keep much."

"Your hand is always open, O Most Generous amongst
Believers! You will not forget your servant who called you
here. Have I not spoken the truth? She has made roast
meat of his heart."

With a horizontal sweep of his arm Abdulla seemed to
push away that last statement, and said slowly, with much
meaning——

"He must be perfectly safe; do you understand?
Perfectly safe—as if he was amongst his own people—
till . . ."

"Till when?" whispered Babalatchi.

"Till I speak," said Abdulla. "As to Omar." He
hesitated for a moment, then went on very low: "He is
very old."

"Haï—ya! Old and sick," murmured Babalatchi, with
sudden melancholy.

"He wanted me to kill that white man. He begged me
to have him killed at once," said Abdulla, contemptuously,
moving again towards the gate.

"He is impatient, like those who feel death near them,"
exclaimed Babalatchi, apologetically.

"Omar shall dwell with me," went on Abdulla, "when
. . . But no matter. Remember! The white man must
be safe."

"He lives in your shadow," answered Babalatchi, solemnly.
"It is enough!" He touched his forehead and fell back
to let Abdulla go first.

And now they are back in the courtyard wherefrom, at their appearance, listlessness vanishes, and all the faces become alert and interested once more. Lakamba approaches his guest, but looks at Babalatchi, who reassures him by a confident nod. Lakamba clumsily attempts a smile, and looking, with natural and ineradicable sulkiness, from under his eyebrows at the man whom he wants to honour, asks whether he would condescend to visit the place of sitting down and take food. Or perhaps he would prefer to give himself up to repose? The house is his, and what is in it, and those many men that stand afar watching the interview are his. Syed Abdulla presses his host's hand to his breast, and informs him in a confidential murmur that his habits are ascetic and his temperament inclines to melancholy. No rest; no food; no use whatever for those many men who are his. Syed Abdulla is impatient to be gone. Lakamba is sorrowful but polite, in his hesitating, gloomy way. Tuan Abdulla must have fresh boatmen, and many, to shorten the dark and fatiguing road. Haï—ya! There! Boats!

By the riverside indistinct forms leap into a noisy and disorderly activity. There are cries, orders, banter, abuse. Torches blaze sending out much more smoke than light, and in their red glare Babalatchi comes up to say that the boats are ready.

Through that lurid glare Syed Abdulla, in his long white gown, seems to glide fantastically, like a dignified apparition attended by two inferior shades, and stands for a moment at the landing-place to take leave of his host and ally—whom he loves. Syed Abdulla says so distinctly before embarking, and takes his seat in the middle of the canoe and under a small canopy of blue calico stretched on four sticks. Before and behind Syed Abdulla, the men squatting by the gunwales hold high the blades of their paddles in readiness for a dip, all together. Ready? Not yet. Hold on all! Syed Abdulla speaks again, while Lakamba and Babalatchi stand close on the bank to hear his words. His words are encouraging. Before the sun rises for the second time they shall meet, and Syed Abdulla's ship shall float on the waters of this river—at last ! Lakamba and Babalatchi have no doubt—if Allah wills. They are in the hands of the Compassionate. No doubt. And so is Syed Abdulla, the great trader who does not know what the word failure means ; and so is the white man—the smartest business man in the islands—who is lying now by Omar's fire with his head on Aïssa's lap, while Syed Abdulla flies down the muddy river with current and paddles between the sombre walls of the sleeping forest ; on his way to the clear and open sea where the " Lord of the Isles " (formerly of Greenock, but condemned, sold, and registered now as of Penang) waits for its owner, and swings erratically at anchor in the currents of the capricious tide, under the crumbling red cliffs of Tanjong Mirrah.

For some time Lakamba, Sahamin, and Bahassoen looked silently into the humid darkness which had swallowed the big canoe that carried Abdulla and his unvarying good fortune. Then the two guests broke into a talk expressive of their joyful anticipations. The venerable Sahamin, as became his advanced age, found his delight in speculation as to the activities of a rather remote future. He would buy praus, he would send expeditions up the river, he would enlarge his trade, and, backed by Abdulla's capital, he would grow rich in a very few years. Very few. Meantime it would be a good thing to interview Almayer to-morrow and, profiting by the last day of the hated man's prosperity, obtain some goods from him on credit. Sahamin thought it could be done by skilful wheedling. After all, that son of Satan was a fool, and the thing was worth doing, because the coming revolution would wipe all debts out. Sahamin did not mind imparting that idea to his companions, with much senile chuckling, while they strolled together from the riverside towards the residence. The bull-necked Lakamba, listening with pouted lips without the sign of a smile, without a gleam in his dull, bloodshot eyes, shuffled slowly across the court-yard between his two guests. But suddenly Bahassoen broke in upon the old man's prattle with the generous enthusiasm of his youth. . . . Trading was very good. But was the change that would make them happy effected yet? The white man should be despoiled with a strong hand! . . . He grew excited, spoke very loud, and his further discourse, delivered with his hand on the hilt of his sword, dealt incoherently with the honourable topics of throat-cutting, fire-raising, and with the far-famed valour of his ancestors.

Babalatchi remained behind, alone with the greatness of his conceptions. The sagacious statesman of Sambir sent a scornful glance after his noble protector and his noble protector's friends, and then stood meditating about that future which to the others seemed so assured. Not so to Babalatchi, who paid the penalty of his wisdom by a vague sense of insecurity that kept sleep at arm's length from his tired body. When he thought at last of leaving the water-side, it was only to strike a path for himself and to creep along the fences, avoiding the middle of the courtyard where small fires glimmered and winked as though the sinister darkness there had reflected the stars of the serene heaven. He slunk past the wicket-gate of Omar's enclosure, and crept on patiently along the light bamboo palisade till he was stopped by the angle where it joined the heavy stockade of Lakamba's private ground. Standing there, he could look over the fence and see Omar's hut and the fire before its door. He could also see the shadow of two human beings sitting between him and the red glow. A man and a woman. The sight seemed to inspire the careworn sage with a frivolous desire to sing. It could hardly be called a song; it was more in the nature of a recitative without any rhythm, delivered rapidly but distinctly in a croaking and unsteady voice; and if Babalatchi considered it a song, then it was a song with a purpose and, perhaps for that reason, artistically defective. It had all the imperfections of unskilful improvisation and its subject was gruesome. It told a tale of shipwreck and of thirst, and of one brother killing another for the sake of a gourd of water. A repulsive story which might have had a purpose but possessed no moral whatever. Yet it must have pleased Babalatchi, for he repeated it twice, the second time even in louder tones than at first, causing a disturbance amongst the white rice-birds and the wild fruit-pigeons which roosted on the boughs of the big tree growing in Omar's compound. There was in the thick foliage above the singer's head a confused beating of wings, sleepy remarks in bird-language, a sharp stir of leaves. The forms by the fire moved; the shadow of the woman altered its shape, and Babalatchi's song was cut short abruptly by a fit of soft and persistent coughing. He did not try to resume his efforts after that interruption, but went away stealthily, to seek—if not sleep—then, at least, repose.

## VI

As soon as Abdulla and his companions had left the enclosure, Aïssa approached Willems and stood by his side. He took no notice of her expectant attitude till she touched him gently, when he turned furiously upon her and, tearing off her face-veil, trampled upon it as though it had been a mortal enemy. She looked at him with the faint smile of patient curiosity, with the puzzled interest of ignorance, watching the running of a complicated piece of machinery. After he had exhausted his rage, he stood again severe and unbending looking down at the fire, but the touch of her fingers at the nape of his neck effaced instantly the hard lines round his mouth; his eyes wavered uneasily; his lips trembled slightly. Starting with the unresisting rapidity of a particle of iron—which, quiescent one moment, leaps in the next to a powerful magnet—he moved forward, caught her in his arms and pressed her violently to his breast. He released her as suddenly, and she stumbled a little, stepped back, breathed quickly through her parted lips, and said in a tone of pleased reproof——

"O Fool-man! And if you had killed me in your strong arms what would you have done?"

"You want to live . . . and to run away from me again," he said gently. "Tell me—do you?"

She moved towards him with very short steps, her head a little on one side, hands on hips, with a slight balancing of her body: an approach more tantalising than an escape. He looked on, eager—charmed. She spoke jestingly.

"What am I to say to a man who has been away three days from me? Three!" she repeated, holding up playfully three fingers before Willems' eyes. He snatched at the hand, but she was on her guard and whisked it behind her back.

"No!" she said. "I cannot be caught. But I will come. I am coming myself because I like. Do not move. Do not touch me with your mighty hands, O child!"

As she spoke she made a step nearer, then another. Willems did not stir. Pressing against him she stood on tiptoe to look into his eyes, and her own seemed to grow bigger, glistening and tender, appealing and promising. With that look she drew the man's soul away from him through his immobile pupils, and from Willems' features the spark of reason vanished under her gaze and was replaced by an appearance of physical well-being, an ecstasy of the senses which had taken possession of his rigid body; an ecstasy that drove out regrets, hesitation and doubt, and proclaimed its terrible work by an appalling aspect of idiotic beatitude. He never stirred a limb, hardly breathed, but stood in stiff immobility, absorbing the delight of her close contact by every pore.

"Closer! Closer!" he murmured.

Slowly she raised her arms, put them over his shoulders, and clasping her hands at the back of his neck, swung off the full length of her arms. Her head fell back, the eyelids dropped slightly, and her thick hair hung straight down: a mass of ebony touched by the red gleams of the fire. He stood unyielding under the strain, as solid and motionless as one of the big trees of the surrounding forests; and his eyes looked at the modelling of her chin, at the outline of her neck, at the swelling lines of her bosom, with the famished and concentrated expression of a starving man looking at food. She drew herself up to him and rubbed her head against his cheek slowly and gently. He sighed. She, with her hands still on his shoulders, glanced up at the placid stars and said——

"The night is half gone. We shall finish it by this fire. By this fire you shall tell me all: your words and Syed Abdulla's words; and listening to you I shall forget the three days—because I am good. Tell me—am I good?"

He said "Yes" dreamily, and she ran off towards the big house.

When she came back, balancing a roll of fine mats on her head, he had replenished the fire and was ready to help her in arranging a couch on the side of it nearest to the hut. She sank down with a quick but gracefully controlled movement, and he threw himself full length with impatient haste, as if he wished to forestall somebody. She took his head on her knees, and when he felt her hands touching his face, her fingers playing with his hair, he had an impression of being taken possession of; he experienced a sense of peace, of rest, of happiness, and of soothing delight. His hands strayed upwards about her neck, and he drew her down so as to have her face above his. Then he whispered—"I wish I could die like this—now!" She looked at him with her big sombre eyes, in which there was no responsive light. His thought was so remote from her understanding that she let the words pass by unnoticed, like the breath of the wind, like the flight of a cloud. Woman though she was, she could not comprehend, in her simplicity, the tremendous compliment of that speech, that whisper of deadly happiness, so sincere, so spontaneous, coming so straight from the heart—like every corruption. It was the voice of madness, of a delirious peace, of happiness that is infamous, cowardly, and so exquisite that the debased mind refuses to contemplate its termination: for to the victims of such happiness the moment of its ceasing is the beginning afresh of that torture which is its price.

With her brows slightly knitted in the determined preoccupation of her own desires, she said——

" Now tell me all. All the words spoken between you and
Syed Abdulla."

Tell what? What words? Her voice recalled back the
consciousness that had departed under her touch, and he
became aware of the passing minutes every one of which was
like a reproach ; of those minutes that falling, slow, reluctant,
irresistible into the past, marked his footsteps on the way to
perdition. Not that he had any conviction about it, any
notion of the possible ending on that painful road. It was
an indistinct feeling, a threat of suffering like the confused
warning of coming disease, an inarticulate monition of evil
made up of fear and pleasure, of resignation and of revolt.
He was ashamed of his state of mind. After all, what was he
afraid of? Were those scruples? Why that hesitation to
think, to speak of what he intended doing? Scruples were
for imbeciles. His clear duty was to make himself happy.
Did he ever take an oath of fidelity to Lingard? No.
Well then—he would not let any interest of that old fool
stand between Willems and Willems' happiness. Happiness? Was he not, perchance, on a false track? Happiness
meant money. Much money. At least he had always
thought so till he had experienced those new sensations
which . . .

Aïssa's question, repeated impatiently, interrupted his
musings, and looking up at her face shining above him in the
dim light of the fire he stretched his limbs luxuriously, and
obedient to her desire, he spoke slowly and hardly above his
breath. She, with her head close to his lips, listened absorbed,
interested, in attentive immobility. The many noises of the
great courtyard were hushed up gradually by the sleep that
stilled all voices and closed all eyes. Then somebody droned
out a song with a nasal drawl at the end of every verse. He
stirred. She put her hand suddenly on his lips and sat
upright. There was a feeble coughing, a rustle of leaves,
and then a complete silence took possession of the land ;
a silence cold, mournful, profound ; more like death than

K 2

peace; more hard to bear than the fiercest tumult. As soon as she removed her hand he hastened to speak, so insupportable to him was that stillness perfect and absolute in which his thoughts seemed to ring with the loudness of shouts.

" Who was there making that noise ! " he asked.

" I do not know. He is gone now," she answered hastily. " Tell me, you will not return to your people; not without me ? Not with me. Do you promise ? "

" I have promised already. I have no people of my own. Have I not told you, that you are everybody to me ? "

" Ah, yes," she said slowly, " but I like to hear you say that again—every day, and every night, whenever I ask; and never to be angry because I ask. I am afraid of white women who are shameless and have fierce eyes." She scanned his features close for a moment and added : " Are they very beautiful ? They must be."

" I do not know," he whispered thoughtfully. " And if I ever did know, looking at you I have forgotten."

" Forgotten ! And for three days and two nights you have forgotten me also ! Why ? Why were you angry with me when I spoke at first of Tuan Abdulla in the days when we lived beside the brook ? You remembered somebody then. Somebody in the land whence you come. Your tongue is false. You are white indeed, and your heart is full of deception. I know it. And yet I cannot help believing you when you talk of your love for me. But I am afraid ! "

He felt flattered and annoyed by her vehemence, and said——

" Well, I am with you now. I did come back. And it was you that went away."

" When you have helped Abdulla against the Rajah Laut, who is the first of white men, I shall not be afraid any more," she whispered.

" You must believe what I say when I tell you that there never was another woman; that there is nothing for me to regret, and nothing but my enemies to remember."

"Where do you come from?" she said, impulsive and inconsequent, in a passionate whisper. "What is that land beyond the great sea from which you come? A land of lies and of evil from which nothing but misfortune ever comes to us—who are not white. Did you not at first ask me to go there with you? That is why I went away."

"I shall never ask you again."

"And there is no woman waiting for you there?"

"No!" said Willems, firmly.

She bent over him. Her lips hovered above his face and her long hair brushed his cheeks.

"You taught me the love of your people which is of the Devil," she murmured, and bending still lower, she said faintly, "Like this?"

"Yes, like this!" he answered very low, in a voice that trembled slightly with eagerness; and she pressed suddenly her lips to his while he closed his eyes in an ecstasy of delight.

There was a long interval of silence. She stroked his head with gentle touches, and he lay dreamily, perfectly happy but for the annoyance of an indistinct vision of a well-known figure; a man going away from him and diminishing in a long perspective of fantastic trees, whose every leaf was an eye looking after that man, who walked away growing smaller, but never getting out of sight for all his steady progress. He felt a desire to see him vanish, a hurried impatience of his disappearance, and he watched for it with a careful and irksome effort. There was something familiar about that figure. Why! Himself! He gave a sudden start and opened his eyes, quivering with the emotion of that quick return from so far, of finding himself back by the fire with the rapidity of a flash of lightning. It had been half a dream; he had slumbered in her arms for a few seconds. Only the beginning of a dream—nothing more. But it was some time before he recovered from the shock of seeing himself go away so deliberately, so definitely, so unguardedly; and going away—where? Now, if he had not woke up in time he would never have come back again from there; from whatever place he was going to. He felt indignant.

It was like an evasion, like a prisoner breaking his parole—that thing slinking off stealthily while he slept. He was very indignant, and was also astonished at the absurdity of his own emotions.

She felt him tremble, and murmuring tender words, pressed his head to her breast. Again he felt very peaceful with a peace that was as complete as the silence round them. He muttered——

"You are tired, Aïssa."

She answered so low that it was like a sigh shaped into faint words.

"I shall watch your sleep, O child!"

He lay very quiet, and listened to the beating of her heart. That sound, light, rapid, persistent and steady; her very life beating against his cheek, gave him a clear perception of secure ownership, strengthened his belief in his possession of that human being, was like an assurance of the vague felicity of the future. There were no regrets, no doubts, no hesitation now. Had there ever been? All that seemed far away, ages ago—as unreal and pale as the fading memory of some delirium. All the anguish, suffering, strife of the past days; the humiliation and anger of his downfall; all that was an infamous nightmare, a thing born in sleep to be forgotten and leave no trace—and true life was this: this dreamy immobility with his head against her heart that beat so steadily.

He was broad awake now, with that tingling wakefulness of the tired body which succeeds to the few refreshing seconds of irresistible sleep, and his wide-open eyes looked absently at the doorway of Omar's hut. The reed walls glistened in the light of the fire, the smoke of which, thin and blue, drifted slanting in a succession of rings and spirals across the doorway, whose empty blackness seemed to him impenetrable and enigmatical like a curtain hiding vast spaces full of unexpected surprises. This was only his fancy, but it was absorbing enough to make him accept the sudden appearance of a head, coming out of the gloom, as part of his idle fantasy or as the beginning of another short dream, of another vagary of his overtired brain. A face with drooping eyelids, old, thin, and yellow, above the scattered white of a long beard that touched the earth. A head without a body, only a foot above the ground, turning slightly from side to side on the edge of the circle of light as if to catch the radiating heat of the fire on either cheek in succession. He watched it in passive amazement, growing distinct, as if coming nearer to him, and the confused outlines of a body crawling on all fours come out, creeping inch by inch towards the fire, with a silent and all but imperceptible movement. He was astounded at the appearance of that blind head dragging that crippled body behind, without a sound, without a change in the composure of the sightless face, which was plain one second, blurred the next in the play of the light that drew it to itself steadily. A mute face with a kriss between its lips. This was no dream. Omar's face. But why? What was he after?

He was too indolent in the happy languor of the moment to answer the question. It darted through his brain and passed out, leaving him free to listen again to the beating of her heart; to that precious and delicate sound which filled the quiet immensity of the night. Glancing upwards he saw the motionless head of the woman looking down at him in a tender gleam of liquid white between the long eyelashes, whose shadow rested on the soft curve of her cheek; and under the caress of that look, the uneasy wonder and the obscure fear of that apparition, crouching and creeping in turns towards the fire that was its guide, were lost—were drowned in the quietude of all his senses, as pain is drowned in the flood of drowsy serenity that follows upon a dose of opium.

He altered the position of his head by ever so little, and now could see easily that apparition which he had seen a minute before and had nearly forgotten already. It had moved closer, gliding and noiseless like the shadow of some nightmare, and now it was there, very near, motionless and still as if listening; one hand and one knee advanced; the neck stretched out and the head turned full towards the fire.

He could see the emaciated face, the skin shiny over the prominent bones, the black shadows of the hollow temples and sunken cheeks, and the two patches of blackness over the eyes, over those eyes that were dead and could not see. What was the impulse which drove out this blind cripple into the night to creep and crawl towards that fire? He looked at him, fascinated, but the face, with its shifting lights and shadows, let out nothing, closed and impenetrable like a walled door.

Omar raised himself to a kneeling posture and sank on his heels, with his hands hanging down before him. Willems, looking out of his dreary numbness, could see plainly the kriss between the thin lips, a bar across the face; the handle on one side where the polished wood caught a red gleam from the fire and the thin line of the blade running to a dull black point on the other. He felt an inward shock, which left his body passive in Aïssa's embrace, but filled his breast with a tumult of powerless fear; and he perceived suddenly that it was his own death that was groping towards him; that it was the hate of himself and the hate of her love for him which drove this helpless wreck, of a once brilliant and resolute pirate, to attempt a desperate deed that would be the glorious and supreme consolation of an unhappy old age. And while he looked, paralysed with dread, at the father who had resumed his cautious advance—blind like fate, persistent like destiny—he listened with greedy eagerness to the heart of the daughter beating light, rapid, and steady against his head.

He was in the grip of horrible fear; of a fear whose cold hand robs its victim of all will and of all power; of all wish to escape, to resist, or to move; which destroys hope and despair alike, and holds the empty and useless carcass as if in a vice under the coming stroke. It was not the fear of death—he had faced danger before—it was not even the fear of that particular form of death. It was not the fear of the end, for he knew that the end would not come then. A movement, a leap, a shout would save him from the feeble hand of the blind old man, from that hand that even now was, with cautious sweeps along the ground, feeling for his body in the darkness. It was the unreasoning fear of this glimpse into the unknown things, into those motives, impulses, desires he had ignored, but that had lived in the breasts of despised men, close by his side, and were revealed to him for a second, to be hidden again behind the black mists of doubt and deception. It was not death that frightened him : it was the horror of bewildered life where he could understand nothing and nobody round him ; where he could guide, control, comprehend nothing and no one—not even himself.

He felt a touch on his side. That contact, lighter than the caress of a mother's hand on the cheek of a sleeping child, had for him the force of a crushing blow. Omar had crept close, and now, kneeling above him, held the kriss in one hand while the other skimmed over his jacket up towards his breast in gentle touches ; but the blind face, still turned to the heat of the fire, was set and immovable in its aspect of stony indifference to things it could not hope to see. With an effort Willems took his eyes off the deathlike mask and turned them up to Aïssa's head. She sat motionless as if she had been part of the sleeping earth, then suddenly he saw her big sombre eyes open out wide in a piercing stare and felt the convulsive pressure of her hands pinning his arms along his body. A second dragged itself out, slow and bitter, like a day of mourning ; a second full of regret and grief for that faith in her which took its flight from the shattered ruins of his trust. She was holding him ! She too ! He felt her heart give a great leap, her head slipped down on her knees, he closed his eyes and there was nothing. Nothing ! It was as if she had died ; as though her heart had leaped out into the night, abandoning him, defenceless and alone, in an empty world.

His head struck the ground heavily as she flung him aside in her sudden rush. He lay as if stunned, face up and, daring not to move, did not see the struggle but heard the piercing shriek of mad fear, her low angry words ; another shriek dying out in a moan. When he got up at last he looked at

Aïssa kneeling over her father, he saw her bent back in the effort of holding him down, Omar's contorted limbs, a hand thrown up above her head and her quick movement grasping the wrist. He made an impulsive step forward, but she turned a wild face to him and called out over her shoulder——

"Keep back! Do not come near! Do not . . ."

And he stopped short, his arms hanging lifelessly by his side, as if those words had changed him into stone. She was afraid of his possible violence, but in the unsettling of all his convictions he was struck with the frightful thought that she preferred to kill her father all by herself; and the last stage of their struggle, at which he looked as though a red fog had filled his eyes, loomed up with an unnatural ferocity, with a sinister meaning; like something monstrous and depraved, forcing its complicity upon him under the cover of that awful night. He was horrified and grateful; drawn irresistibly to her—and ready to run away. He could not move at first—then he did not want to stir. He wanted to see what would happen. He saw her lift, with a tremendous effort, the apparently lifeless body into the hut, and remained standing, after they disappeared, with the vivid image in his eyes of that head swaying on her shoulder, the lower jaw hanging down, collapsed, passive, meaningless, like the head of a corpse.

Then after a while he heard her voice speaking inside, harshly, with an agitated abruptness of tone; and in answer there were groans and broken murmurs of exhaustion. She spoke louder. He heard her saying violently—"No! No! Never!"

And again a plaintive murmur of entreaty as of some one begging for a supreme favour with a last breath. Then she said——

"Never! I would sooner strike it into my own heart."

She came out, stood panting for a short moment in the doorway, and then stepped into the firelight. Behind her, through the darkness came the sound of words calling the vengeance of heaven on her head, rising higher, shrill, strained, repeating the curse over and over again—till the voice cracked in a passionate shriek that died out into hoarse muttering, ending with a deep and prolonged sigh. She stood facing Willems, one hand behind her back, the other raised in a gesture compelling attention, and she listened in that attitude till all was still inside the hut. Then she made another step forward and her hand dropped slowly.

"Nothing but misfortune," she whispered, absently, to herself. "Nothing but misfortune to us who are not white." The anger and excitement died out of her face, and she looked straight at Willems with an intense and mournful gaze.

He recovered his senses and his power of speech with a sudden start.

"Aïssa," he exclaimed, and the words broke out through his lips with hurried nervousness. "Aïssa! How can I live here? Trust me. Believe in me. Let us go away from here. Go very far away! Very far; you and I!"

He did not stop to ask himself whether he could escape and how, and where. He was carried away by the flood of hate, disgust and contempt of a white man for that blood which is not his blood, for that race which is not his race; for the brown skins; for the hearts false like the sea, blacker than night. This feeling of repulsion overmastered his reason in a clear conviction of the impossibility for him to live with her people. He urged her passionately to fly with him because out of all that abhorred crowd he wanted this one woman, but wanted her away from them, away from that race of slaves and cut-throats from which she sprang. He wanted her for himself—far from everybody, in some safe and dumb solitude. And as he spoke his anger and contempt rose, his hate became almost fear; and his desire of her grew immense, burning, illogical and merciless; crying to him through all his senses; louder than his hate, stronger than his fear, deeper than his contempt—irresistible and certain like death itself.

Standing at a little distance, just within the light—but on the threshold of that darkness from which she had come—she listened, one hand still behind her back, the other arm stretched out with the hand half open as if to catch the fleeting words that rang around her, passionate, menacing, imploring, but all tinged with the anguish of his suffering, all hurried by the impatience that gnawed his breast. And while she listened she felt like a slowing down of her heart-beats as the meaning of his appeal grew clearer before her indignant eyes, as she saw with rage and pain the edifice of her love, her own work, crumble slowly to pieces, destroyed by that man's fears, by that man's falseness. Her memory recalled the days by the brook when she had listened to other words—to other thoughts—to promises and to pleadings for other things, which came from that man's lips at the bidding of her look or her smile, at the nod of her head, at the whisper of her lips. Was there then in his heart something else than her image, other desires than the desires of her love, other fears than the fear of losing her? How could that be? Had she grown ugly or old in a moment? She was appalled, surprised and angry with the anger of unexpected humilia-tion; and her eyes looked fixedly, sombre and steady, at that man born in the land of violence and of evil wherefrom nothing but misfortune comes to those who are not white. Instead of thinking of her caresses, instead of forgetting all the world in her embrace, he was thinking yet of his people; of that people that steals every land, masters every sea, that knows no mercy and no truth—knows nothing but its own strength. O man of strong arm and of false heart! Go with him to a far country, be lost in the throng of cold eyes and false hearts—lose him there! Never! He was mad—mad with fear; but he should not escape her! She would keep him here a slave and a master; here where he was alone with her; where he must live for her—or die. She had a right to his love which was of her making, to the love that was in him now, while he spoke those words without sense. She must put between him and other white men a barrier of hate. He must not only stay, but he must also keep his promise to Abdulla, the fulfilment of which would make her safe. . . .

"Aïssa, let us go! With you by my side I would attack

them with my naked hands. Or no! To-morrow we shall
be outside, on board Abdulla's ship. You shall come with
me, and then I could . . . If the ship went ashore by some
chance, then we could steal a canoe and escape in the confusion. . . . You are not afraid of the sea . . . of the sea that
would give me freedom . . ."

He was approaching her gradually with extended arms,
while he pleaded ardently in incoherent words that ran
over and tripped each other in the extreme eagerness of his
speech. She stepped back, keeping her distance, her eyes
on his face, watching on it the play of his doubts and of his
hopes with a piercing gaze, that seemed to search out the
innermost recesses of his thought; and it was as if she had
drawn slowly the darkness round her, wrapping herself in
its undulating folds that made her indistinct and vague. He
followed her step by step till at last they both stopped, facing
each other under the big tree of the enclosure. The solitary
exile of the forests, great, motionless and solemn in his
abandonment, left alone by the life of ages that had been
pushed away from him by those pigmies that crept at his
foot, towered high and straight above their heads. He seemed
to look on, dispassionate and imposing, in his lonely greatness,
spreading his branches wide in a gesture of lofty protection,
as if to hide them in the sombre shelter of innumerable
leaves; as if moved by the disdainful compassion of the
strong, by the scornful pity of an aged giant, to screen this
struggle of two human hearts from the cold scrutiny of
glittering stars.

The last cry of his appeal to her mercy rose loud, vibrated
under the sombre canopy, darted among the boughs startling
the white birds that slept wing to wing—and died without an
echo, strangled in the dense mass of unstirring leaves. He
could not see her face, but he heard her sighs and the distracted murmur of indistinct words. Then, as he listened
holding his breath, she exclaimed suddenly——

"Have you heard him? He has cursed me because I love
you. You brought me suffering and strife—and his curse.
And now you want to take me far away where I would lose

you, lose my life; because your love is my life now. What else is there? Do not move," she cried violently, as he stirred a little—"do not speak! Take this! Sleep in peace!"

He saw a shadowy movement of her arm. Something whizzed past and struck the ground behind him, close to the fire. Instinctively he turned round to look at it. A kriss without its sheath lay by the embers; a sinuous dark object, looking like something that had been alive and was now crushed, dead and very inoffensive; a black wavy outline very distinct and still in the dull red glow. Without thinking he moved to pick it up, stooping with the sad and humble movement of a beggar gathering the alms flung into the dust of the roadside. Was this the answer to his pleading, to the hot and living words that came from his heart? Was this the answer thrown at him like an insult, that thing made of wood and iron, insignificant and venomous, fragile and deadly? He held it by the blade and looked at the handle stupidly for a moment before he let it fall again at his feet; and when he turned round he faced only the night:—the night immense, profound and quiet; a sea of darkness in which she had disappeared without leaving a trace.

He moved forward with uncertain steps, putting out both his hands before him with the anguish of a man blinded suddenly.

"Aïssa!" he cried—"come to me at once."

Let him touch her only; speak to her while he held her in his arms, under the gaze of his eyes, close, face to face! In the tenderness of his caress he would melt her obstinacy, destroy her fears, and talking to her the only language common to them both—that speech without words, the language of the senses—he would make her understand, he would obtain her consent to any wish of his. Again he called out, and this time his voice trembled with eagerness and apprehension——

"Aïssa!"

He peered and listened, but saw nothing, heard nothing. After a while the solid blackness seemed to wave before his eyes like a curtain disclosing movements but hiding forms, and he heard light and hurried footsteps, then the short clatter of the gate leading to Lakamba's private enclosure. He sprang forward and brought up against the rough timber in time to hear the words, "Quick! Quick!" and the sound of the wooden bar dropped on the other side, securing the gate. With his arms thrown up, the palms against the paling, he slid down in a heap on the ground.

"Aïssa," he said, pleadingly, pressing his lips to a chink between the stakes. "Aïssa, do you hear me? Come back! I will do what you want, give you all you desire—if I have to set the whole Sambir on fire and put that fire out with blood. Only come back. Now! At once! Are you there? Do you hear me? Aïssa!"

On the other side there were startled whispers of feminine voices; a frightened little laugh suddenly interrupted; some woman's admiring murmur—"This is brave talk!" Then after a short silence Aïssa cried——

"Sleep in peace—for the time of your going is near. Now I am afraid of you. Afraid of your fear. When you return with Tuan Abdulla you shall be great. You will find me here. And there will be nothing but love. Nothing else!—Always!—Till we die!"

He listened to the shuffle of footsteps going away, and staggered to his feet, mute with the excess of his passionate anger against that being so savage and so charming; loathing her, himself, everybody he had ever known; the earth, the sky, the very air he drew into his oppressed chest; loathing it because it made him live, loathing her because she made him suffer. But he could not leave that gate through which she had passed. He wandered a little way off, then swerved round, came back and fell down again by the stockade only to rise suddenly in another attempt to break away from the spell that held him, that brought him back there, dumb, obedient and furious. And under the immobilised gesture of lofty protection in the branches outspread wide above his head, under the high branches where white birds slept wing to wing in the shelter of countless leaves, he tossed like a grain of dust in a whirlwind—sinking and rising—round and round—always near that gate. All through the languid stillness of that night he fought with the impalpable; he fought with the shadows, with the darkness, with the silence. He fought without a sound, striking futile blows, dashing from side to side; obstinate, hopeless, and always beaten back; like a man bewitched within the invisible sweep of a magic circle.

# PART III

## I

"YES! Cat, dog, anything that can scratch or bite; as
long as it is harmful enough and mangy enough. A sick
tiger would make you happy—of all things. A half-dead
tiger that you could weep over and palm upon some poor
devil in your power, to tend and nurse for you. Never
mind the consequences—to the poor devil. Let him be
mangled or eaten up of course! You haven't any pity to
spare for the victims of your infernal charity. Not you!
Your tender heart bleeds only for what is poisonous and
deadly. I curse the day when you set your benevolent
eyes on him. I curse it . . ."

"Now then! Now then!" growled Lingard in his
moustache. Almayer, who had talked himself up to the
choking point, drew a long breath and went on——

"Yes! It has been always so. Always. As far back
as I can remember. Don't you recollect? What about
that half-starved dog you brought on board in Bankok in
your arms by . . .! It went mad next day
and bit the serang. You don't mean to say you have forgotten? The best serang you ever had! You said so
yourself while you were helping us to lash him down to the
chain-cable, just before he died in his fits. Now, didn't
you? Two wives and ever so many children the man left.
That was your doing. . . . And when you went out of
your way and risked your ship to rescue some Chinamen
from a water-logged junk in Formosa Straits, that was also
a clever piece of business. Wasn't it? Those damned

Chinamen rose on you before forty-eight hours. They were cut-throats, those poor fishermen. You knew they were cut-throats before you made up your mind to run down on a lee shore in a gale of wind to save them. A mad trick! If they hadn't been scoundrels—hopeless scoundrels—you would not have put your ship in jeopardy for them, I know. You would not have risked the lives of your crew—that crew you loved so—and your own life. Wasn't that foolish? And, besides, you were not honest. Suppose you had been drowned? I would have been in a pretty mess then, left alone here with that adopted daughter of yours. Your duty was to myself first. I married that girl because you promised to make my fortune. You know you did! And then three months afterwards you go and do that mad trick—for a lot of Chinamen too. Chinamen! You have no morality. I might have been ruined for the sake of those murderous scoundrels that, after all, had to be driven overboard after killing ever so many of your crew—of your beloved crew! Do you call that honest?"

"Well, well!" muttered Lingard, chewing nervously the stump of his cheroot that had gone out and looking at Almayer—who stamped wildly about the verandah—much as a shepherd might look at a pet sheep in his obedient flock turning unexpectedly upon him in enraged revolt. He seemed disconcerted, contemptuously angry, yet somewhat amused; and also a little hurt as if at some bitter jest at his own expense. Almayer stopped suddenly, and crossing his arms on his breast, bent his body forward and went on speaking.

"I might have been left then in an awkward hole—all on account of your absurd disregard for your safety—yet I bore no grudge. I knew your weaknesses. But now—when I think of it! Now we are ruined. Ruined! Ruined! My poor little Nina. Ruined!"

He slapped his thighs smartly, walked with small steps this way and that, seized a chair, planted it with a bang before Lingard, and sat down staring at the old seaman with haggard eyes. Lingard, returning his stare steadily, dived slowly into various pockets, fished out at last a box of matches and proceeded to light his cheroot carefully, rolling it round and round between his lips, without taking his gaze for a moment off the distressed Almayer. Then from behind a cloud of tobacco smoke he said calmly——

"If you had been in trouble as often as I have, my boy, you wouldn't carry on so. I have been ruined more than once. Well, here I am."

"Yes, here you are," interrupted Almayer. "Much good it is to me. Had you been here a month ago it would have been of some use. But now ! . . . You might as well be a thousand miles off."

"You scold like a drunken fish-wife," said Lingard, serenely. He got up and moved slowly to the front rail of the verandah. The floor shook and the whole house vibrated under his heavy step. For a moment he stood with his back to Almayer, looking out on the river and forest of the east bank, then turned round and gazed mildly down upon him.

"It's very lonely this morning here. Hey ? " he said.

Almayer lifted up his head.

"Ah ! you notice it—don't you ? I should think it is lonely ! Yes, Captain Lingard, your day is over in Sambir. Only a month ago this verandah would have been full of people coming to greet you. Fellows would be coming up those steps grinning and salaaming—to you and to me. But our day is over. And not by my fault either. You can't say that. It's all the doing of that pet rascal of yours. Ah ! He is a beauty ! You should have seen him leading that hellish crowd. You would have been proud of your old favourite."

"Smart fellow that," muttered Lingard, thoughtfully.

Almayer jumped up with a shriek.

"And that's all you have to say ! Smart fellow ! O Lord ! "

"Don't make a show of yourself. Sit down. Let's talk quietly. I want to know all about it. So he led ? "

"He was the soul of the whole thing. He piloted Abdulla's

ship in. He ordered everything and everybody," said Almayer, who sat down again, with a resigned air.

"When did it happen—exactly?"

"On the sixteenth I heard the first rumours of Abdulla's ship being in the river; a thing I refused to believe at first. Next day I could not doubt any more. There was a great council held openly in Lakamba's place where almost everybody in Sambir attended. On the eighteenth the *Lord of the Isles* was anchored in Sambir reach, abreast of my house. Let's see. Six weeks to-day, exactly."

"And all that happened like this? All of a sudden. You never heard anything—no warning. Nothing. Never had an idea that something was up? Come! Almayer."

"Heard! Yes, I used to hear something every day. Mostly lies. Is there anything else in Sambir?"

"You might not have believed them," observed Lingard. "In fact you ought not to have believed everything that was told to you as if you had been a green hand on his first voyage."

Almayer moved in his chair uneasily.

"That scoundrel came here one day," he said. "He had been away from the house for a couple of months living with that woman. I only heard about him now and then from Patalolo's people when they came over. Well, one day, about noon, he appeared in this courtyard, as if he had been jerked up from hell—where he belongs."

Lingard took his cheroot out, and, with his mouth full of white smoke that oozed out through his parted lips, listened, attentive. After a short pause Almayer went on, looking at the floor moodily——

"I must say he looked awful. Had a bad bout of the ague probably. The left shore is very unhealthy. Strange that only the breadth of the river . . ."

He dropped off into deep thoughtfulness as if he had forgotten his grievances in a bitter meditation upon the unsanitary condition of the virgin forests on the left bank. Lingard took this opportunity to expel the smoke in a mighty expiration and threw the stump of his cheroot over his shoulder.

"Go on," he said, after a while. "He came to see you . . ."

"But it wasn't unhealthy enough to finish him, worse luck!" went on Almayer, rousing himself, "and, as I said, he turned up here with his brazen impudence. He bullied me, he threatened vaguely. He wanted to scare me, to blackmail me. Me! And, by heaven! he said you would approve. You! Can you conceive such impudence? I couldn't exactly make out what he was driving at. Had I known, I would have approved him. Yes! With a bang on the head. But how could I guess that he knew enough to pilot a ship through the entrance you always said was so difficult. And, after all, that was the only danger. I could deal with anybody here—but when Abdulla came. . . . That barque of his is armed. He carries twelve brass six-pounders, and about thirty men. Desperate beggars. Sumatra men, from Deli and Acheen. Fight all day and ask for more in the evening. That kind."

"I know, I know," said Lingard, impatiently.

"Of course, then, they were cheeky as much as you please after he anchored abreast of our jetty. Willem brought her up himself in the best berth. I could see him from this verandah standing forward, together with the half-caste master. And that woman was there too. Close to him. I heard they took her on board off Lakamba's place. Willems said he would not go higher without her. Stormed and raged. Frightened them, I believe. Abdulla had to interfere. She came off alone in a canoe, and no sooner on deck than she fell at his feet before all hands, embraced his knees, wept, raved, begged his pardon. Why? I wonder. Everybody in Sambir is talking of it. They never heard tell or saw anything like it. I have all this from Ali, who goes about in the settlement and brings me the news. I had better know what is going on—hadn't I? From what I can make out, they—he and that woman—are looked upon as something mysterious—beyond comprehension. Some think them mad. They live alone with an old woman in a house outside Lakamba's campong and are greatly respected—or feared, I should say rather. At least, he is. He is very violent. She knows nobody, sees nobody, will speak to nobody but him. Never leaves him for a moment. It's the talk of the place. There are other rumours. From what I hear I suspect that Lakamba and Abdulla are tired of him. There's also talk of him going away in the *Lord of the Isles*—when she leaves here for the southward—as a kind of Abdulla's agent. At any rate, he must take the ship out. The half-caste is not equal to it as yet."

Lingard, who had listened absorbed till then, began now to walk with measured steps. Almayer ceased talking, and followed him with his eyes as he paced up and down with a quarter-deck swing, tormenting and twisting his long white beard, his face perplexed and thoughtful.

"So he came to you first of all, did he?" asked Lingard, without stopping.

"Yes. I told you so. He did come. Came to extort money, goods—I don't know what else. Wanted to set up as a trader—the swine! I kicked his hat into the courtyard, and he went after it, and that was the last of him till he showed up with Abdulla. How could I know that he could do harm in that way? Or in any way at that! Any local rising I could put down easy with my own men and with Patalolo's help."

"Oh! yes. Patalolo. No good. Eh? Did you try him at all?"

"Didn't I!" exclaimed Almayer. "I went to see him myself on the twelfth. That was four days before Abdulla entered the river. In fact, same day Willems tried to get at me. I did feel a little uneasy then. Patalolo assured me that there was no human being that did not love me in Sambir. Looked as wise as an owl. Told me not to listen to the lies of wicked people from down the river. He was alluding to that man Bulangi, who lives up the sea reach, and who had sent me word that a strange ship was anchored outside—which, of course, I repeated to Patalolo. He would not believe. Kept on mumbling 'No! No! No!'

like an old parrot, his head all of a tremble, all beslobbered with betel-juice. I thought there was something queer about him. Seemed so restless, and as if in a hurry to get rid of me. Well. Next day that one-eyed malefactor who lives with Lakamba—what's his name—Babalatchi, put in an appearance here. Came about mid-day, casually like, and stood there on this verandah chatting about one thing and another. Asking when I expected you, and so on. Then, incidentally, he mentioned that they—his master and himself—were very much bothered by a ferocious white man —my friend—who was hanging about that woman—Omar's daughter. Asked my advice. Very deferential and proper. I told him the white man was not my friend, and that they had better kick him out. Whereupon he went away salaaming, and protesting his friendship and his master's goodwill. Of course I know now the infernal nigger came to spy and to talk over some of my men. Anyway, eight were missing at the evening muster. Then I took alarm. Did not dare to leave my house unguarded. You know what my wife is, don't you? And I did not care to take the child with me— it being late—so I sent a message to Patalolo to say that we ought to consult; that there were rumours and uneasiness in the settlement. Do you know what answer I got?"

Lingard stopped short in his walk before Almayer, who went on, after an impressive pause, with growing animation.

"Ali brought it: 'The Rajah sends a friend's greeting, and does not understand the message.' That was all. Not a word more could Ali get out of him. I could see that Ali was pretty well scared. He hung about, arranging my hammock—one thing and another. Then just before going away he mentioned that the water-gate of the Rajah's place was heavily barred, but that he could see only very few men about the courtyard. Finally he said, 'There is darkness in our Rajah's house, but no sleep. Only darkness and fear and the wailing of women.' Cheerful, wasn't it? It made me feel cold down my back somehow. After Ali slipped away I stood here—by this table, and listened to the shouting and drumming in the settlement. Racket enough for twenty weddings. It was a little past midnight then."

Again Almayer stopped in his narrative with an abrupt shutting of lips, as if he had said all that there was to tell, and Lingard stood staring at him, pensive and silent. A big bluebottle fly flew in recklessly into the cool verandah, and darted with loud buzzing between the two men. Lingard struck at it with his hat. The fly swerved, and Almayer dodged his head out of the way. Then Lingard aimed another ineffectual blow; Almayer jumped up and waved his arms about. The fly buzzed desperately, and the vibration of minute wings sounded in the peace of the early morning like a far-off string orchestra accompanying the hollow, determined stamping of the two men, who, with heads thrown back and arms gyrating on high, or again bending low with infuriated lunges, were intent upon killing the intruder. But suddenly the buzz died out in a thin thrill away in the open space of the courtyard, leaving Lingard and Almayer standing face to face in the fresh silence of the young day, looking very puzzled and idle, their arms hanging uselessly by their sides—like men disheartened by some portentous failure.

" Look at that ! " muttered Lingard. " Got away after all."

" Nuisance," said Almayer in the same tone. " Riverside is overrun with them. This house is badly placed . . . mosquitoes . . . and these big flies . . . last week stung Nina . . . been ill four days . . . poor child. . . . I wonder what such damned things are made for !"

## II

AFTER a long silence, during which Almayer had moved towards the table and sat down, his head between his hands, staring straight before him, Lingard, who had recommenced walking, cleared his throat and said—

" What was it you were saying ? "

" Ah ! Yes ! You should have seen this settlement that night. I don't think anybody went to bed. I walked down to the point, and could see them. They had a big bonfire in the palm grove, and the talk went on there till the morning. When I came back here and sat in the dark verandah in this quiet house I felt so frightfully lonely that I stole in and took the child out of her cot and brought her here into my hammock. If it hadn't been for her I am sure I would have gone mad ; I felt so utterly alone and helpless. Remember, I hadn't heard from you for four months. Didn't know whether you were alive or dead. Patalolo would have nothing to do with me. My own men were deserting me like rats do a sinking hulk. That was a black night for me, Captain Lingard. A black night as I sat here not knowing what would happen next. They were so excited and rowdy that I really feared they would come and burn the house over my head. I went and brought my revolver. Laid it loaded on the table. There were such awful yells now and then. Luckily the child slept through it, and seeing her so pretty and peaceful steadied me somehow. Couldn't believe there was any violence in this world, looking at her lying so quiet and so unconscious of what went on. But it was very hard. Everything was at an end. You must understand that on that night there was no government in Sambir. Nothing to restrain those fellows. Patalolo had collapsed. I was abandoned by my own people, and all that lot could vent their spite on me if they wanted. They know no gratitude. How many times haven't I saved this settlement from starvation. Absolute starvation. Only three months ago I distributed again a lot of rice on credit. There was nothing to eat in this infernal place. They came begging on their knees. There isn't a man in Sambir, big or little, who is not in debt to Lingard & Co. Not one. You ought to be satisfied. You always said that was the right policy for us. Well, I carried it out. Ah! Captain Lingard, a policy like that should be backed by loaded rifles . . ."

"You had them!" exclaimed Lingard in the midst of his promenade, that went on more rapid as Almayer talked : the headlong tramp of a man hurrying on to do something violent. The verandah was full of dust, oppressive and choking, which rose under the old seaman's feet, and made Almayer cough again and again.

"Yes, I had! Twenty. And not a finger to pull a trigger. It's easy to talk," he spluttered, his face very red.

Lingard dropped into a chair, and leaned back with one hand stretched out at length upon the table, the other thrown over the back of his seat. The dust settled, and the sun surging above the forest flooded the verandah with a clear light. Almayer got up and busied himself in lowering the split rattan screens that hung between the columns of the verandah.

"Phew!" said Lingard, "it will be a hot day. That's right, my boy. Keep the sun out. We don't want to be roasted alive here."

Almayer came back, sat down, and spoke very calmly—

"In the morning I went across to see Patalolo. I took the child with me, of course. I found the water-gate barred, and had to walk round through the bushes. Patalolo received me lying on the floor, in the dark, all the shutters closed. I could get nothing out of him but lamentations and groans. He said you must be dead. That Lakamba was coming now with Abdulla's guns to kill everybody. Said he did not mind being killed, as he was an old man, but that the wish of his heart was to make a pilgrimage. He was tired of men's ingratitude—he had no heirs—he wanted to go to Mecca and die there. He would ask Abdulla to let him go. Then he abused Lakamba—between sobs—and you, a little. You prevented him from asking for a flag that would have been respected—he was right there—and now when his enemies were strong he was weak, and you were not there to help him. When I tried to put some heart into him, telling him he had four big guns—you know the brass six-pounders you left here last year—and that I would get powder, and that, perhaps, together we could make head against Lakamba, he simply howled at me. No matter which way he turned—he shrieked—the white men would be the death of him, while he wanted only to be a pilgrim and be at peace. My belief is," added Almayer, after a short pause, and fixing a dull stare upon Lingard, "that the old fool saw this thing coming for a long time, and was not only too frightened to do anything himself, but actually too scared to let you or me know of his suspicions. Another of your particular pets ! You have a lucky hand, I must say ! "

Lingard struck a sudden blow on the table with his clenched hand. There was a sharp crack of splitting wood. Almayer started up violently, then fell back in his chair and looked at the table.

"There ! " he said moodily, "you don't know your own strength. This table is completely ruined. The only table I had been able to save from my wife. By and by I will have to eat squatting on the floor like a native."

Lingard laughed heartily. "Well, then, don't nag at me like a woman at a drunken husband ! " He became very serious after awhile, and added, "If it hadn't been for the loss of the *Flash* I would have been here three months ago, and all would have been well. No use crying over that. Don't you be uneasy, Kaspar. We will have everything ship-shape here in a very short time."

"What ? You don't mean to expel Abdulla out of here by force ! I tell you, you can't."

"Not I ! " exclaimed Lingard. "That's all over, I am afraid. Great pity. They will suffer for it. He will squeeze them. Great pity. Damn it ! I feel so sorry for them that if I had the *Flash* here I would try force.

L

Eh! Why not? However, the poor *Flash* is gone, and there is an end of it. Poor old hooker. Hey, Almayer? You made a voyage or two with me. Wasn't she a sweet craft? Could make her do anything but talk. She was better than a wife to me. Never scolded. Hey? . . . And to think that it should come to this. That I should leave her poor old bones sticking on a reef as though I had been a damn'd fool of a southern-going man who must have half a mile of water under his keel to be safe! Well! well! It's only those who do nothing that make no mistakes, I suppose. But it's hard. Hard."

He nodded his head sadly, with his eyes on the ground. Almayer looked at him with growing indignation.

"Upon my word, you are heartless," he burst out; "perfectly heartless—and selfish. It does not seem to strike you—in all that—that in losing your ship—by your recklessness, I am sure—you ruin me—us, and my little Nina. What's going to become of me and of her? That's what I want to know. You brought me here, made me your partner, and now, when everything is gone to the devil—through your fault, mind you—you talk about your ship . . . ship! You can get another. But here. This trade. That's gone now, thanks to Willems. . . . Your dear Willems!"

"Never you mind about Willems. I will look after him," said Lingard, severely. "And as to the trade . . . I will make your fortune yet, my boy. Never fear. Have you got any cargo for the schooner that brought me here?"

"The shed is full of rattans," answered Almayer, "and I have about eighty tons of guttah in the well. The last lot I ever will have, no doubt," he added, bitterly.

"So, after all, there was no robbery. You've lost nothing actually. Well, then, you must . . . Hallo! What's the matter! . . . Here! . . ."

"Robbery! No!" screamed Almayer, throwing up his hands.

He fell back in the chair and his face became purple. A little white foam appeared on his lips and trickled down his chin, while he lay back, showing the whites of his upturned eyes. When he came to himself he saw Lingard standing over him, with an empty water-chatty in his hand.

"You had a fit of some kind," said the old seaman with much concern. "What is it? You did give me a fright. So very sudden."

Almayer, his hair all wet and stuck to his head, as if he had been diving, sat up and gasped.

"Outrage! A fiendish outrage. I . . ."

Lingard put the chatty on the table and looked at him in attentive silence. Almayer passed his hand over his forehead and went on in an unsteady tone:

"When I remember that, I lose all control," he said. "I told you he anchored Abdulla's ship abreast our jetty, but over to the other shore, near the Rajah's place. The ship was surrounded with boats. From here it looked as if she had been landed on a raft. Every dugout in Sambir was there. Through my glass I could distinguish the faces of people on the poop—Abdulla, Willems, Lakamba—everybody. That old cringing scoundrel Sahamin was there. I could see quite plain. There seemed to be much talk and discussion. Finally I saw a ship's boat lowered. Some Arab got into her, and the boat went towards Patalolo's landing-place. It seems they had been refused admittance—they say. I think myself that the water-gate was not unbarred quick enough to please the exalted messenger. At any rate I saw the boat come back almost directly. I was looking on, rather interested, when I saw Willems and some more go forward—very busy about something there. That woman was also amongst them. Ah, that woman. . . ."

Almayer choked, and seemed on the point of having a relapse, but by a violent effort regained a comparative composure.

"All of a sudden," he continued—"bang! They fired a shot into Patalolo's gate, and before I had time to catch my breath—I was startled, you may believe—they sent another and burst the gate open. Whereupon, I suppose, they thought they had done enough for a while, and probably felt hungry, for a feast began aft. Abdulla sat amongst them like an idol, cross-legged, his hands on his lap. He's too great altogether to eat when others do, but he presided, you see. Willems kept on dodging about forward, aloof from the crowd, and looking at my house through the ship's long glass. I could not resist it. I shook my fist at him."

"Just so," said Lingard, gravely. "That was the thing to do, of course. If you can't fight a man the best thing is to exasperate him."

Almayer waved his hand in a superior manner, and continued, unmoved :

"You may say what you like. You can't realise my feelings. He saw me, and, with his eye still at the small end of the glass, lifted his arm as if answering a hail. I thought my turn to be shot at would come next after Patalolo, so I ran up the Union Jack to the flagstaff in the yard, I had no other protection. There were only three men besides Ali that stuck to me—three cripples, for that matter, too sick to get away. I would have fought singlehanded, I think, I was that angry, but there was the child. What to do with her ? Couldn't send her up the river with the mother. You know I can't trust my wife. I decided to keep very quiet, but to let nobody land on our shore. Private property, that ; under a deed from Patalolo. I was within my right— wasn't I ? The morning was very quiet. After they had a feed on board the barque with Abdulla most of them went home ; only the big people remained. Towards three o'clock Sahamin crossed alone in a small canoe. I went down on our wharf with my gun to speak to him, but didn't let him land. The old hypocrite said Abdulla sent greetings and wished to talk with me on business ; would I come on board ? I said no ; I would not. Told him that Abdulla may write and I would answer, but no interview, neither on board his ship or on shore. I also said that if anybody attempted to land within my fences I would shoot— no matter whom. On that he lifted his hands to heaven, scandalised, and then paddled away pretty smartly—to report, I suppose. An hour or so afterwards I saw Willems land a boat party at the Rajah's. It was very quiet. Not a shot was fired, and there was hardly any shouting. They tumbled those brass guns you presented to Patalolo last year down the bank into the river. It's deep there close to. The channel runs that way, you know. About five, Willems went back on board, and I saw him join Abdulla by the wheel, aft. He talked a lot, swinging his arms about—seemed to explain things—pointed at my house, then down the reach. Finally, just before sunset, they hove upon the cable and dredged the ship down nearly half a mile to the junction of the two branches of the river—where she is now, as you might have seen."

Lingard nodded.

"That evening, after dark—I am informed—Abdulla landed for the first time in Sambir. He was entertained in Sahamin's house. I sent Ali to the settlement for news. He returned about nine, and reported that Patalolo was sitting on Abdulla's left hand before Sahamin's fire. There was a great council. Ali seemed to think that Patalolo was a prisoner, but he was wrong there. They did the trick very neatly. Before midnight everything was arranged as I can make out. Patalolo went back to his demolished stockade, escorted by a dozen boats with torches. It appears he begged Abdulla to let him have a passage in the *Lord of the Isles* to Penang. From there he would go to Mecca. The firing business was alluded to as a mistake. No doubt it was in a sense. Patalolo never meant resisting. So he is going as soon as the ship is ready for sea. He went on board next day with three women and half a dozen fellows as old as himself. By Abdulla's orders he was received with a salute of seven guns, and he has been living on board ever since—five weeks. I doubt whether he will leave the river alive. At any rate he won't live to reach Penang. Lakamba took over all his goods, and gave him a draft on Abdulla's house, payable in Penang. He is bound to die before he gets there. Don't you see!"

He sat silent for awhile in dejected meditation, then went on:

"Of course there were several rows during the night.

Various fellows took the opportunity of the unsettled state of affairs to pay off old scores and settle old grudges. I passed the night in that chair there, dozing uneasily. Now and then there would be a great tumult and yelling which would make me sit up revolver in hand. However, nobody was killed. A few broken heads—that's all. Early in the morning Willems caused them to make a fresh move which I must say surprised me not a little. As soon as there was daylight they busied themselves in setting up a flag-pole on the open space at the other end of the settlement, where Abdulla is having his houses built now. Shortly after sunrise there was a great gathering at the flag-pole. All went there. Willems was standing leaning against the mast, one arm over that woman's shoulders. They had brought an arm-chair for Patalolo, and Lakamba stood on the right hand of the old man, who made a speech. Everybody in Sambir was there: women, slaves, children—everybody! Then Patalolo spoke. He said that by the mercy of the Most High he was going on a Pilgrimage. The dearest wish of his heart was to be accomplished. Then, turning to Lakamba, he begged him to rule justly during his— Patalolo's—absence. There was a bit of play-acting there. Lakamba said he was unworthy of the honourable burden, and Patalolo insisted. Poor old fool! It must have been bitter to him. They made him actually entreat that scoundrel. Fancy a man compelled to beg of a robber to despoil him! But the old Rajah was so frightened. Anyway, he did it, and Lakamba accepted at last. Then Willems made a speech to the crowd. Said that on his way to the west the Rajah—he meant Patalolo—would see the Great White Ruler in Batavia and obtain his protection for Sambir. Meantime, he went on, I, an Orang Blanda and your friend, hoist the flag under the shadow of which there is safety. With that he ran up a Dutch flag to the mast-head. It was made hurriedly, during the night, of cotton stuffs, and, being heavy, hung down the mast, while the crowd stared. Ali told me there was a great sigh of surprise, but not a word was spoken till Lakamba advanced and proclaimed in a loud voice that during all that day everyone passing by the flagstaff must uncover his head and salaam before the emblem."

"But, hang it all!" exclaimed Lingard—"Abdulla is British!"

"Abdulla wasn't there at all—did not go on shore that day. Yet Ali, who has his wits about him, noticed that the space where the crowd stood was under the guns of the *Lord of the Isles.* They had put a coir warp ashore, and gave the barque a cant in the current, so as to bring the broadside to bear on the flagstaff. Clever! Eh? But nobody dreamt of resistance. When they recovered from the surprise there was a little quiet jeering, and Bahassoen abused Lakamba violently till one of Lakamba's men hit him on the head with a staff. Frightful crack, I am told. Then they left off jeering. Meantime Patalolo went away, and Lakamba sat in the chair at the foot of the flagstaff, while the crowd surged around, as if they could not make up their minds to go. Suddenly there was a great noise behind Lakamba's chair. It was that woman, who went for Willems. Ali says she was like a wild beast, but he twisted her wrist and made her grovel in the dust. Nobody knows exactly what it was about. Some say it was about that flag. He carried her off, flung her into a canoe, and went on board Abdulla's ship. After that Sahamin was the first to salaam to the flag. Others followed suit. Before noon everything was quiet in the settlement, and Ali came back and told me all this."

Almayer drew a long breath. Lingard stretched out his legs.

"Go on!" he said.

Almayer seemed to struggle with himself. At last he spluttered out:

"The hardest is to tell yet. The most unheard-of thing! An outrage! A fiendish outrage!"

### III

"Well! Let's know all about it. I can't imagine . . ." began Lingard, after waiting for some time in silence.

"Can't imagine! I should think you couldn't," interrupted Almayer. "Why! . . . You just listen. When Ali came back I felt a little easier in my mind. There was then some semblance of order in Sambir. I had the Union Jack up since the morning and began to feel safer. Some of my men turned up in the afternoon. I did not ask any questions; set them to work as if nothing had happened. Towards the evening—it might have been five or half-past—I was on our jetty with the child when I heard shouts at the far-off end of the settlement. At first I didn't take much notice. By and by Ali came to me and says, ' Master, give me the child, there is much trouble in the settlement.' So I gave him Nina and went in, took my revolver, and passed through the house into the back courtyard. As I came down the steps I saw all the serving girls clear out from the cooking shed, and I heard a big crowd howling on the other side of the dry ditch which is the limit of our ground. Could not see them on account of the fringe of bushes along the ditch, but I knew that crowd was angry and after somebody. As I stood wondering, that Jim-Eng—you know the Chinaman who settled here a couple of years ago ? "

"He was my passenger; I brought him here," exclaimed Lingard. "A first-class Chinaman that."

"Did you? I had forgotten. Well, that Jim-Eng, he burst through the bush and fell into my arms, so to speak. He told me, panting, that they were after him because he wouldn't take off his hat to the flag. He was not so much scared, but he was very angry and indignant. Of course he had to run for it; there were some fifty men after him— Lakamba's friends—but he was full of fight. Said he was an Englishman, and would not take off his hat to any flag but English. I tried to soothe him while the crowd was shouting on the other side of the ditch. I told him he must take one of my canoes and cross the river. Stop on the other side for a couple of days. He wouldn't! Not he. He was English, and he would fight the whole lot. Says he: 'They are only black fellows. We white men,' meaning me and himself, 'can fight everybody in Sambir.' He was mad with passion. The crowd quieted a little, and I thought I could shelter Jim-Eng without much risk, when all of a sudden I heard Willems' voice. He shouted to me in English: 'Let four men enter your compound to get that Chinaman!' I said nothing. Told Jim-Eng to keep quiet too. Then after a while Willems shouts again: 'Don't resist, Almayer. I give you good advice. I am keeping this crowd back. Don't resist them!' That beggar's voice enraged me; I could not help it. I cried to him: 'You are a liar!' and just then Jim-Eng, who had flung off his jacket and had tucked up his trousers ready for a fight; just then that fellow snatches the revolver out of my hand and lets fly at them through the bush. There was a sharp cry—he must have hit somebody—and a great yell, and before I could wink twice they were over the ditch and through the bush and on top of us! Simply rolled over us! There wasn't the slightest chance to resist. I was trampled under foot, Jim-Eng got a dozen gashes about his body, and we were carried half-way up the yard in the first rush. My eyes and mouth were full of dust; I was on my back with three or four fellows sitting on me. I could hear Jim-Eng trying to shout curses not very far from me. Now and then they would throttle him and he would gurgle. I could hardly breathe myself with two heavy fellows on my chest. Willems came up running and ordered them to raise me, but to keep good hold. They led me into the verandah. I looked round, but did not see either Ali or the child. Felt easier. Struggled a little. . . . Oh, my God!"

Almayer's face was distorted with a passing spasm of rage. Lingard moved in his chair slightly. Almayer went on after a short pause:

"They held me, shouting threats in my face. Willems

L 2

took down my hammock and threw it to them. He pulled out the drawer of this table, and found there a palm and needle and some sail-twine. We were making awnings for your brig, as you had asked me last voyage before you left. He knew, of course, where to look for what he wanted. By his orders they laid me out on the floor, wrapped me in my hammock, and he started to stitch me in, as if I had been a corpse, beginning at the feet. While he worked he laughed wickedly. I called him all the names I could think of. He told them to put their dirty paws over my mouth and nose. I was nearly choked. Whenever I moved they punched me in the ribs. He went on taking fresh needle-fuls as he wanted them, and working steadily. Sewed me up to my throat. Then he rose, saying, ' That will do ; let go.' That woman had been standing by ; they must have been reconciled. She clapped her hands. I lay on the floor like a bale of goods while he stared at me, and the woman shrieked with delight. Like a bale of goods ! There was a grin on every face, and the verandah was full of them. I wished myself dead—'pon my word, Captain Lingard, I did ! I do now whenever I think of it ! "

Lingard's face expressed a sympathetic indignation, but it brought no comfort to Almayer, who dropped his head upon his arms on the table, and spoke in that position in an indistinct and muffled voice, without looking up.

" Finally, by his directions, they flung me into the big rocking-chair. I was sewed in so tight that I was stiff like a piece of wood. He was giving orders in a very loud voice, and that man Babalatchi saw that they were executed. They obeyed him implicitly. Meantime I lay there in the chair like a log, and that woman capered before me and made faces ; snapped her fingers before my nose. Women are bad !—ain't they ? I never saw her before, as far as I know. Never done anything to her. Yet she was perfectly fiendish. Can you understand it ? Now and then she would leave me alone to hang round his neck for awhile, and then she would return before my chair and begin her exercises again. He looked on, indulgent. The perspiration

ran down my face, got into my eyes—my arms were sewn in.
I was blinded half the time; at times I could see better.
She drags him before my chair. 'I am like white women,'
she says, her arms round his neck. You should have seen
the faces of the fellows in the verandah! They were scandalised and ashamed of themselves to see her behaviour. Suddenly she asks him, alluding to me: 'When are you going
to kill him?' Imagine how I felt. I must have swooned;
I don't remember exactly. I fancy there was a row; he
was angry. When I got my wits again he was sitting close
to me, and she was gone. I understood he sent her to my
wife, who was hiding in the back room and never came out
during this affair. Willems says to me—I fancy I can hear
his voice, hoarse and dull—he says to me: 'Not a hair of
your head shall be touched.' I made no sound. Then he
goes on: 'Please remark that the flag you have hoisted—
which, by the by, is not yours—has been respected. Tell
Captain Lingard so when you do see him. But,' he says,
'you first fired at the crowd.' 'You are a liar, you black-
guard!' I shouted. He winced, I am sure. It hurt him
to see I was not frightened. 'Anyways,' he says, 'a shot
had been fired out of your compound and a man was hit.
Still, all your property shall be respected on account of the
Union Jack. Moreover, I have no quarrel with Captain
Lingard, who is the senior partner in this business. As to
you,' he continued, 'you will not forget this day—not if
you live to be a hundred years old—or I don't know your
nature. You will keep the bitter taste of this humiliation
to the last day of your life, and so your kindness to me shall
be repaid. I shall remove all the powder you have. This
coast is under the protection of the Netherlands, and you
have no right to have any powder. There are the Governor's
Orders in Council to that effect, and you know it. Tell me
where the key of the small storehouse is?' I said not a
word, and he waited a little, then rose, saying: 'It's your
own fault if there is any damage done.' He ordered Babalatchi to have the lock of the office-room forced, and went in—
rummaged amongst my drawers—could not find the key.

Then that woman Aïssa asked my wife, and she gave them the key. After awhile they tumbled every barrel into the river. Eighty-three hundredweight! He superintended himself, and saw every barrel roll into the water. There were mutterings. Babalatchi was angry and tried to expostulate, but he gave him a good shaking. I must say he was perfectly fearless with those fellows. Then he came back to the verandah, sat down by me again, and says : ' We found your man Ali with your little daughter hiding in the bushes up the river. We brought them in. They are perfectly safe, of course. Let me congratulate you, Almayer, upon the cleverness of your child. She recognised me at once, and cried " pig " as naturally as you would yourself. Circumstances alter feelings. You should have seen how frightened your man Ali was. Clapped his hands over her mouth. I think you spoil her, Almayer. But I am not angry. Really, you look so ridiculous in this chair that I can't feel angry.' I made a frantic effort to burst out of my hammock to get at that scoundrel's throat, but I only fell off and upset the chair over myself. He laughed and said only : ' I leave you half of your revolver cartridges and take half myself ; they will fit mine. We are both white men, and should back each other up. I may want them.' I shouted at him from under the chair : ' You are a thief,' but he never looked, and went away, one hand round that woman's waist, the other on Babalatchi's shoulder, to whom he was talking— laying down the law about something or other. In less than five minutes there was nobody inside our fences. After awhile Ali came to look for me and cut me free. I haven't seen Willems since—nor anybody else for that matter. I have been left alone. I offered sixty dollars to the man who had been wounded, which were accepted. They released Jim-Eng the next day, when the flag had been hauled down. He sent six cases of opium to me for safe keeping but has not left his house. I think he is safe enough now. Everything is very quiet."

Towards the end of his narrative Almayer lifted his head off the table, and now sat back in his chair and stared at the bamboo rafters of the roof above him. Lingard lolled in his seat with his legs stretched out. In the peaceful gloom of the verandah, with its lowered screens, they heard faint noises from the world outside in the blazing sunshine : a hail on the river, the answer from the shore, the creak of a pulley ; sounds short, interrupted, as if lost suddenly in the brilliance of noonday. Lingard got up slowly, walked to the front rail, and holding one of the screens aside, looked out in silence. Over the water and the empty courtyard came a distinct voice from a small schooner anchored abreast of the Lingard jetty.

"Serang ! Take a pull at the main peak halyards. This gaff is down on the boom."

There was a shrill pipe dying in long-drawn cadence, the song of the men swinging on the rope. The voice said sharply : "That will do !" Another voice—the serang's probably—shouted : "Ikat !" and as Lingard dropped the blind and turned away all was silent again, as if there had been nothing on the other side of the swaying screen ; nothing but the light, brilliant, crude, heavy, lying on a dead land like a pall of fire. Lingard sat down again, facing Almayer, his elbow on the table, in a thoughtful attitude.

"Nice little schooner," muttered Almayer, wearily. "Did you buy her ? "

"No," answered Lingard. "After I lost the *Flash* we got to Palembang in our boats. I chartered her there, for six months. From young Ford, you know. Belongs to him. He wanted a spell ashore, so I took charge myself. Of course all Ford's people on board. Strangers to me. I had to go to Singapore about the insurance ; then I went to Macassar, of course. Had long passages. No wind. It was like a curse on me. I had lots of trouble with old Hudig. That delayed me much."

"Ah ! Hudig ! Why with Hudig ? " asked Almayer, in a perfunctory manner.

"Oh ! about a . . . a woman," mumbled Lingard.

Almayer looked at him with languid surprise. The old seaman had twisted his white beard into a point, and now was busy giving his moustaches a fierce curl. His little red eyes—those eyes that had smarted under the salt sprays of every sea, that had looked unwinking to windward in the gales of all latitudes—now glared at Almayer from behind the lowered eyebrows like a pair of frightened wild beasts crouching in a bush.

" Extraordinary ! So like you ! What can you have to do with Hudig's women ? The old sinner ! " said Almayer, negligently.

" What are you talking about ! Wife of a friend of . . . I mean of a man I know. . . ."

" Still, I don't see . . ." interjected Almayer carelessly.

" Of a man you know too. Well. Very well."

" I knew so many men before you made me bury myself in this hole ! " growled Almayer, unamiably. " If she had anything to do with Hudig—that wife—then she can't be up to much. I would be sorry for the man," added Almayer, brightening up with the recollection of the scandalous tittle-tattle of the past, when he was a young man in the second capital of the Islands—and so well informed, so well informed. He laughed. Lingard's frown deepened.

" Don't talk foolish ! It's Willems' wife."

Almayer grasped the sides of his seat, his eyes and mouth opened wide.

" What ? Why ! " he exclaimed, bewildered.

" Willems'—wife," repeated Lingard distinctly. " You ain't deaf, are you ? The wife of Willems. Just so. As to why ! There was a promise. And I did not know what had happened here."

" What is it ? You've been giving her money, I bet," cried Almayer.

" Well, no ! " said Lingard, deliberately. " Although I suppose I shall have to . . ."

Almayer groaned.

" The fact is," went on Lingard, speaking slowly and steadily, " the fact is that I have . . . I have brought her here. Here. To Sambir."

" In heaven's name ! why ? " shouted Almayer, jumping

up. The chair tilted and fell slowly over. He raised his clasped hands above his head and brought them down jerkily, separating his fingers with an effort, as if tearing them apart. Lingard nodded, quickly, several times.

"I have. Awkward. Hey?" he said, with a puzzled look upwards.

"Upon my word," said Almayer, tearfully. "I can't understand you at all. What will you do next? Willems' wife!"

"Wife and child. Small boy, you know. They are on board the schooner."

Almayer looked at Lingard with sudden suspicion, then turning away busied himself in picking up the chair, sat down in it, turning his back upon the old seaman, and tried to whistle, but gave it up directly. Lingard went on—

"Fact is, the fellow got into trouble with Hudig. Worked upon my feelings. I promised to arrange matters. I did. With much trouble. Hudig was angry with her for wishing to join her husband. Unprincipled old fellow. You know she is his daughter. Well, I said I would see her through it all right; help Willems to a fresh start and so on. I spoke to Craig in Palembang. He is getting on in years, and wanted a manager or partner. I promised to guarantee Willems' good behaviour. We settled all that. Craig is an old crony of mine. Been shipmates in the forties. He's waiting for him now. A pretty mess! What do you think?"

Almayer shrugged his shoulders.

"That woman broke with Hudig on my assurance that all would be well," went on Lingard, with growing dismay. "She did. Proper thing, of course. Wife, husband . . . together . . . as it should be. . . . Smart fellow. . . . Impossible scoundrel. . . . Jolly old go! Oh! damn!"

Almayer laughed spitefully.

"How delighted he will be," he said, softly. "You will make two people happy. Two at least!" He laughed again, while Lingard looked at his shaking shoulders in consternation.

"I am jammed on a lee shore this time, if ever I was," muttered Lingard.

"Send her back quick," suggested Almayer, stifling another laugh.

"What are you sniggering at?" growled Lingard, angrily. "I'll work it out all clear yet. Meantime you must receive her into this house."

"My house!" cried Almayer, turning round.

"It's mine too—a little—isn't it?" said Lingard. "Don't argue," he shouted, as Almayer opened his mouth. "Obey orders and hold your tongue!"

"Oh! If you take it in that tone!" mumbled Almayer, sulkily, with a gesture of assent.

"You are so aggravating too, my boy," said the old seaman, with unexpected placidity. "You must give me time to turn round. I can't keep her on board all the time. I must tell her something. Say, for instance, that he is gone up the river. Expected back every day. That's it. D'ye hear? You must put her on that tack and dodge her along easy, while I take the kinks out of the situation. By God!" he exclaimed, mournfully, after a short pause, "life is foul! Foul like a lee forebrace on a dirty night. And yet. And yet. One must see it clear for running before going below—for good. Now you attend to what I said," he added, sharply, "if you don't want to quarrel with me, my boy."

"I don't want to quarrel with you," murmured Almayer with unwilling deference. "Only I wish I could understand you. I know you are my best friend, Captain Lingard; only, upon my word, I can't make you out sometimes! I wish I could. . . ."

Lingard burst into a loud laugh which ended shortly in a deep sigh. He closed his eyes, tilting his head over the back of his armchair; and on his face, baked by the unclouded suns of many hard years, there appeared for a moment a weariness and a look of age which startled Almayer, like an unexpected disclosure of evil.

"I am done up," said Lingard, gently. "Perfectly done up. All night on deck getting that schooner up the river.

Then talking with you. Seems to me I could go to sleep on a clothes-line. I should like to eat something, though. Just see about that, Kasper."

Almayer clapped his hands, and receiving no response was going to call, when in the central passage of the house, behind the red curtain of the doorway opening upon the verandah, they heard a child's imperious voice speaking shrilly.

"Take me up at once. I want to be carried into the verandah. I shall be very angry. Take me up."

A man's voice answered, subdued, in humble remonstrance. The faces of Almayer and Lingard brightened at once. The old seaman called out—

"Bring the child. Lekas!"

"You will see how she has grown," exclaimed Almayer, in a jubilant tone.

Through the curtained doorway Ali appeared with little Nina Almayer in his arms. The child had one arm round his neck, and with the other she hugged a ripe pumelo nearly as big as her own head. Her little pink, sleeveless robe had half slipped off her shoulders, but the long black hair, that framed her olive face, in which the big black eyes looked out in childish solemnity, fell in luxuriant profusion over her shoulders, all round her and over Ali's arms, like a close-meshed and delicate net of silken threads. Lingard got up to meet Ali, and as soon as she caught sight of the old seaman she dropped the fruit and put out both her hands with a cry of delight. He took her from the Malay, and she laid hold of his moustaches with an affectionate goodwill that brought unaccustomed tears into his little red eyes.

"Not so hard, little one, not so hard," he murmured, pressing with an enormous hand, that covered it entirely, the child's head to his face.

"Pick up my pumelo, O Rajah of the sea!" she said, speaking in a high-pitched, clear voice with great volubility. "There, under the table. I want it quick! Quick! You have been away fighting with many men. Ali says so. You are a mighty fighter. Ali says so. On the great sea far away, away, away."

She waved her hand, staring with dreamy vacancy, while Lingard looked at her, and squatting down groped under the table after the pumelo.

"Where does she get those notions?" said Lingard, getting up cautiously, to Almayer, who had been giving orders to Ali.

"She is always with the men. Many a time I've found her with her fingers in their rice dish, of an evening. She does not care for her mother, though—I am glad to say. How pretty she is—and so sharp. My very image!"

Lingard had put the child on the table, and both men stood looking at her with radiant faces.

"A perfect little woman," whispered Lingard. "Yes, my dear boy, we shall make her somebody. You'll see!"

"Very little chance of that now," remarked Almayer, sadly.

"You do not know!" exclaimed Lingard, taking up the child again, and beginning to walk up and down the verandah. "I have my plans. I have—listen."

And he began to explain to the interested Almayer his plans for the future. He would interview Abdulla and Lakamba. There must be some understanding with those fellows now they had the upper hand. Here he interrupted himself to swear freely, while the child, who had been diligently fumbling about his neck, had found his whistle and blew a loud blast now and then close to his ear—which made him wince and laugh as he put her hands down, scolding her lovingly. Yes—that would be easily settled. He was a man to be reckoned with yet. Nobody knew that better than Almayer. Very well. Then he must patiently try and keep some little trade together. It would be all right. But the great thing—and here Lingard spoke lower, bringing himself to a sudden standstill before the entranced Almayer—the great thing would be the gold hunt up the river. He—Lingard—would devote himself to it. He had been in the interior before. There were immense deposits of alluvial gold there. Fabulous. He felt sure. Had seen places. Dangerous work? Of course! But what a reward! He would explore—and find. Not a shadow of doubt. Hang the danger. They would first get as much as they could for themselves. Keep the thing quiet. Then after a time form a Company. In Batavia or in England. Yes, in England. Much better. Splendid! Why, of course. And that baby would be the richest woman in the world. He— Lingard—would not, perhaps see it—although he felt good for many years yet—but Almayer would. Here was something to live for yet! Hey?

But the richest woman in the world had been for the last five minutes shouting shrilly—"Rajah Laut! Rajah Laut! Haï! Give ear!" while the old seaman had been speaking louder, unconsciously, to make his deep bass heard above the impatient clamour. He stopped now and said tenderly—

"What is it, little woman?"

"I am not a little woman. I am a white child. Anak Putih. A white child; and the white men are my brothers. Father says so. And Ali says so too. Ali knows as much as father. Everything."

Almayer almost danced with paternal delight.

"I taught her. I taught her," he repeated, laughing with tears in his eyes. "Isn't she sharp?"

"I am the slave of the white child," said Lingard, with playful solemnity. "What is the order?"

"I want a house," she warbled, with great eagerness. "I want a house, and another house on the roof, and another on the roof—high. High! Like the places where they dwell—my brothers—in the land where the sun sleeps."

"To the westward," explained Almayer, under his breath. "She remembers everything. She wants you to build a house of cards. You did, last time you were here."

Lingard sat down with the child on his knees, and Almayer pulled out violently one drawer after another, looking for the cards, as if the fate of the world depended upon his haste. He produced a dirty double pack which was only used during Lingard's visits to Sambir, when he would sometimes play— of an evening—with Almayer, a game which he called

Chinese bezique. It bored Almayer, but the old seaman delighted in it, considering it a remarkable product of Chinese genius—a race for which he had an unaccountable liking and admiration.

"Now we will get on, my little pearl," he said, putting together with extreme precaution two cards that looked absurdly flimsy between his big fingers. Little Nina watched him with intense seriousness as he went on erecting the ground floor, while he continued to speak to Almayer with his head over his shoulder so as not to endanger the structure with his breath.

"I know what I am talking about. . . . Been in California in forty-nine. . . . Not that I made much . . . then in Victoria in the early days. . . . I know all about it. Trust me. Moreover a blind man could . . . Be quiet, little sister, or you will knock this affair down. . . . My hand pretty steady yet! Hey, Kaspar? . . . Now, delight of my heart, we shall put a third house on the top of these two . . . keep very quiet. . . . As I was saying, you got only to stoop and gather handfuls of gold . . . dust . . . there. Now here we are. Three houses on top of one another. Grand!"

He leaned back in his chair, one hand on the child's head, which he smoothed mechanically, and gesticulated with the other, speaking to Almayer.

"Once on the spot, there would be only the trouble to pick up the stuff. Then we shall all go to Europe. The child must be educated. We shall be rich. Rich is no name for it. Down in Devonshire where I belong, there was a fellow who built a house near Teignmouth which had as many windows as a three-decker has ports. Made all his money somewhere out here in the good old days. People around said he had been a pirate. We boys—I was a boy in a Brixham trawler then—certainly believed that. He went about in a bath-chair in his grounds. Had a glass eye . . ."

"Higher! Higher!" called out Nina, pulling the old seaman's beard.

"You do worry me—don't you?" said Lingard, gently,

giving her a tender kiss. " What ? One more house on top of all these ? Well ! I will try."

The child watched him breathlessly. When the difficult feat was accomplished she clapped her hands, looked on steadily, and after a while gave a great sigh of content.

" Oh ! Look out ! " shouted Almayer.

The structure collapsed suddenly before the child's light breath. Lingard looked discomposed for a moment. Almayer laughed, but the little girl began to cry.

" Take her," said the old seaman, abruptly. Then, after Almayer went away with the crying child, he remained sitting by the table, looking gloomily at the heap of cards.

" Damn this Willems," he muttered to himself. " But I will do it yet ! "

He got up, and with an angry push of his hand swept the cards off the table. Then he fell back in his chair.

" Tired as a dog," he sighed out, closing his eyes.

## IV

CONSCIOUSLY or unconsciously, men are proud of their firmness, steadfastness of purpose, directness of aim. They go straight towards their desire, to the accomplishment of virtue—sometimes of crime—in an uplifting persuasion of their firmness. They walk the road of life, the road fenced in by their tastes, prejudices, disdains or enthusiasms, generally honest, invariably stupid, and are proud of never losing their way. If they do stop, it is to look for a moment over the hedges that make them safe, to look at the misty valleys, at the distant peaks, at cliffs and morasses, at the dark forests and the hazy plains where other human beings grope their days painfully away, stumbling over the bones of the wise, over the unburied remains of their predecessors who died alone, in gloom or in sunshine, half-way from anywhere. The man of purpose does not understand, and goes on, full of contempt. He never loses his way. He knows where he is going and what he wants. Travelling on, he achieves great length without any breadth, and battered, besmirched, and weary, he touches the goal at last; he grasps the reward of his perseverance, of his virtue, of his healthy optimism : an untruthful tombstone over a dark and soon forgotten grave.

Lingard had never hesitated in his life. Why should he ? He had been a most successful trader, and a man lucky in his fights, skilful in navigation, undeniably first in seamanship in those seas. He knew it. Had he not heard the voice of common consent ? The voice of the world that respected him so much ; the whole world to him—for to us the limits of the universe are strictly defined by those we know. There is nothing for us outside the babble of praise and blame on familiar lips, and beyond our last acquaintance there lies only a vast chaos ; a chaos of laughter and tears which concerns us not ; laughter and tears unpleasant, wicked, morbid, contemptible—because heard imperfectly by ears rebellious to strange sounds. To Lingard—simple himself—all things were simple. He seldom read. Books were not much in his way, and he had to work hard navigating, trading, and also, in obedience to his benevolent instincts, shaping stray lives he found here and there under his busy hand. He remembered the Sunday-school teachings of his native village and the discourses of the black-coated gentleman connected with the Mission to Fishermen and Seamen, whose yawl-rigged boat darting through rain-squalls amongst the coasters wind-bound in Falmouth Bay, was part of those precious pictures of his youthful days that lingered in his memory. " As clever a sky-pilot as you could wish to see," he would say with conviction, " and the best man to handle a boat in any weather I ever did meet ! " Such were the agencies that had roughly shaped his young soul before he went away to see the world in a southern-going ship—before he went, ignorant and happy, heavy of hand, pure in heart, profane in speech, to give himself up to the great sea that took his life and gave him his fortune. When thinking of his rise in the world—commander of ships, then shipowner, then a man of much capital, respected wherever he went, Lingard in a word, the Rajah Laut—he was amazed and awed by his fate, that seemed to his ill-informed mind the most wondrous known in the annals of men. His experience appeared to him immense and conclusive, teaching him the lesson of the simplicity of life. In life—as in seamanship—there were only two ways of doing a thing : the right way and the wrong way. Common sense and experience taught a man the way that was right. The other was for lubbers and fools, and led, in seamanship, to loss of spars and sails or shipwreck ; in life, to loss of money and consideration, or to an unlucky knock on the head. He did not consider it his duty to be angry with rascals. He was only angry with things he could not understand, but for the weaknesses of humanity he could find a contemptuous tolerance. It being manifest that he was wise and lucky—otherwise how could he have been as successful in life as he had been ?—he had an inclination to set right the lives of other people, just as he could hardly refrain—in defiance of nautical etiquette—from interfering with his chief officer when the crew was sending up a new topmast, or generally when busy about, what he called, " a heavy job." He was meddlesome with perfect modesty ; if he knew a thing or two there was no merit in it. " Hard knocks taught me wisdom, my boy," he used to say, " and you had better take the advice of a man who has been a fool in his time. Have another." And " my boy " as a rule took the cool drink, the advice, and the consequent help which Lingard felt himself bound in honour to give, so as to back up his opinion like an honest man. Captain Tom went sailing from island to island, appearing unexpectedly in various localities, beaming, noisy, anecdotal, commendatory or comminatory, but always welcome.

It was only since his return to Sambir that the old seaman had for the first time known doubt and unhappiness. The loss of the *Flash*—planted firmly and for ever on a ledge of rock at the north end of Gaspar Straits in the uncertain light of a cloudy morning—shook him considerably ; and the amazing news which he heard on his arrival in Sambir were not made to soothe his feelings. A good many years ago—prompted by his love of adventure—he, with infinite trouble, had found out and surveyed—for his own benefit only—the entrances to that river, where, as he had heard through native report, a new settlement of Malays was forming. No doubt he thought at the time mostly of personal gain; but, received with hearty friendliness by Patalolo, he soon came to like the ruler and the people, offered his counsel and his help, and—knowing nothing of Arcadia—he dreamed of Arcadian happiness for that little corner of the world which he loved to think all his own. His deep-seated and immovable conviction that only he—he, Lingard—knew what was good for them was characteristic of him, and, after all, not so very far wrong. He would make them happy whether or no, he said, and he meant it. His trade brought prosperity to the young state, and the fear of his heavy hand secured its internal peace for many years.

He looked proudly upon his work. With every passing year he loved more the land, the people, the muddy river that, if he could help it, would carry no other craft but the *Flash* on its unclean and friendly surface. As he slowly warped his vessel up-stream he would scan with knowing looks the riverside clearings, and pronounce solemn judgment upon the prospects of the season's rice-crop. He knew every settler on the banks between the sea and Sambir; he knew their wives, their children; he knew every individual of the multi-coloured groups that, standing on the flimsy platforms of tiny reed dwellings built over the water, waved their hands and shouted shrilly: O ! Kapal layer ! Haï ! " while the *Flash* swept slowly through the populated reach, to enter the lonely stretches of sparkling brown water bordered by the dense and silent forest, whose big trees nodded their outspread boughs gently in the faint, warm breeze—as if in sign of tender but melancholy welcome. He loved it all: the landscape of brown golds and brilliant emeralds under the dome of hot sapphire; the whispering big trees; the loquacious nipa-palms that rattled their leaves volubly in the night breeze, as if in haste to tell him all the secrets of the great forest behind them. He loved the heavy scents of blossoms and black earth, that breath of life and of death which lingered over his brig in the damp air of tepid and peaceful nights. He loved the narrow and sombre creeks, strangers to sunshine : black, smooth, tortuous—like byways of despair. He liked even the troops of sorrowful-faced monkeys that profaned the quiet spots with capricious gambols and insane gestures of inhuman madness. He loved everything there, animated or inanimate; the very mud of the riverside; the very alligators, enormous and stolid, basking on it with impertinent unconcern. Their size was a source of pride to him. "Immense fellows ! Make two of them Palembang reptiles ! I tell you, old man !" he would shout, poking some crony of his playfully in the ribs : "I tell you, big as you are, they could swallow you in one gulp, hat, boots and all ! Magnificent beggars ! Wouldn't you like to see them ? Wouldn't you ! Ha ! ha ! ha !" His thunderous laughter filled the verandah, rolled over the hotel garden, overflowed into the street, paralysing for a short moment the noiseless traffic of bare brown feet; and its loud reverberations would even startle the landlord's tame bird—a shameless mynah—into a momentary propriety of behaviour under the nearest chair. In the big billiard-room perspiring men in thin cotton singlets would stop the game, listen, cue in hand, for a while through the open windows, then nod their moist faces at each other sagaciously and whisper : "The old fellow is talking about his river."

His river ! The whispers of curious men, the mystery of the thing, were to Lingard a source of never-ending delight. The common talk of ignorance exaggerated the profits of his queer monopoly, and, although strictly truthful in general, he liked, on that matter, to mislead speculation still further by boasts full of cold raillery. His river ! By it he was not only rich—he was interesting. This secret of his which made him different to the other traders of those seas gave intimate satisfaction to that desire for singularity which he shared with the rest of mankind, without being aware of its presence within his breast. It was the greater part of his happiness, but he only knew it after its loss, so unforeseen, so sudden and so cruel.

After his conversation with Almayer he went on board the schooner, sent Joanna on shore, and shut himself up in his cabin, feeling very unwell. He made the most of his indisposition to Almayer, who came to visit him twice a day. It was an excuse for doing nothing just yet. He wanted to think. He was very angry. Angry with himself, with Willems. Angry at what Willems had done—and also angry at what he had left undone. The scoundrel was not complete. The conception was perfect, but the execution, unaccountably, fell short. Why? He ought to have cut Almayer's throat and burnt the place to ashes—then cleared out. Got out of his way; of him, Lingard! Yet he didn't. Was it impudence, contempt—or what? He felt hurt at the implied disrespect of his power, and the incomplete rascality of the proceedings disturbed him exceedingly. There was something short, something wanting, something that would have given him a free hand in the work of retribution. The obvious, the right thing to do, was to shoot Willems. Yet how could he? Had the fellow resisted, showed fight, or ran away; had he shown any consciousness of harm done, it would have been more possible, more natural. But no! The fellow actually had sent him a message. Wanted to see him. What for? The thing could not be explained. An unexampled, cold-blooded treachery, awful, incomprehensible. Why did he do it? Why? Why? The old seaman in the stuffy solitude of his little cabin on board the schooner groaned out many times that question, striking with an open palm his perplexed forehead.

During his four days of seclusion he had received two messages from the outer world; from that world of Sambir which had, so suddenly and so finally, slipped from his grasp. One, a few words from Willems written on a torn-out page of a small notebook; the other, a communication from Abdulla caligraphed carefully on a large sheet of paper, nearly as stiff as cardboard, and delivered to him in a green silk wrapper. The first he could not understand. It said:

" Come and see me. I am not afraid. Are you? W."
He tore it up angrily, but before the small bits of dirty paper
had the time to flutter down and settle on the floor, the anger
was gone and was replaced by a sentiment that induced him
to go on his knees, pick up the fragments of the torn message,
piece it together on the top of his chronometer box, and contemplate it long and thoughtfully, as if he had hoped to read
the answer of the horrible riddle in the very form of the
letters that went to make up that fresh insult. Abdulla's
letter he read carefully and rammed it into his pocket, also
with anger, but with anger that ended in a half-resigned,
half-amused smile. He would never give in as long as there
was a chance. " It's generally the safest way to stick to the
ship as long as she will swim," was one of his favourite sayings : " The safest and the right way. To abandon a craft
because it leaks is easy—but poor work. Poor work ! " Yet
he was intelligent enough to know when he was beaten, and
to accept the situation like a man, without repining. When
Almayer came on board that afternoon he handed him the
letter without comment.

Almayer read it, returned it in silence, and leaning over
the taffrail (the two men were on deck) looked down for
some time at the play of the eddies round the schooner's
rudder. At last he said without looking up—

" That's a decent enough letter. Abdulla gives him
up to you. I told you they were getting sick of him. What
are you going to do ? "

Lingard cleared his throat, shuffled his feet, opened his
mouth with great determination, but said nothing for a while.
At last he murmured—

" I'll be hanged if I know—just yet."

" I wish you would do something soon . . ."

" What's the hurry ? " interrupted Lingard. " He can't
get away. As it stands he is at my mercy, as far as I can
see."

" Yes," said Almayer, reflectively—" and very little mercy
he deserves too. Abdulla's meaning—as I can make it out
amongst all those compliments—is : ' Get rid for me of that

white man—and we shall live in peace and share the trade.'"

"You believe that?" asked Lingard, contemptuously.

"Not altogether," answered Almayer. "No doubt we will share the trade for a time—till he can grab the lot. Well, what are you going to do?"

He looked up as he spoke and was surprised to see Lingard's discomposed face.

"You ain't well. Pain anywhere?" he asked, with real solicitude.

"I have been queer—you know—these last few days, but no pain." He struck his broad chest several times, cleared his throat with a powerful "Hem!" and repeated: "No. No pain. Good for a few years yet. But I am bothered with all this, I can tell you!"

"You must take care of yourself," said Almayer. Then after a pause he added: "You will see Abdulla. Won't you?"

"I don't know. Not yet. There's plenty of time," said Lingard, impatiently.

"I wish you would do something," urged Almayer, moodily. "You know, that woman is a perfect nuisance to me. She and her brat! Yelps all day. And the children don't get on together. Yesterday the little devil wanted to fight with my Nina. Scratched her face too. A perfect savage! Like his honourable papa. Yes, really. She worries about her husband, and whimpers from morning to night. When she isn't weeping she is furious with me. Yesterday she tormented me to tell her when he would be back, and cried because he was engaged in such dangerous work. I said something about it being all right—no necessity to make a fool of herself, when she turned upon me like a wild cat. Called me a brute, selfish, heartless; raved about her beloved Peter risking his life for my benefit, while I did not care. Said I took advantage of his generous good-nature to get him to do dangerous work—my work. That he was worth twenty of the likes of me. That she would tell you— open your eyes as to the kind of man I was, and so on. That's

what I've got to put up with for your sake. You really
might consider me a little. I haven't robbed anybody,"
went on Almayer, with an attempt at bitter irony—" or sold
my best friend, but still you ought to have some pity on me.
It's like living in a hot fever. She is out of her wits. You
make my house a refuge for scoundrels and lunatics. It isn't
fair. 'Pon my word it isn't! When she is in her tantrums
she is ridiculously ugly and screeches so—it sets my teeth
on edge. Thank God! my wife got a fit of the sulks and
cleared out of the house. Lives in a riverside hut since that
affair—you know. But this Willems' wife by herself is
almost more than I can bear. And I ask myself why should
I? You are exacting and no mistake. This morning I
thought she was going to claw me. Only think! She
wanted to go prancing about the settlement. She might
have heard something there, so I told her she mustn't. It
wasn't safe outside our fences, I said. Thereupon she rushes
at me with her ten nails up to my eyes. 'You miserable
man,' she yells, ' even this place is not safe, and you've sent
him up this awful river where he may lose his head. If he
dies before forgiving me, Heaven will punish you for your
crime . . .' My crime! I ask myself sometimes whether
I am dreaming! It will make me ill, all this. I've lost my
appetite already."

He flung his hat on deck and laid hold of his hair
despairingly. Lingard looked at him with sympathetic
concern.

"What did she mean by it?" he muttered, thoughtfully.

"Mean! She is crazy, I tell you—and I will be, very soon
if this lasts!"

"Just a little patience, Kaspar," pleaded Lingard. "A
day or so more."

Relieved or tired by his violent outburst, Almayer calmed
down, picked up his hat and, leaning against the bulwark,
commenced to fan himself with it.

"Days do pass," he said, resignedly—" but that kind of
thing makes a man old before his time. What is there to
think about?—I can't imagine! Abdulla says plainly that

if you undertake to pilot his ship out and instruct the half-caste, he will drop Willems like a hot potato and be your friend ever after. I believe him perfectly, as to Willems. It's so natural. As to being your friend it's a lie, of course, but we need not bother about that just yet. You just say yes to Abdulla, and then whatever happens to Willems will be nobody's business."

He interrupted himself and remained silent for a while, glaring about with set teeth and dilated nostrils.

"You leave it to me. I'll see to it that something happens to him," he said at last, with calm ferocity. Lingard smiled faintly.

"The fellow isn't worth a shot. Not the trouble of it," he whispered, as if to himself. Almayer fired up suddenly.

"That's what you think," he cried. "You haven't been sewn up in your hammock to be made a laughing-stock of before a parcel of savages. Why! I daren't look anybody here in the face while that scoundrel is alive. I will . . . I will settle him."

"I don't think you will," growled Lingard.

"Do you think I am afraid of him?"

"Bless you! no!" said Lingard with alacrity. "Afraid! Not you. I know you. I don't doubt your courage. It's your head, my boy, your head that I . . ."

"That's it," said the aggrieved Almayer. "Go on. Why don't you call me a fool at once?"

"Because I don't want to," burst out Lingard, with nervous irritability. "If I wanted to call you a fool, I would do so without asking your leave." He began to walk athwart the narrow quarter-deck, kicking ropes' ends out of his way and growling to himself: "Delicate gentleman . . . what next? . . . I've done man's work before you could toddle. Understand . . . say what I like."

"Well! well!" said Almayer, with affected resignation. "There's no talking to you these last few days." He put on his hat, strolled to the gangway and stopped, one foot on the little inside ladder, as if hesitating, came back and planted himself in Lingard's way, compelling him to stand still and listen.

"Of course you will do what you like. You never take advice—I know that; but let me tell you that it wouldn't be honest to let that fellow get away from here. If you do nothing, that scoundrel will leave in Abdulla's ship for sure. Abdulla will make use of him to hurt you and others elsewhere. Willems knows too much about your affairs. He will cause you lots of trouble. You mark my words. Lots of trouble. To you—and to others perhaps. Think of that, Captain Lingard. That's all I've got to say. Now I must go back on shore. There's lots of work. We will begin loading this schooner to-morrow morning, first thing. All the bundles are ready. If you should want me for anything, hoist some kind of flag on the mainmast. At night two shots will fetch me." Then he added, in a friendly tone, "Won't you come and dine in the house to-night? It can't be good for you to stew on board like that, day after day."

Lingard did not answer. The image evoked by Almayer; the picture of Willems ranging over the islands and disturbing the harmony of the universe by robbery, treachery, and violence, held him silent, entranced—painfully spellbound. Almayer, after waiting for a little while, moved reluctantly towards the gangway, lingered there, then sighed and got over the side, going down step by step. His head disappeared slowly below the rail. Lingard, who had been staring at him absently, started suddenly, ran to the side, and looking over, called out—

"Hey! Kaspar! Hold on a bit!"

Almayer signed to his boatmen to cease paddling, and turned his head towards the schooner. The boat drifted back slowly abreast of Lingard, nearly alongside.

"Look here," said Lingard, looking down—"I want a good canoe with four men to-day."

"Do you want it now?" asked Almayer.

"No! Catch this rope. Oh, you clumsy devil! . . . No, Kaspar," went on Lingard, after the bowman had got hold of the end of the brace he had thrown down into the canoe—" No, Kaspar. The sun is too much for me. And it would be better to keep my affairs quiet, too. Send the canoe—four good paddlers, mind, and your canvas chair for me to sit in. Send it about sunset. D'ye hear ? "

" All right, father," said Almayer, cheerfully—" I will send Ali for a steersman, and the best men I've got. Anything else ? "

" No, my lad. Only don't let them be late."

" I suppose it's no use asking you where you are going," said Almayer, tentatively. " Because if it is to see Abdulla, I . . ."

" I am not going to see Abdulla. Not to-day. Now be off with you."

He watched the canoe dart away shorewards, waved his hand in response to Almayer's nod, and walked to the taffrail smoothing out Abdulla's letter, which he had pulled out of his pocket. He read it over carefully, crumpled it up slowly, smiling the while and closing his fingers firmly over the crackling paper as though he had hold there of Abdulla's throat. Half-way to his pocket he changed his mind, and flinging the ball overboard looked at it thoughtfully as it spun round in the eddies for a moment, before the current bore it away down-stream, towards the sea.

# PART IV

## I

THE night was very dark. For the first time in many months
the East Coast slept unseen by the stars under a veil of
motionless cloud that, driven before the first breath of the
rainy monsoon, had drifted slowly from the eastward all the
afternoon; pursuing the declining sun with its masses of
black and grey that seemed to chase the light with wicked
intent, and with an ominous and gloomy steadiness, as though
conscious of the message of violence and turmoil they carried.
At the sun's disappearance below the western horizon, the
immense cloud, in quickened motion, grappled with the glow
of retreating light, and rolling down to the clear and jagged
outline of the distant mountains, hung arrested above the
steaming forests; hanging low, silent and menacing over the
unstirring tree-tops; withholding the blessing of rain,
nursing the wrath of its thunder; undecided—as if brooding
over its own power for good or for evil.

Babalatchi, coming out of the red and smoky light of his
little bamboo house, glanced upwards, drew in a long breath
of the warm and stagnant air, and stood for a moment with
his good eye closed tightly, as if intimidated by the unwonted
and deep silence of Lakamba's courtyard. When he opened
his eye he had recovered his sight so far, that he could distinguish the various degrees of formless blackness which
marked the places of trees, of abandoned houses, of riverside
bushes, on the dark background of the night. The careworn
sage walked cautiously down the deserted courtyard to the
waterside, and stood on the bank listening to the voice of the

invisible river that flowed at his feet; listening to the soft
whispers, to the deep murmurs, to the sudden gurgles and the
short hisses of the swift current racing along the bank through
the hot darkness.

He stood with his face turned to the river, and it seemed
to him that he could breathe easier with the knowledge of the
clear vast space before him; then, after a while, he leaned
heavily forward on his staff, his chin fell on his breast, and a
deep sigh was his answer to the selfish discourse of the river
that hurried on unceasing and fast, regardless of joy or sorrow,
of suffering and of strife, of failures and triumphs that lived
on its banks. The brown water was there, ready to carry
friends or enemies, to nurse love or hate on its submissive
and heartless bosom, to help or to hinder, to save life or give
death; the great and rapid river: a deliverance, a prison, a
refuge or a grave.

Perchance such thoughts as these caused Babalatchi to send
another mournful sigh into the trailing mists of the uncon-
cerned Pantai. The barbarous politician had forgotten the
recent success of his plottings in the melancholy contemplation of a sorrow that made the night blacker, the clammy
heat more oppressive, the still air more heavy, the dumb
solitude more significant of torment than of peace. He had
spent the night before by the side of the dying Omar, and
now, after twenty-four hours, his memory persisted in
returning to that low and sombre reed hut from which the
fierce spirit of the incomparably accomplished pirate took its
flight, to learn too late, in a worse world, the error of its
earthly ways. The mind of the savage statesman, chastened
by bereavement, felt for a moment the weight of his loneliness
with keen perception worthy even of a sensibility exasperated
by all the refinements of tender sentiment that a glorious
civilisation brings in its train, among other blessings and
virtues, into this excellent world. For the space of about
thirty seconds, a half-naked, betel-chewing pessimist stood
upon the bank of the tropical river, on the edge of the still
and immense forests; a man angry, powerless, empty-
handed, with a cry of bitter discontent ready on his lips;

a cry that, had it come out, would have rung through the
virgin solitudes of the woods, as true, as great, as profound
as any philosophical shriek that ever came from the depths of
an easy-chair to disturb the impure wilderness of chimneys
and roofs.

For half a minute and no more did Babalatchi face the gods
in the sublime privilege of his revolt, and then the one-eyed
puller of wires became himself again, full of care and wisdom
and far-reaching plans, and a victim to the tormenting
superstitions of his race. The night, no matter how quiet,
is never perfectly silent to attentive ears, and now Babalatchi fancied he could detect in it other noises than those
caused by the ripples and eddies of the river. He turned his
head sharply to the right and to the left in succession, and
then spun round quickly in a startled and watchful manner,
as if he had expected to see the blind ghost of his departed
leader wandering in the obscurity of the empty courtyard
behind his back. Nothing there. Yet he had heard a noise ;
a strange noise ! No doubt a ghostly voice of a complaining
and angry spirit. He listened. Not a sound. Reassured,
Babalatchi made a few paces towards his house, when a very
human noise, that of hoarse coughing, reached him from the
river. He stopped, listened attentively, but now without
any sign of emotion, and moving briskly back to the waterside
stood expectant with parted lips, trying to pierce with his
eye the wavering curtain of mist that hung low over the water.
He could see nothing, yet some people in a canoe must have
been very near, for he heard words spoken in an ordinary
tone.

"Do you think this is the place, Ali ? I can see nothing."

"It must be near here, Tuan," answered another voice.
"Shall we try the banks ? "

"No ! . . . Let drift a little. If you go poking into the
bank in the dark you might stove the canoe on some log.
We must be careful. . . . Let drift ! Let drift ! . . .
This does seem to be a clearing of some sort. We may see a
light by and by from some house or other. In Lakamba's
campong there are many houses ? Hey ? "

"A great number, Tuan . . . I do not see any light."

"Nor I," grumbled the first voice again, this time nearly abreast of the silent Babalatchi, who looked uneasily towards his own house, the doorway of which glowed with the dim light of a torch burning within. The house stood end on to the river, and its doorway faced down-stream, so Babalatchi reasoned rapidly that the strangers on the river could not see the light from the position their boat was in at the moment. He could not make up his mind to call out to them, and while he hesitated he heard the voices again, but now some way below the landing-place where he stood.

"Nothing. This cannot be it. Let them give way, Ali! Dayong there!"

That order was followed by the splash of paddles, then a sudden cry—

"I see a light. I see it! Now I know where to land, Tuan."

There was more splashing as the canoe was paddled sharply round and came back up-stream close to the bank.

"Call out," said very near a deep voice, which Babalatchi felt sure must belong to a white man. "Call out—and somebody may come with a torch. I can't see anything."

The loud hail that succeeded these words was emitted nearly under the silent listener's nose. Babalatchi, to preserve appearances, ran with long but noiseless strides half-way up the courtyard, and only then shouted in answer and kept on shouting as he walked slowly back again towards the river bank. He saw there an indistinct shape of a boat, not quite alongside the landing-place.

"Who speaks on the river?" asked Babalatchi, throwing a tone of surprise into his question.

"A white man," answered Lingard from the canoe. "Is there not one torch in rich Lakamba's campong to light a guest on his landing?"

"There are no torches and no men. I am alone here," said Babalatchi, with some hesitation.

"Alone!" exclaimed Lingard. "Who are you?"

"Only a servant of Lakamba. But land, Tuan Putih, and

see my face. Here is my hand. No! Here! . . . By
your mercy. . . . Ada! . . . Now you are safe."

"And you are alone here?" said Lingard, moving with
precaution a few steps into the courtyard. "How dark it
is," he muttered to himself—"one would think the world
had been painted black."

"Yes. Alone. What more did you say, Tuan? I did
not understand your talk."

"It is nothing. I expected to find here . . . But where
are they all?"

"What matters where they are?" said Babalatchi,
gloomily. "Have you come to see my people? The last
departed on a long journey—and I am alone. To-morrow
I go too."

"I came to see a white man," said Lingard, walking on
slowly. "He is not gone, is he?"

"No!" answered Babalatchi, at his elbow. "A man with
a red skin and hard eyes," he went on, musingly, "whose
hand is strong, and whose heart is foolish and weak. A white
man indeed . . . But still a man."

They were now at the foot of the short ladder which led
to the split-bamboo platform surrounding Babalatchi's
habitation. The faint light from the doorway fell down upon
the two men's faces as they stood looking at each other
curiously.

"Is he there?" asked Lingard, in a low voice, with a wave
of his hand upwards.

Babalatchi, staring hard at his long-expected visitor, did
not answer at once.

"No, not there," he said at last, placing his foot on the
lowest rung and looking back. "Not there, Tuan—yet not
very far. Will you sit down in my dwelling? There may be
rice and fish and clear water—not from the river, but from
a spring . . ."

"I am not hungry," interrupted Lingard, curtly, "and
I did not come here to sit in your dwelling. Lead me
to the white man who expects me. I have no time to
lose."

"The night is long, Tuan," went on Babalatchi, softly, "and there are other nights and other days. Long. Very long . . . How much time it takes for a man to die! O Rajah Laut!"

Lingard started.

"You know me!" he exclaimed.

"Ay—wa! I have seen your face and felt your hand before—many years ago," said Babalatchi, holding on half-way up the ladder, and bending down from above to peer into Lingard's upturned face. "You do not remember—but I have not forgotten. There are many men like me : there is only one Rajah Laut."

He climbed with sudden agility the last few steps, and stood on the platform waving his hand invitingly to Lingard, who followed after a short moment of indecision.

The elastic bamboo floor of the hut bent under the heavy weight of the old seaman, who, standing within the threshold, tried to look into the smoky gloom of the low dwelling. Under the torch, thrust into the cleft of a stick, fastened at a right angle to the middle stay of the ridge pole, lay a red patch of light, showing a few shabby mats and a corner of a big wooden chest the rest of which was lost in shadow. In the obscurity of the more remote parts of the house a lance-head, a brass tray hung on the wall, the long barrel of a gun leaning against the chest, caught the stray rays of the smoky illumination in trembling gleams that wavered, disappeared, reappeared, went out, came back—as if engaged in a doubtful struggle with the darkness that, lying in wait in distant corners, seemed to dart out viciously towards its feeble enemy. The vast space under the high pitch of the roof was filled with a thick cloud of smoke, whose under-side—level like a ceiling—reflected the light of the swaying dull flame, while at the top it oozed out through the imperfect thatch of dried palm leaves. An indescribable and complicated smell, made up of the exhalation of damp earth below, of the taint of dried fish and of the effluvia of rotting vegetable matter, pervaded the place and caused Lingard to sniff strongly as he strode over, sat on the chest, and, leaning his elbows on his knees, took his head between his hands and stared at the doorway thoughtfully.

Babalatchi moved about in the shadows, whispering to an indistinct form or two that flitted about at the far end of the hut. There was a noiseless vibration of cautious footsteps, subdued exclamations, a sigh, an impatient louder word, directly repressed—then silence in which the breathing of several persons was distinctly audible to Lingard. Without stirring he glanced sideways, and caught sight of muffled-up human shapes that hovered for a moment near the edge of light and retreated suddenly back into the darkness. Babalatchi approached, and sat at Lingard's feet on a rolled-up bundle of mats.

"Will you eat rice and drink sagueir?" he said. "I have waked up my household."

"My friend," said Lingard, without looking at him, "when I come to see Lakamba, or any of Lakamba's servants, I am never hungry and never thirsty. Tau! Savee! Never! Do you think I am devoid of reason? That there is nothing there?"

He sat up, and, fixing abruptly his eyes on Babalatchi, tapped his own forehead significantly.

"Tse! Tse! Tse! How can you talk like that, Tuan!" exclaimed Babalatchi, in a horrified tone.

"I talk as I think. I have lived many years," said Lingard, stretching his arm negligently to take up the gun, which he began to examine knowingly, cocking it, and easing down the hammer several times. "This is good. Mataram make. Old, too," he went on.

"Haï!" broke in Babalatchi, eagerly. "I got it when I was young. He was an Aru trader, a man with a big stomach and a loud voice, and brave—very brave. When we came up with his prau in the grey morning, he stood aft shouting to his men and fired this gun at us once. Only once!" . . . He paused, laughed softly, and went on in a low, dreamy voice. "In the grey morning we came up: forty silent men in a swift Sulu prau; and when the sun was so high"— here he held up his hands about three feet apart—"when the sun was only so high, Tuan, our work was done—and there was a feast ready for the fishes of the sea."

"Aye! aye!" muttered Lingard, nodding his head slowly. "I see. You should not let it get rusty like this," he added.

He let the gun fall between his knees, and moving back on his seat, leaned his head against the wall of the hut, crossing his arms on his breast.

"A good gun," went on Babalatchi. "Carry far and true. Better than this—there."

With the tips of his fingers he touched gently the butt of a revolver peeping out of the right pocket of Lingard's white jacket.

"Take your hand off," said Lingard sharply, but in a good-humoured tone and without making the slightest movement.

Babalatchi smiled and hitched his seat a little further off.

For some time they sat in silence. Lingard, with his head tilted back, looked downwards with lowered eyelids at Babalatchi, who was tracing invisible lines with his finger on the mat between his feet. Outside, they could hear Ali and the other boatmen chattering and laughing round the fire they had lighted in the big and deserted courtyard.

"Well, what about that white man?" said Lingard, quietly.

It seemed as if Babalatchi had not heard the question. He went on tracing elaborate patterns in the floor for a good while. Lingard waited motionless. At last the Malay lifted his head.

"Haï! The white man. I know!" he murmured absently. "This white man or another. . . . Tuan," he said aloud with unexpected animation, "you are a man of the sea?"

"You know me. Why ask?" said Lingard, in a low tone.

"Yes. A man of the sea—even as we are. A true Orang Laut," went on Babalatchi, thoughtfully, "not like the rest of the white men."

"I am like other whites, and do not wish to speak many words when the truth is short. I came here to see the white man that helped Lakamba against Patalolo, who is my friend. Show me where that white man lives; I want him to hear my talk."

"Talk only? Tuan! Why hurry? The night is long and death is swift—as you ought to know; you who have dealt it to so many of my people. Many years ago I have faced you, arms in hand. Do you not remember? It was in Carimata—far from here."

"I cannot remember every vagabond that came in my way," protested Lingard, seriously.

"Haï! Haï!" continued Babalatchi, unmoved and dreamy, "many years ago. Then all this"—and looking up suddenly at Lingard's beard, he flourished his fingers below his own beardless chin—"then all this was like gold in sunlight, now it is like the foam of an angry sea."

"Maybe, maybe," said Lingard, patiently, paying the involuntary tribute of a faint sigh to the memories of the past evoked by Babalatchi's words.

He had been living with Malays so long and so close that the extreme deliberation and deviousness of their mental proceedings had ceased to irritate him much. To-night, perhaps, he was less prone to impatience than ever. He was disposed, if not to listen to Babalatchi, then to let him talk. It was evident to him that the man had something to say, and he hoped that from the talk a ray of light would shoot through the thick blackness of inexplicable treachery, to show him clearly—if only for a second—the man upon whom he would have to execute the verdict of justice. Justice only! Nothing was further from his thoughts than such an useless thing as revenge. Justice only. It was his duty that justice should be done—and by his own hand. He did not like to think how. To him, as to Babalatchi, it seemed that the night would be long enough for the work he had to do. But he did not define to himself the nature of the work, and he sat very still, and willingly dilatory, under the fearsome oppression of his call. What was the good to think about it? It was inevitable, and its time was near. Yet he could not command his memories that came crowding

M 2

round him in that evil-smelling hut, while Babalatchi talked on in a flowing monotone, nothing of him moving but the lips, in the artificially inanimated face. Lingard, like an anchored ship that had broken her sheer, darted about here and there on the rapid tide of his recollections. The subdued sound of soft words rang around him, but his thoughts were lost, now in the contemplation of the past sweetness and strife of Carimata days, now in the uneasy wonder at the failure of his judgment; at the fatal blindness of accident that had caused him, many years ago, to rescue a half-starved runaway from a Dutch ship in Samarang roads. How he had liked the man : his assurance, his push, his desire to get on, his conceited good-humour and his selfish eloquence. He had liked his very faults—those faults that had so many, to him, sympathetic sides. And he had always dealt fairly by him from the very beginning; and he would deal fairly by him now—to the very end. This last thought darkened Lingard's features with a responsive and menacing frown. The doer of justice sat with compressed lips and a heavy heart, while in the calm darkness outside the silent world seemed to be waiting breathlessly for that justice he held in his hand— in his strong hand :—ready to strike—reluctant to move.

## II

BABALATCHI ceased speaking. Lingard moved his feet a little, uncrossed his arms, and shook his head slowly. The narrative of the events in Sambir, related from the point of view of the astute statesman, the sense of which had been caught here and there by his inattentive ears, had been yet like a thread to guide him out of the sombre labyrinth of his thoughts ; and now he had come to the end of it, out of the tangled past into the pressing necessities of the present. With the palms of his hands on his knees, his elbows squared out, he looked down on Babalatchi, who sat in a stiff attitude, inexpressive and mute as a talking doll the mechanism of which had at length run down.

"You people did all this," said Lingard at last, "and you will be sorry for it before the dry wind begins to blow again. Abdulla's voice will bring the Dutch rule here."

Babalatchi waved his hand towards the dark doorway.

"There are forests there. Lakamba rules the land now. Tell me, Tuan, do you think the big trees know the name of the ruler? No. They are born, they grow, they live and they die—yet know not, feel not. It is their land."

"Even a big tree may be killed by a small axe," said Lingard, drily. "And, remember, my one-eyed friend, that axes are made by white hands. You will soon find that out, since you have hoisted the flag of the Dutch."

"Ay—wa!" said Babalatchi, slowly. "It is written that the earth belongs to those who have fair skins and hard but foolish hearts. The farther away is the master, the easier it is for the slave, Tuan! You were too near. Your voice rang in our ears always. Now it is not going to be so. The great Rajah in Batavia is strong, but he may be deceived. He must speak very loud to be heard here. But if we have need to shout, then he must hear the many voices that call for protection. He is but a white man."

"If I ever spoke to Patalolo, like an elder brother, it was for your good—for the good of all," said Lingard with great earnestness.

"This is a white man's talk," exclaimed Babalatchi, with bitter exultation. "I know you. That is how you all talk while you load your guns and sharpen your swords; and when you are ready, then to those who are weak you say: 'Obey me and be happy, or die!' You are strange, you white men. You think it is only your wisdom and your virtue and your happiness that are true. You are stronger than the wild beasts, but not so wise. A black tiger knows when he is not hungry—you do not. He knows the difference between himself and those that can speak; you do not understand the difference between yourselves and us—who are men. You are wise and great—and you shall always be fools."

He threw up both hands, stirring the sleeping cloud of smoke that hung above his head, and brought the open palms on the flimsy floor on each side of his outstretched legs. The whole hut shook. Lingard looked at the excited statesman curiously.

"Apa! Apa! What's the matter?" he murmured, soothingly. "Whom did I kill here? Where are my guns? What have I done? What have I eaten up?"

Babalatchi calmed down, and spoke with studied courtesy.

"You, Tuan, are of the sea, and more like what we are. Therefore I speak to you all the words that are in my heart. . . . Only once has the sea been stronger than the Rajah of the sea."

"You know it; do you?" said Lingard, with pained sharpness.

"Haï! We have heard about your ship—and some rejoiced. Not I. Amongst the whites, who are devils, you are a man."

"Trima kassi! I give you thanks," said Lingard, gravely.

Babalatchi looked down with a bashful smile, but his face became saddened directly, and when he spoke again it was in a mournful tone.

"Had you come a day sooner, Tuan, you would have seen an enemy die. You would have seen him die poor, blind, unhappy—with no son to dig his grave and speak of his wisdom and courage. Yes; you would have seen the man that fought you in Carimata many years ago, die alone—but for one friend. A great sight to you."

"Not to me," answered Lingard, "I did not even remember him till you spoke his name just now. You do not understand us. We fight, we vanquish—and we forget."

"True, true," said Babalatchi, with polite irony; "you whites are so great that you disdain to remember your enemies. No! No!" he went on, in the same tone, "you have so much mercy for us, that there is no room for any remembrance. Oh, you are great and good! But it is in my mind that amongst yourselves you know how to remember. Is it not so, Tuan?"

Lingard said nothing. His shoulders moved imperceptibly. He laid his gun across his knees and stared at the
flint lock absently.

"Yes," went on Babalatchi, falling again into a mournful
mood, "yes, he died in darkness. I sat by his side and held
his hand, but he could not see the face of him who watched
the faint breath of his lips. She, whom he had cursed because of the white man, was there too, and wept with covered
face. The white man walked about the courtyard making
many noises. Now and then he would come to the doorway
and glare at us who mourned. He stared with wicked eyes,
and then I was glad that he who was dying was blind. This
is true talk. I was glad; for a white man's eyes are not
good to see when the devil that lives within is looking out
through them."

"Devil! Hey?" said Lingard, half aloud to himself, as
if struck with the obviousness of some novel idea. Babalatchi
went on :

"At the first hour of the morning he sat up—he so weak—
and said plainly some words that were not meant for human
ears. I held his hand tightly, but it was time for the leader
of brave men to go amongst the Faithful who are happy.
They of my household brought a white sheet, and I began to
dig a grave in the hut in which he died. She mourned aloud.
The white man came to the doorway and shouted. He was
angry. Angry with her because she beat her breast, and tore
her hair, and mourned with shrill cries as a woman should.
Do you understand what I say, Tuan? That white man
came inside the hut with great fury, and took her by the
shoulder, and dragged her out. Yes, Tuan. I saw Omar
dead, and I saw her at the feet of that white dog who has
deceived me. I saw his face grey, like the cold mist of the
morning; I saw his pale eyes looking down at Omar's
daughter beating her head on the ground at his feet. At the
feet of him who is Abdulla's slave. Yes, he lives by Abdulla's
will. That is why I held my hand while I saw all this. I held
my hand because we are now under the flag of the Orang
Blanda, and Abdulla can speak into the ears of the great.

We must not have any trouble with white men. Abdulla has spoken—and I must obey."

"That's it, is it?" growled Lingard in his moustache. Then in Malay, "It seems that you are angry, O Baba-latchi!"

"No; I am not angry, Tuan," answered Babalatchi, descending from the insecure heights of his indignation into the insincere depths of safe humility. "I am not angry. What am I to be angry? I am only an Orang Laut, and I have fled before your people many times. Servants of this one—protected of another: I have given my counsel here and there for a handful of rice. What am I, to be angry with a white man? What is anger without the power to strike? But you whites have taken all: the land, the sea, and the power to strike! And there is nothing left for us in the islands but your white men's justice; your great justice that knows not anger."

He got up and stood for a moment in the doorway, sniffing the hot air of the courtyard, then turned back and leaned against the stay of the ridge pole, facing Lingard, who kept his seat on the chest. The torch, consumed nearly to the end, burned noisily. Small explosions took place in the heart of the flame, driving through its smoky blaze strings of hard, round puffs of white smoke, no bigger than peas, which rolled out of doors in the faint draught that came from invisible cracks of the bamboo walls. At times a spark would wander hesitatingly downwards, die on the road, and add on the floor-mat at the foot of the pole another minute black speck to the grimy record of sparks that went out before. Round Lingard the pungent taint of unclean things below and about the hut grew heavier, weighing down his resolution and his thoughts in an irresistible numbness of the brain. He thought drowsily of himself and of that man who wanted to see him—who waited to see him. Who waited! Night and day. Waited. . . . A spiteful but vaporous idea floated through his brain that such waiting could not be very pleasant to the fellow. Well, let him wait. He would see him soon enough. And for how long? Five seconds—

five minutes—say nothing—say something. What? No! Just give him time to take one good look, and then . . .

Suddenly Babalatchi began to speak in a soft voice. Lingard blinked, cleared his throat—sat up straight.

"You know all now, Tuan. Lakamba dwells in the stockaded house of Patalolo; Abdulla has begun to build godowns of plank and stone; and now that Omar is dead, I myself shall depart from this place and live with Lakamba and speak in his ear. I have served many. The best of them all sleeps in the ground in a white sheet, with nothing to mark his grave but the ashes of the hut in which he died. Yes, Tuan! the white man destroyed it himself. With a blazing brand in his hand he strode around, shouting to me to come out—shouting to me, who was throwing earth on the body of a great leader. Yes; swearing to me by the name of your God and ours that he would burn me and her in there if we did not make haste. . . . Haï! The white nen are very masterful and wise. I dragged her out quickly!"

"Oh, damn it!" exclaimed Lingard—then went on in Malay, speaking earnestly. "Listen. That man is not like other white men. You know he is not. He is not a man at all. He is . . . I don't know."

Babalatchi lifted his hand deprecatingly. His eye twinkled, and his red-stained big lips, parted by an expressionless grin, uncovered a stumpy row of black teeth filed evenly to the gums.

"Haï! Haï! Not like you. Not like you," he said, increasing the softness of his tones as he neared the object uppermost in his mind during that much-desired interview. "Not like you, Tuan, who are like ourselves, only wiser and stronger. Yet he, also, is full of great cunning, and speaks of you without any respect, after the manner of white men when they talk of one another."

Lingard leaped in his seat as if he had been prodded.

"He speaks! What does he say?" he shouted.

"Nay, Tuan," protested the composed Babalatchi; "what matters his talk if he is not a man? I am nothing before you—why should I repeat words of one white man about another ? He did boast to Abdulla of having learned much from your wisdom in years past. Other words I have forgotten. Indeed, Tuan, I have . . ."

Lingard cut short Babalatchi's protestations by a contemptuous wave of the hand and reseated himself with dignity.

" I shall go," said Babalatchi, " and the white man will remain here, alone with the spirit of the dead and with her who has been the delight of his heart. He, being white, cannot hear the voice of those that died. . . . Tell me, Tuan," he went on, looking at Lingard with curiosity— " tell me, Tuan, do you white people ever hear the voices of the invisible ones ? "

" We do not," answered Lingard, " because those that we cannot see do not speak."

" Never speak ! And never complain with sounds that are not words ? " exclaimed Babalatchi, doubtingly. " It may be so—or your ears are dull. We Malays hear many sounds near the places where men are buried. To-night I heard . . . Yes, even I have heard. . . . I do not want to hear any more," he added, nervously. " Perhaps I was wrong when I . . . There are things I regret. The trouble was heavy in his heart when he died. Sometimes I think I was wrong . . . but I do not want to hear the complaint of invisible lips. Therefore I go, Tuan. Let the unquiet spirit speak to his enemy the white man who knows not fear, or love, or mercy— knows nothing but contempt and violence. I have been wrong ! I have ! Haï ! Haï ! "

He stood for a while with his elbow in the palm of his left hand, the fingers of the other over his lips as if to stifle the expression of inconvenient remorse ! then after glancing at the torch, burnt out nearly to its end, he moved towards the wall by the chest, fumbled about there and suddenly flung open a large shutter of attaps woven in a light framework of sticks. Lingard swung his legs quickly round the corner of his seat.

" Hallo ! " he said, surprised.

The cloud of smoke stirred, and a slow wisp curled out through the new opening. The torch flickered, hissed, and went out, the glowing end falling on the mat, whence Babalatchi snatched it up and tossed it outside through the open square. It described a vanishing curve of red light, and lay below, shining feebly in the vast darkness. Babalatchi remained with his arm stretched out into the empty night.

"There," he said, "you can see the white man's courtyard, Tuan, and his house."

"I can see nothing," answered Lingard, putting his head through the shutter-hole. "It's too dark."

"Wait, Tuan," urged Babalatchi. "You have been looking long at the burning torch. You will soon see. Mind the gun, Tuan. It is loaded."

"There is no flint in it. You could not find a fire-stone for a hundred miles round this spot," said Lingard, testily. "Foolish thing to load that gun."

"I have a stone. I had it from a man wise and pious that lives in Menang Kabau. A very pious man—very good fire. He spoke words over that stone that make its sparks good. And the gun is good—carries straight and far. Would carry from here to the door of the white man's house, I believe, Tuan."

"Tida apa. Never mind your gun," muttered Lingard, peering into the formless darkness. "Is that the house—that black thing over there?" he asked.

"Yes," answered Babalatchi; "that is his house. He lives there by the will of Abdulla, and shall live there till . . . From where you stand, Tuan, you can look over the fence and across the courtyard straight at the door—at the door from which he comes out every morning, looking like a man that had seen Jehannum in his sleep."

Lingard drew his head in. Babalatchi touched his shoulder with a groping hand.

"Wait a little, Tuan. Sit still. The morning is not far off now—a morning without sun after a night without stars. But there will be light enough to see the man who said not many days ago that he alone has made you less than a child in Sambir."

He felt a slight tremor under his hand, but took it off directly and began feeling all over the lid of the chest, behind Lingard's back, for the gun.

" What are you at ? " said Lingard, impatiently. " You do worry about that rotten gun. You had better get a light."

" A light ! I tell you, Tuan, that the light of heaven is very near," said Babalatchi, who had now obtained possession of the object of his solicitude, and grasping it strongly by its long barrel, grounded the stock at his feet.

" Perhaps it is near," said Lingard, leaning both his elbows on the lower cross-piece of the primitive window and looking out. " It is very black outside yet," he remarked carelessly.

Babalatchi fidgeted about.

" It is not good for you to sit where you may be seen," he muttered.

" Why not ? " asked Lingard.

" The white man sleeps, it is true," explained Babalatchi, softly ; " yet he may come out early, and he has arms."

" Ah ! he has arms ? " said Lingard.

" Yes ; a short gun that fires many times—like yours here. Abdulla had to give it to him."

Lingard heard Babalatchi's words, but made no movement. To the old adventurer the idea that fire-arms could be dangerous in other hands than his own did not occur readily, and certainly not in connection with Willems. He was so busy with the thoughts about what he considered his own sacred duty, that he could not give any consideration to the probable actions of the man of whom he thought—as one may think of an executed criminal—with wondering indignation tempered by scornful pity. While he sat staring into the darkness, that every minute grew thinner before his pensive eyes, like a dispersing mist, Willems appeared to him as a figure belonging already wholly to the past—a figure that could come in no way into his life again. He had made up his mind, and the thing was as well as done. In his weary thoughts he had closed this fatal, inexplicable, and horrible episode in his life. The worst had happened. The coming days would see the retribution.

He had removed an enemy once or twice before, out of his path; he had paid off some very heavy scores a good many times. Captain Tom had been a good friend to many: but it was generally understood, from Honolulu round about to Diego Suarez, that Captain Tom's enmity was rather more than any man single-handed could easily manage. He would not, as he said often, hurt a fly as long as the fly left him alone; yet a man does not live for years beyond the pale of civilised laws without evolving for himself some queer notions of justice. Nobody of those he knew had ever cared to point out to him the errors of his conceptions. It was not worth anybody's while to run counter to Lingard's idea of the fitness of things—that fact was acquired to the floating wisdom of the South Seas, of the Eastern Archipelago, and was nowhere better understood than in out-of-the-way nooks of the world; in those nooks which filled, unresisted and masterful, with the echoes of the noisy presence. There is not much use in arguing with a man who boasts of never having regretted a single action of his life, whose answer to a mild criticism is a good-natured shout—" You know nothing about it. I would do it again. Yes, sir ! " His associates and his acquaintances accepted him, his opinions, his actions like things preordained and unchangeable; looked upon his many-sided manifestations with passive wonder not unmixed with that admiration which is only the rightful due of a successful man. But nobody had ever seen him in the mood he was in now. Nobody had seen Lingard doubtful and giving way to doubt, unable to make up his mind and unwilling to act; Lingard timid and hesitating one minute, angry yet inactive the next; Lingard puzzled, in a word, because, confronted with a situation that discomposed him by its unprovoked malevolence, by its ghastly injustice, that to his rough but unsophisticated palate tasted distinctly of sulphurous fumes from the deepest hell.

He had never thought about a line of conduct so much in his life—thought so bitterly and to so little purpose. He could understand a thief, a murderer, a liar, a pirate : even a mutineer—that greatest sinner of all—and he knew how to deal with any of them; how to defend himself, how to punish, how to avenge either his own wrongs or outraged justice. But now it seemed to him that he would have to confront the very devil himself, and he had a kind of a glimmer of consciousness within him that he might prove unequal to the task. He felt suddenly old, worn out and tired with his night travelling and with Babalatchi's talk; disgusted with mankind and sick of his work, past and to come. For the first time in his life he ceased to be himself, and consequently felt profoundly unhappy.

The smooth darkness filling the shutter-hole grew paler and became blotchy with ill-defined shapes, as if a new universe was being evolved out of sombre chaos. Then outlines came out, defining forms without any details, indicating here a tree, there a bush; a black belt of forest far off ; the straight lines of a house, the ridge of a high roof near by. Inside the hut, Babalatchi, who lately had been only a persuasive voice, became a human shape leaning its chin imprudently on the muzzle of a gun and rolling an uneasy eye over the reappearing world. The day came rapidly, dismal and oppressed by the fog of the river and by the heavy vapours of the sky—a day without colour and without sunshine : incomplete, disappointing, and sad.

Babalatchi twitched gently Lingard's sleeve, and when the old seaman had lifted up his head interrogatively, he stretched out an arm and a pointing forefinger towards Willems' house, now plainly visible to the right and beyond the big tree of the courtyard.

" Look, Tuan ! " he said. " He lives there. That is the door—his door. Through it he will appear soon, with his hair in disorder and his mouth full of curses. That is so. He is a white man, and never satisfied. It is in my mind he is angry even in his sleep. A dangerous man. As Tuan may observe," he went on, obsequiously, " his door faces this opening, where you condescend to sit, which is concealed from all eyes. Faces it—straight—and not far. Observe, Tuan, not at all far."

"Yes, yes; I can see. I shall see him when he wakes."

"No doubt, Tuan. When he wakes. . . . If you remain here he will not see you. That is good. No eye will see you. I shall withdraw quickly and prepare my canoe myself. I am only a poor man, and must go to Sambir to greet Lakamba when he opens his eyes. I must bow before Abdulla, who has strength—even more strength than you. Now if you remain here, you shall easily behold the man who boasted to Abdulla that he had been your friend, even while he prepared to fight those who called you protector. Yes, he plotted with Abdulla for that cursed flag. Lakamba was blind then, and I was deceived. But you, Tuan! Remember, he deceived you more. Of that he boasted before all men."

He leaned the gun quietly against the wall close to the window, and said softly: "Shall I go now, Tuan? Be careful of the gun. I have put the fire-stone in. The fire-stone of the wise man, which never fails."

Lingard's eyes were fastened on the distant doorway. Across his line of sight, in the grey emptiness of the court-yard, a big fruit-pigeon flapped languidly towards the forests with a loud booming cry, like the note of a deep gong: a brilliant bird looking in the gloom of threatening day as black as a crow. A serried flock of white rice birds rose above the trees with a faint scream, and hovered, swaying in a disordered mass that suddenly scattered in all directions, as if burst asunder by a silent explosion. Behind his back Lingard heard a shuffle of feet—women leaving the hut. In the other courtyard a voice was heard complaining of cold, and coming very feeble, but exceedingly distinct, out of the vast silence of the abandoned houses and clearings. Baba-latchi coughed discreetly. From under the house the thumping of wooden pestles husking the rice started with unexpected abruptness. The weak but clear voice in the yard again urged, "Blow up the embers, O brother!"

Another voice answered, drawling in modulated, thin sing-song, " Do it yourself, O shivering pig ! " and the drawl of the last word stopped short, as if the man had fallen into a deep hole. Babalatchi coughed again a little impatiently, and said in a confidential tone—

" Do you think it is time for me to go, Tuan ? Will you take care of my gun, Tuan ? I am a man that knows how to obey ; even obey Abdulla, who has deceived me. Nevertheless this gun carries far and true—if you would want to know, Tuan. And I have put in a double measure of powder and three slugs. Yes, Tuan. Now—perhaps—I go."

When Babalatchi commenced speaking, Lingard turned slowly round and gazed upon him with the dull and unwilling look of a sick man waking to another day of suffering. As the astute statesman proceeded, Lingard's eyebrows came close, his eyes became animated, and a big vein stood out on his forehead, accentuating a lowering frown. When speaking his last words Babalatchi faltered, then stopped, confused, before the steady gaze of the old seaman.

Lingard rose. His face cleared, and he looked down at the anxious Babalatchi with sudden benevolence.

" So ! That's what you were after," he said, laying a heavy hand on Babalatchi's yielding shoulder. " You thought I came here to murder him. Hey ? Speak ! You faithful dog of an Arab trader ! "

" And what else, Tuan ? " shrieked Babalatchi, exasperated into sincerity. " What else, Tuan ! Remember what he has done ; he poisoned our ears with his talk about you. You are a man. If you did not come to kill, Tuan, then either I am a fool or. . . ." He paused, struck his naked breast with his open palm, and finished in a discouraged whisper—" or, Tuan, you are."

Lingard looked down at him with scornful serenity. After his long and painful gropings amongst the obscure abominations of Willems' conduct, the logical if tortuous evolutions of Babalatchi's diplomatic mind were to him welcome as daylight. There was something at last he could understand—the clear effect of a simple cause. He felt indulgent towards the disappointed sage.

" So you are angry with your friend, O one-eyed one ! " he said slowly, nodding his fierce countenance close to Babalatchi's discomfited face. " It seems to me that you must have had much to do with what happened in Sambir lately. Hey ? You son of a burnt father."

" May I perish under your hand, O Rajah of the sea, if my words are not true ! " said Babalatchi, with reckless excitement. " You are here in the midst of your enemies. He the greatest. Abdulla would do nothing without him, and I could do nothing without Abdulla. Strike me—so that you strike all ! "

" Who are you," exclaimed Lingard contemptuously— " who are you to dare call yourself my enemy ! Dirt ! Nothing ! Go out first," he went on severely. " Lakas ! quick. March out ! "

He pushed Babalatchi through the doorway and followed him down the short ladder into the courtyard. The boat-men squatting over the fire turned their slow eyes with apparent difficulty towards the two men ; then, uncon-cerned, huddled close together again, stretching forlornly their hands over the embers. The women stopped in their work and with uplifted pestles flashed quick and curious glances from the gloom under the house.

" Is that the way ? " asked Lingard with a nod of his head towards the little wicket-gate of Willems' enclosure.

" If you seek death, that is surely the way," answered Babalatchi in a dispassionate voice, as if he had exhausted all the emotions. " He lives there : he who destroyed your friends ; who hastened Omar's death ; who plotted with Abdulla first against you, then against me. I have been like a child. O shame ! . . . But go, Tuan. Go there."

" I go where I like," said Lingard, emphatically, " and you may go to the devil ; I do not want you any more. The islands of these seas will sink before I, Rajah Laut, serve the will of any of your people. Tau ? But I tell you this :

I do not care what you do with him after to-day. And I say that because I am merciful."

"Tida! I do nothing," said Babalatchi, shaking his head with bitter apathy. "I am in Abdulla's hand and care not, even as you do. No! no!" he added, turning away, "I have learned much wisdom this morning. There are no men anywhere. You whites are cruel to your friends and merciful to your enemies—which is the work of fools."

He went away towards the riverside, and, without once looking back, disappeared in the low bank of mist that lay over the water and the shore. Lingard followed him with his eyes thoughtfully. After awhile he roused himself and called out to his boatmen—

"Haï—ya there! After you have eaten rice, wait for me with your paddles in your hands. You hear?"

"Ada, Tuan!" answered Ali through the smoke of the morning fire that was spreading itself, low and gentle, over the courtyard—"we hear!"

Lingard opened slowly the little wicket-gate, made a few steps into the empty enclosure, and stopped. He had felt about his head the short breath of a puff of wind that passed him, made every leaf of the big tree shiver—and died out in a hardly perceptible tremor of branches and twigs. Instinctively he glanced upwards with a seaman's impulse. Above him, under the grey motionless waste of a stormy sky, drifted low black vapours, in stretching bars, in shapeless patches, in sinuous wisps and tormented spirals. Over the courtyard and the house floated a round, sombre, and lingering cloud, dragging behind a tail of tangled and filmy streamers—like the dishevelled hair of a mourning woman.

## III

" Beware ! "

The tremulous effort and the broken, inadequate tone of
the faint cry surprised Lingard more than the unexpected
suddenness of the warning conveyed, he did not know by
whom and to whom. Besides himself there was no one in
the courtyard as far as he could see. The cry was not
renewed, and his watchful eyes, scanning warily the misty
solitude of Willems' enclosure, were met everywhere only
by the stolid impassiveness of inanimate things : the big
sombre-looking tree, the shut-up, sightless house, the glistening bamboo fences, the damp and drooping bushes further
off—all these things, that condemned to look for ever at the
incomprehensible afflictions or joys of mankind, assert in
their aspect of cold unconcern the high dignity of lifeless
matter that surrounds, incurious and unmoved, the restless
mysteries of the ever-changing, of the never-ending life.

Lingard, stepping aside, put the trunk of the tree between himself and the house, then, moving cautiously round
one of the projecting buttresses, had to tread short in order
to avoid scattering a small heap of black embers upon which
he came unexpectedly on the other side. A thin, wizened,
little old woman, who, standing behind the tree, had been
looking at the house, turned towards him with a start, gazed
with faded, expressionless eyes at the intruder, then made
a limping attempt to get away. She seemed, however, to
realise directly the hopelessness or the difficulty of the
undertaking, stopped, hesitated, tottered back slowly ; then,
after blinking dully, fell suddenly on her knees amongst the
white ashes, and, bending over the heap of smouldering
coals, distended her sunken cheeks in a steady effort to blow
up the hidden sparks into a useful blaze. Lingard looked
down on her, but she seemed to have made up her mind that
there was not enough life left in her lean body for anything

else than the discharge of the simple domestic duty, and, apparently, she begrudged him the least moment of attention. After waiting for awhile, Lingard asked—

"Why did you call, O daughter?"

"I saw you enter," she croaked feebly, still grovelling with her face near the ashes and without looking up, "and I called—the cry of warning. It was her order. Her order," she repeated, with a moaning sigh.

"And did she hear?" pursued Lingard, with gentle composure.

Her projecting shoulder-blades moved uneasily under the thin stuff of the tight body jacket. She scrambled up with difficulty to her feet, and hobbled away, muttering peevishly to herself, towards a pile of dry brushwood heaped up against the fence.

Lingard, looking idly after her, heard the rattle of loose planks that led from the ground to the door of the house. He moved his head beyond the shelter of the tree and saw Aïssa coming down the inclined way into the courtyard. After making a few hurried paces towards the tree, she stopped with one foot advanced in an appearance of sudden terror, and her eyes glanced wildly right and left. Her head was uncovered. A blue cloth wrapped her from her head to foot in close slanting folds, with one end thrown over her shoulder. A tress of her black hair strayed across her bosom. Her bare arms pressed down close to her body, with hands open and outstretched fingers; her slightly elevated shoulders and the backward inclination of her torso gave her the aspect of one defiant yet shrinking from a coming blow. She had closed the door of the house behind her; and as she stood solitary in the unnatural and threatening twilight of the murky day, with everything unchanged around her, she appeared to Lingard as if she had been made there, on the spot, out of the black vapours of the sky and of the sinister gleams of feeble sunshine that struggled, through the thickening clouds, into the colourless desolation of the world.

After a short but attentive glance towards the shut-up house, Lingard stepped out from behind the tree and

advanced slowly towards her. The sudden fixity of her—
till then—restless eyes and a slight twitch of her hands were
the only signs she gave at first of having seen him; but as
he went on, as if to pass her on his way to the house, she made
a long stride forward, and putting herself right in his path,
stretched her arms across; her black eyes opened wide, her
lips parted as if in an uncertain attempt to speak—but no
sound came out to break the significant silence of their
meeting. Somewhat embarrassed, Lingard stopped and
looked at her with stern curiosity. After a while he said
composedly—

"Let me pass. I came here to talk to a man. Does he
hide? Has he sent you?"

She made a step nearer, her arms fell by her side, then she
put them straight out nearly touching Lingard's breast.

"He knows not fear," she said, speaking low, with a
forward throw of her head, in a voice trembling but distinct.
"It is my own fear that has sent me here. He sleeps."

"He has slept long enough," said Lingard, in measured
tones. "I am come—and now is the time of his waking.
Go and tell him this—or else my own voice will call him up.
A voice he knows well."

He put her hands down firmly and again made as if to
pass by her.

"Do not!" she exclaimed, and fell at his feet as if she had
been cut down by a scythe. The unexpected suddenness
of her movement startled Lingard, who stepped back.

"What's this?" he exclaimed in a wondering whisper—
then added in a tone of sharp command: "Stand up!"

She rose at once and stood looking at him, obedient and
resisting—timorous and fearless: hesitating, as if she longed
to flee, yet with a fire of recklessness burning in her eyes that
made clear her resolve to pursue her purpose—even to the
death. Lingard went on in a severe voice—

"Go out of my path. You are Omar's daughter, and
you ought to know that when men meet in daylight women
must be silent and abide their fate."

"Women!" she retorted, with subdued vehemence.

"Yes, I am a woman! Your eyes see that, O Rajah Laut, but can you see my life? I also have heard—O man of many fights—I also have heard the voice of fire-arms; I also have felt the rain of young twigs and of leaves cut up by bullets fall down upon my head; I also know how to look in silence at angry faces and at strong hands raised high grasping sharp steel. I also saw men fall dead around me without a cry of fear and of mourning; and I have watched the sleep of weary fugitives, and looked at night shadows full of menace and death with eyes that knew nothing but watchfulness. And," she went on, with a mournful drop in her voice, " I have faced the heartless sea, held on my lap the heads of those who died raving from thirst, and from their cold hands took the paddle and worked so that those with me did not know that one man more was dead. I did all this. What more have you done? That was my life. What has been yours? "

The matter and the manner of her speech held Lingard motionless, attentive and approving against his will. When she ceased speaking she drew a long breath, and from her staring black eyes that glittered, big, steady and round, with a narrow border of white above and below, a double ray of her very soul streamed out in a fierce desire to light up the most obscure designs of his heart. After a long silence, which served to emphasise the meaning of her words, she added in the whisper of bitter regret—

" And I have knelt at your feet! And I am afraid! "

" You," said Lingard deliberately, and returning her look with an interested gaze, " you are a woman whose heart, I believe, is great enough to fill a man's breast: but still you are a woman, and to you, I, Rajah Laut, have nothing to say."

She listened bending her head in a movement of forced attention; and his voice sounded to her unexpected, far off, with the distant and unearthly ring of voices that we hear in dreams, saying faintly things startling, cruel or absurd, to which there is no possible reply. To her he had nothing to say! She wrung her hands, glanced over the courtyard with that eager and distracted look that sees nothing, then looked up at the hopeless sky of livid grey and drifting black; at the unquiet mourning of the hot and brilliant heaven that had seen the beginning of her love, that had heard his entreaties and her answers, that had seen his desire and her fear; that had seen her joy, her surrender—and his defeat. Lingard moved a little, and this slight stir near her precipitated her disordered and shapeless thoughts into hurried words.

"Wait!" she exclaimed in a stifled voice, and went on disconnectedly and rapidly—"Stay. I have heard. Men often spoke by the fires . . . men of my people. And they said of you—the first on the sea—they said that to men's cries you were deaf in battle, but after . . . No! even while you fought, your ears were open to the voice of children and women. They said . . . that. Now I, a woman, I . . ."

She broke off suddenly and stood before him with dropped eyelids and parted lips, so still now that she seemed to have been changed into a breathless, an unhearing, an unseeing figure, without knowledge of fear or hope, of anger or despair. In the astounding repose that came on her face unexpected, desperate and firm, nothing moved but the delicate nostrils that expanded and collapsed quickly, flutteringly, in interrupted beats, like the wings of a snared bird.

"I am white," said Lingard, proudly, looking at her with a steady gaze where simple curiosity was giving way to a pitying annoyance, "and men you have heard, spoke only what is true over the evening fires. My ears are open to your prayers. But listen to me before you speak. For yourself you need not be afraid. You can come even now with me and you shall find refuge in the household of Syed Abdulla—who is of your own faith. And this also you must know: nothing that you may say will change my purpose towards the man who is sleeping—or hiding—in that house."

Again she gave him the look that was like a stab, not of anger but of desire; of the intense, overpowering desire to see in, to see through, to understand everything: every thought, emotion, purpose; every impulse, every hesitation inside that man; inside that white-clad foreign being who looked at her, who spoke to her, who breathed before her like any other man, but bigger, red-faced, white-haired and mysterious. It was the future clothed in flesh; the to-morrow; the day after; all the days, all the years of her life standing there before her alive and secret, with all their good or evil shut up within the breast of that man; of that man who could be persuaded, cajoled, entreated, perhaps touched, worried; frightened—who knows?—if only first he could be understood! She had seen a long time ago whither events were tending. She had noted the contemp-tuous yet menacing coldness of Abdulla; she had heard—alarmed yet unbelieving—Babalatchi's gloomy hints, covert allusions and veiled suggestions to abandon the useless white man whose fate would be the price of the peace secured by the wise and good who had no need of him any more. And he—himself! She clung to him. There was nobody else. Nothing else. She would try to cling to him always—all her life! And yet he was far from her. Further every day. Every day he seemed more distant, and she followed him patiently, hopefully, blindly, but steadily, through all the devious wanderings of his mind. She followed as well as she could. Yet at times—very often lately—she had felt lost like one strayed in the thickets of tangled undergrowth in the great forest—pushing on till he can go no further, and held at last in the maze of branches and creepers, seeing nothing but thick leaves, tough green twigs, obstinate tendrils, clinging parasites; seeing all the interlaced con-fusion of those many things close before his eyes—yet unable to see the ground on which he stands. She was like one lost in a wilderness impenetrable and heavy, in a wilderness devoid of hope but full of surprises; one held captive amongst the restlessness of unseen forces that are silent and destructive, dangerous and indifferent, incomprehensible and strong. To her the ex-clerk of old Hudig appeared as remote, as brilliant, as terrible, as necessary as the sun that gives life to these lands: the sun of unclouded skies that dazzles and withers; the sun beneficent and wicked—the giver of light, perfume, and pestilence. She had watched him—watched him close; fascinated by love, fascinated by danger. He was alone now—but for her; and she saw—she thought she saw—that he was like a man afraid of something. Was it possible? He afraid? Of what? Was it of that old white man who was coming? Who had come! Possibly. She had heard of that man ever since she could remember. The bravest were afraid of him! And now what was in the mind of this old, old man who looked so strong? What was he going to do with the light of her life? Put it out? Take it away? Take it away for ever!—for ever!—and leave her in darkness :—not in the stirring, whispering, expectant night in which the hushed world awaits the return of sunshine; but in the night without end, the night of the grave, where nothing breathes, nothing moves, nothing thinks— the last darkness of cold and silence without hope of another sunrise.

She cried—"Your purpose! You know nothing. I must . . ."

He interrupted—unreasonably excited, as if she had, by her look, inoculated him with some of her own distress.

" I know enough."

She approached, and stood facing him at arm's length, with both her hands on his shoulders; and he, surprised by that audacity, closed and opened his eyes two or three times, aware of some emotion arising within him, from her words, her tone, her contact; an emotion unknown, singular, penetrating and sad—at the close sight of that strange woman, of that being savage and tender, strong and delicate, fearful and resolute, that had got entangled so fatally between their two lives—his own and that other white man's, the abominable scoundrel.

" How can you know? " she went on, in a persuasive tone that seemed to flow out of her very heart—" how can you know? I live with him all the days. All the nights. I look at him; I see his every breath, every glance of his eyes, every movement of his lips. I see nothing else! What else

is there? And even I do not understand. I do not understand him!—Him!—My life! Him who to me is so great
that his presence hides the earth and the water from my
sight!"

Lingard stood straight, with his hands deep in the pockets
of his jacket. His eye winked quickly, because she spoke
very close to his face. She disturbed him much, and he
had a sense of the efforts he was making to get hold of her
meaning, while all the time he could not help telling himself
that all this was of no use.

She added after a pause—" There has been a time when I
could understand him. When I knew what was in his mind
better than he knew it himself. When I felt him. When
I held him. . . . And now he has escaped."

" Escaped? What? Gone!" shouted Lingard.

" Escaped from me," she said; " left me alone. Alone.
And I am ever near him. Yet alone."

Her hands slipped slowly off Lingard's shoulders and her
arms fell by her side, listless, discouraged, as if to her—to her,
the savage, violent, and ignorant creature—had been revealed
clearly in that moment the tremendous fact of our isolation,
of the loneliness impenetrable and transparent, elusive and
everlasting; of the indestructible loneliness that surrounds,
envelops, clothes every human soul from the cradle to the
grave, and, perhaps, beyond.

" Aye! Very well! I understand. His face is turned
away from you," said Lingard. " Now, what do you want?"

" I want . . . I have looked—for help . . . everywhere
. . . against men. . . . All men . . . I do not know.
First they came, the invisible whites, and dealt death from
afar . . . then he came. He came to me who was alone and
sad. He came; angry with his brothers; great amongst his
own people; angry with those I have not seen: with the
people where men have no mercy and women have no shame.
He was of them, and great amongst them. For he was
great?"

Lingard shook his head slightly. She frowned at him, and
went on in disordered haste—

" Listen. I saw him. I have lived by the side of brave men . . . of chiefs. When he came I was the daughter of a beggar—of a blind man without strength and hope. He spoke to me as if I had been brighter than the sunshine— more delightful than the cool water of the brook by which we met—more . . ."

Her anxious eyes saw some shade of expression pass on her listener's face that made her hold her breath for a second, and then explode into pained fury so violent that it drove Lingard back a pace, like an unexpected blast of wind. He lifted both his hands, incongruously paternal in his venerable aspect, bewildered and soothing, while she stretched her neck forward and shouted at him.

" I tell you I was all that to him. I know it ! I saw it ! . . . There are times when even you white men speak the truth. I saw his eyes. I felt his eyes, I tell you ! I saw him tremble when I came near—when I spoke—when I touched him. Look at me ! You have been young. Look at me. Look, Rajah Laut ! "

She stared at Lingard with provoking fixity, then, turning her head quickly, she sent over her shoulder a glance, full of humble fear, at the house that stood high behind her back—dark, closed, rickety and silent on its crooked posts.

Lingard's eyes followed her look, and remained gazing expectantly at the house. After a minute or so he muttered, glancing at her suspiciously—

" If he has not heard your voice now, then he must be far away—or dead."

" He is there," she whispered, a little calmed but still anxious—" he is there. For three days he waited. Waited for you night and day. And I waited with him. I waited, watching his face, his eyes, his lips ; listening to his words.— To the words I could not understand.—To the words he spoke in daylight ; to the words he spoke at night in his short sleep. I listened. He spoke to himself walking up and down here—by the river ; by the bushes. And I followed. I wanted to know—and I could not ! He was

N

tormented by things that made him speak in the words of his own people. Speak to himself—not to me. Not to me! What was he saying? What was he going to do? Was he afraid of you?—Of death? What was in his heart? . . . Fear? . . . Or anger? . . . What desire? . . . What sadness? He spoke; spoke; many words. All the time! And I could not know! I wanted to speak to him. He was deaf to me. I followed him everywhere, watching for some word I could understand; but his mind was in the land of his people—away from me. When I touched him he was angry—so!"

She imitated the movement of some one shaking off roughly an importunate hand, and looked at Lingard with tearful and unsteady eyes.

After a short interval of laboured panting, as if she had been out of breath with running or fighting, she looked down and went on—

"Day after day, night after night, I lived watching him—seeing nothing. And my heart was heavy—heavy with the presence of death that dwelt amongst us. I could not believe. I thought he was afraid. Afraid of you! Then I, myself, knew fear. . . . Tell me, Rajah Laut, do you know the fear without voice—the fear of silence—the fear that comes when there is no one near—when there is no battle, no cries, no angry faces or armed hands anywhere? . . . The fear from which there is no escape!"

She paused, fastened her eyes again on puzzled-looking Lingard, and hurried on in a tone of despair—

"And I knew then he would not fight you! Before—many days ago—I went away twice to make him obey my desire; to make him strike at his own people so that he could be mine—mine! O calamity! His hand was false as your white hearts. It struck forward, pushed by my desire—by his desire of me. . . . It struck that strong hand, and—O shame!—it killed nobody! Its fierce and lying blow woke up hate without any fear. Round me all was lies. His strength was a lie. My own people lied to me—and to him. And to meet you—you, the great!—he had no one but me?

But me—with my rage, my pain, my weakness. Only me! And to me he would not even speak. The fool!"

She came up close to Lingard, with the wild and stealthy aspect of a lunatic longing to whisper out an insane secret— one of those misshapen, heartrending, and ludicrous secrets; one of those thoughts that, like monsters—cruel, fantastic, and mournful, wander about terrible and unceasing in the night of madness. Lingard looked at her, astounded but unflinching. She spoke in his face, very low.

"He is all! Everything. He is my breath, my light, my heart. . . . Go away. . . . Forget him. . . . He has no courage and no wisdom any more . . . and I have lost my power. . . . Go away and forget. There are other enemies. . . . Leave him to me. He has been a man once. . . . You are too great. Nobody can withstand you. . . . I tried. . . . I know now. . . . I cry for mercy. Leave him to me and go away."

The fragments of her supplicating sentences were as if tossed on the crest of her sobs; of sobs long, rolling, and deep like the waves of the open sea under the tormenting breath of strong winds; the miserable wreckage of her passion, her thoughts, her desires rising and falling and beating, black, sinister and torn up, in the white foam at the foot of hard rocks that belong to the solid and motionless earth. Lingard, standing outwardly impassible, with his eyes fixed on the house, felt the recoil of all the fibres of his being before that prayer; experienced that feeling of condemnation, deep-seated, persuasive, and masterful; that illogical impulse of disapproval which is half disgust, half vague fear, and that wakes up in our hearts in the presence of anything new or unusual, of anything that is not run into the mould of our own conscience; the accursed feeling made up of disdain, of anger, and of the sense of superior virtue that leaves us deaf, blind, contemptuous and stupid before anything which is not like ourselves.

He answered, not looking at her at first, but speaking towards the house that fascinated him—

"I go away! He wanted me to come—he himself did!

. . . You must go away. You do not know what you ask.
Look. He is done. Go to your own people. Leave him.
He is . . ."

He paused, looked down at her with his steady red eyes;
hesitated, as if seeking an adequate expression; then snapped
his fingers, and said—

" Finish."

She stepped back, her eyes on the ground, and pressed her
temples with both her hands, which she raised to her head
in a slow and ample movement full of unconscious tragedy.
The tone of her words was gentle and vibrating, like a loud
meditation. She said—

" Tell the brook not to run to the river; tell the river not
to run to the sea. Speak loud. Speak angrily. Maybe they
will obey. But it is in my mind that the brook will not care.
The brook that springs out of the hillside and runs to the
great river. He would not care for your words: he that
cares not for the very mountain that gave him life; he that
tears the earth from which he springs. Tears it, eats it,
destroys it—to hurry faster to the river—to the river in
which he is lost for ever. . . . O Rajah Laut ! . . . I do
not care."

She drew close again to Lingard, approaching slowly,
reluctantly, as if pushed by an invisible hand, and added in
words that seemed to be torn out of her—

" I cared not for my own father. For him that died. I
would have rather . . . You do not know what I have done
. . . I . . ."

" You shall have his life," said Lingard, hastily.

They stood together, crossing their glances ; she suddenly
appeased, and Lingard thoughtful and uneasy under a vague
sense of defeat. And yet there was no defeat. He never
intended to kill the fellow—not after the first moment of
anger, a long time ago. The days of bitter wonder had
killed anger ; had left only a bitter indignation and a bitter
wish for complete justice. He felt discontented and surprised.
Unexpectedly he had come upon a human being—a woman
at that—who had made him disclose his will before its time.

This was a matter strictly between Willems and himself. He had an unpleasant notion of having been cheated. Never before in all his life had he been induced to let a mortal creature know in advance of any design of his. When the thing was done they would see. And now he went and told her. That woman! Why? He did not know. He thought he must be getting old—and soft; unaware that some vague remnant of the fisher-boy lurking within him had suddenly revolted, had been honestly ready to imagine the worst and so would not let him hear all she had to say : a horrible confession. He heard like an indistinct voice speaking between him and her ; a voice saying that if she had committed some horrible crime for that scoundrel, and the scoundrel let her, then the scoundrel must at once die— which would be less than justice. But had she? Oh! Nonsense. What was she going to tell when he . . . She must be told, she must know that for such men as Willems there was no favour and no grace.

"Understand," he said slowly, "that I give you his life not in mercy but in punishment."

She started, watched every word on his lips, and after he finished speaking she remained still and mute in astonished immobility. A single big drop of rain, a drop enormous, pellucid and heavy—like a superhuman tear coming straight and rapid from above, as if it had torn its way through the sombre sky—struck loudly the dry ground between them in a starred splash. She wrung her hands in the bewilderment of the new and incomprehensible fear. The anguish of her whisper was more piercing than the shrillest cry.

"What punishment! Will you take him away? Away from me? Listen to what I have done. . . . It is I who . . ."

"Ah!" exclaimed Lingard, who had been looking at the house.

"Don't you believe her, Captain Lingard," shouted Willems from the doorway, where he appeared with swollen eyelids and bared breast. He stood for a while, his hands grasping the lintels on each side of the door, and writhed about, glaring wildly, as if he had been crucified there. Then he made a sudden rush head foremost down the plankway that responded with hollow, short noises to every footstep.

She heard him. A slight thrill passed on her face and the words that were on her lips fell back unspoken into her benighted heart; fell back amongst the mud, the stones—and the flowers, that are at the bottom of every heart.

## IV

When he felt the solid ground of the courtyard under his feet, Willems pulled himself up in his headlong rush and moved forward with a moderate gait. He paced stiffly, looking with extreme exactitude at Lingard's face; looking neither to the right nor to the left but at the face only, as if there was nothing in the world but those features familiar and dreaded; that white-haired, rough and severe head upon which he gazed in a fixed effort of his eyes, like a man trying to read small print at the full range of human vision. As soon as Willems' feet had left the planks, the silence which had been lifted up by the jerky rattle of his footsteps fell down again upon the courtyard; the silence of the cloudy sky and of the windless air, the sullen silence of the earth oppressed by the aspect of coming turmoil, the silence of the world collecting its faculties to withstand the storm.

Through this silence Willems pushed his way, feeling its resistance at every step, feeling it grow heavy, thick, troublesome to get through—impenetrable and solid at last like a sheet of iron. He stopped about six feet from Lingard. He stopped simply because he could go no further. He had started from the door with the reckless purpose of clapping the old fellow on the shoulder. He had no idea that the man would turn out to be so tall, so big and so unapproachable. It seemed to him that he had never, never in his life, seen Lingard.

He tried to say—

" Do not believe . . ."

A fit of coughing checked his sentence in a faint splutter ;
a fit of soft, low coughing that could not be kept in to save
his life and that shook him from head to foot, irresistible and
gentle, like the warning of great strength to extreme weakness. Directly afterwards he swallowed—as it were—a couple
of pebbles, throwing his chin up in the act ; and Lingard,
who looked at him narrowly, saw a bone, sharp and triangular
like the head of a snake, dart up and down twice under the
skin of his throat. Then that, too, did not move. Nothing
moved.

" Well," said Lingard, and with that word he came unexpectedly to the end of his speech. His hand in his pocket
closed firmly round the butt of his revolver bulging his
jacket on the hip, and he thought how soon and how quickly
he could terminate his quarrel with that man who had been
so anxious to deliver himself into his hands—and how
inadequate would be that ending ! He could not bear the
idea of that man escaping from him by going out of life ;
escaping from fear, from doubt, from remorse into the peaceful certitude of death. He held him now. And he was
not going to let him go—to let him disappear for ever in the
faint blue smoke of a pistol shot. His anger grew within
him. He felt a touch as of a burning hand on his heart.
Not on the flesh of his breast, but a touch on his heart itself,
on the palpitating and untiring particle of matter that responds to every emotion of the soul ; that leaps with joy,
with terror, or with anger.

He drew a long breath. He could see before him the
bare chest of the man expanding and collapsing under the
wide-open jacket. He glanced aside, and saw the bosom
of the woman near him rise and fall in quick respirations
that moved slightly up and down her hand, which was
pressed to her breast with all the fingers spread out and a
little curved, as if grasping something too big for its span.
They stood all three under the low sky, inhaling painfully
the tepid, misty and perfidious air ; the air poisonous and

corrupted; the breath of death that trailed about them under the heavy clouds, crept towards them from the forests, from the marshes, from the uncovered mud-flats of the starved river. And nearly a minute passed. One of those minutes that stand out forbidding and sombre like barren islets in the sea of time—ready for harm, useless for refuge. One of those minutes when the voice is silenced, while the thoughts flutter in the head, like captive birds inside a cage, in rushes desperate, exhausting and vain.

During that minute of silence Lingard's anger kept rising, immense and towering, such as a crested wave running over the troubled shallows of the sands. Its roar filled his ears; a roar so powerful and distracting that, it seemed to him, his head must burst directly with the expanding volume of that sound. He looked at that man. That thing! That infamous figure upright on its feet, still, rigid, with stony eyes, as if its rotten soul had departed that moment and the carcass hadn't had the time yet to topple over. For the fraction of a second he had the illusion and the fear of the damned scoundrel having died there before the enraged glance of his eyes. Willems' eyelids fluttered, and the unconscious and passing tremor in that stiffly erect body exasperated Lingard like a fresh outrage. The fellow dared to stir! Dare to wink, to breathe, to exist; here, right before his eyes! His grip on the revolver relaxed gradually. As the transport of his rage increased, so also his contempt for the instruments that pierce or stab, that interpose themselves between the hand and the object of hate. He wanted another kind of satisfaction. Naked hands, by heaven! No firearms. Hands that could take him by the throat, beat down his defence, batter his face into shapeless flesh; hands that could feel all the desperation of his resistance and overpower it in the violent delight of a contact lingering and furious, intimate and brutal.

He let go the revolver altogether, stood hesitating, then throwing his hands out, strode forward—and everything passed from his sight. He could not see the man, the woman, the earth, the sky—saw nothing, as if in that one stride he

had left the visible world behind to step into a black and
deserted space. He heard screams round him in that
obscurity, screams like the melancholy and pitiful cries of
sea-birds that dwell on the lonely reefs of great oceans. Then
suddenly a face appeared within a few inches of his own.
His face. He felt something in his left hand. His throat.
. . . Ah! the thing like a snake's head that darts up and
down . . . He squeezed hard. He was back in the world.
He could see the quick beating of eyelids over a pair of eyes
that were all whites, the grin of a drawn-up lip, a row of
teeth gleaming through the drooping hair of a moustache . . .
Strong white teeth. Knock them down his lying throat . . .
He drew back his right hand, the fist up to the shoulder,
knuckles out. From under his feet rose the screams of
sea-birds. Thousands of them. Something held his legs. . .
What the devil . . . He delivered his blow straight from
the shoulder, felt the jar right up his arm, and realised
suddenly that he was striking something passive and unresisting. His heart sank within him with disappointment,
with rage, with mortification. He pushed with his left
arm, opening the hand with haste, as if he had just perceived
that he got hold by accident of something repulsive—and
he watched with stupefied eyes Willems tottering backwards
in groping strides, the white sleeve of his jacket across his
face. He watched his distance from that man increase,
while he remained motionless, without being able to account
to himself for the fact that so much empty space had come
in between them. It should have been the other way.
They ought to have been very close, and . . . Ah! He
wouldn't fight, he wouldn't resist, he wouldn't defend
himself! A cur! Evidently a cur! . . . He was amazed
and aggrieved—profoundly—bitterly—with the immense
and blank desolation of a small child robbed of a toy. He
shouted—unbelieving:

" Will you be a cheat to the end ? "

He waited for some answer. He waited anxiously with
an impatience that seemed to lift him off his feet. He
waited like one that sees coming out of the future an un-

N 2

heard-of fortune or sudden disaster. He waited for some word, some sign; for some threatening stir. Nothing! Only two unwinking eyes glittered intently at him above the white sleeve. He saw the raised arm detach itself from the face and sink along the body. A white-clad arm, with a big stain on the white sleeve. A red stain. There was a cut on the cheek. It bled. The nose bled too. The blood ran down, made one moustache look like a dark rag stuck over the lip, and went on in a wet streak down the clipped beard on one side of the chin. A drop of blood hung on the end of some hairs that were glued together; it hung for a while and took a leap down to the ground. Many more followed, leaping one after another in close file. One alighted on the breast and glided down instantly with devious vivacity, like a small insect running away; it left a narrow dark track on the white skin. He looked at it, looked at the tiny and active drops, looked at what he had done, with obscure satisfaction, with anger, with regret. This wasn't much like an act of justice. He had a desire to go up nearer to the man, to hear him speak, to hear him say something atrocious and wicked that would justify the violence of the blow. He made an attempt to move, and became aware of a close embrace round both his legs, just above the ankles. Instinctively, he kicked out with his foot, broke through the close bond and felt at once the clasp transferred to his other leg; the clasp warm, desperate and soft, of human arms. He looked down bewildered. He saw the body of the woman stretched at length, flattened on the ground like a dark-blue rag. She trailed face downwards, clinging to his leg with both arms in a tenacious hug. He saw the top of her head, the long black hair streaming over his foot, all over the beaten earth, around his boot. He couldn't see his foot for it. He heard the short and repeated moaning of her breath. He imagined the invisible face close to his heel. With one kick into that face he could free himself. He dared not stir, and shouted down—

"Let go! Let go! Let go!"

The only result of his shouting was a tightening of the

pressure of her arms. With a tremendous effort he tried
to bring his right foot up to his left, and succeeded partly.
He heard distinctly the rub of her body on the ground as he
jerked her along. He tried to disengage himself by drawing
up his foot. He stamped. He heard a voice saying sharply—

"Steady, Captain Lingard, steady!"

His eyes flew back to Willems at the sound of that voice,
and, in the quick awakening of sleeping memories, Lingard
stood suddenly still, appeased by the clear ring of familiar
words. Appeased as in days of old, when they were trading
together, when Willems was his trusted and helpful companion in out-of-the-way and dangerous places; when that
fellow, who could keep his temper so much better than he
could himself, had spared him many a difficulty, had saved
him from many an act of hasty violence by the timely and
good-humoured warning, whispered or shouted, "Steady,
Captain Lingard, steady." A smart fellow. He had
brought him up. The smartest fellow in the islands. If he
had only stayed with him, then all this . . . He called out
to Willems—

"Tell her to let me go or . . ."

He heard Willems shouting something, waited for awhile,
then glanced vaguely down and saw the woman still stretched
out perfectly mute and unstirring, with her head at his feet.
He felt a nervous impatience that, somehow, resembled
fear.

"Tell her to let go, to go away, Willems, I tell you. I've
had enough of this," he cried.

"All right, Captain Lingard," answered the calm voice of
Willems, "she has let go. Take your foot off her hair; she
can't get up."

Lingard leaped aside, clean away, and spun round quickly.
He saw her sit up and cover her face with both hands, then
he turned slowly on his heel and looked at the man. Willems
held himself very straight, but was unsteady on his feet, and
moved about nearly on the same spot, like a tipsy man
attempting to preserve his balance. After gazing at him for
a while, Lingard called, rancorous and irritable—

" What have you got to say for yourself ? "

Willems began to walk towards him. He walked slowly, reeling a little before he took each step, and Lingard saw him put his hand to his face, then look at it holding it up to his eyes, as if he had there, concealed in the hollow of the palm, some small object which he wanted to examine secretly. Suddenly he drew it, with a brusque movement, down the front of his jacket and left a long smudge.

" That's a fine thing to do," said Willems.

He stood in front of Lingard, one of his eyes sunk deep in the increasing swelling of his cheek, still repeating mechanically the movement of feeling his damaged face ; and every time he did this he pressed the palm to some clean spot on his jacket, covering the white cotton with bloody imprints as of some deformed and monstrous hand. Lingard said nothing, looking on. At last Willems left off staunching the blood and stood, his arms hanging by his side, with his face stiff and distorted under the patches of coagulated blood ; and he seemed as though he had been set up there for a warning : an incomprehensible figure marked all over with some awful and symbolic signs of deadly import. Speaking with difficulty, he repeated in a reproachful tone—

" That was a fine thing to do."

" After all," answered Lingard, bitterly, " I had too good an opinion of you."

" And I of you. Don't you see that I could have had that fool over there killed and the whole thing burnt to the ground, swept off the face of the earth ? You wouldn't have found as much as a heap of ashes had I liked. I could have done all that. And I wouldn't."

" You—could—not. You dared not. You scoundrel ! " cried Lingard.

" What's the use of calling me names ? "

" True," retorted Lingard—" there's no name bad enough for you."

There was a short interval of silence. At the sound of their rapidly exchanged words, Aïssa had got up from the ground where she had been sitting, in a sorrowful and dejected pose, and approached the two men. She stood on one side and looked on eagerly. Her eyes would watch on the moving lips the quiver of last words, then would leap in a flash to the other face, forestalling the first tremor of the lips that were going to speak. She looked on helpless, bewildered, in a desperate effort of her brain, with the quick and distracted eyes of a person trying for her life to penetrate the meaning of sentences uttered in a foreign tongue : the meaning portentous and fateful that lurks in the sounds of mysterious words ; in the sounds surprising, unknown and strange.

Willems let the last speech of Lingard pass by ; seemed by a slight movement of his hand to help it on its way to join the other shadows of the past. Then he said—

" You have struck me ; you have insulted me . . ."

" Insulted you ! " interrupted Lingard, passionately. " Who—what can insult you . . . you . . ."

He choked, advanced a step.

" Steady ! steady ! " said Willems, calmly. " I tell you I sha'n't fight. Is it clear enough to you that I sha'n't ? I—shall—not—lift—a—finger."

As he spoke, slowly punctuating each word with a slight jerk of his head, he stared at Lingard, his right eye open and big, the left small and nearly closed by the swelling of one half of his face, that appeared all drawn out on one side like faces seen in a concave glass. And they stood exactly opposite each other : one tall, slight and disfigured ; the other tall, heavy and severe.

Willems went on—

" If I had wanted to hurt you—if I had wanted to destroy you, it was easy. I stood in the doorway long enough to pull a trigger—and you know I shoot straight."

" You would have missed," said Lingard, with assurance. " There is, under heaven, such a thing as justice."

The sound of that word on his own lips made him pause, confused, like an unexpected and unanswerable rebuke. The anger of his outraged pride, the anger of his outraged heart, had gone out in the blow ; and there remained nothing but the sense of some immense infamy—of something vague, disgusting and terrible, which seemed to surround him on all sides, hover about him with shadowy and stealthy movements, like a band of assassins in the darkness of vast and unsafe places. Was there, under heaven, such a thing as justice? He looked at the man before him with such an intensity of prolonged glance that he seemed to see right through him, that at last he saw but a floating and unsteady mist in human shape. Would it blow away before the first breath of the breeze and leave nothing behind? Nothing to lay hold of? No motive, no reason, no cause, nothing to justify to his simple heart the strange workings of Providence that allowed such a thing to live, to lie, to do harm; that gave it eyes to search out, lips to deceive, a brain to plan infamous treacheries. To plan them, to execute them—and to go on breathing, moving, confronting men, speaking to them—impudent and safe. He, himself, felt an intolerable shame when looking at that creature before him. He felt somehow the weight of his responsibility for its continued existence; and he was so appalled by the thought that had the world that moment come to an end, had it crumbled to pieces, dissolved, drifted away in fragments from under his feet, he would not have felt the slightest surprise.

The sound of Willems' voice made him start violently. Willems was saying—

" I have always led a virtuous life; you know I have. You always praised me for my steadiness; you know you have. You know also I never stole—if that's what you're thinking of. I borrowed. You know how much I repaid. It was an error of judgment. But then consider my position there. I had been a little unlucky in my private affairs, and had debts. Could I let myself go under before the eyes of all those men who envied me? But that's all over. It was an error of judgment. I've paid for it. An error of judgment."

Lingard, astounded into perfect stillness, looked down. He looked down at Willems' bare feet. Then, as the other had paused, he repeated in a blank tone—

" An error of judgment . . ."

"Yes," drawled out Willems, thoughtfully, and went on with increasing animation: "As I said, I have always led a virtuous life. More so than Hudig—than you. Yes, than you. I drank a little, I played cards a little. Who doesn't? But I had principles from a boy. Yes, principles. Business is business, and I never was an ass. I never respected fools. They had to suffer for their folly when they dealt with me. The evil was in them, not in me. But as to principles, it's another matter. I kept clear of women. It's forbidden— I had no time—and I despised them. Now I hate them!"

He put his tongue out a little; a tongue whose pink and moist end ran here and there, like something independently alive, under his swollen and blackened lip; he touched with the tips of his fingers the cut on his cheek, felt all round it with precaution: and the unharmed side of his face appeared for a moment to be preoccupied and uneasy about the state of that other side which was so very sore and stiff.

He recommenced speaking, and his voice vibrated as though with repressed emotion of some kind.

"You ask my wife, when you see her in Macassar, whether I have no reason to hate her. She was nobody, and I made her Mrs. Willems. A half-caste girl! You ask her how she showed her gratitude to me. You ask . . . Never mind that. Well, you came and dumped me here like a load of rubbish; dumped me here and left me with nothing to do— nothing good to remember—and damn little to hope for. You left me here at the mercy of that fool, Almayer, who suspected me of something. Of what? Devil only knows. But he suspected and hated me from the first; I suppose because you befriended me. Oh! I could read him like a book. He isn't very deep, your Sambir partner, Captain Lingard, but he knows how to be disagreeable. Months passed. I thought I would die of sheer weariness, of my thoughts, of my regrets. And then . . ."

He made a quick step nearer to Lingard, and as if moved by the same thought, by the same instinct, by the impulse of his will, Aïssa also stepped nearer to them. They stood in a close group, and the two men could feel the calm air between their faces stirred by the light breath of the anxious woman who enveloped them both in the uncomprehending, in the despairing and wondering glances of her wild and mournful eyes.

## V

WILLEMS turned a little from her and spoke lower.

"Look at that," he said, with an almost imperceptible movement of his head towards the woman to whom he was presenting his shoulder. "Look at that! Don't believe her! What has she been saying to you? What? I have been asleep. Had to sleep at last. I've been waiting for you three days and nights. I had to sleep some time. Hadn't I? I told her to remain awake and watch for you, and call me at once. She did watch. You can't believe her. You can't believe any woman. Who can tell what's inside their heads? No one. You can know nothing. The only thing you can know is that it isn't anything like what comes through their lips. They live by the side of you. They seem to hate you, or they seem to love you; they caress or torment you; they throw you over or stick to you closer than your skin for some inscrutable and awful reason of their own—which you can never know! Look at her—and look at me. At me!—her infernal work. What has she been saying?"

His voice had sunk to a whisper. Lingard listened with great attention, holding his chin in his hand, which grasped a great handful of his white beard. His elbow was in the palm of his other hand, and his eyes were still fixed on the ground. He murmured, without looking up—

"She begged me for your life—if you want to know—as if the thing was worth giving or taking!"

"And for three days she begged me to take yours," said Willems quickly. "For three days she wouldn't give me any peace. She was never still. She planned ambushes. She has been looking for places all over here where I could hide and drop you with a safe shot as you walked up. It's true. I give you my word."

"Your word," muttered Lingard, contemptuously.

Willems took no notice.

"Ah! She is a ferocious creature," he went on. "You don't know . . . I wanted to pass the time—to do something —to have something to think about—to forget my troubles till you came back. And . . . look at her . . . she took me as if I did not belong to myself. She did. I did not know there was something in me she could get hold of. She, a savage. I, a civilised European, and clever! She that knew no more than a wild animal! Well, she found out something in me. She found it out, and I was lost. I knew it. She tormented me. I was ready to do anything. I resisted— but I was ready. I knew that too. That frightened me more than anything; more than my own sufferings; and that was frightful enough, I assure you."

Lingard listened, fascinated and amazed like a child listening to a fairy tale, and, when Willems stopped for breath, he shuffled his feet a little.

"What does he say?" cried out Aïssa, suddenly.

The two men looked at her quickly, and then looked at one another.

Willems began again, speaking hurriedly—

"I tried to do something. Take her away from those people. I went to Almayer; the biggest blind fool that you ever . . . Then Abdulla came—and she went away. She took away with her something of me which I had to get back. I had to do it. As far as you are concerned, the change here had to happen sooner or later; you couldn't be master here for ever. It isn't what I have done that torments me. It is the why. It's the madness that drove me to it. It's that thing that came over me. That may come again some day."

"It will do no harm to anybody then, I promise you," said Lingard, significantly.

Willems looked at him for a second with a blank stare, then went on—

"I fought against her. She goaded me to violence and to murder. Nobody knows why. She pushed me to it persistently, desperately, all the time. Fortunately Abdulla had sense. I don't know what I wouldn't have done. She held me then. Held me like a nightmare that is terrible and sweet. By and by it was another life. I woke up. I found myself beside an animal as full of harm as a wild cat. You don't know through what I have passed. Her father tried to kill me—and she very nearly killed him. I believe she would have stuck at nothing. I don't know which was more terrible! She would have stuck at nothing to defend her own. And when I think that it was me—me—Willems . . . I hate her. To-morrow she may want my life. How can I know what's in her? She may want to kill me next!"

He paused in great trepidation, then added in a scared tone—

"I don't want to die here."

"Don't you?" said Lingard, thoughtfully.

Willems turned towards Aïssa and pointed at her with a bony forefinger.

"Look at her! Always there. Always near. Always watching, watching . . . for something. Look at her eyes. Ain't they big? Don't they stare? You wouldn't think she can shut them like human beings do. I don't believe she ever does. I go to sleep, if I can, under their stare, and when I wake up I see them fixed on me and moving no more than the eyes of a corpse. While I am still they are still. By God! she can't move them till I stir, and then they follow me like a pair of jailers. They watch me; when I stop they seem to wait patient and glistening till I am off my guard—for to do something. To do something horrible. Look at them! You can see nothing in them. They are big, menacing—and empty. The eyes of a savage; of a damned mongrel, half-Arab, half-Malay. They hurt me! I am white! I swear to you I can't stand this! Take me away. I am white! All white!"

He shouted towards the sombre heaven, proclaiming desperately under the frown of thickening clouds the fact of his pure and superior descent. He shouted, his head thrown up, his arms swinging about wildly; lean, ragged, disfigured; a tall madman making a great disturbance about something invisible; a being absurd, repulsive, pathetic, and droll. Lingard, who was looking down as if absorbed in deep thought, gave him a quick glance from under his eyebrows: Aïssa stood with clasped hands. At the other end of the courtyard the old woman, like a vague and decrepit apparition, rose noiselessly to look, then sank down again with a stealthy movement and crouched low over the small glow of the fire. Willems' voice filled the enclosure, rising louder with every word, and then, suddenly, at its very loudest, stopped short— like water stops running from an overturned vessel. As soon as it had ceased the thunder seemed to take up the burden in a low growl coming from the inland hills. The noise approached in confused mutterings which kept on increasing, swelling into a roar that came nearer, rushed down the river, passed close in a tearing crash—and instantly sounded faint, dying away in monotonous and dull repetitions amongst the endless sinuosities of the lower reaches. Over the great forests, over all the innumerable people of unstirring trees— over all that living people immense, motionless, and mute— the silence, that had rushed in on the track of the passing tumult, remained suspended as deep and complete as if it had never been disturbed from the beginning of remote ages. Then, through it, after a time, came to Lingard's ears the voice of the running river: a voice low, discreet, and sad, like the persistent and gentle voices that speak of the past in the silence of dreams.

He felt a great emptiness in his heart. It seemed to him that there was within his breast a great space without any light, where his thoughts wandered forlornly, unable to escape, unable to rest, unable to die, to vanish—and to relieve him from the fearful oppression of their existence. Speech, action, anger, forgiveness, all appeared to him alike useless and vain, appeared to him unsatisfactory, not worth the effort of hand or brain that was needed to give them effect. He could not see why he should not remain standing there, without ever doing anything, to the end of time. He felt something, something like a heavy chain, that held him there. This wouldn't do. He backed away a little from Willems and Aïssa, leaving them close together, then stopped and looked at both. The man and the woman appeared to him much further than they really were. He had made only about three steps backward, but he believed for a moment that another step would take him out of earshot for ever. They appeared to him slightly under life size, and with a great cleanness of outlines, like figures carved with great precision of detail and highly finished by a skilful hand. He pulled himself together. The strong consciousness of his own personality came back to him. He had a notion of surveying them from a great and inaccessible height.

He said slowly : " You have been possessed of a devil."

" Yes," answered Willems gloomily, and looking at Aïssa. " Isn't it pretty ? "

" I've heard this kind of talk before," said Lingard, in a scornful tone ; then paused, and went on steadily after a while : " I regret nothing. I picked you up by the water-side, like a starving cat—by God. I regret nothing ; nothing that I have done. Abdulla—twenty others—no doubt Hudig himself, were after me. That's business—for them. But that you should . . . Money belongs to him who picks it up and is strong enough to keep it—but this thing was different. It was part of my life. . . . I am an old fool."

He was. The breath of his words, of the very words he spoke, fanned the spark of divine folly in his breath, the spark that made him—the hard-headed, heavy-handed adventurer —stand out from the crowd, from the sordid, from the joyous, unscrupulous, and noisy crowd of men that were so much like himself.

Willems said hurriedly : " It wasn't me. The evil was not in me, Captain Lingard."

" And where else—confound you ! Where else ? " interrupted Lingard, raising his voice. " Did you ever see me cheat and lie and steal ? Tell me that. Did you ? Hey ? I wonder where in perdition you came from when I found you under my feet. . . . No matter. You will do no more harm."

Willems moved nearer, gazing upon him anxiously. Lingard went on with distinct deliberation—

" What did you expect when you asked me to see you ? What ? You know me. I am Lingard. You lived with me. You've heard men speak. You knew what you had done. Well ! What did you expect ? "

" How can I know ? " groaned Willems, wringing his hands ; " I was alone in that infernal savage crowd. I was delivered into their hands. After the thing was done, I felt so lost and weak that I would have called the devil himself to my aid if it had been any good—if he hadn't put in all his work already. In the whole world there was only one man that had ever cared for me. Only one white man. You ! Hate is better than being alone ! Death is better ! I expected . . . anything. Something to expect. Something to take me out of this. Out of her sight ! "

He laughed. His laugh seemed to be torn out from him against his will, seemed to be brought violently on the surface from under his bitterness, his self-contempt, from under his despairing wonder at his own nature.

" When I think that when I first knew her it seemed to me that my whole life wouldn't be enough to . . . And now when I look at her ! She did it all. I must have been mad. I was mad. Every time I look at her I remember my madness. It frightens me. . . . And when I think that of all my life, of all my past, of all my future, of my intelligence, of my work, there is nothing left but she, the cause of my ruin, and you whom I have mortally offended . . ."

He hid his face for a moment in his hands, and when he took them away he had lost the appearance of comparative calm and gave way to a wild distress.

" Captain Lingard . . . anything . . . a deserted island . . . anywhere . . . I promise. . . ."

" Shut up ! " shouted Lingard, roughly.

He became dumb, suddenly, completely.

The wan light of the clouded morning retired slowly from the courtyard, from the clearings, from the river, as if it had gone unwillingly to hide in the enigmatical solitudes of the gloomy and silent forests. The clouds over their heads thickened into a low vault of uniform blackness. The air was still and inexpressibly oppressive. Lingard unbuttoned his jacket, flung it wide open, and, inclining his body sideways a little, wiped his forehead with his hand, which he jerked sharply afterwards. Then he looked at Willems and said—

" No promise of yours is any good to me. I am going to take your conduct into my own hands. Pay attention to what I am going to say. You are my prisoner."

Willems' head moved imperceptibly ; then he became rigid and still. He seemed not to breathe,

" You shall stay here," continued Lingard, with sombre deliberation. " You are not fit to go amongst people. Who could suspect, who could guess, who could imagine what's in you ? I couldn't ! You are my mistake. I shall hide you here. If I let you out you would go amongst unsuspecting men, and lie, and steal, and cheat for a little money or for some woman. I don't care about shooting you. It would be the safest way though. But I won't. Do not expect me to forgive you. To forgive one must have been angry and become contemptuous, and there is nothing in me now—no anger, no contempt, no disappointment. To me you are not Willems, the man I befriended and helped through thick and thin, and thought much of. . . . You are not a human being that may be destroyed or forgiven. You are a bitter thought, a something without a body and that must be hidden. . . . You are my shame."

He ceased and looked slowly round. How dark it was ! It seemed to him that the light was dying prematurely out of the world and that the air was already dead. Again his big, hairy hand swept the perspiration from his forehead, and he shook the moisture off the fingers, projecting his arm clear away from his body.

"Of course," he went on, " I shall see to it that you don't starve."

"You don't mean to say that I must live here, Captain Lingard?" said Willems, in a kind of mechanical voice without any inflections.

"Did you ever hear me say something I did not mean?" asked Lingard. "You said you didn't want to die here— well, you must live . . . Unless you change your mind," he added, as if in involuntary afterthought.

He looked at Willems narrowly, then shook his head.

"You are alone," he went on. "Nothing can help you. Nobody will. You are neither white nor brown. You have no colour as you have no heart. Your accomplices have abandoned you to me because I am still somebody to be reckoned with. You are alone but for that woman there. You say you did this for her. Well, you have her."

Willems mumbled something, and then suddenly caught his hair with both his hands and remained standing so. Aïssa, who had been looking at him, turned to Lingard.

"What did you say, Rajah Laut?" she cried.

There was a slight stir amongst the filmy threads of her disordered hair, the bushes by the river sides trembled, the big tree nodded precipitately over them with an abrupt rustle, as if waking with a start from a troubled sleep—and the breath of hot breeze passed, light, rapid, and scorching, under the clouds that whirled round, unbroken but un-dulating, like a restless phantom of a sombre sea.

Lingard looked at her pityingly before he said—

"I have told him that he must live here all his life . . . and with you."

The sun seemed to have gone out at last like a flickering light away up beyond the clouds, and in the stifling gloom of the courtyard the three figures stood colourless and shadowy, as if surrounded by a black and superheated mist. Aïssa looked at Willems, who remained still, as though he had been changed into stone in the very act of tearing his hair. Then she turned her head towards Lingard and shouted—

"You lie! You lie! . . . White man. Like you all do. You . . . whom Abdulla made small. You lie!"

Her words rang out shrill and venomous with her secret scorn, with her overpowering desire to wound regardless of consequences; in her woman's reckless desire to cause suffering at any cost, to cause it by the sound of her own voice— by her own voice, that would carry the poison of her thought into the hated heart.

Willems let his hands fall, and began to mumble again. Lingard turned his ear towards him instinctively, caught something that sounded like "Very well"—then some more mumbling—then a sigh.

"As far as the rest of the world is concerned," said Lingard, after waiting for awhile in an attentive attitude, "your life is finished. Nobody will be able to throw any of your villainies in my teeth; nobody will be able to point at you and say, 'Here goes a scoundrel of Lingard's up-bringing.' You are buried here."

"And you think that I will stay . . . that I will submit?" exclaimed Willems, as if he had suddenly recovered the power of speech.

"You needn't stay here—on this spot," said Lingard, drily. "There are the forests—and here is the river. You may swim. Fifteen miles up, or forty down. At one end you will meet Almayer, at the other the sea. Take your choice."

He burst into a short, joyless laugh, then added with severe gravity—

"There is also another way."

"If you want to drive my soul into damnation by trying to drive me to suicide you will not succeed," said Willems in wild excitement. "I will live. I shall repent. I may escape. . . . Take that woman away—she is sin."

A hooked dart of fire tore in two the darkness of the distant horizon and lit up the gloom of the earth with a dazzling and ghastly flame. Then the thunder was heard far away, like an incredibly enormous voice muttering menaces.

Lingard said—

"I don't care what happens, but I may tell you that without that woman your life is not worth much—not twopence. There is a fellow here who . . . and Abdulla himself wouldn't stand on any ceremony. Think of that! And then she won't go."

He began, even while he spoke, to walk slowly down towards the little gate. He didn't look, but he felt as sure that Willems was following him as if he had been leading him by a string. Directly he had passed through the wicket-gate into the big courtyard he heard a voice, behind his back, saying—

"I think she was right. I ought to have shot you. I couldn't have been worse off."

"Time yet," answered Lingard, without stopping or looking back. "But, you see, you can't. There is not even that in you."

"Don't provoke me, Captain Lingard," cried Willems.

Lingard turned round sharply. Willems and Aïssa stopped. Another forked flash of lightning split up the clouds overhead, and threw upon their faces a sudden burst of light—of light violent, sinister and fleeting; and in the same instant they were deafened by a near, single crash of thunder, which was followed by a rushing noise, like a frightened sigh of the startled earth.

"Provoke you!" said the old adventurer, as soon as he could make himself heard. "Provoke you! Hey! What's there in you to provoke? What do I care?"

"It is easy to speak like that when you know that in the whole world—in the whole world—I have no friend," said Willems.

"Whose fault?" said Lingard, sharply.

Their voices, after the deep and tremendous noise, sounded to them very unsatisfactory—thin and frail, like the voices of pigmies—and they became suddenly silent, as if on that account. From up the courtyard Lingard's boatmen came down and passed them, keeping step in a single file, their paddles on shoulder, and holding their heads straight with their eyes fixed on the river. Ali, who was walking last, stopped before Lingard, very stiff and upright. He said—

"That one-eyed Babalatchi is gone, with all his women. He took everything. All the pots and boxes. Big. Heavy. Three boxes."

He grinned as if the thing had been amusing, then added with an appearance of anxious concern, "Rain coming."

"We return," said Lingard. "Make ready."

"Aye, aye, sir!" ejaculated Ali with precision, and moved on. He had been quartermaster with Lingard before making up his mind to stay in Sambir as Almayer's head man. He strutted towards the landing-place thinking proudly that he was not like those other ignorant boatmen, and knew how to answer properly the very greatest of white captains.

"You have misunderstood me from the first, Captain Lingard," said Willems.

"Have I? It's all right, as long as there is no mistake about my meaning," answered Lingard, strolling slowly to the landing-place. Willems followed him, and Aïssa followed Willems.

Two hands were extended to help Lingard in embarking. He stepped cautiously and heavily into the long and narrow canoe, and sat in the canvas folding-chair that had been placed in the middle. He leaned back and turned his head to the two figures that stood on the bank a little above him. Aïssa's eyes were fastened on his face in a visible impatience to see him gone. Willems' look went straight above the canoe, straight at the forest on the other side of the river.

"All right, Ali," said Lingard, in a low voice.

A slight stir animated the faces, and a faint murmur ran along the line of paddlers. The foremost man pushed with the point of his paddle, canted the fore end out of the dead water into the current; and the canoe fell rapidly off before the rush of brown water, the stern rubbing gently against the low bank.

"We shall meet again, Captain Lingard!" cried Willems, in an unsteady voice.

"Never!" said Lingard, turning half round in his chair to look at Willems. His fierce red eyes glittered remorselessly over the high back of his seat.

"Must cross the river. Water less quick over there," said Ali.

He pushed in his turn now with all his strength, throwing his body recklessly right out over the stern. Then he recovered himself just in time into the squatting attitude of a monkey perched on a high shelf, and shouted: "Dayong!"

The paddles struck the water together. The canoe darted forward and went on steadily crossing the river with a sideways motion made up of its own speed and the downward drift of the current.

Lingard watched the shore astern. The woman shook her hand at him, and then squatted at the feet of the man who stood motionless. After a while she got up and stood beside him, reaching up to his head—and Lingard saw then that she had wetted some part of her covering and was trying to wash the dried blood off the man's immovable face, which did not seem to know anything about it. Lingard turned away and threw himself back in his chair, stretching his legs out with a sigh of fatigue. His head fell forward; and under his red face the white beard lay fan-like on his breast, the ends of fine long hairs all astir in the faint draught made by the rapid motion of the craft that carried him away from his prisoner—from the only thing in his life he wished to hide.

In its course across the river the canoe came into the line of Willems' sight and his eyes caught the image, followed it eagerly as it glided, small but distinct, on the dark background of the forest. The low canoe itself was almost invisible, appearing only like a narrow, dark, and progressing stroke on the light brown surface of the river, but he could see plainly the figure of the man sitting in the middle. All his life he had felt that man behind his back, a reassuring presence ready with help, with commendation, with advice; friendly

in reproof, enthusiastic in approbation; a man inspiring
confidence by his strength, by his fearlessness, by the very
weakness of his simple heart. Seeing him go away beyond
his reach, Willems realised how much of himself belonged to
that man; what an immense place that man had in his life,
in his thoughts, in his belief in his own future; in all his
actions and in all his hopes. In his struggles with himself,
with temptation; in his revolt and in his defeat, in his
recklessness and in his remorse, he had always looked unconsciously towards the image of that man. And now that
man was going away. He must call him back.

He shouted, and his words, which he wanted to throw
across the river, seemed to fall helplessly at his feet. Aïssa
put her hand on his arm in a restraining attempt, but he
shook it off. He wanted to call back his very life that was
going away from him. He shouted again—and this time he
did not even hear himself. No use. He would never return.
And he stood in sullen silence looking at the white figure
over there, lying back in the chair in the middle of the boat;
a figure that struck him suddenly as very terrible, heartless
and astonishing, with its unnatural appearance of running
over the water in an attitude of languid repose.

For a time nothing on earth stirred, seemingly, but the
canoe, which glided up-stream with a motion so even and
smooth that it did not convey any sense of movement; and
the craft's change of place along the succession of perpendicular trunks in the forest on its other side seemed to be
only a persistent and inexplicable error of the eye. Overhead, the massed clouds appeared solid and steady as if held
there in a powerful grip, but on their uneven surface there
was a continuous and trembling glimmer, a faint reflection
of the distant lightning from the thunderstorm that had
broken already on the coast and was working its way up the
river with low and angry growls. Willems looked on, as
motionless as everything round him and above him. Only
his eyes seemed to live, as they followed the canoe on its
course that carried it away from him, steadily, unhesitatingly,
finally; as if it was going, not up the great river into the

momentous excitement of Sambir, but straight into the past, into the past crowded yet empty, like an old cemetery full of neglected graves, where lie dead hopes that never return.

From time to time he felt on his face the passing, warm touch of an immense breath coming from beyond the forest, like the short panting of an oppressed world. Then the heavy air round him, the air full of heat, odorous and sickly, was pierced by a sharp gust of wind, bringing with it the fresh, damp feel of the falling rain; and all the innumerable tree-tops of the forests before his eyes, swayed to the left and sprang back again in a tumultuous balancing of nodding branches and shuddering leaves. A light frown ran over the river, the clouds stirred slowly, changing their aspect but not their place, as if they had turned ponderously over; and when the sudden movement had died out in a quickened tremor of the slenderest twigs, there was a short period of formidable immobility above and below, during which the voice of the thunder was heard, speaking in a sustained, emphatic and vibrating roll, with violent louder bursts of crashing sound, like a wrathful and threatening discourse of an angry god. For a moment it died out, and then another gust of wind passed, driving before it a white mist which filled the space with a cloud of water-dust that hid suddenly from Willems the canoe, the forests, the river itself; that woke him up from his numbness in a forlorn shiver; that made him look round despairingly to see nothing but the whirling drift of rain spray before the freshening breeze, while through it the heavy big drops fell about him with sonorous and rapid beats upon the dry earth. He made a few hurried steps up the courtyard and was arrested by an immense sheet of water that fell all at once on him, fell sudden and overwhelming from the clouds, cutting his respiration, streaming over his head, clinging to him, running down his body, off his arms, off his legs. He stood gasping while the water beat him in a vertical downpour, drove on him slanting in squalls, and he felt the drops striking him from above, from everywhere; drops thick, pressed and dashing at him as if flung from all sides by a mob of infuriated hands. From under his feet a great vapour of broken water floated up, and he felt the ground become soft—melt under him—and saw the water spring out from the dry earth to meet the water that fell from the sombre heaven. An insane dread took possession of him, the dread of all that water around him, of the water that ran down the courtyard towards him, of the water that pressed him on every side, of the slanting water that drove across his face in wavering sheets which gleamed pale red with the flicker of lightning streaming through them, as if fire and water were falling together, monstrously mixed, upon the stunned earth; were falling continuous and mingled in a piercing hiss—a hiss, loud, prolonged, persistent and indestructible—that vanished in every burst of crashing and tearing noise amongst the invisible clouds : only to return and fill the waste of falling water with the sound of its distinct and passionless whisper.

He wanted to run away, but when he moved it was to slide about painfully and slowly upon that earth which had become mud so suddenly under his feet. He fought his way up the courtyard like a man pushing through a crowd, his head down, one shoulder forward, stopping often, and sometimes carried back a pace or two in the rush of water which his heart was not stout enough to face. Aïssa followed him step by step, stopping when he stopped, recoiling with him, moving forward with him in his toilsome way up the slippery declivity of the courtyard, of that courtyard from which everything seemed to have been swept away by the first rush of the mighty downpour. They could see nothing. The tree, the bushes, the house, and the fences—all had disappeared in the thickness of the falling rain; and they seemed to progress into an infinite space full only of deafening sound, of blinding fire, and of water falling vertical and heavy. Their hair stuck, streaming, to their heads; their clothing clung to them, beaten close to their bodies; water ran off them, off their heads over their shoulders, as they moved, patient, upright, slow and dark, in the gleam clear or fiery of the falling drops, under the roll of unceasing thunder which they seemed not to hear. And they appeared like two wandering ghosts of the drowned that, condemned to haunt the water for ever, had come up from the river to look at the world under a deluge.

On the left the tree seemed to step out to meet them, appearing vaguely, high, motionless and patient; with a rustling plaint of its innumerable leaves through which every drop of water tore its separate way with cruel haste. And then, to the right, the house surged up in the mist, very black, and clamorous with the patter of rain on its high-pitched roof—the quick, loud patter that rang sharp and distracting above the steady plash of the water running off the eaves. Down the plankway leading to the door flowed a thin and pellucid stream, and when Willems began his ascent it broke over his foot as if he were going up a steep ravine in the bed of a rapid and shallow torrent. Behind his heels two streaming smudges of mud stained for an instant the purity of the rushing water, and then he splashed his way up with a spurt and stood on the bamboo platform before the open door under the shelter of the overhanging eaves—under shelter at last !

A low moan ending in a broken and plaintive mutter arrested Willems on the threshold. He peered round in the half-light under the roof and saw the old woman crouching close to the wall in a shapeless heap, and while he looked he felt a touch of two arms on his shoulders. Aïssa ! He had forgotten her. He turned quickly, and she clasped him round the neck instantly, pressing close to him as if afraid of violence or escape. He stiffened himself in repulsion, in horror, in the mysterious revolt of his heart; while she clung to him—clung to him as if he was a refuge from misery, from storm, from weariness, from fear, from despair; and it was on the part of that being an embrace terrible, enraged and mournful, in which all her strength went out to make him captive, to hold him for ever.

He said nothing. He looked into her eyes while he struggled with her fingers about the nape of his neck, and suddenly he tore her hands apart, holding her arms up in a strong grip of her wrists, and bending his swollen face close over hers, he said—

"It is all your doing. You . . ."

She did not understand him—not a word. He spoke in the language of his people—of his people that know no mercy and no shame. And he was angry. Alas! he was always angry now, and always speaking words that she could not understand. She stood in silence, with dolorous wonder looking at him through her patient eyes, while he shook her arms a little and then flung them down.

"Don't go in there!" he shouted. "I want to be alone —I mean to be left alone!"

He went in, leaving the door open.

She did not move. What need to understand the words when they are spoken in such a voice? In that voice which did not seem to be his voice—his voice when he spoke by the brook, when he was never angry and always smiling! Her eyes were fixed upon the dark doorway, but her hands strayed mechanically upwards; she took up all her hair, and, inclining her head slightly over her shoulder, wrung out the long black tresses, twisting them persistently, while she stood, sad and absorbed, like one listening to an inward voice—the voice of bitter, of unavailing regret. The thunder had ceased, the wind had died out, and the rain fell perpendicular and steady through a great pale clearness—the light of remote sun coming victorious from amongst the dissolving blackness of the clouds. She stood near the doorway. He was there— alone. She could hear his breathing in the gloom of the dwelling. He was there. He spoke not. What was in his mind now? What fear? What desire? Not the desire of her as in the days when he used to smile . . . How could she know? . . .

And a sigh, coming from the bottom of her heart, flew out into the world through her parted lips. A sigh faint, profound, and broken; a sigh full of pain and fear, like the sigh of those who are about to face the unknown: to face it in loneliness, in doubt, and without hope. She let go her hair, that fell scattered over her shoulders like a funeral veil, and she sank down suddenly by the door. Her hands clasped her ankles; she rested her head on her drawn-up knees, and remained still, very still, under the streaming mourning of her hair. She was thinking of him; of the days by the brook; she was thinking of all that had been their love—and she sat in the abandoned posture of those who sit weeping by the dead, of those who watch and mourn over a corpse.

# PART V

## I

ALMAYER sat alone on the verandah of his house, with both his elbows on the table, and holding his head between his hands, stared before him, away over the stretch of sprouting young grass in his courtyard, and over the short jetty with its cluster of small canoes, amongst which his big whaleboat floated high, like a white mother of all that dark and aquatic brood. He stared on the river, past the schooner anchored in mid-stream, past the forests of the left bank; he stared through and past the illusion of the material world; and his gaze glided over, glided between the crowd of tangible things—things indifferent, solid, and unnecessary—which appeared to him offensive in their ignorance of the thought that dwelt amongst them, beyond them, above them; of the thought intangible and real, invisible and tenacious; of the thought that, born in his brain, had flowed out into the world and lay now, like a film transparent and disquieting, upon the colour, upon the movement, upon the form of all things alive and dead.

The sun was sinking. Under the sky was stretched a network of white threads, a network fine and close-meshed, where here and there were caught thicker white vapours of globular shape; and to the eastward, above the ragged barrier of the forests, surged the summits of a chain of great clouds, growing bigger slowly, in imperceptible motion, as they climbed up above the tree-tops, climbed noiseless and gentle, as if careful not to disturb the glowing stillness of the earth and of the sky. Abreast of the house the river was empty but for the motionless schooner. Higher up, a solitary log came out from the bend above and went on drifting slowly down the straight reach : a dead and wandering tree going out to its grave in the sea, between two ranks of trees motionless and living.

And Almayer sat, his chin in his hands, looking on and hating all this : the muddy river; the faded blue of the sky; the black log passing by on its first and last voyage; the green sea of leaves—the sea that glowed, shimmered, and stirred above the uniform and impenetrable gloom of the forests—the joyous sea of living green powdered with the brilliant dust of oblique sunrays. He hated all this; he begrudged every day—every minute—of his life spent amongst all these things, of his life that went in payment of his future; he begrudged it bitterly, angrily, with enraged and immense regret, like a miser compelled to give up some of his treasure to a near relation. And yet all this was very precious to him. It was the present sign of a splendid future.

He pushed the table away impatiently, got up, made a few steps aimlessly, then stood by the balustrade and again looked at the river—at that river which would have been the instrument for the making of his fortune if . . . if . . .

"What an abominable brute ! " he said.

He was alone, but he spoke aloud, as one is apt to do under the impulse of a strong, of an overmastering thought.

"What a brute ! " he muttered again.

The river was dark now, and the schooner lay on it, a black, a lonely, and a graceful form, with the slender masts darting upwards from it in two frail and raking lines. The shadows of the evening crept up the trees, crept up from bough to bough, till at last the long sunbeams coursing from the western horizon skimmed lightly over the topmost branches, then flew upwards amongst the piled-up clouds, giving them a sombre and fiery aspect in the last flush of light. And suddenly the light disappeared as if lost in the immensity of the great, blue, and empty hollow overhead. The sun had set : and the forests became a straight wall of formless blackness. Above them, on the edge of lingering clouds, a single star glimmered fitfully, obscured now and then by the rapid flight of high and invisible vapours.

Almayer fought with the uneasiness within his breast. He heard Ali, who moved behind him preparing his evening meal, and he listened with strange attention to the sounds the man made—to the short, dry bang of the plate put upon the table, to the clink of glass and the metallic rattle of knife and fork. The man went away. Now he was coming back. He would speak directly; and Almayer, notwithstanding the absorbing gravity of his thoughts, listened for the sound of expected words. He heard them, spoken in English with painstaking distinctness.

" Ready, sir ! "

" All right," said Almayer, curtly. He did not move. He remained pensive, with his back to the table upon which stood the lighted lamp brought by Ali. He was thinking : Where was Lingard now ? Half-way down the river probably, in Abdulla's ship. He would be back in about three days—perhaps less. And then ? Then the schooner would have to be got out of the river, and when that craft was gone they—he and Lingard—would remain here ; alone with the constant thought of that other man, that other man living near them ! What an extraordinary idea to keep him there for ever. For ever ! What did that mean—for ever ? Perhaps a year, perhaps ten years. Preposterous ! Keep him there ten years—or maybe twenty ! The fellow was capable of living more than twenty years. And for all that time he would have to be watched, fed, looked after. There was nobody but Lingard to have such insane notions. Twenty years ! Why, no ! In less than ten years their fortune would be made and they would leave this place, first for Batavia—yes, Batavia—and then for Europe. England, no doubt. Lingard would want to go to England. And would they leave that man here ? How would that fellow look in ten years ? Very old probably. Well, devil take him. Nina would be fifteen. She would be rich and very pretty, and he himself would not be so old then . . ."

Almayer smiled into the night.

. . . Yes, rich! Why! Of course! Captain Lingard was a resourceful man, and he had plenty of money even now. They were rich already; but not enough. Decidedly not enough. Money brings money. That gold business was good. Famous! Captain Lingard was a remarkable man. He said the gold was there—and it was there. Lingard knew what he was talking about. But he had queer ideas. For instance, about Willems. Now what did he want to keep him alive for? Why?

"That scoundrel," muttered Almayer again.

"Makan Tuan!" ejaculated Ali suddenly, very loud in a pressing tone.

Almayer walked to the table, sat down, and his anxious visage dropped from above into the light thrown down by the lamp-shade. He helped himself absently, and began to eat in great mouthfuls.

. . . Undoubtedly, Lingard was the man to stick to! The man undismayed, masterful and ready. How quickly he had planned a new future when Willems' treachery destroyed their established position in Sambir! And the position even now was not so bad. What an immense prestige that Lingard had with all those people—Arabs, Malays and all. Ah, it was good to be able to call a man like that father. Fine! Wonder how much money really the old fellow had. People talked—they exaggerated surely, but if he had only half of what they said . . .

He drank, throwing his head up, and fell to again.

. . . Now if that Willems had known how to play his cards well, had he stuck to the old fellow he would have been in his position, he would be now married to Lingard's adopted daughter with his future assured—splendid . . .

"The beast!" growled Almayer, between two mouthfuls.

Ali stood rigidly straight with an uninterested face, his gaze lost in the night which pressed round the small circle of light that shone on the table, on the glass, on the bottle, and on Almayer's head as he leaned over his plate moving his jaws.

. . . A famous man Lingard—yet you never knew what he would do next. It was notorious that he had shot a

white man once for less than Willems had done. For less?
. . . Why, for nothing, so to speak! It was not even his
own quarrel. It was about some Malay returning from
pilgrimage with wife and children. Kidnapped, or robbed,
or something. A stupid story—an old story. And now he
goes to see that Willems and—nothing. Comes back talking
big about his prisoner; but after all he said very little.
What did that Willems tell him? What passed between
them? The old fellow must have had something in his
mind when he let that scoundrel off. And Joanna! She
would get round the old fellow. Sure. Then he would
forgive perhaps. Impossible. But at any rate he would
waste a lot of money on them. The old man was tenacious
in his hates, but also in his affections. He had known that
beast Willems from a boy. They would make it up in a
year or so. Everything is possible: why did he not rush
off at first and kill the brute? That would have been more
like Lingard. . . .

Almayer laid down his spoon suddenly, and pushing his
plate away, threw himself back in the chair.

. . . Unsafe. Decidedly unsafe. He had no mind to
share Lingard's money with anybody. Lingard's money was
Nina's money in a sense. And if Willems managed to become
friendly with the old man it would be dangerous for him—
Almayer. Such an unscrupulous scoundrel! He would
oust him from his position. He would lie and slander.
Everything would be lost. Lost. Poor Nina! What
would become of her? Poor child! For her sake he must
remove that Willems. Must. But how? Lingard wanted
to be obeyed. Impossible to kill Willems. Lingard might
be angry. Incredible, but so it was. He might . . .

A wave of heat passed through Almayer's body, flushed
his face, and broke out of him in copious perspiration. He
wriggled in his chair, and pressed his hands together under
the table. What an awful prospect. He fancied he could
see Lingard and Willems reconciled and going away arm-in-
arm, leaving him alone in this God-forsaken hole—in Sambir
—in this deadly swamp! And all his sacrifices, the sacrifice

of his independence, of his best years, his surrender to Lingard's fancies and caprices, would go for nothing! Horrible! Then he thought of his little daughter—his daughter!— and the ghastliness of his supposition overpowered him. He had a deep emotion, a sudden emotion that made him feel quite faint at the idea of that young life spoiled before it had fairly begun. His dear child's life! Lying back in his chair he covered his face with both his hands.

Ali glanced down at him and said, unconcernedly— "Master finish?"

Almayer was lost in the immensity of his commiseration for himself, for his daughter, who was—perhaps—not going to be the richest woman in the world—notwithstanding Lingard's promises. He did not understand the other's question, and muttered through his fingers in a doleful tone—

"What did you say? What? Finish what?"

"Clear up meza," explained Ali.

"Clear up!" burst out Almayer, with incomprehensible exasperation. "Devil take you and the table. Go! Stupid! Chatterer! Chelakka! Go! go!"

He leaned forward, glaring at his head man, then sank back in his seat with his arms hanging straight down on each side of the chair. And he sat motionless in a meditation so concentrated and so absorbing, with all his power of thought so deep within himself, that all expression disappeared from his face in an aspect of staring vacancy.

Ali was clearing the table. He dropped negligently the tumbler into the greasy dish, flung there the spoon and fork, then slipped in the plate with a push amongst the remnants of food. He took up the dish, tucked up the bottle under his armpit, and went off.

"My hammock!" shouted Almayer after him.

"Ada! I come soon," answered Ali from the doorway in an offended tone, looking back over his shoulder. . . . How could he clear the table and hang the hammock at the same time. Ya—wa! Those white men were all alike. Wanted everything at once. Like children . . .

The indistinct murmur of his criticism went away, faded and died out together with the soft footfall of his bare feet in the dark passage.

For some time Almayer did not move. His thoughts were busy at work shaping a momentous resolution, and in the perfect silence of the house he believed that he could hear the noise of the operation as if the work had been done with a hammer. He certainly felt a thumping of strokes, faint, profound, and startling, somewhere low down in his breast; and he was aware of a sound of dull knocking, abrupt and rapid, in his ears. Now and then he held his breath, unconsciously, too long, and had to relieve himself by a deep expiration that whistled dully through his pursed lips. The lamp standing on the far side of the table threw a section of a lighted circle on the floor, where his outstretched legs stuck out from under the table with feet rigid and turned up like the feet of a corpse; and his set face with fixed eyes would have been also like the face of the dead, but for its vacant yet conscious aspect; the hard, the stupid, the stony aspect of one not dead, but only buried under the dust, ashes, and corruption of personal thoughts, of base fears, of selfish desires.

" I will do it ! "

Not till he heard his own voice did he know that he had spoken. It startled him. He stood up. The knuckles of his hand, somewhat behind him, were resting on the edge of the table as he remained still with one foot advanced, his lips a little open, and thought : It would not do to fool with Lingard. But I must risk it. It's the only way I can see. I must tell her. She has some little sense. I wish they were a thousand miles off already. A hundred thousand miles. I do. And if it fails. And she blabs out then to Lingard ? She seemed a fool. No ; probably they will get away. And if they did, would Lingard believe me ? Yes. I never lied to him. He would believe. I don't know . . . Perhaps he won't. . . . " I must do it. Must ! " he argued aloud to himself.

For a long time he stood still, looking before him with an

intense gaze, a gaze rapt and immobile, that seemed to watch the minute quivering of a delicate balance, coming to a rest.

To the left of him, in the whitewashed wall of the house that formed the back of the verandah, there was a closed door. Black letters were painted on it proclaiming the fact that behind that door there was the office of Lingard & Co. The interior had been furnished by Lingard when he had built the house for his adopted daughter and her husband, and it had been furnished with reckless prodigality. There was an office desk, a revolving chair, bookshelves, a safe : all to humour the weakness of Almayer, who thought all those paraphernalia necessary to successful trading. Lingard had laughed, but had taken immense trouble to get the things. It pleased him to make his *protégé*, his adopted son-in-law, happy. It had been the sensation of Sambir some five years ago. While the things were being landed, the whole settlement literally lived on the river bank in front of the Rajah Laut's house, to look, to wonder, to admire. . . . What a big meza, with many boxes fitted all over it and under it ! What did the white man do with such a table ? And look, look, O Brothers ! There is a green square box, with a gold plate on it, a box so heavy that those twenty men cannot drag it up the bank. Let us go, brothers, and help pull at the ropes, and perchance we may see what's inside. Treasure, no doubt. Gold is heavy and hard to hold, O Brothers ! Let us go and earn a recompense from the fierce Rajah of the Sea who shouts over there, with a red face. See ! There is a man carrying a pile of books from the boat ! What a number of books. What were they for ? . . . And an old invalided jurumudi, who had travelled over many seas and had heard holy men speak in far-off countries, explained to a small knot of unsophisticated citizens of Sambir that those books were books of magic—of magic that guides the white men's ships over the seas, that gives them their wicked wisdom and their strength ; of magic that makes them great, powerful, and irresistible while they live, and—praise be to Allah !— the victims of Satan, the slaves of Jehannum when they die.

And when he saw the room furnished, Almayer had felt proud. In his exultation of an empty-headed quill-driver, he thought himself, by the virtue of that furniture, at the head of a serious business. He had sold himself to Lingard for these things—married the Malay girl of his adoption for the reward of these things and of the great wealth that must necessarily follow upon conscientious book-keeping. He found out very soon that trade in Sambir meant something entirely different. He could not guide Patalolo, control the irrepressible old Sahamin, or restrain the youthful vagaries of the fierce Bahassoen with pen, ink, and paper. He found no successful magic in the blank pages of his ledgers; and gradually he lost his old point of view in the saner appreciation of his situation. The room known as the office became neglected then like a temple of an exploded superstition. At first, when his wife reverted to her original savagery, Almayer, now and again, had sought refuge from her there; but after their child began to speak, to know him, he became braver, for he found courage and consolation in his unreasoning and fierce affection for his daughter—in the impenetrable mantle of selfishness he wrapped round both their lives: round himself, and that young life that was also his.

When Lingard ordered him to receive Joanna into his house, he had a truckle bed put into the office—the only room he could spare. The big office desk was pushed on one side, and Joanna came with her little shabby trunk and with her child and took possession in her dreamy, slack, half-asleep way; took possession of the dust, dirt, and squalor, where she appeared naturally at home, where she dragged a melancholy and dull existence; an existence made up of sad remorse and frightened hope, amongst the hopeless disorder—the senseless and vain decay of all these emblems of civilised commerce. Bits of white stuff; rags yellow, pink, blue: rags limp, brilliant and soiled trailed on the floor, lay on the desk amongst the sombre covers of books soiled, grimy, but stiff-backed, in virtue, perhaps, of their European origin. The biggest set of bookshelves was partly hidden by a petticoat, the waistband of which was caught upon the back of a slender book pulled a little out of the row so as to make an improvised clothes-peg. The folding canvas bedstead stood nearly in the middle of the room, stood anyhow, parallel to no wall, as if it had been, in the process of transportation to some remote place, dropped casually there by tired bearers. And on the tumbled blankets that lay in a disordered heap on its edge Joanna sat almost all day with her stockingless feet upon one of the bed pillows that were somehow always kicking about the floor. She sat there, vaguely tormented at times by the thought of her absent husband, but most of the time thinking tearfully of nothing at all, looking with swimming eyes at her little son—at the big-headed, pasty-faced and sickly Louis Willems—who rolled a glass inkstand, solid with dried ink, about the floor, and tottered after it with the portentous gravity of demeanour and absolute absorption by the business in hand that characterise the pursuits of early childhood. Through the half-open shutter a ray of sunlight, a ray merciless and crude, came into the room, beat in the early morning upon the safe in the far-off corner, then, travelling against the sun, cut at midday the big desk in two with its solid and clean-edged brilliance; with its hot brilliance in which a swarm of flies hovered in dancing flight over some dirty plate forgotten there amongst yellow papers for many a day. And towards the evening the cynical ray seemed to cling to the ragged petticoat, lingered on it with wicked enjoyment of that misery it had exposed all day; lingered on the corner of the dusty book-shelf, in a red glow intense and mocking, till it was suddenly snatched by the setting sun out of the way of the coming night. And the night entered the room. The night abrupt, impenetrable and all-filling with its flood of darkness; the night cool and merciful; the blind night that saw nothing, but could hear the fretful whimpering of the child, the creak of the bedstead, Joanna's deep sighs as she turned over, sleepless, in the confused conviction of her wickedness, thinking of that man masterful, fairheaded, and strong—a man hard perhaps, but her husband; her clever and handsome husband to whom she had acted so cruelly on the advice of bad people, if her own people; and of her poor, dear, deceived mother.

To Almayer, Joanna's presence was a constant worry, a worry unobtrusive yet intolerable; a constant, but mostly mute, warning of possible danger. In view of the absurd softness of Lingard's heart, every one in whom Lingard manifested the slightest interest was to Almayer a natural enemy. He was quite alive to that feeling, and in the intimacy of the secret intercourse with his inner self had often congratulated himself upon his own wide-awake comprehension of his position. In that way, and impelled by that motive, Almayer had hated many and various persons at various times. But he never had hated and feared anybody so much as he did hate and fear Willems. Even after Willems' treachery, which seemed to remove him beyond the pale of all human sympathy, Almayer mistrusted the situation and groaned in spirit every time he caught sight of Joanna.

He saw her very seldom in the daytime. But in the short and opal-tinted twilights, or in the azure dusk of starry evenings, he often saw, before he slept, the slender and tall figure trailing to and fro the ragged tail of its white gown over the dried mud of the riverside in front of the house. Once or twice when he sat late on the verandah, with his feet upon the deal table on a level with the lamp, reading the seven months' old copy of the *North China Herald*, brought by Lingard, he heard the stairs creak, and, looking round the paper, he saw her frail and meagre form rise step by step and toil across the verandah, carrying with difficulty the big, fat child, whose head, lying on the mother's bony shoulder, seemed of the same size as Joanna's own. Several times she had assailed him with tearful clamour or mad entreaties : asking about her husband, wanting to know where he was, when he would be back; and ending every such outburst with despairing and incoherent self-reproaches that were absolutely incomprehensible to Almayer. On one or two occasions she had overwhelmed her host with vituperative abuse, making him responsible for her husband's absence. Those scenes, begun without any warning, ended abruptly in a sobbing flight and a bang of the door; stirred the house with a sudden, a fierce, and an evanescent disturbance; like those inexplicable whirlwinds that rise, run, and vanish without apparent cause upon the sun-scorched dead level of arid and lamentable plains.

But to-night the house was quiet, deadly quiet, while Almayer stood still, watching that delicate balance where he was weighing all his chances : Joanna's intelligence, Lingard's credulity, Willems' reckless audacity, desire to escape, readiness to seize an unexpected opportunity. He weighed, anxious and attentive, his fears and his desires against the tremendous risk of a quarrel with Lingard. . . . Yes. Lingard would be angry. Lingard might suspect him of some connivance in his prisoner's escape—but surely he would not quarrel with him—Almayer—about those people once they were gone—gone to the devil in their own way. And then he had hold of Lingard through the little girl. Good. What an annoyance. A prisoner ! As if one could keep him in there. He was bound to get away some time or other. Of course. A situation like that can't last. Anybody could see that. Lingard's eccentricity passed all bounds. You may kill a man, but you mustn't torture him. It was almost criminal. It caused worry, trouble and unpleasantness. . . . Almayer for a moment felt very angry with Lingard. He made him responsible for the anguish he suffered from, for the anguish of doubt and fear ; for compelling him—the practical and innocent Almayer—to such painful efforts of mind in order to find out some issue for absurd situations created by the unreasonable sentimentality of Lingard's unpractical impulses.

" Now if the fellow were dead it would be all right," said Almayer to the verandah.

He stirred a little, and, scratching his nose thoughtfully, revelled in a short flight of fancy, showing him his own image crouching in a big boat, that floated arrested—say fifty yards off—abreast of Willems' landing-place. In the bottom of the boat there was a gun. A loaded gun. One of the boatmen would shout, and Willems would answer—from the bushes. The rascal would be suspicious. Of course. Then the man would wave a piece of paper urging Willems to come to the landing-place and receive an important message. " From the Rajah Laut," the man would yell as the boat edged in-shore, and that would fetch Willems out. Wouldn't it? Rather! And Almayer saw himself jumping up at the right moment, taking aim, pulling the trigger—and Willems tumbling over, his head in the water—the swine!

He seemed to hear the report of the shot. It made him thrill from head to foot where he stood. . . . How simple! . . . Unfortunately . . . Lingard . . . He sighed, shook his head. Pity. Couldn't be done. And couldn't leave him there either! Suppose the Arabs were to get hold of him again—for instance to lead an expedition up the river! Goodness only knows what harm would come of it. . . .

The balance was at rest now and inclining to the side of immediate action. Almayer walked to the door, walked up very close to it, knocked loudly, and turned his head away, looking frightened for a moment at what he had done. After waiting for a while he put his ear against the panel and listened. Nothing. He composed his features into an agreeable expression while he stood listening and thinking to himself : I hear her. Crying. Eh? I believe she has lost the little wits she had and is crying night and day since I began to prepare her for the news of her husband's death—as Lingard told me. I wonder what she thinks. It's just like father to make me invent all these stories for nothing at all. Out of kindness. Kindness! Damn! . . . She isn't deaf, surely.

He knocked again, then said in a friendly tone, grinning benevolently at the closed door—

" It's me, Mrs. Willems. I want to speak to you. I have . . . have . . . important news. . . ."

" What is it ? "

" News," repeated Almayer, distinctly. " News about

your husband. Your husband! . . . Damn him!" he added, under his breath.

He heard a stumbling rush inside. Things were overturned. Joanna's agitated voice cried—

"News! What? What? I am coming out."

"No," shouted Almayer. "Put on some clothes, Mrs. Willems, and let me in. It's . . . very confidential. You have a candle, haven't you?"

She was knocking herself about blindly amongst the furniture in that room. The candlestick was upset. Matches were struck ineffectually. The matchbox fell. He heard her drop on her knees and grope over the floor while she kept on moaning in maddened distraction.

"Oh, my God! News! Yes . . . yes. . . . Ah! where . . . where . . . candle. Oh, my God! . . . I can't find . . . Don't go away, for the love of Heaven . . ."

"I don't want to go away," said Almayer, impatiently, through the keyhole; "but look sharp. It's confi . . . it's pressing."

He stamped his foot lightly, waiting with his hand on the door-handle. He thought anxiously: The woman's a perfect idiot. Why should I go away? She will be off her head. She will never catch my meaning. She's too stupid.

She was moving now inside the room hurriedly and in silence. He waited. There was a moment of perfect stillness in there, and then she spoke in an exhausted voice, in words that were shaped out of an expiring sigh—out of a sigh light and profound, like words breathed out by a woman before going off into a dead faint—

"Come in."

He pushed the door. Ali, coming through the passage with an armful of pillows and blankets pressed to his breast high up under his chin, caught sight of his master before the door closed behind him. He was so astonished that he dropped his bundle and stood staring at the door for a long time. He heard the voice of his master talking. Talking to that Sirani woman! Who was she? He had never thought about that really. He speculated for a while hazily upon things in general. She was a Sirani woman—and ugly. He made a disdainful grimace, picked up the bedding, and went about his work, slinging the hammock between two uprights of the verandah. . . . Those things did not concern him. She was ugly, and brought here by the Rajah Laut, and his master spoke to her in the night. Very well. He, Ali, had his work to do. Sling the hammock—go round and see that the watchmen were awake—take a look at the moorings of the boats, at the padlock of the big storehouse—then go to sleep. To sleep! He shivered pleasantly. He leaned with both arms over his master's hammock and fell into a light doze.

A scream, unexpected, piercing—a scream beginning at once in the highest pitch of a woman's voice and then cut short, so short that it suggested the swift work of death—caused Ali to jump on one side away from the hammock, and the silence that succeeded seemed to him as startling as the awful shriek. He was thunderstruck with surprise. Almayer came out of the office, leaving the door ajar, passed close to his servant without taking any notice, and made straight for the water-chatty hung on a nail in a draughty place. He took it down and came back, missing the petrified Ali by an inch. He moved with long strides, yet, notwithstanding his haste, stopped short before the door, and, throwing his head back poured a thin stream of water down his throat. While he came and went, while he stopped to drink, while he did all this, there came steadily from the dark room the sound of feeble and persistent crying, the crying of a sleepy and frightened child. After he had drunk, Almayer went in, closing the door carefully.

Ali did not budge. That Sirani woman shrieked! He felt an immense curiosity very unusual to his stolid disposition. He could not take his eyes off the door. Was she dead in there? How interesting and funny! He stood with open mouth till he heard again the rattle of the door-handle. Master coming out. He pivoted on his heels with great rapidity and made believe to be absorbed in the contemplation of the night outside. He heard Almayer moving about behind his back. Chairs were displaced. His master sat down.

"Ali," said Almayer.

His face was gloomy and thoughtful. He looked at his head man, who had approached the table, then he pulled out his watch. It was going. Whenever Lingard was in Sambir Almayer's watch was going. He would set it by the cabin clock, telling himself every time that he must really keep that watch going for the future. And every time, when Lingard went away, he would let it run down and would measure his weariness by sunrises and sunsets in an apathetic indifference to mere hours; to hours only; to hours that had no importance in Sambir life, in the tired stagnation of empty days; when nothing mattered to him but the quality of guttah and the size of rattans; where there were no small hopes to be watched for; where to him there was nothing interesting, nothing supportable, nothing desirable to expect; nothing bitter but the slowness of the passing days; nothing sweet but the hope, the distant and glorious hope—the hope wearying, aching and precious, of getting away.

He looked at the watch. Half-past eight. Ali waited stolidly.

"Go to the settlement," said Almayer, "and tell Mahmat Banjer to come and speak to me to-night."

Ali went off muttering. He did not like his errand. Banjer and his two brothers were Bajow vagabonds who had appeared lately in Sambir and had been allowed to take possession of a tumbledown abandoned hut, on three posts, belonging to Lingard & Co., and standing just outside their fence. Ali disapproved of the favour shown to those strangers. Any kind of dwelling was valuable in Sambir at that time, and if master did not want that old rotten house he might have given it to him, Ali, who was his servant, instead of bestowing it upon those bad men. Everybody knew they were bad. It was well known that they had stolen a boat from Hinopari, who was very aged and feeble and had no sons ; and that afterwards, by the truculent recklessness of their demeanour, they had frightened the poor old man into holding his tongue about it. Yet everybody knew of it. It was one of the tolerated scandals of Sambir, disapproved and accepted, a manifestation of that base acquiescence in success, of that inexpressed and cowardly toleration of strength, that exists, infamous and irremediable, at the bottom of all hearts, in all societies ; whenever men congregate ; in bigger and more virtuous places than Sambir, and in Sambir also, where, as in other places, one man could steal a boat with impunity while another would have no right to look at a paddle.

Almayer, leaning back in his chair, meditated. The more he thought, the more he felt convinced that Banjer and his brothers were exactly the men he wanted. Those fellows were sea gipsies, and could disappear without attracting notice ; and if they returned, nobody—and Lingard least of all—would dream of seeking information from them. Moreover, they had no personal interest of any kind in Sambir affairs—had taken no sides—would know nothing anyway.

He called in a strong voice : " Mrs. Willems ! "

She came out quickly, almost startling him, so much did she appear as though she had surged up through the floor, on the other side of the table. The lamp was between them, and Almayer moved it aside, looking up at her from his chair. She was crying. She was crying gently, silently, in a ceaseless welling up of tears that did not fall in drops, but seemed to overflow in a clear sheet from under her eyelids—seemed to flow at once all over her face, her cheeks, and over her chin that glistened with moisture in the light. Her breast and her shoulders were shaken repeatedly by a convulsive and noiseless catching in her breath, and after every spasmodic sob her sorrowful little head, tied up in a red kerchief, trembled on her long neck, round which her bony hands gathered and clasped the disarranged dress.

" Compose yourself, Mrs. Willems," said Almayer.

She emitted an inarticulate sound that seemed to be a

faint, very far off, a hardly audible cry of mortal distress. Then the tears went on flowing in profound stillness.

"You must understand that I have told you all this because I am your friend—real friend," said Almayer, after looking at her for some time with visible dissatisfaction. "You, his wife, ought to know the danger he is in. Captain Lingard is a terrible man, you know."

She blubbered out, sniffing and sobbing together.

"Do you . . . you . . . speak . . . the . . . the truth now ? "

"Upon my word of honour. On the head of my child," protested Almayer. "I had to deceive you till now because of Captain Lingard. But I couldn't bear it. Think only what a risk I run in telling you—if ever Lingard was to know ! Why should I do it ? Pure friendship. Dear Peter was my colleague in Macassar for years, you know."

"What shall I do . . . what shall I do ! " she exclaimed, faintly, looking around on every side as if she could not make up her mind which way to rush off.

"You must help him to clear out, now Lingard is away. He offended Lingard, and that's no joke. Lingard said he would kill him. He will do it, too," said Almayer, earnestly.

She wrung her hands. "Oh ! the wicked man. The wicked, wicked man ! " she moaned, swaying her body from side to side.

"Yes. Yes ! He is terrible," assented Almayer. "You must not lose any time. I say ! Do you understand me, Mrs. Willems ? Think of your husband. Of your poor husband. How happy he will be. You will bring him life— actually his life. Think of him."

She ceased her swaying movements, and now, with her head sunk between her shoulders, she hugged herself with both her arms ; and she stared at Almayer with wild eyes, while her teeth chattered, rattling violently and uninter- ruptedly, with a very loud sound, in the deep peace of the house.

"Oh ! Mother of God ! " she wailed. " I am a miserable woman. Will he forgive me ? The poor, innocent man.

Will he forgive me? Oh, Mr. Almayer, he is so severe. Oh! help me. . . . I dare not. . . . You don't know what I've done to him. . . . I daren't! . . . I can't! . . . God help me!"

The last words came in a despairing cry. Had she been flayed alive she could not have sent to heaven a more terrible, a more heartrending and anguished plaint.

"Sh! Sh!" hissed Almayer, jumping up. "You will wake up everybody with your shouting."

She kept on sobbing then without any noise, and Almayer stared at her in boundless astonishment. The idea that, maybe, he had done wrong by confiding in her upset him so much that for a moment he could not find a connected thought in his head.

At last he said: "I swear to you that your husband is in such a position that he would welcome the devil . . . listen well to me . . . the devil himself if the devil came to him in a canoe. Unless I am much mistaken," he added, under his breath. Then again, loudly: "If you have any little difference to make up with him, I assure you—I swear to you—this is your time!"

The ardently persuasive tone of his words—he thought—would have carried irresistible conviction to a graven image. He noticed with satisfaction that Joanna seemed to have got some inkling of his meaning. He continued, speaking slowly—

"Look here, Mrs. Willems. I can't do anything. Daren't. But I will tell you what I will do. There will come here in about ten minutes a Bugis man—you know the language; you are from Macassar. He has a large canoe; he can take you there. To the new Rajah's clearing, tell him. They are three brothers, ready for anything if you pay them . . . you have some money. Haven't you?"

She stood—perhaps listening—but giving no sign of intelligence, and stared at the floor in sudden immobility, as if the horror of the situation, the overwhelming sense of her own wickedness and of her husband's great danger, had stunned her brain, her heart, her will—had left her no faculty but that of breathing and of keeping on her feet. Almayer swore to himself with much mental profanity that he had never seen a more useless, a more stupid being.

"D'ye hear me?" he said, raising his voice. "Do try to understand. Have you any money? Money. Dollars. Guilders. Money! What's the matter with you?"

Without raising her eyes she said, in a voice that sounded weak and undecided as if she had been making a desperate effort of memory—

"The house has been sold. Mr. Hudig was angry."

Almayer gripped the edge of the table with all his strength. He resisted manfully an almost uncontrollable impulse to fly at her and box her ears.

"It was sold for money, I suppose," he said with studied and incisive calmness. "Have you got it? Who has got it?"

She looked up at him, raising her swollen eyelids with a great effort, in a sorrowful expression of her drooping mouth, of her whole besmudged and tear-stained face. She whispered resignedly—

"Leonard had some. He wanted to get married. And uncle Antonio; he sat at the door and would not go away. And Aghostina—she is so poor . . . and so many, many children—little children. And Luiz the engineer. He never said a word against my husband. Also our cousin Martha. She came and shouted, and my head was so bad, and my heart was worse. Then cousin Salvator and old Daniel da Souza, who . . ."

Almayer had listened to her speechless with rage. He thought: I must give money now to that idiot. Must! Must get her out of the way now before Lingard is back. He made two attempts to speak before he managed to burst out—

"I don't want to know their blasted names! Tell me, did all those infernal people leave you anything? To you! That's what I want to know!"

"I have two hundred and fifteen dollars," said Joanna, in a frightened tone.

Almayer breathed freely. He spoke with great friendliness—

"That will do. It isn't much, but it will do. Now when
the man comes I will be out of the way. You speak to him.
Give him some money; only a little, mind! And promise
more. Then when you get there you will be guided by
your husband, of course. And don't forget to tell him that
Captain Lingard is at the mouth of the river—the northern
entrance. You will remember. Won't you? The northern
branch. Lingard is—death."

Joanna shivered. Almayer went on rapidly—

"I would have given you money if you had wanted it.
'Pon my word! Tell your husband I've sent you to him.
And tell him not to lose any time. And also say to him
from me that we shall meet—some day. That I could not
die happy unless I met him once more. Only once. I
love him, you know. I prove it. Tremendous risk to me—
this business is!"

Joanna snatched his hand and before he knew what she
would be at, pressed it to her lips.

"Mrs. Willems! Don't. What are you . . ." cried the
abashed Almayer, tearing his hand away.

"Oh, you are good!" she cried, with sudden exaltation.
"You are noble . . . I shall pray every day. . . . to all the
saints . . . I shall . . ."

"Never mind . . . never mind!" stammered out Almayer, confusedly, without knowing very well what he was
saying. "Only look out for Lingard. . . . I am happy to
be able . . . in your sad situation . . . believe me. . . ."

They stood with the table between them, Joanna looking
down, and her face, in the half-light above the lamp, appeared
like a soiled carving of old ivory—a carving, with accentuated
anxious hollows, of old, very old ivory. Almayer looked at
her, mistrustful, hopeful. He was saying to himself: How
frail she is! I could upset her by blowing at her. She
seems to have got some idea of what must be done, but will
she have the strength to carry it through? I must trust to
luck now!

Somewhere far in the back courtyard Ali's voice rang suddenly in angry remonstrance—

"Why did you shut the gate, O father of all mischief! You a watchman! You are only a wild man. Did I not tell you I was coming back? You . . ."

"I am off, Mrs. Willems," exclaimed Almayer. "That man is here—with my servant. Be calm. Try to . . ."

He heard the footsteps of the two men in the passage, and without finishing his sentence ran rapidly down the steps towards the riverside.

## II

For the next half-hour Almayer, who wanted to give Joanna plenty of time, stumbled amongst the lumber in distant parts of his enclosure, sneaked along the fences, or held his breath, flattened against grass walls behind various outhouses: all this to escape Ali's inconveniently zealous search for his master. He heard him talk with the head watchman —sometimes quite close to him in the darkness—then moving off, coming back, wondering, and, as the time passed, growing uneasy.

"He did not fall into the river ?—say, thou blind watcher!" Ali was growling in a bullying tone, to the other man. "He told me to fetch Mahmat, and when I came back swiftly I found him not in the house. There is that Sirani woman there, so that Mahmat cannot steal anything, but it is in my mind, the night will be half gone before I rest."

He shouted—

"Master! O master! O mast . . ."

"What are you making that noise for ? " said Almayer, with severity, stepping out close to them.

The two Malays leaped away from each other in their surprise.

"You may go. I don't want you any more to-night, Ali," went on Almayer. "Is Mahmat there ? "

"Unless the ill-behaved savage got tired of waiting. Those men know not politeness. They should not be spoken to by white men," said Ali, resentfully.

Almayer went towards the house, leaving his servants to wonder where he had sprung from so unexpectedly. The watchman hinted obscurely at powers of invisibility possessed by the master, who often at night . . . Ali interrupted him with great scorn. Not every white man had the power. Now, the Rajah Laut could make himself invisible. Also, he could be in two places at once, as everybody knew; except he—the useless watchman—who knew no more about white men than a wild pig! Ya-wa!

And Ali strolled towards his hut yawning loudly.

As Almayer ascended the steps he heard the noise of a door flung to, and when he entered the verandah he saw only Mahmat there, close to the doorway of the passage. Mahmat seemed to be caught in the very act of slinking away, and Almayer noticed that with satisfaction. Seeing the white man, the Malay gave up his attempt and leaned against the wall. He was a short, thick, broad-shouldered man with very dark skin and a wide, stained, bright red mouth that uncovered, when he spoke, a close row of black and glistening teeth. His eyes were big, prominent, dreamy and restless. He said sulkily, looking all over the place from under his eyebrows—

"White Tuan, you are great and strong—and I a poor man. Tell me what is your will, and let me go in the name of God. It is late."

Almayer examined the man thoughtfully. How could he find out whether . . . He had it! Lately he had employed that man and his two brothers as extra boatmen to carry stores, provisions, and new axes to a camp of rattan cutters some distance up the river. A three days' expedition. He would test him now in that way. He said negligently—

"I want you to start at once for the camp, with a surat for the Kavitan. One dollar a day."

The man appeared plunged in dull hesitation, but Almayer,

who knew his Malays, felt pretty sure from his aspect that nothing would induce the fellow to go. He urged—

"It is important—and if you are swift I shall give two dollars for the last day."

"No, Tuan. We do not go," said the man, in a hoarse whisper.

"Why?"

"We start on another journey."

"Where?"

"To a place we know of," said Mahmat, a little louder, in a stubborn manner, and looking at the floor.

Almayer experienced a feeling of immense joy. He said, with affected annoyance—

"You men live in my house—and it is as if it were your own. I may want my house soon."

Mahmat looked up.

"We are men of the sea and care not for a roof when we have a canoe that will hold three, and a paddle apiece. The sea is our house. Peace be with you, Tuan."

He turned and went away rapidly, and Almayer heard him directly afterwards in the courtyard calling to the watchman to open the gate. Mahmat passed through the gate in silence, but before the bar had been put up behind him he had made up his mind that if the white man ever wanted to eject him from his hut, he would burn it and also as many of the white man's other buildings as he could safely get at. And he began to call his brothers before he was inside the dilapidated dwelling.

"All's well!" muttered Almayer to himself, taking some loose Java tobacco from a drawer in the table. "Now if anything comes out I am clear. I asked the man to go up the river. I urged him. He will say so himself. Good."

He began to charge the china bowl of his pipe, a pipe with a long cherry stem and a curved mouth-piece, pressing the tobacco down with his thumb and thinking: No. I sha'n't see her again. Don't want to. I will give her a good start, then go in chase—and send an express boat after father. Yes! that's it.

He approached the door of the office and said, holding his pipe away from his lips—

"Good luck to you, Mrs. Willems. Don't lose any time. You may get along by the bushes; the fence there is out of repair. Don't lose time. Don't forget that it is a matter of . . . life and death. And don't forget that I know nothing. I trust you."

He heard inside a noise as of a chest-lid falling down. She made a few steps. Then a sigh, profound and long, and some faint words which he did not catch. He moved away from the door on tiptoe, kicked off his slippers in a corner of the verandah, then entered the passage puffing at his pipe; entered cautiously in a gentle creaking of planks and turned into a curtained entrance to the left. There was a big room. On the floor a small binnacle lamp—that had found its way to the house years ago from the lumber-room of the *Flash*—did duty for a night-light. It glimmered very small and dull in the great darkness. Almayer walked to it, and picking it up revived the flame by pulling the wick with his fingers, which he shook directly after with a grimace of pain. Sleeping shapes, covered—head and all—with white sheets, lay about on the mats on the floor. In the middle of the room a small cot, under a square white mosquito net, stood—the only piece of furniture between the four walls—looking like an altar of transparent marble in a gloomy temple. A woman, half-lying on the floor with her head dropped on her arms, which were crossed on the foot of the cot, woke up as Almayer strode over her outstretched legs. She sat up without a word, leaning forward, and, clasping her knees, stared down with sad eyes, full of sleep.

Almayer, the smoky light in one hand, his pipe in the other, stood before the curtained cot looking at his daughter —at his little Nina—at that part of himself, at that small and unconscious particle of humanity that seemed to him to contain all his soul. And it was as if he had been bathed in a bright and warm wave of tenderness, in a tenderness greater than the world, more precious than life; the only thing real, living, sweet, tangible, beautiful and safe amongst the elusive, the distorted and menacing shadows of existence. On his face, lit up indistinctly by the short yellow flame of the lamp, came a look of rapt attention while he looked into her future. And he could see things there! Things charming and splendid passing before him in a magic unrolling of resplendent pictures; pictures of events brilliant, happy, inexpressibly glorious, that would make up her life. He would do it! He would do it. He would! He would —for that child! And as he stood in the still night, lost in his enchanting and gorgeous dreams, while the ascending, thin thread of tobacco smoke spread into a faint bluish cloud above his head, he appeared strangely impressive and ecstatic: like a devout and mystic worshipper, adoring, transported and mute; burning incense before a shrine, a diaphanous shrine of a child-idol with closed eyes; before a pure and vaporous shrine of a small god—fragile, powerless, unconscious and sleeping.

When Ali, roused by loud and repeated shouting of his name, stumbled outside the door of his hut, he saw a narrow streak of trembling gold above the forests and a pale sky with faded stars overhead: signs of the coming day. His master stood before the door waving a piece of paper in his hand and shouting excitedly—" Quick, Ali! Quick!" When he saw his servant he rushed forward, and pressing the paper on him objurgated him, in tones which induced Ali to think that something awful had happened, to hurry up and get the whale-boat ready to go immediately—at once, at once—after Captain Lingard. Ali remonstrated, agitated also, having caught the infection of distracted haste.

" If must go quick, better canoe. Whale-boat no can catch, same as small canoe."

" No, no! Whale-boat! whale-boat! You dolt! you wretch!" howled Almayer, with all the appearance of having gone mad. " Call the men! Go! Fly!"

And Ali rushed about the courtyard kicking the doors of

huts open to put his head in and yell frightfully inside;
and as he dashed from hovel to hovel, men shivering and
sleepy were coming out, looking after him stupidly, while
they scratched their ribs with bewildered apathy. It was
hard work to put them in motion. They wanted time to
stretch themselves and to shiver a little. Some wanted
food. One said he was sick. Nobody knew where the
rudder was. Ali darted here and there, ordering, abusing,
pushing one, then another, and stopping in his exertions at
times to wring his hands hastily and groan, because the
whale-boat was much slower than the worst canoe and his
master would not listen to his protestations.

Almayer saw the boat go off at last, pulled anyhow by
men that were cold, hungry, and sulky; and he remained
on the jetty watching it down the reach. It was broad
day then, and the sky was perfectly cloudless. Almayer
went up to the house for a moment. His household was
all astir and wondering at the strange disappearance of the
Sirani woman, who had taken her child and had left her
luggage. Almayer spoke to no one, got his revolver, and
went down to the river again. He jumped into a small
canoe and paddled himself towards the schooner. He
worked very leisurely, but as soon as he was nearly alongside
he began to hail the silent craft with the tone and appearance
of a man in a tremedous hurry.

" Schooner ahoy ! schooner ahoy ! " he shouted.

A row of blank faces popped up above the bulwark.
After a while a man with a woolly head of hair said—

" Sir ! "

" The mate ! the mate ! Call him, steward ! " said
Almayer, excitedly, making a frantic grab at a rope thrown
down to him by somebody.

In less than a minute the mate put his head over. He
asked, surprised—

" What can I do for you, Mr. Almayer ? "

" Let me have the gig at once, Mr. Swan—at once. I
ask in Captain Lingard's name. I must have it. Matter
of life and death."

The mate was impressed by Almayer's agitation.

"You shall have it, sir. . . Man the gig there! Bear a hand, serang! . . . It's hanging astern, Mr. Almayer," he said, looking down again. "Get into it, sir. The men are coming down by the painter."

By the time Almayer had clambered over into the stern sheets, four calashes were in the boat and the oars were being passed over the taffrail. The mate was looking on. Suddenly he said—

"Is it dangerous work? Do you want any help? I would come . . ."

"Yes, yes!" cried Almayer. "Come along. Don't lose a moment. Go and get your revolver. Hurry up! hurry up!"

Yet, notwithstanding his feverish anxiety to be off, he lolled back very quiet and unconcerned till the mate got in and, passing over the thwarts, sat down by his side. Then he seemed to wake up, and called out—

"Let go—let go the painter!"

"Let go the painter—the painter!" yelled the bowman, jerking at it.

People on board also shouted, "Let go!" to one another, till it occurred at last to somebody to cast off the rope; and the boat drifted rapidly away from the schooner in the sudden silencing of all voices.

Almayer steered. The mate sat by his side, pushing the cartridges into the chambers of his revolver. When the weapon was loaded he asked—

"What is it? Are you after somebody?"

"Yes," said Almayer, curtly, with his eyes fixed ahead on the river. "We must catch a dangerous man."

"I like a bit of a chase myself," declared the mate, and then, discouraged by Almayer's aspect of severe thoughtfulness, said nothing more.

Nearly an hour passed. The calashes stretched forward head first and lay back with their faces to the sky, alternatively, in a regular swing that sent the boat flying through the water; and the two sitters, very upright in the stern sheets, swayed rhythmically a little at every stroke of the long oars plied vigorously.

The mate observed: "The tide is with us."

"The current always runs down in this river," said Almayer.

"Yes—I know," retorted the other; "but it runs faster on the ebb. Look by the land at the way we go over the ground! A five-knot current here, I should say."

"H'm!" growled Almayer. Then suddenly: "There is a passage between two islands that will save us four miles. But at low water the two islands, in the dry season, are like one with only a mud ditch between them. Still, it's worth trying."

"Ticklish job that, on a falling tide," said the mate, coolly. "You know best whether there's time to get through."

"I will try," said Almayer, watching the shore intently. "Look out now!"

He tugged hard at the starboard yoke-line.

"Lay in your oars!" shouted the mate.

The boat swept round and shot through the narrow opening of a creek that broadened out before the craft had time to lose its way.

"Out oars! . . . Just room enough," muttered the mate.

It was a sombre creek of black water speckled with gold, with the gold of scattered sunlight falling through the boughs that met overhead in a soaring, restless arch full of gentle whispers passing, tremulous, aloft amongst the thick leaves. The creepers climbed up the trunks of serried trees that leaned over, looking insecure and undermined by floods which had eaten away the earth from under their roots. And the pungent, acrid smell of rotting leaves, of flowers, of blossoms and plants dying in that poisonous and cruel gloom, where they pined for sunshine in vain, seemed to lay heavy, to press upon the shiny and stagnant water in its tortuous windings amongst the everlasting and invincible shadows.

Almayer looked anxious. He steered badly. Several times

the blades of the oars got foul of the bushes on one side or the other, checking the way of the gig. During one of those occurrences, while they were getting clear, one of the calashes said something to the others in a rapid whisper. They looked down at the water. So did the mate.

"Hallo!" he exclaimed. "Eh, Mr. Almayer! Look! The water is running out. See there! We will be caught."

"Back! back! We must go back!" cried Almayer.

"Perhaps better go on."

"No; back! back!"

He pulled at the steering line, and ran the nose of the boat into the bank. Time was lost again in getting clear.

"Give way, men! give way!" urged the mate, anxiously.

The men pulled with set lips and dilated nostrils, breathing hard.

"Too late," said the mate, suddenly. "The oars touch the bottom already. We are done."

The boat stuck. The men laid in the oars, and sat, panting, with crossed arms.

"Yes, we are caught," said Almayer, composedly. "That is unlucky!"

The water was falling round the boat. The mate watched the patches of mud coming to the surface. Then in a moment he laughed, and pointing his finger at the creek—

"Look!" he said; "the blamed river is running away from us. Here's the last drop of water clearing out round that bend."

Almayer lifted his head. The water was gone, and he looked only at a curved track of mud—of mud soft and black, hiding fever, rottenness, and evil under its level and glazed surface.

"We are in for it till the evening," he said, with cheerful resignation. "I did my best. Couldn't help it."

"We must sleep the day away," said the mate. "There's nothing to eat," he added, gloomily.

Almayer stretched himself in the stern sheets. The Malays curled down between thwarts.

"Well, I'm jiggered!" said the mate, starting up after

a long pause. " I was in a devil of a hurry to go and pass the day stuck in the mud. Here's a holiday for you ! Well ! well ! "

They slept or sat unmoving and patient. As the sun mounted higher the breeze died out, and perfect stillness reigned in the empty creek. A troop of long-nosed monkeys appeared, and, crowding on the outer boughs, contemplated the boat and the motionless men in it with grave and sorrowful intensity, disturbed now and then by irrational outbreaks of mad gesticulation. A little bird with sapphire breast balanced a slender twig across a slanting beam of light and flashed it to and fro like a gem dropped from the sky. His minute round eye stared at the strange and tranquil creatures in the boat. After a while he sent out a thin twitter that sounded impertinent and funny in the solemn silence of the great wilderness ; in the great silence full of struggle and death.

### III

On Lingard's departure solitude and silence closed round Willems ; the cruel solitude of one abandoned by men ; the reproachful silence which surrounds an outcast rejected by his kind, the silence unbroken by the slightest whisper of hope ; an immense and impenetrable silence that swallows up without echo the murmur of regret and the cry of revolt. The bitter peace of the abandoned clearings entered his heart, in which nothing could live now but the memory and hate of his past. Not remorse. In the breast of a man possessed by the masterful consciousness of his individuality with its desires and its rights ; by the immovable conviction of his own importance, of an importance so indisputable and final that it clothes all his wishes, endeavours, and mistakes with the dignity of unavoidable fate, there could be no place for such a feeling as that of remorse.

The days passed. They passed unnoticed, unseen, in the rapid blaze of glaring sunrises, in the short glow of tender sunsets, in the crushing oppression of high noons without a cloud. How many days? Two—three—or more? He did not know. To him, since Lingard had gone, the time seemed to roll on in profound darkness. All was night within him. All was gone from his sight. He walked about blindly in the deserted courtyards, amongst the empty houses that, perched high on their posts, looked down inimically on him, a white stranger, a man from other lands; seemed to look hostile and mute out of all the memories of native life that lingered between their decaying walls. His wandering feet stumbled against the blackened brands of extinct fires, kicking up a light black dust of cold ashes that flew in drifting clouds and settled to leeward on the fresh grass sprouting from the hard ground, between the shade trees. He moved on, and on; ceaseless, unresting, in widening circles, in zigzagging paths that led to no issue; and the marks of his footsteps, pressed deep into the soft mud of the bank, were filled slowly behind by the percolating water of the rising river, caught the light and shone in a chain of small reflected suns along the broad expanse of black slime, of the dull and quivering mire where he struggled on, objectless, unappeased : struggled on wearily with a set, distressed face behind which, in his tired brain, seethed his thoughts : restless, sombre, tangled, chilling, horrible and venomous, like a nestful of snakes.

From afar, the bleared eyes of the old serving woman, the sombre gaze of Aïssa followed the gaunt and tottering figure in its unceasing prowl along the fences, between the houses, amongst the wild luxuriance of riverside thickets. Those three human beings abandoned by all were like shipwrecked people left on an insecure and slippery ledge by the retiring tide of an angry sea—listening to its distant roar, living anguished between the menace of its return and the hopeless horror of their solitude—in the midst of a tempest of passion, of regret, of disgust, of despair. The breath of the storm had cast two of them there, robbed of everything

P

—even of resignation. The third, the decrepit witness of their struggle and their torture, accepted her own dull conception of facts; of strength and youth gone; of her useless old age; of her last servitude; of being thrown away by her chief, by her nearest, to use up the last and worthless remnant of flickering life between those two incomprehensible and sombre outcasts: a shrivelled, an unmoved, a passive companion of their disaster.

To the river Willems turned his eyes like a captive that looks fixedly at the door of his cell. If there was any hope in the world it would come from the river, by the river. For hours together he would stand in sunlight while the sea breeze sweeping over the lonely reach fluttered his ragged garments; the keen salt breeze that made him shiver now and then under the flood of intense heat. He looked at the brown and sparkling solitude of the flowing water, of the water flowing ceaseless and free in a soft, cool murmur of ripples at his feet; and he tried to find a promise of release in the vivid glitter of innumerable suns reflected by the running wavelets of the stream. The world seemed to end there. The forests of the other bank appeared unattainable, enigmatical, for ever beyond reach like the stars of heaven—and as indifferent. Above and below, the forests on his side of the river came down to the water in a serried multitude of tall, immense trees towering in a great spread of twisted boughs above the thick undergrowth; great, solid trees, looking sombre, severe, and malevolently stolid, like a giant crowd of pitiless enemies pressing round silently to witness his slow agony. He was alone, small, crushed. He thought of escape—of something to be done. What? A raft! He imagined himself working at it, feverishly, desperately; cutting down trees, fastening the logs together and then drifting down with the current, down to the sea into the straits. There were ships there—ships, help, white men. Men like himself. Good men who would rescue him, take him away, take him far away where there was trade, and houses, and other men that could understand him exactly, appreciate his capabilities; where there was proper food, and money; where there were beds, knives, forks, carriages, brass bands, cool drinks, churches with well-dressed people praying in them. He would pray also. The superior land of refined delights where he could sit on a chair, eat his tiffin off a white tablecloth, nod to fellows—good fellows; he would be popular; always was—where he could be virtuous, correct, do business, draw a salary, smoke cigars, buy things in shops—have boots . . . be happy, free, become rich. O God! What was wanted? Cut down a few trees. No! One would do. They used to make canoes by burning out a tree trunk, he had heard. Yes! One would do. One tree to cut down . . . He rushed forward, and suddenly stood still as if rooted in the ground. He had a pocket-knife.

And he would throw himself down on the ground by the riverside. He was tired, exhausted; as if that raft had been made, the voyage accomplished, the fortune attained. A glaze came over his staring eyes, over his eyes that gazed hopelessly at the rising river where big logs and uprooted trees drifted in the shine of mid-stream: a long procession of black and ragged specks. He could swim out and drift away on one of these trees. Anything to escape! Anything! Any risk! He could fasten himself up between the dead branches. He was torn by desire, by fear; his heart was wrung by the faltering of his courage. He turned over, face downwards, his head on his arms. He had a terrible vision of shadowless horizons where the blue sky and the blue sea met; of a circular and blazing emptiness where a dead tree and a dead man drifted together, endlessly, up and down, upon the brilliant undulations of the straits. No ships there. Only death. And the river led to it.

He sat up with a profound groan.

Yes, death. Why should he die? No! Better solitude, better hopeless waiting, alone. Alone. No! he was not alone, he saw death looking at him from everywhere; from the bushes, from the clouds—he heard her speaking to him in the murmur of the river, filling the space, touching his heart, his brain with a cold hand. He could see and think of nothing else. He saw it—the sure death—everywhere. He saw it so close that he was always on the point of throwing out his arms to keep it off. It poisoned all he saw, all he did; the miserable food he ate, the muddy water he drank; it gave a frightful aspect to sunrises and sunsets, to the brightness of hot noon, to the cooling shadows of the evenings. He saw the horrible form among the big trees, in the network of creepers, in the fantastic outlines of leaves, of the great indented leaves that seemed to be so many enormous hands with big broad palms, with stiff fingers outspread to lay hold of him; hands gently stirring, or hands arrested in a frightful immobility, with a stillness attentive and watching for the opportunity to take him, to enlace him, to strangle him, to hold him till he died; hands that would hold him dead, that would never let go, that would cling to his body for ever till it perished—disappeared in their frantic and tenacious grasp.

And yet the world was full of life. All the things, all the men he knew, existed, moved, breathed; and he saw them in a long perspective, far off, diminished, distinct, desirable, unattainable, precious . . . lost for ever. Round him, ceaselessly, there went on without a sound the mad turmoil of tropical life. After he had died all this would remain! He wanted to clasp, to embrace solid things; he had an immense craving for sensations; for touching, pressing, seeing, handling, holding on, to all these things. All this would remain—remain for years, for ages, for ever. After he had miserably died there, all this would remain, would live, would exist in joyous sunlight, would breathe in the coolness of serene nights. What for, then? He would be dead. He would be stretched upon the warm moisture of the ground, feeling nothing, seeing nothing, knowing nothing; he would lie stiff, passive, rotting slowly; while over him, under him, through him—unopposed, busy, hurried—the endless and minute throngs of insects, little shining monsters of repulsive shapes, with horns, with claws, with pincers, would swarm in streams, in rushes, in eager struggle for his body; would swarm countless, persistent, ferocious and greedy—till there would remain nothing but the white gleam of bleaching bones in the long grass; in the long grass that would shoot its feathery heads between the bare and polished ribs. There would be that only left of him; nobody would miss him; no one would remember him.

Nonsense! It could not be. There were ways out of this. Somebody would turn up. Some human beings would come. He would speak, entreat—use force to extort help from them. He felt strong; he was very strong. He would . . . The discouragement, the conviction of the futility of his hopes would return in an acute sensation of pain in his heart. He would begin again his aimless wanderings. He tramped till he was ready to drop, without being able to calm by bodily fatigue the trouble of his soul. There was no rest, no peace within the cleared grounds of his prison. There was no relief but in the black release of sleep, of sleep without memory and without dreams; in the sleep coming brutal and heavy, like the lead that kills. To forget in annihilating sleep; to tumble headlong, as if stunned, out of daylight into the night of oblivion, was for him the only, the rare respite from this existence which he lacked the courage to endure—or to end.

He lived, he struggled with the inarticulate delirium of his thoughts under the eyes of the silent Aïssa. She shared his torment in the poignant wonder, in the acute longing, in the despairing inability to understand the cause of his anger and of his repulsion; the hate of his looks; the mystery of his silence; the menace of his rare words—of those words in the speech of white people that were thrown at her with rage, with contempt, with the evident desire to hurt her; to hurt her who had given herself, her life—all she had to give—to that white man; to hurt her who had wanted to show him the way to true greatness, who had tried to help him, in her woman's dream of everlasting, enduring, unchangeable affection. From the short contact with the whites in the crashing collapse of her old life, there remained with her the imposing idea of irresistible power and of ruthless strength. She had found a man of their race—and with all their qualities. All whites are alike. But this man's heart was full of anger against his own people, full of anger existing there by the side of his desire of her. And to her it had been an intoxication of hope for great things born in the proud and tender consciousness of her influence. She had heard the passing whisper of wonder and fear in the presence of his hesitation, of his resistance, of his compromises; and yet with a woman's belief in the durable steadfastness of hearts, in the irresistible charm of her own personality, she had pushed him forward, trusting the future, blindly, hopefully; sure to attain by his side the ardent desire of her life, if she could only push him far beyond the possibility of retreat. She did not know, and could not conceive, anything of his—so exalted—ideals. She thought the man a warrior and a chief, ready for battle, violence, and treachery to his own people—for her. What more natural? Was he not a great, strong man? Those two, surrounded each by the impenetrable wall of their aspirations, were hopelessly alone, out of sight, out of earshot of each other; each the centre of dissimilar and distant horizons; standing each on a different earth, under a different sky. She remembered his words, his eyes, his trembling lips, his outstretched hands; she remembered the great, the immeasurable sweetness of her surrender, that beginning of her power which was to last until death. He remembered the quaysides and the warehouses; the excitement of a life in a whirl of silver coins; the glorious uncertainty of a money hunt; his numerous successes, the lost possibilities of wealth and consequent glory. She, a woman, was the victim of her heart, of her woman's belief that there is nothing in the world but love—the everlasting thing. He was the victim of his strange principles, of his continence, of his blind belief in himself, of his solemn veneration for the voice of his boundless ignorance.

In a moment of his idleness, of suspense, of discouragement, she had come—that creature—and by the touch of her hand had destroyed his future, his dignity of a clever and civilised man; had awakened in his breast the infamous thing which had driven him to what he had done, and to end miserably in the wilderness and be forgotten, or else remembered with hate or contempt. He dared not look at her, because now whenever he looked at her his thoughts seemed to touch crime, like an outstretched hand. She could only look at him—and at nothing else. What else was there? She followed him with a timorous gaze, with a gaze for ever expecting, patient and entreating. And in her eyes there was the wonder and desolation of an animal that knows only suffering, of the incomplete soul that knows pain but knows not hope; that can find no refuge from the facts of life in the illusory conviction of its dignity, of an exalted destiny beyond; in the heavenly consolation of a belief in the momentous origin of its hate.

For the first three days after Lingard went away he would not even speak to her. She preferred his silence to the sound of hated and incomprehensible words he had been lately addressing to her with a wild violence of manner, passing at once into complete apathy. And during these three days he hardly ever left the river, as if on that muddy bank he had felt himself nearer to his freedom. He would stay late; he would stay till sunset; he would look at the glow of gold passing away amongst sombre clouds in a bright red flush, like a splash of warm blood. It seemed to him ominous and ghastly with a foreboding of violent death that beckoned him from everywhere—even from the sky.

One evening he remained by the riverside long after sunset, regardless of the night mist that had closed round him, had wrapped him up and clung to him like a wet winding-sheet. A slight shiver recalled him to his senses, and he walked up the courtyard towards his house. Aïssa rose from before the fire, that glimmered red through its own smoke, which hung thickening under the boughs of the big tree. She approached him from the side as he neared the plankway of the house. He saw her stop to let him begin his ascent. In the darkness her figure was like the shadow of a woman with clasped hands put out beseechingly. He stopped—could not help glancing at her. In all the sombre gracefulness of the straight figure, her limbs, features—all was indistinct and vague but the gleam of her eyes in the faint starlight. He turned his head away and moved on. He could feel her footsteps behind him on the bending planks, but he walked up without turning his head. He knew what she wanted. She wanted to come in there. He shuddered at the thought of what might happen in the impenetrable darkness of that house if they were to find themselves alone—even for a moment. He stopped in the doorway, and heard her say—

"Let me come in. Why this anger? Why this silence? . . . Let me watch . . by your side. . . . Have I not watched faithfully? Did harm ever come to you when you closed your eyes while I was by? . . . I have waited . . . I have waited for your smile, for your words. . . . I can wait no more. . . . Look at me . . . speak to me. Is there a bad spirit in you? A bad spirit that has eaten up your courage and your love? Let me touch you. Forget all. . . . All. Forget the wicked hearts, the angry faces . . . and remember only the day I came to you . . . to you! O! my heart! O! my life!"

The pleading sadness of her appeal filled the space with the tremor of her low tones, that seemed to carry tenderness and tears into the great peace of the sleeping world. All around them the forests, the clearings, the river, covered by the silent veil of night, seemed to wake up and listen to her words in attentive stillness. After the sound of her voice had died out in a stifled sigh they appeared to listen yet; and nothing stirred among the shapeless shadows but the innumerable fireflies that twinkled in changing clusters, in gliding pairs, in wandering and solitary points—like the glimmering drift of scattered star-dust.

Willems turned round slowly, reluctantly, as if compelled by main force. Her face was hidden in her hands, and he looked above her bent head, into the sombre brilliance of the night. It was one of those nights that give the impression of extreme vastness, when the sky seems higher, when the passing puffs of tepid breeze seem to bring with them faint whispers from beyond the stars. The air was full of sweet scent, of the scent charming, penetrating and violent like the impulse of love. He looked into that great dark place odorous with the breath of life, with the mystery of existence, renewed, fecund, indestructible; and he felt afraid of his solitude, of the solitude of his body, of the loneliness of his soul in the presence of this unconscious and ardent struggle; of this lofty indifference; of this merciless and mysterious purpose, perpetuating strife and death through the march of ages. For the second time in his life he felt, in a sudden sense of his insignificance, the need to send a cry for help into the wilderness, and for the second time he realised the hopelessness of its unconcern. He could shout for help on every side—and nobody would answer. He could stretch out his hands, he could call for aid, for support, for sympathy, for relief—and nobody would come. Nobody. There was no one there—but that woman.

His heart was moved, softened with a pity at his own abandonment. His anger against her, against her who was the cause of all his misfortunes, vanished before his extreme need for some kind of consolation. Perhaps—if he must resign himself to his fate—she might help him to forget. To forget! For a moment, in an access of despair so profound that it seemed like the beginning of peace, he planned the deliberate descent from his pedestal, the throwing away of his superiority, of all his hopes, of old ambitions, of the ungrateful civilisation. For a moment, forgetfulness in her arms seemed possible; and lured by that possibility the semblance of renewed desire possessed his breast in a burst of reckless contempt for everything outside himself—in a savage disdain of Earth and of Heaven. He said to himself that he would not repent. The punishment for his only sin was too heavy. There was no mercy under heaven. He did not want any. He thought, desperately, that if he could find with her again the madness of the past, the strange delirium that had changed him, that had worked

P 2

his undoing, he would be ready to pay for it with an eternity of perdition. He was intoxicated by the subtle perfumes of the night; he was carried away by the suggestive stir of the warm breeze; he was possessed by the exaltation of the solitude, of the silence, of his memories, in the presence of that figure offering herself in a submissive and patient devotion; coming to him in the name of the past, in the name of those days when he could see nothing, think of nothing, desire nothing—but her embrace.

He took her suddenly in his arms, and she clasped her hands round his neck with a low cry of joy and surprise. He took her in his arms and waited for the transport, for the madness, for the sensations remembered and lost; and while she sobbed gently on his breast he felt her and felt cold, sick, tired, exasperated with his failure—and ended by cursing himself. She clung to him trembling with the intensity of her happiness and her love. He heard her whispering—her face hidden on his shoulder—of past sorrow, of coming joy that would last for ever; of her unshaken belief in his love. She had always believed. Always! Even while his face was turned away from her in the dark days while his mind was wandering in his own land, amongst his own people. But it would never wander away from her any more, now it had come back. He would forget the cold faces and the hard hearts of the cruel people. What was there to remember? Nothing? Was it not so? . . .

He listened hopelessly to the faint murmur. He stood still and rigid, pressing her mechanically to his breast while he thought that there was nothing for him in the world. He was robbed of everything; robbed of his passion, of his liberty, of forgetfulness, of consolation. She, wild with delight, whispered on rapidly, of love, of light, of peace, of long years. . . . He looked drearily above her head down into the deeper gloom of the courtyard. And, all at once, it seemed to him that he was peering into a sombre hollow, into a deep black hole full of decay and of whitened bones; into an immense and inevitable grave full of corruption where sooner or later he must, unavoidably, fall.

In the morning he came out early, and stood for a time in the doorway, listening to the light breathing behind him—in the house. She slept. He had not closed his eyes through all that night. He stood swaying—then leaned against the lintel of the door. He was exhausted, done up; fancied himself hardly alive. He had a disgusted horror of himself that, as he looked into the level sea of mist at his feet, faded quickly into dull indifference. It was like a sudden and final decrepitude of his senses, of his body, of his thoughts. Standing on the high platform, he looked over the expanse of low night fog above which, here and there, stood out the feathery heads of tall bamboo clumps and the round tops of single trees, resembling small islets emerging black and solid from a ghostly and impalpable sea. Further on, upon the faintly luminous background of the eastern sky, the sombre line of the great forests bounded that smooth sea of white vapours with an appearance of a fantastic and unattainable shore. He looked without seeing anything—thinking of himself. Before his eyes the light of the rising sun burst above the forest with the suddenness of an explosion. He saw nothing. Then, after a time, he murmured with conviction—speaking half aloud to himself in the shock of the penetrating thought:

" I am a lost man."

He shook his hand above his head in a gesture careless and tragic, then walked down into the mist that closed above him in shining undulations under the first breath of the morning breeze.

## IV

WILLEMS moved languidly towards the river, then retraced his steps to the tree and let himself fall on the seat under its shade. On the other side of the immense trunk he could hear the old woman moving about, sighing loudly, muttering to herself, snapping dry sticks, blowing up the fire. After a while a whiff of smoke drifted round to where he sat. It made him feel hungry, and that feeling was like a new indignity added to an intolerable load of humiliations. He felt inclined to cry. He felt very weak. He held up his arm before his eyes and watched for a little while the trembling of the lean limb. Skin and bone, by God! How thin he was! . . . He had suffered from fever a good deal, and now he thought with tearful dismay that Lingard, although he had sent him food—and what food, great Lord: a little rice and dried fish; quite unfit for a white man—had not sent him any medicine. Did the old savage think that he was like the wild beasts that are never ill? He wanted quinine.

He leaned the back of his head against the tree and closed his eyes. He thought feebly that if he could get hold of Lingard he would like to flay him alive; but it was only a blurred, a short and a passing thought. His imagination, exhausted by the repeated delineations of his own fate, had not enough strength left to grip the idea of revenge. He was not indignant and rebellious. He was cowed. He was cowed by the immense cataclysm of his disaster. Like most men, he had carried solemnly within his breast the whole universe, and the approaching end of all things in the destruction of his own personality filled him with paralysing awe. Everything was toppling over. He blinked his eyes quickly, and it seemed to him that the very sunshine of the morning disclosed in its brightness a suggestion of some hidden and sinister meaning. In his unreasoning fear he tried to hide within himself. He drew his feet up, his head sank between his shoulders, his arms hugged his sides. Under the high and enormous tree soaring superbly out of the mist in a vigorous spread of lofty boughs, with a restless and eager flutter of its innumerable leaves in the clear sunshine, he remained motionless, huddled up on his seat : terrified and still. He looked like a heap of soiled rags thrown over a lot of bones and topped by a mournful and fleshless head with a pair of big, shining eyes, that moved slowly in their sockets : wandering and stupid.

Willems' gaze roamed over the ground, and then he watched with idiotic fixity half a dozen black ants entering courageously a tuft of long grass which, to them, must have appeared a dark and a dangerous jungle. Suddenly he thought : There must be something dead in there. Some dead insect. Death everywhere ! He closed his eyes again in an accesss of trembling panic. Death everywhere— wherever one looks. He did not want to see the ants. He did not want to see anybody or anything. He sat in the darkness of his own making, reflecting bitterly that there was no peace for him. He heard voices now. . . . Illusion ! Misery ! Torment ! Who would come ? Who would speak to him ? What business had he to hear voices ? . . . yet he heard them faintly, from the river. Faintly, as if shouted far off over there, came the words : "We come back soon." . . . Delirium and mockery ! Who would come back ? Nobody ever comes back ! Fever comes back. He had it on him this morning. That was it. . . . He heard unexpectedly the old woman muttering something near by. She had come round to his side of the tree. He opened his eyes and saw her bent back before him. She stood, with her hand shading her eyes, looking towards the landing-place. Then she glided away. She had seen—and now she was going back to her cooking ; a woman incurious ; expecting nothing ; without fear and without hope.

She had gone back behind the tree, and now Willems could see a human figure on the path to the landing-place.

It appeared to him to be a woman, in a red gown, holding some heavy bundle in her arms; it was an apparition unexpected, familiar and odd. He cursed through his teeth . . . It had wanted only this! See things like that in broad daylight! He was very bad—very bad. . . . He was horribly scared at this awful symptom of the desperate state of his health.

This scare lasted for the space of a flash of lightning, and in the next moment it was revealed to him that the woman was real; that she was coming towards him; that she was his wife! He put his feet down to the ground quickly, but made no other movement. His eyes opened wide. He was so amazed that for a time he absolutely forgot his own existence. The only idea in his head was: Why on earth did she come here?

Joanna was coming up the courtyard with eager, hurried steps. She carried in her arms the child, wrapped up in one of Almayer's white blankets that she had snatched off the bed at the last moment, before leaving the house. She seemed to be dazed by the sun in her eyes; bewildered by her strange surroundings. She moved on, looking quickly right and left in impatient expectation of seeing her husband at any moment. Then, approaching the tree, she perceived suddenly a kind of dried-up, yellow corpse, sitting very stiff on a bench in the shade and looking at her with big eyes that were alive. That was her husband.

She stopped dead short. They stared at one another in profound stillness, with astounded eyes, with eyes maddened by the memories of things far off that seemed lost in the lapse of time. Their looks crossed, passed each other, and appeared to dart at them through fantastic distances, to come straight from the Incredible.

Looking at him steadily she came nearer, and deposited the blanket with the child in it on the bench. Little Louis, after howling with terror in the darkness of the river most of the night, now slept soundly and did not wake. Willems' eyes followed his wife, his head turning slowly after her. He accepted her presence there with a tired acquiescence in its fabulous improbability. Anything might happen. What did she come for? She was part of the general scheme of his misfortune. He half expected that she would rush at him, pull his hair, and scratch his face. Why not? Anything might happen! In an exaggerated sense of his great bodily weakness he felt somewhat apprehensive of possible assault. At any rate, she would scream at him. He knew her of old. She could screech. He had thought that he was rid of her for ever. She came now probably to see the end. . . .

Suddenly she turned, and embracing him slid gently to the ground. This startled him. With her forehead on his knees she sobbed noiselessly. He looked down dismally at the top of her head. What was she up to? He had not the strength to move—to get away. He heard her whispering something, and bent over to listen. He caught the word " Forgive."

That was what she came for! All that way. Women are queer. Forgive. Not he! . . . All at once this thought darted through his brain: How did she come? In a boat. Boat—boat!

He shouted " Boat!" and jumped up, knocking her over. Before she had time to pick herself up he pounced upon her and was dragging her up by the shoulders. No sooner had she regained her feet than she clasped him tightly round the neck, covering his face, his eyes, his mouth, his nose with desperate kisses. He dodged his head about, shaking her arms, trying to keep her off, to speak, to ask her. . . . She came in a boat, boat, boat! . . . They struggled and swung round, tramping in a semicircle. He blurted out, " Leave off. Listen," while he tore at her hands. This meeting of lawful love and sincere joy resembled a fight. Louis Willems slept peacefully under his blanket.

At last Willems managed to free himself, and held her off, pressing her arms down. He looked at her. He had half a suspicion that he was dreaming. Her lips trembled; her eyes wandered unsteadily, always coming back to his face. He saw her the same as ever, in his presence. She appeared startled, tremulous, ready to cry. She did not inspire him with confidence. He shouted—

"How did you come?"

She answered in hurried words, looking at him intently—

"In a big canoe with three men. I know everything. Lingard's away. I come to save you. I know. . . . Almayer told me."

"Canoe!—Almayer—Lies. Told you—You!" stammered Willems in a distracted manner. "Why you?—Told what?"

Words failed him. He stared at his wife, thinking with fear that she—stupid woman—had been made a tool in some plan of treachery . . . in some deadly plot.

She began to cry—

"Don't look at me like that, Peter. What have I done? I come to beg—to beg—forgiveness. . . . Save—Lingard—danger."

He trembled with impatience, with hope, with fear. She looked at him and sobbed out in a fresh outburst of grief—

"Oh! Peter. What's the matter?—Are you ill? . . . Oh! you look so ill. . . ."

He shook her violently into a terrified and wondering silence.

"How dare you!—I am well—perfectly well. . . . Where's that boat? Will you tell me where that boat is—at last? The boat, I say. . . . You! . . ."

"You hurt me," she moaned.

He let her go, and, mastering her terror, she stood quivering and looking at him with strange intensity. Then she made a movement forward, but he lifted his finger, and she restrained herself with a long sigh. He calmed down suddenly and surveyed her with cold criticism, with the same appearance as when, in the old days, he used to find fault with the household expenses. She found a kind of fearful delight in this abrupt return into the past, into her old subjection.

He stood outwardly collected now, and listened to her disconnected story. Her words seemed to fall round him

with the distracting clatter of stunning hail. He caught
the meaning here and there, and straightway would lose
himself in a tremendous effort to shape out some intelligible
theory of events. There was a boat. A boat. A big boat
that could take him to sea if necessary. That much was
clear. She brought it. Why did Almayer lie to her so?
Was it a plan to decoy him into some ambush? Better
than that hopeless solitude. She had money. The men
were ready to go anywhere . . . she said.

He interrupted her—

" Where are they now ? "

" They are coming directly," she answered, tearfully.
" Directly. There are some fishing stakes near here—they
said. They are coming directly."

Again she was talking and sobbing together. She wanted
to be forgiven. Forgiven? What for? Ah! the scene
in Macassar. As if he had time to think of that! What
did he care what she had done months ago? He seemed to
struggle in the toils of complicated dreams where everything
was impossible, yet a matter of course, where the past took
the aspects of the future and the present lay heavy on his
heart—seemed to take him by the throat like the hand of
an enemy. And while she begged, entreated, kissed his
hands, wept on his shoulder, adjured him in the name of
God, to forgive, to forget, to speak the word for which she
longed, to look at his boy, to believe in her sorrow and in
her devotion—his eyes, in the fascinated immobility of shining
pupils, looked far away, far beyond her, beyond the river,
beyond this land, through days, weeks, months ; looked into
liberty, into the future, into his triumph . . . into a great
possibility of a startling revenge.

He felt a sudden desire to dance and shout. He
shouted—

" After all, we shall meet again, Captain Lingard."

" Oh, no ! No ! " she cried, joining her hands.

He looked at her with surprise. He had forgotten she
was there till the break of her cry in the monotonous tones
of her prayer recalled him into that courtyard from the

glorious turmoil of his dreams. It was very strange to see her there—near him. He felt almost affectionate towards her. After all, she came just in time. Then he thought: That other one. I must get away without a scene. Who knows; she may be dangerous! . . . And all at once he felt he hated Aïssa with an immense hatred that seemed to choke him. He said to his wife—

" Wait a moment."

She, obedient, seemed to gulp down some words which wanted to come out. He muttered : " Stay here," and disappeared round the tree.

The water in the iron pan on the cooking fire boiled furiously, belching out volumes of white steam that mixed with the thin black thread of smoke. The old woman appeared to him through this as if in a fog, squatting on her heels, impassive and weird.

Willems came up near and asked, " Where is she ? "

The woman did not even lift her head, but answered at once, readily, as though she had expected the question for a long time.

" When you were asleep under the tree, before the strange canoe came, she went out of the house. I saw her look at you and pass on with a great light in her eyes. A great light. And she went towards the place where our master Lakamba had his fruit trees. When we were many here. Many, many. Men with arms by their side. Many . . . men. And talk . . . and songs . . ."

She went on like that, raving gently to herself for a long time after Willems had left her.

Willems went back to his wife. He came up close to her and found he had nothing to say. Now all his faculties were concentrated upon his wish to avoid Aïssa. She might stay all the morning in that grove. Why did those rascally boatmen go ? He had a physical repugnance to set eyes on her. And somewhere, at the very bottom of his heart, there was a fear of her. Why ? What else could she do ? Nothing on earth could stop him now. He felt strong, reckless, pitiless, and superior to everything. He wanted

to preserve before his wife the lofty purity of his character.
He thought: She does not know. Almayer held his tongue
about Aïssa. But if she finds out, I am lost. If it hadn't
been for the boy I would . . . free of both of them. . . .
The idea darted through his head. Not he! Married. . . .
Swore solemnly. No . . . sacred tie. . . . Looking on his
wife, he felt for the first time in his life something approaching remorse. Remorse, arising from his conception of the
awful nature of an oath before the altar. . . . She mustn't
find out. . . . Oh for that boat! He must go and get his
revolver. Couldn't think of trusting himself unarmed with
those Bajow fellows. Get it now while she is away. Oh
for that boat! . . . He dared not go to the river and hail.
He thought: She might hear me. . . . I'll go and get . . .
cartridges . . . then will be all ready . . . nothing else.
No.

And while he stood meditating profoundly before he could
make up his mind to run to the house, Joanna pleaded,
holding to his arm—pleaded despairingly, broken-hearted,
hopeless whenever she glanced up at his face, which to her
seemed to wear the aspect of unforgiving rectitude, of
virtuous severity, of merciless justice. And she pleaded
humbly—abashed before him, before the unmoved appearance of the man she had wronged in defiance of human
and divine laws. He heard not a word of what she said
till she raised her voice in a final appeal—

" . . . Don't you see I loved you always? They told me
horrible things about you. . . . My own mother! They
told me—you have been—you have been unfaithful to me,
and I . . ."

" It's a damned lie! " shouted Willems, waking up for a
moment into righteous indignation.

" I know! I know—Be generous.—Think of my misery
since you went away—Oh! I could have torn my tongue
out. . . . I will never believe anybody—Look at the boy—
Be merciful—I could never rest till I found you. . . . Say—
a word—one word . . ."

" What the devil do you want? " exclaimed Willems,

looking towards the river. "Where's that damned boat?
Why did you let them go away? You stupid!"

"Oh, Peter!—I know that in your heart you have forgiven me—You are so generous—I want to hear you say
so. . . . Tell me—do you?"

"Yes! yes!" said Willems, impatiently. "I forgive
you. Don't be a fool."

"Don't go away. Don't leave me here alone. Where
is the danger? I am so frightened. . . . Are you alone
here? Sure? . . . Let us go away!"

"That's sense," said Willems, still looking anxiously
towards the river.

She sobbed gently, leaning on his arm.

"Let me go," he said.

He had seen above the steep bank the heads of three
men glide along smoothly. Then, where the shore shelved
down to the landing-place, appeared a big canoe which
came slowly to land.

"Here they are," he went on, briskly. "I'll go and get
my revolver."

He made a few hurried paces towards the house, but
seemed to catch sight of something, turned short round and
came back to his wife. She stared at him, alarmed by the
sudden change in his face. He appeared much discomposed.
He stammered a little as he began to speak.

"Go. Take the child. Go down to the boat and tell
them to drop it out of sight, quick, behind the bushes.
Do you hear? Hurry! I will come to you there directly.
Hurry up!"

"Peter! What is it? I won't leave you. There is
some danger in this horrible place."

"Will you go?" said Willems, in an irritable whisper.
"I tell you I am coming. Run! I tell you."

"No! no! no! I won't leave you. I will not lose you
again. Tell me, what is it?"

From beyond the house came a faint voice singing.
Willems shook his wife by the shoulder.

"Do what I tell you! Go at once!"

She gripped his arm and clung to him desperately. He looked up to heaven as if taking it to witness of that woman's infernal folly. The song grew louder, then ceased suddenly, and Aïssa appeared in sight, walking slowly, her hands full of flowers.

She had turned the corner of the house, coming out into the full sunshine, and the light seemed to leap upon her in a stream brilliant, tender, and caressing, as if attracted by the radiant happiness of her face. She had dressed herself for a festive day, for the memorable day of his return to her, of his return to an affection that would last for ever. The rays of the morning sun were caught by the oval clasp of the embroidered belt that held the silk sarong round her waist. The dazzling white stuff of her body jacket was crossed by a bar of yellow and silver of her scarf, and in the black hair twisted high on her small head shone the round balls of gold pins amongst crimson blossoms and white star-shaped flowers, with which she had crowned herself to charm his eyes; those eyes that were henceforth to see nothing in the world but her own resplendent image. And she moved slowly, bending her face over the mass of pure white champakas and jasmine pressed to her breast, in a dreamy intoxication of sweet scents and of sweeter hopes.

She did not seem to see anything, stopped for a moment at the foot of the plankway leading to the house, then, leaving her high-heeled wooden sandals there, ascended the planks in a light run; straight, graceful, flexible and noiseless, as if she had soared up to the door on invisible wings. Willems pushed his wife roughly behind the tree, and made up his mind quickly for a rush to the house, to get his revolver and . . . Thoughts, doubts, expedients seemed to boil in his brain. He had a flashing vision of delivering a stunning blow, of tying up that flower-bedecked woman in the dark house—a vision of things done swiftly with enraged haste—to save his prestige, his superiority—something of immense importance. . . . He had not made two steps when Joanna bounded after him, caught the back of his ragged jacket, tore out a big piece, and instantly hooked herself with both hands to the collar, nearly dragging him down on his back. Although taken by surprise, he managed to keep his feet. From behind she panted into his ear—

"That woman! Who's that woman? Ah! that's what those boatmen were talking about. I heard them . . . heard them . . . heard . . . in the night. They spoke about some woman. I dared not understand. I would not ask . . . listen . . . believe! How could I? Then it's true. No. Say no. . . . Who's that woman?"

He swayed, tugging forward. She jerked at him till the button gave way, and then he slipped half out of his jacket and, turning round, remained strangely motionless. His heart seemed to beat in his throat. He choked—tried to speak—could not find any words. He thought with fury: I will kill both of them.

For a second nothing moved about the courtyard in the great vivid clearness of the day. Only down by the landing-place a waringan-tree, all in a blaze of clustering red berries, seemed alive with the stir of little birds that filled with the feverish flutter of their feathers the tangle of overloaded branches. Suddenly the variegated flock rose spinning in a soft whir and dispersed, slashing the sunlit haze with the sharp outlines of stiffened wings. Mahmat and one of his brothers appeared coming up from the landing-place, their lances in their hands, to look for their passengers.

Aïssa coming now empty-handed out of the house, caught sight of the two armed men. In her surprise she emitted a faint cry, vanished back and in a flash reappeared in the doorway with Willems' revolver in her hand. To her the presence of any man there could only have an ominous meaning. There was nothing in the outer world but enemies. She and the man she loved were alone, with nothing round them but menacing dangers. She did not mind that, for if death came, no matter from what hand, they would die together.

Her resolute eyes took in the courtyard in a circular glance. She noticed that the two strangers had ceased to advance and now were standing close together leaning on the polished shafts of their weapons. The next moment she saw Willems, with his back towards her, apparently struggling under the tree with someone. She saw nothing distinctly, and, unhesitating, flew down the plankway calling out : " I come ! "

He heard her cry, and with an unexpected rush drove his wife backwards to the seat. She fell on it; he jerked himself altogether out of his jacket, and she covered her face with the soiled rags. He put his lips close to her, asking—

" For the last time, will you take the child and go ? "

She groaned behind the unclean ruins of his upper garment. She mumbled something. He bent lower to hear. She was saying—

" I won't go. Order that woman away. I can't look at her ! "

" You fool ! "

He seemed to spit the words at her, then, making up his mind, spun round to face Aïssa. She was coming towards them slowly now, with a look of unbounded amazement on her face. Then she stopped and stared at him—who stood there, stripped to the waist, bareheaded and sombre.

Some way off, Mahmat and his brother exchanged rapid words in calm undertones. . . . This was the strong daughter of the holy man who had died. The white man is very tall. There would be three women and the child to take in the boat, besides that white man who had the money. . . . The brother went away back to the boat, and Mahmat remained looking on. He stood like a sentinel, the leaf-shaped blade of his lance glinting above his head ; somnolent and upright under the cataract of sun-rays.

Willems spoke suddenly.

" Give me this," he said, stretching his hand towards the revolver.

Aïssa stepped back. Her lips trembled. She said very low : " Your people ? "

He nodded slightly. She shook her head thoughtfully,

and a few delicate petals of the flowers dying in her hair fell like big drops of crimson and white at her feet.

" Did you know ? " she whispered.

" No ! " said Willems. " They sent for me."

" Tell them to go. They are accursed. What is there between them and you—and you who carry my life in your heart ! "

Willems said nothing. He stood before her looking down on the ground and repeating to himself : I must get that revolver away from her, at once, at once. I can't think of trusting myself with those men without firearms. I must have it.

She asked, after gazing in silence at Joanna, who was sobbing gently—

" Who is she ? "

" My wife," answered Willems, without looking up. " My wife according to our white law, which comes from God ! "

" Your law ! Your God ! " murmured Aïssa, contemptuously.

" Give me that revolver," said Willems, in a peremptory tone. He felt an unwillingness to close with her, to get it by force.

She took no notice and went on—

" Your law . . . or your lies ? What am I to believe ? I came—I ran to defend you when I saw the strange men. You lied to me with your lips, with your eyes. You crooked heart ! . . . Ah ! " she added, after an abrupt pause. " She is the first ! Am I then to be a slave ? "

" You may be what you like," said Willems, brutally. " I am going."

Her gaze was fastened on the blanket under which she had detected a slight movement. She made a long stride towards it. Willems turned half round. His legs seemed to him to be made of lead. He felt faint and so weak that, for a moment, the fear of dying there where he stood, before he could make escape from sin and disaster, passed through his mind in a wave of despair.

She lifted up one corner of the blanket, and when she saw the sleeping child a sudden quick shudder shook her as though she had seen something inexpressibly horrible. She looked at Louis Willems with eyes fixed in an unbelieving and terrified stare. Then her fingers opened slowly, and a shadow seemed to settle on her face as if something obscure and fatal had come between her and the sunshine. She stood looking down, absorbed, as though she had watched at the bottom of a gloomy abyss the mournful procession of her thoughts.

Willems did not move. All his faculties were concentrated upon the idea of his release. And it was only then, in that minute, when the assurance of it came to him with such force that he seemed to hear a loud voice shouting in the heavens that all was over, that in another five, ten minutes, he would step into another existence; that all this, the woman, the madness, the sin, the regrets, all would go, rush into the past, disappear, become as dust, as smoke, as drifting clouds—as nothing! Yes! All would vanish in the unappeasable past which would swallow up all—even the very memory of his temptation and of his downfall. Nothing mattered. He cared for nothing. He had forgotten Aïssa, his wife, Lingard, Hudig—everybody, in the rapid vision of his hopeful future.

After a while he heard Aïssa saying—

"A child! A child! What have I done to be made to devour this sorrow and this grief? And while your man-child and the mother lived you told me there was nothing for you to remember in the land from which you came! And I thought you could be mine. I thought that I would . . ."

Her voice ceased in a broken murmur, and with it, in her heart, seemed to die the greater and most precious hope of her new life. She had hoped that in the future the frail arms of a child would bind their two lives together in a bond which nothing on earth could break, a bond of affection, of gratitude, of tender respect. She the first—the only one! But in the instant she saw the son of that other woman she felt herself removed into the cold, the darkness, the silence of a solitude impenetrable and immense—very far from him, beyond the possibility of any hope, into an infinity of wrongs without any redress.

She strode nearer to Joanna. She felt towards that woman anger, envy, jealousy. Before her she felt humiliated and enraged. She seized the hanging sleeve of the jacket in which Joanna was hiding her face and tore it out of her hands, exclaiming loudly—

"Let me see the face of her before whom I am only a servant and a slave. Ya-wa! I see you!"

Her unexpected shout seemed to fill the sunlit space of cleared grounds, rise high and run on far into the land over the unstirring tree-tops of the forests. She stood in sudden stillness, looking at Joanna with surprised contempt.

"A Sirani woman!" she said, slowly, in a tone of wonder.

Joanna rushed at Willems—clung to him, shrieking: "Defend me, Peter! Defend me from that woman!"

"Be quiet. There is no danger," muttered Willems, thickly.

Aïssa looked at them with scorn. "God is great! I sit in the dust at your feet," she exclaimed jeeringly, joining her hands above her head in a gesture of mock humility. "Before you I am as nothing." She turned to Willems fiercely, opening her arms wide. "What have you made of me?" she cried, "you lying child of an accursed mother! What have you made of me? The slave of a slave. Don't speak! Your words are worse than the poison of snakes. A Sirani woman. A woman of a people despised by all."

She pointed her finger at Joanna, stepped back, and began to laugh.

"Make her stop, Peter!" screamed Joanna. "That heathen woman. Heathen! Heathen! Beat her, Peter."

Willems caught sight of the revolver which Aïssa had laid on the seat near the child. He spoke in Dutch to his wife, without moving his head.

"Go. Snatch the boy—and my revolver there. See. Run to the boat. I will keep her back. Now's the time."

Aïssa came nearer. She stared at Joanna, while between the short gusts of broken laughter she raved, fumbling distractedly at the buckle of her belt.

"To her! To her—the mother of him who will speak of your wisdom, of your courage. All to her. I have nothing! Nothing. Take, take."

She tore the belt off and threw it at Joanna's feet. She flung down with haste the armlets, the gold pins, the flowers; and the long hair, released, fell scattered over her shoulders, framing in its blackness the wild exaltation of her face.

"Drive her off, Peter. Drive off the heathen savage," persisted Joanna. She seemed to have lost her head altogether. She stamped, clinging to Willems' arm with both her hands.

"Look," cried Aïssa. "Look at the mother of your son! She is afraid. Why does she not go from before my face? Look at her. She is ugly."

Joanna seemed to understand the scornful tone of the words. As Aïssa stepped back again nearer to the tree she let go her husband's arm, rushed at her madly, slapped her face, then, swerving round, darted at the child, who, unnoticed, had been wailing for some time, and, snatching him up, flew down to the waterside, sending shriek after shriek in an access of insane terror.

Willems made for the revolver. Aïssa passed swiftly, giving him an unexpected push that sent him staggering away from the tree. She caught up the weapon, put it behind her back, and cried—

"You shall not have it. Go after her. Go to meet danger. . . . Go to meet death. . . . Go unarmed. . . . Go with empty hands and sweet words . . . as you came to me. . . . Go helpless and lie to the forests, to the sea . . . to the death that waits for you. . . ."

She ceased as if strangled. She saw in the horror of the passing seconds the half-naked, wild-looking man before her; she heard the faint shrillness of Joanna's insane shrieks for help somewhere down by the riverside. The sunlight streamed on her, on him, on the mute land, on the murmuring river—the gentle brilliance of a serene morning that, to her, seemed traversed by ghastly flashes of uncertain darkness. Hate filled the world, filled the space between them—the hate of race, the hate of hopeless diversity, the hate of blood; the hate against the man born in the land of lies and of evil from which nothing but misfortune comes to those who are not white. And as she stood, maddened, she heard a whisper near her, the whisper of the dead Omar's voice saying in her ear: "Kill! Kill!"

She cried, seeing him move—

"Do not come near me . . . or you die now! Go while I remember yet . . . remember. . . ."

Willems pulled himself together for a struggle. He dared not go unarmed. He made a long stride, and saw her raise the revolver. He noticed that she had not cocked it, and said to himself that, even if she did fire, she would surely miss. Go too high; it was a stiff trigger. He made a step nearer—saw the long barrel moving unsteadily at the end of her extended arm. He thought: This is my time. . . . He bent his knees slightly, throwing his body forward, and took off with a long bound for a tearing rush.

He saw a burst of red flame before his eyes, and was deafened by a report that seemed to him louder than a clap of thunder. Something stopped him short, and he stood aspiring in his nostrils the acrid smell of the blue smoke that drifted from before his eyes like an immense cloud. . . . Missed, by Heaven! . . . Thought so! . . . And he saw her very far off, throwing her arms up, while the revolver, very small, lay on the ground between them. . . . Missed! . . . He would go and pick it up now. Never before did he understand, as in that second, the joy, the triumphant delight of sunshine and of life. His mouth was full of something salt and warm. He tried to cough; spat out. . . . Who shrieks: In the name of God, he dies!—he dies!— Who dies?—Must pick up—Night!—What? . . . Night already. . . .

\*        \*        \*        \*        \*

Many years afterwards Almayer was telling the story of

the great revolution in Sambir to a chance visitor from Europe. He was a Roumanian, half naturalist, half orchid-hunter for commercial purposes, who used to declare to everybody, in the first five minutes of acquaintance, his intention of writing a scientific book about tropical countries. On his way to the interior he had quartered himself upon Almayer. He was a man of some education, but he drank his gin neat, or only, at most, would squeeze the juice of half a small lime into the raw spirit. He said it was good for his health, and, with that medicine before him, he would relate to the surprised Almayer the wonders of European capitals; while Almayer, in exchange, bored him by ex-pounding, with gusto, his unfavourable opinions of Sambir's social and political life. They talked far into the night, across the deal table on the verandah, while, between them, clear-winged, small, and flabby insects, dissatisfied with moonlight, streamed in and perished in thousands round the smoky light of the evil-smelling lamp.

Almayer, his face flushed, was saying—

"Of course, I did not see that. I told you I was stuck in the creek on account of father's—Captain Lingard's—susceptible temper. I am sure I did it all for the best in trying to facilitate the fellow's escape; but Captain Lingard was that kind of man—you know—one couldn't argue with. Just before sunset the water was high enough, and we got out of the creek. We got to Lakamba's clearing about dark. All very quiet; I thought they were gone, of course, and felt very glad. We walked up the courtyard—saw a big heap of something lying in the middle. Out of that she rose and rushed at us. By God. . . . You know those stories of faithful dogs watching their masters' corpses . . . don't let anybody approach . . . got to beat them off—and all that. . . . Well, 'pon my word we had to beat her off. Had to ! She was like a fury. Wouldn't let us touch him. Dead—of course. Should think so. Shot through the lung, on the left side, rather high up, and at pretty close quarters too, for the two holes were small. Bullet came out through the shoulder-blade. After we had overpowered her—you can't imagine how strong that woman was; it took three of us—we got the body into the boat and shoved off. We thought she had fainted then, but she got up and rushed into the water. Well, I let her clamber in. What could I do? The river's full of alligators, and she would swim after us. I will never forget that pull up-stream in the night as long as I live. She sat in the bottom of the boat, holding his head in her lap, and now and again wiping his face with her hair. There was a lot of blood dried about his mouth and chin. And for all the six hours of that journey she kept on whispering tenderly to that corpse! . . . I had the mate of the schooner with me. The man said afterwards that he wouldn't go through it again—not for a handful of diamonds. And I believed him—I did. It makes me shiver. Do you think he heard? No! I mean somebody—something—heard? . . ."

"I am a materialist," declared the man of science, tilting the bottle shakily over the emptied glass.

Almayer shook his head and went on—

"Nobody saw how it really happened but that man Mahmat. He always said that he was no further off from them than two lengths of his lance. It appears the two women rowed each other while that Willems stood between them. Then Mahmat says that when Joanna struck her and ran off, the other two seemed to become suddenly mad together. They rushed here and there. Mahmat says—those were his very words: 'I saw her standing holding the pistol that fires many times and pointing it all over the campong. I was afraid—lest she might shoot me, and jumped on one side. Then I saw the white man coming at her swiftly. He came like our master the tiger when he rushes out of the jungle at the spears held by men. She did not take aim. The barrel of her weapon went like this—from side to side, but in her eyes I could see suddenly a great fear. There was only one shot. She shrieked while the white man stood blinking his eyes and very straight, till you could count slowly one, two, three; then he coughed and fell on his face. The daughter of Omar shrieked without drawing breath, till he fell. I went away then and left silence behind me. These things did not concern me, and in my boat there was that other woman who had promised me money. We left directly, paying no attention to her cries. We are only poor men, and had but a small reward for our trouble ! ' That's what Mahmat said. Never varied. You ask him yourself. He's the man you hired the boats from, for your journey up the river."

"The most rapacious thief I ever met ! " exclaimed the traveller, thickly.

"Ah ! He is a respectable man. His two brothers got themselves speared—served them right. They went in for robbing Dyak graves. Gold ornaments in them, you know. Serve them right. But he kept respectable and got on. Aye ! Everybody got on—but I. And all through that scoundrel who brought the Arabs here."

"De mortuis nil ni . . . num," muttered Almayer's guest.

"I wish you would speak English instead of jabbering in your own language, which no one can understand," said Almayer, sulkily.

"Don't be angry," hiccoughed the other. "It's Latin, and it's wisdom. It means: Don't waste your breath in abusing shadows. No offence there. I like you. You have a quarrel with Providence—so have I. I was meant to be a professor, while—look."

His head nodded. He sat grasping the glass. Almayer walked up and down, then stopped suddenly.

"Yes, they all got on but I. Why ? I am better than any of them. Lakamba calls himself a Sultan, and when I go to see him on business sends that one-eyed fiend of his—Babalatchi—to tell me that the ruler is asleep ; and shall sleep for a long time. And that Babalatchi ! He is the Shahbandar of the State—if you please. Oh Lord ! Shahbandar ! The pig ! A vagabond I wouldn't let come up these steps when he first came here. . . . Look at Abdulla now. He lives here because—he says—here is away from white men. But he has hundreds of thousands. Has a house in Penang. Ships. What did he not have when he stole my trade from me! He knocked everything here into a cocked hat; drove father to gold-hunting—then to Europe, where he disappeared. Fancy a man like Captain Lingard disappearing as though he had been a common coolie. Friends of mine wrote to London asking about him. Nobody ever heard of him there! Fancy! Never heard of Captain Lingard!"

The learned gatherer of orchids lifted his head.

"He was a sen—sentimen—tal old buc—buccaneer," he stammered out, "I like him. I'm sent—tal myself."

He winked slowly at Almayer, who laughed.

"Yes! I told you about that gravestone. Yes! Another hundred and twenty dollars thrown away. Wish I had them now. He would do it. And the inscription. Ha! ha! ha! 'Peter Willems, Delivered by the Mercy of God from his Enemy.' What enemy—unless Captain Lingard himself? And then it has no sense. He was a great man—father was—but strange in many ways. . . . You haven't seen the grave? On the top of that hill, there, on the other side of the river. I must show you. We will go there."

"Not I!" said the other. "No interest—in the sun—too tiring. . . . Unless you carry me there."

As a matter of fact he was carried there a few months afterwards, and his was the second white man's grave in Sambir; but at present he was alive if rather drunk. He asked abruptly—

"And the woman?"

"Oh! Lingard, of course, kept her and her ugly brat in Macassar. Sinful waste of money—that! Devil only knows what became of them since father went home. I had my daughter to look after. I shall give you a word to Mrs. Vinck in Singapore when you go back. You shall see my Nina there. Lucky man. She is beautiful, and I hear so accomplished, so . . ."

"I have heard already twenty . . . a hundred times about your daughter. What ab—about—that—that other one, Aï . . . ssa?"

"She! Oh! we kept her here. She was mad for a long time in a quiet sort of way. Father thought a lot of her. We gave her a house to live in, in my campong. She wandered about, speaking to nobody unless she caught sight of Abdulla, when she would have a fit of fury, and shriek and curse like anything. Very often she would disappear—and then we all had to turn out and hunt for her, because father would worry till she was brought back. Found her in all kinds of places. Once in the abandoned campong of Lakamba. Sometimes simply wandering in the bush. She had one favourite spot we always made for at first. It was ten to one on finding her there—a kind of a grassy glade on the banks of a small brook. Why she preferred that place, I can't imagine! And such a job to get her away from there. Had to drag her away by main force. Then, as the time passed, she became quieter and more settled, like. Still, all my people feared her greatly. It was my Nina that tamed her. You see the child was naturally fearless, and used to have her own way, so she would go to her and pull at her sarong, and order her about, as she did everybody. Finally she, I verily believe, came to love the child. Nothing could resist that little one—you know. She made a capital nurse. Once when the little devil ran away from me and fell into the river off the end of the jetty, she jumped in and pulled her out in no time. I very nearly died of fright. Now of course she lives with my serving girls, but does what she likes. As long as I have a handful of rice or a piece of cotton in the store she sha'n't want for anything. You have seen her. She brought in the dinner with Ali."

"What! That doubled-up crone?"

"Ah!" said Almayer. "They age quickly here. And long foggy nights spent in the bush will soon break the strongest backs—as you will find out yourself soon."

"Dis . . . disgusting," growled the traveller.

He dozed off. Almayer stood by the balustrade looking out at the bluish sheen of the moonlit night. The forests, unchanged and sombre, seemed to hang over the water,

Q

listening to the unceasing whisper of the great river; and above their dark wall the hill on which Lingard had buried the body of his late prisoner rose in a black, rounded mass, upon the silver paleness of the sky. Almayer looked for a long time at the clean-cut outline of the summit, as if trying to make out through darkness and distance the shape of that expensive tombstone. When he turned round at last he saw his guest sleeping, his arms on the table, his head on his arms.

"Now, look here!" he shouted, slapping the table with the palm of his hand.

The naturalist woke up, and sat all in a heap, staring owlishly.

"Here!" went on Almayer, speaking very loud and thumping the table, "I want to know. You, who say you have read all the books, just tell me . . . why such damned things are ever born. Here I am! Done harm to nobody, lived an honest life . . . and a scoundrel like that is born in Rotterdam or some such damn'd place at the other end of the world somewhere, travels out here, robs his employer, runs away from his wife, and ruins me and Nina—he ruined me, I tell you—and gets himself shot at last by a poor miserable savage, that knows nothing at all about him really. Where's the sense of all this? Where's your Providence? Where's the good for anybody in all this? The world's a swindle! A swindle! Why should I suffer? What have I done to be treated so?"

He howled out his string of questions, and suddenly became silent. The man who ought to have been a professor made a tremendous effort to articulate distinctly—

"My dear fellow, don't—don't you see that the ba— bare fac—the fact of your existence is off—offensive. . . . I—I like you—like . . ."

He fell forward on the table, and ended his remarks by an unexpected and prolonged snore.

Almayer shrugged his shoulders and walked back to the balustrade. He drank his own trade gin very seldom, but, when he did, a ridiculously small quantity of the stuff could induce him to assume a rebellious attitude towards the scheme of the universe. And now, throwing his body over the rail, he shouted impudently into the night, turning his face towards that far-off and invisible slab of imported granite upon which Lingard had thought fit to record God's mercy and Willems' escape.

"Father was wrong—wrong!" he yelled. "I want you to smart for it. You must smart for it! Where are you, Willems? Hey? . . . Hey? . . . Where there is no mercy for you—I hope!"

"Hope," repeated in a whispering echo the startled forests, the river and the hills; but Almayer, who stood waiting with his head on one side and a smile of tipsy attention on his lips, heard no other answer.

# THE ARROW OF GOLD

# FIRST NOTE

THE pages which follow have been extracted from a pile of manuscript which was apparently meant for the eye of one woman only. She seems to have been the writer's childhood's friend. They had parted as children, or very little more than children. Years passed. Then something recalled to the woman the companion of her young days and she wrote to him: " I have been hearing of you lately. I know where life has brought you. You certainly selected your own road. But to us, left behind, it always looked as if you had struck out into a pathless desert. We always regarded you as a person that must be given up for lost. But you have turned up again; and though we may never see each other, my memory welcomes you and I confess to you I should like to know the incidents on the road which has led you to where you are now."

And he answers her: " I believe you are the only one now alive who remembers me as a child. I have heard of you from time to time, but I wonder what sort of person you are now. Perhaps if I did know I wouldn't dare put pen to paper. But I don't know. I, only remember that we were great chums. In fact, I chummed with you even more than with your brothers. But I am like the pigeon that went away in the fable of the Two Pigeons. If I once start to tell you I would want you to feel that you have been there yourself. I may overtax your patience with the story of my life so different from yours, not only in all the facts but altogether in spirit. You may not understand. You may even be shocked. I say all this to myself; but I know I shall succumb! I have a distinct recollection that in the old days, when you were about fifteen, you always could make me do whatever you liked."

He succumbed. He begins his story for her with the minute narration of this adventure which took about twelve months to develop. In the form in which it is presented here it has been pruned of all allusions to their common past, of all asides, disquisitions, and explanations addressed directly to the friend of his childhood. And even as it is the whole thing is of considerable length. It seems that he had not only a memory but that he also knew how to remember. But as to that opinions may differ.

This, his first great adventure, as he calls it, begins in Marseilles. It ends there, too. Yet it might have happened anywhere. This does not mean that the people concerned could have come together in pure space. The locality had a definite importance. As to the time, it is easily fixed by the events at about the middle years of the seventies, when Don Carlos de Bourbon, encouraged by the general reaction of all Europe against the excesses of communistic Republicanism, made his attempt for the throne of Spain, arms in hand, amongst the hills and gorges of Guipuzcoa. It is perhaps the last instance of a Pretender's adventure for a Crown that History will have to record with the usual grave moral disapproval tinged by a shamefaced regret for the departing romance. Historians are very much like other people.

However, History has nothing to do with this tale. Neither is the moral justification or condemnation of conduct aimed at here. If anything it is perhaps a little sympathy that the writer expects for his buried youth, as he lives it over again at the end of his insignificant course on this earth. Strange person—yet perhaps not so very different from ourselves.

A few words as to certain facts may be added.

It may seem that he was plunged very abruptly into this long adventure. But from certain passages (suppressed here because mixed up with irrelevant matter) it appears clearly that at the time of the meeting in the café, Mills had already gathered, in various quarters, a definite view of the eager youth who had been introduced to him in that ultra-legitimist salon. What Mills had learned represented him as a young gentleman who had arrived furnished with proper credentials and who apparently was doing his best to waste his life in an eccentric fashion, with a bohemian set (one poet at least, emerged out of it later) on one side, and on the other making friends with the people of the Old Town, pilots, coasters, sailors, workers of all sorts. He pretended rather absurdly to be a seaman himself and was already credited with an ill-defined and vaguely illegal enterprise in the Gulf of Mexico. At once it occurred to Mills that this eccentric youngster was the very person for what the legitimist sympathizers had very much at heart just then : to organize a supply by sea of arms and ammunition to the Carlist detachments in the South. It was precisely to confer on that matter with Doña Rita that Captain Blunt had been despatched from Headquarters.

Mills got in touch with Blunt at once and put the suggestion before him. The Captain thought this the very thing. As a matter of fact, on that evening of Carnival, those two, Mills and Blunt, had been actually looking everywhere for our man. They had decided that he should be drawn into the affair if it could be done. Blunt naturally wanted to see him first. He must have estimated him a promising person, but, from another point of view, not dangerous. Thus lightly was the notorious (and at the same time mysterious) Monsieur George brought into the world ; out of the contact of two minds which did not give a single thought to his flesh and blood.

Their purpose explains the intimate tone given to their first conversation and the sudden introduction of Doña Rita's history. Mills, of course, wanted to hear all about it. As to Captain Blunt I suspect that, at the time, he was thinking of nothing else. In addition it was Doña Rita who would have to do the persuading ; for, after all, such an enterprise with its ugly and desperate risks was not a trifle to put before a man—however young.

It cannot be denied that Mills seems to have acted somewhat unscrupulously. He himself appears to have had some doubt about it, at a given moment, as they were driving to

Q 2

the Prado.   But perhaps Mills, with his penetration, understood very well the nature he was dealing with.   He might
even have envied it.   But it's not my business to excuse
Mills.   As to him whom we may regard as Mills' victim it
is obvious that he has never harboured a single reproachful
thought.   For him Mills is not to be criticized.   A remarkable instance of the great power of mere individuality over
the young.

# PART ONE

## I

CERTAIN streets have an atmosphere of their own, a sort of universal fame and the particular affection of their citizens. One of such streets is the Cannebière, and the jest : "If Paris had a Cannebière it would be a little Marseilles" is the jocular expression of municipal pride. I, too, I have been under the spell. For me it has been a street leading into the unknown.

There was a part of it where one could see as many as five big cafés in a resplendent row. That evening I strolled into one of them. It was by no means full. It looked deserted, in fact, festal and overlighted, but cheerful. The wonderful street was distinctly cold (it was an evening of carnival), I was very idle, and I was feeling a little lonely. So I went in and sat down.

The carnival time was drawing to an end. Everybody, high and low, was anxious to have the last fling. Companies of masks with linked arms and whooping like red Indians swept the streets in crazy rushes while gusts of cold mistral swayed the gas lights as far as the eye could reach. There was a touch of bedlam in all this.

Perhaps it was that which made me feel lonely, since I was neither masked, nor disguised, nor yelling, nor in any other way in harmony with the bedlam element of life. But I was not sad. I was merely in a state of sobriety. I had just returned from my second West Indies voyage. My eyes were still full of tropical splendour, my memory of my experiences, lawful and lawless, which had their charm and their thrill ; for they had startled me a little and had amused me considerably. But they had left me untouched. Indeed they were other men's adventures, not mine. Except for a little habit of responsibility which I had acquired they had not matured me. I was as young as before. Inconceivably young—still beautifully unthinking—infinitely receptive.

You may believe that I was not thinking of Don Carlos and his fight for a kingdom. Why should I? You don't want to think of things which you meet every day in the newspapers and in conversation. I had paid some calls since my return and most of my acquaintance were legitimists and intensely interested in the events of the frontier of Spain, for political, religious, or romantic reasons. But I was not interested. Apparently I was not romantic enough. Or was it that I was even more romantic than all those good people? The affair seemed to me commonplace. That man was attending to his business of a Pretender.

On the front page of the illustrated paper I saw lying on a table near me, he looked picturesque enough, seated on a boulder, a big strong man with a square-cut beard, his hands resting on the hilt of a cavalry sabre—and all around him a landscape of savage mountains. He caught my eye on that spiritedly composed woodcut. (There were no inane snap-shot-reproductions in those days.) It was the obvious romance for the use of royalists but it arrested my attention.

Just then some masks from outside invaded the café, dancing hand in hand in a single file led by a burly man with a cardboard nose. He gambolled in wildly and behind him twenty others perhaps, mostly Pierrots and Pierrettes holding each other by the hand and winding in and out between the chairs and tables: eyes shining in the holes of cardboard faces, breasts panting; but all preserving a mysterious silence.

They were people of the poorer sort (white calico with red spots, costumes), but amongst them there was a girl in a black dress sewn over with gold half moons, very high in the neck and very short in the skirt. Most of the ordinary clients of the café didn't even look up from their games or papers. I, being alone and idle, stared abstractedly. The girl costumed as Night wore a small black velvet mask, what is

called in French a "*loup*." What made her daintiness join
that obviously rough lot I can't imagine. Her uncovered
mouth and chin suggested refined prettiness.

They filed past my table; the Night noticed perhaps
my fixed gaze and throwing her body forward out of the
wriggling chain shot out at me a slender tongue like a pink
dart. I was not prepared for this, not even to the extent of
an appreciative "*Très joli*," before she wriggled and hopped
away. But having been thus distinguished I could do no
less than follow her with my eyes to the door where the chain
of hands being broken all the masks were trying to get out at
once. Two gentlemen coming in out of the street stood
arrested in the crush. The Night (it must have been her
idiosyncrasy) put her tongue out at them, too. The taller
of the two (he was in evening clothes under a light wide-
open overcoat) with great presence of mind chucked her
under the chin, giving me the view at the same time of a
flash of white teeth in his dark, lean face. The other man
was very different; fair, with smooth, ruddy cheeks and burly
shoulders. He was wearing a grey suit, obviously bought
ready-made, for it seemed too tight for his powerful frame.

That man was not altogether a stranger to me. For the
last week or so I had been rather on the look-out for him in
all the public places where in a provincial town men may
expect to meet each other. I saw him for the first time
(wearing that same grey ready-made suit) in a legitimist
drawing-room where, clearly, he was an object of interest,
especially to the women. I had caught his name as Monsieur Mills. The lady who had introduced me took the
earliest opportunity to murmur into my ear : "A relation
of Lord X." (*Un proche parent de Lord X.*) And then she
added, casting up her eyes : "A good friend of the King."
Meaning Don Carlos of course.

I looked at the *proche parent*; not on account of the
parentage but marvelling at his air of ease in that cumbrous
body and in such tight clothes, too. But presently the same
lady informed me further : "He has come here amongst us
*un naufragé*."

I became then really interested. I had never seen a ship-wrecked person before. All the boyishness in me was aroused. I considered a shipwreck as an unavoidable event sooner or later in my future.

Meantime the man thus distinguished in my eyes glanced quietly about and never spoke unless addressed directly by one of the ladies present. There were more than a dozen people in that drawing-room, mostly women eating fine pastry and talking passionately. It might have been a Carlist committee meeting of a particularly fatuous character. Even my youth and inexperience were aware of that. And I was by a long way the youngest person in the room. That quiet Monsieur Mills intimidated me a little by his age (I suppose he was thirty-five), his massive tranquillity, his clear, watchful eyes. But the temptation was too great— and I addressed him impulsively on the subject of that shipwreck.

He turned his big fair face towards me with surprise in his keen glance, which (as though he had seen through me in an instant and found nothing objectionable) changed subtly into friendliness. On the matter of the shipwreck he did not say much. He only told me that it had not occurred in the Mediterranean, but on the other side of Southern France—in the Bay of Biscay. "But this is hardly the place to enter on a story of that kind," he observed, looking round at the room with a faint smile as attractive as the rest of his rustic but well-bred personality.

I expressed my regret. I should have liked to hear all about it. To this he said that it was not a secret and that perhaps next time we met . . .

"But where can we meet?" I cried. "I don't come often to this house, you know."

"Where? Why, on the Cannebière to be sure. Everybody meets everybody else at least once a day on the pavement opposite the *Bourse*."

This was absolutely true. But though I looked for him on each succeeding day he was nowhere to be seen at the usual times. The companions of my idle hours (and all my hours were idle just then) noticed my preoccupation and chaffed me about it in a rather obvious way. They wanted to know whether she, whom I expected to see, was dark or fair; whether that fascination which kept me on tenter-hooks of expectation was one of my aristocrats or one of my marine beauties: for they knew I had a footing in both these—shall we say circles? As to themselves they were the bohemian circle, not very wide—half a dozen of us led by a sculptor whom we called Prax for short. My own nick-name was "Young Ulysses." I liked it.

But chaff or no chaff they would have been surprised to see me leave them for the burly and sympathetic Mills. I was ready to drop any easy company of equals to approach that interesting man with every mental deference. It was not precisely because of that shipwreck. He attracted and interested me the more because he was not to be seen. The fear that he might have departed suddenly for England—(or for Spain)—caused me a sort of ridiculous depression as though I had missed a unique opportunity. And it was a joyful reaction which emboldened me to signal to him with a raised arm across that café.

I was abashed immediately afterwards, when I saw him advance towards my table with his friend. The latter was eminently elegant. He was exactly like one of those figures one can see of a fine May evening in the neighbourhood of the Opera-house in Paris. Very Parisian indeed. And yet he struck me as not so perfectly French as he ought to have been, as if one's nationality were an accomplishment with varying degrees of excellence. As to Mills, he was perfectly insular. There could be no doubt about him. They were both smiling faintly at me. The burly Mills attended to the introduction: "Captain Blunt."

We shook hands. The name didn't tell me much. What surprised me was that Mills should have remembered mine so well. I don't want to boast of my modesty but it seemed to me that two or three days was more than enough for a man like Mills to forget my very existence. As to the Cap-tain, I was struck on closer view by the perfect correctness of his personality. Clothes, slight figure, clear-cut, thin, sun-tanned face, pose, all this was so good that it was saved from the danger of banality only by the mobile black eyes of a keenness that one doesn't meet every day in the south of France and still less in Italy. Another thing was that, viewed as an officer in mufti, he did not look sufficiently professional. That imperfection was interesting, too.

You may think that I am subtilizing my impressions on purpose, but you may take it from a man who has lived a rough, a very rough life, that it is the subtleties of personalities, and contacts, and events, that count for interest and memory—and pretty well nothing else. This—you see—is the last evening of that part of my life in which I did not know that woman. These are like the last hours of a previous existence. It isn't my fault that they are associated with nothing better at the decisive moment than the banal splendours of a gilded café and the bedlamite yells of carnival in the street.

We three, however (almost complete strangers to each other), had assumed attitudes of serious amiability round our table. A waiter approached for orders and it was then, in relation to my order for coffee, that the absolutely first thing I learned of Captain Blunt was the fact that he was a sufferer from insomnia. In his immovable way Mills began charging his pipe. I felt extremely embarrassed all at once, but became positively annoyed when I saw our Prax enter the café in a sort of mediæval costume very much like what Faust wears in the third act. I have no doubt it was meant for a purely operatic Faust. A light mantle floated from his shoulders. He strode theatrically up to our table and addressing me as "Young Ulysses" proposed I should go outside on the fields of asphalt and help him gather a few marguerites to decorate a truly infernal supper which was being organized across the road at the Maison Dorée—upstairs. With expostulatory shakes of the head and indignant glances I called his attention to the fact that I was not alone. He stepped back a pace as if astonished by the discovery, took off his plumed velvet toque with a low obeisance so that the feathers swept the floor, and swaggered off the stage with his left hand resting on the hilt of the property dagger at his belt.

Meantime the well-connected but rustic Mills had been busy lighting his briar and the distinguished Captain sat smiling to himself. I was horribly vexed and apologized for that intrusion, saying that the fellow was a future great sculptor and perfectly harmless; but he had been swallowing lots of night air which had got into his head apparently.

Mills peered at me with his friendly but awfully searching blue eyes through the cloud of smoke he had wreathed about his big head. The slim, dark Captain's smile took on an amiable expression. Might he know why I was addressed as "Young Ulysses" by my friend? and immediately he added the remark with urbane playfulness that Ulysses was an astute person. Mills did not give me time for a reply. He struck in: "That old Greek was famed as a wanderer—the first historical seaman." He waved his pipe vaguely at me.

"Ah! *Vraiment!*" The polite Captain seemed incredulous and as if weary. "Are you a seaman? In what sense, pray?" We were talking French and he used the term *homme de mer*.

Again Mills interfered quietly. "In the same sense in which you are a military man." (*Homme de guerre.*)

It was then that I heard Captain Blunt produce one of his striking declarations. He had two of them, and this was the first.

"I live by my sword."

It was said in an extraordinary dandified manner which in conjunction with the matter made me forget my tongue in my head. I could only stare at him. He added more naturally: "2nd Reg. Castille Cavalry." Then with marked stress in Spanish, "*En las filas legitimas.*"

Mills was heard, unmoved, like Jove in his cloud: "He's on leave here."

"Of course I don't shout that fact on the housetops," the Captain addressed me pointedly, "any more than our friend his shipwreck adventure. We must not strain the toleration

of the French authorities too much! It wouldn't be correct
—and not very safe either."

I became suddenly extremely delighted with my company.
A man who "lived by his sword," before my eyes, close at
my elbow! So such people did exist in the world yet! I
had not been born too late! And across the table with his
air of watchful, unmoved benevolence, enough in itself to
arouse one's interest, there was the man with the story
of a shipwreck that mustn't be shouted on housetops.
Why?

I understood very well why, when he told me that he had
joined in the Clyde, a small steamer chartered by a relative
of his, " a very wealthy man," he observed (probably Lord X,
I thought), to carry arms and other supplies to the Carlist
army. And it was not a shipwreck in the ordinary sense.
Everything went perfectly well to the last moment when
suddenly the *Numancia* (a Republican ironclad) had appeared
and chased them ashore on the French coast below Bayonne.
In a few words, but with evident appreciation of the adventure, Mills described to us how he swam to the beach clad
simply in a money belt and a pair of trousers. Shells were
falling all round till a tiny French gunboat came out of
Bayonne and shooed the *Numancia* away out of territorial
waters.

He was very amusing and I was fascinated by the mental
picture of that tranquil man rolling in the surf and emerging
breathless, in the costume you know, on the fair land of
France, in the character of a smuggler of war material.
However, they had never arrested or expelled him, since he
was there before my eyes. But how and why did he get so
far from the scene of his sea adventure was an interesting
question. And I put it to him with most naïve indiscretion
which did not shock him visibly. He told me that the ship
being only stranded, not sunk, the contraband cargo aboard
was doubtless in good condition. The French custom-house
men were guarding the wreck. If their vigilance could be—
h'm—removed by some means, or even merely reduced, a
lot of these rifles and cartridges could be taken off quietly at

night by certain Spanish fishing boats. In fact, salved for the Carlists, after all. He thought it could be done. . . .

I said with professional gravity that given a few perfectly quiet nights (rare on that coast) it could certainly be done.

Mr. Mills was not afraid of the elements. It was the highly inconvenient zeal of the French custom-house people that had to be dealt with in some way.

"Heavens!" I cried, astonished. "You can't bribe the French Customs. This isn't a South-American republic."

"Is it a republic?" he murmured, very absorbed in smoking his wooden pipe.

"Well, isn't it?"

He murmured again, "Oh, so little." At this I laughed, and a faintly humorous expression passed over Mills' face. No. Bribes were out of the question, he admitted. But there were many legitimist sympathies in Paris. A proper person could set them in motion and a mere hint from high quarters to the officials on the spot not to worry over-much about that wreck. . . .

What was most amusing was the cool, reasonable tone of this amazing project. Mr. Blunt sat by very detached, his eyes roamed here and there all over the café; and it was while looking upward at the pink foot of a fleshy and very much foreshortened goddess of some sort depicted on the ceiling in an enormous composition in the Italian style that he let fall casually the words, "She will manage it for you quite easily."

"Every Carlist agent in Bayonne assured me of that," said Mr. Mills. "I would have gone straight to Paris only I was told she had fled here for a rest; tired, discontented. Not a very encouraging report."

"These flights are well known," muttered Mr. Blunt. "You shall see her all right."

"Yes. They told me that you . . ."

I broke in: "You mean to say that you expect a woman to arrange that sort of thing for you?"

"A trifle for her," Mr. Blunt remarked indifferently.

"At that sort of thing women are best. They have less scruples."

"More audacity," interjected Mr. Mills almost in a whisper.

Mr. Blunt kept quiet for a moment, then : "You see," he addressed me in a most refined tone, "a mere man may suddenly find himself being kicked down the stairs."

I don't know why I should have felt shocked by that statement. It could not be because it was untrue. The other did not give me time to offer any remark. He inquired with extreme politeness what did I know of South American republics? I confessed that I knew very little of them. Wandering about the Gulf of Mexico I had a look-in here and there; and amongst others I had a few days in Haiti which was of course unique, being a negro republic. On this Captain Blunt began to talk of negroes at large. He talked of them with knowledge, intelligence, and a sort of contemptuous affection. He generalized, he particularized about the black; he told anecdotes. I was interested, a little incredulous, and considerably surprised. What could this man with such a boulevardier exterior that he looked positively like an exile in a provincial town, and with his drawing-room manner—what could he know of negroes?

Mills, sitting silent with his air of watchful intelligence, seemed to read my thoughts, waved his pipe slightly and explained : "The Captain is from South Carolina."

"Oh," I murmured, and then after the slightest of pauses I heard the second of Mr. J. K. Blunt's declarations.

"Yes," he said. "*Je suis Américain, catholique et gentil-homme*," in a tone contrasting so strongly with the smile, which, as it were, underlined the uttered words, that I was at a loss whether to return the smile in kind or acknowledge the words with a grave little bow. Of course I did neither and there fell on us an odd, equivocal silence. It marked our final abandonment of the French language. I was the one to speak first, proposing that my companions should sup with me, not across the way, which would be riotous with more than one "infernal" supper, but in another much

more select establishment in a side street away from the
Cannebière.   It flattered my vanity a little to be able to
say that I had a corner table always reserved in the Salon
des Palmiers, otherwise Salon Blanc, where the atmosphere
was legitimist and extremely decorous besides—even in Carnival time.   "Nine-tenths of the people there," I said,
"would be of your political opinions, if that's an induce-
ment.   Come along.   Let's be festive," I encouraged them.

I didn't feel particularly festive.   What I wanted was to
remain in my company and break an inexplicable feeling of
constraint of which I was aware.   Mills looked at me steadily
with a faint, kind smile.

"No," said Blunt.   "Why should we go there?   They
will be only turning us out in the small hours, to go home
and face insomnia.   Can you imagine anything more disgusting?

He was smiling all the time, but his deep-set eyes did not
lend themselves to the expression of whimsical politeness
which he tried to achieve.   He had another suggestion to
offer.   Why shouldn't we adjourn to his rooms?   He had
there materials for a dish of his own invention for which he
was famous all along the line of the Royal Cavalry outposts,
and he would cook it for us.   There were also a few bottles
of some white wine, quite possible, which we could drink
out of Venetian cut-glass goblets.   A *bivouac* feast, in fact.
And he wouldn't turn us out in the small hours.   Not he.
He couldn't sleep.

Need I say I was fascinated by the idea?   Well, yes.
But somehow I hesitated and looked towards Mills, so much
my senior.   He got up without a word.   This was decisive:
for no obscure premonition, and of something indefinite at
that, could stand against the example of his tranquil personality.

## II

THE street in which Mr. Blunt lived presented itself to our
eyes, narrow, silent, empty, and dark, but with enough gas-
lamps in it to disclose its most striking feature : a quantity
of flag-poles sticking out above many of its closed portals.
It was the street of Consuls and I remarked to Mr. Blunt
that coming out in the morning he could survey the flags
of all nations almost—except his own. (The U.S. consulate
was on the other side of the town.) He mumbled through
his teeth that he took good care to keep clear of his own
consulate.

"Are you afraid of the consul's dog ? " I asked jocularly.
The consul's dog weighed about a pound and a half and was
known to the whole town as exhibited on the consular forearm in all places, at all hours, but mainly at the hour of the
fashionable promenade on the Prado.

But I felt my jest misplaced when Mills growled low in my
ear : "They are all Yankees there."

I murmured a confused "Of course."

Books are nothing. I discovered that I had never been
aware before that the Civil War in America was not printed
matter but a fact only about ten years old. Of course. He
was a South Carolinian gentleman. I was a little ashamed of
my want of tact. Meantime, looking like the conventional
conception of a fashionable reveller, with his opera-hat
pushed off his forehead, Captain Blunt was having some slight
difficulty with his latch-key ; for the house before which we
had stopped was not one of those many-storied houses that
made up the greater part of the street. It had only one row
of windows above the ground floor. Dead walls abutting on
to it indicated that it had a garden. Its dark front presented
no marked architectural character, and in the flickering light
of a street lamp it looked a little as though it had gone down
in the world. The greater then was my surprise to enter a
hall paved in black and white marble and in its dimness
appearing of palatial proportions. Mr. Blunt did not turn

up the small solitary gas-jet, but led the way across the black
and white pavement past the end of the staircase, past a door
of gleaming dark wood with a heavy bronze handle. It gave
access to his rooms he said ; but he took us straight on to the
studio at the end of the passage.

It was rather a small place tacked on in the manner of a
lean-to to the garden side of the house. A large lamp was
burning brightly there. The floor was of mere flagstones
but the few rugs scattered about though extremely worn were
very costly. There was also there a beautiful sofa upholstered in pink figured silk, an enormous divan with many
cushions, some splendid arm-chairs of various shapes (but all
very shabby), a round table, and in the midst of these fine
things a small common iron stove. Somebody must have
been attending it lately, for the fire roared and the warmth
of the place was very grateful after the bone-searching cold
blasts of mistral outside.

Mills without a word flung himself on the divan and,
propped on his arm, gazed thoughtfully at a distant corner
where in the shadow of a monumental carved wardrobe an
articulated dummy without head or hands but with beautifully shaped limbs composed in a shrinking attitude, seemed
to be embarrassed by his stare.

As we sat enjoying the *bivouac* hospitality (the dish was
really excellent and our host in a shabby grey jacket still
looked the accomplished man-about-town) my eyes kept on
straying towards that corner. Blunt noticed this and
remarked that I seemed to be attracted by the Empress.

" It's disagreeable," I said. " It seems to lurk there like
a shy skeleton at the feast. But why do you give the name
of Empress to that dummy ? "

" Because it sat for days and days in the robes of a Byzantine Empress to a painter. . . . I wonder where he discovered these priceless stuffs. . . . You knew him, I
believe ? "

Mills lowered his head slowly, then tossed down his throat
some wine out of a Venetian goblet.

" This house is full of costly objects. So are all his other houses, so is his place in Paris—that mysterious Pavilion hidden away in Passy somewhere."

Mills knew the Pavilion. The wine had, I suppose, loosened his tongue. Blunt, too, lost something of his reserve. From their talk I gathered the notion of an eccentric personality, a man of great wealth, not so much solitary as difficult of access, a collector of fine things, a painter known only to very few people and not at all to the public market. But as meantime I had been emptying my Venetian goblet with a certain regularity (the amount of heat given out by that iron stove was amazing; it parched one's throat, and the straw-coloured wine didn't seem much stronger than so much pleasantly flavoured water) the voices and the impressions they conveyed acquired something fantastic to my mind. Suddenly I perceived that Mills was sitting in his shirt-sleeves. I had not noticed him taking off his coat. Blunt had unbuttoned his shabby jacket, exposing a lot of starched shirt-front with the white tie under his dark shaved chin. He had a strange air of insolence—or so it seemed to me. I addressed him much louder than I intended really.

"Did you know that extraordinary man?"

"To know him personally one had to be either very distinguished or very lucky. Mr. Mills here . . ."

"Yes, I have been lucky," Mills struck in. "It was my cousin who was distinguished. That's how I managed to enter his house in Paris—it was called the Pavilion—twice."

"And saw Doña Rita twice, too?" asked Blunt with an indefinite smile and a marked emphasis. Mills was also emphatic in his reply but with a serious face.

"I am not an easy enthusiast where women are concerned, but she was without doubt the most admirable find of his amongst all the priceless items he had accumulated in that house—the most admirable . . ."

"Ah! But, you see, of all the objects there she was the only one that was alive," pointed out Blunt with the slightest possible flavour of sarcasm.

"Immensely so," affirmed Mills. "Not because she was

restless, indeed she hardly ever moved from that couch between the windows—you know."

"No. I don't know. I've never been in there," announced Blunt with that flash of white teeth so strangely without any character of its own that it was merely disturbing.

"But she radiated life," continued Mills. "She had plenty of it, and it had a quality. My cousin and Henry Allègre had a lot to say to each other and so I was free to talk to her. At the second visit we were like old friends, which was absurd considering that all the chances were that we would never meet again in this world or in the next. I am not meddling with theology but it seems to me that in the Elysian fields she'll have her place in a very special company."

All this in a sympathetic voice and in his unmoved manner. Blunt produced another disturbing white flash and muttered :

"I should say mixed." Then louder : "As for instance . . ."

"As for instance Cleopatra," answered Mills quietly. He added after a pause : "Who was not exactly pretty."

"I should have thought rather a La Vallière," Blunt dropped with an indifference of which one did not know what to make. He may have begun to be bored with the subject. But it may have been put on, for the whole personality was not clearly definable. I, however, was not indifferent. A woman is always an interesting subject and I was thoroughly awake to that interest. Mills pondered for a while with a sort of dispassionate benevolence, at last :

"Yes, Doña Rita as far as I know her is so varied in her simplicity that even that is possible," he said. "Yes. A romantic resigned La Vallière . . . who had a big mouth."

I felt moved to make myself heard.

"Did you know La Vallière, too ? " I asked impertinently. Mills only smiled at me. "No. I am not quite so old as that," he said. "But it's not very difficult to know facts of that kind about a historical personage. There were some

ribald verses made at the time, and Louis XIV was congratulated on the possession—I really don't remember how
it goes—on the possession of :

> " . . . de ce bec amoureux
> Qui d'unc oreille à l'autre va,
> Tra là là."

or something of the sort. It needn't be from ear to ear,
but it's a fact that a big mouth is often a sign of a certain
generosity of mind and feeling. Young man, beware of
women with small mouths. Beware of the others, too, of
course ; but a small mouth is a fatal sign. Well, the royalist
sympathizers can't charge Doña Rita with any lack of generosity from what I hear. Why should I judge her ? I have
known her for, say, six hours altogether. It was enough to
feel the seduction of her native intelligence and of her splendid
physique. And all that was brought home to me so quickly,"
he concluded, " because she had what some Frenchman has
called the ' terrible gift of familiarity.' "

Blunt had been listening moodily. He nodded assent.

" Yes ! " Mills' thoughts were still dwelling in the past.
" And when saying good-bye she could put in an instant an
immense distance between herself and you. A slight stiffening of that perfect figure, a change of the physiognomy : it
was like being dismissed by a person born in the purple.
Even if she did offer you her hand—as she did to me—it was
as if across a broad river. Trick of manner or a bit of truth
peeping out ? Perhaps she's really one of those inaccessible
beings. What do you think, Blunt ? "

It was a direct question which for some reason (as if my
range of sensitiveness had been increased already) displeased
or rather disturbed me strangely. Blunt seemed not to have
heard it. But after a while he turned to me.

" That thick man," he said in a tone of perfect urbanity,
" is as fine as a needle. All these statements about the
seduction and then this final doubt expressed after only two
visits which could not have included more than six hours
altogether and this some three years ago ! But it is Henry
Allègre that you should ask this question, Mr. Mills."

"I haven't the secret of raising the dead," answered Mills good-humouredly. "And if I had I would hesitate. It would seem such a liberty to take with a person one had known so slightly in life."

"And yet Henry Allègre is the only person to ask about her, after all this uninterrupted companionship of years, ever since he discovered her; all the time, every breathing moment of it, till, literally, his very last breath. I don't mean to say she nursed him. He had his confidential man for that. He couldn't bear women about his person. But then apparently he couldn't bear this one out of his sight. She's the only woman who ever sat to him, for he would never suffer a model inside his house. That's why the 'Girl in the Hat' and the 'Byzantine Empress' have that family air, though neither of them is really a likeness of Doña Rita. . . . You know my mother?"

Mills inclined his body slightly and a fugitive smile vanished from his lips. Blunt's eyes were fastened on the very centre of his empty plate.

"Then perhaps you know my mother's artistic and literary associations," Blunt went on in a subtly changed tone. "My mother has been writing verse since she was a girl of fifteen. She's still writing verse. She's still fifteen— a spoiled girl of genius. So she requested one of her poet friends—no less than Versoy himself—to arrange for a visit to Henry Allègre's house. At first he thought he hadn't heard aright. You must know that for my mother a man that doesn't jump out of his skin for any woman's caprice is not chivalrous. But perhaps you do know? . . ."

Mills shook his head with an amused air. Blunt, who had raised his eyes from his plate to look at him, started afresh with great deliberation.

"She gives no peace to herself or her friends. My mother's exquisitely absurd. You understand that all these painters, poets, art collectors (and dealers in bric-à-brac, he interjected through his teeth) of my mother are not in my way; but Versoy lives more like a man of the world. One day I met him at the fencing school. He was furious. He asked me to tell my mother that this was the last effort of his chivalry. The jobs she gave him to do were too difficult. But I daresay he had been pleased enough to show the influence he had in that quarter. He knew my mother would tell the world's wife all about it. He's a spiteful, gingery little wretch. The top of his head shines like a billiard ball. I believe he polishes it every morning with a cloth. Of course they didn't get further than the big drawing-room on the first floor, an enormous drawing-room with three pairs of columns in the middle. The double doors on the top of the staircase had been thrown wide open, as if for a visit from royalty. You can picture to yourself my mother, with her white hair done in some 18th century fashion and her sparkling black eyes, penetrating into those splendours attended by a sort of bald-headed, vexed squirrel—and Henry Allègre coming forward to meet them like a severe prince with the face of a tombstone Crusader, big white hands, muffled silken voice, half-shut eyes, as if looking down at them from a balcony. You remember that trick of his, Mills ? "

Mills emitted an enormous cloud of smoke out of his distended cheeks.

" I daresay he was furious, too," Blunt continued dispassionately. " But he was extremely civil. He showed her all the ' treasures ' in the room, ivories, enamels, miniatures, all sorts of monstrosities from Japan, from India, from Timbuctoo . . . for all I know. . . . He pushed his condescension so far as to have the ' Girl in the Hat ' brought down into the drawing-room—half length, unframed. They put her on a chair for my mother to look at. The ' Byzantine Empress ' was already there, hung on the end wall—full length, gold frame weighing half a ton. My mother first overwhelms the ' Master ' with thanks, and then absorbs herself in the adoration of the ' Girl in the Hat.' Then she sighs out : ' It should be called Diaphanéité, if there is such a word. Ah ! This is the last expression of modernity ! ' She puts up suddenly her face-à-main and looks towards the end wall. ' And that—Byzantium itself ! Who was she, this sullen and beautiful Empress ? '

" ' The one I had in my mind was Theodosia ! ' Allègre consented to answer. ' Originally a slave girl—from somewhere.'

" My mother can be marvellously indiscreet when the whim takes her. She finds nothing better to do than to ask the ' Master ' why he took his inspiration for those two faces from the same model. No doubt she was proud of her discerning eye. It was really clever of her. Allègre, however, looked on it as a colossal impertinence ; but he answered in his silkiest tones :

" ' Perhaps it is because I saw in that woman something of the women of all time.'

" My mother might have guessed that she was on thin ice there. She is extremely intelligent. Moreover, she ought to have known. But women can be miraculously dense sometimes. So she exclaims, ' Then she is a wonder ! ' And with some notion of being complimentary goes on to say that only the eyes of the discoverer of so many wonders of art could have discovered something so marvellous in life. I suppose Allègre lost his temper altogether then ; or perhaps he only wanted to pay my mother out, for all these ' Masters ' she had been throwing at his head for the last two hours. He insinuates with the utmost politeness :

" ' As you are honouring my poor collection with a visit you may like to judge for yourself as to the inspiration of these two pictures. She is upstairs changing her dress after our morning ride. But she wouldn't be very long. She might be a little surprised at first to be called down like this, but with a few words of preparation and purely as a matter of art . . .'

" There were never two people more taken aback. Versoy himself confesses that he dropped his tall hat with a crash. I am a dutiful son, I hope, but I must say I should have liked to have seen the retreat down the great staircase. Ha ! Ha ! Ha ! "

He laughed most undutifully and then his face twitched grimly.

" That implacable brute Allègre followed them down cere-

moniously and put my mother into the fiacre at the door with
the greatest deference. He didn't open his lips though, and
made a great bow as the fiacre drove away. My mother
didn't recover from her consternation for three days. I
lunch with her almost daily and I couldn't imagine what was
the matter. Then one day . . ."

He glanced round the table, jumped up and with a word
of excuse left the studio by a small door in a corner. This
startled me into the consciousness that I had been as if I had
not existed for these two men. With his elbows propped
on the table Mills had his hands in front of his face clasping
the pipe from which he extracted now and then a puff of
smoke, staring stolidly across the room.

I was moved to ask in a whisper :

" Do you know him well ? "

" I don't know what he is driving at," he answered drily.
" But as to his mother she is not as volatile as all that. I
suspect it was business. It may have been a deep plot to
get a picture out of Allègre for somebody. My cousin as
likely as not. Or simply to discover what he had. The
Blunts lost all their property and in Paris there are various
ways of making a little money, without actually breaking
anything. Not even the law. And Mrs. Blunt really had
a position once—in the days of the Second Empire—and
so . . ."

I listened open-mouthed to these things into which my
West-Indian experiences could not have given me an insight.
But Mills checked himself and ended in a changed tone.

" It's not easy to know what she would be at, either, in
any given instance. For the rest, spotlessly honourable. A
delightful, aristocratic old lady. Only poor."

A bump at the door silenced him and immediately Mr.
John Blunt, Captain of Cavalry in the Army of Legitimity,
first-rate cook (as to one dish at least), and generous host,
entered clutching the necks of four more bottles between the
fingers of his hand.

" I stumbled and nearly smashed the lot," he remarked
casually. But even I, with all my innocence, never for a

moment believed he had stumbled accidentally. During the uncorking and the filling up of glasses a profound silence reigned; but neither of us took it seriously—any more than his stumble.

"One day," he went on again in that curiously flavoured voice of his, "my mother took a heroic decision and made up her mind to get up in the middle of the night. You must understand my mother's phraseology. It meant that she would be up and dressed by nine o'clock. This time it was not Versoy that was commanded for attendance, but I. You may imagine how delighted I was. . . ."

It was very plain to me that Blunt was addressing himself exclusively to Mills : Mills the mind, even more than Mills the man. It was as if Mills represented something initiated and to be reckoned with. I, of course, could have no such pretensions. If I represented anything it was a perfect freshness of sensations and a refreshing ignorance, not so much of what life may give one (as to that I had some ideas at least) but of what it really contains. I knew very well that I was utterly insignificant in these men's eyes. Yet my attention was not checked by that knowledge. It's true they were talking of a woman, but I was yet at the age when this subject by itself is not of overwhelming interest. My imagination would have been more stimulated probably by the adventures and fortunes of a man. What kept my interest from flagging was Mr. Blunt himself. The play of the white gleams of his smile round the suspicion of grimness of his tone fascinated me like a moral incongruity.

So at the age when one sleeps well indeed but does feel sometimes as if the need of sleep were a mere weakness of a distant old age, I kept easily awake; and in my freshness I was kept amused by the contrast of personalities, of the disclosed facts and moral outlook with the rough initiations of my West-Indian experience. And all these things were dominated by a feminine figure which to my imagination had only a floating outline, now invested with the grace of girlhood, now with the prestige of a woman; and indistinct in both these characters. For these two men had *seen* her,

while to me she was only being "presented," elusively, in
vanishing words, in the shifting tones of an unfamiliar voice.

She was being presented to me now in the Bois de Boulogne
at the early hour of the ultra-fashionable world (so I understood), on a light bay "bit of blood" attended on the off
side by that Henry Allègre mounted on a dark brown powerful weight carrier; and on the other by one of Allègre's
acquaintances (the man had no real friends), distinguished
frequenters of that mysterious Pavilion. And so that side
of the frame in which that woman appeared to one down the
perspective of the great Allée was not permanent. That
morning when Mr. Blunt had to escort his mother there for
the gratification of her irresistible curiosity (of which he
highly disapproved) there appeared in succession, at that
woman's or girl's bridle-hand, a cavalry general in red
breeches, on whom she was smiling; a rising politician in a
grey suit, who talked to her with great animation but left
her side abruptly to join a personage in a red fez and mounted
on a white horse; and then, some time afterwards, the vexed
Mr. Blunt and his indiscreet mother (though I really couldn't
see where the harm was) had one more chance of a good
stare. The third party that time was the Royal Pretender
(Allègre had been painting his portrait lately), whose hearty,
sonorous laugh was heard long before the mounted trio came
riding very slowly abreast of the Blunts. There was colour
in the girl's face. She was not laughing. Her expression
was serious and her eyes thoughtfully downcast. Blunt
admitted that on that occasion the charm, brilliance, and
force of her personality was adequately framed between
those magnificently mounted, paladin-like attendants, one
older than the other but the two composing together admirably in the different stages of their manhood. Mr. Blunt
had never before seen Henry Allègre so close. Allègre was
riding nearest to the path on which Blunt was dutifully
giving his arm to his mother (they had got out of their fiacre)
and wondering if that confounded fellow would have the
impudence to take off his hat. But he did not. Perhaps he
didn't notice. Allègre was not a man of wandering glances.

There were silver hairs in his beard but he looked as solid as a statue. Less than three months afterwards he was gone.

"What was it?" asked Mills, who had not changed his pose for a very long time.

"Oh, an accident. But he lingered. They were on their way to Corsica. A yearly pilgrimage. Sentimental perhaps. It was to Corsica that he carried her off—I mean first of all."

There was the slightest contraction of Mr. Blunt's facial muscles. Very slight; but I, staring at the narrator after the manner of all simple souls, noticed it; the twitch of a pain which surely must have been mental. There was also a suggestion of effort before he went on: "I suppose you know how he got hold of her?" in a tone of ease which was astonishingly ill-assumed for such a worldly, self-controlled, drawing-room person.

Mills changed his attitude to look at him fixedly for a moment. Then he leaned back in his chair and with interest —I don't mean curiosity, I mean interest: "Does anybody know besides the two parties concerned?" he asked, with something as it were renewed (or was it refreshed?) in his unmoved quietness. "I ask because one has never heard any tales. I remember one evening in a restaurant seeing a man come in with a lady—a beautiful lady—very particularly beautiful, as though she had been stolen out of Mahomet's paradise. With Doña Rita it can't be anything as definite as that. But speaking of her in the same strain, I've always felt that she looked as though Allègre had caught her in the precincts of some temple . . . in the mountains."

I was delighted. I had never heard before a woman spoken about in that way, a real live woman that is, not a woman in a book. For this was no poetry and yet it seemed to put her in the category of visions. And I would have lost myself in it if Mr. Blunt had not, most unexpectedly, addressed himself to me.

"I told you that man was as fine as a needle." . . . And then to Mills: "Out of a temple? We know what that

R

means." His dark eyes flashed : " And must it be really in
the mountains ? " he added.

" Or in a desert," conceded Mills, " if you prefer that.
There have been temples in deserts, you know."

Blunt had calmed down suddenly and assumed a nonchalant pose.

" As a matter of fact, Henry Allègre caught her very early
one morning in his own old garden full of thrushes and other
small birds. She was sitting on a stone, a fragment of some
old balustrade, with her feet in the damp grass, and reading
a tattered book of some kind. She had on a short, black,
two-penny frock (*une petite robe de deux sous*) and there was
a hole in one of her stockings. She raised her eyes and saw
him looking down at her thoughtfully over that ambrosian
beard of his, like Jove at a mortal. They exchanged a good
long stare, for at first she was too startled to move ; and then
he murmured, " *Restez donc.*" She lowered her eyes again
on her book and after a while heard him walk away on the
path. Her heart thumped while she listened to the little
birds filling the air with their noise. She was not frightened.
I am telling you this positively because she has told me the
tale herself. What better authority can you have . . . ? "
Blunt paused.

" That's true. She's not the sort of person to lie about
her own sensations," murmured Mills above his clasped hands.

" Nothing can escape his penetration," Blunt remarked to
me with that equivocal urbanity which made me always feel
uncomfortable on Mills' account. " Positively nothing."
He turned to Mills again. " After some minutes of immobility—she told me—she arose from her stone and walked
slowly on the track of that apparition. Allègre was nowhere
to be seen by that time. Under the gateway of the extremely
ugly tenement house, which hides the Pavilion and the
garden from the street, the wife of the porter was waiting
with her arms akimbo. At once she cried out to Rita :
' You were caught by our gentleman.'

" As a matter of fact, that old woman, being a friend of
Rita's aunt, allowed the girl to come into the garden when-

ever Allègre was away.  But Allègre's goings and comings
were sudden and unannounced; and that morning, Rita,
crossing the narrow, thronged street, had slipped in through
the gateway in ignorance of Allègre's return and unseen by
the porter's wife.

"The child, she was but little more than that then,
expressed her regret of having perhaps got the kind porter's
wife into trouble.

"The old woman said with a peculiar smile : 'Your face
is not of the sort that gets other people into trouble.  My
gentleman wasn't angry.  He says you may come in any
morning you like.'

"Rita, without saying anything to this, crossed the street
back again to the warehouse full of oranges where she spent
most of her waking hours.  Her dreaming, empty, idle,
thoughtless, unperturbed hours, she calls them.  She crossed
the street with a hole in her stocking.  She had a hole in her
stocking not because her uncle and aunt were poor (they had
around them never less than eight thousand oranges, mostly
in cases) but because she was then careless and untidy and
totally unconscious of her personal appearance.  She told me
herself that she was not even conscious then of her personal
existence.  She was a mere adjunct in the twilight life of her
aunt, a Frenchwoman, and her uncle, the orange merchant,
a Basque peasant, to whom her other uncle, the great man
of the family, the priest of some parish in the hills near
Tolosa, had sent her up at the age of thirteen or thereabouts
for safe keeping.  She is of peasant stock, you know.  This is
the true origin of the 'Girl in the Hat' and of the 'Byzantine
Empress' which excited my dear mother so much; of the
mysterious girl that the privileged personalities great in art,
in letters, in politics, or simply in the world, could see on
the big sofa during the gatherings in Allègre's exclusive
Pavilion : the Doña Rita of their respectful addresses, manifest and mysterious, like an object of art from some unknown
period; the Doña Rita of the initiated Paris.  Doña Rita
and nothing more—unique and indefinable."  He stopped
with a disagreeable smile.

"And of peasant stock?" I exclaimed in the strangely conscious silence that fell between Mills and Blunt.

"Oh! All these Basques have been ennobled by Don Sanche II," said Captain Blunt moodily. "You see coats of arms carved over the doorways of the most miserable *caserios*. As far as that goes she's Doña Rita right enough whatever else she is or is not in herself or in the eyes of others. In your eyes, for instance, Mills. Eh?"

For a time Mills preserved that conscious silence.

"Why think about it at all?" he murmured coldly at last.

"A strange bird is hatched sometimes in a nest in an un-accountable way and then the fate of such a bird is bound to be ill-defined, uncertain, questionable. And so that is how Henry Allègre saw her first? And what happened next?"

"What happened next?" repeated Mr. Blunt, with an affected surprise in his tone. "Is it necessary to ask that question? If you had asked *how* the next happened. . . . But as you may imagine she hasn't told me anything about that. She didn't," he continued with polite sarcasm, "enlarge upon the facts. That confounded Allègre, with his impudent assumption of princely airs, must have (I shouldn't wonder) made the fact of his notice appear as a sort of favour dropped from Olympus. I really can't tell how the minds and the imaginations of such aunts and uncles are affected by such rare visitations. Mythology may give us a hint. There is the story of Danae, for instance."

"There is," remarked Mills calmly, "but I don't remember any aunt or uncle in that connection."

"And there are also certain stories of the discovery and acquisition of some unique objects of art. The sly approaches, the astute negotiations, the lying and the circumventing . . . for the love of beauty, you know."

With his dark face and with the perpetual smiles playing about his grimness, Mr. Blunt appeared to me positively satanic. Mills' hand was toying absently with an empty glass. Again they had forgotten my existence altogether.

"I don't know how an object of art would feel," went on Blunt, in an unexpectedly grating voice, which, however, recovered its tone immediately. "I don't know. But I do know that Rita herself was not a Danae, never, not at any time of her life. She didn't mind the holes in her stockings. She wouldn't mind holes in her stockings now. . . . That is if she manages to keep any stockings at all," he added, with a sort of suppressed fury so funnily unexpected that I would have burst into a laugh if I hadn't been lost in astonishment of the simplest kind.

"No—really !" There was a flash of interest from the quiet Mills.

"Yes, really," Blunt nodded and knitted his brows very devilishly indeed. "She may yet be left without a single pair of stockings."

"The world's a thief," declared Mills, with the utmost composure. "It wouldn't mind robbing a lonely traveller."

"He is so subtle." Blunt remembered my existence for the purpose of that remark and as usual it made me very uncomfortable. "Perfectly true. A lonely traveller. They are all in the scramble from the lowest to the highest. Heavens ! What a gang ! There was even an Archbishop in it."

"*Vous plaisantez*," said Mills, but without any marked show of incredulity.

"I joke very seldom," Blunt protested earnestly. "That's why I haven't mentioned His Majesty—whom God preserve. That would have been an exaggeration. . . . However, the end is not yet. We were talking about the beginning. I have heard that some dealers in fine objects, quite mercenary people of course (my mother has an experience in that world), show sometimes an astonishing reluctance to part with some specimens, even at a good price. It must be very funny. It's just possible that the uncle and the aunt have been rolling in tears on the floor, amongst their oranges, or beating their heads against the walls from rage and despair. But I doubt it. And in any case Allègre is not the sort of person that gets into any vulgar trouble. And it's just possible that those people stood open-mouthed at all that magnificence. They weren't poor, you know; therefore it wasn't incumbent on them to be honest. They are still there in the old respectable warehouse, I understand. They have kept their position in their *quartier*, I believe. But they didn't keep their niece. It might have been an act of sacrifice! For I seem to remember hearing that after attending for a while some school round the corner the child had been set to keep the books of that orange business. However it might have been, the first fact in Rita's and Allègre's common history is a journey to Italy, and then to Corsica. You know Allègre had a house in Corsica somewhere. She has it now as she has everything he ever had; and that Corsican palace is the portion that will stick the longest to Doña Rita, I imagine. Who would want to buy a place like that? I suppose nobody would take it for a gift. The fellow was having houses built all over the place. This very house where we are sitting belonged to him. Doña Rita has given it to her sister, I understand. Or at any rate the sister runs it. She is my landlady . . ."

"Her sister here!" I exclaimed. "Her sister!"

Blunt turned to me politely, but only for a long mute gaze. His eyes were in deep shadow and it struck me for the first time then that there was something fatal in that man's aspect as soon as he fell silent. I think the effect was purely physical, but in consequence whatever he said seemed inadequate, and as if produced by a commonplace, if uneasy, soul.

"Doña Rita brought her down from her mountains on purpose. She is asleep somewhere, in this house, in one of the vacant rooms. She lets them, you know, at extortionate prices, that is, if people will pay them, for she is easily intimidated. You see, she has never seen such an enormous town before in her life, nor yet so many strange people. She has been keeping house for the uncle-priest in some mountain gorge for years and years. It's extraordinary he should have let her go. There is something mysterious there, some reason or other. It's either theology or Family. The saintly uncle in his wild parish would know nothing of any other reasons. She wears a rosary at her waist. Directly

she had seen some real money she developed a love of it. If
you stay with me long enough, and I hope you will (I really
can't sleep), you will see her going out to mass at half-past
six; but there is nothing remarkable in her; just a peasant
woman of thirty-four or so. A rustic nun. . . ."

I may as well say at once that we didn't stay as long as
that. It was not that morning that I saw for the first time
Therese of the whispering lips and downcast eyes slipping
out to an early mass from the house of iniquity into the early
winter murk of the city of perdition, in a world steeped in
sin. No. It was not on that morning that I saw Doña
Rita's incredible sister with her brown, dry face, her gliding
motion, and her really nun-like dress, with a black handkerchief enfolding her head tightly, with the two pointed ends
hanging down her back. Yes, nun-like enough. And yet
not altogether. People would have turned round after her
if those dartings out to the half-past six mass hadn't been the
only occasion on which she ventured into the impious streets.
She was frightened of the streets, but in a particular way,
not as if of a danger but as if of a contamination. Yet she
didn't fly back to her mountains because at bottom she had
an indomitable character, a peasant tenacity of purpose,
predatory instincts. . . .

No, we didn't remain long enough with Mr. Blunt to see
even as much as her back glide out of the house on her
prayerful errand. She was prayerful. She was terrible.
Her one-idead peasant mind was as inaccessible as a closed
iron safe. She was fatal. . . . It's perfectly ridiculous to
confess that they all seem fatal to me now; but writing to
you like this in all sincerity I don't mind appearing ridiculous.
I suppose fatality must be expressed, embodied, like other
forces of this earth; and if so why not in such people as well
as in other more glorious or more frightful figures?

We remained, however, long enough to let Mr. Blunt's
half-hidden acrimony develop itself or prey on itself in
further talk about the man Allègre and the girl Rita. Mr.
Blunt, still addressing Mills with that story, passed on to
what he called the second act, the disclosure, with, what he

called, the characteristic Allègre impudence—which surpassed the impudence of kings, millionaires, or tramps, by
many degrees—the revelation of Rita's existence to the
world at large.   It wasn't a very large world, but then it was
most choicely composed.   How is one to describe it shortly ?
In a sentence it was the world that rides in the morning in
the Bois.

In something less than a year and a half from the time he
found her sitting on a broken fragment of stone-work buried
in the grass of his wild garden, full of thrushes, starlings, and
other innocent creatures of the air, he had given her amongst
other accomplishments the art of sitting admirably on a
horse, and directly they returned to Paris he took her out
with him for their first morning ride.

"I leave you to judge of the sensation," continued Mr.
Blunt, with a faint grimace, as though the words had an
acrid taste in his mouth.   "And the consternation," he
added venomously.   "Many of those men on that great
morning had some one of their womenkind with them.   But
their hats had to go off all the same, especially the hats of
the fellows who were under some sort of obligation to
Allègre.   You would be astonished to hear the names of
people, of real personalities in the world, who, not to mince
matters, owed money to Allègre.   And I don't mean in the
world of art only.   In the first rout of the surprise some
story of an adopted daughter was set abroad hastily, I believe.
You know ' adopted ' with a peculiar accent on the word—
and it was plausible enough.   I have been told that at that
time she looked extremely youthful by his side, I mean
extremely youthful in expression, in the eyes, in the smile.
She must have been . . ."

Blunt pulled himself up short, but not so short as not to
let the confused murmur of the word " adorable " reach our
attentive ears.

The heavy Mills made a slight movement in his chair.
The effect on me was more inward, a strange emotion which
left me perfectly still ; and for the moment of silence Blunt
looked more fatal than ever.

"I understand it didn't last very long," he addressed us politely again. "And no wonder! The sort of talk she would have heard during that first springtime in Paris would have put an impress on a much less receptive personality; for of course Allègre didn't close his doors to his friends and this new apparition was not of the sort to make them keep away. After that first morning she always had somebody to ride at her bridle hand. Old Doyen, the sculptor, was the first to approach them. At that age a man may venture on anything. He rides a strange animal like a circus horse. Rita had spotted him out of the corner of her eye as he passed them, putting up his enormous paw in a still more enormous glove, airily, you know, like this" (Blunt waved his hand above his head), "to Allègre. He passes on. All at once he wheels his fantastic animal round and comes trotting after them. With the merest casual 'Bonjour, Allègre' he ranges close to her on the other side and addresses her, hat in hand, in that booming voice of his like a deferential roar of the sea very far away. His articulation is not good and the first words she really made out were 'I am an old sculptor. . . . Of course there is that habit. . . . But I can see you through all that. . . .'

"He put his hat on very much on one side. 'I am a great sculptor of women,' he declared. 'I gave up my life to them, poor unfortunate creatures, the most beautiful, the wealthiest, the most loved. . . . Two generations of them. . . . Just look at me full in the eyes, *mon enfant.*'

"They stared at each other. Doña Rita confessed to me that the old fellow made her heart beat with such force that she couldn't manage to smile at him. And she saw his eyes run full of tears. He wiped them simply with the back of his hand and went on booming faintly. 'Thought so. You are enough to make one cry. I thought my artist's life was finished, and here you come along from devil knows where with this young friend of mine, who isn't a bad smearer of canvases—but it's marble and bronze that you want. . . . I shall finish my artist's life with your face; but I shall want a bit of those shoulders, too. . . . You hear, Allègre, I must

R 2

have a bit of her shoulders, too.    I can see through the cloth
that they are divine.    If they aren't divine I will eat my hat.
Yes, I will do your head and then—*nunc dimittis.*'

" These were the first words with which the world greeted
her, or should I say civilization did ; already both her native
mountains and the cavern of oranges belonged to a pre-
historic age.    ' Why don't you ask him to come this afternoon ? '    Allègre's voice suggested gently.    ' He knows the
way to the house.'

" The old man said with extraordinary fervour, ' Oh, yes
I will,' pulled up his horse and they went on.    She told me
that she could feel her heart-beats for a long time.    The
remote power of that voice, those old eyes full of tears, that
noble and ruined face, had affected her extraordinarily she
said.    But perhaps what affected her was the shadow, the
still living shadow of a great passion in the man's heart.

" Allègre remarked to her calmly :  ' He has been a little
mad all his life.' "

### III

Mills lowered the hands holding the extinct and even cold
pipe before his big face.

" H'm, shoot an arrow into that old man's heart like this ?
But was there anything done ? "

" A terra-cotta bust, I believe.    Good ?  I don't know.
I rather think it's in this house.    A lot of things have been
sent down from Paris here, when she gave up the Pavilion.
When she goes up now she stays in hotels, you know.    I
imagine it is locked up in one of these things," went on
Blunt, pointing towards the end of the studio where amongst
the monumental presses of dark oak lurked the shy dummy
which had worn the stiff robes of the Byzantine Empress and
the amazing hat of the " Girl," rakishly.    I wondered
whether that dummy had travelled from Paris, too, and
whether with or without its head.    Perhaps that head had

been left behind, having rolled into a corner of some empty room in the dismantled Pavilion. I represented it to myself very lonely, without features, like a turnip, with a mere peg sticking out where the neck should have been. . . . And Mr. Blunt was talking on.

"There are treasures behind these locked doors, brocades, old jewels, unframed pictures, bronzes, chinoiseries, Japoneries." . . .

He growled as much as a man of his accomplished manner and voice could growl. " I don't suppose she gave away all that to her sister, but I shouldn't be surprised if that timid rustic didn't lay a claim to the lot for the love of God and the good of the Church. . . . And held on with her teeth, too," he added graphically.

Mills' face remained grave. Very grave. I was amused at those little venomous outbreaks of the fatal Mr. Blunt. Again I knew myself utterly forgotten. But I didn't feel dull and I didn't even feel sleepy. That last strikes me as strange at this distance of time, in regard of my tender years and of the depressing hour which precedes the dawn. We had been drinking that straw-coloured wine, too, I won't say like water (nobody would have drunk water like that) but, well . . . and the haze of tobacco smoke was like the blue mist of great distances seen in dreams.

Yes, that old sculptor was the first who joined them in the sight of all Paris. It was that old glory that opened the series of companions of those morning rides ; a series which extended through three successive Parisian spring-times and comprised a famous physiologist, a fellow who seemed to hint that mankind could be made immortal or at least everlastingly old ; a fashionable philosopher and psychologist who used to lecture to enormous audiences of women with his tongue in his cheek (but never permitted himself anything of the kind when talking to Rita) ; that surly dandy Cabanel (but he only once, from mere vanity), and everybody else at all distinguished including also a celebrated person who turned out later to be a swindler. But he was really a genius. . . . All this according to Mr. Blunt, who

gave us all those details with a sort of languid zest covering a
secret irritation.

"Apart from that, you know," went on Mr. Blunt, "all
she knew of the world of men and women (I mean till
Allègre's death) was what she had seen of it from the saddle
two hours every morning during four months of the year or
so. Absolutely all, with Allègre self-denyingly on her right
hand, with that impenetrable air of guardianship. Don't
touch ! He didn't like his treasures to be touched unless he
actually put some unique object into your hands with a sort
of triumphant murmur, 'Look close at that.' Of course I
only have heard all this. I am much too small a person, you
understand, to even . . ."

He flashed his white teeth at us most agreeably, but the
upper part of his face, the shadowed setting of his eyes, and
the slight drawing in of his eyebrows gave a fatal suggestion.
I thought suddenly of the definition he applied to himself :
" Américain, catholique et gentilhomme " completed by that
startling " I live by my sword " uttered in a light drawing-
room tone tinged by a flavour of mockery lighter even than air.

He insisted to us that the first and only time he had seen
Allègre a little close was that morning in the Bois with his
mother. His Majesty (whom God preserve), then not even
an active Pretender, flanked the girl, still a girl, on the other
side, the usual companion for a month past or so. Allègre
had suddenly taken it into his head to paint his portrait. A
sort of intimacy had sprung up. Mrs. Blunt's remark was
that of the two striking horsemen Allègre looked the more
kingly.

"The son of a confounded millionaire soap-boiler," commented Mr. Blunt through his clenched teeth. "A man
absolutely without parentage. Without a single relation in
the world. Just a freak."

"That explains why he could leave all his fortune to her,"
said Mills.

"The will, I believe," said Mr. Blunt moodily, "was
written on a half sheet of paper, with his device of an Assyrian
bull at the head. What the devil did he mean by it ?

Anyway it was the last time that she surveyed the world of men and women from the saddle. Less than three months later . . ."

" Allègre died and . . ." murmured Mills in an interested manner.

" And she had to dismount," broke in Mr. Blunt grimly. " Dismount right into the middle of it. Down to the very ground, you understand. I suppose you can guess what that would mean. She didn't know what to do with herself. She had never been on the ground. She . . ."

" Aha ! " said Mills.

" Even eh ! eh ! if you like," retorted Mr. Blunt, in an unrefined tone, that made me open my eyes, which were well opened before, still wider.

He turned to me with that horrible trick of his of commenting upon Mills as though that quiet man whom I admired, whom I trusted, and for whom I had already something resembling affection had been as much of a dummy as that other one lurking in the shadows, pitiful and headless in its attitude of alarmed chastity.

" Nothing escapes his penetration. He can perceive a haystack at an enormous distance when he is interested."

I thought this was going rather too far, even to the borders of vulgarity ; but Mills remained untroubled and only reached for his tobacco pouch.

" But that's nothing to my mother's interest. She can never see a haystack, therefore she is always so surprised and excited. Of course Doña Rita was not a woman about whom the newspapers insert little paragraphs. But Allègre was the sort of man. A lot came out in print about him and a lot was talked in the world about her ; and at once my dear mother perceived a haystack and naturally became unreasonably absorbed in it. I thought her interest would wear out. But it didn't. She had received a shock and had received an impression by means of that girl. My mother has never been treated with impertinence before, and the æsthetic impression must have been of extraordinary strength. I must suppose that it amounted to a sort of moral revolution,

I can't account for her proceedings in any other way. When
Rita turned up in Paris a year and a half after Allègre's death
some shabby journalist (smart creature) hit upon the notion
of alluding to her as the heiress of Mr. Allègre. ' The
heiress of Mr. Allègre has taken up her residence again
amongst the treasures of art in that Pavilion so well known
to the élite of the artistic, scientific, and political world, not
to speak of the members of aristocratic and even royal
families. . . .' You know the sort of thing. It appeared
first in the *Figaro*, I believe. And then at the end a little
phrase : ' She is alone.' She was in a fair way of becoming
a celebrity of a sort. Daily little allusions and that sort of
thing. Heaven only knows who stopped it. There was a
rush of ' old friends ' into that garden, enough to scare all
the little birds away. I suppose one or several of them,
having influence with the press, did it. But the gossip didn't
stop, and the name stuck, too, since it conveyed a very certain
and very significant sort of fact, and of course the Venetian
episode was talked about in the houses frequented by my
mother. It was talked about from a royalist point of view
with a kind of respect. It was even said that the inspiration
and the resolution of the war going on now over the Pyrenees
had come out from that head. . . . Some of them talked as
if she were the guardian angel of Legitimacy. You know
what royalist gush is like."

Mr. Blunt's face expressed sarcastic disgust. Mills moved
his head the least little bit. Apparently he knew.

" Well, speaking with all possible respect, it seems to have
affected my mother's brain. I was already with the royal
army and of course there could be no question of regular
postal communications with France. My mother hears or
overhears somewhere that the heiress of Mr. Allègre is contemplating a secret journey. All the noble Salons were full
of chatter about that secret naturally. So she sits down and
pens an autograph : ' Madame, Informed that you are proceeding to the place on which the hopes of all the right
thinking people are fixed, I trust to your womanly sympathy
with a mother's anxious feelings, etc., etc.,' and ending with

a request to take messages to me and bring news of me. . . . The coolness of my mother!"

Most unexpectedly Mills was heard murmuring a question which seemed to me very odd.

"I wonder how your mother addressed that note?"

A moment of silence ensued.

"Hardly in the newspaper style, I should think," retorted Mr. Blunt, with one of his grins that made me doubt the stability of his feelings and the consistency of his outlook in regard to his whole tale. "My mother's maid took it in a fiacre very late one evening to the Pavilion and brought an answer scrawled on a scrap of paper: 'Write your messages at once' and signed with a big capital R. So my mother sat down again to her charming writing desk and the maid made another journey in a fiacre just before midnight; and ten days later or so I got a letter thrust into my hand at the *avanzadas* just as I was about to start on a night patrol, together with a note asking me to call on the writer so that she might allay my mother's anxieties by telling her how I looked.

"It was signed R only, but I guessed at once and nearly fell off my horse with surprise."

"You mean to say that Doña Rita was actually at the Royal Headquarters lately?" exclaimed Mills, with evident surprise. "Why, we—everybody—thought that all this affair was over and done with."

"Absolutely. Nothing in the world could be more done with than that episode. Of course the rooms in the hotel at Tolosa were retained for her by an order from Royal Headquarters. Two garret-rooms, the place was so full of all sorts of court people; but I can assure you that for the three days she was there she never put her head outside the door. General Mongroviejo called on her officially from the King. A general, not anybody of the household, you see. That's a distinct shade of the present relation. He stayed just five minutes. Some personage from the Foreign department at Headquarters was closeted for about a couple of hours. That was of course business. Then two officers from the staff came together with some explanations or instructions to her. Then Baron H., a fellow with a pretty wife, who had made so many sacrifices for the cause, raised a great to-do about seeing her and she consented to receive him for a moment. They say he was very much frightened by her arrival, but after the interview went away all smiles. Who else? Yes, the Archbishop came. Half an hour. This is more than is necessary to give a blessing, and I can't conceive what else he had to give her. But I am sure he got something out of her. Two peasants from the upper valley were sent for by military authorities and she saw them, too. That friar who hangs about the court has been in and out several times. Well, and lastly, I myself. I got leave from the outposts. That was the first time I talked to her. I would have gone that evening back to the regiment, but the friar met me in the corridor and informed me that I would be ordered to escort that most loyal and noble lady back to the French frontier as a personal mission of the biggest honour. I was inclined to laugh at him. He himself is a cheery and jovial person and he laughed with me quite readily—but I got the order before dark all right. It was rather a job, as the Alphonsists were attacking the right flank of our whole front and there was some considerable disorder there. I mounted her on a mule and her maid on another. We spent one night in a ruined old tower occupied by some of our infantry and got away at daybreak under the Alphonsist shells. The maid nearly died of fright and one of the troopers with us was wounded. To smuggle her back across the frontier was another job but it wasn't my job. It wouldn't have done for her to appear in sight of French frontier posts in the company of Carlist uniforms. She seems to have a fearless streak in her nature. At one time as we were climbing a slope absolutely exposed to artillery fire I asked her on purpose, being provoked by the way she looked about at the scenery, 'A little emotion, eh?' And she answered me in a low voice: 'Oh, yes! I am moved. I used to run about these hills when I was little.' And note, just then the trooper close behind us had been wounded by a shell fragment. He was swearing awfully and fighting with his horse. The shells were falling around us about two to the minute.

"Luckily the Alphonsist shells are not much better than our own. But women are funny. I was afraid the maid would jump down and clear out amongst the rocks, in which case we should have had to dismount and catch her. But she didn't do that; she sat perfectly still on her mule and shrieked. Just simply shrieked. Ultimately we came to a curiously shaped rock at the end of a short wooded valley. It was very still there and the sunshine was brilliant. I said to Doña Rita : 'We will have to part in a few minutes. I understand that my mission ends at this rock.' And she said : 'I know this rock well. This is my country.'

"Then she thanked me for bringing her there and presently three peasants appeared, waiting for us, two youths and one shaven old man, with a thin nose like a sword blade and perfectly round eyes, a character well known to the whole Carlist army. The two youths stopped under the trees at a distance, but the old fellow came quite close up and gazed at her, screwing up his eyes as if looking at the sun. Then he raised his arm very slowly and took his red *boina* off his bald head. I watched her smiling at him all the time. I daresay she knew him as well as she knew the old rock. Very old rock. The rock of ages—and the aged man—landmarks of her youth. Then the mules started walking smartly forward, with the three peasants striding alongside of them, and vanished between the trees. These fellows were most likely sent out by her uncle the Cura.

"It was a peaceful scene, the morning light, the bit of open country, framed in steep stony slopes, a high peak or two in the distance, the thin smoke of some invisible *caserios*, rising straight up here and there. Far away behind us the guns had ceased and the echoes in the gorges had died out. I never knew what peace meant before. . . .

"Nor since," muttered Mr. Blunt after a pause and then went on. "The little stone church of her uncle, the holy man of the family, might have been round the corner of the

next spur of the nearest hill. I dismounted to bandage
the shoulder of my trooper. It was only a nasty long scratch.
While I was busy about it a bell began to ring in the distance.
The sound fell deliciously on the ear, clear like the morning
light. But it stopped all at once. You know how a distant
bell stops suddenly. I never knew before what stillness
meant. While I was wondering at it the fellow holding
our horses was moved to uplift his voice. He was a Spaniard,
not a Basque, and he trolled out in Castilian that song you
know,

> " ' Oh bells of my native village,
>      I am going away . . . good-bye ! ' "

He had a good voice. When the last note had floated away
I remounted, but there was a charm in the spot, something
particular and individual because while we were looking at
it before turning our horses' heads away the singer said :
' I wonder what is the name of this place,' and the other man
remarked : ' Why, there is no village here,' and the first one
insisted : ' No, I mean this spot, this very place.' The
wounded trooper decided that it had no name probably.
But he was wrong. It had a name. The hill, or the rock,
or the wood, or the whole had a name. I heard of it by
chance later. It was—Lastaola."

A cloud of tobacco smoke from Mills' pipe drove between
my head and the head of Mr. Blunt, who, strange to say,
yawned slightly. It seemed to me an obvious affectation
on the part of that man of perfect manners, and, moreover,
suffering from distressing insomnia.

"This is how we first met and how we first parted," he
said in a weary, indifferent tone. "It's quite possible that
she did see her uncle on the way. It's perhaps on this
occasion that she got her sister to come out of the wilderness.
I have no doubt she had a pass from the French Government
giving her the completest freedom of action. She must
have got it in Paris before leaving."

Mr. Blunt broke out into worldly, slightly cynical smiles.

"She can get anything she likes in Paris. She could get

a whole army over the frontier if she liked. She could get herself admitted into the Foreign Office at one o'clock in the morning if it so pleased her. Doors fly open before the heiress of Mr Allègre. She has inherited the old friends, the old connections. . . . Of course, if she were a toothless old woman. . . . But, you see, she isn't. The ushers in all the ministries bow down to the ground therefore, and voices from the innermost sanctums take on an eager tone when they say, ' *Faites entrer*.' My mother knows something about it. She has followed her career with the greatest attention. And Rita herself is not even surprised. She accomplishes most extraordinary things, as naturally as buying a pair of gloves. People in the shops are very polite and people in the world are like people in the shops. What did she know of the world ? She had seen it only from the saddle. Oh, she will get your cargo released for you all right. How will she do it ? . . . Well, when it's done—you follow me, Mills ? —when it's done she will hardly know herself."

" It's hardly possible that she shouldn't be aware," Mills pronounced calmly.

" No, she isn't an idiot," admitted Mr. Blunt, in the same matter-of-fact voice. " But she confessed to myself only the other day that she suffered from a sense of unreality. I told her that at any rate she had her own feelings surely. And she said to me : Yes, there was one of them at least about which she had no doubt; and you will never guess what it was. Don't try. I happen to know, because we are pretty good friends."

At that moment we all changed our attitude slightly. Mills' staring eyes moved for a glance towards Blunt, I, who was occupying the divan, raised myself on the cushions a little and Mr. Blunt, with half a turn, put his elbow on the table.

" I asked her what it was. I don't see," went on Mr. Blunt, with a perfectly horrible gentleness, " why I should have shown particular consideration to the heiress of Mr. Allègre. I don't mean to that particular mood of hers. It was the mood of weariness. And so she told me. It's fear. I will say it once again : Fear. . . ."

He added after a pause, " There can be not the slightest doubt of her courage.  But she distinctly uttered the word fear."

There was under the table the noise of Mills stretching his legs.

" A person of imagination," he began, " a young, virgin intelligence, steeped for nearly five years in the talk of Allègre's studio, where every hard truth had been cracked and every belief had been worried into shreds.  They were like a lot of intellectual dogs, you know . . ."

" Yes, yes, of course," Blunt interrupted hastily, " the intellectual personality altogether adrift, a soul without a home . . . but I, who am neither very fine nor very deep, I am convinced that the fear is material."

" Because she confessed to it being that ? " insinuated Mills.

" No, because she didn't," contradicted Blunt, with an angry frown and in an extremely suave voice.  " In fact, she bit her tongue.  And considering what good friends we are (under fire together and all that) I conclude that there is nothing there to boast of.  Neither is my friendship, as a matter of fact."

Mills' face was the very perfection of indifference.  But I who was looking at him, in my innocence, to discover what it all might mean, I had a notion that it was perhaps a shade too perfect.

" My leave is a farce," Captain Blunt burst out, with a most unexpected exasperation.  " As an officer of Don Carlos, I have no more standing than a bandit.  I ought to have been interned in those filthy old barracks in Avignon a long time ago. . . . Why am I not ?  Because Doña Rita exists and for no other reason on earth.  Of course it's known that I am about.  She has only to whisper over the wires to the Minister of the Interior, ' Put that bird in a cage for me,' and the thing would be done without any more formalities than that. . . . Sad world this," he commented in a changed tone.  " Nowadays a gentleman who lives by his sword is exposed to that sort of thing."

It was then for the first time I heard Mr. Mills laugh. It was a deep, pleasant, kindly note, not very loud and altogether free from that quality of derision that spoils so many laughs and gives away the secret hardness of hearts. But neither was it a very joyous laugh.

"But the truth of the matter is that I am '*en mission*,'" continued Captain Blunt. "I have been instructed to settle some things, to set other things going, and, by my instructions, Doña Rita is to be the intermediary for all those objects. And why? Because every bald head in this Republican Government gets pink at the top whenever her dress rustles outside the door. They bow with immense deference when the door opens, but the bow conceals a smirk because of those Venetian days. That confounded Versoy shoved his nose into that business; he says accidentally. He saw them together on the Lido and (those writing fellows are horrible) he wrote what he calls a vignette (I suppose accidentally, too) under that very title. There was in it a Prince and a lady and a big dog. He described how the Prince on landing from the gondola emptied his purse into the hands of a picturesque old beggar, while the lady, a little way off, stood gazing back at Venice with the dog romantically stretched at her feet. One of Versoy's beautiful prose vignettes in a great daily that has a literary column. But some other papers that didn't care a cent for literature rehashed the mere fact. And that's the sort of fact that impresses your political man, especially if the lady is, well, such as she is . . ."

He paused. His dark eyes flashed fatally, away from us, in the direction of the shy dummy; and then he went on with cultivated cynicism.

"So she rushes down here. Overdone, weary, rest for her nerves. Nonsense. I assure you she has no more nerves than I have."

I don't know how he meant it, but at that moment, slim and elegant, he seemed a mere bundle of nerves himself, with the flitting expressions on his thin, well-bred face, with the restlessness of his meagre brown hands amongst the objects on the table. With some pipe ash amongst a little spilt wine his forefinger traced a capital R. Then he looked into an empty glass profoundly. I have a notion that I sat there staring and listening like a yokel at a play. Mills' pipe was lying quite a foot away in front of him, empty, cold. Perhaps he had no more tobacco. Mr. Blunt assumed his dandified air—nervously.

" Of course her movements are commented on in the most exclusive drawing-rooms and also in other places, also exclusive, but where the gossip takes on another tone. There they are probably saying that she has got a ' *coup de cœur* ' for some one. Whereas I think she is utterly incapable of that sort of thing. That Venetian affair, the beginning of it and the end of it, was nothing but a *coup de tete*, and all those activities in which I am involved, as you see (by order of Headquarters, ha, ha, ha !), are nothing but that, all this connection, all this intimacy into which I have dropped. . . . Not to speak of my mother, who is delightful, but as irresponsible as one of those crazy princesses that shock their Royal families. . . ."

He seemed to bite his tongue and I observed that Mills' eyes seemed to have grown wider than I had ever seen them before. In that tranquil face it was a great play of feature. " An intimacy," began Mr. Blunt, with an extremely refined grimness of tone, " an intimacy with the heiress of Mr. Allègre on the part of . . . on my part, well, it isn't exactly . . . it's open . . . well, I leave it to you, what does it look like ? "

" Is there anybody looking on ? " Mills let fall, gently, through his kindly lips.

" Not actually, perhaps, at this moment. But I don't need to tell a man of the world, like you, that such things cannot remain unseen. And that they are, well, compromising, because of the mere fact of the fortune."

Mills got on his feet, looked for his jacket and after getting into it made himself heard while he looked for his hat.

" Whereas the woman herself is, so to speak, priceless."

Mr. Blunt muttered the word " Obviously."

By then we were all on our feet. The iron stove glowed

no longer and the lamp, surrounded by empty bottles and empty glasses, had grown dimmer.

I know that I had a great shiver on getting away from the cushions of the divan.

"We will meet again in a few hours," said Mr. Blunt. "Don't forget to come," he said, addressing me. "Oh, yes, do. Have no scruples. I am authorized to make invitations."

He must have noticed my shyness, my surprise, my embarrassment. And indeed I didn't know what to say.

"I assure you there isn't anything incorrect in your coming," he insisted, with the greatest civility. "You will be introduced by two good friends, Mills and myself. Surely you are not afraid of a very charming woman. . . ."

I was not afraid, but my head swam a little and I only looked at him mutely.

"Lunch precisely at midday. Mills will bring you along. I am sorry you two are going. I shall throw myself on the bed for an hour or two, but I am sure I won't sleep."

He accompanied us along the passage into the black-and-white hall, where the low gas flame glimmered forlornly. When he opened the front door the cold blast of the mistral rushing down the street of the Consuls made me shiver to the very marrow of my bones.

Mills and I exchanged but a few words as we walked down towards the centre of the town. In the chill tempestuous dawn he strolled along musingly, disregarding the discomfort of the cold, the depressing influence of the hour, the desolation of the empty streets in which the dry dust rose in whirls in front of us, behind us, flew upon us from the side streets. The masks had gone home and our footsteps echoed on the flagstones with unequal sound as of men without purpose, without hope.

"I suppose you will come," said Mills suddenly.

"I really don't know," I said.

"Don't you? Well, remember I am not trying to persuade you; but I am staying at the Hôtel de Louvre and I shall leave there at a quarter to twelve for that lunch. At a quarter to twelve, not a minute later. I suppose you can sleep ? "

I laughed.

" Charming age, yours," said Mills, as we came out on the quays. Already dim figures of the workers moved in the biting dawn and the masted forms of ships were coming out dimly, as far as the eye could reach down the old harbour.

" Well," Mills began again, " you may oversleep yourself."

This suggestion was made in a cheerful tone, just as we shook hands at the lower end of the Cannebière. He looked very burly as he walked away from me. I went on towards my lodgings. My head was very full of confused images, but I was really too tired to think.

# PART TWO

## I

Sometimes I wonder yet whether Mills wished me to over-sleep myself or not : that is, whether he really took sufficient interest to care. His uniform kindliness of manner made it impossible for me to tell. And I can hardly remember my own feelings. Did I care? The whole recollection of that time of my life has such a peculiar quality that the beginning and the end of it are merged in one sensation of profound emotion, continuous and overpowering, containing the extremes of exultation, full of careless joy and of an invincible sadness—like a day-dream. The sense of all this having been gone through as if in one great rush of imagination is all the stronger in the distance of time, because it had something of that quality even then : of fate unprovoked, of events that didn't cast any shadow before.

Not that those events were in the least extraordinary. They were, in truth, commonplace. What to my backward glance seems startling and a little awful is their punctual-ness and inevitability. Mills was punctual. Exactly at a quarter to twelve he appeared under the lofty portal of the Hôtel de Louvre, with his fresh face, his ill-fitting grey suit, and enveloped in his own sympathetic atmosphere.

How could I have avoided him? To this day I have a shadowy conviction of his inherent distinction of mind and heart, far beyond any man I have ever met since. He was unavoidable : and of course I never tried to avoid him. The first sight on which his eyes fell was a victoria pulled up before the hotel door, in which I sat with no sentiment I can remember now but that of some slight shyness. He got in without a moment's hesitation, his friendly glance took me in from head to foot and (such was his peculiar gift) gave me a pleasurable sensation.

After we had gone a little way I couldn't help saying to him with a bashful laugh : " You know, it seems very extraordinary that I should be driving out with you like this."

He turned to look at me and in his kind voice :

" You will find everything extremely simple," he said. " So simple that you will be quite able to hold your own. I suppose you know that the world is selfish, I mean the majority of the people in it, often unconsciously I must admit, and especially people with a mission, with a fixed idea, with some fantastic object in view, or even with only some fantastic illusion. That doesn't mean that they have no scruples. And I don't know that at this moment I myself am not one of them."

" That, of course, I can't say," I retorted.

" I haven't seen her for years," he said, " and in comparison with what she was then she must be very grown up by now. From what we heard from Mr. Blunt she had experiences which would have matured her more than they would teach her. There are of course people that are not teachable. I don't know that she is one of them. But as to maturity that's quite another thing. Capacity for suffering is developed in every human being worthy of the name."

" Captain Blunt doesn't seem to be a very happy person," I said. " He seems to have a grudge against everybody. People make him wince. The things they do, the things they say. He must be awfully mature."

Mills gave me a sidelong look. It met mine of the same character and we both smiled without openly looking at each other. At the end of the Rue de Rome the violent chilly breath of the mistral enveloped the victoria in a great widening of brilliant sunshine without heat. We turned to the right, circling at a stately pace about the rather mean obelisk which stands at the entrance to the Prado.

" I don't know whether you are mature or not," said Mills humorously. " But I think you will do. You . . ."

" Tell me," I interrupted, " what is really Captain Blunt's position there ? "

And I nodded at the alley of the Prado opening before us between the rows of the perfectly leafless trees.

" Thoroughly false, I should think. It doesn't accord either with his illusions or his pretensions, or even with the real position he has in the world. And so what between his mother and the General Headquarters and the state of his own feelings he . . ."

" He is in love with her," I interrupted again.

" That wouldn't make it any easier. I'm not at all sure of that. But if so it can't be a very idealistic sentiment. All the warmth of his idealism is concentrated upon a certain ' *Américain, Catholique et gentilhomme. . . .* ' "

The smile which for a moment dwelt on his lips was not unkind.

" At the same time he has a very good grip of the material conditions that surround, as it were, the situation."

" What do you mean ? That Doña Rita " (the name came strangely familiar to my tongue) " is rich, that she has a fortune of her own ? "

" Yes, a fortune," said Mills. " But it was Allègre's fortune before. . . . And then there is Blunt's fortune : he lives by his sword. And there is the fortune of his mother, I assure you a perfectly charming, clever, and most aristocratic old lady, with the most distinguished connections. I really mean it. She doesn't live by her sword. She . . . she lives by her wits. I have a notion that those two dislike each other heartily at times. . . . Here we are."

The victoria stopped in the side alley, bordered by the low walls of private grounds. We got out before a wrought-iron gateway which stood half open and walked up a circular drive to the door of a large villa of a neglected appearance. The mistral howled in the sunshine, shaking the bare bushes quite furiously. And everything was bright and hard, the air was hard, the light was hard, the ground under our feet was hard.

The door at which Mills rang came open almost at once.

The maid who opened it was short, dark, and slightly pock-marked. For the rest, an obvious "*femme-de-chambre*," and very busy. She said quickly, "Madame has just returned from her ride," and went up the stairs leaving us to shut the front door ourselves.

The staircase had a crimson carpet. Mr. Blunt appeared from somewhere in the hall. He was in riding breeches and a black coat with ample square skirts. This get-up suited him but it also changed him extremely by doing away with the effect of flexible slimness he produced in his evening clothes. He looked to me not at all himself but rather like a brother of the man who had been talking to us the night before. He carried about him a delicate perfume of scented soap. He gave us a flash of his white teeth and said :

"It's a perfect nuisance. We have just dismounted. I will have to lunch as I am. A lifelong habit of beginning her day on horseback. She pretends she is unwell unless she does. I daresay, when one thinks there has been hardly a day for five or six years that she didn't begin with a ride. That's the reason she is always rushing away from Paris where she can't go out in the morning alone. Here, of course, it's different. And as I, too, am a stranger here I can go out with her. Not that I particularly care to do it."

These last words were addressed to Mills specially, with the addition of a mumbled remark : "It's a confounded position." Then calmly to me with a swift smile : "We have been talking of you this morning. You are expected with impatience."

"Thank you very much," I said, "but I can't help asking myself what I am doing here."

The upward cast in the eyes of Mills who was facing the staircase made us both, Blunt and I, turn round. The woman of whom I had heard so much, in a sort of way in which I had never heard a woman spoken of before, was coming down the stairs, and my first sensation was that of profound astonishment at this evidence that she did really exist. And even then the visual impression was more of colour in a picture than of the forms of actual life. She was wearing a wrapper, a sort of dressing-gown of pale blue silk embroidered with black and gold designs round the neck and down the front, lapped round her and held together by a broad belt of the same material. Her slippers were of the same colour, with black bows at the instep. The white stairs, the deep crimson of the carpet, and the light blue of the dress made an effective combination of colour to set off the delicate carnation of that face, which, after the first glance given to the whole person, drew irresistibly your gaze to itself by an indefinable quality of charm beyond all analysis and made you think of remote races, of strange generations, of the faces of women sculptured on immemorial monuments and of those lying unsung in their tombs. While she moved downwards from step to step with slightly lowered eyes there flashed upon me suddenly the recollection of words heard at night, of Allègre's words about her, of there being in her "something of the women of all time."

At the last step she raised her eyelids, treated us to an exhibition of teeth as dazzling as Mr. Blunt's and looking even stronger; and indeed, as she approached us she brought home to our hearts (but after all I am speaking only for myself) a vivid sense of her physical perfection in beauty of limb and balance of nerves, and not so much of grace, probably, as of absolute harmony.

She said to us, "I am sorry I kept you waiting." Her voice was low pitched, penetrating, and of the most seductive gentleness. She offered her hand to Mills very frankly as to an old friend. Within the extraordinarily wide sleeve, lined with black silk, I could see the arm, very white, with a pearly gleam in the shadow. But to me she extended her hand with a slight stiffening, as it were a recoil of her person, combined with an extremely straight glance. It was a finely shaped, capable hand. I bowed over it, and we just touched fingers. I did not look then at her face.

Next moment she caught sight of some envelopes lying on the round marble-topped table in the middle of the hall. She seized one of them with a wonderfully quick, almost feline, movement and tore it open, saying to us, "Excuse me, I must. . . . Do go into the dining-room. Captain Blunt, show the way."

Her widened eyes stared at the paper. Mr. Blunt threw one of the doors open, but before we passed through it we heard a petulant exclamation accompanied by childlike stamping with both feet and ending in a laugh which had in it a note of contempt.

The door closed behind us; we had been abandoned by Mr. Blunt. He had remained on the other side, possibly to soothe. The room in which we found ourselves was long like a gallery and ended in a rotunda with many windows. It was long enough for two fireplaces of red polished granite. A table laid out for four occupied very little space. The floor inlaid in two kinds of wood in a bizarre pattern was highly waxed, reflecting objects like still water.

Before very long Doña Rita and Blunt rejoined us and we sat down around the table; but before we could begin to talk a dramatically sudden ring at the front door stilled our incipient animation. Doña Rita looked at us all in turn, with surprise and, as it were, with suspicion. "How did he know I was here?" she whispered after looking at the card which was brought to her. She passed it to Blunt, who passed it to Mills, who made a faint grimace, dropped it on the table-cloth, and only whispered to me, "A journalist from Paris."

"He has run me to earth," said Doña Rita. "One would bargain for peace against hard cash if these fellows weren't always ready to snatch at one's very soul with the other hand. It frightens me."

Her voice floated mysterious and penetrating from her lips, which moved very little. Mills was watching her with sympathetic curiosity. Mr. Blunt muttered: "Better not make the brute angry." For a moment Doña Rita's face, with its narrow eyes, its wide brow, and high cheek bones, became very still; then her colour was a little heightened. "Oh," she said softly, "let him come in. He would be really dangerous if he had a mind—you know," she said to Mills.

The person who had provoked all those remarks and as much hesitation as though he had been some sort of wild beast astonished me on being admitted, first by the beauty of his white head of hair and then by his paternal aspect and the innocent simplicity of his manner. They laid a cover for him between Mills and Doña Rita, who quite openly removed the envelopes she had brought with her, to the other side of her plate. As openly the man's round china-blue eyes followed them in an attempt to make out the handwriting of the addresses.

He seemed to know, at least slightly, both Mills and Blunt. To me he gave a stare of stupid surprise. He addressed our hostess.

"Resting? Rest is a very good thing. Upon my word, I thought I would find you alone. But you have too much sense. Neither man nor woman has been created to live alone. . . ." After this opening he had all the talk to himself. It was left to him pointedly, and I verily believe that I was the only one who showed an appearance of interest. I couldn't help it. The others, including Mills, sat like a lot of deaf and dumb people. No. It was even something more detached. They sat rather like a very superior lot of waxworks, with the fixed but indetermined facial expression and with that odd air wax figures have of being aware of their existence being but a sham.

I was the exception; and nothing could have marked better my status of a stranger, the completest possible stranger in the moral region in which those people lived, moved, enjoying or suffering their incomprehensible emotions. I was as much of a stranger as the most hopeless castaway stumbling in the dark upon a hut of natives and finding them in the grip of some situation appertaining to the mentalities, prejudices, and problems of an undiscovered country—of a country of which he had not even had one single clear glimpse before.

It was even worse in a way. It ought to have been more disconcerting. For, pursuing the image of the castaway blundering upon the complications of an unknown scheme of life, it was I, the castaway, who was the savage, the simple, innocent child of nature. Those people were obviously more civilized than I was. They had more rites, more ceremonies, more complexity in their sensations, more knowledge of evil, more varied meanings to the subtle phrases of their language. Naturally! I was still so young! And yet I assure you, that just then I lost all sense of inferiority. And why? Of course the carelessness and the ignorance of youth had something to do with that. But there was something else besides. Looking at Doña Rita, her head leaning on her hand, with her dark lashes lowered on the slightly flushed cheek, I felt no longer alone in my youth. That woman of whom I had heard these things I have set down with all the exactness of unfailing memory, that woman was revealed to me young, younger than anybody I had ever seen, as young as myself (and my sensation of my youth was then very acute); revealed with something peculiarly intimate in the conviction, as if she were young exactly in the same way in which I felt myself young; and that therefore no misunderstanding between us was possible and there could be nothing more for us to know about each other. Of course this sensation was momentary, but it was illuminating; it was a light which could not last, but it left no darkness behind. On the contrary, it seemed to have kindled magically somewhere within me a glow of assurance, of unaccountable confidence in myself: a warm, steady, and eager sensation of my individual life beginning for good there, on that spot, in that sense of solidarity, in that seduction.

## II

FOR this, properly speaking wonderful, reason I was the only one of the company who could listen without constraint to the unbidden guest with that fine head of white hair, so beautifully kept, so magnificently waved, so artistically arranged that respect could not be felt for it any more than for a very expensive wig in the window of a hair-dresser. In fact, I had an inclination to smile at it. This proves how unconstrained I felt. My mind was perfectly at liberty; and so of all the eyes in that room mine was the only pair able to look about in easy freedom. All the other listeners' eyes were cast down, including Mills' eyes, but that I am sure was only because of his perfect and delicate sympathy. He could not have been concerned otherwise.

The intruder devoured the cutlets—if they were cutlets. Notwithstanding my perfect liberty of mind I was not aware of what we were eating. I have a notion that the lunch was a mere show, except of course for the man with the white hair, who was really hungry and who, besides, must have had the pleasant sense of dominating the situation. He stooped over his plate and worked his jaw deliberately while his blue eyes rolled incessantly; but as a matter of fact he never looked openly at any one of us. Whenever he laid down his knife and fork he would throw himself back and start retailing in a light tone some Parisian gossip about prominent people.

He talked first about a certain politician of mark. His "dear Rita" knew him. His costume dated back to '48, he was made of wood and parchment and still swathed his neck in a white cloth; and even his wife had never been seen in a low-necked dress. Not once in her life. She was buttoned up to the chin like her husband. Well, that man had confessed to him that when he was engaged in political controversy, not on a matter of principle but on some special measure in debate, he felt ready to kill everybody.

He interrupted himself for a comment. " I am something like that myself. I believe it's a purely professional feeling. Carry one's point whatever it is. Normally I couldn't kill a fly. My sensibility is too acute for that. My heart is too tender also. Much too tender. I am a Republican. I am a Red. As to all our present masters and governors, all those people you are trying to turn round

your little finger, they are all horrible Royalists in disguise.
They are plotting the ruin of all the institutions to which I
am devoted.   But I have never tried to spoil your little game,
Rita.   After all, it's but a little game.   You know very well
that two or three fearless articles, something in my style,
you know, would soon put a stop to all that underhand back-
ing of your king.   I am calling him king because I want to
be polite to you.   He is an adventurer, a blood-thirsty,
murderous adventurer, for me, and nothing else.   Look
here, my dear child, what are you knocking yourself about
for ?   For the sake of that bandit ?   *Allons donc !*   A pupil of
Henry Allègre can have no illusions of that sort about any
man.   And such a pupil, too !   Ah, the good old days in the
Pavilion !   Don't think I claim any particular intimacy.
It was just enough to enable me to offer my services to you,
Rita, when our poor friend died.   I found myself handy
and so I came.   It so happened that I was the first.   You
remember, Rita ?   What made it possible for everybody to
get on with our poor dear Allègre was his complete, equable,
and impartial contempt for all mankind.   There is nothing
in that against the purest democratic principles ; but that
you, Rita, should elect to throw so much of your life away
for the sake of a Royal adventurer, it really knocks me over.
For you don't love him.   You never loved him, you know."

He made a snatch at her hand, absolutely pulled it away
from under her head (it was quite startling) and retaining it
in his grasp, proceeded to a paternal patting of the most
impudent kind.   She let him go on with apparent insensibility.   Meanwhile his eyes strayed round the table over our
faces.   It was very trying.   The stupidity of that wandering stare had a paralysing power.   He talked at large with
husky familiarity.

" Here I come, expecting to find a good sensible girl who
had seen at last the vanity of all those things ; half-light
in the rooms ; surrounded by the works of her favourite
poets, and all that sort of thing.   I say to myself : I must
just run in and see the dear wise child, and encourage her in
her good resolutions. . . . And I fall into the middle of an

*intime* lunch-party. For I suppose it is *intime.* . . . Eh ? Very ? H'm, yes. . . .

He was really appalling. Again his wandering stare went round the table, with an expression incredibly incongruous with the words. It was as though he had borrowed those eyes from some idiot for the purpose of that visit. He still held Doña Rita's hand, and, now and then, patted it.

" It's discouraging," he cooed. " And I believe not one of you here is a Frenchman. I don't know what you are all about. It's beyond me. But if we were a Republic —you know I am an old Jacobin, sans-culotte and terrorist —if this were a real Republic with the Convention sitting and a Committee of Public Safety attending to national business, you would all get your heads cut off. Ha, ha. . . . I am joking, ha, ha ! . . . and serve you right, too. Don't mind my little joke."

While he was still laughing he released her hand, and she leaned her head on it again without haste. She had never looked at him once.

During the rather humiliating silence that ensued he got a leather cigar case like a small valise out of his pocket, opened it and looked with critical interest at the six cigars it contained. The tireless *femme-de-chambre* set down a tray with coffee cups on the table. We each (glad, I suppose, of something to do) took one, but he, to begin with, sniffed at his. Doña Rita continued leaning on her elbow, her lips closed in a reposeful expression of peculiar sweetness. There was nothing drooping in her attitude. Her face with the delicate carnation of a rose and downcast eyes was as if veiled in firm immobility and was so appealing that I had an insane impulse to walk round and kiss the forearm on which it was leaning ; that strong, well-shaped forearm, gleaming not like marble but with a living and warm splendour. So familiar had I become already with her in my thoughts ! Of course I didn't do anything of the sort. It was nothing uncontrollable, it was but a tender longing of a most respectful and purely sentimental kind. I performed the act in my thought quietly, almost solemnly, while the creature with the silver hair leaned back in his chair, puffing at his cigar, and began to speak again.

It was all apparently very innocent talk. He informed his " dear Rita " that he was really on his way to Monte Carlo. A lifelong habit of his at this time of the year ; but he was ready to run back to Paris if he could do anything for his " *chère enfant*," run back for a day, for two days, for three days, for any time ; miss Monte Carlo this year altogether, if he could be of the slightest use and save her going herself. For instance he could see to it that proper watch was kept over the Pavilion stuffed with all these art treasures. What was going to happen to all those things ? . . . Making herself heard for the first time Doña Rita murmured without moving that she had made arrangements with the police to have it properly watched. And I was enchanted by the almost imperceptible play of her lips.

But the anxious creature was not reassured. He pointed out that things had been stolen out of the Louvre, which was, he dared say, even better watched. And there was that marvellous cabinet on the landing, black lacquer with silver herons, which alone would repay a couple of burglars. A wheelbarrow, some old sacking, and they could trundle it off under people's noses.

" Have you thought it all out ? " she asked in a cold whisper, while we three sat smoking to give ourselves a countenance (it was certainly no enjoyment) and wondering what we would hear next.

No, he had not. But he confessed that for years and years he had been in love with that cabinet. And anyhow what *was* going to happen to the things ? The world was greatly exercised by that problem. He turned slightly his beautifully groomed white head so as to address Mr. Blunt directly.

" I had the pleasure of meeting your mother lately."

Mr. Blunt took his time to raise his eyebrows and flash his teeth at him before he dropped negligently, " I can't imagine where you could have met my mother."

" Why, at Bing's, the curio-dealer, " said the other with

an air of the heaviest possible stupidity. And yet there was something in these few words which seemed to imply that if Mr. Blunt was looking for trouble he would certainly get it. "Bing was bowing her out of his shop, but he was so angry about something that he was quite rude even to me afterwards. I don't think it's very good for *Madame votre mère* to quarrel with Bing. He is a Parisian personality. He's quite a power in his sphere. All these fellows' nerves are upset from worry as to what will happen to the Allègre collection. And no wonder they are nervous. A big art event hangs on your lips, my dear, great Rita. And by the way, you too ought to remember that it isn't wise to quarrel with people. What have you done to that poor Azzolati? Did you really tell him to get out and never come near you again, or something awful like that? I don't doubt that he was of use to you or to your king. A man who gets invitations to shoot with the President at Rambouillet! I saw him only the other evening; I heard he had been winning immensely at cards; but he looked perfectly wretched, the poor fellow. He complained of your conduct— oh, very much! He told me you had been perfectly brutal with him. He said to me: 'I am no good for anything, *mon cher*. The other day at Rambouillet, whenever I had a hare at the end of my gun I would think of her cruel words and my eyes would run full of tears. I missed every shot' . . . You are not fit for diplomatic work, you know, *ma chère*. You are a mere child at it. When you want a middle-aged gentleman to do anything for you, you don't begin by reducing him to tears. I should have thought any woman would have known that much. A nun would have known that much. What do you say? Shall I run back to Paris and make it up for you with Azzolati?"

He waited for her answer. The compression of his thin lips was full of significance. I was surprised to see our hostess shake her head negatively the least bit, for indeed by her pose, by the thoughtful immobility of her face she seemed to be a thousand miles away from us all, lost in an infinite reverie.

He gave it up. "Well, I must be off. The express for Nice passes at four o'clock. I will be away about three weeks and then you shall see me again. Unless I strike a run of bad luck and get cleaned out, in which case you shall see me before then."

He turned to Mills suddenly.

"Will your cousin come south this year, to that beautiful villa of his at Cannes?"

Mills hardly deigned to answer that he didn't know anything about his cousin's movements.

"A *grand seigneur* combined with a great connoisseur," opined the other heavily. His mouth had gone slack and he looked a perfect and grotesque imbecile under his wig-like crop of white hair. Positively I thought he would begin to slobber. But he attacked Blunt next.

"Are you on your way down, too? A little flutter. . . . It seems to me you haven't been seen in your usual Paris haunts of late. Where have you been all this time?"

"Don't you know where I have been?" said Mr. Blunt with great precision.

"No, I only ferret out things that may be of some use to me," was the unexpected reply, uttered with an air of perfect vacancy and swallowed by Mr. Blunt in blank silence.

At last he made ready to rise from the table. "Think over what I have said, my dear Rita."

"It's all over and done with," was Doña Rita's answer, in a louder tone than I had ever heard her use before. It thrilled me while she continued: "I mean, this thinking." She was back from the remoteness of her meditation, very much so indeed. She rose and moved away from the table, inviting by a sign the other to follow her; which he did at once, yet slowly and as it were warily.

It was a conference in the recess of a window. We three remained seated round the table from which the dark maid was removing the cups and the plates with brusque movements. I gazed frankly at Doña Rita's profile, irregular, animated, and fascinating in an undefinable way, at her well-

shaped head with the hair twisted high up and apparently
held in its place by a gold arrow with a jewelled shaft. We
couldn't hear what she said, but the movement of her lips
and the play of her features were full of charm, full of
interest, expressing both audacity and gentleness. She spoke
with fire without raising her voice. The man listened
round-shouldered, but seeming much too stupid to understand. I could see now and then that he was speaking, but
he was inaudible. At one moment Doña Rita turned her
head to the room and called out to the maid, " Give me my
hand-bag off the sofa."

At this the other was heard plainly, " No, no," and then
a little lower, " You have no tact, Rita. . . ." Then came
her argument in a low, penetrating voice which I caught,
" Why not ? Between such old friends." However, she
waved away the hand-bag, he calmed down, and their voices
sank again. Presently I saw him raise her hand to his lips,
while with her back to the room she continued to contemplate out of the window the bare and untidy garden. At last
he went out of the room, throwing to the table an airy
" *Bonjour, bonjour,*" which was not acknowledged by any of
us three.


### III

MILLS got up and approached the figure at the window. To
my extreme surprise, Mr. Blunt, after a moment of obviously
painful hesitation, hastened out after the man with the
white hair.

In consequence of these movements I was left to myself
and I began to be uncomfortably conscious of it when
Doña Rita, near the window, addressed me in a raised voice.

" We have no confidences to exchange, Mr. Mills and I."

I took this for an encouragement to join them. They
were both looking at me. Doña Rita added, " Mr. Mills
and I are friends from old times, you know."

Bathed in the softened reflection of the sunshine, which did not fall directly into the room, standing very straight with her arms down, before Mills, and with a faint smile directed to me, she looked extremely young, and yet mature. There was even, for a moment, a slight dimple in her cheek.

" How old, I wonder ? " I said, with an answering smile.

" Oh, for ages, for ages," she exclaimed hastily, frowning a little, then she went on addressing herself to Mills, apparently in continuation of what she was saying before.

. . . " This man's is an extreme case, and yet perhaps it isn't the worst. But that's the sort of thing. I have no account to render to anybody, but I don't want to be dragged along all the gutters where that man picks up his living."

She had thrown her head back a little but there was no scorn, no angry flash under the dark-lashed eyelids. The words did not ring. I was struck for the first time by the even, mysterious quality of her voice.

" Will you let me suggest," said Mills, with a grave, kindly face, " that being what you are, you have nothing to fear ? "

" And perhaps nothing to lose," she went on without bitterness. " No. It isn't fear. It's a sort of dread. You must remember that no nun could have had a more protected life. Henry Allègre had his greatness. When he faced the world he also masked it. He was big enough for that. He filled the whole field of vision for me."

" You found that enough ? " asked Mills.

" Why ask now ? " she remonstrated. " The truth—the truth is that I never asked myself. Enough or not there was no room for anything else. He was the shadow and the light and the form and the voice. He would have it so. The morning he died they came to tell me at four o'clock. I ran into his room bare-footed. He recognized me and whispered, ' You are flawless.' I was very frightened. He seemed to think, and then said very plainly, ' Such is my character. I am like that.' These were the last words he spoke. I hardly noticed them then. I was thinking that he was lying in a very uncomfortable position and I asked him if I should lift him up a little higher on the pillows. You know I am very strong. I could have done it. I had done it before. He raised his hand off the blanket just enough to make a sign that he didn't want to be touched. It was the last gesture he made. I hung over him and then—and then I nearly ran out of the house just as I was, in my night-gown. I think if I had been dressed I would have run out of the garden, into the street—run away altogether. I had never seen death. I may say I had never heard of it. I wanted to run from it."

She paused for a long, quiet breath. The harmonized sweetness and daring of her face was made pathetic by her downcast eyes.

" *Fuir la mort,*" she repeated, meditatively, in her mysterious voice.

Mills' big head had a little movement, nothing more. Her glance glided for a moment towards me like a friendly recognition of my right to be there, before she began again.

" My life might have been described as looking at mankind from a fourth-floor window for years. When the end came it was like falling out of a balcony into the street. It was as sudden as that. Once I remember somebody was telling us in the pavilion a tale about a girl who jumped down from a fourth-floor window. . . . For love, I believe," she interjected very quickly, " and came to no harm. Her guardian angel must have slipped his wings under her just in time. He must have. But as to me, all I know is that I didn't break anything—not even my heart. Don't be shocked, Mr. Mills. It's very likely that you don't understand."

" Very likely," Mills assented, unmoved. " But don't be too sure of that."

" Henry Allègre had the highest opinion of your intelligence," she said unexpectedly and with evident seriousness. " But all this is only to tell you that when he was gone I found myself down there unhurt, but dazed, bewildered, not sufficiently stunned. It so happened that that creature was somewhere in the neighbourhood. How he found out.

s 2

. . . But it's his business to find out things.   And he knows, too, how to worm his way in anywhere.   Indeed, in the first days he was useful and somehow he made it look as if Heaven itself had sent him.   In my distress I thought I could never sufficiently repay. . . .   Well, I have been paying ever since."

"What do you mean?" asked Mills softly.   "In hard cash?"

"Oh, it's really so little," she said.   "I told you it wasn't the worst case.   I stayed on in that house from which I nearly ran away in my nightgown.   I stayed on because I didn't know what to do next.   He vanished as he had come on the track of something else, I suppose.   You know he really has got to get his living some way or other.   But don't think I was deserted.   On the contrary.   People were coming and going, all sorts of people that Henry Allègre used to know—or had refused to know.   I had a sensation of plotting and intriguing around me all the time.   I was feeling morally bruised, sore all over, when, one day, Don Rafael de Villarel sent in his card.   A grandee.   I didn't know him, but, as you are aware, there was hardly a personality of mark or position that hasn't been talked about in the Pavilion before me.   Of him I had only heard that he was a very austere and pious person, always at Mass, and that sort of thing.   I saw a frail little man with a long, yellow face and sunken fanatical eyes, an Inquisitor, an unfrocked monk.   One missed a rosary from his thin fingers.   He gazed at me terribly and I couldn't imagine what he might want.   I waited for him to pull out a crucifix and sentence me to the stake there and then.   But no; he dropped his eyes and in a cold, righteous sort of voice informed me that he had called on behalf of the prince—he called him His Majesty.   I was amazed by the change.   I wondered now why he didn't slip his hands into the sleeves of his coat, you know, as begging Friars do when they come for a sub-scription.   He explained that the Prince asked for per-mission to call and offer me his condolences in person.   We had seen a lot of him our last two months in Paris that year.   Henry Allègre had taken a fancy to paint his portrait.   He used to ride with us nearly every morning. Almost without thinking I said I should be pleased. Don Rafael was shocked at my want of formality, but bowed to me in silence, very much as a monk bows, from the waist. If he had only crossed his hands flat on his chest it would have been perfect. Then, I don't know why, something moved me to make him a deep curtsey as he backed out of the room, leaving me suddenly impressed, not only with him but with myself too. I had my door closed to everybody else that afternoon and the Prince came with a very proper sorrowful face, but five minutes after he got into the room he was laughing as usual, made the whole little house ring with it. You know his big, irresistible laugh. . . ."

" No," said Mills, a littls abruptly, " I have never seen him."

" No," she said, surprised, " and yet you . . ."

" I understand," interrupted Mills. " All this is purely accidental. You must know that I am a solitary man of books but with a secret taste for adventure which somehow came out ; surprising even me."

She listened with that enigmatic, still, under the eyelids glance, and a friendly turn of the head.

" I know you for a frank and loyal gentleman. . . . Adventure—and books ? Ah, the books ! Haven't I turned stacks of them over ! Haven't I ? . . ."

" Yes," murmured Mills. " That's what one does."

She put out her hand and laid it lightly on Mills' sleeve.

" Listen, I don't need to justify myself, but if I had known a single woman in the world, if I had only had the opportunity to observe a single one of them, I would have been perhaps on my guard. But you know I hadn't. The only woman I had anything to do with was myself, and they say that one can't know oneself. It never entered my head to be on my guard against his warmth and his terrible obviousness. You and he were the only two, infinitely different, people, who didn't approach me as if I had been a precious object in a collection, an ivory carving or a piece of Chinese porcelain. That's why I have kept you in my memory so well. Oh! you were not obvious! As to him —I soon learned to regret I was not some object, some beautiful, carved object of bone or bronze; a rare piece of porcelain, *pâte dure*, not *pâte tendre*. A pretty specimen."

"Rare, yes. Even unique," said Mills, looking at her steadily with a smile. "But don't try to depreciate yourself. You were never pretty. You are not pretty. You are worse."

Her narrow eyes had a mischievous gleam. "Do you find such sayings in your books?" she asked.

"As a matter of fact I have," said Mills, with a little laugh, "found this one in a book. It was a woman, who said that of herself. A woman far from common, who died some few years ago. She was an actress. A great artist."

"A great! . . . Lucky person! She had that refuge, that garment, while I stand here with nothing to protect me from evil fame; a naked temperament for any wind to blow upon. Yes, greatness in art is a protection. I wonder if there would have been anything in me if I had tried? But Henry Allègre would never let me try. He told me that whatever I could achieve would never be good enough for what I was. The perfection of flattery! Was it that he thought I had not talent of any sort? It's possible. He would know. I've had the idea since that he was jealous. He wasn't jealous of mankind any more than he was afraid of thieves for his collection; but he may have been jealous of what he could see in me, of some passion that could be aroused. But if so he never repented. I shall never forget his last words. He saw me standing beside his bed, defenceless, symbolic and forlorn, and all he found to say was, ' Well, I am like that.' "

I forgot myself in watching her. I had never seen anybody speak with less play of facial muscles. In the fullness of its life her face preserved a sort of immobility. The words seemed to form themselves, fiery or pathetic, in the air, outside her lips. Their design was hardly disturbed; a design of sweetness, gravity, and force as if born from the inspiration of some artist; for I had never seen anything to come up to it in nature before or since.

All this was part of the enchantment she cast over me; and I seemed to notice that Mills had the aspect of a man under a spell. If he too was a captive then I had no reason to feel ashamed of my surrender.

"And you know," she began again abruptly, "that I have been accustomed to all the forms of respect."

"That's true," murmured Mills, as if involuntarily.

"Well, yes," she reaffirmed. "My instinct may have told me that my only protection was obscurity, but I didn't know how and where to find it. Oh, yes, I had that instinct. . . . But there were other instincts and . . . How am I to tell you? I don't know how to be on guard against myself, either. Not a soul to speak to, or to get a warning from. Some woman soul that would have known, in which perhaps I could have seen my own reflection. I assure you the only woman that ever addressed me directly, and that was in writing, was . . ."

She glanced aside, saw Mr. Blunt returning from the hall and added rapidly in a lowered voice,

"His mother."

The bright, mechanical smile of Mr. Blunt gleamed at us right down the room, but he didn't, as it were, follow it in his body. He swerved to the nearest of the two big fireplaces and finding some cigarettes on the mantelpiece remained leaning on his elbow in the warmth of the bright wood fire. I noticed then a bit of mute play. The heiress of Henry Allègre, who could secure neither obscurity nor any other alleviation to that invidious position, looked as if she would speak to Blunt from a distance; but in a moment the confident eagerness of her face died out as if killed by a sudden thought. I didn't know then her shrinking from all falsehood and evasion; her dread of insincerity and disloyalty of every kind. But even then I felt that at the very last moment her being had recoiled before some shadow of a suspicion. And it occurred to me, too, to wonder what sort of business Mr. Blunt could have had to transact with our odious visitor, of a nature so urgent as to make him run out after him into the hall ? Unless to beat him a little with one of the sticks that were to be found there ? White hair so much like an expensive wig could not be considered a serious protection. But it couldn't have been that. The transaction, whatever it was, had been much too quiet. I must say that none of us had looked out of the window and that I didn't know when the man did go or if he was gone at all. As a matter of fact he was already far away ; and I may just as well say here that I never saw him again in my life. His passage across my field of vision was like that of other figures of that time : not to be forgotten, a little fantastic, infinitely enlightening for my contempt, darkening for my memory which struggles still with the clear lights and the ugly shadows of those unforgotten days.

## IV

It was past four o'clock before I left the house, together with Mills. Mr. Blunt, still in his riding costume, escorted us to the very door. He asked us to send him the first fiacre we met on our way to town. " It's impossible to walk in this get-up through the streets," he remarked, with his brilliant smile.

At this point I propose to transcribe some notes I made at the time in little black books which I have hunted up in the litter of the past ; very cheap, common little notebooks that by the lapse of years have acquired a touching dimness of aspect, the frayed, worn-out dignity of documents.

Expression on paper has never been my forte. My life had been a thing of outward manifestations. I never had been secret or even systematically taciturn about my simple occupations which might have been foolish but had never required either caution or mystery. But in those four hours since midday a complete change had come over me. For good or evil I left that house committed to an enterprise that could not be talked about; which would have appeared to many senseless and perhaps ridiculous, but was certainly full of risks, and apart from that, commanded discretion on the ground of simple loyalty. It would not only close my lips but it would to a certain extent cut me off from my usual haunts and from the society of my friends; especially of the light-hearted, young, harum-scarum kind. This was unavoidable. It was because I felt myself thrown back upon my own thoughts and forbidden to seek relief amongst other lives—it was perhaps only for that reason at first that I started an irregular, fragmentary record of my days.

I made these notes not so much to preserve the memory (one cared not for any to-morrow then) but to help me to keep a better hold of the actuality. I scribbled them on shore and I scribbled them on the sea; and in both cases they are concerned not only with the nature of the facts but with the intensity of my sensations. It may be, too, that I learned to love the sea for itself only at that time. Woman and the sea revealed themselves to me together, as it were: two mistresses of life's values. The illimitable greatness of the one, the unfathomable seduction of the other working their immemorial spells from generation to generation fell upon my heart at last: a common fortune, an unforgettable memory of the sea's formless might and of the sovereign charm in that woman's form wherein there seemed to beat the pulse of divinity rather than blood.

I begin here with the notes written at the end of that very day.

—Parted with Mills on the quay. We had walked side by side in absolute silence. The fact is he is too old for me to talk to him freely. For all his sympathy and seriousness I don't know what note to strike and I am not at all certain what he thinks of all this. As we shook hands at parting, I asked him how much longer he expected to stay. And he answered me that it depended on R. She was making arrangements for him to cross the frontier. He wanted to see the very ground on which the Principle of Legitimacy was actually asserting itself arms in hand. It sounded to my positive mind the most fantastic thing in the world, this elimination of personalities from what seemed but the merest political, dynastic adventure. So it wasn't Doña Rita, it wasn't Blunt, it wasn't the Pretender with his big infectious laugh, it wasn't all that lot of politicians, archbishops, and generals, of monks, guerrilleros, and smugglers by sea and land, of dubious agents and shady speculators and undoubted swindlers, who were pushing their fortunes at the risk of their precious skins. No. It was the Legitimist Principle asserting itself! Well, I would accept the view but with one reservation. All the others might have been merged into the idea, but I, the latest recruit, I would not be merged in the Legitimist Principle. Mine was an act of independent assertion. Never before had I felt so intensely aware of my personality. But I said nothing of that to Mills. I only told him I thought we had better not be seen very often together in the streets. He agreed. Hearty handshake. Looked affectionately after his broad back. It never occurred to him to turn his head. What was I in comparison with the Principle of Legitimacy?

Late that night I went in search of Dominic. That Mediterranean sailor was just the man I wanted. He had a great experience of all unlawful things that can be done on the seas and he brought to the practice of them much wisdom and audacity. That I didn't know where he lived was nothing since I knew where he loved. The proprietor of a small, quiet café on the quay, a certain Madame Léonore, a woman of thirty-five with an open Roman face and intelligent black eyes, had captivated his heart years ago. In that café with our heads close together over a marble table, Dominic and I held an earnest and endless confabulation while Madame Léonore, rustling a black silk skirt, with gold ear-rings, with her raven hair elaborately dressed and something nonchalant in her movements, would take occasion, in passing to and fro, to rest her hand for a moment on Dominic's shoulder. Later when the little café had emptied itself of its habitual customers, mostly people connected with the work of ships and cargoes, she came

quietly to sit at our table and looking at me very hard with
her black, sparkling eyes asked Dominic familiarly what had
happened to his Signorino. It was her name for me. I
was Dominic's Signorino. She knew me by no other; and
our connection has always been somewhat of a riddle to her.
She said that I was somehow changed since she saw me last.
In her rich voice she urged Dominic only to look at my eyes.
I must have had some piece of luck come to me either in
love or at cards, she bantered. But Dominic answered half
in scorn that I was not of the sort that runs after that kind
of luck. He stated generally that there were some young
gentlemen very clever in inventing new ways of getting rid of
their time and their money. However, if they needed a
sensible man to help them he had no objection himself to
lend a hand. Dominic's general scorn for the beliefs, and
activities, and abilities of upper-class people covered the
Principle of Legitimacy amply; but he could not resist the
opportunity to exercise his special faculties in a field he knew
of old. He had been a desperate smuggler in his younger
days. We settled the purchase of a fast sailing craft. Agreed
that it must be a balancelle and something altogether out
of the common. He knew of one suitable but she was in
Corsica. Offered to start for Bastia by mail-boat in the
morning. All the time the handsome and mature Madame
Léonore sat by, smiling faintly, amused at her great man
joining like this in a frolic of boys. She said the last words
of that evening: "You men never grow up," touching
lightly the grey hair above his temple.

A fortnight later.

. . . In the afternoon to the Prado. Beautiful day.
At the moment of ringing at the door a strong emotion
of an anxious kind. Why? Down the length of the dining-
room in the rotunda part full of afternoon light Doña R.,
sitting cross-legged on the divan in the attitude of a very
old idol or a very young child and surrounded by many
cushions, waves her hand from afar pleasantly surprised,
exclaiming: "What! Back already!" I give her all the
details and we talk for two hours across a large brass bowl

containing a little water placed between us, lighting cigarettes and dropping them, innumerable, puffed at, yet untasted in the overwhelming interest of the conversation. Found her very quick in taking the points and very intelligent in her suggestions. All formality soon vanished between us and before very long I discovered myself sitting cross-legged, too, while I held forth on the qualities of different Mediterranean sailing craft and on the romantic qualifications of Dominic for the task. I believe I gave her the whole history of the man, mentioning even the existence of Madame Léonore, since the little café would have to be the headquarters of the marine part of the plot.

She murmured, "*Ah! Une belle Romaine,*" thoughtfully. She told me that she liked to hear people of that sort spoken of in terms of our common humanity. She observed also that she wished to see Dominic some day; to set her eyes for once on a man who could be absolutely depended on. She wanted to know whether he had engaged himself in this adventure solely for my sake.

I said that no doubt it was partly that. We had been very close associates in the West Indies from where we had returned together, and he had a notion that I could be depended on, too. But mainly, I suppose, it was from taste. And there was in him also a fine carelessness as to what he did and a love of venturesome enterprise.

"And you," she said. "Is it carelessness, too?"

"In a measure," I said. "Within limits."

"And very soon you will get tired."

"When I do I will tell you. But I may also get frightened. I suppose you know there are risks, I mean apart from the risk of life."

"As for instance," she said.

"For instance, being captured, tried, and sentenced to what they call ' the galleys,' in Ceuta."

"And all this from that love for . . ."

"Not for Legitimacy," I interrupted the inquiry lightly. "But what's the use asking such questions? It's like asking the veiled figure of fate. It doesn't know its own mind nor its own heart. It has no heart. But what if I were to start asking you—who have a heart and are not veiled to my sight?" She dropped her charming adolescent head, so firm in modelling, so gentle in expression. Her uncovered neck was round like the shaft of a column. She wore the same wrapper of thick blue silk. At that time she seemed to live either in her riding habit or in that wrapper folded tightly round her and open low to a point in front. Because of the absence of all trimming round the neck and from the deep view of her bare arms in the wide sleeve this garment seemed to be put directly on her skin and gave one the impression of one's nearness to her body which would have been troubling but for the perfect unconsciousness of her manner. That day she carried no barbarous arrow in her hair. It was parted on one side, brushed back severely, and tied with a black ribbon, without any bronze mist about her forehead or temple. This smoothness added to the many varieties of her expression also that of child-like innocence.

Great progress in our intimacy brought about unconsciously by our enthusiastic interest in the matter of our discourse and, in the moments of silence, by the sympathetic current of our thoughts. And this rapidly growing familiarity (truly, she had a terrible gift for it) had all the varieties of earnestness : serious, excited, ardent, and even gay. She laughed in contralto ; but her laugh was never very long ; and when it had ceased, the silence of the room with the light dying in all its many windows seemed to lie about me warmed by its vibration.

As I was preparing to take my leave after a longish pause into which we had fallen as into a vague dream, she came out of it with a start and a quiet sigh. She said, " I had forgotten myself." I took her hand and was raising it naturally, without premeditation, when I felt suddenly the arm to which it belonged become insensible, passive, like a stuffed limb, and the whole woman go inanimate all over ! Brusquely I dropped the hand before it reached my lips ; and it was so lifeless that it fell heavily on to the divan.

I remained standing before her. She raised to me not

her eyes but her whole face, inquisitively—perhaps in appeal.

"No! This isn't good enough for me," I said.

The last of the light gleamed in her long enigmatic eyes as if they were precious enamel in that shadowy head which in its immobility suggested a creation of a distant past : immortal art, not transient life. Her voice had a profound quietness. She excused herself.

"It's only habit—or instinct—or what you like. I have had to practise that in self-defence lest I should be tempted sometimes to cut the arm off."

I remembered the way she had abandoned this very arm and hand to the white-haired ruffian. It rendered me gloomy and idiotically obstinate.

"Very ingenious. But this sort of thing is of no use to me," I declared.

"Make it up," suggested her mysterious voice, while her shadowy figure remained unmoved, indifferent amongst the cushions.

I didn't stir either. I refused in the same low tone.

"No. Not before you give it to me yourself, some day."

"Yes—some day," she repeated in a breath in which there was no irony but rather hesitation, reluctance—what did I know ?

I walked away from the house in a curious state of gloomy satisfaction with myself.

And this is the last extract. A month afterwards.

—This afternoon going up to the Villa I was for the first time accompanied in my way by some misgivings. To-morrow I sail.

First trip and therefore in the nature of a trial trip ; and I can't overcome a certain gnawing emotion, for it is a trip that *mustn't* fail. In that sort of enterprise there is no room for mistakes. Of all the individuals engaged in it will every one be intelligent enough, faithful enough, bold enough ? Looking upon them as a whole it seems impossible ; but as each has got only a limited part to play they may be

found sufficient each for his particular trust.    And will they
be all punctual, I wonder ?    An enterprise that hangs on
the punctuality of many people, no matter how well disposed
and even heroic, hangs on a thread.    This I have perceived
to be also the greatest of Dominic's concerns.    He, too,
wonders.    And when he breathes his doubts the smile lurking under the dark curl of his moustaches is not reassuring.

But there is also something exciting in such speculations
and the road to the Villa seemed to me shorter than ever
before.

Let in by the silent, ever-active, dark lady's maid, who
is always on the spot and always on the way somewhere
else, opening the door with one hand, while she passes on,
turning on one for a moment her quick, black eyes, which
just miss being lustrous, as if some one had breathed on
them lightly.

On entering the long room I perceive Mills established
in an armchair which he had dragged in front of the divan.
I do the same to another and there we sit side by side facing
R., tenderly amiable yet somehow distant among her
cushions, with an immemorial seriousness in her long, shaded
eyes and her fugitive smile hovering about but never settling
on her lips.    Mills, who is just back from over the frontier,
must have been asking R. whether she had been worried
again by her devoted friend with the white hair.    At least I
concluded so because I found them talking of the heart-
broken Azzolati.    And after having answered their greetings
I sit and listen to Rita addressing Mills earnestly.

" No, I assure you Azzolati had done nothing to me.    I
knew him.    He was a frequent visitor at the Pavilion, though
I, personally, never talked with him very much in Henry
Allègre's lifetime.    Other men were more interesting, and
he himself was rather reserved in his manner to me.    He was
an international politician and financier—a nobody.    He,
like many others, was admitted only to feed and amuse
Henry Allègre's scorn of the world, which was insatiable—
I tell you."

" Yes," said Mills.    " I can imagine."

"But I know. Often when we were alone Henry Allègre used to pour it into my ears. If ever anybody saw mankind stripped of its clothes as the child sees the king in the German fairy tale, it's I! Into my ears! A child's! Too young to die of fright. Certainly not old enough to understand—or even to believe. But then his arm was about me. I used to laugh, sometimes. Laugh! At this destruction —at these ruins!"

"Yes," said Mills, very steady before her fire. "But you have at your service the everlasting charm of life; you are a part of the indestructible."

"Am I? . . . But there is no arm about me now. The laugh! Where is my laugh? Give me back my laugh. . . ."

And she laughed a little on a low note. I don't know about Mills, but the subdued shadowy vibration of it echoed in my breast which felt empty for a moment and like a large space that makes one giddy.

"The laugh is gone out of my heart, which at any rate used to feel protected. That feeling's gone, too. And I myself will have to die some day."

"Certainly," said Mills in an unaltered voice. "As to this body you . . ."

"Oh, yes! Thanks. It's a very poor jest. Change from body to body as travellers used to change horses at post houses. I've heard of this before. . . ."

"I've no doubt you have." Mills put on a submissive air. "But are we to hear any more about Azzolati?"

"You shall. Listen. I had heard that he was invited to shoot at Rambouillet—a quiet party, not one of these great shoots. I hear a lot of things. I wanted to have a certain information, also certain hints conveyed to a diplomatic personage who was to be there, too. A personage that would never let me get in touch with him though I had tried many times."

"Incredible!" mocked Mills solemnly.

"The personage mistrusts his own susceptibility. Born cautious," explained Doña Rita crisply with the slightest possible quiver of her lips. "Suddenly I had the inspira-

tion to make use of Azzolati, who had been reminding me
by a constant stream of messages that he was an old friend.
I never took any notice of those pathetic appeals before.
But in this emergency I sat down and wrote a note asking
him to come and dine with me in my hotel. I suppose you
know I don't live in the Pavilion. I can't bear the Pavilion
now. When I have to go there I begin to feel after an
hour or so that it is haunted. I seem to catch sight of
somebody I know behind columns, passing through doorways, vanishing here and there. I hear light footsteps behind
closed doors. . . . My own ! "

Her eyes, her half-parted lips, remained fixed till Mills
suggested softly, " Yes, but Azzolati."

Her rigidity vanished like a flake of snow in the sunshine.
" Oh ! Azzolati. It was a most solemn affair. It had
occurred to me to make a very elaborate toilet. It was most
successful. Azzolati looked positively scared for a moment
as though he had got into the wrong suite of rooms. He
had never before seen me *en toilette*, you understand. In
the old days once out of my riding habit I would never dress.
I draped myself, you remember, Monsieur Mills. To go
about like that suited my indolence, my longing to feel free
in my body, as at that time when I used to herd goats. . . .
But never mind. My aim was to impress Azzolati. I
wanted to talk to him seriously."

There was something whimsical in the quick beat of her
eyelids and in the subtle quiver of her lips. " And behold !
the same notion had occurred to Azzolati. Imagine that
for this tête-à-tête dinner the creature had got himself up
as if for a reception at court. He displayed a brochette
of all sorts of decorations on the lapel of his *frac* and had a
broad ribbon of some order across his shirt front. An
orange ribbon. Bavarian, I should say. Great Roman
Catholic, Azzolati. It was always his ambition to be the
banker of all the Bourbons in the world. The last remnants
of his hair were dyed jet black and the ends of his moustache were like knitting needles. He was disposed to be as
soft as wax in my hands. Unfortunately I had had some

irritating interviews during the day. I was keeping down sudden impulses to smash a glass, throw a plate on the floor, do something violent to relieve my feelings. His submissive attitude made me still more nervous. He was ready to do anything in the world for me providing that I would promise him that he would never find my door shut against him as long as he lived. You understand the impudence of it, don't you? And his tone was positively abject, too. I snapped back at him that I had no door, that I was a nomad. He bowed ironically till his nose nearly touched his plate but begged me to remember that to his personal knowledge I had four houses of my own about the world. And you know this made me feel a homeless outcast more than ever—like a little dog lost in the street—not knowing where to go. I was ready to cry, and there the creature sat in front of me with an imbecile smile as much as to say 'here is a poser for you. . . .' I gnashed my teeth at him. Quietly, you know. . . . I suppose you two think that I am stupid."

She paused as if expecting an answer but we made no sound and she continued with a remark.

"I have days like that. Often one must listen to false protestations, empty words, strings of lies all day long, so that in the evening one is not fit for anything, not even for truth if it comes in one's way. That idiot treated me to a piece of brazen sincerity which I couldn't stand. First of all he began to take me into his confidence; he boasted of his great affairs, then started groaning about his overstrained life which left him no time for the amenities of existence, for beauty, or sentiment, or any sort of ease of heart. His heart! He wanted me to sympathize with his sorrows. Of course I ought to have listened. One must pay for service. Only I was nervous and tired. He bored me. I told him at last that I was surprised that a man of such immense wealth should still keep on going like this reaching for more and more. I suppose he must have been sipping a good deal of wine while we talked and all at once he let out an atrocity which was too much for me. He had been moaning and sentimentalizing but then suddenly he showed me his fangs. 'No,' he cries, 'you can't imagine what a satisfaction it is to feel all that penniless, beggarly lot of the dear, honest, meritorious poor wriggling and slobbering under one's boots.' You may tell me that he is a contemptible animal anyhow, but you should have heard the tone ! I felt my bare arms go cold like ice. A moment before I had been hot and faint with sheer boredom. I jumped up from the table, rang for Rose, and told her to bring me my fur cloak. He remained in his chair leering at me curiously. When I had the fur on my shoulders and the girl had gone out of the room I gave him the surprise of his life. 'Take yourself off instantly,' I said. 'Go trample on the poor if you like but never dare speak to me again.' At this he leaned his head on his arm and sat so long at the table shading his eyes with his hand that I had to ask, calmly—you know— whether he wanted me to have him turned out into the corridor. He fetched an enormous sigh. ' I have only tried to be honest with you, Rita.' But by the time he got to the door he had regained some of his impudence. 'You know how to trample on a poor fellow, too,' he said. ' But I don't mind being made to wriggle under your pretty shoes, Rita. I forgive you. I thought you were free from all vulgar sentimentalism and that you had a more independent mind. I was mistaken in you, that's all.' With that he pretends to dash a tear from his eye—crocodile !—and goes out, leaving me in my fur by the blazing fire, my teeth going like castanets. . . . Did you ever hear of anything so stupid as this affair ? " she concluded in a tone of extreme candour and a profound unreadable stare that went far beyond us both. And the stillness of her lips was so perfect directly she ceased speaking that I wondered whether all this had come through them or only had formed itself in my mind.

Presently she continued as if speaking for herself only. " It's like taking the lids off boxes and seeing ugly toads staring at you. In every one. Every one. That's what it is having to do with men more than mere—Good morning— Good evening. And if you try to avoid meddling with their lids, some of them will take them off themselves. And they don't even know, they don't even suspect what they are showing you. Certain confidences—they don't see it—are the bitterest kind of insult. I suppose Azzolati imagines himself a noble beast of prey. Just as some others imagine themselves to be most delicate, noble, and refined gentlemen. And as likely as not they would trade on a woman's troubles—and in the end make nothing of that either. Idiots!"

The utter absence of all anger in this spoken meditation gave it a character of touching simplicity. And as if it had been truly only a meditation we conducted ourselves as though we had not heard it. Mills began to speak of his experiences during his visit to the army of the Legitimist King. And I discovered in his speeches that this man of books could be graphic and picturesque. His admiration for the devotion and bravery of the army was combined with the greatest distaste for what he had seen of the way its great qualities were misused. In the conduct of this great enterprise he had seen a deplorable levity of outlook, a fatal lack of decision, an absence of any reasoned plan.

He shook his head.

"I feel that you of all people, Doña Rita, ought to be told the truth. I don't know exactly what you have at stake."

She was rosy like some impassive statue in a desert in the flush of the dawn.

"Not my heart," she said quietly. "You must believe that."

"I do. Perhaps it would have been better if you . . ."

"No, *Monsieur le Philosophe*. It would not have been better. Don't make that serious face at me," she went on with tenderness in a playful note, as if tenderness had been her inheritance of all time and playfulness the very fibre of her being. "I suppose you think that a woman who has acted as I did and has not staked her heart on it is . . . How do you know to what the heart responds as it beats from day to day?"

"I wouldn't judge you. What am I before the knowledge you were born to? You are as old as the world."

She accepted this with a smile. I who was innocently watching them was amazed to discover how much a fleeting thing like that could hold of seduction without the help of any other feature and with that unchanging glance.

"With me it is *pun d'onor*. To my first independent friend."

"You were soon parted," ventured Mills, while I sat still under a sense of oppression.

"Don't think for a moment that I have been scared off," she said. "It is they who were frightened. I suppose you heard a lot of Headquarters gossip?"

"Oh, yes," Mills said meaningly. "The fair and the dark are succeeding each other like leaves blown in the wind dancing in and out. I suppose you have noticed that leaves blown in the wind have a look of happiness."

"Yes," she said, "that sort of leaf is dead. Then why shouldn't it look happy? And so I suppose there is no uneasiness, no occasion for fears amongst the 'responsibles.'"

"Upon the whole not. Now and then a leaf seems as if it would stick. There is for instance Madame . . ."

"Oh, I don't want to know, I understand it all, I am as old as the world."

"Yes," said Mills thoughtfully, "you are not a leaf, you might have been a tornado yourself."

"Upon my word," she said, "there was a time that they thought I could carry him off, away from them all—beyond them all. Verily, I am not very proud of their fears. There was nothing reckless there worthy of a great passion. There was nothing sad there worthy of a great tenderness."

"And is *this* the word of the Venetian riddle?" asked Mills, fixing her with his keen eyes.

"If it pleases you to think so, Señor," she said indifferently. The movement of her eyes, their veiled gleam, became mischievous when she asked, "And Don Juan Blunt, have you seen him over there?"

"I fancy he avoided me. Moreover, he is always with his regiment at the outposts. He is a most valorous captain. I heard some people describe him as foolhardy."

"Oh, he needn't seek death," she said in an indefinable tone. "I mean as a refuge. There will be nothing in his life great enough for that."

"You are angry. You miss him, I believe, Doña Rita."

"Angry? No! Weary. But of course it's very inconvenient. I can't very well ride out alone. A solitary amazon swallowing the dust and the salt spray of the Corniche promenade would attract too much attention. And then I don't mind you two knowing that I am afraid of going out alone."

"Afraid?" we both exclaimed together.

"You men are extraordinary. Why do you want me to be courageous? Why shouldn't I be afraid? Is it because there is no one in the world to care what would happen to me?"

There was a deep-down vibration in her tone for the first time. We had not a word to say. And she added after a long silence:

"There is a very good reason. There is a danger."

With wonderful insight Mills affirmed at once:

"Something ugly."

She nodded slightly several times. Then Mills said with conviction:

"Ah! Then it can't be anything in yourself. And if so . . ."

I was moved to extravagant advice.

"You should come out with me to sea then. There may be some danger there but there's nothing ugly to fear."

She gave me a startled glance quite unusual with her, more than wonderful to me; and suddenly as though she had seen me for the first time she exclaimed in a tone of compunction:

"Oh! And there is this one, too! Why! Oh, why should he run his head into danger for those things that will all crumble into dust before long?"

I said: "*You* won't crumble into dust."

And Mills chimed in:

"That young enthusiast will always have his sea."

We were all standing up now. She kept her eyes on me, and repeated with a sort of whimsical enviousness:

"The sea! The violet sea—and he is longing to rejoin it! . . . At night! Under the stars! . . . A lovers' meeting," she went on, thrilling me from head to foot with those two words, accompanied by a wistful smile pointed by a suspicion of mockery. She turned away. "And you, Monsieur Mills?" she asked.

"I am going back to my books," he declared with a very serious face. "My adventure is over."

"Each one to his love," she bantered us gently. "Didn't I love books, too, at one time! They seemed to contain all wisdom and hold a magic power, too. Tell me, Monsieur Mills, have you found amongst them in some black-letter volume the power of foretelling a poor mortal's destiny, the power to look into the future? Anybody's future . . ." Mills shook his head. . . . "What, not even mine?" she coaxed as if she really believed in a magic power to be found in books.

Mills shook his head again. "No, I have not the power," he said. "I am no more a great magician, than you are a poor mortal. You have your ancient spells. You are as old as the world. Of us two it's you that are more fit to foretell the future of the poor mortals on whom you happen to cast your eyes."

At these words she cast her eyes down and in the moment of deep silence I watched the slight rising and falling of her breast. Then Mills pronounced distinctly:

"Good-bye, old Enchantress."

They shook hands cordially. "Good-bye, poor Magician," she said.

Mills made as if to speak but seemed to think better of it. Doña Rita returned my distant bow with a slight, charmingly ceremonious inclination of her body.

"*Bon voyage* and a happy return," she said formally.

I was following Mills through the door when I heard her voice behind us raised in recall:

"Oh, a moment . . . I forgot . . ."

I turned round. The call was for me, and I walked slowly back wondering what she could have forgotten. She waited in the middle of the room with lowered head, with a mute gleam in her deep blue eyes. When I was near enough she extended to me without a word her bare white arm and suddenly pressed the back of her hand against my lips. I was too startled to seize it with rapture. It detached itself from my lips and fell slowly by her side. We had made it up and there was nothing to say. She turned away to the window and I hurried out of the room.

# PART THREE

## I

It was on our return from that first trip that I took Dominic up to the Villa to be presented to Doña Rita. If she wanted to look on the embodiment of fidelity, resource, and courage, she could behold it all in that man. Apparently she was not disappointed. Neither was Dominic disappointed. During the half-hour's interview they got into touch with each other in a wonderful way as if they had some common and secret standpoint in life. Maybe it was their common lawlessness, and their knowledge of things as old as the world. Her seduction, his recklessness, were both simple, masterful and, in a sense, worthy of each other.

Dominic was, I won't say awed by this interview. No woman could awe Dominic. But he was, as it were, rendered thoughtful by it, like a man who had not so much an experience as a sort of revelation vouchsafed to him. Later, at sea, he used to refer to La Señora in a particular tone and I knew that henceforth his devotion was not for me alone. And I understood the inevitability of it extremely well. As to Doña Rita she, after Dominic left the room, had turned to me with animation and said : " But he is perfect, this man." Afterwards she often asked after him and used to refer to him in conversation. More than once she said to me : " One would like to put the care of one's personal safety into the hands of that man. He looks as if he simply couldn't fail one." I admitted that this was very true, especially at sea. Dominic couldn't fail. But at the same time I rather chaffed Rita on her preoccupation as to personal safety that so often cropped up in her talk.

" One would think you were a crowned head in a revolutionary world," I used to tell her.

" That would be different. One would be standing then for something, either worth or not worth dying for. One could even run away then and be done with it. But I can't run away unless I got out of my skin and left that behind. Don't you understand ? You are very stupid . . ." But she has the grace to add, " On purpose."

I don't know about the on purpose. I am not certain about the stupidity. Her words bewildered one often and bewilderment is a sort of stupidity. I remedied it by simply disregarding the sense of what she said. The sound was there and also her poignant heart-gripping presence giving occupation enough to one's faculties. In the power of those things over one there was mystery enough. It was more absorbing than the mere obscurity of her speeches. But I daresay she couldn't understand that.

Hence, at times, the amusing outbreaks of temper in word and gesture that only strengthened the natural, the invincible force of the spell. Sometimes the brass bowl would get upset or the cigarette box would fly up, dropping a shower of cigarettes on the floor. We would pick them up, re-establish everything, and fall into a long silence, so close that the sound of the first word would come with all the pain of a separation.

It was at that time, too, that she suggested I should take up my quarters in her house in the street of the Consuls. There were certain advantages in that move. In my present abode my sudden absences might have been in the long run subject to comment. On the other hand, the house in the street of Consuls was a known outpost of Legitimacy. But then it was covered by the occult influence of her who was referred to in confidential talks, secret communications, and discreet whispers of Royalist salons as : " Madame de Lastaola."

That was the name which the heiress of Henry Allègre had decided to adopt when, according to her own expression, she had found herself precipitated at a moment's notice into the crowd of mankind. It is strange how the death of Henry Allègre, which certainly the poor man had not planned, acquired in my view the character of a heartless desertion. It gave one a glimpse of amazing egoism in a sentiment to which one could hardly give a name, a mysterious appropriation of one human being by another as if in defiance of unexpressed things and for an unheard-of satisfaction of an inconceivable pride. If he had hated her he could not have flung that enormous fortune more brutally at her head. And his unrepentant death seemed to lift for a moment the curtain on something lofty and sinister like an Olympian's caprice.

Doña Rita said to me once with humorous resignation : "You know, it appears that one must have a name. That's what Henry Allègre's man of business told me. He was quite impatient with me about it. But my name, *amigo*, Henry Allègre had taken from me like all the rest of what I had been once. All that is buried with him in his grave. It wouldn't have been true. That is how I felt about it. So I took that one." She whispered to herself : "Lastaola," not as if to test the sound but as if in a dream.

To this day I am not quite certain whether it was the name of any human habitation, a lonely *caserio* with a half-effaced carving of a coat of arms over its door, or of some hamlet at the dead end of a ravine with a stony slope at the back. It might have been a hill for all I know or perhaps a stream. A wood, or perhaps a combination of all these : just a bit of the earth's surface. Once I asked her where exactly it was situated and she answered, waving her hand cavalierly at the dead wall of the room : "Oh, over there." I thought that this was all that I was going to hear but she added moodily, "I used to take my goats there, a dozen or so of them, for the day. From after my uncle had said his Mass till the ringing of the evening bell."

I saw suddenly the lonely spot, sketched for me some time ago by a few words from Mr. Blunt, populated by the agile, bearded beasts with cynical heads, and a little misty figure dark in the sunlight with a halo of dishevelled rust-coloured hair about its head.

T

The epithet of rust-coloured comes from her. It was really tawny. Once or twice in my hearing she had referred to " my rust-coloured hair " with laughing vexation. Even then it was unruly, abhorring the restraints of civilization, and often in the heat of a dispute getting into the eyes of Madame de Lastaola, the possessor of coveted art treasures, the heiress of Henry Allègre. She proceeded in a reminiscent mood, with a faint flash of gaiety all over her face, except her dark blue eyes that moved so seldom out of their fixed scrutiny of things invisible to other human beings.

" The goats were very good. We clambered amongst the stones together. They beat me at that game. I used to catch my hair in the bushes."

" Your rust-coloured hair," I whispered.

" Yes, it was always this colour. And I used to leave bits of my frock on thorns here and there. It was pretty thin, I can tell you. There wasn't much at that time between my skin and the blue of the sky. My legs were as sunburnt as my face ; but really I didn't tan very much. I had plenty of freckles though. There were no looking-glasses in the Presbytery but uncle had a piece not bigger than my two hands for his shaving. One Sunday I crept into his room and had a peep at myself. And wasn't I startled to see my own eyes looking at me ! But it was fascinating, too. I was about eleven years old then, and I was very friendly with the goats, and I was as shrill as a cicada and as slender as a match. Heavens ! When I overhear myself speaking sometimes, or look at my limbs, it doesn't seem to be possible. And yet it is the same one. I do remember every single goat. They were very clever. Goats are no trouble really ; they don't scatter much. Mine never did even if I had to hide myself out of their sight for ever so long."

It was but natural to ask her why she wanted to hide, and she uttered vaguely what was rather a comment on my question :

" It was like fate." But I chose to take it otherwise, teasingly, because we were often like a pair of children.

" Oh, really," I said, " you talk like a pagan. What

could you know of fate at that time? What was it like?
Did it come down from Heaven?"

"Don't be stupid. It used to come along a cart-track
that was there and it looked like a boy. Wasn't he a little
devil though. You understand, I couldn't know that.
He was a wealthy cousin of mine. Round there we are
all related, all cousins—as in Brittany. He wasn't much
bigger than myself but he was older, just a boy in blue
breeches and with good shoes on his feet, which of course
interested and impressed me. He yelled to me from below,
I screamed to him from above, he came up and sat down
near me on a stone, never said a word, let me look at him for
half an hour before he condescended to ask me who I was.
And the airs he gave himself! He quite intimidated me
sitting there perfectly dumb. I remember trying to hide
my bare feet under the edge of my skirt as I sat below him
on the ground.

"*C'est comique, eh!*" she interrupted herself to comment in a melancholy tone. I looked at her sympathetically
and she went on:

"He was the only son from a rich farmhouse two miles
down the slope. In winter they used to send him to school
at Tolosa. He had an enormous opinion of himself; he was
going to keep a shop in a town by and by and he was about
the most dissatisfied creature I have ever seen. He had an
unhappy mouth and unhappy eyes and he was always
wretched about something: about the treatment he received,
about being kept in the country and chained to work. He
was moaning and complaining and threatening all the world,
including his father and mother. He used to curse God,
yes, that boy, sitting there on a piece of rock like a wretched
little Prometheus with a sparrow pecking at his miserable
little liver. And the grand scenery of mountains all round,
ha, ha, ha!"

She laughed in contralto: a penetrating sound with
something generous in it; not infectious, but in others
provoking a smile.

"Of course I, poor little animal, I didn't know what to

make of it, and I was even a little frightened. But at first because of his miserable eyes I was sorry for him, almost as much as if he had been a sick goat. But, frightened or sorry, I don't know how it is, I always wanted to laugh at him, too, I mean from the very first day when he let me admire him for half an hour. Yes, even then I had to put my hand over my mouth more than once for the sake of good manners, you understand. And yet, you know, I was never a laughing child.

"One day he came up and sat down very dignified a little bit away from me and told me he had been thrashed for wandering in the hills.

"'To be with me?' I asked. And he said: 'To be with you! No. My people don't know what I do.' I can't tell why, but I was annoyed. So instead of raising a clamour of pity over him, which I suppose he expected me to do, I asked him if the thrashing hurt very much. He got up, he had a switch in his hand, and walked up to me, saying, 'I will soon show you.' I went stiff with fright; but instead of slashing at me he dropped down by my side and kissed me on the cheek. Then he did it again, and by that time I was gone dead all over and he could have done what he liked with the corpse but he left off suddenly and then I came to life again and I bolted away. Not very far. I couldn't leave the goats altogether. He chased me round and about the rocks, but of course I was too quick for him in his nice town boots. When he got tired of that game he started throwing stones. After that he made my life very lively for me. Sometimes he used to come on me unawares and then I had to sit still and listen to his miserable ravings, because he would catch me round the waist and hold me very tight. And yet I often felt inclined to laugh. But if I caught sight of him at a distance and tried to dodge out of the way he would start stoning me into a shelter I knew of and then sit outside with a heap of stones at hand so that I daren't show the end of my nose for hours. He would sit there and rave and abuse me till I would burst into a crazy laugh in my hole; and then I could see him

through the leaves rolling on the ground and biting his fists
with rage. Didn't he hate me! At the same time I was
often terrified. I am convinced now that if I had started
crying he would have rushed in and perhaps strangled me
there. Then as the sun was about to set he would make me
swear that I would marry him when I was grown up. ' Swear
you little wretched beggar,' he would yell to me. And I
would swear. I was hungry, and I didn't want to be made
black and blue all over with stones. Oh, I swore ever so
many times to be his wife. Thirty times a month for two
months. I couldn't help myself. It was no use complaining
to my sister Therese. When I showed her my bruises and
tried to tell her a little about my trouble she was quite
scandalized. She called me a sinful girl, a shameless creature.
I assure you it puzzled my head so that, between Therese
my sister and José the boy, I lived in a state of idiocy almost.
But luckily at the end of the two months they sent him away
from home for good. Curious story to happen to a goatherd
living all her days out under God's eye, as my uncle the Cura
might have said. My sister Therese was keeping house in
the Presbytery. She's a terrible person."

" I have heard of your sister Therese," I said.

" Oh, you have ! Of my big sister Therese, six, ten years
older than myself perhaps ? She just comes a little above
my shoulder, but then I was always a long thing. I never
knew my mother. I don't even know how she looked.
There are no paintings or photographs in our farmhouses
amongst the hills. I haven't even heard her described
to me. I believe I was never good enough to be told these
things. Therese decided that I was a lump of wickedness,
and now she believes that I will lose my soul altogether unless
I take some steps to save it. Well, I have no particular taste
that way. I suppose it is annoying to have a sister going fast
to eternal perdition, but there are compensations. The
funniest thing is that it's Therese, I believe, who managed
to keep me out of the Presbytery when I went out of my way
to look in on them on my return from my visit to the *Quartel
Real* last year. I couldn't have stayed much more than half

an hour with them anyway, but still I would have liked to get over the old doorstep. I am certain that Therese persuaded my uncle to go out and meet me at the bottom of the hill. I saw the old man a long way off and I understood how it was. I dismounted at once and met him on foot. We had half an hour together walking up and down the road. He is a peasant priest, he didn't know how to treat me. And of course I was uncomfortable, too. There wasn't a single goat about to keep me in countenance. I ought to have embraced him. I was always fond of the stern, simple old man. But he drew himself up when I approached him and actually took off his hat to me. So simple as that! I bowed my head and asked for his blessing. And he said: ' I would never refuse a blessing to a good Legitimist.' So stern as that! And when I think that I was perhaps the only girl of the family or in the whole world that he ever in his priest's life patted on the head! When I think of that! . . . I believe at that moment I was as wretched as he was himself. I handed him an envelope with a big red seal which quite startled him. I had asked the Marquis de Villarel to give me a few words for him, because my uncle has a great influence in his district; and the Marquis penned with his own hand some compliments and an inquiry about the spirit of the population. My uncle read the letter, looked up at me with an air of mournful awe, and begged me to tell his excellency that the people were all for God, their lawful King and their old privileges. I said to him then, after he had asked me about the health of His Majesty in an awfully gloomy tone—I said then : ' There is only one thing that remains for me to do, uncle, and that is to give you two pounds of the very best snuff I have brought here for you.' What else could I have got for the poor old man? I had no trunks with me. I had to leave behind a spare pair of shoes in the hotel to make room in my little bag for that snuff. And fancy! That old priest absolutely pushed the parcel away. I could have thrown it at his head; but I thought suddenly of that hard, prayerful life, knowing nothing of any ease or pleasure in the world, absolutely nothing but a pinch of snuff now and then. I remembered how wretched he used to be when he lacked a copper or two to get some snuff with. My face was hot with indignation, but before I could fly out at him I remembered how simple he was. So I said with great dignity that as the present came from the King and as he wouldn't receive it from my hand there was nothing else for me to do but to throw it into the brook ; and I made as if I were going to do it, too. He shouted : ' Stay, unhappy girl ! Is it really from His Majesty, whom God preserve ? ' I said contemptuously, ' Of course.' He looked at me with great pity in his eyes, sighed deeply, and took the little tin from my hand. I suppose he imagined me in my abandoned way wheedling the necessary cash out of the King for the purchase of that snuff. You can't imagine how simple he is. Nothing was easier than to deceive him ; but don't imagine I deceived him from the vainglory of a mere sinner. I lied to the dear man, simply because I couldn't bear the idea of him being deprived of the only gratification his big, ascetic, gaunt body ever knew on earth. As I mounted my mule to go away he murmured coldly : ' God guard you, Señora ! ' Señora ! What sternness ! We were off a little way already when his heart softened and he shouted after me in a terrible voice : ' The road to Heaven is repentance ! ' And then, after a silence, again the great shout ' Repentance ! ' thundered after me. Was that sternness or simplicity, I wonder ? Or a mere unmeaning superstition, a mechanical thing ? If there lives anybody completely honest in this world, surely it must be my uncle. And yet—who knows ?

" Would you guess what was the next thing I did ? Directly I got over the frontier I wrote from Bayonne asking the old man to send me out my sister here. I said it was for the service of the King. You see, I had thought suddenly of that house of mine in which you once spent the night talking with Mr. Mills and Don Juan Blunt. I thought it would do extremely well for Carlist officers coming this way on leave or on a mission. In hotels they might have been molested, but I knew that I could get protection for my house. Just a word from the ministry in Paris to the Prefect. But I wanted a woman to manage it for me. And where was I to find a trustworthy woman? How was I to know one when I saw her? I don't know how to talk to women. Of course my Rose would have done for me that or anything else; but what could I have done myself without her? She has looked after me from the first. It was Henry Allègre who got her for me eight years ago. I don't know whether he meant it for a kindness but she's the only human being on whom I can lean. She knows. . . . What doesn't she know about me! She has never failed to do the right thing for me unasked. I couldn't part with her. And I couldn't think of anybody else but my sister.

"After all it was somebody belonging to me. But it seemed the wildest idea. Yet she came at once. Of course I took care to send her some money. She likes money. As to my uncle there is nothing that he wouldn't have given up for the service of the King. Rose went to meet her at the railway station. She told me afterwards that there had been no need for me to be anxious about her recognizing Mademoiselle Therese. There was nobody else in the train that could be mistaken for her. I should think not! She had made for herself a dress of some brown stuff like a nun's habit and had a crooked stick and carried all her belongings tied up in a handkerchief. She looked like a pilgrim to a saint's shrine. Rose took her to the house. She asked when she saw it: 'And does this big place really belong to our Rita?' My maid of course said that it was mine. 'And how long did our Rita live here?'—'Madame has never seen it unless perhaps the outside, as far as I know. I believe Mr. Allègre lived here for some time when he was a young man.'—'The sinner that's dead?'—'Just so,' says Rose. You know nothing ever startles Rose. 'Well, his sins are gone with him,' said my sister, and began to make herself at home.

"Rose was going to stop with her for a week but on the third day she was back with me with the remark that Mlle. Therese knew her way about very well already and preferred to be left to herself. Some little time afterwards I went to see that sister of mine. The first thing she said to me, 'I wouldn't have recognized you, Rita,' and I said, 'What a funny dress you have, Therese, more fit for the portress of a convent than for this house.'—'Yes,' she said, ' and unless you give this house to me, Rita, I will go back to our country. I will have nothing to do with your life, Rita. Your life is no secret for me.'

" I was going from room to room and Therese was follow- ing me. ' I don't know that my life is a secret to anybody,' I said to her, ' but how do you know anything about it ?' And then she told me that it was through a cousin of ours, that horrid wretch of a boy, you know. He had finished his schooling and was a clerk in a Spanish commercial house of some kind, in Paris, and apparently had made it his business to write home whatever he could hear about me or ferret out from those relations of mine with whom I lived as a girl. I got suddenly very furious. I raged up and down the room (we were alone upstairs), and Therese scuttled away from me as far as the door. I heard her say to herself, ' It's the evil spirit in her that makes her like this.' She was absolutely convinced of that. She made the sign of the cross in the air to protect herself. I was quite astounded. And then I really couldn't help myself. I burst into a laugh. I laughed and laughed ; I really couldn't stop till Therese ran away. I went downstairs still laughing and found her in the hall with her face to the wall and her fingers in her ears kneeling in a corner. I had to pull her out by the shoulders from there. I don't think she was frightened ; she was only shocked. But I don't suppose her heart is desperately bad, because when I dropped into a chair feeling very tired she came and knelt in front of me and put her arms round my waist and entreated me to cast off from me my evil ways with the help of saints and priests. Quite a little programme for a reformed sinner. I got away at last. I left her sunk on her heels before the empty chair looking after me. ' I pray for you every night and morning, Rita,' she said.—'Oh, yes. I know you are a good sister,' I said to her. I was letting myself out when she called after me, ' And what about this house, Rita ?' I said to her, ' Oh, you may keep it till the day I reform and

T 2

enter a convent.' The last I saw of her she was still on her knees looking after me with her mouth open. I have seen her since several times, but our intercourse is, at any rate on her side, as of a frozen nun with some great lady. But I believe she really knows how to make men comfortable. Upon my word I think she likes to look after men. They don't seem to be such great sinners as women are. I think you could do worse than take up your quarters at number 10. She will no doubt develop a saintly sort of affection for you, too."

I don't know that the prospect of becoming a favourite of Doña Rita's peasant sister was very fascinating to me. If I went to live very willingly at No. 10 it was because everything connected with Doña Rita had for me a peculiar fascination. She had only passed through the house once as far as I knew ; but it was enough. She was one of those beings that leave a trace. I am not unreasonable—I mean for those that knew her. That is, I suppose, because she was so unforgettable. Let us remember the tragedy of Azzolati the ruthless, the ridiculous financier with a criminal soul (or shall we say heart) and facile tears. No wonder, then, that for me, who may flatter myself without undue vanity with being much finer than that grotesque international intriguer, the mere knowledge that Doña Rita had passed through the very rooms in which I was going to live between the strenuous times of the sea-expeditions, was enough to fill my inner being with a great content. Her glance, her darkly brilliant blue glance, had run over the walls of that room which most likely would be mine to slumber in. Behind me, somewhere near the door, Therese, the peasant sister, said in a funnily compassionate tone and in an amazingly landlady-of-a-boarding-house spirit of false persuasiveness :

"You will be very comfortable here, Señor. It is so peaceful here in the street. Sometimes one may think oneself in a village. It's only a hundred and twenty-five francs for the friends of the King. And I shall take such good care of you that your very heart will be able to rest."

## II

Doña Rita was curious to know how I got on with her peasant sister and all I could say in return for that inquiry was that the peasant sister was in her own way amiable. At this she clicked her tongue amusingly and repeated a remark she had made before : " She likes young men. The younger the better." The mere thought of those two women being sisters aroused one's wonder. Physically they were altogether of different design. It was also the difference between living tissue of glowing loveliness with a divine breath, and a hard hollow figure of baked clay.

Indeed Therese did somehow resemble an achievement, wonderful enough in its way, in unglazed earthenware. The only gleam perhaps that one could find on her was that of her teeth, which one used to get between her dull lips unexpectedly, startlingly, and a little inexplicably, because it was never associated with a smile. She smiled with compressed mouth. It was indeed difficult to conceive of those two birds coming from the same nest. And yet . . . Contrary to what generally happens, it was when one saw those two women together that one lost all belief in the possibility of their relationship near or far. It extended even to their common humanity. One, as it were, doubted it. If one of the two was representative, then the other was either something more or less than human. One wondered whether these two women belonged to the same scheme of creation. One was secretly amazed to see them standing together, speaking to each other, having words in common, understanding each other. And yet ! . . . Our psychological sense is the crudest of all ; we don't know, we don't perceive how superficial we are. The simplest shades escape us, the secret of changes, of relations. No, upon the whole, the only feature (and yet with enormous differences) which Therese had in common with her sister, as I told Doña Rita, was amiability.

" For, you know, you are a most amiable person yourself,"

I went on. " It's one of your characteristics, of course much more precious than in other people. You transmute the commonest traits into gold of your own; but after all there are no new names. You are amiable. You were most amiable to me when I first saw you."

" Really. I was not aware. Not specially . . ."

" I had never the presumption to think that it was special. Moreover, my head was in a whirl. I was lost in astonishment first of all at what I had been listening to all night. Your history, you know, a wonderful tale with a flavour of wine in it and wreathed in clouds, with that amazing decapitated, mutilated dummy of a woman lurking in a corner, and with Blunt's smile gleaming through a fog, the fog in my eyes, from Mills' pipe, you know. I was feeling quite inanimate as to body and frightfully stimulated as to mind all the time. I had never heard anything like that talk about you before. Of course I wasn't sleepy, but still I am not used to do altogether without sleep like Blunt . . ."

" Kept awake all night listening to my story ! " She marvelled.

" Yes. You don't think I am complaining, do you ? I wouldn't have missed it for the world. Blunt in a ragged old jacket and a white tie and that incisive polite voice of his seemed strange and weird. It seemed as though he were inventing it all rather angrily. I had doubts as to your existence."

" Mr. Blunt is very much interested in my story."

" Anybody would be," I said. " I was. I didn't sleep a wink. I was expecting to see you soon—and even then I had my doubts."

" As to my existence ? "

" It wasn't exactly that, though of course I couldn't tell that you weren't a product of Captain Blunt's sleeplessness. He seemed to dread exceedingly to be left alone and your story might have been a device to detain us . . ."

" He hasn't enough imagination for that," she said.

" It didn't occur to me. But there was Mills, who apparently believed in your existence. I could trust Mills.

en ck.
a New Yor
during the fir
rviving are his
two sons, Stephen

ther obituaries on preced

ut the propriety. I couldn't see any
g taken to see you. Strange that it
on with the sea which brought me here

pected perhaps."

No. I mean particularly strange and significant."

" Why ? "

" Because my friends are in the habit of telling me (and each other) that the sea is my only love. They were always chaffing me because they couldn't see or guess in my life at any woman, open or secret. . . ."

" And is that really so ? " she inquired negligently.

" Why, yes. I don't mean to say that I am like an innocent shepherd in one of those interminable stories of the eighteenth century. But I don't throw the word love about indiscriminately. It may be all true about the sea ; but some people would say that they love sausages."

" You are horrible."

" I am surprised."

" I mean your choice of words."

" And you have never uttered a word yet that didn't change into a pearl as it dropped from your lips. At least not before me."

She glanced down deliberately and said, " This is better. But I don't see any of them on the floor."

" It's you who are horrible in the implications of your language. Don't see any on the floor ! Haven't I caught up and treasured them all in my heart ? I am not the animal from which sausages are made."

She looked at me suavely and then with the sweetest possible smile breathed out the word : " No."

And we both laughed very loud. O ! days of innocence ! On this occasion we parted from each other on a light-hearted note. But already I had acquired the conviction that there was nothing more lovable in the world than that woman ; nothing more life-giving, inspiring, and illuminating than the emanation of her charm. I meant it absolutely —not excepting the light of the sun.

From this there was only one step further to take. The step into a conscious surrender; the open perception that this charm, warming like a flame, was also all-revealing like a great light; giving new depth to shades, new brilliance to colours, an amazing vividness to all sensations and vitality to all thoughts; so that all that had been lived before seemed to have been lived in a drab world and with a languid pulse.

A great revelation this. I don't mean to say it was soul-shaking. The soul was already a captive before doubt, anguish, or dismay could touch its surrender and its exaltation. But all the same the revelation turned many things into dust; and, amongst others, the sense of the careless freedom of my life. If that life ever had any purpose or any aim outside itself I would have said that it threw a shadow across its path. But it hadn't. There had been no path. But there was a shadow, the inseparable companion of all light. No illumination can sweep all mystery out of the world. After the departed darkness the shadows remain, more mysterious because as if more enduring; and one feels a dread of them from which one was free before. What if they were to be victorious at the last? They, or what perhaps lurks in them: fear, deception, desire, disillusion——all silent at first before the song of triumphant love vibrating in the light. Yes. Silent. Even desire itself! All silent. But not for long!

This was, I think, before the third expedition. Yes, it must have been the third, for I remember that it was boldly planned and that it was carried out without a hitch. The tentative period was over; all our arrangements had been perfected. There was, so to speak, always an unfailing smoke on the hill and an unfailing lantern on the shore. Our friends, mostly bought for hard cash and therefore valuable, had acquired confidence in us. This, they seemed to say, is no unfathomable roguery of penniless adventurers. This is but the reckless enterprise of men of wealth and sense and needn't be inquired into. The young *caballero* has got real gold pieces in the belt he wears next his skin; and the man with the heavy moustaches and unbelieving eyes is indeed very much of a man. They gave to Dominic all their respect and to me a great show of deference; for I had all the money, while they thought that Dominic had all the sense. That judgment was not exactly correct. I had my share of judgment and audacity which surprises me now that the years have chilled the blood without dimming the memory. I remember going about the business with a light-hearted, clear-headed recklessness which, according as its decisions were sudden or considered, made Dominic draw his breath through his clenched teeth, or look hard at me before he gave me either a slight nod of assent or a sarcastic " Oh, certainly "—just as the humour of the moment prompted him.

One night as we were lying on a bit of dry sand under the lee of a rock, side by side, watching the light of our little vessel dancing away at sea in the windy distance, Dominic spoke suddenly to me.

" I suppose Alphonso and Carlos, Carlos and Alphonso, they are nothing to you, together or separately ? "

I said : " Dominic, if they were both to vanish from the earth together or separately it would make no difference to my feelings."

He remarked : " Just so. A man mourns only for his friends. I suppose they are no more friends to you than they are to me. Those Carlists make a great consumption of cartridges. That is well. But why should we do all those mad things that you will insist on us doing till my hair," he pursued with grave, mocking exaggeration, " till my hair tries to stand up on my head ? and all for that Carlos, let God and the devil each guard his own, for that Majesty as they call him, but after all a man like another and—no friend."

" Yes, why ? " I murmured, feeling my body nestled at ease in the sand.

It was very dark under the overhanging rock on that night of clouds and of wind that died and rose and died again. Dominic's voice was heard speaking low between the short gusts.

" Friend of the Señora, eh ? "

" That's what the world says, Dominic."

"Half of what the world says are lies," he pronounced dogmatically. "For all his majesty he may be a good enough man. Yet he is only a king in the mountains and to-morrow he may be no more than you. Still a woman like that—one, somehow, would grudge her to a better king. She ought to be set up on a high pillar for people that walk on the ground to raise their eyes up to. But you are otherwise, you gentlemen. You, for instance, Monsieur, you wouldn't want to see her set up on a pillar."

"That sort of thing, Dominic," I said, "that sort of thing, you understand me, ought to be done early."

He was silent for a time. And then his manly voice was heard in the shadow of the rock.

"I see well enough what you mean. I spoke of the multitude, that only raise their eyes. But for kings and suchlike that is not enough. Well, no heart need despair; for there is not a woman that wouldn't at some time or other get down from her pillar for no bigger bribe perhaps than just a flower which is fresh to-day and withered to-morrow. And then, what's the good of asking how long any woman has been up there? There is a true saying that lips that have been kissed do not lose their freshness."

I don't know what answer I could have made. I imagine Dominic thought himself unanswerable. As a matter of fact, before I could speak, a voice came to us down the face of the rock crying secretly, "Olà, down there! All is safe ashore."

It was the boy who used to hang about the stable of a muleteer's inn in a little shallow valley with a shallow little stream in it, and where we had been hiding most of the day before coming down to the shore. We both started to our feet and Dominic said, "A good boy that. You didn't hear him either come or go above our heads. Don't reward him with more than one peseta, Señor, whatever he does. If you were to give him two he would go mad at the sight of so much wealth and throw up his job at the Fonda, where he is so useful to run errands, in that way he has of skimming along the paths without displacing a stone."

Meantime he was busying himself with striking a fire to set alight a small heap of dry sticks he had made ready beforehand on that spot which in all the circuit of the Bay was perfectly screened from observation from the land side.

The clear flame shooting up revealed him in the black cloak with a hood of a Mediterranean sailor. His eyes watched the dancing dim light to seaward. And he talked the while.

"The only fault you have, Señor, is being too generous with your money. In this world you must give sparingly. The only things you may deal out without counting, in this life of ours which is but a little fight and a little love, is blows to your enemy and kisses to a woman. . . . Ah! here they are coming in."

I noticed the dancing light in the dark west much closer to the shore now. Its motion had altered. It swayed slowly as it ran towards us, and, suddenly, the darker shadow as of a great pointed wing appeared gliding in the night. Under it a human voice shouted something confidently.

"*Bueno*," muttered Dominic. From some receptacle I didn't see he poured a lot of water on the blaze, like a magician at the end of a successful incantation that had called out a shadow and a voice from the immense space of the sea. And his hooded figure vanished from my sight in a great hiss and the warm feel of ascending steam.

"That's all over," he said, "and now we go back for more work, more toil, more trouble, more exertion with hands and feet, for hours and hours. And all the time the head turned over the shoulder, too."

We were climbing a precipitous path sufficiently dangerous in the dark, Dominic, more familiar with it, going first and I scrambling close behind in order that I might grab at his cloak if I chanced to slip or miss my footing. I remonstrated against this arrangement as we stopped to rest. I had no doubt I would grab at his cloak if I felt myself falling. I couldn't help doing that. But I would probably only drag him down with me.

With one hand grasping a shadowy bush above his head, he

growled that all this was possible, but that it was all in the bargain, and urged me onwards.

When we got on to the level that man whose even breathing no exertion, no danger, no fear or anger could disturb, remarked as we strode side by side :

" I will say this for us, that we are carrying out all this deadly foolishness as conscientiously as though the eyes of the Señora were on us all the time.   And as to risk, I suppose we take more than she would approve of, I fancy, if she ever gave a moment's thought to us out here.   Now, for instance, in the next half hour, we may come any moment on three carabineers who would let off  their pieces without asking questions.   Even your way of flinging money about cannot make safety for men set in defying a whole big country for the sake of—what is it exactly ?—the blue eyes, or the white arms of the Señora."

He kept his voice equably low.   It was a lonely spot and but for a vague shape of a dwarf tree here and there we had only the flying clouds for company.   Very far off a tiny light twinkled a little way up the seaward shoulder of an invisible mountain.   Dominic moved on.

" Fancy yourself lying here, on this wild spot, with a leg smashed by a shot or perhaps with a bullet in your side.   It might happen.   A star might fall.   I have watched stars falling in scores on clear nights in the Atlantic.   And it was nothing.   The flash of a pinch of gunpowder in your face may be a bigger matter.   Yet somehow it's pleasant as we stumble in the dark to think of our Señora in that long room with a shiny floor and all that lot of glass at the end, sitting on that divan, you call it, covered with carpets as if expecting a king indeed.   And very still . . ."

He remembered her—whose image could not be dismissed. I laid my hand on his shoulder.

" That light on the mountain side flickers exceedingly, Dominic.   Are we in the path ? "

He addressed me then in French, which was between us the language of more formal moments

" *Prenez mon bras, monsieur*.   Take a firm hold, or I will have you stumbling again and falling into one of those beastly holes, with a good chance to crack your head. And there is no need to take offence. For, speaking with all respect, why should you, and I with you, be here on this lonely spot, barking our shins in the dark on the way to a confounded flickering light where there will be no other supper but a piece of a stale sausage and a draught of leathery wine out of a stinking skin ? Pah ! "

I had good hold of his arm. Suddenly he dropped the formal French and pronounced in his inflexible voice :

" For a pair of white arms, Señor. *Bueno.*"

He could understand.


### III

On our return from that expedition we came gliding into the old harbour so late that Dominic and I, making for the café kept by Madame Léonore, found it empty of customers, except for two rather sinister fellows playing cards together at a corner table near the door. The first thing done by Madame Léonore was to put her hands on Dominic's shoulders and look at arm's length into the eyes of that man of audacious deeds and wild stratagems who smiled straight at her from under his heavy and, at that time, uncurled moustaches.

Indeed we didn't present a neat appearance, our faces unshaven, with the traces of dried salt sprays on our smarting skins and the sleeplessness of full forty hours filming our eyes. At least it was so with me who saw as through a mist Madame Léonore moving with her mature nonchalant grace, setting before us wine and glasses with a faint swish of her ample black skirt. Under the elaborate structure of black hair her jet-black eyes sparkled like good-humoured stars and even I could see that she was tremendously excited at having this lawless wanderer Dominic within her reach and as it were in her power. Presently she sat down by us, touched lightly Dominic's curly head silvered on the temples (she couldn't really help it), gazed at me for a while with a quizzical smile, observed that I looked very tired, and asked Dominic whether for all that I was likely to sleep soundly to-night.

" I don't know," said Dominic. " He's young. And there is always the chance of dreams."

" What do you men dream of in those little barques of yours tossing for months on the water ? "

" Mostly of nothing," said Dominic. " But it has happened to me to dream of furious fights."

" And of furious loves, too, no doubt," she caught him up in a mocking voice.

" No, that's for the waking hours," Dominic drawled, basking sleepily with his head between his hands in her ardent gaze. " The waking hours are longer."

" They must be, at sea," she said, never taking her eyes off him. " But I suppose you do talk of your loves sometimes."

" You may be sure, Madame Léonore," I interjected, noticing the hoarseness of my voice, " that you at any rate are talked about a lot at sea."

" I am not so sure of that now. There is that strange lady from the Prado that you took him to see, Signorino. She went to his head like a glass of wine into a tender youngster's. He is such a child, and I suppose that I am another. Shame to confess it, the other morning I got a friend to look after the café for a couple of hours, wrapped up my head, and walked out there to the other end of the town. . . . Look at these two sitting up ! And I thought they were so sleepy and tired, the poor fellows ! "

She kept our curiosity in suspense for a moment.

" Well, I have seen your marvel, Dominic," she continued in a calm voice. " She came flying out of the gate on horseback and it would have been all I would have seen of her if—and this is for you, Signorino—if she hadn't pulled up in the main alley to wait for a very good-looking cavalier. He had his moustaches so, and his teeth were very white when he smiled at her. But his eyes are too deep in his head for my taste. I didn't like it. It reminded me of a certain very severe priest who used to come to our village when I was young; younger even than your marvel, Dominic."

"It was no priest in disguise, Madame Léonore," I said, amused by her expression of disgust. "That's an American."

"Ah! *Un Americano!* Well, never mind him. It was her that I went to see."

"What! Walked to the other end of the town to see Doña Rita!" Dominic addressed her in a low bantering tone. "Why, you were always telling me you couldn't walk further than the end of the quay to save your life— or even mine, you said."

"Well, I did; and I walked back again and between the two walks, I had a good look. And you may be sure—that will surprise you both—that on the way back—oh, Santa Madre, wasn't it a long way, too—I wasn't thinking of any man at sea or on shore in that connection."

"No. And you were not thinking of yourself, either, I suppose," I said. Speaking was a matter of great effort for me, whether I was too tired or too sleepy, I can't tell. "No, you were not thinking of yourself. You were thinking of a woman, though."

"*Si.* As much a woman as any of us that ever breathed in the world. Yes, of her! Of that very one! You see, we women are not like you men, indifferent to each other unless by some exception. Men say we are always against one another but that's only men's conceit. What can she be to me? I am not afraid of the big child here," and she tapped Dominic's forearm on which he rested his head with a fascinated stare. "With us two it is for life and death, and I am rather pleased that there is something yet in him that can catch fire on occasion. I would have thought less of him if he hadn't been able to get out of hand a little, for something really fine. As for you, Signorino," she turned on me with an unexpected and sarcastic sally, "I am not in love with you yet." She changed her tone from sarcasm to a soft and even dreamy note. "A head like a gem," went on that woman born in some by-street of Rome, and a plaything for years of God knows what obscure fates. "Yes, Dominic! *Antica.* I haven't been haunted by a face since—since I was sixteen years old. It was the face of a young cavalier in the street. He was on horseback, too. He never looked at me, I never saw him again, and I loved him for—for days and days and days. That was the sort of face he had. And her face is of the same sort. She had a man's hat, too, on her head. So high!"

"A man's hat on her head," remarked with profound displeasure Dominic, to whom this wonder, at least, of all the wonders of the earth, was apparently unknown.

"*Si.* And her face has haunted me. Not so long as that other but more touchingly because I am no longer sixteen and this is a woman. Yes, I did think of her. I myself was once that age and I, too, had a face of my own to show to the world, though not so superb. And I, too, didn't know why I had come into the world any more than she does."

"And now you know," Dominic growled softly, with his head still between his hands.

She looked at him for a long time, opened her lips but in the end only sighed lightly.

"And what do you know of her, you who have seen her so well as to be haunted by her face?" I asked.

I wouldn't have been surprised if she had answered me with another sigh. For she seemed only to be thinking of herself and looked not in my direction. But suddenly she roused up.

"Of her?" she repeated in a louder voice. "Why should I talk of another woman? And then she is a great lady."

At this I could not repress a smile which she detected at once.

"Isn't she? Well, no, perhaps she isn't; but you may be sure of one thing, that she is both flesh and shadow more than any one that I have seen. Keep that well in your mind: She is for no man! She would be vanishing out of their hands like water that cannot be held."

I caught my breath. "Inconstant," I whispered.

"I don't say that. Maybe too proud, too wilful, too full of pity. Signorino, you don't know much about women. And you may learn something yet or you may not; but what you learn from her you will never forget."

"Not to be held," I murmured; and she whom the quayside called Madame Léonore closed her outstretched hand before my face and opened it at once to show its emptiness in illustration of her expressed opinion. Dominic never moved.

I wished good-night to these two and left the café for the fresh air and the dark spaciousness of the quays augmented by all the width of the old Port where between the trails of light the shadows of heavy hulls appeared very black, merging their outlines in a great confusion. I left behind me the end of the Cannebière, a wide vista of tall houses and much-lighted pavements losing itself in the distance with an extinction of both shapes and lights. I slunk past it with only a side glance and sought the dimness of quiet streets away from the centre of the usual night gaieties of the town. The dress I wore was just that of a sailor come ashore from some coaster, a thick blue woollen shirt or rather a sort of jumper with a knitted cap like a tam-o'-shanter worn very much on one side and with a red tuft of wool in the centre. This was even the reason why I had lingered so long in the café. I didn't want to be recognized in the streets in that costume and still less to be seen entering the house in the street of the Consuls. At that hour when the performances were over and all the sensible citizens in their beds I didn't hesitate to cross the Place of the Opera. It was dark, the audience had already dispersed. The rare passers-by I met hurrying on their last affairs of the day paid no attention to me at all. The street of the Consuls I expected to find empty, as usual at that time of the night. But as I turned a corner into it I overtook three people who must have belonged to the locality. To me, somehow, they appeared strange. Two girls in dark cloaks walked ahead of a tall man in a top hat. I slowed down, not wishing to pass them by, the more so that the door of the house was only a few yards distant. But to my intense surprise those people stopped at it and the man in the top hat, producing a latchkey, let his two companions through, followed them, and with a heavy slam cut himself off from my astonished self and the rest of mankind.

In the stupid way people have I stood and meditated on the sight, before it occurred to me that this was the most useless thing to do. After waiting a little longer to let the others get away from the hall I entered in my turn. The small gas-jet seemed not to have been touched ever since that distant night when Mills and I trod the black-and-white marble hall for the first time on the heels of Captain Blunt— who lived by his sword. And in the dimness and solitude which kept no more trace of the three strangers than if they had been the merest ghosts I seemed to hear the ghostly murmur, " *Américain, Catholique et gentilhomme. Amer . . .*" Unseen by human eye I ran up the flight of steps swiftly and on the first floor stepped into my sitting-room of which the door was open . . . " *et gentilhomme.*" I tugged at the bell pull and somewhere down below a bell rang as unexpected for Therese as a call from a ghost.

I had no notion whether Therese could hear me. I seemed to remember that she slept in any bed that happened to be vacant. For all I knew she might have been asleep in mine. As I had no matches on me I waited for a while in the dark. The house was perfectly still. Suddenly without the slightest preliminary sound light fell into the room and Therese stood in the open door with a candlestick in her hand.

She had on her peasant brown skirt. The rest of her was concealed in a black shawl which covered her head, her shoulders, arms, and elbows completely, down to her waist. The hand holding the candle protruded from that envelope which the other invisible hand clasped together under her very chin. And her face looked like a face in a painting. She said at once :

" You startled me, my young Monsieur."

She addressed me most frequently in that way as though she liked the very word " young." Her manner was certainly peasant-like with a sort of plaint in the voice, while the face was that of a serving Sister in some small and rustic convent.

"I meant to do it," I said. "I am a very bad person."

"The young are always full of fun," she said as if she were gloating over the idea. "It is very pleasant."

"But you are very brave," I chaffed her, "for you didn't expect a ring, and after all it might have been the devil who pulled the bell."

"It might have been. But a poor girl like me is not afraid of the devil. I have a pure heart. I have been to confession last evening. No. But it might have been an assassin that pulled the bell ready to kill a poor harmless woman. This is a very lonely street. What could prevent you to kill me now and then walk out again free as air?"

While she was talking like this she had lighted the gas and with the last words she glided through the bedroom door leaving me thunderstruck at the unexpected character of her thoughts.

I couldn't know that there had been during my absence a case of atrocious murder which had affected the imagination of the whole town; and though Therese did not read the papers (which she imagined to be full of impieties and immoralities invented by godless men) yet if she spoke at all with her kind, which she must have done at least in shops, she could not have helped hearing of it. It seems that for some days people could talk of nothing else. She returned gliding from the bedroom hermetically sealed in her black shawl just as she had gone in, with the protruding hand holding the lighted candle and relieved my perplexity as to her morbid turn of mind by telling me something of the murder story in a strange tone of indifference even while referring to its most horrible features. "That's what carnal sin (*pêché de chair*) leads to," she commented severely and passed her tongue over her thin lips. "And then the devil furnishes the occasion."

"I can't imagine the devil inciting me to murder you, Therese," I said, "and I didn't like that ready way you took me for an example, as it were. I suppose pretty near every lodger might be a potential murderer, but I expected to be made an exception."

With the candle held a little below her face, with that face of one tone and without relief she looked more than ever as though she had come out of an old, cracked, smoky painting, the subject of which was altogether beyond human conception. And she only compressed her lips.

"All right," I said, making myself comfortable on a sofa after pulling off my boots. "I suppose any one is liable to commit murder all of a sudden. Well, have you got many murderers in the house?"

"Yes," she said, "it's pretty good. Upstairs and down-stairs," she sighed. "God sees to it."

"And by the by, who is that grey-headed murderer in a tall hat whom I saw shepherding two girls into this house?"

She put on a candid air in which one could detect a little of her peasant cunning.

"Oh, yes. They are two dancing girls at the Opera, sisters, as different from each other as I and our poor Rita. But they are both virtuous and that gentleman, their father, is very severe with them. Very severe indeed, poor mother-less things. And it seems to be such a sinful occupation."

"I bet you make them pay a big rent, Therese. With an occupation like that . . ."

She looked at me with eyes of invincible innocence and began to glide towards the door, so smoothly that the flame of the candle hardly swayed. "Good-night," she murmured.

"Good-night, Mademoiselle."

Then in the very doorway she turned right round as a marionette would turn.

"Oh, you ought to know, my dear young Monsieur, that Mr. Blunt, the dear handsome man, has arrived from Navarre three days ago or more. Oh," she added with a priceless air of compunction, "he is such a charming gentleman."

And the door shut after her.

## IV

THAT night I passed in a state, mostly open-eyed, I believe, but always on the border between dreams and waking. The only thing absolutely absent from it was the feeling of rest. The usual sufferings of a youth in love had nothing to do with it. I could leave her, go away from her, remain away from her, without an added pang or any augmented consciousness of that torturing sentiment of distance so acute that often it ends by wearing itself out in a few days. Far or near was all one to me, as if one could never get any further but also never any nearer to her secret : the state like that of some strange wild faiths that get hold of mankind with the cruel mystic grip of unattainable perfection, robbing them of both liberty and felicity on earth.  A faith presents one with some hope, though.  But I had no hope, and not even desire as a thing outside myself, that would come and go, exhaust or excite.  It was in me just like life was in me; that life of which a popular saying affirms that " it is sweet." For the general wisdom of mankind will always stop short on the limit of the formidable.

What is best in a state of brimful, equable suffering is that it does away with the gnawings of petty sensations. Too far gone to be sensible to hope and desire I was spared the inferior pangs of elation and impatience.  Hours with her or hours without her were all alike, all in her possession ! But still there are shades and I will admit that the hours of that morning were perhaps a little more difficult to get through than the others.  I had sent word of my arrival of course.  I had written a note.  I had rung the bell.  Therese had appeared herself in her brown garb and as monachal as ever.  I had said to her :

" Have this sent off at once."

She had gazed at the addressed envelope, smiled (I was looking up at her from my desk), and at last took it up with an effort of sanctimonious repugnance.  But she remained with it in her hand looking at me as though she were piously gloating over something she could read in my face.

"Oh, that Rita, that Rita," she murmured. "And you too! Why are you trying, you, too, like the others, to stand between her and the mercy of God? What's the good of all this to you? And you such a nice, dear, young gentleman. For no earthly good only making all the kind saints in heaven angry, and our mother ashamed in her place amongst the blessed."

"Mademoiselle Therese," I said, "*vous êtes folle.*"

I believed she was crazy. She was cunning, too. I added an imperious: "*Allez,*" and with a strange docility she glided out without another word. All I had to do then was to get dressed and wait till eleven o'clock.

The hour struck at last. If I could have plunged into a light wave and been transported instantaneously to Doña Rita's door it would no doubt have saved me an infinity of pangs too complex for analysis; but as this was impossible I elected to walk from end to end of that long way. My emotions and sensations were childlike and chaotic inasmuch that they were very intense and primitive, and that I lay very helpless in their unrelaxing grasp. If one could have kept a record of one's physical sensations it would have been a fine collection of absurdities and contradictions. Hardly touching the ground and yet leaden-footed; with a sinking heart and an excited brain; hot and trembling with a secret faintness, and yet as firm as a rock and with a sort of indifference to it all, I did reach the door which was frightfully like any other commonplace door, but at the same time had a fateful character: a few planks put together—and an awful symbol; not to be approached without awe—and yet coming open in the ordinary way to the ring of the bell.

It came open. Oh, yes, very much as usual. But in the ordinary course of events the first sight in the hall should have been the back of the ubiquitous, busy, silent maid hurrying off and already distant. But not at all! She actually waited for me to enter. I was extremely taken aback and I believe spoke to her for the first time in my life.

" *Bonjour*, Rose."

She dropped her dark eyelids over those eyes that ought to have been lustrous but were not, as if somebody had breathed on them the first thing in the morning. She was a girl without smiles. She shut the door after me, and not only did that but in the incredible idleness of that morning she, who had never a moment to spare, started helping me off with my overcoat. It was positively embarrassing from its novelty. While busying herself with those trifles she murmured without any marked intention :

" Captain Blunt is with Madame."

This didn't exactly surprise me. I knew he had come up to town ; I only happened to have forgotten his existence for the moment. I looked at the girl also without any particular intention. But she arrested my movement towards the dining-room door by a low, hurried, if perfectly unemotional appeal :

" Monsieur George ! "

That of course was not my name. It served me then as it will serve for this story. In all sorts of strange places I was alluded to as " that young gentleman they call Monsieur George." Orders came from " Monsieur George " to men who nodded knowingly. Events pivoted about " Monsieur George." I haven't the slightest doubt that in the dark and tortuous streets of the old Town there were fingers pointed at my back : there goes " Monsieur George." I had been introduced discreetly to several considerable persons as " Monsieur George." I had learned to answer to the name quite naturally ; and to simplify matters I was also " Monsieur George " in the street of the Consuls and in the Villa on the Prado. I verily believe that at that time I had the feeling that the name of George really belonged to me. I waited for what the girl had to say. I had to wait some time, though during that silence she gave no sign of distress or agitation. It was for her obviously a moment of reflection. Her lips were compressed a little in a characteristic, capable manner. I looked at her with a friendliness I really felt towards her slight, unattractive, and dependable person.

" Well," I said at last, rather amused by this mental hesitation. I never took it for anything else. I was sure it was not distrust. She appreciated men and things and events solely in relation to Doña Rita's welfare and safety. And as to that I believed myself above suspicion. At last she spoke.

" Madame is not happy." This information was given to me not emotionally but as it were officially. It hadn't even a tone of warning. A mere statement. Without waiting to see the effect she opened the dining-room door, not to announce my name in the usual way but to go in and shut it behind her. In that short moment I heard no voices inside. Not a sound reached me while the door remained shut ; but in a few seconds it came open again and Rose stood aside to let me pass.

Then I heard something : Doña Rita's voice raised a little on an impatient note (a very, very rare thing) finishing some phrase of protest with the words :

" . . . Of no consequence."

I heard them as I would have heard any other words, for she had that kind of voice which carries a long distance. But the maid's statement occupied all my mind. " Madame *n'est pas heureuse.*" It had a dreadful precision. . . . " Not happy . . ." This unhappiness had almost a concrete form—something resembling a horrid bat. I was tired, excited, and generally overwrought. My head felt empty. What were the appearances of unhappiness ? I was still naïve enough to associate them with tears, lamentations, extraordinary attitudes of the body and some sort of facial distortion, all very dreadful to behold. I didn't know what I should see ; but in what I did see there was nothing startling, at any rate from that nursery point of view which apparently I had not yet outgrown.

With immense relief the apprehensive child within me beheld Captain Blunt warming his back at the more distant of the two fireplaces ; and as to Doña Rita there was nothing extraordinary in her attitude either, except perhaps that her hair was all loose about her shoulders. I hadn't the slightest doubt they had been riding together that morning, but she, with her impatience of all costume (and yet she could dress herself admirably and wore her dresses triumphantly), had divested herself of her riding habit and sat cross-legged enfolded in that ample blue robe like a young savage chieftain in a blanket. It covered her very feet. And before the normal fixity of her enigmatical eyes the smoke of the cigarette ascended ceremonially, straight up, in a slender shiral.

"How are you," was the greeting of Captain Blunt with the usual smile which would have been more amiable if his teeth hadn't been, just then, clenched quite so tight. How he managed to force his voice through that shining barrier I could never understand. Doña Rita tapped the couch engagingly by her side but I sat down instead in the armchair nearly opposite her, which, I imagine, must have been just vacated by Blunt. She inquired with that particular gleam of the eyes in which there was something immemorial and gay:

"Well?"

"Perfect success."

"I could hug you."

At any time her lips moved very little but in this instance the intense whisper of these words seemed to form itself right in my very heart; not as a conveyed sound but as an imparted emotion vibrating there with an awful intimacy of delight. And yet it left my heart heavy.

"Oh, yes, for joy," I said bitterly but very low; "for your Royalist, Legitimist, joy." Then with that trick of very precise politeness which I must have caught from Mr. Blunt I added:

"I don't want to be embraced—for the King."

And I might have stopped there. But I didn't. With a perversity which should be forgiven to those who suffer night and day and are as if drunk with an exalted unhappiness, I went on: "For the sake of an old cast-off glove; for I suppose a disdained love is not much more than a soiled flabby thing that finds itself on a private rubbish heap because it has missed the fire."

She listened to me unreadable, unmoved, narrowed eyes, closed lips, slightly flushed face, as if carved six thousand years ago in order to fix for ever that something secret and obscure which is in all women.    Not the gross immobility of a Sphinx proposing roadside riddles but the finer immobility, almost sacred, of a fateful figure seated at the very source of the passions that have moved men from the dawn of ages.

Captain Blunt, with his elbow on the high mantelpiece, had turned away a little from us and his attitude expressed excellently the detachment of a man who does not want to hear.    As a matter of fact, I don't suppose he could have heard.    He was too far away, our voices were too contained.    Moreover, he didn't want to hear.    There could be no doubt about it; but she addressed him unexpectedly.

"As I was saying to you, Don Juan, I have the greatest difficulty in getting myself, I won't say understood, but simply believed."

No pose of detachment could avail against the warm waves of that voice.    He had to hear.    After a moment he altered his position as it were reluctantly, to answer her.

"That's a difficulty that women generally have."

"Yet I have always spoken the truth."

"All women speak the truth," said Blunt imperturbably. And this annoyed her.

"Where are the men I have deceived?" she cried.

"Yes, where?" said Blunt in a tone of alacrity as though he had been ready to go out and look for them outside.

"No!    But show me one.    I say—where is he?"

He threw his affectation of detachment to the winds, moved his shoulders slightly, very slightly made a step nearer to the couch, and looked down on her with an expression of amused courtesy.

"Oh, I don't know.    Probably nowhere.    But if such a man could be found I am certain he would turn out a very stupid person.    You can't be expected to furnish every one who approaches you with a mind.    To expect that would be too much, even from you who know how to work wonders at such little cost to yourself."

"To myself," she repeated in a loud tone.

"Why this indignation? I am simply taking your word for it."

"Such little cost!" she exclaimed under her breath.

"I mean to your person."

"Oh, yes," she murmured, glanced down, as it were upon herself, then added very low : "This body."

"Well, it is you," said Blunt with visibly contained irritation. "You don't pretend it's somebody else's. It can't be. You haven't borrowed it. . . . It fits you too well," he ended between his teeth.

"You take pleasure in tormenting yourself," she remonstrated, suddenly placated ; "and I would be sorry for you if I didn't think it's the mere revolt of your pride. And you know you are indulging your pride at my expense. As to the rest of it, as to my living, acting, working wonders at a little cost . . . it has all but killed me morally. Do you hear? Killed."

"Oh, you are not dead yet," he muttered.

"No," she said with gentle patience. "There is still some feeling left in me ; and if it is any satisfaction to you to know it, you may be certain that I shall be conscious of the last stab."

He remained silent for a while and then with a polite smile and a movement of the head in my direction he warned her.

"Our audience will get bored."

"I am perfectly aware that Monsieur George is here, and that he has been breathing a very different atmosphere from what he gets in this room. Don't you find this room extremely confined?" she asked me.

The room was very large but it is a fact that I felt oppressed at that moment. This mysterious quarrel between those two people, revealing something more close in their intercourse than I had ever before suspected, made me so profoundly unhappy that I didn't even attempt to answer. And she continued :

U

" More space. More air. Give me air, air." She seized the embroidered edges of her blue robe under her white throat and made as if to tear them apart, to fling it open on her breast, recklessly, before our eyes. We both remained perfectly still. Her hands dropped nervelessly by her side. " I envy you, Monsieur George. If I am to go under I should prefer to be drowned in the sea with the wind on my face. What luck, to feel nothing less than all the world closing over one's head ! "

A short silence ensued before Mr. Blunt's drawing-room voice was heard with playful familiarity.

" I have often asked myself whether you weren't really a very ambitious person, Doña Rita."

" And I ask myself whether you have any heart." She was looking straight at him and he gratified her with the usual cold white flash of his even teeth before he answered.

" Asking yourself ? That means that you are really asking me. But why do it so publicly ? I mean it. One single, detached presence is enough to make a public. One alone. Why not wait till he returns to those regions of space and air—from which he came."

His particular trick of speaking of any third person as of a lay figure was exasperating. Yet at the moment I did not know how to resent it, in any case, Doña Rita would not have given me time. Without a moment's hesitation she cried out :

" I only wish he could take me out there with him."

For a moment Mr. Blunt's face became as still as a mask and then instead of an angry it assumed an indulgent expression. As to me I had a rapid vision of Dominic's astonishment, awe, and sarcasm which was always as tolerant as it is possible for sarcasm to be. But what a charming, gentle, gay, and fearless companion she would have made ! I believed in her fearlessness in any adventure that would interest her. It would be a new occasion for me, a new viewpoint for that faculty of admiration she had awakened in me at sight—at first sight—before she opened her lips—before she ever turned her eyes on me. She would have to wear some sort of sailor costume, a blue woollen shirt open at the throat. . . . Dominic's hooded cloak would envelop her amply, and her face under the black hood would have a luminous quality, adolescent charm, and an enigmatic expression. The confined space of the little vessel's quarter-deck would lend itself to her cross-legged attitudes, and the blue sea would balance gently her characteristic immobility that seemed to hide thoughts as old and profound as itself. As restless, too—perhaps.

But the picture I had in my eye, coloured and simple like an illustration to a nursery-book tale of two venture-some children's escapade, was what fascinated me most. Indeed I felt that we two were like children under the gaze of a man of the world—who lived by his sword. And I said recklessly :

"Yes, you ought to come along with us for a trip. You would see a lot of things for yourself."

Mr. Blunt's expression had grown even more indulgent if that were possible. Yet there was something incradicably ambiguous about that man. I did not like the indefinable tone in which he observed :

"You are perfectly reckless in what you say, Doña Rita. It has become a habit with you of late."

"While with you reserve is a second nature, Don Juan."

This was uttered with the gentlest, almost tender, irony. Mr. Blunt waited a while before he said :

"Certainly. . . . Would you have liked me to be other-wise ? "

She extended her hand to him on a sudden impulse.

"Forgive me ! I may have been unjust, and you may only have been loyal. The falseness is not in us. The fault is in life itself, I suppose. I have been always frank with you."

"And I obedient," he said, bowing low over her hand. He turned away, paused to look at me for some time and finally gave me the correct sort of nod. But he said nothing and went out, or rather lounged out with his worldly manner of perfect ease under all conceivable circumstances. With her head lowered Doña Rita watched him till he actually shut the door behind him. I was facing her and only heard the door close.

"Don't stare at me," were the first words she said.

It was difficult to obey that request. I didn't know exactly where to look, while I sat facing her. So I got up, vaguely full of goodwill, prepared even to move off as far as the window, when she commanded :

"Don't turn your back on me."

I chose to understand it symbolically.

"You know very well I could never do that. I couldn't. Not even if I wanted to." And I added : "It's too late now."

"Well, then, sit down. Sit down on this couch."

I sat down on the couch. Unwillingly ? Yes. I was at that stage when all her words, all her gestures, all her silences were a heavy trial to me, put a stress on my resolution, on that fidelity to myself and to her which lay like a leaden weight on my untried heart. But I didn't sit down very far away from her, though that soft and billowy couch was big enough, God knows ! No, not very far from her. Self-control, dignity, hopelessness itself, have their limits. The halo of her tawny hair stirred as I let myself drop by her side. Whereupon she flung one arm round my neck, leaned her temple against my shoulder and began to sob ; but that I could only guess from her slight, convulsive movements because in our relative positions I could only see the mass of her tawny hair brushed back, yet with a halo of escaped hair which as I bent my head over her tickled my lips, my cheek, in a maddening manner.

We sat like two venturesome children in an illustration to a tale, scared by their adventure. But not for long. As I instinctively, yet timidly, sought for her other hand I felt a tear strike the back of mine, big and heavy as if fallen from a great height. It was too much for me. I must have given a nervous start. At once I heard a murmur : "You had better go away now."

I withdrew myself gently from under the light weight of

her head, from this unspeakable bliss and inconceivable
misery, and had the absurd impression of leaving her suspended in the air.  And I moved away on tiptoe.

Like an inspired blind man led by Providence I found
my way out of the room but really I saw nothing, till in the
hall the maid appeared by enchantment before me holding
up my overcoat.  I let her help me into it.  And then (again
as if by enchantment) she had my hat in her hand.

"No.  Madame isn't happy," I whispered to her distractedly.

She let me take my hat out of her hand, and while I was
putting it on my head I heard an austere whisper:

"Madame should listen to her heart."

Austere is not the word; it was almost freezing, this
unexpected, dispassionate rustle of words.  I had to repress
a shudder, and as coldly as herself I murmured:

"She has done that once too often."

Rose was standing very close to me and I caught distinctly the note of scorn in her indulgent compassion.

"Oh, that ! . . . Madame is like a child."

It was impossible to get the bearing of that utterance
from that girl who, as Doña Rita herself had told me, was
the most taciturn of human beings; and yet of all human
beings the one nearest to herself.  I seized her head in my
hands and turning up her face I looked straight down into
her black eyes which should have been lustrous.  Like a
piece of glass breathed upon they reflected no light, revealed
no depths, and under my ardent gaze remained tarnished,
mistic, unconscious.

"Will Monsieur kindly let me go ?  Monsieur shouldn't
play the child, either." (I let her go.)  "Madame could
have the world at her feet.  Indeed she has it there; only
she doesn't care for it."

How talkative she was, this maid with unsealed lips !
For some reason or other this last statement of hers brought
me immense comfort.

"Yes ? " I whispered breathlessly.

"Yes !  But in that case what's the use of living in fear

and torment ? " she went on, revealing a little more of herself to my astonishment. She opened the door for me and added :

"Those that don't care to stoop ought at least make themselves happy."

I turned in the very doorway : "There is something which prevents that ? " I suggested.

"To be sure there is. *Bonjour*, Monsieur."

# PART FOUR

## I

'Such a charming lady in a grey silk dress and a hand as white as snow. She looked at me through such funny glasses on the end of a long handle. A very great lady but her voice was as kind as the voice of a saint. I have never seen anything like that. She made me feel so timid."

The voice uttering these words was the voice of Therese and I looked at her from a bed draped heavily in brown silk curtains fantastically looped up from ceiling to floor. The glow of a sunshiny day was toned down by closed jalousies to a mere transparency of darkness. In this thin medium Therese's form appeared flat, without detail, as if cut out of black paper. It glided towards the window and with a click and a scrape let in the full flood of light which smote my aching eyeballs painfully.

In truth all that night had been the abomination of desolation to me. After wrestling with my thoughts, if the acute consciousness of a woman's existence may be called a thought, I had apparently dropped off to sleep only to go on wrestling with a nightmare, a senseless and terrifying dream of being in bonds which, even after waking, made me feel powerless in all my limbs. I lay still, suffering acutely from a renewed sense of existence, unable to lift an arm, and wondering why I was not at sea, how long I had slept, how long Therese had been talking before her voice had reached me in that purgatory of hopeless longing and unanswerable questions to which I was condemned.

It was Therese's habit to begin talking directly she entered the room with the tray of morning coffee. This was her method for waking me up. I generally regained the consciousness of the external world on some pious phrase asserting

615

the spiritual comfort of early mass, or on angry lamentations about the unconscionable rapacity of the dealers in fish and vegetables ; for after mass it was Therese's practice to do the marketing for the house. As a matter of fact the necessity of having to pay, to actually give money to people, infuriated the pious Therese. But the matter of this morning's speech was so extraordinary that it might have been the prolongation of a nightmare : a man in bonds having to listen to weird and unaccountable speeches against which, he doesn't know why, his very soul revolts.

In sober truth my soul remained in revolt though I was convinced that I was no longer dreaming. I watched Therese coming away from the window with that helpless dread a man bound hand and foot may be excused to feel. For in such a situation even the absurd may appear ominous. She came up close to the bed and folding her hands meekly in front of her turned her eyes up to the ceiling.

" If I had been her daughter she couldn't have spoken more softly to me," she said sentimentally.

I made a great effort to speak.

" Mademoiselle Therese, you are raving."

" She addressed me as Mademoiselle, too, so nicely. I was struck with veneration for her white hair but her face, believe me, my dear young Monsieur, has not so many wrinkles as mine."

She compressed her lips with an angry glance at me as if I could help her wrinkles, then she sighed.

" God sends wrinkles, but what is our face ? " she digressed in a tone of great humility. " We shall have glorious faces in Paradise. But meantime God has permitted me to preserve a smooth heart."

" Are you going to keep on like this much longer ? " I fairly shouted at her. " What are you talking about ? "

" I am talking about the sweet old lady who came in a carriage. Not a fiacre. I can tell a fiacre. In a little carriage shut in with glass all in front. I suppose she is very rich. The carriage was very shiny outside and all beautiful grey stuff inside. I opened the door to her myself.

She got out slowly like a queen. I was struck all of a heap. Such a shiny beautiful little carriage. There were blue silk tassels inside, beautiful silk tassels."

Obviously Therese had been very much impressed by a brougham, though she didn't know the name for it. Of all the town she knew nothing but the streets which led to a neighbouring church frequented only by the poorer classes, and the humble quarter around, where she did her marketing. Besides, she was accustomed to glide along the walls with her eyes cast down ; for her natural boldness would never show itself through that nun-like mien except when bargaining, if only on a matter of threepence. Such a turn-out had never been presented to her notice before. The traffic in the street of the Consuls was mostly pedestrian and far from fashionable. And anyhow Therese never looked out of the window. She lurked in the depths of the house like some kind of spider that shuns attention. She used to dart at one from some dark recesses which I never explored.

Yet it seemed to me that she exaggerated her raptures for some reason or other. With her it was very difficult to distinguish between craft and innocence.

" Do you mean to say," I asked suspiciously, " that an old lady wants to hire an apartment here ? I hope you told her there was no room, because, you know, this house is not exactly the thing for venerable old ladies."

" Don't make me angry, my dear young Monsieur. I have been to confession this morning. Aren't you comfortable ? Isn't the house appointed richly enough for anybody ? "

That girl with a peasant-nun's face had never seen the inside of a house other than some half-ruined *caserio* in her native hills.

I pointed out to her that this was not a matter of splendour or comfort but of " convenances." She pricked up her ears at that word which probably she had never heard before ; but with woman's uncanny intuition I believe she understood perfectly what I meant. Her air of saintly patience became so pronounced that with my own poor intuition I perceived that she was raging at me inwardly. Her weather-tanned

U 2

complexion, already affected by her confined life, took on an extraordinary clayey aspect which reminded me of a strange head painted by El Greco which my friend Prax has hung on one of his walls and used to rail at; yet not without a certain respect.

Therese, with her hands still meekly folded about her waist, had mastered the feelings of anger so unbecoming to a person whose sins had been absolved only about three hours before, and asked me with an insinuating softness whether she wasn't an honest girl enough to look after any old lady belonging to a world which after all was sinful. She reminded me that she had kept house ever since she was " so high " for her uncle the priest : a man well-known for his saintliness in a large district extending even beyond Pampeluna. The character of a house depended upon the person who ruled it. She didn't know what impenitent wretches had been breathing within these walls in the time of that godless and wicked man who had planted every seed of perdition in " our Rita's " ill-disposed heart. But he was dead and she, Therese, knew for certain that wickedness perished utterly, because of God's anger (*la colère du bon Dieu*). She would have no hesitation in receiving a bishop, if need be, since " our Rita," with her poor, wretched, unbelieving heart, had nothing more to do with the house.

All this came out of her like an unctuous trickle of some acrid oil. The low, voluble delivery was enough by itself to compel my attention.

" You think you know your sister's heart ? " I asked.

She made small eyes at me to discover if I was angry. She seemed to have an invincible faith in the virtuous dispositions of young men. And as I had spoken in measured tones and hadn't got red in the face she let herself go.

" Black, my dear young Monsieur. Black. I always knew it. Uncle, poor saintly man, was too holy to take notice of anything. He was too busy with his thoughts to listen to anything I had to say to him. For instance as to her shamelessness. She was always ready to run half naked about the hills . . ."

"Yes. After your goats. All day long. Why didn't you mend her frocks?"

"Oh, you know about the goats. My dear young Monsieur, I could never tell when she would fling over her pretended sweetness and put her tongue out at me. Did she tell you about a boy, the son of pious and rich parents, whom she tried to lead astray into the wildness of thoughts like her own, till the poor dear child drove her off because she outraged his modesty? I saw him often with his parents at Sunday mass. The grace of God preserved him and made him quite a gentleman in Paris. Perhaps it will touch Rita's heart, too, some day. But she was awful then. When I wouldn't listen to her complaints she would say: 'All right, sister, I would just as soon go clothed in rain and wind.' And such a bag of bones, too, like the picture of a devil's imp. Ah, my dear young Monsieur, you don't know how wicked her heart is. You aren't bad enough for that yourself. I don't believe you are evil at all in your innocent little heart. I never heard you jeer at holy things. You are only thoughtless. For instance, I have never seen you make the sign of the cross in the morning. Why don't you make a practice of crossing yourself directly you open your eyes. It's a very good thing. It keeps Satan off for the day."

She proffered that advice in a most matter-of-fact tone as if it were a precaution against a cold, compressed her lips, then returning to her fixed idea, "But the house is mine," she insisted very quietly with an accent which made me feel that Satan himself would never manage to tear it out of her hands.

"And so I told the great lady in grey. I told her that my sister had given it to me and that surely God would not let her take it away again."

"You told that grey-headed lady, an utter stranger! You are getting more crazy every day. You have neither good sense nor good feeling, Mademoiselle Therese, let me tell you. Do you talk about your sister to the butcher and the greengrocer, too? A downright savage would have more restraint. What's your object? What do you expect from

it? What pleasure do you get from it? Do you think you
please God by abusing your sister? What do you think
you are?"

"A poor lone girl amongst a lot of wicked people. Do you
think I wanted to go forth amongst those abominations?
It's that poor sinful Rita that wouldn't let me be where
I was, serving a holy man, next door to a church, and sure
of my share of Paradise. I simply obeyed my uncle. It's he
who told me to go forth and attempt to save her soul, bring
her back to us, to a virtuous life. But what would be the
good of that? She is given over to worldly, carnal thoughts.
Of course we are a good family and my uncle is a great man
in the country, but where is the reputable farmer or God-
fearing man of that kind that would dare to bring such a girl
into his house to his mother and sister. No, let her give
her ill-gotten wealth up to the deserving and devote the rest
of her life to repentance."

She uttered these righteous reflections and presented this
programme for the salvation of her sister's soul in a reasonable
convinced tone which was enough to give goose flesh to one
all over.

"Mademoiselle Therese," I said, "you are nothing less
than a monster."

She received that true expression of my opinion as though
I had given her a sweet of a particularly delicious kind. She
liked to be abused. It pleased her to be called names. I did
let her have that satisfaction to her heart's content. At last
I stopped because I could do no more, unless I got out of bed
to beat her. I have a vague notion that she would have liked
that, too, but I didn't try. After I had stopped she waited
a little before she raised her downcast eyes.

"You are a dear, ignorant, flighty young gentleman,"
she said. "Nobody can tell what a cross my sister is to me
except the good priest in the church where I go every day."

"And the mysterious lady in grey," I suggested sar-
castically.

"Such a person might have guessed it," answered Therese,
seriously, "but I told her nothing except that this house

had been given me in full property by our Rita. And I
wouldn't have done that if she hadn't spoken to me of my
sister first. I can't tell too many people about that. One
can't trust Rita. I know she doesn't fear God but perhaps
human respect may keep her from taking this house back
from me. If she doesn't want me to talk about her to people
why doesn't she give me a properly stamped piece of paper
for it?"

She said all this rapidly in one breath and at the end had
a sort of anxious gasp which gave me the opportunity to
voice my surprise. It was immense.

"That lady, the strange lady, spoke to you of your sister
first!" I cried.

"The lady asked me, after she had been in a little time,
whether really this house belonged to Madame de Lastaola.
She had been so sweet and kind and condescending that I
did not mind humiliating my spirit before such a good
Christian. I told her that I didn't know how the poor sinner
in her mad blindness called herself, but that this house had
been given to me truly enough by my sister. She raised her
eyebrows at that but she looked at me at the same time so
kindly, as much as to say, 'Don't trust much to that, my dear
girl,' that I couldn't help taking up her hand, soft as down,
and kissing it. She took it away pretty quick but she was not
offended. But she only said, That's very generous on your
sister's part,' in a way that made me run cold all over. I
suppose all the world knows our Rita for a shameless girl. It
was then that the lady took up those glasses on a long gold
handle and looked at me through them till I felt very much
abashed. She said to me, 'There is nothing to be unhappy
about. Madame de Lastaola is a very remarkable person who
has done many surprising things. She is not to be judged
like other people and as far as I know she has never wronged a
single human being. . . .' That put heart into me, I can
tell you; and the lady told me then not to disturb her son.
She would wait till he woke up. She knew he was a bad
sleeper. I said to her: 'Why, I can hear the dear sweet
gentleman this moment having his bath in the fencing-room,'

and I took her into the studio.    They are there now and they
are going to have their lunch together at twelve o'clock."

"Why on earth didn't you tell me at first that the lady
was Mrs. Blunt?"

"Didn't I?  I thought I did," she said innocently.  I
felt a sudden desire to get out of that house, to fly from the
reinforced Blunt element which was to me so oppressive.

"I want to get up and dress, Mademoiselle Therese," I said.
She gave a slight start and without looking at me again
glided out of the room, the many folds of her brown skirt
remaining undisturbed as she moved.

I looked at my watch; it was ten o'clock.  Therese had
been late with my coffee.    The delay was clearly caused by
the unexpected arrival of Mr. Blunt's mother, which might
or might not have been expected by her son.    The existence
of those Blunts made me feel uncomfortable in a peculiar
way as though they had been the denizens of another planet
with a subtly different point of view and something in the
intelligence which was bound to remain unknown to me.    It
caused in me a feeling of inferiority which I intensely disliked.    This did not arise from the actual fact that those
people originated in another continent.    I had met Americans
before.    And the Blunts were Americans.    But so little!
That was the trouble.    Captain Blunt might have been a
Frenchman as far as languages, tones, and manners went.
But you could not have mistaken him for one. . . . Why?
You couldn't tell.    It was something indefinite.    It occurred
to me while I was towelling hard my hair, face, and the back
of my neck, that I could not meet J. K. Blunt on equal terms
in any relation of life except perhaps arms in hand, and in
preference with pistols, which are less intimate, acting at a
distance—but arms of some sort.    For physically his life,
which could be taken away from him, was exactly like mine,
held in the same terms and of the same vanishing quality.

I would have smiled at my absurdity if all, even the most
intimate, vestige of gaiety had not been crushed out of my
heart by the intolerable weight of my love for Rita.    It
crushed, it overshadowed, too, it was immense.    If there

were any smiles in the world (which I didn't believe) I could not have seen them. Love for Rita . . . if it was love, I asked myself despairingly, while I brushed my hair before a glass. It did not seem to have any sort of beginning as far as I could remember. A thing the origin of which you cannot trace cannot be seriously considered. It is an illusion. Or perhaps mine was a physical state, some sort of disease akin to melancholia which is a form of insanity? The only moments of relief I could remember were when she and I would start squabbling like two passionate infants in a nursery, over anything under heaven, over a phrase, a word sometimes, in the great light of the glass rotunda, disregarding the quiet entrances and exits of the ever-active Rose, in great bursts of voices and peals of laughter. . . .

I felt tears come into my eyes at the memory of her laughter, the true memory of the senses almost more penetrating than the reality itself. It haunted me. All that appertained to her haunted me with the same awful intimacy, her whole form in the familiar pose, her very substance in its colour and texture, her eyes, her lips, the gleam of her teeth, the tawny mist of her hair, the smoothness of her forehead, the faint scent that she used, the very shape, feel, and warmth of her high-heeled slipper that would sometimes in the heat of the discussion drop on the floor with a crash, and which I would (always in the heat of the discussion) pick up and toss back on the couch without ceasing to argue. And besides being haunted by what was Rita on earth I was haunted also by her waywardness, her gentleness and her flame, by that which the high gods called Rita when speaking of her amongst themselves. Oh, yes, certainly I was haunted by her but so was her sister Therese—who was crazy. It proved nothing. As to her tears, since I had not caused them, they only aroused my indignation. To put her head on my shoulder, to weep these strange tears, was nothing short of an outrageous liberty. It was a mere emotional trick. She would have just as soon leaned her head against the over-mantel of one of those tall, red granite chimney-pieces in order to weep comfortably. And then when she had no longer any need of support she dispensed with it by simply telling me to go away. How convenient! The request had sounded pathetic, almost sacredly so, but then it might have been the exhibition of the coolest possible impudence. With her one could not tell. Sorrow, indifference, tears, smiles, all with her seemed to have a hidden meaning. Nothing could be trusted. . . . "Heavens! Am I as crazy as Therese?" I asked myself with a passing chill of fear, while occupied in equalizing the ends of my neck-tie.

I felt suddenly that "this sort of thing" would kill me. The definition of the cause was vague, but the thought itself was no mere morbid artificiality of sentiment but a genuine conviction. "That sort of thing" was what I would have to die from. It wouldn't be from the innumerable doubts. Any sort of certitude would be also deadly. It wouldn't be from a stab—a kiss would kill me as surely. It would not be from a frown or from any particular word or any particular act—but from having to bear them all, together and in succession—from having to live with "that sort of thing." About the time I finished with my neck-tie I had done with life too. I absolutely did not care because I couldn't tell whether, mentally and physically, from the roots of my hair to the soles of my feet—whether I was more weary or unhappy.

And now my toilet was finished, my occupation was gone. An immense distress descended upon me. It has been observed that the routine of daily life, that arbitrary system of trifles, is a great moral support. But my toilet was finished, I had nothing more to do of those things consecrated by usage and which leave you no option. The exercise of any kind of volition by a man whose consciousness is reduced to the sensation that he is being killed by "that sort of thing" cannot be anything but mere trifling with death, an insincere pose before himself. I wasn't capable of it. It was then that I discovered that being killed by "that sort of thing," I mean the absolute conviction of it, was, so to speak, nothing in itself. The horrible part was the waiting. That was the cruelty, the tragedy, the bitterness of it. "Why the devil don't I drop dead now?" I asked myself peevishly, taking a clean handkerchief out of the drawer and stuffing it in my pocket.

This was absolutely the last thing, the last ceremony of an imperative rite. I was abandoned to myself now and it was terrible. Generally I used to go out, walk down to the port, take a look at the craft I loved with a sentiment that was extremely complex, being mixed up with the image of a woman; perhaps go on board, not because there was anything for me to do there but just for nothing, for happiness, simply as a man will sit contented in the companionship of the beloved object. For lunch I had the choice of two places, one Bohemian, the other select, even aristocratic, where I had still my reserved table in the *petit salon*, up the white staircase. In both places I had friends who treated my erratic appearances with discretion, in one case tinged with respect, in the other with a certain amused tolerance. I owed this tolerance to the most careless, the most confirmed of those Bohemians (his beard had streaks of grey amongst its many other tints) who, once bringing his heavy hand down on my shoulder, took my defence against the charge of being disloyal and even foreign to that milieu of earnest visions taking beautiful and revolutionary shapes in the smoke of pipes, in the jingle of glasses.

" That fellow (*ce garçon*) is a primitive nature, but he may be an artist in a sense. He has broken away from his conventions. He is trying to put a special vibration and his own notion of colour into his life; and perhaps even to give it a modelling according to his own ideas. And for all you know he may be on the track of a masterpiece; but observe: if it happens to be one nobody will see it. It can be only for himself. And even he won't be able to see it in its completeness except on his death-bed. There is something fine in that."

I had blushed with pleasure; such fine ideas had never entered my head. But there was something fine. . . . How far all this seemed ! How mute and how still ! What a phantom he was, that man with a beard of at least seven tones of brown. And those shades of the other kind such as

Baptiste with the shaven diplomatic face, the *maître d'hôtel* in charge of the *petit salon*, taking my hat and stick from me with a deferential remark : " Monsieur is not very often seen nowadays." And those other well-groomed heads raised and nodding at my passage—" *Bonjour*." " *Bonjour* "— following me with interested eyes ; these young X.'s and Z.'s, low-toned, markedly discreet, lounging up to my table on their way out with murmurs : " Are you well ? " —" Will one see you anywhere this evening ? "—not from curiosity, God forbid, but just from friendliness ; and passing on almost without waiting for an answer. What had I to do with them, this elegant dust, these moulds of provincial fashion ?

I also often lunched with Doña Rita without invitation. But that was now unthinkable. What had I to do with a woman who allowed somebody else to make her cry and then with an amazing lack of good feeling did her offensive weeping on my shoulder ? Obviously I could have nothing to do with her. My five minutes' meditation in the middle of the bedroom came to an end without even a sigh. The dead don't sigh, and for all practical purposes I was that, except for the final consummation, the growing cold, the *rigor mortis*—that blessed state ! With measured steps I crossed the landing to my sitting-room.


II


THE windows of that room gave out on the street of the Consuls which as usual was silent. And the house itself below me and above me was soundless, perfectly still. In general the house was quiet, dumbly quiet, without reso-nances of any sort, something like what one would imagine the interior of a convent would be. I suppose it was very solidly built. Yet that morning I missed in the stillness that feeling of security and peace which ought to have been associated with it. It is, I believe, generally admitted that the dead are glad to be at rest. But I wasn't at rest. What was wrong with that silence? There was something incongruous in that peace. What was it that had got into that stillness? Suddenly I remembered: the mother of Captain Blunt.

Why had she come all the way from Paris? And why should I bother my head about it? H'm—the Blunt atmosphere, the reinforced Blunt vibration stealing through the walls, through the thick walls and the almost more solid stillness. Nothing to me, of course—the movements of Mme. Blunt, *mère*. It was maternal affection which had brought her south by either the evening or morning Rapide, to take anxious stock of the ravages of that insomnia. Very good thing, insomnia, for a cavalry officer perpetually on outpost duty, a real god-send, so to speak; but on leave a truly devilish condition to be in.

The above sequence of thoughts was entirely unsympathetic and it was followed by a feeling of satisfaction that I, at any rate, was not suffering from insomnia. I could always sleep in the end. In the end. Escape into a nightmare. Wouldn't he revel in that if he could! But that wasn't for him. He had to toss about open-eyed all night and get up weary, weary. But oh, wasn't I weary, too, waiting for a sleep without dreams.

I heard the door behind me open. I had been standing with my face to the window and, I declare, not knowing what I was looking at across the road—the Desert of Sahara or a wall of bricks, a landscape of rivers and forests or only the Consulate of Paraguay. But I had been thinking, apparently, of Mr. Blunt with such intensity that when I saw him enter the room it didn't really make much difference. When I turned about the door behind him was already shut. He advanced towards me, correct, supple, hollow-eyed, and smiling; and as to his costume ready to go out except for the old shooting jacket which he must have affectioned particularly, for he never lost any time in getting into it at every opportunity. Its material was some tweed mixture; it had gone inconceivably shabby, it was

shrunk from old age, it was ragged at the elbows; but any
one could see at a glance that it had been made in London
by a celebrated tailor, by a distinguished specialist. Blunt
came towards me in all the elegance of his slimness and
affirming in every line of his face and body, in the correct
set of his shoulders and the careless freedom of his movements, the superiority, the inexpressible superiority, the
unconscious, the unmarked, the not-to-be-described, and
even not-to-be-caught, superiority of the naturally born
and the perfectly finished man of the world, over the simple
young man. He was smiling, easy, correct, perfectly
delightful, fit to kill.

He had come to ask me, if I had no other engagement,
to lunch with him and his mother in about an hour's time.
He did it in a most *dégagé* tone. His mother had given
him a surprise. The completest . . . The foundation of
his mother's psychology was her delightful unexpectedness.
She could never let things be (this in a peculiar tone which
he checked at once) and he really would take it very kindly
of me if I came to break the tête-à-tête for a while (that is
if I had no other engagement.   Flash of teeth).   His mother
was exquisitely and tenderly absurd.   She had taken it
into her head that his health was endangered in some way.
And when she took anything into her head . . . Perhaps I
might find something to say which would reassure her.
His mother had two long conversations with Mills on his
passage through Paris and had heard of me (I knew how
that thick man could speak of people, he interjected am-
biguously), and his mother, with an insatiable curiosity for
anything that was rare (filially humorous accent here and a
softer flash of teeth), was very anxious to have me presented
to her (courteous intonation, but no teeth).   He hoped I
wouldn't mind if she treated me a little as an " interesting
young man."   His mother had never got over her seven-
teenth year, and the manner of the spoilt beauty of at least
three counties at the back of the Carolinas.   That again
got overlaid by the *sans-façon* of a *grande dame* of the Second
Empire.

I accepted the invitation with a worldly grin and a perfectly just intonation, because I really didn't care what I did. I only wondered vaguely why that fellow required all the air in the room for himself. There did not seem enough left to go down my throat. I didn't say that I would come with pleasure or that I would be delighted, but I said that I would come. He seemed to forget his tongue in his head, put his hands in his pockets and moved about vaguely. "I am a little nervous this morning," he said in French, stopping short and looking me straight in the eyes. His own were deep sunk, dark, fatal. I asked with some malice, that no one could have detected in my intonation, "How's that sleeplessness?"

He muttered through his teeth, "*Mal. Je ne dors plus.*" He moved off to stand at the window with his back to the room. I sat down on a sofa that was there and put my feet up, and silence took possession of the room.

"Isn't this street ridiculous?" said Blunt suddenly, and crossing the room rapidly waved his hand to me, "*A bientôt donc,*" and was gone. He had seared himself into my mind. I did not understand him nor his mother then; which made them more impressive; but I have discovered since that those two figures required no mystery to make them memorable. Of course it isn't every day that one meets a mother that lives by her wits and a son that lives by his sword, but there was a perfect finish about their ambiguous personalities which is not to be met twice in a life-time. I shall never forget that grey dress with ample skirts and long corsage yet with infinite style, the ancient as if ghostly beauty of outlines, the black lace, the silver hair, the harmonious, restrained movements of those white, soft hands like the hands of a queen—or an abbess; and in the general fresh effect of her person the brilliant eyes like two stars with the calm reposeful way they had of moving on and off one, as if nothing in the world had the right to veil itself before their once sovereign beauty. Captain Blunt with smiling formality introduced me by name, adding with a certain relaxation of the formal tone the comment: "The

'Monsieur George' whose fame you tell me has reached even Paris." Mrs. Blunt's reception of me, glance, tones, even to the attitude of the admirably corseted figure, was most friendly, approaching the limit of half-familiarity. I had the feeling that I was beholding in her a captured idea. No common experience! But I didn't care. It was very lucky perhaps for me that in a way I was like a very sick man who has yet preserved all his lucidity. I was not even wondering to myself at what on earth I was doing there. She breathed out: "*Comme c'est romantique*," at large to the dusty studio as it were; then pointing to a chair at her right hand, and bending slightly towards me she said:

"I have heard this name murmured by pretty lips in more than one royalist salon."

I didn't say anything to that ingratiating speech. I had only an odd thought that she could not have had such a figure, nothing like it, when she was seventeen and wore snowy muslin dresses on the family plantation in South Carolina, in pre-abolition days.

"You won't mind, I am sure, if an old woman whose heart is still young elects to call you by it," she declared.

"Certainly, Madame. It will be more romantic," I assented with a respectful bow.

She dropped a calm: "Yes—there is nothing like romance while one is young. So I will call you Monsieur George," she paused and then added, "I could never get old," in a matter-of-fact final tone as one would remark, "I could never learn to swim," and I had the presence of mind to say in a tone to match, "*C'est évident*, Madame." It was evident. She couldn't get old; and across the table her thirty-year-old son who couldn't get sleep sat listening with courteous detachment and the narrowest possible line of white underlining his silky black moustache.

"Your services are immensely appreciated," she said with an amusing touch of importance as of a great official lady. "Immensely appreciated by people in a position to understand the great significance of the Carlist movement in the South. There it has to combat anarchism, too. I who have lived through the Commune . . ."

Therese came in with a dish, and for the rest of the lunch the conversation so well begun drifted amongst the most appalling inanities of the religious-royalist-legitimist order. The ears of all the Bourbons in the world must have been burning. Mrs. Blunt seemed to have come into personal contact with a good many of them and the marvellous insipidity of her recollections was astonishing to my inexperience. I looked at her from time to time thinking: She has seen slavery, she has seen the Commune, she knows two continents, she has seen a civil war, the glory of the Second Empire, the horrors of two sieges; she has been in contact with marked personalities, with great events, she has lived on her wealth, on her personality, and there she is with her plumage unruffled, as glossy as ever, unable to get old:—a sort of Phœnix free from the slightest signs of ashes and dust, all complacent amongst those inanities as if there had been nothing else in the world. In my youthful haste I asked myself what sort of airy soul she had.

At last Therese put a dish of fruit on the table, a small collection of oranges, raisins, and nuts. No doubt she had bought that lot very cheap and it did not look at all inviting. Captain Blunt jumped up. " My mother can't stand tobacco smoke. Will you keep her company, *mon cher*, while I take a turn with a cigar in that ridiculous garden ? The brougham from the hotel will be here very soon."

He left us in the white flash of an apologetic grin. Almost directly he reappeared, visible from head to foot through the glass side of the studio, pacing up and down the central path of that " ridiculous " garden : for its elegance and its air of good breeding the most remarkable figure that I have ever seen before or since. He had changed his coat. Madame Blunt *mère* lowered the long-handled glasses through which she had been contemplating him with an appraising, absorbed expression which had nothing material in it. But what she said to me was :

"You understand my anxieties while he is campaigning with the King."

She had spoken in French and she had used the expression "*mes transes*" but for all the rest, intonation, bearing, solemnity, she might have been referring to one of the Bourbons. I am sure that not a single one of them looked half as aristocratic as her son.

"I understand perfectly, Madame. But then that life is so romantic."

"Hundreds of young men belonging to a certain sphere are doing that," she said very distinctly, "only their case is different. They have their positions, their families to go back to; but we are different. We are exiles, except of course for the ideals, the kindred spirit, the friendships of old standing we have in France. Should my son come out unscathed he has no one but me and I have no one but him. I have to think of his life. Mr. Mills (what a distinguished mind that is!) has reassured me as to my son's health. But he sleeps very badly, doesn't he?"

I murmured something affirmative in a doubtful tone and she remarked quaintly, with a certain curtness, "It's so unnecessary, this worry! The unfortunate position of an exile has its advantages. At a certain height of social position (wealth has got nothing to do with it, we have been ruined in a most righteous cause), at a certain established height one can disregard narrow prejudices. You see examples in the aristocracies of all the countries. A chivalrous young American may offer his life for a remote ideal which yet may belong to his familial tradition. We, in our great country, have every sort of tradition. But a young man of good connections and distinguished relations must settle down some day, dispose of his life."

"No doubt, Madame," I said, raising my eyes to the figure outside—"*Américain, Catholique et gentilhomme*"—walking up and down the path with a cigar which he was not smoking. "For myself, I don't know anything about those necessities. I have broken away for ever from those things."

" Yes, Mr. Mills talked to me about you. What a golden heart that is. His sympathies are infinite."

I thought suddenly of Mills pronouncing on Mme. Blunt, whatever his text on me might have been : " She lives by her wits." Was she exercising her wits on me for some purpose of her own ? And I observed coldly :

" I really know your son so very little."

" Oh, *voyons*," she protested. " I am aware that you are very much younger, but the similitudes of opinions, origins and perhaps at bottom, faintly, of character, of chivalrous devotion—no, you must be able to understand him in a measure. He is infinitely scrupulous and recklessly brave."

I listened deferentially to the end yet with every nerve in my body tingling in hostile response to the Blunt vibration, which seemed to have got into my very hair.

" I am convinced of it, Madame. I have even heard of your son's bravery. It's extremely natural in a man who, in his own words, ' lives by his sword.' "

She suddenly departed from her almost inhuman perfection, betrayed " nerves " like a common mortal, of course very slightly, but in her it meant more than a blaze of fury from a vessel of inferior clay. Her admirable little foot, marvellously shod in a black shoe, tapped the floor irritably. But even in that display there was something exquisitely delicate. The very anger in her voice was silvery, as it were, and more like the petulance of a seventeen-year-old beauty.

" What nonsense ! A Blunt doesn't hire himself."

" Some princely families," I said, " were founded by men who have done that very thing. The great Condottieri, you know."

It was in an almost tempestuous tone that she made me observe that we were not living in the fifteenth century. She gave me also to understand with some spirit that there was no question here of founding a family. Her son was very far from being the first of the name. His importance lay rather in being the last of a race which had totally perished, she added in a completely drawing-room tone, "in our Civil War."

She had mastered her irritation and through the glass side of the room sent a wistful smile to his address, but I noticed the yet unextinguished anger in her eyes full of fire under her beautiful white eyebrows. For she was growing old! Oh, yes, she was growing old, and secretly weary, and perhaps desperate.


### III

WITHOUT caring much about it I was conscious of sudden illumination. I said to myself confidently that these two people had been quarrelling all the morning. I had discovered the secret of my invitation to that lunch. They did not care to face the strain of some obstinate, inconclusive discussion for fear, maybe, of it ending in a serious quarrel. And so they had agreed that I should be fetched downstairs to create a diversion. I cannot say I felt annoyed. I didn't care. My perspicacity did not please me either. I wished they had left me alone—but nothing mattered. They must have been in their superiority accustomed to make use of people, without compunction. From necessity, too. She especially. She lived by her wits. The silence had grown so marked that I had at last to raise my eyes; and the first thing I observed was that Captain Blunt was no longer to be seen in the garden. Must have gone indoors. Would rejoin us in a moment. Then I would leave mother and son to themselves.

The next thing I noticed was that a great mellowness had descended upon the mother of the last of his race. But these terms, irritation, mellowness, appeared gross when applied to her. It is impossible to give an idea of the refinement and subtlety of all her transformations. She smiled faintly at me.

"But all this is beside the point. The real point is that my son, like all fine natures, is a being of strange contradictions which the trials of life have not yet reconciled in him. With me it is a little different. The trials fell mainly to my share—and of course I have lived longer. And then men are much more complex than women, much more difficult, too. And you, Monsieur George? Are you complex, with unexpected resistances and difficulties in your *être intime*—your inner self? I wonder now . . ."

The Blunt atmosphere seemed to vibrate all over my skin. I disregarded the symptom. "Madame," I said, "I have never tried to find out what sort of being I am."

"Ah, that's very wrong. We ought to reflect on what manner of beings we are. Of course we are all sinners. My John is a sinner like the others," she declared further, with a sort of proud tenderness as though our common lot must have felt honoured and to a certain extent purified by this condescending recognition.

"You are too young perhaps as yet . . . But as to my John," she broke off, leaning her elbow on the table and supporting her head on her old, impeccably shaped, white fore-arm emerging from a lot of precious, still older, lace trimming the short sleeve. "The trouble is that he suffers from a profound discord between the necessary reactions to life and even the impulses of nature and the lofty idealism of his feelings; I may say, of his principles. I assure you that he won't even let his heart speak uncontradicted."

I am sure I don't know what particular devil looks after the associations of memory, and I can't even imagine the shock which it would have been for Mrs. Blunt to learn that the words issuing from her lips had awakened in me the visual perception of a dark-skinned, hard-driven lady's maid with tarnished eyes; even of the tireless Rose handing me my hat while breathing out the enigmatic words: "Madame should listen to her heart." A wave from the atmosphere of another house rolled in, overwhelming and fiery, seductive and cruel, through the Blunt vibration, bursting through it as through tissue paper and filling my heart with sweet murmurs and distracting images, till it seemed to break, leaving an empty stillness in my breast.

After that for a long time I heard Mme. Blunt *mère* talking with extreme fluency and I even caught the individual words, but I could not in the revulsion of my feelings get hold of the sense. She talked apparently of life in general, of its difficulties, moral and physical, of its surprising turns, of its unexpected contacts, of the choice and rare personalities that drift on it as if on the sea ; of the distinction that letters and art gave to it, the nobility and consolations there are in æsthetics, of the privileges they confer on individuals and (this was the first connected statement I caught) that Mills agreed with her in the general point of view as to the inner worth of individualities and in the particular instance of it on which she had opened to him her innermost heart. Mills had a universal mind. His sympathy was universal, too. He had that large comprehension—oh, not cynical, not at all cynical, in fact rather tender—which was found in its perfection only in some rare, very rare Englishmen. The dear creature was romantic, too. Of course he was reserved in his speech but she understood Mills perfectly. Mills apparently liked me very much.

It was time for me to say something. There was a challenge in the reposeful black eyes resting upon my face. I murmured that I was very glad to hear it. She waited a little, then uttered meaningly, " Mr. Mills is a little bit uneasy about you."

" It's very good of him," I said. And indeed I thought that it was very good of him, though I did ask myself vaguely in my dulled brain why he should be uneasy. Somehow it didn't occur to me to ask Mrs. Blunt. Whether she had expected me to do so or not I don't know but after a while she changed the pose she had kept so long and folded her wonderfully preserved white arms. She looked a perfect picture in silver and grey, with touches of black here and there. Still I said nothing more in my dull misery. She waited a little longer, then she woke me up with a crash.

It was as if the house had fallen, and yet she had only asked
me :

"I believe you are received on very friendly terms by
Madame de Lastaola on account of your common exertions
for the cause. Very good friends, are you not?"

"You mean Rita," I said stupidly, but I felt stupid, like
a man who wakes up only to be hit on the head.

"Oh, Rita," she repeated with unexpected acidity, which
somehow made me feel guilty of an incredible breach of
good manners. "H'm, Rita. . . . Oh, well, let it be
Rita—for the present. Though why she should be deprived
of her name in conversation about her, really I don't understand. Unless a very special intimacy . . ."

She was distinctly annoyed. I said sulkily, "It isn't her
name."

"It is her choice, I understand, which seems almost a
better title to recognition on the part of the world. It
didn't strike you so before? Well, it seems to me that
choice has got more right to be respected than heredity or
law. Moreover, Mme. de Lastaola," she continued in an
insinuating voice, "that most rare and fascinating young
woman is, as a friend like you cannot deny, outside legality
altogether. Even in that she is an exceptional creature.
For she is exceptional—you agree?"

I had gone dumb, I could only stare at her.

"Oh, I see, you agree. No friend of hers could deny."

"Madame," I burst out, "I don't know where a question of friendship comes in here with a person whom you
yourself call so exceptional. I really don't know how she
looks upon me. Our intercourse is of course very close and
confidential. Is that also talked about in Paris?"

"Not at all, not in the least," said Mrs. Blunt, easy,
equable, but with her calm, sparkling eyes holding me in
angry subjection. "Nothing of the sort is being talked
about. The references to Mme. de Lastaola are in a very
different tone, I can assure you, thanks to her discretion in
remaining here. And, I must say, thanks to the discreet
efforts of her friends. I am also a friend of Mme. de Lastaola,

you must know. Oh, no, I have never spoken to her in my life and have seen her only twice, I believe. I wrote to her though, that I admit. She or rather the image of her has come into my life, into that part of it where art and letters reign undisputed like a sort of religion of beauty to which I have been faithful through all the vicissitudes of my existence. Yes, I did write to her and I have been preoccupied with her for a long time. It arose from a picture, from two pictures and also from a phrase pronounced by a man, who in the science of life and in the perception of æsthetic truth had no equal in the world of culture. He said that there was something in her of the women of all time. I suppose he meant the inheritance of all the gifts that make up an irresistible fascination—a great personality. Such women are not born often. Most of them lack opportunities. They never develop. They end obscurely. Here and there one survives to make her mark—even in history. . . . And even that is not a very enviable fate. They are at another pole from the so-called dangerous women who are merely coquettes. A coquette has got to work for her success. The others have nothing to do but simply exist. You perceive the view I take of the difference ? "

I perceived the view. I said to myself that nothing in the world could be more aristocratic. This was the slave-owning woman who had never worked, even if she had been reduced to live by her wits. She was a wonderful old woman. She made me dumb. She held me fascinated by the well-bred attitude, something sublimely aloof in her air of wisdom.

I just simply let myself go admiring her as though I had been a mere slave of æsthetics : the perfect grace, the amazing poise of that venerable head, the assured as if royal—yes, royal—even flow of the voice. . . . But what was it she was talking about now ? These were no longer considerations about fatal women. She was talking about her son again. My interest turned into mere bitterness of contemptuous attention. For I couldn't withhold it though I tried to let the stuff go by. Educated in the most aristocratic college in Paris . . . at eighteen . . . call of duty . . . with General Lee to the very last cruel minute . . . after that catastrophe—end of the world—return to France—to old friendships, infinite kindness—but a life hollow, without occupation. . . . Then 1870—and chivalrous response to adopted country's call and again emptiness, the chafing of a proud spirit without aim and handicapped not exactly by poverty but by lack of fortune. And she, the mother, having to look on at this wasting of a most accomplished man, of a most chivalrous nature that practically had no future before it.

"You understand me well, Monsieur George. A nature like this ! It is the most refined cruelty of fate to look at. I don't know whether I suffered more in times of war or in times of peace. You understand ? "

I bowed my head in silence. What I couldn't understand was why he delayed so long in joining us again. Unless he had had enough of his mother ? I thought without any great resentment that I was being victimized; but then it occurred to me that the cause of his absence was quite simple. I was familiar enough with his habits by this time to know that he often managed to snatch an hour's sleep or so during the day. He had gone and thrown himself on his bed.

"I admire him exceedingly," Mrs. Blunt was saying in a tone which was not at all maternal. "His distinction, his fastidiousness, the earnest warmth of his heart. I know him well. I assure you that I would never have dared to suggest," she continued with an extraordinary haughtiness of attitude and tone that aroused my attention, "I would never have dared to put before him my views of the extra-ordinary merits and the uncertain fate of the exquisite woman of whom we speak, if I had not been certain that, partly by my fault, I admit, his attention has been attracted to her and his—his—his heart engaged."

It was as if some one had poured a bucket of cold water over my head. I woke up with a great shudder to the acute perception of my own feelings and of that aristocrat's incredible purpose. How it could have germinated, grown and matured in that exclusive soil was inconceivable. She had been inciting her son all the time to undertake wonderful salvage work by annexing the heiress of Henry Allègre—the woman and the fortune.

There must have been an amazed incredulity in my eyes, to which her own responded by an unflinching black brilliance which suddenly seemed to develop a scorching quality even to the point of making me feel extremely thirsty all of a sudden. For a time my tongue literally clove to the roof of my mouth. I don't know whether it was an illusion but it seemed to me that Mrs. Blunt had nodded at me twice as if to say: "You are right, that's so." I made an effort to speak but it was very poor. If she did hear me it was because she must have been on the watch for the faintest sound.

"His heart engaged. Like two hundred others, or two thousand, all around," I mumbled.

"Altogether different. And it's no disparagement to a woman surely. Of course her great fortune protects her in a certain measure."

"Does it?" I faltered out and that time I really doubt whether she heard me. Her aspect in my eyes had changed. Her purpose being disclosed, her well-bred ease appeared sinister, her aristocratic repose a treacherous device, her venerable graciousness a mask of unbounded contempt for all human beings whatever. She was a terrible old woman with those straight, white wolfish eyebrows. How blind I had been! Those eyebrows alone ought to have been enough to give her away. Yet they were as beautifully smooth as her voice when she admitted: "That protection naturally is only partial. There is the danger of her own self, poor girl. She requires guidance."

I marvelled at the villainy of my tone as I spoke, but it was only assumed.

"I don't think she has done badly for herself, so far," I forced myself to say. "I suppose you know that she began life by herding the village goats."

In the course of that phrase I noticed her wince just the least bit. Oh, yes, she winced; but at the end of it she smiled easily.

"No, I didn't know. So she told you her story! Oh, well, I suppose you are very good friends. A goatherd—really? In the fairy tale I believe the girl that marries the prince is—what is it?—*a gardeuse d'oies*. And what a thing to drag out against a woman. One might just as soon reproach any of them for coming unclothed into the world. They all do, you know. And then they become—what you will discover when you have lived longer, Monsieur George—for the most part futile creatures, without any sense of truth and beauty, drudges of all sorts, or else dolls to dress. In a word—ordinary."

The implication of scorn in her tranquil manner was immense. It seemed to condemn all those that were not born in the Blunt connection. It was the perfect pride of Republican aristocracy, which has no gradations and knows no limit, and, as if created by the grace of God, thinks it ennobles everything it touches : people, ideas, even passing tastes !

"How many of them," pursued Mrs. Blunt, "have had the good fortune, the leisure to develop their intelligence and their beauty in æsthetic conditions as this charming woman had? Not one in a million. Perhaps not one in an age."

"The heiress of Henry Allègre," I murmured.

"Precisely. But John wouldn't be marrying the heiress of Henry Allègre."

It was the first time that the frank word, the clear idea, came into the conversation and it made me feel ill with a sort of enraged faintness.

"No," I said. "It would be Mme. de Lastaola then."

"Mme. la Comtesse de Lastaola as soon as she likes after the success of this war."

"And you believe in its success ? "

"Do you ? "

"Not for a moment," I declared, and was surprised to see her look pleased.

x

She was an aristocrat to the tips of her fingers; she really didn't care for anybody. She had passed through the Empire, she had lived through a siege, had rubbed shoulders with the Commune, had seen everything, no doubt, of what men are capable in the pursuit of their desires or in the extremity of their distress, for love, for money, and even for honour; and in her precarious connection with the very highest spheres she had kept her own honourability unscathed while she had lost all her prejudices. She was above all that. Perhaps "the world" was the only thing that could have the slightest checking influence; but when I ventured to say something about the view it might take of such an alliance she looked at me for a moment with visible surprise.

"My dear Monsieur George, I have lived in the great world all my life. It's the best that there is, but that's only because there is nothing merely decent anywhere. It will accept anything, forgive anything, forget anything in a few days. And after all who will he be marrying? A charming, clever, rich and altogether uncommon woman. What did the world hear of her? Nothing. The little it saw of her was in the Bois for a few hours every year, riding by the side of a man of unique distinction and of exclusive tastes, devoted to the cult of æsthetic impressions; a man of whom, as far as aspect, manner, and behaviour goes, she might have been the daughter. I have seen her myself. I went on purpose. I was immensely struck. I was even moved. Yes. She might have been—except for that something radiant in her that marked her apart from all the other daughters of men. The few remarkable personalities that count in society and who were admitted into Henry Allègre's Pavilion treated her with punctilious reserve. I know that, I have made enquiries. I know she sat there amongst them like a marvellous child, and for the rest what can they say about her? That when abandoned to herself by the death of Allègre she has made a mistake? I think that any woman ought to be allowed one mistake in her life. The worst they can say of her is that she discovered it, that she had sent away a man in love directly she found out that his love was not worth having; that she had told him to go and look for his crown, and that, after dismissing him, she had remained generously faithful to his cause, in her person and fortune. And this, you will allow, is rather uncommon upon the whole."

"You make her out very magnificent," I murmured, looking down upon the floor.

"Isn't she?" exclaimed the aristocratic Mrs. Blunt, with an almost youthful ingenuousness, and in those black eyes which looked at me so calmly there was a flash of the Southern beauty, still naïve and romantic, as if altogether untouched by experience. "I don't think there is a single grain of vulgarity in all her enchanting person. Neither is there in my son. I suppose you won't deny that he is uncommon." She paused.

"Absolutely," I said in a perfectly conventional tone. I was now on my mettle that she should not discover what there was humanly common in my nature. She took my answer at her own valuation and was satisfied.

"They can't fail to understand each other on the very highest level of idealistic perceptions. Can you imagine my John thrown away on some enamoured white goose out of a stuffy old salon? Why, she couldn't even begin to understand what he feels or what he needs."

"Yes," I said impenetrably, "he is not easy to understand."

"I have reason to think," she said with a suppressed smile, "that he has a certain power over women. Of course I don't know anything about his intimate life but a whisper or two have reached me, like that, floating in the air, and I could hardly suppose that he would find an exceptional resistance in that quarter of all others. But I should like to know the exact degree."

I disregarded an annoying tendency to feel dizzy that came over me and was very careful in managing my voice.

"May I ask, Madame, why you are telling me all this?"

"For two reasons," she condescended graciously. "First

of all because Mr. Mills told me that you were much more mature than one would expect. In fact you look much younger than I was prepared for."

"Madame," I interrupted her, "I may have a certain capacity for action and for responsibility, but as to the regions into which this very unexpected conversation has taken me I am a great novice. They are outside my interest. I have had no experience."

"Don't make yourself out so hopeless," she said in a spoilt-beauty tone. "You have your intuitions. At any rate you have a pair of eyes. You are everlastingly over there, so I understand. Surely you have seen how far they are . . ."

I interrupted again and this time bitterly, but always in a tone of polite enquiry :

"You think her facile, Madame ? "

She looked offended. " I think her most fastidious. It is my son who is in question here."

And I understood then that she looked on her son as irresistible. For my part I was just beginning to think that it would be impossible for me to wait for his return. I figured him to myself lying dressed on his bed sleeping like a stone. But there was no denying that the mother was holding me with an awful, tortured interest. Twice Therese had opened the door, had put her small head in and drawn it back like a tortoise. But for some time I had lost the sense of us two being quite alone in the studio. I had perceived the familiar dummy in its corner but it lay now on the floor as if Therese had knocked it down angrily with a broom for a heathen idol. It lay there prostrate, handless, without its head, pathetic, like the mangled victim of a crime.

"John is fastidious, too," began Mrs. Blunt again. "Of course you wouldn't suppose anything vulgar in his resistances to a very real sentiment. One has got to understand his psychology. He can't leave himself in peace. He is exquisitely absurd."

I recognized the phrase. Mother and son talked of each

other in identical terms. But perhaps " exquisitely absurd " was the Blunt family saying? There are such sayings in families and generally there is some truth in them. Perhaps this old woman was simply absurd. She continued :

" We had a most painful discussion all this morning. He is angry with me for suggesting the very thing his whole being desires. I don't feel guilty. It's he who is tormenting himself with his infinite scrupulosity."

" Ah," I said, looking at the mangled dummy like the model of some atrocious murder. " Ah, the fortune. But that can be left alone."

" What nonsense ! How is it possible ? It isn't contained in a bag, you can't throw it into the sea. And moreover, it isn't her fault. I am astonished that you should have thought of that vulgar hypocrisy. No, it isn't her fortune that checks my son ; it's something much more subtle. Not so much her history as her position. He is absurd. It isn't what has happened in her life. It's her very freedom that makes him torment himself and her, too— as far as I can understand."

I suppressed a groan and said to myself that I must really get away from there.

Mrs. Blunt was fairly launched now.

" For all his superiority he is a man of the world and shares to a certain extent its current opinions. He has no power over her. She intimidates him. He wishes he had never set eyes on her. Once or twice this morning he looked at me as if he could find it in his heart to hate his old mother. There is no doubt about it—he loves her, Monsieur George. He loves her, this poor, luckless, perfect *homme du monde.*"

The silence lasted for some time and then I heard a murmur : " It's a matter of the utmost delicacy between two beings so sensitive, so proud. It has to be managed."

I found myself suddenly on my feet and saying with the utmost politeness that I had to beg her permission to leave her alone as I had an engagement ; but she motioned me simply to sit down—and I sat down again.

" I told you I had a request to make," she said. " I

have understood from Mr. Mills that you have been to the West Indies, that you have some interests there."

I was astounded. "Interests! I certainly have been there," I said, "but . . ."

She caught me up. "Then why not go there again? I am speaking to you frankly because . . ."

"But, Madame, I am engaged in this affair with Doña Rita, even if I had any interests elsewhere. I won't tell you about the importance of my work. I didn't suspect it but you brought the news of it to me, and so I needn't point it out to you."

And now we were frankly arguing with each other.

"But where will it lead you in the end? You have all your life before you, all your plans, prospects, perhaps dreams, at any rate your own tastes and all your life-time before you. And would you sacrifice all this to—the Pretender? A mere figure for the front page of illustrated papers."

"I never think of him," I said curtly, "but I suppose Doña Rita's feelings, instincts, call it what you like—or only her chivalrous fidelity to her mistakes——"

"Doña Rita's presence here in this town, her withdrawal from the possible complications of her life in Paris has produced an excellent effect on my son. It simplifies infinite difficulties, I mean moral as well as material. It's extremely to the advantage of her dignity, of her future, and of her peace of mind. But I am thinking, of course, mainly of my son. He is most exacting."

I felt extremely sick at heart. "And so I am to drop everything and vanish," I said, rising from my chair again. And this time Mrs. Blunt got up, too, with a lofty and inflexible manner but she didn't dismiss me yet.

"Yes," she said distinctly. "All this, my dear Monsieur George, is such an accident. What have you got to do here? You look to me like somebody who would find adventures wherever he went as interesting and perhaps less dangerous than this one."

She slurred over the word dangerous but I picked it up.

"What do you know of its dangers, Madame, may I ask?" But she did not condescend to hear.

"And then you, too, have your chivalrous feelings," she went on, unswerving, distinct, and tranquil. "You are not absurd. But my son is. He would shut her up in a convent for a time if he could."

"He isn't the only one," I muttered.

"Indeed!" She was startled; then lower, "Yes. That woman must be the centre of all sorts of passions," she mused audibly. "But what have you got to do with all this? It's nothing to you."

She waited for me to speak.

"Exactly, Madame," I said, "and therefore I don't see why I should concern myself in all this one way or another."

"No," she assented with a weary air, "except that you might ask yourself what is the good of tormenting a man of noble feelings, however absurd. His Southern blood makes him very violent sometimes. I fear——" And then for the first time during this conversation, for the first time since I left Doña Rita the day before, for the first time I laughed.

"Do you mean to hint, Madame, that Southern gentlemen are dead shots? I am aware of that—from novels."

I spoke looking her straight in the face and I made that exquisite, aristocratic old woman positively blink by my directness. There was a faint flush on her delicate old cheeks but she didn't move a muscle of her face. I made her a most respectful bow and went out of the studio.


## IV

THROUGH the great arched window of the hall I saw the hotel brougham waiting at the door. On passing the door of the front room (it was originally meant for a drawing-room but a bed for Blunt was put in there) I banged with my fist on the panel and shouted: "I am obliged to go out.

Your mother's carriage is at the door." I didn't think he was asleep. My view now was that he was aware beforehand of the subject of the conversation, and if so I did not wish to appear as if I had slunk away from him after the interview. But I didn't stop—I didn't want to see him—and before he could answer I was already half way up the stairs running noiselessly up the thick carpet which also covered the floor of the landing. Therefore opening the door of my sitting-room quickly I caught by surprise the person who was in there watching the street half concealed by the window curtain. It was a woman. A totally unexpected woman. A perfect stranger. She came away quickly to meet me. Her face was veiled and she was dressed in a dark walking costume and a very simple form of hat. She murmured : " I had an idea that Monsieur was in the house," raising a gloved hand to lift her veil. It was Rose and she gave me a shock. I had never seen her before but with her little black silk apron and a white cap with ribbons on her head. This outdoor dress was like a disguise. I asked anxiously :

" What has happened to Madame ? "

" Nothing. I have a letter," she murmured, and I saw it appear between the fingers of her extended hand, in a very white envelope which I tore open impatiently. It consisted of a few lines only. It began abruptly :

" If you are gone to sea then I can't forgive you for not sending the usual word at the last moment. If you are not gone why don't you come ? Why did you leave me yesterday ? You leave me crying—I who haven't cried for years and years, and you haven't the sense to come back within the hour, within twenty hours ! This conduct is idiotic "—and a sprawling signature of the four magic letters at the bottom.

While I was putting the letter in my pocket the girl said in an earnest undertone : " I don't like to leave Madame by herself for any length of time."

" How long have you been in my room ? " I asked.

" The time seemed long. I hope Monsieur won't mind

the liberty. I sat for a little in the hall but then it struck me I might be seen. In fact, Madame told me not to be seen if I could help it."

"Why did she tell you that?"

"I permitted myself to suggest that to Madame. It might have given a false impression. Madame is frank and open like the day but it won't do with everybody. There are people who would put a wrong construction on anything. Madame's sister told me Monsieur was out."

"And you didn't believe her?"

"*Non*, Monsieur. I have lived with Madame's sister for nearly a week when she first came into this house. She wanted me to leave the message, but I said I would wait a little. Then I sat down in the big porter's chair in the hall and after a while, everything being very quiet, I stole up here. I know the disposition of the apartments. I reckoned Madame's sister would think that I got tired of waiting and let myself out."

"And you have been amusing yourself watching the street ever since?"

"The time seemed long," she answered evasively. "An empty *coupé* came to the door about an hour ago and it's still waiting," she added, looking at me inquisitively. "It seems strange."

"There are some dancing girls staying in the house," I said negligently. "Did you leave Madame alone?"

"There's the gardener and his wife in the house."

"Those people keep at the back. Is Madame alone? That's what I want to know."

"Monsieur forgets that I have been three hours away; but I assure Monsieur that here in this town it's perfectly safe for Madame to be alone."

"And wouldn't it be anywhere else? It's the first I hear of it."

"In Paris, in our apartments in the hotel, it's all right, too; but in the Pavilion, for instance, I wouldn't leave Madame by herself, not for half an hour."

"What is there in the Pavilion?" I asked.

"It's a sort of feeling I have," she murmured reluctantly.
. . . "Oh! There's that *coupé* going away."

She made a movement towards the window but checked
herself. I hadn't moved. The rattle of wheels on the
cobble-stones died out almost at once.

"Will Monsieur write an answer?" Rose suggested after
a short silence.

"Hardly worth while," I said. "I will be there very
soon after you. Meantime, please tell Madame from me
that I am not anxious to see any more tears. Tell her this
just like that, you understand. I will take the risk of not
being received."

She dropped her eyes, said: "*Oui*, Monsieur," and at
my suggestion waited, holding the door of the room half
open, till I went downstairs to see the road clear.

It was a kind of deaf-and-dumb house. The black-and-
white hall was empty and everything was perfectly still.
Blunt himself had no doubt gone away with his mother in
the brougham, but as to the others, the dancing girls,
Therese, or anybody else that its walls may have contained,
they might have been all murdering each other in perfect
assurance that the house would not betray them by indulging
in any unseemly murmurs. I emitted a low whistle which
didn't seem to travel in that peculiar atmosphere more than
two feet away from my lips, but all the same Rose came
tripping down the stairs at once. With just a nod to my
whisper: "Take a fiacre," she glided out and I shut the
door noiselessly behind her.

The next time I saw her she was opening the door of the
house on the Prado to me, with her cap and the little black
silk apron on, and with that marked personality of her own,
which had been concealed so perfectly in the dowdy walking
dress, very much to the fore.

"I have given Madame the message," she said in her
contained voice, swinging the door wide open. Then after
relieving me of my hat and coat she announced me with the
simple words: "*Voilà*, Monsieur," and hurried away.
Directly I appeared Doña Rita, away there on the couch,

passed the tips of her fingers over her eyes and holding her hands up palms outwards on each side of her head, shouted to me down the whole length of the room : " The dry season has set in." I glanced at the pink tips of her fingers perfunctorily and then drew back. She let her hands fall negligently as if she had no use for them any more and put on a serious expression.

" So it seems," I said, sitting down opposite her. " For how long, I wonder."

" For years and years. One gets so little encouragement. First you bolt away from my tears, then you send an impertinent message, and then when you come at last you pretend to behave respectfully, though you don't know how to do it. You should sit much nearer the edge of the chair and hold yourself very stiff, and make it quite clear that you don't know what to do with your hands."

All this in a fascinating voice with a ripple of badinage that seemed to play upon the sober surface of her thoughts. Then seeing that I did not answer she altered the note a bit.

" *Amigo* George," she said, " I take the trouble to send for you and here I am before you, talking to you and you say nothing."

" What am I to say ? "

" How can I tell? You might say a thousand things. You might, for instance, tell me that you were sorry for my tears."

" I might also tell you a thousand lies. What do I know about your tears ? I am not a susceptible idiot. It all depends upon the cause. There are tears of quiet happiness. Peeling onions also will bring tears."

" Oh, you are not susceptible," she flew out at me. " But you are an idiot all the same."

" Is it to tell me this you have written to me to come ? " I asked with a certain animation.

" Yes. And if you had as much sense as the talking parrot I owned once you would have read between the lines that all I wanted you here for was to tell you what I think of you."

"Well, tell me what you think of me."

"I would in a moment if I could be half as impertinent as you are."

"What unexpected modesty," I said.

"These, I suppose, are your sea manners."

"I wouldn't put up with half that nonsense from anybody at sea. Don't you remember you told me yourself to go away? What was I to do?"

"How stupid you are. I don't mean that you pretend. You really are. Do you understand what I say? I will spell it for you. S-t-u-p-i-d. Ah, now I feel better. Oh, *amigo* George, my dear fellow-conspirator for the king—the king. Such a king! *Vive le Roi!* Come, why don't you shout *Vive le Roi*, too?"

"I am not your parrot," I said.

"No, he never sulked. He was a charming, good-mannered bird, accustomed to the best society, whereas you, I suppose, are nothing but a heartless vagabond like myself."

"I daresay you are, but I suppose nobody had the insolence to tell you that to your face."

"Well, very nearly. It was what it amounted to. I am not stupid. There is no need to spell out simple words for me. It just came out. Don Juan struggled desperately to keep the truth in. It was most pathetic. And yet he couldn't help himself. He talked very much like a parrot."

"Of the best society," I suggested.

"Yes, the most honourable of parrots. I don't like parrot-talk. It sounds so uncanny. Had I lived in the Middle Ages I am certain I would have believed that a talking bird must be possessed by the devil. I am sure Therese would believe that now. My own sister! She would cross herself many times and simply quake with terror."

"But you were not terrified," I said. "May I ask when that interesting communication took place?"

"Yesterday, just before you blundered in here of all days in the year. I was sorry for him."

"Why tell me this? I couldn't help noticing it. I regretted I hadn't my umbrella with me."

"Those unforgiven tears! Oh, you simple soul! Don't you know that people never cry for anybody but themselves? . . . *Amigo* George, tell me—what are we doing in this world?"

"Do you mean all the people, everybody?"

"No, only people like you and me. Simple people, in this world which is eaten up with charlatanism of all sorts so that even we, the simple, don't know any longer how to trust each other."

"Don't we? Then why don't you trust him? You are dying to do so, don't you know?"

She dropped her chin on her breast and from under her straight eyebrows the deep blue eyes remained fixed on me, impersonally, as if without thought.

"What have you been doing since you left me yesterday?" she asked.

"The first thing I remember I abused your sister horribly this morning."

"And how did she take it?"

"Like a warm shower in spring. She drank it all in and unfolded her petals."

"What poetical expressions he uses! That girl is more perverted than one would think possible, considering what she is and whence she came. It's true that I, too, come from the same spot."

"She is slightly crazy. I am a great favourite with her. I don't say this to boast."

"It must be very comforting."

"Yes, it has cheered me immensely. Then after a morning of delightful musings on one thing and another I went to lunch with a charming lady and spent most of the afternoon talking with her."

Doña Rita raised her head.

"A lady! Women seem such mysterious creatures to me.

I don't know them. Did you abuse her? Did she—how did you say that?—unfold her petals, too? Was she really and truly . . . ?"

"She is simply perfection in her way and the conversation was by no means banal. I fancy that if your late parrot had heard it, he would have fallen off his perch. For after all, in that Allègre Pavilion, my dear Rita, you were but a crowd of glorified *bourgeois*."

She was beautifully animated now. In her motionless blue eyes like melted sapphires, around those red lips that almost without moving could breathe enchanting sounds into the world, there was a play of light, that mysterious ripple of gaiety that seemed always to run and faintly quiver under her skin even in her gravest moods; just as in her rare moments of gaiety its warmth and radiance seemed to come to one through infinite sadness, like the sunlight of our life hiding the invincible darkness in which the universe must work out its impenetrable destiny.

"Now I think of it! . . . Perhaps that's the reason I never could feel perfectly serious while they were demolishing the world about my ears. I fancy now that I could tell beforehand what each of them was going to say. They were repeating the same words over and over again, those great clever men, very much like parrots who also seem to know what they say. That doesn't apply to the master of the house, who never talked much. He sat there mostly silent and looming up three sizes bigger than any of them."

"The ruler of the aviary," I muttered viciously.

"It annoys you that I should talk of that time?" she asked in a tender voice. "Well, I won't, except for once to say that you must not make a mistake: in that aviary he was the man. I know because he used to talk to me afterwards sometimes. Strange! For six years he seemed to carry all the world and me with it in his hand. . . ."

"He dominates you yet," I shouted.

She shook her head innocently as a child would do.

"No, no. You brought him into the conversation yourself. You think of him much more than I do." Her voice drooped sadly to a hopeless note. " I hardly ever do. He is not the sort of person to merely flit through one's mind and so I have no time. Look. I had eleven letters this morning and there were also five telegrams before midday which have tangled up everything. I am quite frightened."

And she explained to me that one of them—the long one on the top of the pile, on the table over there—seemed to contain ugly references directed at herself in a menacing way. She begged me to read it and see what I could make of it.

I knew enough of the general situation to see at a glance that she had misunderstood it thoroughly and even amazingly. I proved it to her very quickly. But her mistake was so ingenious in its wrongheadedness and arose so obviously from the distraction of an acute mind, that I couldn't help looking at her admiringly.

" Rita," I said, " you are a marvellous idiot."

" Am I ? Imbecile," she retorted with an enchanting smile of relief. " But perhaps it only seems so to you in contrast with the lady so perfect in her way. What is her way ? "

" Her way, I should say, lies somewhere between her sixtieth and seventieth year, and I have walked tête-à-tête with her for some little distance this afternoon."

" Heavens," she whispered, thunderstruck. " And meantime I had the son here. He arrived about five minutes after Rose left with that note for you," she went on in a tone of awe. " As a matter of fact, Rose saw him across the street but she thought she had better go on to you."

" I am furious with myself for not having guessed that much," I said bitterly. " I suppose you got him out of the house about five minutes after you heard I was coming here. Rose ought to have turned back when she saw him on his way to cheer your solitude. That girl is stupid after all, though she has got a certain amount of low cunning which no doubt is very useful at times."

" I forbid you to talk like this about Rose. I won't have it. Rose is not to be abused before me."

"I only mean to say that she failed in this instance to read your mind, that's all."

"This is, without exception, the most unintelligent thing you have said ever since I have known you. You may understand a lot about running contraband and about the minds of a certain class of people, but as to Rose's mind let me tell you that in comparison with hers yours is absolutely infantile, my adventurous friend. It would be contemptible if it weren't so—what shall I call it?—babyish. You ought to be slapped and put to bed." There was an extraordinary earnestness in her tone and when she ceased I listened yet to the seductive inflexions of her voice, that no matter in what mood she spoke seemed only fit for tenderness and love. And I thought suddenly of Azzolati being ordered to take himself off from her presence for ever, in that voice the very anger of which seemed to twine itself gently round one's heart. No wonder the poor wretch could not forget the scene and couldn't restrain his tears on the plain of Rambouillet. My moods of resentment against Rita, hot as they were, had no more duration than a blaze of straw. So I only said :

"Much *you* know about the management of children."

The corners of her lips stirred quaintly ; her animosity, especially when provoked by a personal attack upon herself, was always tinged by a sort of wistful humour of the most disarming kind.

"Come, *amigo* George, let us leave poor Rose alone. You had better tell me what you heard from the lips of the charming old lady. Perfection, isn't she? I have never seen her in my life, though she says she has seen me several times. But she has written to me on three separate occasions and every time I answered her as if I were writing to a queen. *Amigo* George, how does one write to a queen? How should a goatherd that could have been mistress of a king, how should she write to an old queen from very far away ; from over the sea ? "

"I will ask you as I have asked the old queen : why do you tell me all this, Doña Rita ? "

"To discover what's in your mind," she said, a little impatiently.

"If you don't know that yet!" I exclaimed under my breath.

"No, not in your mind. Can any one ever tell what is in a man's mind? But I see you won't tell."

"What's the good? You have written to her before, I understand. Do you think of continuing the correspondence?"

"Who knows?" she said in a profound tone. "She is the only woman that ever wrote to me. I returned her three letters to her with my last answer, explaining humbly that I preferred her to burn them herself. And I thought that would be the end of it. But an occasion may still arise."

"Oh, if an occasion arises," I said, trying to control my rage, "you may be able to begin your letter by the words *Chère Maman.*"

The cigarette box, which she had taken up without removing her eyes from me, flew out of her hand and opening in mid-air scattered cigarettes for quite a surprising distance all over the room. I got up at once and wandered off picking them up industriously. Doña Rita's voice behind me said indifferently:

"Don't trouble, I will ring for Rose."

"No need," I growled, without turning my head, "I can find my hat in the hall by myself, after I've finished picking up . . ."

"Bear!"

I returned with the box and placed it on the divan near her. She sat cross-legged, leaning back on her arms, in the blue shimmer of her embroidered robe and with the tawny halo of her unruly hair about her face which she raised to mine with an air of resignation.

"George, my friend," she said, "we have no manners."

"You would never have made a career at court, Doña Rita," I observed. "You are too impulsive."

"This is not bad manners, that's sheer insolence. This

has happened to you before. If it happens again, as I can't be expected to wrestle with a savage and desperate smuggler single-handed, I will go upstairs and lock myself in my room till you leave the house. Why did you say this to me ? "

" Oh, just for nothing, out of a full heart."

" If your heart is full of things like that, then my dear friend, you had better take it out and give it to the crows. No ! you said that for the pleasure of appearing terrible. And you see you are not terrible at all, you are rather amusing. Go on, continue to be amusing. Tell me something of what you heard from the lips of that aristocratic old lady who thinks that all men are equal and entitled to the pursuit of happiness."

" I hardly remember now. I heard something about the unworthiness of certain white geese out of stuffy drawing-rooms. It sounds mad, but the lady knows exactly what she wants. I also heard your praises sung. I sat there like a fool not knowing what to say."

" Why ? You might have joined in the singing."

" I didn't feel in the humour, because, don't you see, I had been incidentally given to understand that I was an insignificant and superfluous person who had better get out of the way of serious people."

" Ah, *par exemple !* "

" In a sense, you know, it was flattering ; but for the moment it made me feel as if I had been offered a pot of mustard to sniff."

She nodded with an amused air of understanding and I could see that she was interested. " Anything more ? " she asked, with a flash of radiant eagerness in all her person and bending slightly forward towards me.

" Oh, it's hardly worth mentioning. It was a sort of threat wrapped up, I believe, in genuine anxiety as to what might happen to my youthful insignificance. If I hadn't been rather on the alert just then I wouldn't even have perceived the meaning. But really an allusion to ' hot Southern blood ' could have only one meaning. Of course I laughed at it, but only ' *pour l'honneur* ' and to show I understood perfectly. In reality it left me completely indifferent."

Doña Rita looked very serious for a minute.

"Indifferent to the whole conversation?"

I looked at her angrily.

"To the whole. . . . You see I got up rather out of sorts this morning. Unrefreshed, you know. As if tired of life."

The liquid blue in her eyes remained directed at me without any expression except that of its usual mysterious immobility, but all her face took on a sad and thoughtful cast. Then as if she had made up her mind under the pressure of necessity:

"Listen, *amigo*," she said, "I have suffered domination and it didn't crush me because I have been strong enough to live with it; I have known caprice, you may call it folly if you like, and it left me unharmed because I was great enough not to be captured by anything that wasn't really worthy of me. My dear, it went down like a house of cards before my breath. There is something in me that will not be dazzled by any sort of prestige in this world, worthy or unworthy. I am telling you this because you are younger than myself."

"If you want me to say that there is nothing petty or mean about you, Doña Rita, then I do say it."

She nodded at me with an air of accepting the rendered justice and went on with the utmost simplicity.

"And what is it that is coming to me now with all the airs of virtue? All the lawful conventions are coming to me, all the glamours of respectability! And nobody can say that I have made as much as the slightest little sign to them. Not so much as lifting my little finger. I suppose you know that?"

"I don't know. I do not doubt your sincerity in anything you say. I am ready to believe. You are not one of those who have to work."

"Have to work—what do you mean?"

"It's a phrase I have heard. What I meant was that it isn't necessary for you to make any signs."

She seemed to meditate over this for a while.

"Don't be so sure of that," she said, with a flash of mischief, which made her voice sound more melancholy than before. "I am not so sure myself," she continued with a curious, vanishing, intonation of despair. "I don't know the truth about myself because I never had an opportunity to compare myself to anything in the world. I have been offered mock adulation, treated with mock reserve or with mock devotion, I have been fawned upon with an appalling earnestness of purpose, I can tell you; but these later honours, my dear, came to me in the shape of a very loyal and very scrupulous gentleman. For he is all that. And as a matter of fact I was touched."

"I know. Even to tears," I said provokingly. But she wasn't provoked, she only shook her head in negation (which was absurd) and pursued the trend of her spoken thoughts.

"That was yesterday," she said. "And yesterday he was extremely correct and very full of extreme self-esteem which expressed itself in the exaggerated delicacy with which he talked. But I know him in all his moods, I have known him even playful. I didn't listen to him. I was thinking of something else. Of things that were neither correct nor playful and that had to be looked at steadily with all the best that was in me. And that was why, in the end—I cried—yesterday."

"I saw it yesterday and I had the weakness of being moved by those tears for a time."

"If you want to make me cry again I warn you you won't succeed."

"No, I know. He has been here to-day and the dry season has set in."

"Yes, he has been here. I assure you it was perfectly unexpected. Yesterday he was railing at the world at large, at me who certainly have not made it, at himself and even at his mother. All this rather in parrot language, in the words of tradition and morality as understood by the members of that exclusive club to which he belongs. And yet when I thought that all this, those poor hackneyed words, expressed a sincere passion I could have found in my heart to be sorry for him. But he ended by telling me that one couldn't believe a single word I said, or something like that. You were here then, you heard it yourself."

"And it cut you to the quick," I said. "It made you depart from your dignity to the point of weeping on any shoulder that happened to be there. And considering that it was some more parrot talk after all (men have been saying that sort of thing to women from the beginning of the world) this sensibility seems to me childish."

"What perspicacity," she observed, with an indulgent, mocking smile, then changed her tone. "Therefore he wasn't expected to-day when he turned up, whereas you, who were expected, remained subject to the charms of conversation in that studio. It never occurred to you . . . did it? No! What had become of your perspicacity?"

"I tell you I was weary of life," I said in a passion.

She had another faint smile of a fugitive and unrelated kind as if she had been thinking of far-off things, then roused herself to grave animation.

"He came in full of smiling playfulness. How well I know that mood! Such self-command has its beauty; but it's no great help for a man with such fateful eyes. I could see he was moved in his correct, restrained way, and in his own way, too, he tried to move me with something that would be very simple. He told me that ever since we became friends, we two, he had not an hour of continuous sleep, unless perhaps when coming back dead-tired from outpost duty, and that he longed to get back to it and yet hadn't the courage to tear himself away from here. He was as simple as that. He's a *très galant homme* of absolute probity, even with himself. I said to him: The trouble is, Don Juan, that it isn't love but mistrust that keeps you in torment. I might have said jealousy, but I didn't like to use that word. A parrot would have added that I had given him no right to be jealous. But I am no parrot. I recognized the rights of his passion which I could very well see. He is jealous. He is not jealous of my past or of the future;

but he is jealously mistrustful of *me*, of what I am, of my very soul. He believes in a soul in the same way Therese does, as something that can be touched with grace or go to perdition ; and he doesn't want to be damned with me before his own judgment seat. He is a most noble and loyal gentleman, but I have my own Basque peasant soul and don't want to think that every time he goes away from my feet— yes, *mon cher*, on this carpet, look for the marks of scorching— that he goes away feeling tempted to brush the dust off his moral sleeve. That ! Never ! "

With brusque movements she took a cigarette out of the box, held it in her fingers for a moment, then dropped it unconsciously.

" And then, I don't love him," she uttered slowly as if speaking to herself and at the same time watching the very quality of that thought. " I never did. At first he fascinated me with his fatal aspect and his cold society smiles. But I have looked into those eyes too often. There are too many disdains in this aristocratic republican without a home. His fate may be cruel, but it will always be commonplace. While he sat there trying in a worldly tone to explain to me the problems, the scruples, of his suffering honour, I could see right into his heart and I was sorry for him. I was sorry enough for him to feel that if he had suddenly taken me by the throat and strangled me slowly, *avec délices*, I could forgive him while I choked. How correct he was ! But bitterness against me peeped out of every second phrase. At last I raised my hand and said to him, ' Enough.' I believe he was shocked by my plebeian abruptness but he was too polite to show it. His conventions will always stand in the way of his nature. I told him that everything that had been said and done during the last seven or eight months was inexplicable unless on the assumption that he was in love with me,—and yet in everything there was an implication that he couldn't forgive me my very existence. I did ask him whether he didn't think that it was absurd on his part . . ."

" Didn't you say that it was exquisitely absurd ? " I asked.

"Exquisitely ! . . ." Doña Rita was surprised at my question. "No. Why should I say that?"

"It would have reconciled him to your abruptness. It's their family expression. It would have come with a familiar sound and would have been less offensive."

"Offensive," Doña Rita repeated earnestly. "I don't think he was offended; he suffered in another way, but I didn't care for that. It was I that had become offended in the end, without spite, you understand, but past bearing. I didn't spare him. I told him plainly that to want a woman formed in mind and body, mistress of herself, free in her choice, independent in her thoughts; to love her apparently for what she is and at the same time to demand from her the candour and the innocence that could be only a shocking pretence; to know her such as life had made her and at the same time to despise her secretly for every touch with which her life had fashioned her—that was neither generous nor high minded; it was positively frantic. He got up and went away to lean against the mantelpiece, there, on his elbow and with his head in his hand. You have no idea of the charm and the distinction of his pose. I couldn't help admiring him : the expression, the grace, the fatal suggestion of his immobility. Oh, yes, I am sensible to æsthetic impressions, I have been educated to believe that there is a soul in them."

With that enigmatic, under the eyebrows glance fixed on me she laughed her deep contralto laugh without mirth but also without irony, and profoundly moving by the mere purity of the sound.

"I suspect he was never so disgusted and appalled in his life. His self-command is the most admirable worldly thing I have ever seen. What made it beautiful was that one could feel in it a tragic suggestion as in a great work of art."

She paused with an inscrutable smile that a great painter might have put on the face of some symbolic figure for the speculation and wonder of many generations. I said :

"I always thought that love for you could work great wonders. And now I am certain."

" Are you trying to be ironic ? " she said sadly and very much as a child might have spoken.

" I don't know," I answered in a tone of the same simplicity. " I find it very difficult to be generous."

" I, too," she said with a sort of funny eagerness. " I didn't treat him very generously. Only I didn't say much more. I found I didn't care what I said—and it would have been like throwing insults at a beautiful composition. He was well inspired not to move. It has spared him some disagreeable truths and perhaps I would even have said more than the truth. I am not fair. I am no more fair than other people. I would have been harsh. My very admiration was making me more angry. It's ridiculous to say of a man got up in correct tailor clothes, but there was a funereal grace in his attitude so that he might have been reproduced in marble on a monument to some woman in one of those atrocious Campo Santos : the bourgeois conception of an aristocratic mourning lover. When I came to that conclusion I became glad that I was angry or else I would have laughed right out before him."

" I have heard a woman say once, a woman of the people— do you hear me, Doña Rita ?—therefore deserving your attention, that one should never laugh at love."

" My dear," she said gently, " I have been taught to laugh at most things by a man who never laughed himself ; but it's true that he never spoke of love to me, love as a subject that is. So perhaps . . . But why ? "

" Because (but maybe that old woman was crazy), because, she said, there was death in the mockery of love."

Doña Rita moved slightly her beautiful shoulders and went on :

" I am glad, then, I didn't laugh. And I am also glad I said nothing more. I was feeling so little generous that if I had known something then of his mother's allusion to ' white geese ' I would have advised him to get one of them and lead it away on a beautiful blue ribbon. Mrs. Blunt was wrong, you know, to be so scornful. A white goose is exactly what her son wants. But look how badly the world is arranged. Such white birds cannot be got for nothing and he has not enough money even to buy a ribbon. Who knows! Maybe it was this which gave that tragic quality to his pose by the mantelpiece over there. Yes, that was it. Though no doubt I didn't see it then. As he didn't offer to move after I had done speaking I became quite unaffectedly sorry and advised him very gently to dismiss me from his mind definitely. He moved forward then and said to me in his usual voice and with his usual smile that it would have been excellent advice but unfortunately I was one of those women who can't be dismissed at will. And as I shook my head he insisted rather darkly : ' Oh, yes, Doña Rita, it is so. Cherish no illusions about that fact.' It sounded so threatening that in my surprise I didn't even acknowledge his parting bow. He went out of that false situation like a wounded man retreating after a fight. No, I have nothing to reproach myself with. I did nothing. I led him into nothing. Whatever illusions have passed through my head I kept my distance, and he was so loyal to what he seemed to think the redeeming proprieties of the situation that he has gone from me for good without so much as kissing the tips of my fingers. He must have felt like a man who had betrayed himself for nothing. It's horrible. It's the fault of that enormous fortune of mine, and I wish with all my heart that I could give it to him ; for he couldn't help his hatred of the thing that is : and as to his love, which is just as real, well—could I have rushed away from him to shut myself up in a convent? Could I ? After all I have a right to my share of daylight."

## V

I took my eyes from her face and became aware that dusk was beginning to steal into the room. How strange it seemed. Except for the glazed rotunda part its long walls, divided into narrow panels separated by an order of flat pilasters, presented, depicted on a black background and in vivid colours, slender women with butterfly wings and lean youths with narrow birds' wings. The effect was supposed to be Pompeiian and Rita and I had often laughed at the delirious fancy of some enriched shopkeeper. But still it was a display of fancy, a sign of grace; but at that moment these figures appeared to me weird and intrusive and strangely alive in their attenuated grace of unearthly beings concealing a power to see and hear.

Without words, without gestures, Doña Rita was heard again. "It may have been as near coming to pass as this." She showed me the breadth of her little finger nail. "Yes, as near as that. Why? How? Just like that, for nothing. Because it had come up. Because a wild notion had entered a practical old woman's head. Yes. And the best of it is that I have nothing to complain of. Had I surrendered I would have been perfectly safe with these two. It is they or rather he who couldn't trust me, or rather that something which I express, which I stand for. Mills would never tell me what it was. Perhaps he didn't know exactly himself. He said it was something like genius. My genius! Oh, I am not conscious of it, believe me, I am not conscious of it. But if I were I wouldn't pluck it out and cast it away. I am ashamed of nothing, of nothing! Don't be stupid enough to think that I have the slightest regret. There is no regret. First of all because I am I—and then because . . . My dear, believe me, I have had a horrible time of it myself lately."

This seemed to be the last word. Outwardly quiet, all the time, it was only then that she became composed enough to light an enormous cigarette of the same pattern as those made specially for the king—*por el Rey!* After a time, tipping the ash into the bowl on her left hand, she asked me in a friendly, almost tender, tone:

"What are you thinking of, *amigo?*"

"I was thinking of your immense generosity. You want to give a crown to one man, a fortune to another. That is very fine. But I suppose there is a limit to your generosity somewhere."

"I don't see why there should be any limit—to fine intentions! Yes, one would like to pay ransom and be done with it all."

"That's the feeling of a captive; and yet somehow I can't think of you as ever having been anybody's captive."

"You do display some wonderful insight sometimes. My dear, I begin to suspect that men are rather conceited about their powers. They think they dominate us. Even exceptional men will think that; men too great for mere vanity, men like Henry Allègre for instance, who by his consistent and serene detachment was certainly fit to dominate all sorts of people. Yet for the most part they can only do it because women choose more or less consciously to let them do so. Henry Allègre, if any man, might have been certain of his own power; and yet, look: I was a chit of a girl, I was sitting with a book where I had no business to be, in his own garden, when he suddenly came upon me, an ignorant girl of seventeen, a most uninviting creature with a tousled head, in an old black frock and shabby boots. I could have run away. I was perfectly capable of it. But I stayed looking up at him and—in the end it was HE who went away and it was I who stayed."

"Consciously?" I murmured.

"Consciously? You may just as well ask my shadow that lay so still by me on the young grass in that morning sunshine. I never knew before how still I could keep. It wasn't the stillness of terror. I remained, knowing perfectly well that if I ran he was not the man to run after me. I remember perfectly his deep-toned, politely indifferent '*Restez donc.*' He was mistaken. Already then I hadn't the slightest intention to move. And if you ask me again how far conscious all this was the nearest answer I can make you is this: that I remained on purpose, but I didn't know for what purpose I remained. Really, that couldn't be expected. . . . Why do you sigh like this? Would you have preferred me to be idiotically innocent or abominably wise?"

"These are not the questions that trouble me," I said. "If I sighed it is because I am weary."

"And getting stiff, too, I should say, in this Pompeiian armchair. You had better get out of it and sit on this couch as you always used to do. That, at any rate, is not Pompeiian. You have been growing of late extremely formal, I don't know why. If it is a pose then for goodness' sake drop it. Are you going to model yourself on Captain Blunt? You couldn't, you know. You are too young."

"I don't want to model myself on anybody," I said. "And anyway Blunt is too romantic; and, moreover, he has been and is yet in love with you—a thing that requires some style, an attitude, something of which I am altogether incapable."

"You know it isn't so stupid, this what you have just said. Yes, there is something in this."

"I am not stupid," I protested, without much heat.

"Oh, yes, you are. You don't know the world enough to judge. You don't know how wise men can be. Owls are nothing to them. Why do you try to look like an owl? There are thousands and thousands of them waiting for me outside the door : the staring, hissing beasts. You don't know what a relief of mental ease and intimacy you have been to me in the frankness of gestures and speeches and thoughts, sane or insane, that we have been throwing at each other. I have known nothing of this in my life but with you. There had always been some fear, some constraint, lurking in the background behind everybody, everybody—except you, my friend."

"An unmannerly, Arcadian state of affairs. I am glad you like it. Perhaps it's because you were intelligent enough to perceive that I was not in love with you in any sort of style."

"No, you were always your own self, unwise and reckless and with something in it kindred to mine, if I may say so without offence."

"You may say anything without offence. But has it

never occurred to your sagacity that I just, simply, loved you ? "

" Just—simply," she repeated in a wistful tone.

" You didn't want to trouble your head about it, is that it ? "

" My poor head. From your tone one might think you yearned to cut it off. No, my dear, I have made up my mind not to lose my head."

" You would be astonished to know how little I care for your mind."

" Would I ? Come and sit on the couch all the same," she said after a moment of hesitation. Then, as I did not move at once, she added with indifference : " You may sit as far away as you like, it's big enough, goodness knows."

The light was ebbing slowly out of the rotunda and to my bodily eyes she was beginning to grow shadowy. I sat down on the couch and for a long time no word passed between us. We made no movement. We did not even turn towards each other. All I was conscious of was the softness of the seat which seemed somehow to cause a relaxation of my stern mood, I won't say against my will but without any will on my part. Another thing I was conscious of, strangely enough, was the enormous brass bowl for cigarette ends. Quietly, with the least possible action, Doña Rita moved it to the other side of her motionless person. Slowly, the fantastic women with butterflies' wings and the slender-limbed youths with the gorgeous pinions on their shoulders were vanishing into their black backgrounds with an effect of silent discretion, leaving us to ourselves.

I felt suddenly extremely exhausted, absolutely overcome with fatigue since I had moved ; as if to sit on that Pompeiian chair had been a task almost beyond human strength, a sort of labour that must end in collapse. I fought against it for a moment and then my resistance gave way. Not all at once but as if yielding to an irresistible pressure (for I was not conscious of any irresistible attraction) I found myself with my head resting, with a weight I felt must be crushing, on Doña Rita's shoulder which yet did not give way, did not flinch at all. A faint scent of violets filled the tragic emptiness of my head and it seemed impossible to me that I should not cry from sheer weakness. But I remained dry-eyed. I only felt myself slipping lower and lower and I caught her round the waist clinging to her not from any intention but purely by instinct. All that time she hadn't stirred. There was only the slight movement of her breathing that showed her to be alive; and with closed eyes I imagined her to be lost in thought, removed by an incredible meditation while I clung to her, to an immense distance from the earth. The distance must have been immense because the silence was so perfect, the feeling as if of eternal stillness. I had a distinct impression of being in contact with an infinity that had the slightest possible rise and fall, was pervaded by a warm, delicate scent of violets and through which came a hand from somewhere to rest lightly on my head. Presently my ear caught the faint and regular pulsation of her heart, firm and quick, infinitely touching in its persistent mystery, disclosing itself into my very ear—and my felicity became complete.

It was a dreamlike state combined with a dreamlike sense of insecurity. Then in that warm and scented infinity, or eternity, in which I rested lost in bliss but ready for any catastrophe, I heard the distant, hardly audible, and fit to strike terror into the heart, ringing of a bell. At this sound the greatness of spaces departed. I felt the world close about me; the world of darkened walls, of very deep grey dusk against the panes, and I asked in a pained voice :

" Why did you ring, Rita ? "

There was a bell rope within reach of her hand. I had not felt her move, but she said very low :

" I rang for the lights."

" You didn't want the lights."

" It was time," she whispered secretly.

Somewhere within the house a door slammed. I got away from her feeling small and weak as if the best part of me had been torn away and irretrievably lost. Rose must have been somewhere near the door.

"It's abominable," I murmured to the still, idol-like shadow on the couch.

The answer was a hurried, nervous whisper : " I tell you it was time.  I rang because I had no strength to push you away."

I suffered a moment of giddiness before the door opened, light streamed in, and Rose entered, preceding a man in a green baize apron whom I had never seen, carrying on an enormous tray three Argand lamps fitted into vases of Pompeiian form.  Rose distributed them over the room.  In the flood of soft light the winged youths and the butterfly women reappeared on the panels, affected, gorgeous, callously unconscious of anything having happened during their absence. Rose attended to the lamp on the nearest mantelpiece, then turned about and asked in a confident undertone.

" Monsieur dine ? "

I had lost myself with my elbows on my knees and my head in my hands, but I heard the words distinctly.  I heard also the silence which ensued.  I sat up and took the responsibility of the answer on myself.

"Impossible.  I am going to sea this evening."

This was perfectly true only I had totally forgotten it till then.  For the last two days my being was no longer composed of memories but exclusively of sensations of the most absorbing, disturbing, exhausting nature.  I was like a man who has been buffeted by the sea or by a mob till he loses all hold on the world in the misery of his helplessness.  But now I was recovering.  And naturally the first thing I remembered was the fact that I was going to sea.

"You have heard, Rose," Doña Rita said at last with some impatience.

The girl waited a moment longer before she said :

"Oh, yes !  There is a man waiting for Monsieur in the hall.  A seaman."

It could be no one but Dominic.  It dawned upon me that since the evening of our return I had not been near him or the ship, which was completely unusual, unheard of and well calculated to startle Dominic.

"I have seen him before," continued Rose, "and as he told me he has been pursuing Monsieur all the afternoon and didn't like to go away without seeing Monsieur for a moment, I proposed to him to wait in the hall till Monsieur was at liberty."

I said : "Very well," and with a sudden resumption of her extremely busy, not-a-moment-to-lose manner Rose departed from the room. I lingered in an imaginary world full of tender light, of unheard-of colours, with a mad riot of flowers and an inconceivable happiness under the sky arched above its yawning precipices, while a feeling of awe enveloped me like its own proper atmosphere. But everything vanished at the sound of Doña Rita's loud whisper full of boundless dismay, such as to make one's hair stir on one's head.

"*Mon Dieu !* And what is going to happen now ? "

She got down from the couch and walked to a window. When the lights had been brought into the room all the panes had turned inky black; for the night had come and the garden was full of tall bushes and trees screening off the gas lamps of the main alley of the Prado. Whatever the question meant she was not likely to see an answer to it outside. But her whisper had offended me, had hurt something infinitely deep, infinitely subtle and infinitely clear-eyed in my nature. I said after her from the couch on which I had remained, "Don't lose your composure. You will always have some sort of bell at hand."

I saw her shrug her uncovered shoulders impatiently. Her forehead was against the very blackness of the panes ; pulled upward from the beautiful, strong nape of her neck, the twisted mass of her tawny hair was held high upon her head by the arrow of gold.

"You set up for being unforgiving," she said without anger.

I sprang to my feet while she turned about and came towards me bravely, with a wistful smile on her bold, adolescent face.

"It seems to me," she went on in a voice like a wave of

love itself, "that one should try to understand before one sets up for being unforgiving. Forgiveness is a very fine word. It is a fine invocation."

"There are other fine words in the language such as fascination, fidelity, also frivolity; and as for invocations there are plenty of them, too; for instance: alas, heaven help me."

We stood very close together, her narrow eyes were as enigmatic as ever, but that face, which, like some ideal conception of art, was incapable of anything like untruth and grimace, expressed by some mysterious means such a depth of infinite patience that I felt profoundly ashamed of myself.

"This thing is beyond words altogether," I said. "Beyond forgiveness, beyond forgetting, beyond anger or jealousy. . . . There is nothing between us two that could make us act together."

"Then we must fall back perhaps on something within us. that—you admit it?—we have in common."

"Don't be childish," I said. "You give one with a perpetual and intense freshness feelings and sensations that are as old as the world itself, and you imagine that your enchantment can be broken off anywhere, at any time! But it can't be broken. And forgetfulness, like everything else, can only come from you. It's an impossible situation to stand up against."

She listened with slightly parted lips as if to catch some further resonances.

"There is a sort of generous ardour about you," she said, "which I don't really understand. No, I don't know it. Believe me, it is not of myself I am thinking. And you—you are going out to-night to make another landing."

"Yes, it is a fact that before many hours I will be sailing away from you to try my luck once more."

"Your wonderful luck," she breathed out.

"Oh, yes, I am wonderfully lucky. Unless the luck really is yours—in having found somebody like me, who

Y

cares at the same time so much and so little for what you have at heart."

" "What time will you be leaving the harbour ? " she asked.

"Some time between midnight and daybreak. Our men may be a little late in joining, but certainly we will be gone before the first streak of light."

"What freedom ! " she murmured enviously. " It's something I shall never know. . . ."

" Freedom ! " I protested. " I am a slave to my word. There will be a string of carts and mules on a certain part of the coast, and a most ruffianly lot of men, men you understand, men with wives and children and sweethearts, who from the very moment they start on a trip risk a bullet in the head at any moment, but who have a perfect conviction that I will never fail them. That's my freedom. I wonder what they would think if they knew of your existence."

" I don't exist," she said.

" That's easy to say. But I will go as if you didn't exist— yet only because you do exist. You exist in me. I don't know where I end and you begin. You have got into my heart and into my veins and into my brain."

" Take this fancy out and trample it down in the dust," she said in a tone of timid entreaty.

" Heroically," I suggested with the sarcasm of despair.

" Well, yes, heroically," she said ; and there passed between us dim smiles, I have no doubt of the most touching imbecility on earth. We were standing by then in the middle of the room with its vivid colours on a black background, with its multitude of winged figures with pale limbs, with hair like halos or flames, all strangely tense in their strained, decorative attitudes. Doña Rita made a step towards me, and as I attempted to seize her hand she flung her arms round my neck. I felt their strength drawing me towards her and by a sort of blind and desperate effort I resisted. And all the time she was repeating with nervous insistence :

" But it is true that you will go. You will surely. Not

because of those people but because of me. You will go away because you feel you must."

With every word urging me to get away, her clasp tightened, she hugged my head closer to her breast. I submitted, knowing well that I could free myself by one more effort which it was in my power to make. But before I made it, in a sort of desperation, I pressed a long kiss into the hollow of her throat. And lo—there was no need for any effort. With a stifled cry of surprise her arms fell off me as if she had been shot. I must have been giddy, and perhaps we both were giddy, but the next thing I knew there was a good foot of space between us in the peaceful glow of the ground-glass globes, in the everlasting stillness of the winged figures. Something in the quality of her exclamation, something utterly unexpected, something I had never heard before, and also the way she was looking at me with a sort of incredulous, concentrated attention, disconcerted me exceedingly. I knew perfectly well what I had done and yet I felt that I didn't understand what had happened. I became suddenly abashed and I muttered that I had better go and dismiss that poor Dominic. She made no answer, gave no sign. She stood there lost in a vision—or was it a sensation?—of the most absorbing kind. I hurried out into the hall, shamefaced, as if I were making my escape while she wasn't looking. And yet I felt her looking fixedly at me, with a sort of stupefaction on her features—in her whole attitude—as though she had never even heard of such a thing as a kiss in her life.

A dim lamp (of Pompeiian form) hanging on a long chain left the hall practically dark. Dominic, advancing towards me from a distant corner, was but a little more opaque shadow than the others. He had expected me on board every moment till about three o'clock, but as I didn't turn up and gave no sign of life in any other way he started on his hunt. He sought news of me from the *garçons* at the various cafés, from the *cochers de fiacre* in front of the Exchange, from the tobacconist lady at the counter of the fashionable *Débit de Tabac*, from the old man who sold papers outside the *cercle*, and from the flower-girl at the door of the fashionable restaurant where I had my table. That young woman, whose business name was Irma, had come on duty about mid-day. She said to Dominic: " I think I've seen all his friends this morning but I haven't seen him for a week. What has become of him ? "

" That's exactly what I want to know," Dominic replied in a fury and then went back to the harbour on the chance that I might have called either on board or at Madame Léonore's café.

I expressed to him my surprise that he should fuss about me like an old hen over a chick. It wasn't like him at all. And he said that " *en effet* " it was Madame Léonore who wouldn't give him any peace. He hoped I wouldn't mind, it was best to humour women in little things ; and so he started off again, made straight for the street of the Consuls, was told there that I wasn't at home but the woman of the house looked so funny that he didn't know what to make of it. Therefore, after some hesitation, he took the liberty to inquire at this house, too, and being told that I couldn't be disturbed, had made up his mind not to go on board without actually setting his eyes on me and hearing from my own lips that nothing was changed as to sailing orders.

" There is nothing changed, Dominic," I said.

" No change of any sort ? " he insisted, looking very sombre and speaking gloomily from under his black moustaches in the dim glow of the alabaster lamp hanging above his head. He peered at me in an extraordinary manner as if he wanted to make sure that I had all my limbs about me. I asked him to call for my bag at the other house, on his way to the harbour, and he departed reassured, not, however, without remarking ironically that ever since she saw that American cavalier Madame Léonore was not easy in her mind about me.

As I stood alone in the hall, without a sound of any sort, Rose appeared before me.

" Monsieur will dine after all," she whispered calmly.

" My good girl, I am going to sea to-night."

" What am I going to do with Madame ? " she murmured to herself. " She will insist on returning to Paris."

" Oh, have you heard of it ? "

" I never get more than two hours' notice," she said. " But I know how it will be," her voice lost its calmness. " I can look after Madame up to a certain point but I cannot be altogether responsible. There is a dangerous person who is everlastingly trying to see Madame alone. I have managed to keep him off several times but there is a beastly old journalist who is encouraging him in his attempts, and I daren't even speak to Madame about it."

" What sort of person do you mean ? "

" Why, a man," she said scornfully.

I snatched up my coat and hat.

" Aren't there dozens of them ? "

" Oh ! But this one is dangerous. Madame must have given him a hold on her in some way. I ought not to talk like this about Madame and I wouldn't to anybody but Monsieur. I am always on the watch, but what is a poor girl to do ? . . . Isn't Monsieur going back to Madame ? "

" No, I am not going back. Not this time." A mist seemed to fall before my eyes. I could hardly see the girl standing by the closed door of the Pompeiian room with extended hand, as if turned to stone. But my voice was firm enough. " Not this time," I repeated, and became aware of the great noise of the wind amongst the trees, with the lashing of a rain squall against the door. " Perhaps some other time," I added.

I heard her say twice to herself : " *Mon Dieu ! Mon Dieu !* " and then a dismayed : " What can Monsieur expect me to do ? " But I had to appear insensible to her distress and that not altogether because, in fact, I had no option but to go away. I remember also a distinct wilfulness in my attitude and something half-contemptuous in my words as I laid my hand on the knob of the front door.

" You will tell Madame that I am gone. It will please her. Tell her that I am gone—heroically."

Rose had come up close to me. She met my words by

a despairing outward movement of her hands as though she were giving everything up.

"I see it clearly now that Madame has no friends," she declared with such a force of restrained bitterness that it nearly made me pause. But the very obscurity of actuating motives drove me on and I stepped out through the doorway muttering : "Everything is as Madame wishes it."

She shot at me a swift : "You should resist," of an extra-ordinary intensity, but I strode on down the path. Then Rose's schooled temper gave way at last and I heard her angry voice screaming after me furiously through the wind and rain : "No! Madame has no friends. Not one!"

# PART FIVE

## I

THAT night I didn't get on board till just before midnight and Dominic could not conceal his relief at having me safely there. Why he should have been so uneasy it was impossible to say but at the time I had a sort of impression that my inner destruction (it was nothing less) had affected my appearance, that my doom was as it were written on my face. I was a mere receptacle for dust and ashes, a living testimony to the vanity of all things. My very thoughts were like a ghostly rustle of dead leaves. But we had an extremely successful trip, and for most of the time Dominic displayed an unwonted jocularity of a dry and biting kind with which, he maintained, he had been infected by no other person than myself. As, with all his force of character, he was very responsive to the moods of those he liked I have no doubt he spoke the truth. But I know nothing about it. The observer, more or less alert, whom each of us carries in his own consciousness, failed me altogether, had turned away his face in sheer horror, or else had fainted from the strain. And thus I had to live alone, unobserved even by myself.

But the trip had been successful. We re-entered the harbour very quietly as usual and when our craft had been moored unostentatiously amongst the plebeian stone-carriers, Dominic, whose grim joviality had subsided in the last twenty-four hours of our homeward run, abandoned me to myself as though indeed I had been a doomed man. He only stuck his head for a moment into our little cuddy where I was changing my clothes and being told in answer to his question that I had no special orders to give went ashore without waiting for me.

679

Generally we used to step on the quay together and I never failed to enter for a moment Madame Léonore's café. But this time when I got on the quay Dominic was nowhere to be seen. What was it? Abandonment—discretion— or had he quarrelled with his Léonore before leaving on the trip?

My way led me past the café and through the glass panes I saw that he was already there. On the other side of the little marble table Madame Léonore, leaning with mature grace on her elbow, was listening to him absorbed. Then I passed on and—what would you have!—I ended by making my way into the street of the Consuls. I had nowhere else to go. There were my things in the apartment on the first floor. I couldn't bear the thought of meeting anybody I knew.

The feeble gas flame in the hall was still there, on duty, as though it had never been turned off since I last crossed the hall at half-past eleven in the evening to go to the harbour. The small flame had watched me letting myself out; and now, exactly of the same size, the poor little tongue of light (there was something wrong with that burner) watched me letting myself in, as indeed it had done many times before. Generally the impression was that of entering an untenanted house, but this time before I could reach the foot of the stairs Therese glided out of the passage leading into the studio. After the usual exclamations she assured me that everything was ready for me upstairs, had been for days, and offered to get me something to eat at once. I accepted and said I would be down in the studio in half an hour. I found her there by the side of the laid table ready for conversation. She began by telling me— the dear, poor young Monsieur—in a sort of plaintive chant, that there were no letters for me, no letters of any kind, no letters from anybody. Glances of absolutely terrifying tenderness mingled with flashes of cunning swept over me from head to foot while I tried to eat.

"Are you giving me Captain Blunt's wine to drink?" I asked, noting the straw-coloured liquid in my glass.

She screwed up her mouth as if she had a twinge of tooth-ache and assured me that the wine belonged to the house. I would have to pay her for it. As far as personal feelings go, Blunt, who addressed her always with polite seriousness, was not a favourite with her. The "charming, brave Monsieur" was now fighting for the King and religion against the impious Liberals. He went away the very morning after I had left and, oh! she remembered, he had asked her before going away whether I was still in the house. Wanted probably to say good-bye to me, shake my hand, the dear, polite Monsieur.

I let her run on in dread expectation of what she would say next but she stuck to the subject of Blunt for some time longer. He had written to her once about some of his things which he wanted her to send to Paris to his mother's address; but she was going to do nothing of the kind. She announced this with a pious smile; and in answer to my questions I discovered that it was a stratagem to make Captain Blunt return to the house.

"You will get yourself into trouble with the police, Mademoiselle Therese, if you go on like that," I said. But she was as obstinate as a mule and assured me with the utmost confidence that many people would be ready to defend a poor honest girl. There was something behind this attitude which I could not fathom. Suddenly she fetched a deep sigh.

"Our Rita, too, will end by coming to her sister."

The name for which I had been waiting deprived me of speech for the moment. The poor mad sinner had rushed off to some of her wickednesses in Paris. Did I know? No? How could she tell whether I did know or not? Well! I had hardly left the house, so to speak, when Rita was down with her maid behaving as if the house did really still belong to her. . . .

"What time was it?" I managed to ask. And with the words my life itself was being forced out through my lips. But Therese, not noticing anything strange about me, said it was something like half-past seven in the morning. The "poor sinner" was all in black as if she were going to church (except for her expression, which was enough to shock any honest person), and after ordering her with frightful menaces not to let anybody know she was in the house she rushed upstairs and locked herself up in my bedroom, while "that French creature" (whom she seemed to love more than her own sister) went into my salon and hid herself behind the window curtain.

I had recovered sufficiently to ask in a quiet natural voice whether Doña Rita and Captain Blunt had seen each other. Apparently they had not seen each other. The polite captain had looked so stern while packing up his kit that Therese dared not speak to him at all. And he was in a hurry, too. He had to see his dear mother off to Paris before his own departure. Very stern. But he shook her hand with a very nice bow.

Therese elevated her right hand for me to see. It was broad and short with blunt fingers, as usual. The pressure of Captain Blunt's handshake had not altered its unlovely shape.

"What was the good of telling him that our Rita was here?" went on Therese. "I would have been ashamed of her coming here and behaving as if the house belonged to her! I had already said some prayers at his intention at the half-past six mass, the brave gentleman. That maid of my sister Rita was upstairs watching him drive away with her evil eyes, but I made a sign of the cross after the fiacre, and then I went upstairs and banged at your door, my dear kind young Monsieur, and shouted to Rita that she had no right to lock herself in any of my *locataires'* rooms. At last she opened it—and what do you think? All her hair was loose over her shoulders. I suppose it all came down when she flung her hat on your bed. I noticed when she arrived that her hair wasn't done properly. She used your brushes to do it up again in front of your glass."

"Wait a moment," I said, and jumped up, upsetting my wine to run upstairs as fast as I could. I lighted the gas, all the three jets in the middle of the room, the jet by the bedside and two others flanking the dressing-table. I had been struck by the wild hope of finding a trace of Rita's passage, a sign or something. I pulled out all the drawers violently, thinking that perhaps she had hidden there a scrap of paper, a note. It was perfectly mad. Of course there was no chance of that. Therese would have seen to it. I picked up one after another all the various objects on the dressing-table. On laying my hands on the brushes I had a profound emotion, and with misty eyes I examined them meticulously with the new hope of finding one of Rita's tawny hairs entangled amongst the bristles by a miraculous chance. But Therese would have done away with that chance, too. There was nothing to be seen, though I held them up to the light with a beating heart. It was written that not even *that* trace of her passage on the earth should remain with me; not to help but, as it were, to soothe the memory. Then I lighted a cigarette and came downstairs slowly. My unhappiness became dulled, as the grief of those who mourn for the dead gets dulled in the overwhelming sensation that everything is over, that a part of themselves is lost beyond recall taking with it all the savour of life.

I discovered Therese still on the very same spot of the floor, her hands folded over each other and facing my empty chair before which the spilled wine had soaked a large portion of the table-cloth. She hadn't moved at all. She hadn't even picked up the overturned glass. But directly I appeared she began to speak in an ingratiating voice.

"If you have missed anything of yours upstairs, my dear young Monsieur, you mustn't say it's me. You don't know what our Rita is."

"I wish to goodness," I said, "that she had taken something."

And again I became inordinately agitated as though it were my absolute fate to be everlastingly dying and reviving to the tormenting fact of her existence. Perhaps she had taken something? Anything. Some small object. I thought suddenly of a Rhenish-stone match-box. Perhaps

it was that. I didn't remember having seen it when upstairs.
I wanted to make sure at once. At once. But I commanded
myself to sit still.

"And she so wealthy," Therese went on. "Even you
with your dear generous little heart can do nothing for our
Rita. No man can do anything for her—except perhaps
one, but she is so evilly disposed towards him that she
wouldn't even see him, if in the goodness of his forgiving
heart he were to offer his hand to her. It's her bad conscience that frightens her. He loves her more than his
life, the dear, charitable man."

"You mean some rascal in Paris that I believe persecutes
Doña Rita. Listen, Mademoiselle Therese, if you know
where he hangs out you had better let him have word to
be careful. I believe he, too, is mixed up in the Carlist
intrigue. Don't you know that your sister can get him shut
up any day or get him expelled by the police?"

Therese sighed deeply and put on a look of pained
virtue.

"Oh, the hardness of her heart. She tried to be tender
with me. She is awful. I said to her, 'Rita, have you sold
your soul to the Devil?' and she shouted like a fiend:
'For happiness! Ha, ha, ha!' She threw herself backwards on that couch in your room and laughed and laughed
and laughed as if I had been tickling her, and she drummed
on the floor with the heels of her shoes. She is possessed.
Oh, my dear innocent young Monsieur, you have never
seen anything like that. That wicked girl who serves her
rushed in with a tiny glass bottle and put it to her nose;
but I had a mind to run out and fetch the priest from the
church where I go to early mass. Such a nice, stout, severe
man. But that false, cheating creature (I am sure she is
robbing our Rita from morning to night), she talked to our
Rita very low and quieted her down. I am sure I don't
know what she said. She must be leagued with the devil.
And then she asked me if I would go down and make a cup
of chocolate for her Madame. Madame—that's our Rita.
Madame! It seems they were going off directly to Paris

and her Madame had had nothing to eat since the morning
of the day before.   Fancy me being ordered to make chocolate for our Rita !   However, the poor thing looked so
exhausted and white-faced that I went.   Ah !  the devil
can give you an awful shake up if he likes."

Therese fetched another deep sigh and raising her eyes
looked at me with great attention.   I preserved an inscrutable expression, for I wanted to hear all she had to tell me
of Rita.   I watched her with the greatest anxiety composing
her face into a cheerful expression.

"So Doña Rita is gone to Paris ? " I asked negligently.

"Yes, my dear Monsieur.  I believe she went straight
to the railway station from here.   When she first got up
from the couch she could hardly stand.   But before, while
she was drinking the chocolate which I made for her, I
tried to get her to sign a paper giving over the house to
me, but she only closed her eyes and begged me to try and
be a good sister and leave her alone for half an hour.   And
she lying there looking as if she wouldn't live a day.   But
she always hated me."

I said bitterly, "You needn't have worried her like this.
If she had not lived for another day you would have had
this house and everything else besides ;  a bigger bit than
even your wolfish throat can swallow, Mademoiselle Therese."

I then said a few more things indicative of my disgust
with her rapacity, but they were quite inadequate, as I
wasn't able to find words strong enough to express my
real mind.   But it didn't matter really because I don't
think Therese heard me at all.   She seemed lost in rapt
amazement.

"What do you say, my dear Monsieur ?   What !   All
for me without any sort of paper ? "

She appeared distracted by my curt : "Yes."   Therese
believed in my truthfulness.   She believed me implicitly,
except when I was telling her the truth about herself,
mincing no words, when she used to stand smilingly bashful
as if I were overwhelming her with compliments.   I expected
her to continue the horrible tale but apparently she had

found something to think about which checked the flow. She fetched another sigh and muttered :

"Then the law can be just, if it does not require any paper. After all, I am her sister."

"It's very difficult to believe that—at sight," I said roughly.

"Ah, but that I could prove. There are papers for that."

After this declaration she began to clear the table, preserving a thoughtful silence.

I was not very surprised at the news of Doña Rita's departure for Paris. It was not necessary to ask myself why she had gone. I didn't even ask myself whether she had left the leased Villa on the Prado for ever. Later talking again with Therese, I learned that her sister had given it up for the use of the Carlist cause and that some sort of unofficial Consul, a Carlist agent of some sort, either was going to live there or had already taken possession. This, Rita herself had told her before her departure on that agitated morning spent in the house—in my rooms. A close investigation demonstrated to me that there was nothing missing from them. Even the wretched match-box which I really hoped was gone turned up in a drawer after I had, delightedly, given it up. It was a great blow. She might have taken that at least ! She knew I used to carry it about with me constantly while ashore. She might have taken it ! Apparently she meant that there should be no bond left even of that kind ; and yet it was a long time before I gave up visiting and revisiting all the corners of all possible receptacles for something that she might have left behind on purpose. It was like the mania of those disordered minds who spend their days hunting for a treasure. I hoped for a forgotten hairpin, for some tiny piece of ribbon. Sometimes at night I reflected that such hopes were altogether insensate ; but I remember once getting up at two in the morning to search for a little cardboard box in the bathroom, into which, I remembered, I had not looked before. Of course it was empty ; and, anyway, Rita could not possibly have known of its existence. I got back to bed shivering violently, though the night was warm, and with a distinct impression that this thing would end by making me mad. It was no longer a question of " this sort of thing " killing me. The moral atmosphere of this torture was different. It would make me mad. And at that thought great shudders ran down my prone body, because, once, I had visited a famous lunatic asylum where they had shown me a poor wretch who was mad, apparently, because he thought he had been abominably fooled by a woman. They told me that his grievance was quite imaginary. He was a young man with a thin fair beard, huddled up on the edge of his bed, hugging himself forlornly; and his incessant and lamentable wailing filled the long bare corridor, striking a chill into one's heart long before one came to the door of his cell.

And there was no one from whom I could hear, to whom I could speak, with whom I could evoke the image of Rita. Of course I could utter that word of four letters to Therese; but Therese for some reason took it into her head to avoid all topics connected with her sister. I felt as if I could pull out great handfuls of her hair hidden modestly under the black handkerchief of which the ends were sometimes tied under her chin. But, really, I could not have given her any intelligible excuse for that outrage. Moreover, she was very busy from the very top to the very bottom of the house, which she persisted in running alone because she couldn't make up her mind to part with a few francs every month to a servant. It seemed to me that I was no longer such a favourite with her as I used to be. That, strange to say, was exasperating, too. It was as if some idea, some fruitful notion had killed in her all the softer and more humane emotions. She went about with brooms and dusters wearing an air of sanctimonious thoughtfulness.

The man who to a certain extent took my place in Therese's favour was the old father of the dancing girls inhabiting the ground floor. In a tall hat and a well-to-do dark blue overcoat he allowed himself to be buttonholed in the hall by

Therese who would talk to him interminably with downcast eyes. He smiled gravely down at her, and meanwhile tried to edge towards the front door. I imagine he didn't put a great value on Therese's favour. Our stay in harbour was prolonged this time and I kept indoors like an invalid. One evening I asked that old man to come in and drink and smoke with me in the studio. He made no difficulties to accept, brought his wooden pipe with him, and was very entertaining in a pleasant voice. One couldn't tell whether he was an uncommon person or simply a ruffian, but in any case with his white beard he looked quite venerable. Naturally he couldn't give me much of his company as he had to look closely after his girls and their admirers; not that the girls were unduly frivolous, but of course being very young they had no experience. They were friendly creatures with pleasant, merry voices and he was very much devoted to them. He was a muscular man with a high colour and silvery locks curling round his bald pate and over his ears, like a *barocco* apostle. I had an idea that he had had a lurid past and had seen some fighting in his youth. The admirers of the two girls stood in great awe of him, from instinct no doubt, because his behaviour to them was friendly and even somewhat obsequious, yet always with a certain truculent glint in his eye that made them pause in everything but their generosity—which was encouraged. I sometimes wondered whether those two careless, merry hard-working creatures understood the secret moral beauty of the situation.

My real company was the dummy in the studio and I can't say it was exactly satisfying. After taking possession of the studio I had raised it tenderly, dusted its mangled limbs and insensible, hard-wood bosom, and then had propped it up in a corner where it seemed to take on, of itself, a shy attitude. I knew its history. It was not an ordinary dummy. One day, talking with Doña Rita about her sister, I had told her that I thought Therese used to knock it down on purpose with a broom, and Doña Rita had laughed very much. This, she had said, was an instance of dislike from mere instinct. That dummy had been made to measure years before. It had to wear for days and days the Imperial Byzantine robes in which Doña Rita sat only once or twice herself; but of course the folds and bends of the stuff had to be preserved as in the first sketch. Doña Rita described amusingly how she had to stand in the middle of her room while Rose walked around her with a tape measure noting the figures down on a small piece of paper which was then sent to the maker, who presently returned it with an angry letter stating that those proportions were altogether impossible in any woman. Apparently Rose had muddled them all up; and it was a long time before the figure was finished and sent to the Pavilion in a long basket to take on itself the robes and the hieratic pose of the Empress. Later, it wore with the same patience the marvellous hat of the "Girl in the Hat." But Doña Rita couldn't understand how the poor thing ever found its way to Marseilles minus its turnip head. Probably it came down with the robes and a quantity of precious brocades which she herself had sent down from Paris. The knowledge of its origin, the contempt of Captain Blunt's references to it, with Therese's shocked dislike of the dummy, invested that summary reproduction with a sort of charm, gave me a faint and miserable illusion of the original, less artificial than a photograph, less precise, too. . . . But it can't be explained. I felt positively friendly to it as if it had been Rita's trusted personal attendant. I even went so far as to discover that it had a sort of grace of its own. But I never went so far as to address set speeches to it where it lurked shyly in its corner, or drag it out from there for contemplation. I left it in peace. I wasn't mad. I was only convinced that I soon would be.

## II

NOTWITHSTANDING my misanthropy I had to see a few
people on account of all these Royalist affairs which I couldn't
very well drop, and in truth did not wish to drop. They
were my excuse for remaining in Europe, which somehow
I had not the strength of mind to leave for the West Indies,
or elsewhere. On the other hand, my adventurous pursuit
kept me in contact with the sea where I found occupation,
protection, consolation, the mental relief of grappling with
concrete problems, the sanity one acquires from close contact with simple mankind, a little self-confidence born from
the dealings with the elemental powers of nature. I couldn't
give all that up. And besides all this was related to Doña
Rita. I had, as it were, received it all from her own hand,
from that hand the clasp of which was as frank as a man's
and yet conveyed a unique sensation. The very memory
of it would go through me like a wave of heat. It was
over that hand that we first got into the habit of quarrelling,
with the irritability of sufferers from some obscure pain and
yet half unconscious of their disease. Rita's own spirit
hovered over the troubled waters of Legitimity. But as
to the sound of the four magic letters of her name I was
not very likely to hear it fall sweetly on my ears. For
instance, the distinguished personality in the world of
finance with whom I had to confer several times, alluded
to the irresistible seduction of the power which reigned
over my heart and my mind ; which had a mysterious and
unforgettable face, the brilliance of sunshine together with
the unfathomable splendour of the night as—Madame
de Lastaola. That's how that steel-grey man called the
greatest mystery of the universe. When uttering that
assumed name he would make for himself a guardedly
solemn and reserved face as though he were afraid lest I
should presume to smile, lest he himself should venture to
smile, and the sacred formality of our relations should be
outraged beyond mending.

He would refer in a studiously grave tone to Madame de Lastaola's wishes, plans, activities, instructions, movements; or picking up a letter from the usual litter of paper found on such men's desks, glance at it to refresh his memory; and, while the very sight of the handwriting would make my lips go dry, would ask me in a bloodless voice whether perchance I had "a direct communication from—er—Paris lately." And there would be other maddening circumstances connected with those visits. He would treat me as a serious person having a clear view of certain eventualities, while at the very moment my vision could see nothing but streaming across the wall at his back, abundant and misty, unearthly and adorable, a mass of tawny hair that seemed to have hot sparks tangled in it. Another nuisance was the atmosphere of Royalism, of Legitimacy, that pervaded the room, thin as air, intangible, as though no Legitimist of flesh and blood had ever existed to the man's mind except perhaps myself. He, of course, was just simply a banker, a very distinguished, a very influential, and a very impeccable banker. He persisted also in deferring to my judgment and sense with an over-emphasis called out by my perpetual surprise at my youth. Though he had seen me many times (I even knew his wife) he could never get over my immature age. He himself was born about fifty years old, all complete, with his iron-grey whiskers and his bilious eyes, which he had the habit of frequently closing during a conversation. On one occasion he said to me: "By the by, the Marquis of Villarel is here for a time. He inquired after you the last time he called on me. May I let him know that you are in town?"

I didn't say anything to that. The Marquis of Villarel was the Don Rafael of Rita's own story. What had I to do with Spanish grandees? And for that matter what had she, the woman of all time, to do with all the villainous or splendid disguises human dust takes upon itself? All this was in the past, and I was acutely aware that for me there was no present, no future, nothing but a hollow pain, a vain passion of such magnitude that being locked up

within my breast it gave me an illusion of lonely greatness
with my miserable head uplifted amongst the stars. But
when I made up my mind (which I did quickly, to be done
with it) to call on the banker's wife, almost the first thing
she said to me was that the Marquis de Villarel was " amongst
us." She said it joyously. If in her husband's room at
the bank legitimism was a mere unpopulated principle, in
her salon Legitimacy was nothing but persons. " *Il m'a
causé beaucoup de vous,*" she said as if there had been a joke
in it of which I ought to be proud. I slunk away from her.
I couldn't believe that the grandee had talked to her about me.
I had never felt myself part of the great Royalist enterprise.
I confess that I was so indifferent to everything, so profoundly demoralized, that having once got into that drawing-
room I hadn't the strength to get away ; though I could
see perfectly well my volatile hostess going from one to
another of her acquaintances in order to tell them with a
little gesture, " Look ! Over there—in that corner. That's
the notorious Monsieur George." At last she herself drove
me out by coming to sit by me vivaciously and going into
ecstasies over " *ce cher* Monsieur Mills " and that magnificent
Lord X ; and ultimately, with a perfectly odious snap in
the eyes and drop in the voice, dragging in the name of
Madame de Lastaola and asking me whether I was really
so much in the confidence of that astonishing person. " *Vous
devez bien regretter son départ pour Paris,*" she cooed, looking
with affected bashfulness at her fan. . . . How I got out
of the room I really don't know. There was also a staircase. I did not fall down it head first—that much I am
certain of ; and I also remember that I wandered for a long
time about the seashore and went home very late, by the
way of the Prado, giving in passing a fearful glance at the
Villa. It showed not a gleam of light through the thin
foliage of its trees.

I spent the next day with Dominic on board the little
craft watching the shipwrights at work on her deck. From
the way they went about their business those men must
have been perfectly sane ; and I felt greatly refreshed by

my company during the day. Dominic, too, devoted himself to his business, but his taciturnity was sardonic. Then
I dropped in at the café and Madame Léonore's loud " Eh,
Signorino, here you are at last ! " pleased me by its resonant
friendliness. But I found the sparkle of her black eyes, as
she sat down for a moment opposite me while I was having
my drink, rather difficult to bear. That man and that
woman seemed to know something. What did they know ?
At parting she pressed my hand significantly. What did
she mean ? But I didn't feel offended by these manifestations. The souls within these people's breasts were not
volatile in the manner of slightly scented and inflated
bladders. Neither had they the impervious skins which
seem the rule in the fine world that wants only to get on.
Somehow they had sensed that there was something wrong ;
and whatever impression they might have formed for themselves I had the certitude that it would not be for them a
matter of grins at my expense.

That day on returning home I found Therese looking out
for me, a very unusual occurrence of late. She handed me
a card bearing the name of the Marquis de Villarel.

" How did you come by this ? " I asked. She turned on
at once the tap of her volubility and I was not surprised to
learn that the grandee had not done such an extraordinary
thing as to call upon me in person. A young gentleman
had brought it. Such a nice young gentleman, she interjected with her piously ghoulish expression. He was not
very tall. He had a very smooth complexion (that woman
was incorrigible) and a nice, tiny black moustache. Therese
was sure that he must have been an officer *en las filas legitimas*.
With that notion in her head she had asked him about the
welfare of that other model of charm and elegance, Captain
Blunt. To her extreme surprise the charming young gentleman with beautiful eyes had apparently never heard of
Blunt. But he seemed very much interested in his surroundings, looked all round the hall, noted the costly wood
of the door panels, paid some attention to the silver statuette
holding up the defective gas burner at the foot of the stairs,

and, finally, asked whether this was in very truth the house of the most excellent Señora Doña Rita de Lastaola. The question staggered Therese, but with great presence of mind she answered the young gentleman that she didn't know what excellence there was about it, but that the house was her property, having been given to her by her own sister. At this the young gentleman looked both puzzled and angry, turned on his heel, and got back into his fiacre. Why should people be angry with a poor girl who had never done a single reprehensible thing in her whole life?

"I suppose our Rita does tell people awful lies about her poor sister." She sighed deeply (she had several kinds of sighs and this was the hopeless kind) and added reflectively, "Sin on sin, wickedness on wickedness! And the longer she lives the worse it will be. It would be better for our Rita to be dead."

I told "Mademoiselle Therese" that it was really impossible to tell whether she was more stupid or atrocious; but I wasn't really very much shocked. These outbursts did not signify anything in Therese. One got used to them. They were merely the expression of her rapacity and her righteousness; so that our conversation ended by my asking her whether she had any dinner ready for me that evening.

"What's the good of getting you anything to eat, my dear young Monsieur?" she quizzed me tenderly. "You just only peck like a little bird. Much better let me save the money for you." It will show the super-terrestrial nature of my misery when I say that I was quite surprised at Therese's view of my appetite. Perhaps she was right. I certainly did not know. I stared hard at her and in the end she admitted that the dinner was in fact ready that very moment.

The new young gentleman within Therese's horizon didn't surprise me very much. Villarel would travel with some sort of suite, a couple of secretaries at least. I had heard enough of Carlist headquarters to know that the man had been (very likely was still) Captain General of the Royal Bodyguard and was a person of great political (and domestic) influence at Court. The card was, under its social form, a mere command to present myself before the grandee. No Royalist devoted by conviction, as I must have appeared to him, could have mistaken the meaning. I put the card in my pocket and after dining or not dining —I really don't remember—spent the evening smoking in the studio, pursuing thoughts of tenderness and grief, visions exalting and cruel. From time to time I looked at the dummy. I even got up once from the couch on which I had been writhing like a worm and walked towards it as if to touch it, but refrained, not from sudden shame but from sheer despair. By and by Therese drifted in. It was then late and, I imagine, she was on her way to bed. She looked the picture of cheerful, rustic innocence and started propounding to me a conundrum which began with the words :

" If our Rita were to die before long . . ."

She didn't get any further because I had jumped up and frightened her by shouting : " Is she ill? What has happened? Have you had a letter ? "

She had had a letter. I didn't ask her to show it to me, though I daresay she would have done so. I had an idea that there was no meaning in anything, at least no meaning that mattered. But the interruption had made Therese apparently forget her sinister conundrum. She observed me with her shrewd, unintelligent eyes for a bit, and then with the fatuous remark about the Law being just she left me to the horrors of the studio. I believe I went to sleep there from sheer exhaustion. Some time during the night I woke up chilled to the bone and in the dark. These were horrors and no mistake. I dragged myself upstairs to bed past the indefatigable statuette holding up the ever-miserable light. The black-and-white hall was like an ice-house.

The main consideration which induced me to call on the Marquis of Villarel was the fact that after all I was a discovery of Doña Rita's, her own recruit. My fidelity and steadfastness had been guaranteed by her and no one else. I couldn't bear the idea of her being criticized by every empty-headed chatterer belonging to the Cause. And as, apart from that, nothing mattered much, why, then—I would get this over.

But it appeared that I had not reflected sufficiently on all the consequences of that step. First of all the sight of the Villa looking shabbily cheerful in the sunshine (but not containing her any longer) was so perturbing that I very nearly went away from the gate. Then when I got in after much hesitation—being admitted by the man in the green baize apron who recognized me—the thought of entering that room, out of which she was gone as completely as if she had been dead, gave me such an emotion that I had to steady myself against the table till the faintness was past. Yet I was irritated as at a treason when the man in the baize apron instead of letting me into the Pompeiian dining-room crossed the hall to another door not at all in the Pompeiian style (more Louis XV rather—that Villa was like a *Salade Russe* of styles) and introduced me into a big, light room full of very modern furniture. The portrait *en pied* of an officer in a sky-blue uniform hung on the end wall. The officer had a small head, a black beard cut square, a robust body, and leaned with gauntleted hands on the simple hilt of a straight sword. That striking picture dominated a massive mahogany desk, and, in front of his desk, a very roomy, tall-backed armchair of dark green velvet. I thought I had been announced into an empty room till glancing along the extremely loud carpet I detected a pair of feet under the armchair.

I advanced towards it and discovered a little man, who had made no sound or movement till I came into his view, sunk deep in the green velvet. He altered his position slowly and rested his hollow, black, quietly burning eyes on my face in prolonged scrutiny. I detected something comminatory in his yellow, emaciated countenance, but I believe now he was simply startled by my youth. I bowed profoundly. He extended a meagre little hand.

"Take a chair, Don Jorge."

He was very small, frail, and thin, but his voice was not

languid, though he spoke hardly above his breath. Such was the envelope and the voice of the fanatical soul belonging to the Grand-master of Ceremonies and Captain General of the Bodyguard at the Headquarters of the Legitimist Court, now detached on a special mission. He was all fidelity, inflexibility, and sombre conviction, but like some great saints he had very little body to keep all these merits in.

"You are very young," he remarked, to begin with. "The matters on which I desired to converse with you are very grave."

"I was under the impression that your Excellency wished to see me at once. But if your Excellency prefers it I will return in, say, seven years' time when I may perhaps be old enough to talk about grave matters."

He didn't stir hand or foot and not even the quiver of an eyelid proved that he had heard my shockingly unbecoming retort.

"You have been recommended to us by a noble and loyal lady, in whom His Majesty—whom God preserve—reposes an entire confidence. God will reward her as she deserves and you, too, Señor, according to the disposition you bring to this great work which has the blessing (here he crossed himself) of our Holy Mother the Church."

"I suppose your Excellency understands that in all this I am not looking for reward of any kind."

At this he made a faint, almost ethereal grimace.

"I was speaking of the spiritual blessing which rewards the service of religion and will be of benefit to your soul," he explained with a slight touch of acidity. "The other is perfectly understood and your fidelity is taken for granted. His Majesty—whom God preserve—has been already pleased to signify his satisfaction with your services to the most noble and loyal Doña Rita by a letter in his own hand."

Perhaps he expected me to acknowledge this announcement in some way, speech, or bow, or something, because before my immobility he made a slight movement in his chair which smacked of impatience. "I am afraid, Señor, that you are affected by the spirit of scoffing and irreverence which pervades this unhappy country of France in which both you and I are strangers, I believe. Are you a young man of that sort?"

"I am a very good gun-runner, your Excellency," I answered quietly.

He bowed his head gravely. "We are aware. But I was looking for the motives which ought to have their pure source in religion."

"I must confess frankly that I have not reflected on my motives," I said. "It is enough for me to know that they are not dishonourable and that anybody can see they are not the motives of an adventurer seeking some sordid advantage."

He had listened patiently and when he saw that there was nothing more to come he ended the discussion.

"Señor, we should reflect upon our motives. It is salutary for our conscience and is recommended (he crossed himself) by our Holy Mother the Church. I have here certain letters from Paris on which I would consult your young sagacity which is accredited to us by the most loyal Doña Rita."

The sound of that name on his lips was simply odious. I was convinced that this man of forms and ceremonies and fanatical royalism was perfectly heartless. Perhaps he reflected on his motives; but it seemed to me that his conscience could be nothing else but a monstrous thing which very few actions could disturb appreciably. Yet for the credit of Doña Rita I did not withhold from him my young sagacity. What he thought of it I don't know. The matters we discussed were not of course of high policy, though from the point of view of the war in the south they were important enough. We agreed on certain things to be done, and finally, always out of regard for Doña Rita's credit, I put myself generally at his disposition or of any Carlist agent he would appoint in his place; for I did not suppose that he would remain very long in Marseilles. He got out of the chair laboriously, like a sick child might have done. The audience was over but he noticed my eyes wandering to the portrait and he said in his measured, breathed-out tones :

"I owe the pleasure of having this admirable work here to the gracious attention of Madame de Lastaola, who, knowing my attachment to the royal person of my Master, has sent it down from Paris to greet me in this house which has been given up for my occupation also through her generosity to the Royal Cause. Unfortunately she, too, is touched by the infection of this irreverent and unfaithful age. But she is young yet. She is young."

These last words were pronounced in a strange tone of menace as though he were supernaturally aware of some suspended disasters. With his burning eyes he was the image of an Inquisitor with an unconquerable soul in that frail body. But suddenly he dropped his eyelids and the conversation finished as characteristically as it had begun : with a slow, dismissing inclination of the head and an " Adios, Señor—may God guard you from sin."

## III

I MUST say that for the next three months I threw myself into my unlawful trade with a sort of desperation, dogged and hopeless, like a fairly decent fellow who takes deliberately to drink. The business was getting dangerous. The bands in the South were not very well organized, worked with no very definite plan, and now were beginning to be pretty closely hunted. The arrangements for the transport of supplies were going to pieces; our friends ashore were getting scared; and it was no joke to find after a day of skilful dodging that there was no one at the landing place and have to go out again with our compromising cargo, to slink and lurk about the coast for another week or so, unable to trust anybody and looking at every vessel we met with suspicion. Once we were ambushed by a lot of " rascally Carabineers," as Dominic called them, who hid themselves among the rocks after disposing a train of mules well in view on the seashore. Luckily, on evidence which I could never understand, Dominic detected something suspicious. Perhaps it was by virtue of some sixth sense that men born for unlawful occupations may be gifted with. "There is a smell of treachery about this," he remarked suddenly, turning at his oar. (He and I were pulling alone in a little boat to reconnoitre.) I couldn't detect any smell and I regard to this day our escape on that occasion as, properly speaking, miraculous. Surely some supernatural power must have struck upwards the barrels of the Carabineers' rifles, for they missed us by yards. And as the Carabineers have the reputation of shooting straight, Dominic, after swearing most horribly, ascribed our escape to the particular guardian angel that looks after crazy young gentlemen. Dominic believed in angels in a conventional way, but laid no claim to having one of his own. Soon afterwards, while sailing quietly at night, we found ourselves suddenly near a small coasting vessel, also without lights, which all at once treated us to a volley of rifle fire. Dominic's mighty and inspired yell: "*A plat ventre !*" and also an unexpected roll to windward saved all our lives. Nobody got a scratch. We were past in a moment and in a breeze then blowing we had the heels of anything likely to give us chase. But an hour afterwards, as we stood side by side peering into the darkness, Dominic was heard to mutter through his teeth: "*Le métier se gâte.*" I, too, had the feeling that the trade, if not altogether spoiled, had seen its best days. But I did not care. In fact, for my purpose it was rather better, a more potent influence; like the stronger intoxication of raw spirit. A volley in the dark after all was not such a bad thing. Only a moment before we had received it, there, in that calm night of the sea full of freshness and soft whispers, I had been looking at an enchanting turn of a head in a faint light of its own, the tawny hair with snared red sparks brushed up from the nape of a white neck and held up on high by an arrow of gold feathered with brilliants and with ruby gleams all along its shaft. That jewelled ornament, which I remember often telling Rita was of a very Philistinish conception (it was in some way connected with a tortoiseshell comb) occupied an undue place in my memory, tried to come into some sort of significance even in my sleep. Often I dreamed of her with white limbs shimmering in the gloom like a nymph haunting a riot of foliage and raising a perfect round arm to take an arrow of gold out of her hair to throw it at me by hand, like a dart. It came on, a whizzing trail of light, but I always woke up before it struck. Always. Invariably. It never had a chance. A volley of small arms was much more likely to do the business some day—or night.

At last came the day when everything slipped out of my grasp. The little vessel, broken and gone like the only toy of a lonely child, the sea itself, which had swallowed it, throwing me on shore after a shipwreck that instead of a fair fight left in me the memory of a suicide. It took away all that there was in me of independent life, but just failed to take me out of the world, which looked then indeed like Another World fit for no one else but unrepentant sinners. Even Dominic failed me, his moral entity destroyed by what to him was a most tragic ending of our common enterprise. The lurid swiftness of it all was like a stunning thunder-clap—and, one evening, I found myself weary, heartsore, my brain still dazed and with awe in my heart entering Marseilles by way of the railway station, after many adventures, one more disagreeable than another, involving privations, great exertions, a lot of difficulties with all sorts of people who looked upon me evidently more as a discreditable vagabond deserving the attentions of gendarmes than a respectable (if crazy) young gentleman attended by a guardian angel of his own. I must confess that I slunk out of the railway station shunning its many lights as if, invariably, failure made an outcast of a man. I hadn't any money in my pocket. I hadn't even the bundle and the stick of a destitute wayfarer. I was unshaven and unwashed, and my heart was faint within me. My attire was such that I daren't approach the rank of fiacres, where indeed I could perceive only two pairs of lamps, of which one suddenly drove away while I looked. The other I gave up to the fortunate of this earth. I didn't believe in my power of persuasion. I had no powers. I slunk on and on, shivering with cold, through the uproarious streets. Bedlam was loose in them. It was the time of Carnival.

Small objects of no value have the secret of sticking to a man in an astonishing way. I had nearly lost my liberty and even my life, I had lost my ship, a money-belt full of gold, I had lost my companions, had parted from my friend; my occupation, my only link with life, my touch with the sea, my cap and jacket were gone—but a small penknife and a latchkey had never parted company with me. With the latchkey I opened the door of refuge. The hall wore its deaf-and-dumb air, its black-and-white stillness.

The sickly gas-jet still struggled bravely with adversity at the end of the raised silver arm of the statuette which had kept to a hair's breadth its graceful pose on the toes of its left foot; and the staircase lost itself in the shadows above. Therese was parsimonious with the lights. To see all this was surprising. It seemed to me that all the things I had known ought to have come down with a crash at the moment of the final catastrophe on the Spanish coast. And there was Therese herself descending the stairs, frightened but plucky. Perhaps she thought that she would be murdered this time for certain. She had a strange, unemotional conviction that the house was particularly convenient for a crime. One could never get to the bottom of her wild notions which she held with the stolidity of a peasant allied to the outward serenity of a nun. She quaked all over as she came down to her doom, but when she recognized me she got such a shock that she sat down suddenly on the lowest step. She did not expect me for another week at least, and, besides, she explained, the state I was in made her blood take "one turn."

Indeed my plight seemed either to have called out or else repressed her true nature. But who had ever fathomed her nature! There was none of her treacly volubility. There were none of her "dear young gentlemans" and "poor little hearts" and references to sin. In breathless silence she ran about the house getting my room ready, lighting fires and gas-jets and even hauling at me to help me up the stairs. Yes, she did lay hands on me for that charitable purpose. They trembled. Her pale eyes hardly left my face. "What brought you here like this?" she whispered once.

"If I were to tell you, Mademoiselle Therese, you would see there the hand of God."

She dropped the extra pillow she was carrying and then nearly fell over it. "Oh, dear heart," she murmured, and ran off to the kitchen.

I sank into bed as into a cloud and Therese reappeared very misty and offering me something in a cup. I believe it was hot milk, and after I drank it she took the cup and stood looking at me fixedly. I managed to say with difficulty: "Go away," whereupon she vanished as if by magic before the words were fairly out of my mouth. Immediately afterwards the sunlight forced through the slats of the jalousies its diffused glow, and Therese was there again as if by magic, saying in a distant voice: "It's midday." . . . Youth will have its rights. I had slept like a stone for seventeen hours.

I suppose an honourable bankrupt would know such an awakening: the sense of catastrophe, the shrinking from the necessity of beginning life again, the faint feeling that there are misfortunes which must be paid for by a hanging. In the course of the morning Therese informed me that the apartment usually occupied by Mr. Blunt was vacant and added mysteriously that she intended to keep it vacant for a time, because she had been instructed to do so. I couldn't imagine why Blunt should wish to return to Marseilles. She told me also that the house was empty except for myself and the two dancing girls with their father. Those people had been away for some time, as the girls had engagements in some Italian summer theatres, but apparently they had secured a re-engagement for the winter and were now back. I let Therese talk because it kept my imagination from going to work on subjects which, I had made up my mind, were no concern of mine. But I went out early to perform an unpleasant task. It was only proper that I should let the Carlist agent ensconced in the Prado Villa know of the sudden ending of my activities. It would be grave enough news for him, and I did not like to be its bearer for reasons which were mainly personal. I resembled Dominic in so far that I, too, disliked failure.

The Marquis of Villarel had of course gone long before. The man who was there was another type of Carlist altogether, and his temperament was that of a trader. He was the chief purveyor of the Legitimist armies, an honest broker of stores, and enjoyed a great reputation for cleverness. His important task kept him, of course, in France, but his young wife, whose beauty and devotion to her King were well known, represented him worthily at Headquarters, where his own appearances were extremely rare. The dissimilar but united loyalties of those two people had been rewarded by the title of baron and the ribbon of some order or other. The gossip of the Legitimist circles appreciated those favours with smiling indulgence. He was the man who had been so distressed and frightened by Doña Rita's first visit to Tolosa. He had an extreme regard for his wife. And in that sphere of clashing arms and unceasing intrigue nobody would have smiled then at his agitation if the man himself hadn't been somewhat grotesque.

He must have been startled when I sent in my name, for he didn't of course expect to see me yet—nobody expected me. He advanced soft-footed down the room. With his jutting nose, flat-topped skull and sable garments he recalled an obese raven, and when he heard of the disaster he manifested his astonishment and concern in a most plebeian manner by a low and expressive whistle. I, of course, could not share his consternation. My feelings in that connection were of a different order; but I was annoyed at his unintelligent stare.

" I suppose," I said, " you will take it on yourself to advise Doña Rita, who is greatly interested in this affair."

"Yes, but I was given to understand that Madame de Lastaola was to leave Paris either yesterday or this morning."

It was my turn to stare dumbly before I could manage to ask : " For Tolosa ? " in a very knowing tone.

Whether it was the droop of his head, play of light, or some other subtle cause, his nose seemed to have grown perceptibly longer.

" That, Señor, is the place where the news has got to be conveyed without undue delay," he said in an agitated wheeze. " I could, of course, telegraph to our agent in Bayonne who would find a messenger. But I don't like, I don't like ! The Alphonsists have agents, too, who hang about the telegraph offices. It's no use letting the enemy get that news."

He was obviously very confused, unhappy, and trying to think of two different things at once.

" Sit down, Don George, sit down." He absolutely forced a cigar on me. " I am extremely distressed. That—I mean Doña Rita is undoubtedly on her way to Tolosa. This is very frightful."

I must say, however, that there was in the man some sense of duty. He mastered his private fears. After some cogitation he murmured : " There is another way of getting the news to Headquarters. Suppose you write me a formal letter just stating the facts, the unfortunate facts, which I will be able to forward. There is an agent of ours, a fellow I have been employing for purchasing supplies, a perfectly honest man. He is coming here from the north by the ten o'clock train with some papers for me of a confidential nature. I was rather embarrassed about it. It wouldn't do for him to get into any sort of trouble. He is not very intelligent. I wonder, Don George, whether you would consent to meet him at the station and take care of him generally till to-morrow. I don't like the idea of him going about alone. Then, to-morrow night, we would send him on to Tolosa by the west coast route, with the news ; and

z

then he can also call on Doña Rita who will no doubt be already there. . . ." He became again distracted all in a moment and actually went so far as to wring his fat hands. " Oh, yes, she will be there ! " he exclaimed in most pathetic accents.

I was not in the humour to smile at anything, and he must have been satisfied with the gravity with which I beheld his extraordinary antics. My mind was very far away. I thought : Why not ? Why shouldn't I also write a letter to Doña Rita, telling her that now nothing stood in the way of my leaving Europe, because, really, the enterprise couldn't be begun again ; that things that come to an end can never be begun again. The idea—never again—had complete possession of my mind. I could think of nothing else. Yes, I would write. The worthy Commissary General of the Carlist forces was under the impression that I was looking at him ; but what I had in my eye was a jumble of butterfly women and winged youths and the soft sheen of Argand lamps gleaming on an arrow of gold in the hair of a head that seemed to evade my outstretched hand.

" Oh, yes," I said, " I have nothing to do and even nothing to think of just now. I will meet your man as he gets off the train at ten o'clock to-night. What's he like ? "

" Oh, he has a black moustache and whiskers, and his chin is shaved," said the newly-fledged baron cordially. " A very honest fellow. I always found him very useful. His name is José Ortega."

He was perfectly self-possessed now, and walking soft-footed accompanied me to the door of the room. He shook hands with a melancholy smile. " This is a very frightful situation. My poor wife will be quite distracted. She is such a patriot. Many thanks, Don George. You relieve me greatly. The fellow is rather stupid and rather bad-tempered. Queer creature, but very honest ! Oh, very honest ! "

## IV

It was the last evening of Carnival. The same masks, the same yells, the same mad rushes, the same bedlam of disguised humanity blowing about the streets in the great gusts of mistral that seemed to make them dance like dead leaves on an earth where all joy is watched by death.

It was exactly twelve months since that other carnival evening when I had felt a little weary and a little lonely but at peace with all mankind. It must have been—to a day or two. But on this evening it wasn't merely loneliness that I felt. I felt bereaved with a sense of a complete and universal loss in which there was perhaps more resentment than mourning; as if the world had not been taken away from me by an august decree but filched from my innocence by an underhand fate at the very moment when it had disclosed to my passion its warm and generous beauty. This consciousness of universal loss had this advantage that it induced something resembling a state of philosophic indifference. I walked up to the railway station caring as little for the cold blasts of wind as though I had been going to the scaffold. The delay of the train did not irritate me in the least. I had finally made up my mind to write a letter to Doña Rita; and this "honest fellow" for whom I was waiting would take it to her. He would have no difficulty in Tolosa in finding Madame de Lastaola. The General Headquarters, which was also a Court, would be buzzing with comments on her presence. Most likely that "honest fellow" was already known to Doña Rita. For all I knew he might have been her discovery just as I was. Probably I, too, was regarded as an "honest fellow" enough; but stupid—since it was clear that my luck was not inexhaustible. I hoped that while carrying my letter the man would not let himself be caught by some Alphonsist guerilla who would, of course, shoot him. But why should he? I, for instance, had escaped with my life from a much more dangerous enterprise than merely passing through the frontier line in charge of some trustworthy guide. I pictured the fellow to myself trudging over the stony slopes and scrambling down wild ravines with my letter to Doña Rita in his pocket. It would be such a letter of farewell as no lover had ever written, no woman in the world had ever read, since the beginning of love on earth. It would be worthy of the woman. No experience, no memories, no dead traditions of passion or language would inspire it. She herself would be its sole inspiration. She would see her own image in it as in a mirror; and perhaps then she would understand what it was I was saying farewell to on the very threshold of my life. A breath of vanity passed through my brain. A letter as moving as her mere existence was moving would be something unique. I regretted I was not a poet.

I woke up to a great noise of feet, a sudden influx of people through the doors of the platform. I made out my man's whiskers at once—not that they were enormous, but because I had been warned beforehand of their existence by the excellent Commissary General. At first I saw nothing of him but his whiskers: they were black and cut somewhat in the shape of a shark's fin and so very fine that the least breath of air animated them into a sort of playful restlessness. The man's shoulders were hunched up and when he had made his way clear of the throng of passengers I perceived him as an unhappy and shivery being. Obviously he didn't expect to be met, because when I murmured an enquiring, " Señor Ortega ? " into his ear he swerved away from me and nearly dropped a little handbag he was carrying. His complexion was uniformly pale, his mouth was red, but not engaging. His social status was not very definite. He was wearing a dark blue overcoat of no particular cut, his aspect had no relief; yet those restless side-whiskers flanking his red mouth and the suspicious expression of his black eyes made him noticeable. This I regretted the more because I caught sight of two skulking fellows, looking very much like policemen in plain clothes, watching us from a corner of the great hall. I hurried my man into a fiacre. He had been travelling from early morning on cross-country lines and after we got on terms a little confessed to being very hungry and cold. His red lips trembled and I noted an underhand, cynical curiosity when he had occasion to raise his eyes to my face. I was in some doubt how to dispose of him but as we rolled on at a jog trot I came to the conclusion that the best thing to do would be to organize for him a shake-down in the studio. Obscure lodging houses are precisely the places most looked after by the police, and even the best hotels are bound to keep a register of arrivals. I was very anxious that nothing should stop his projected mission of courier to head-quarters. As we passed various street corners where the mistral blast struck at us fiercely I could feel him shivering by my side. However, Therese would have lighted the iron stove in the studio before retiring for the night, and, anyway, I would have to turn her out to make up a bed on the couch. Service of the King! I must say that she was amiable and didn't seem to mind anything one asked her to do. Thus while the fellow slumbered on the divan I would sit upstairs in my room setting down on paper those great words of passion and sorrow that seethed in my brain and even must have forced themselves in murmurs on to my lips, because the man by my side suddenly asked me : "What did you say? "—" Nothing," I answered, very much surprised. In the shifting light of the street lamps he looked the picture of bodily misery with his chattering teeth and his whiskers blown back flat over his ears. But somehow he didn't arouse my compassion. He was swearing to himself, in French and Spanish, and I tried to soothe him by the assurance that we had not much farther to go. " I am starving," he remarked acidly, and I felt a little compunction. Clearly, the first thing to do was to feed him. We were then entering the Cannebière and as I didn't care to show myself with him in the fashionable restaurant where a new face (and such a face, too) would be remarked, I pulled up the fiacre at the door of the Maison Dorée. That was more of a place of general resort where, in the multitude of casual patrons, he would pass unnoticed.

For this last night of carnival the big house had decorated

all its balconies with rows of coloured paper lanterns right
up to the roof. I led the way to the grand salon, for as to
private rooms they had been all retained days before. There
was a great crowd of people in costume, but by a piece of
good luck we managed to secure a little table in a corner.
The revellers, intent on their pleasure, paid no attention to
us. Señor Ortega trod on my heels and after sitting down
opposite me threw an ill-natured glance at the festive scene.
It might have been about half-past ten, then.

Two glasses of wine he drank one after another did not
improve his temper. He only ceased to shiver. After he
had eaten something it must have occurred to him that he
had no reason to bear me a grudge and he tried to assume a
civil and even friendly manner. His mouth, however,
betrayed an abiding bitterness. I mean when he smiled.
In repose it was a very expressionless mouth, only it was too
red to be altogether ordinary. The whole of him was like
that: the whiskers too black, the hair too shiny, the forehead too white, the eyes too mobile; and he lent you his
attention with an air of eagerness which made you uncomfortable. He seemed to expect you to give yourself away
by some unconsidered word that he would snap up with
delight. It was that peculiarity that somehow put me on
my guard. I had no idea who I was facing across the table
and as a matter of fact I did not care. All my impressions
were blurred; and even the promptings of my instinct were
the haziest thing imaginable. Now and then I had acute
hallucinations of a woman with an arrow of gold in her hair.
This caused alternate moments of exaltation and depression
from which I tried to take refuge in conversation; but
Señor Ortega was not stimulating. He was preoccupied
with personal matters. When suddenly he asked me whether
I knew why he had been called away from his work (he had
been buying supplies from peasants somewhere in Central
France), I answered that I didn't know what the reason was
originally, but I had an idea that the present intention was
to make of him a courier, bearing certain messages from Baron
H. to the Quartel Real in Tolosa.

He glared at me like a basilisk. "And why have I been met like this?" he enquired with an air of being prepared to hear a lie.

I explained that it was the Baron's wish, as a matter of prudence and to avoid any possible trouble which might arise from enquiries by the police.

He took it badly. "What nonsense." He was—he said—an employé (for several years) of Hernandez Brothers in Paris, an importing firm, and he was travelling on their business—as he could prove. He dived into his side pocket and produced a handful of folded papers of all sorts which he plunged back again instantly.

And even then I didn't know whom I had there, opposite me, busy now devouring a slice of paté de foie gras. Not in the least. It never entered my head. How could it? The Rita that haunted me had no history; she was but the principle of life charged with fatality. Her form was only a mirage of desire decoying one step by step into despair.

Señor Ortega gulped down some more wine and suggested I should tell him who I was. "It's only right I should know," he added.

This could not be gainsaid; and to a man connected with the Carlist organization the shortest way was to introduce myself as that "Monsieur George" of whom he had probably heard.

He leaned far over the table, till his very breast-bone was over the edge, as though his eyes had been stilettos and he wanted to drive them home into my brain. It was only much later that I understood how near death I had been at that moment. But the knives on the tablecloth were the usual restaurant knives with rounded ends and about as deadly as pieces of hoop-iron. Perhaps in the very gust of his fury he remembered what a French restaurant knife is like and something sane within him made him give up the sudden project of cutting my heart out where I sat. For it could have been nothing but a sudden impulse. His settled purpose was quite other. It was not my heart that he was after. His fingers indeed were groping amongst the knife handles by the side of his plate but what captivated my attention for a moment were his red lips which were formed into an odd, sly, insinuating smile. Heard! To be sure he had heard! The chief of the great arms smuggling organization!

"Oh!" I said, "that's giving me too much importance." The person responsible and whom I looked upon as chief of all the business was, as he might have heard, too, a certain noble and loyal lady.

"I am as noble as she is," he snapped peevishly, and I put him down at once as a very offensive beast. "And as to being loyal, what is that? It is being truthful! It is being faithful! I know all about her."

I managed to preserve an air of perfect unconcern. He wasn't a fellow to whom one could talk of Doña Rita. "You are a Basque," I said.

He admitted rather contemptuously that he was a Basque and even then the truth did not dawn upon me. I suppose that with the hidden egoism of a lover I was thinking of myself, of myself alone in relation to Doña Rita, not of Doña Rita herself. He, too, obviously. He said : "I am an educated man, but I know her people, all peasants. There is a sister, an uncle, a priest, a peasant, too, and perfectly unenlightened. One can't expect much from a priest (I am a free-thinker of course), but he is really too bad, more like a brute beast. As to all her people, mostly dead now, they never were of any account. There was a little land, but they were always working on other people's farms, a barefooted gang, a starved lot. I ought to know because we are distant relations. Twentieth cousins or something of the sort. Yes, I am related to that most loyal lady. And what is she, after all, but a Parisian woman with innumerable lovers, as I have been told."

"I don't think your information is very correct," I said, affecting to yawn slightly. "This is mere gossip of the gutter and I am surprised at you, who really know nothing about it——"

But the disgusting animal had fallen into a brown study.

The hair of his very whiskers was perfectly still. I had now given up all idea of the letter to Rita. Suddenly he spoke again :

"Women are the origin of all evil. One should never trust them. They have no honour. No honour ! " he repeated, striking his breast with his closed fist on which the knuckles stood out very white. " I left my village many years ago and of course I am perfectly satisfied with my position and I don't know why I should trouble my head about this loyal lady. I suppose that's the way women get on in the world."

I felt convinced that he was no proper person to be a messenger to headquarters. He struck me as altogether untrustworthy and perhaps not quite sane. This was confirmed by him saying suddenly with no visible connection and as if it had been forced from him by some agonizing process : " I was a boy once," and then stopping dead short with a smile. He had a smile that frightened one by its association of malice and anguish.

"Will you have anything more to eat ? " I asked.

He declined dully. He had had enough. But he drained the last of a bottle into his glass and accepted a cigar which I offered him. While he was lighting it I had a sort of confused impression that he wasn't such a stranger to me as I had assumed he was ; and yet, on the other hand, I was perfectly certain I had never seen him before. Next moment I felt that I could have knocked him down if he hadn't looked so amazingly unhappy, while he came out with the astounding question : " Señor, have you ever been a lover in your young days ? "

"What do you mean ? " I asked. " How old do you think I am ? "

" That's true," he said, gazing at me in a way in which the damned gaze out of their cauldrons of boiling pitch at some soul walking scot free in the place of torment. " It's true, you don't seem to have anything on your mind." He assumed an air of ease, throwing an arm over the back of his chair and blowing the smoke through the gash of his

z 2

twisted red mouth. " Tell me," he said, " between men,
you know, has this wonderful celebrity—what does she call
herself ? How long has she been your mistress ? "

I reflected rapidly, that if I knocked him over, chair and
all, by a sudden blow from the shoulder it would bring about
infinite complications beginning with a visit to the Com-
missaire de Police on night-duty, and ending in God knows
what scandal and disclosures of political kind ; because there
was no telling what, or how much, this outrageous brute
might choose to say and how many people he might not
involve in a most undesirable publicity. He was smoking his
cigar with a poignantly mocking air and not even looking at me.
One can't hit like that a man who isn't even looking at one ;
and then, just as I was looking at him swinging his leg with a
caustic smile and stony eyes, I felt sorry for the creature. It
was only his body that was there in that chair. It was
manifest to me that his soul was absent in some hell of its
own. At that moment I attained the knowledge of who it
was I had before me. This was the man of whom both
Doña Rita and Rose were so much afraid. It remained then
for me to look after him for the night and then arrange with
Baron H. that he should be sent away the very next day—
and anywhere but to Tolosa. Yes, evidently, I mustn't lose
sight of him. I proposed in the calmest tone that we should
go on where he could get his much-needed rest. He rose
with alacrity, picked up his little hand-bag, and, walking out
before me, no doubt looked a very ordinary person to all eyes
but mine. It was then past eleven, not much, because we
had not been in that restaurant quite an hour, but the
routine of the town's night-life being upset during the
Carnival the usual row of fiacres outside the Maison Doree
was not there ; in fact, there were very few carriages about.
Perhaps the coachmen had assumed Pierrot costumes and
were rushing about the streets on foot yelling with the rest
of the population. " We will have to walk," I said after a
while.—" Oh, yes, let us walk," assented Señor Ortega, " or
I will be frozen here." It was like a plaint of unutterable
wretchedness. I had a fancy that all his natural heat had

abandoned his limbs and gone to his brain. It was otherwise with me; my head was cool but I didn't find the night really so very cold. We stepped out briskly side by side. My lucid thinking was, as it were, enveloped by the wide shouting of the consecrated Carnival gaiety. I have heard many noises since, but nothing that gave me such an intimate impression of the savage instincts hidden in the breast of mankind; these yells of festivity suggested agonizing fear, rage of murder, ferocity of lust, and the irremediable joylessness of human condition: yet they were emitted by people who were convinced that they were amusing themselves supremely, traditionally, with the sanction of ages, with the approval of their conscience—and no mistake about it whatever! Our appearance, the soberness of our gait made us conspicuous. Once or twice, by common inspiration, masks rushed forward and forming a circle danced round us uttering discordant shouts of derision; for we were an outrage to the peculiar proprieties of the hour, and besides we were obviously lonely and defenceless. On those occasions there was nothing for it but to stand still till the flurry was over. My companion, however, would stamp his feet with rage, and I must admit that I myself regretted not having provided for our wearing a couple of false noses, which would have been enough to placate the just resentment of those people. We might have also joined in the dance, but for some reason or other it didn't occur to us; and I heard once a high, clear woman's voice stigmatizing us for a "species of swelled heads" (espèce d'enflés). We proceeded sedately, my companion muttered with rage, and I was able to resume my thinking. It was based on the deep persuasion that the man at my side was insane with quite another than Carnivalesque lunacy which comes on at one stated time of the year. He was fundamentally mad, though not perhaps completely; which of course made him all the greater, I won't say danger, but nuisance.

I remember once a young doctor expounding the theory that most catastrophes in family circles, surprising episodes in public affairs and disasters in private life, had their origin in the fact that the world was full of half-mad people. He asserted that they were the real majority. When asked whether he considered himself as belonging to the majority, he said frankly that he didn't think so; unless the folly of voicing this view in a company, so utterly unable to appreciate all its horror, could be regarded as the first symptom of his own fate. We shouted down him and his theory, but there is no doubt that it had thrown a chill on the gaiety of our gathering.

We had now entered a quieter quarter of the town and Señor Ortega had ceased his muttering. For myself I had not the slightest doubt of my own sanity. It was proved to me by the way I could apply my intelligence to the problem of what was to be done with Señor Ortega. Generally, he was unfit to be trusted with any mission whatever. The unstability of his temper was sure to get him into a scrape. Of course carrying a letter to Headquarters was not a very complicated matter; and as to that I would have trusted willingly a properly trained dog. My private letter to Doña Rita, the wonderful, the unique letter of farewell, I had given up for the present. Naturally I thought of the Ortega problem mainly in the terms of Doña Rita's safety. Her image presided at every council, at every conflict of my mind, and dominated every faculty of my senses. It floated before my eyes, it touched my elbow, it guarded my right side and my left side; my ears seemed to catch the sound of her footsteps behind me, she enveloped me with passing whiffs of warmth and perfume, with filmy touches of the hair on my face. She penetrated me, my head was full of her. . . . And his head, too, I thought suddenly with a side glance at my companion. He walked quietly with hunched-up shoulders carrying his little hand-bag and he looked the most commonplace figure imaginable.

Yes. There was between us a most horrible fellowship; the association of his crazy torture with the sublime suffering of my passion. We hadn't been a quarter of an hour together when that woman had surged up fatally between us; between this miserable wretch and myself. We were haunted by the same image. But I was sane! I was sane! Not because I was certain that the fellow must not be allowed to go to Tolosa, but because I was perfectly alive to the difficulty of stopping him from going there, since the decision was absolutely in the hands of Baron H.

If I were to go early in the morning and tell that fat, bilious man: "Look here, your Ortega's mad," he would certainly think at once that I was, get very frightened, and . . . one couldn't tell what course he would take. He would eliminate me somehow out of the affair. And yet I could not let the fellow proceed to where Doña Rita was, because, obviously, he had been molesting her, had filled her with uneasiness and even alarm, was an unhappy element and a disturbing influence in her life—incredible as the thing appeared! I couldn't let him go on to make himself a worry and a nuisance, drive her out from a town in which she wished to be (for whatever reason) and perhaps start some explosive scandal. And that girl Rose seemed to fear something graver even than a scandal. But if I were to explain the matter fully to H. he would simply rejoice in his heart. Nothing would please him more than to have Doña Rita driven out of Tolosa. What a relief from his anxieties (and his wife's, too); and if I were to go further, if I even went so far as to hint at the fears which Rose had not been able to conceal from me, why then—I went on thinking coldly with a stoical rejection of the most elementary faith in mankind's rectitude—why then, that accommodating husband would simply let the ominous messenger have his chance. He would see there only his natural anxieties being laid to rest for ever. Horrible? Yes. But I could not take the risk. In a twelvemonth I had travelled a long way in my mistrust of mankind.

We paced on steadily. I thought: "How on earth am I going to stop you?" Had this arisen only a month before, when I had the means at hand and Dominic to confide in, I would have simply kidnapped the fellow. A little trip to sea would not have done Señor Ortega any harm; though no doubt it would have been abhorrent to his feelings. But now I had not the means. I couldn't even tell where my poor Dominic was hiding his diminished head.

Again I glanced at him sideways. I was the taller of the two and as it happened I met in the light of the street lamp his own stealthy glance directed up at me with an agonized expression, an expression that made me fancy I could see the man's very soul writhing in his body like an impaled worm. In spite of my utter inexperience I had some notion of the images that rushed into his mind at the sight of any man who had approached Doña Rita. It was enough to awaken in any human being a movement of horrified compassion; but my pity went out not to him but to Doña Rita. It was for her that I felt sorry; I pitied her for having that damned soul on her track. I pitied her with tenderness and indignation, as if this had been both a danger and a dishonour.

I don't mean to say that those thoughts passed through my head consciously. I had only the resultant, settled feeling. I had, however, a thought, too. It came on me suddenly, and I asked myself with rage and astonishment: " Must I then kill that brute ? " There didn't seem to be any alternative. Between him and Doña Rita I couldn't hesitate. I believe I gave a slight laugh of desperation. The suddenness of this sinister conclusion had in it something comic and unbelievable. It loosened my grip on my mental processes. A Latin tag came into my head about the facile descent into the abyss. I marvelled at its aptness, and also that it should have come to me so pat. But I believe now that it was suggested simply by the actual declivity of the street of the Consuls which lies on a gentle slope. We had just turned the corner. All the houses were dark and in a perspective of complete solitude our two shadows dodged about and wheeled about our feet.

" Here we are," I said.

He was an extraordinarily chilly devil. When we stopped I could hear his teeth chattering again. I don't know what came over me, I had a sort of nervous fit, was incapable of finding my pockets, let alone the latchkey. I had the illusion of a narrow streak of light on the wall of the house as if it had been cracked. "I hope we will be able to get in," I murmured.

Señor Ortega stood waiting patiently with his hand-bag, like a rescued wayfarer. "But you live in this house, don't you?" he observed.

"No," I said, without hesitation. I didn't know how that man would behave if he were aware that I was staying under the same roof. He was half mad. He might want to talk all night, try crazily to invade my privacy. How could I tell? Moreover, I wasn't so sure that I would remain in the house. I had some notion of going out again and walking up and down the street of the Consuls till daylight. "No, an absent friend lets me use . . . I had that latchkey this morning. . . . Ah! here it is."

I let him go in first. The sickly gas flame was there on duty, undaunted, waiting for the end of the world to come and put it out. I think that the black-and-white hall surprised Ortega. I had closed the front door without noise and stood for a moment listening, while he glanced about furtively. There were only two other doors in the hall, right and left. Their panels of ebony were decorated with bronze applications in the centre. The one on the left was of course Blunt's door. As the passage leading beyond it was dark at the further end I took Señor Ortega by the hand and led him along, unresisting, like a child. For some reason or other I moved on tip-toe and he followed my example. The light and the warmth of the studio impressed him favourably; he laid down his little bag, rubbed his hands together, and produced a smile of satis-faction; but it was such a smile as a totally ruined man would perhaps force on his lips, or a man condemned to a short shrift by his doctor. I begged him to make himself at home and said that I would go at once and hunt up the woman of the house who would make him up a bed on the big couch there. He hardly listened to what I said. What were all those things to him! He knew that his destiny was to sleep on a bed of thorns, to feed on adders. But he tried to show a sort of polite interest. He asked : " What is this place ? "

" It used to belong to a painter," I mumbled.

" Ah, your absent friend," he said, making a wry mouth. " I detest all those artists, and all those writers, and all politicos who are thieves ; and I would go even farther and higher, laying a curse on all idle lovers of women. You think perhaps I am a Royalist ? No. If there was anybody in heaven or hell to pray to I would pray for a revolution—a red revolution everywhere."

" You astonish me," I said, just to say something.

" No ! But there are half a dozen people in the world with whom I would like to settle accounts. One could shoot them like partridges and no questions asked. That's what revolution would mean to me."

" It's a beautifully simple view," I said. " I imagine you are not the only one who holds it ; but I really must look after your comforts. You mustn't forget that we have to see Baron H. early to-morrow morning." And I went out quietly into the passage wondering in what part of the house Therese had elected to sleep that night. But, lo and behold, when I got to the foot of the stairs there was Therese coming down from the upper regions in her nightgown, like a sleep-walker. However, it wasn't that, because, before I could exclaim, she vanished off the first floor landing like a streak of white mist and without the slightest sound. Her attire made it perfectly clear that she could not have heard us coming in. In fact, she must have been certain that the house was empty, because she was as well aware as myself that the Italian girls after their work at the opera were going to a masked ball to dance for their own amusement, attended of course by their conscientious father. But what thought, need, or sudden impulse had driven Therese out of bed like this was something I couldn't conceive.

I didn't call out after her. I felt sure that she would return. I went up slowly to the first floor and met her coming down again, this time carrying a lighted candle.

She had managed to make herself presentable in an extraordinarily short time.

"Oh, my dear young Monsieur, you have given me a fright."

"Yes. And I nearly fainted, too," I said. "You looked perfectly awful. What's the matter with you? Are you ill?"

She had lighted by then the gas on the landing and I must say that I had never seen exactly that manner of face on her before. She wriggled, confused and shifty-eyed, before me; but I ascribed this behaviour to her shocked modesty and without troubling myself any more about her feelings I informed her that there was a Carlist downstairs who must be put up for the night. Most unexpectedly she betrayed ridiculous consternation, but only for a moment. Then she assumed at once that I would give him hospitality upstairs where there was a camp-bedstead in my dressing-room. I said:

"No. Give him a shake-down in the studio, where he is now. It's warm in there. And remember! I charge you strictly not to let him know that I sleep in this house. In fact, I don't know myself that I will; I have certain matters to attend to this very night. You will also have to serve him his coffee in the morning. I will take him away before ten o'clock."

All this seemed to impress her more than I had expected. As usual when she felt curious, or in some other way excited, she assumed a saintly, detached expression, and asked:

"The dear gentleman is your friend, I suppose?"

"I only know he is a Spaniard and a Carlist," I said: "and that ought to be enough for you."

Instead of the usual effusive exclamations she murmured: "Dear me, dear me," and departed upstairs with the candle to get together a few blankets and pillows, I suppose. As for me I walked quietly downstairs on my way to the studio. I had a curious sensation that I was acting in a preordained manner, that life was not at all what I had thought it to be, or else that I had been altogether changed sometime during the day, and that I was a different person from the man whom I remembered getting out of my bed in the morning.

Also feelings had altered all their values. The words, too, had become strange. It was only the inanimate surroundings that remained what they had always been. For instance the studio. . . .

During my absence Señor Ortega had taken off his coat and I found him as it were in the air, sitting in his shirt sleeves on a chair which he had taken pains to place in the very middle of the floor. I repressed an absurd impulse to walk round him as though he had been some sort of exhibit. His hands were spread over his knees and he looked perfectly insensible. I don't mean strange, or ghastly, or wooden, but just insensible—like an exhibit. And that effect persisted even after he raised his black suspicious eyes to my face. He lowered them almost at once. It was very mechanical. I gave him up and became rather concerned about myself. My thought was that I had better get out of that before any more queer notions came into my head. So I only remained long enough to tell him that the woman of the house was bringing down some bedding and that I hoped that he would have a good night's rest. And directly I spoke it struck me that this was the most extraordinary speech that ever was addressed to a figure of that sort. He, however, did not seem startled by it or moved in any way. He simply said :

"Thank you."

In the darkest part of the long passage outside I met Therese with her arms full of pillows and blankets.

## V

COMING out of the bright light of the studio I didn't make out Therese very distinctly. She, however, having groped in dark cupboards, must have had her pupils sufficiently dilated to have seen that I had my hat on my head. This has its importance because after what I had said to her upstairs it must have convinced her that I was going out on some midnight business. I passed her without a word and heard behind me the door of the studio close with an unexpected crash. It strikes me now that under the circumstances I might have without shame gone back to listen at the keyhole. But truth to say the association of events was not so clear in my mind as it may be to the reader of this story. Neither were the exact connections of persons present to my mind. And, besides, one doesn't listen at a keyhole but in pursuance of some plan ; unless one is afflicted by a vulgar and fatuous curiosity. But that vice is not in my character. As to plan, I had none. I moved along the passage between the dead wall and the black-and-white marble elevation of the staircase with hushed footsteps, as though there had been a mortally sick person somewhere in the house. And the only person that could have answered to that description was Señor Ortega. I moved on, stealthy, absorbed, undecided ; asking myself earnestly : " What on earth am I going to do with him ? " That exclusive preoccupation of my mind was as dangerous to Señor Ortega as typhoid fever would have been. It strikes me that this comparison is very exact. People recover from typhoid fever, but generally the chance is considered poor. This was precisely his case. His chance was poor ; though I had no more animosity towards him than a virulent disease has against the victim it lays low. He really would have nothing to reproach me with ; he had run up against me, unwittingly, as a man enters an infected place, and now he was very ill, very ill indeed. No, I had no plans against him. I had only the feeling that he was in mortal danger.

I believe that men of the most daring character (and I make no claim to it) often do shrink from the logical processes of thought. It is only the devil, they say, that loves logic. But I was not a devil. I was not even a victim of the devil. It was only that I had given up the direction of my intelligence before the problem ; or rather that the problem had dispossessed my intelligence and reigned in its stead side by side with a superstitious awe. A dreadful order seemed to lurk in the darkest shadows of life. The madness of that Carlist with the soul of a Jacobin, the vile fears of Baron H., that excellent organizer of supplies, the contact of their two ferocious stupidities, and last, by a remote disaster at sea, my love brought into direct contact with the situation : all that was enough to make one shudder—not at the chance, but at the design.

For it was my love that was called upon to act here, and nothing else. And love which elevates us above all safeguards, above restraining principles, above all littlenesses of self-possession, yet keeps its feet always firmly on earth, remains marvellously practical in its suggestions.

I discovered that however much I had imagined I had given up Rita, that whatever agonies I had gone through, my hope of her had never been lost. Plucked out, stamped down, torn to shreds, it had remained with me secret, intact, invincible. Before the danger of the situation it sprang, full of life, up in arms—the undying child of immortal love. What incited me was independent of honour and compassion ; it was the prompting of a love supreme, practical, remorseless in its aim ; it was the practical thought that no woman need be counted as lost for ever, unless she be dead !

This excluded for the moment all considerations of ways and means and risks and difficulties. Its tremendous intensity robbed it of all direction and left me adrift in the big black-and-white hall as on a silent sea. It was not, properly speaking, irresolution. It was merely hesitation as to the next immediate step, and that step even of no great importance : hesitation merely as to the best way I could spend the rest of the night. I didn't think further forward for many reasons, more or less optimistic, but mainly because I have no homicidal vein in my composition. The disposition to gloat over homicide was in that miserable creature in the studio, the potential Jacobin ; in that confounded buyer of agricultural produce, the punctual employé of Hernandez Brothers, the jealous wretch with an obscene tongue and an imagination of the same kind to drive him mad. I thought of him without pity but also without contempt. I reflected that there were no means of sending a warning to Doña Rita in Tolosa; for of course no postal communication existed with the Headquarters. And moreover what would a warning be worth in this particular case, supposing it would reach her, that she would believe it, and that she would know what to do? How could I communicate to another that certitude which was in my mind, the more absolute because without proofs that one could produce?

The last expression of Rose's distress rang again in my ears: "Madame has no friends. Not one!" and I saw Doña Rita's complete loneliness beset by all sorts of insincerities, surrounded by pitfalls; her greatest dangers within herself, in her generosity, in her fears, in her courage, too. What I had to do first of all was to stop that wretch at all costs. I became aware of a great mistrust of Therese. I didn't want her to find me in the hall, but I was reluctant to go upstairs to my rooms from an unreasonable feeling that there I would be too much out of the way; not sufficiently on the spot. There was the alternative of a livelong night of watching outside, before the dark front of the house. It was a most distasteful prospect. And then it occurred to me that Blunt's former room would be an extremely good place to keep a watch from. I knew that room. When Henry Allègre gave the house to Rita in the early days (long before he made his will) he had planned a complete renovation and this room had been meant for the drawing-room. Furniture had been made for it specially, upholstered in beautiful ribbed stuff, made to order, of dull gold colour with a pale blue tracery of arabesques and oval medallions enclosing Rita's monogram, repeated on the backs of chairs and sofas, and on the heavy curtains reaching from ceiling to floor. To the same time belonged the ebony and bronze doors, the silver statuette at the foot of the stairs, the forged iron balustrade reproducing right up the marble staircase Rita's decorative monogram in its complicated design. Afterwards the work was stopped and the house had fallen into disrepair. When Rita devoted it to the Carlist cause a bed was put into that drawing-room, just simply the bed. The room next to that yellow salon had been in Allègre's young days fitted as a fencing-room containing also a bath, and a complicated system of all sorts of shower and jet arrangements, then quite up to date. That room was very large, lighted from the top, and one wall of it was covered by trophies of arms of all sorts, a choice collection of cold steel disposed on a background of Indian mats and rugs. Blunt used it as a dressing-room. It communicated by a small door with the studio.

I had only to extend my hand and make one step to reach the magnificent bronze handle of the ebony door, and if I didn't want to be caught by Therese there was no time to lose. I made the step and extended the hand, thinking that it would be just like my luck to find the door locked. But the door came open to my push. In contrast to the dark hall the room was most unexpectedly dazzling to my eyes, as if illuminated *a giorno* for a reception. No voice came from it, but nothing could have stopped me now. As I turned round to shut the door behind me noiselessly. I caught sight of a woman's dress on a chair, of other articles of apparel scattered about. The mahogany bed with a piece of light silk which Therese found somewhere and used for a counter-pane was a magnificent combination of white and crimson between the gleaming surfaces of dark wood; and the whole room had an air of splendour with marble consoles, gilt carvings, long mirrors and a sumptuous Venetian lustre depending from the ceiling : a darkling mass of icy pendants catching a spark here and there from the candles of an eight-branched candelabra standing on a little table near the head of a sofa which had been dragged round to face the fireplace. The faintest possible whiff of a familiar perfume made my head swim with its suggestion.

I grabbed the back of the nearest piece of furniture and the splendour of marbles and mirrors, of cut crystals and carvings, swung before my eyes in the golden mist of walls and draperies round an extremely conspicuous pair of black stockings thrown over a music stool which remained motionless. The silence was profound. It was like being in an enchanted place. Suddenly a voice began to speak, clear, detached, infinitely touching in its calm weariness.

"Haven't you tormented me enough to-day?" it said. . . . My head was steady now but my heart began to beat violently. I listened to the end without moving. "Can't you make up your mind to leave me alone for to-night?" It pleaded with an accent of charitable scorn.

The penetrating quality of these tones which I had not heard for so many, many days made my eyes run full of tears. I guessed easily that the appeal was addressed to the atrocious Therese. The speaker was concealed from me by the high back of the sofa, but her apprehension was perfectly justified. For was it not I who had turned back Therese the pious, the insatiable, coming downstairs in her nightgown to torment her sister some more? Mere surprise at Doña Rita's presence in the house was enough to paralyze me; but I was also overcome by an enormous sense of relief, by the assurance of security for her and for myself. I didn't even ask myself how she came there. It was enough for me that she was not in Tolosa. I could have smiled at the thought that all I had to do now was to hasten the departure of that abominable lunatic—for Tolosa: an easy task, almost no task at all. Yes, I would have smiled, had not I felt outraged by the presence of Señor Ortega under the same roof with Doña Rita. The mere fact was repugnant to me, morally revolting; so that I should have liked to rush at him and throw him out into the street. But that was not to be done for various reasons. One of them was pity. I was suddenly at peace with all mankind, with all nature. I felt as if I couldn't hurt a fly. The intensity of my emotion sealed my lips. With a fearful joy tugging at my heart I moved round the head of the couch without a word.

In the wide fireplace on a pile of white ashes the logs had a deep crimson glow; and turned towards them Doña Rita reclined on her side enveloped in the skins of wild beasts like a charming and savage young chieftain before a camp fire. She never even raised her eyes, giving me the opportunity to contemplate mutely that adolescent, delicately masculine head, so mysteriously feminine in the power of instant seduction, so infinitely suave in its firm design, almost child-like in the freshness of detail : altogether ravishing in the inspired strength of the modelling. That precious head reposed in the palm of her hand ; the face was slightly flushed (with anger perhaps). She kept her eyes obstinately fixed on the pages of a book which she was holding with her other hand. I had the time to lay my infinite adoration at her feet whose white insteps gleamed below the dark edge of the fur out of quilted blue silk bedroom slippers, embroid-ered with small pearls. I had never seen them before ; I mean the slippers. The gleam of the insteps, too, for that matter. I lost myself in a feeling of deep content, something like a foretaste of a time of felicity which must be quiet or it couldn't be eternal. I had never tasted such pefect quietness before. It was not of this earth. I had gone far beyond. It was as if I had reached the ultimate wisdom beyond all dreams and all passions. She was That which is to be contemplated to all Infinity.

The perfect stillness and silence made her raise her eyes at last, reluctantly, with a hard, defensive expression which I had never seen in them before. And no wonder ! The glance was meant for Therese and assumed in self-defence. For some time its character did not change and when it did it turned into a perfectly stony stare of a kind which I also had never seen before. She had never wished so much to be left in peace. She had never been so astonished in her life. She had arrived by the evening express only two hours before Señor Ortega, had driven to the house, and after having something to eat had become for the rest of the evening the helpless prey of her sister who had fawned and scolded and wheedled and threatened in a way that outraged all Rita's feelings. Seizing this unexpected occasion Therese had displayed a distracting versatility of sentiment : rapacity, virtue, piety, spite, and false tenderness—while, characteristically enough, she unpacked the dressing-bag, helped the sinner to get ready for bed, brushed her hair, and finally, as a climax, kissed her hands, partly by surprise and partly by violence. After that she had retired from the field of battle slowly, undefeated, still defiant, firing as a last shot the impudent question : " Tell me only, have you made your will, Rita ? " To this poor Doña Rita with the spirit of opposition strung to the highest pitch answered : " No, and I don't mean to "— being under the impression that this was what her sister wanted her to do. There can be no doubt, however, that all Therese wanted was the information.

Rita, much too agitated to expect anything but a sleepless night, had not the courage to get into bed. She thought she would remain on the sofa before the fire and try to compose herself with a book. As she had no dressing-gown with her she put on her long fur coat over her night-gown, threw some logs on the fire, and lay down. She didn't hear the slightest noise of any sort till she heard me shut the door gently. Quietness of movement was one of Therese's accomplishments, and the harassed heiress of the Allègre millions naturally thought it was her sister coming again to renew the scene. Her heart sank within her. In the end she became a little frightened at the long silence, and raised her eyes. She didn't believe them for a long time. She concluded that I was a vision. In fact, the first word which I heard her utter was a low, awed " No," which, though I understood its meaning, chilled my blood like an evil omen.

It was then that I spoke. " Yes," I said, " it's me that you see," and made a step forward. She didn't start; only her other hand flew to the edges of the fur coat, gripping them together over her breast. Observing this gesture I sat down in the nearest chair. The book she had been reading slipped with a thump on the floor.

" How is it possible that you should be here ? " she said, still in a doubting voice.

" I am really here," I said.  " Would you like to touch my hand ? "

She didn't move at all; her fingers still clutched the fur coat.

" What has happened ? "

" It's a long story, but you may take it from me that all is over.  The tie between us is broken.  I don't know that it was ever very close.  It was an external thing.  The true misfortune is that I have ever seen you."

This last phrase was provoked by an exclamation of sympathy on her part.  She raised herself on her elbow and looked at me intently.  " All over," she murmured.

" Yes, we had to wreck the little vessel.  It was awful. I feel like a murderer.  But she had to be killed."

" Why ? "

" Because I loved her too much.  Don't you know that love and death go very close together ? "

" I could feel almost happy that it is all over, if you hadn't had to lose your love.  Oh, *amigo* George, it was a safe love for you."

" Yes," I said.  " It was a faithful little vessel.  She would have saved us all from any plain danger.  But this was a betrayal.  It was—never mind.  All that's past. The question is what will the next one be."

" Why should it be that ? "

" I don't know.  Life seems but a series of betrayals. There are so many kinds of them.  This was a betrayed plan, but one can betray confidence, and hope and—desire, and the most sacred . . ."

" But what are you doing here ? " she interrupted.

" Oh, yes !  The eternal why.  Till a few hours ago I didn't know what I was here for.  And what are you here for ? "  I asked point blank and with a bitterness she disregarded.  She even answered my question quite readily with many words out of which I could make very little.  I only learned that for at least five mixed reasons, none of which impressed me profoundly, Doña Rita had started at a moment's notice from Paris with nothing but a dressing-bag, and permitting Rose to go and visit her aged parents for two days, and then follow her mistress. That girl of late had looked so perturbed and worried that the sensitive Rita, fearing that she was tired of her place, proposed to settle a sum of money on her which would have enabled her to devote herself entirely to her aged parents. And did I know what that extraordinary girl said? She had said: "Don't let Madame think that I would be too proud to accept anything whatever from her; but I can't even dream of leaving Madame. I believe Madame has no friends. Not one." So instead of a large sum of money Doña Rita gave the girl a kiss and as she had been worried by several people who wanted her to go to Tolosa she bolted down this way just to get clear of all those busybodies. "Hide from them," she went on with ardour. "Yes, I came here to hide," she repeated twice as if delighted at last to have hit on that reason among so many others. "How could I tell that you would be here?" Then with sudden fire which only added to the delight with which I had been watching the play of her physiognomy she added: "Why did you come into this room?"

She enchanted me. The ardent modulations of the sound, the slight play of the beautiful lips, the still, deep sapphire gleam in those long eyes inherited from the dawn of ages and that seemed always to watch unimaginable things, that underlying faint ripple of gaiety that played under all her moods as though it had been a gift from the high gods moved to pity for this lonely mortal, all this within the four walls and displayed for me alone gave me the sense of almost intolerable joy. The words didn't matter. They had to be answered, of course.

"I came in for several reasons. One of them is that I didn't know you were here."

"Therese didn't tell you?"

"No."

"Never talked to you about me?"

I hesitated only for a moment. "Never," I said. Then I asked in my turn, "Did she tell you I was here?"

"No," she said.

"It's very clear she did not mean us to come together again."

"Neither did I, my dear."

"What do you mean by speaking like this, in this tone, in these words? You seem to use them as if they were a sort of formula. Am I a dear to you? Or is anybody? . . . or everybody? . . ."

She had been for some time raised on her elbow, but then as if something had happened to her vitality she sank down till her head rested again on the sofa cushion.

"Why do you try to hurt my feelings?" she asked.

"For the same reason for which you call me dear at the end of a sentence like that: for want of something more amusing to do. You don't pretend to make me believe that you do it for any sort of reason that a decent person would confess to."

The colour had gone from her face: but a fit of wickedness was on me and I pursued, "What are the motives of your speeches? What prompts your actions? On your own showing your life seems to be a continuous running away. You have just run away from Paris. Where will you run to-morrow? What are you everlastingly running from— or is it that you are running after something? What is it? A man, a phantom—or some sensation that you don't like to own to?"

Truth to say, I was abashed by the silence which was her only answer to this sally. I said to myself that I would not let my natural anger, my just fury be disarmed by any assumption of pathos or dignity. I suppose I was really out of my mind and what in the middle ages would have been called "possessed" by an evil spirit. I went on enjoying my own villainy.

"Why aren't you in Tolosa? You ought to be in Tolosa. Isn't Tolosa the proper field for your abilities, for your sympathies, for your profusions, for your generosities—the king without a crown, the man without a fortune! But here there is nothing worthy of your talents. No, there is no longer anything worth any sort of trouble here. There isn't even that ridiculous Monsieur George. I understand that the talk of the coast from here to Cette is that Monsieur George is drowned. Upon my word I believe he is. And serve him right, too. There's Therese, but I don't suppose that your love for your sister . . ."

"For goodness' sake don't let her come in and find you here."

Those words recalled me to myself, exorcised the evil spirit by the mere enchanting power of the voice. They were also impressive by their suggestion of something practical, utilitarian, and remote from sentiment. The evil spirit left me and I remained taken aback slightly.

"Well," I said, "if you mean that you want me to leave the room I will confess to you that I can't very well do it yet. But I could lock both doors if you don't mind that."

"Do what you like as long as you keep her out. You two together would be too much for me to-night. Why don't you go and lock those doors? I have a feeling she is on the prowl."

I got up at once saying, "I imagine she has gone to bed by this time." I felt absolutely calm and responsible. I turned the keys one after another so gently that I couldn't hear the click of the locks myself. This done I recrossed the room with measured steps, with downcast eyes, and approaching the couch without raising them from the carpet I sank down on my knees and leaned my forehead on its edge. That penitential attitude had but little remorse in it. I detected no movement and heard no sound from her. In one place a bit of the fur coat touched my cheek softly, but no forgiving hand came to rest on my bowed head. I only breathed deeply the faint scent of violets, her own particular fragrance enveloping my body, penetrating my very heart with an inconceivable intimacy, bringing me closer to her than the closest embrace, and yet so subtle that I sensed her existence in me only as a great, glowing, indeterminate tenderness, something like the evening light disclosing after the white passion of the day infinite depths in the colours of the sky and an unsuspected soul of peace in the protean forms of life. I had not known such quietness for months; and I detected in myself an immense fatigue, a longing to remain where I was without changing my position to the end of time. Indeed to remain seemed to me a complete solution for all the problems that life presents—even as to the very death itself.

Only the unwelcome reflection that this was impossible made me get up at last with a sigh of deep grief at the end of the dream. But I got up without despair. She didn't murmur, she didn't stir. There was something august in the stillness of the room. It was a strange peace which she shared with me in this unexpected shelter full of disorder in its neglected splendour. What troubled me was the sudden, as it were material, consciousness of time passing as water flows. It seemed to me that it was only the tenacity of my sentiment that held that woman's body, extended and tranquil above the flood. But when I ventured at last to look at her face I saw her flushed, her teeth clenched—it was visible—her nostrils dilated, and in her narrow, level-glancing eyes a look of inward and frightened ecstasy. The edges of the fur coat had fallen open and I was moved to turn away. I had the same impression as on the evening we parted that something had happened which I did not understand; only this time I had not touched her at all. I really didn't understand. At the slightest whisper I would now have gone out without a murmur, as though that emotion had given her the right to be obeyed. But there was no whisper; and for a long time I stood leaning on my arm, looking into the fire and feeling distinctly between the four walls of that locked room the unchecked time flow past our two stranded personalities.

And suddenly she spoke. She spoke in that voice that was so profoundly moving without ever being sad, a little wistful perhaps and always the supreme expression of her grace. She asked as if nothing had happened:

"What are you thinking of, *amigo* ?"

I turned about. She was lying on her side, tranquil above the smooth flow of time, again closely wrapped up in her fur, her head resting on the old-gold sofa cushion bearing like everything else in that room the decoratively enlaced letters of her monogram; her face a little pale now, with the crimson lobe of her ear under the tawny mist of her loose hair, the lips a little parted, and her glance of melted sapphire level and motionless, darkened by fatigue.

"Can I think of anything but you?" I murmured, taking a seat near the foot of the couch. "Or rather it isn't thinking, it is more like the consciousness of you always being present in me, complete to the last hair, to the faintest shade of expression, and that not only when we are apart but when we are together, alone, as close as this. I see you now lying on this couch but that is only the insensible phantom of the real you that is in me. And it is the easier for me to feel this because that image which others see and call by your name—how am I to know that it is anything else but an enchanting mist? You have always eluded me except in one or two moments which seem still more dream-like than the rest. Since I came into this room you have done nothing to destroy my conviction of your unreality apart from myself. You haven't offered me your hand to touch. Is it because you suspect that apart from me you are but a mere phantom, and that you fear to put it to the test?"

One of her hands was under the fur and the other under her cheek. She made no sound. She didn't offer to stir. She didn't move her eyes, not even after I had added after waiting for a while,

"Just what I expected. You are a cold illusion."

She smiled mysteriously, right away from me, straight at the fire, and that was all.

## VI

I HAD a momentary suspicion that I had said something stupid. Her smile amongst many other things seemed to have meant that, too. And I answered it with a certain resignation :

"Well, I don't know that you are so much mist. I remember once hanging on to you like a drowning man. . . . But perhaps I had better not speak of this. It wasn't so very long ago, and you may . . ."

"I don't mind. Well . . ."

"Well, I have kept an impression of great solidity, I'll admit that. A woman of granite."

"A doctor once told me that I was made to last for ever," she said.

"But essentially it's the same thing," I went on. "Granite too, is insensible."

I watched her profile against the pillow and there came on her face an expression I knew well when with an indignation full of suppressed laughter she used to throw at me the word "Imbecile." I expected it to come, but it didn't come. I must say, though, that I was swimmy in my head and now and then had a noise as of the sea in my ears, so I might not have heard it. The woman of granite, built to last for ever, continued to look at the glowing logs which made a sort of fiery ruin on the white pile of ashes. "I will tell you how it is," I said. "When I have you before my eyes there is such a projection of my whole being towards you that I fail to see you distinctly. It was like that from the beginning. I may say that I never saw you distinctly till after we had parted and I thought you had gone from my sight for ever. It was then that you took body in my imagination and that my mind seized on a definite form of you for all its adorations—for its profanations, too. Don't imagine me grovelling in spiritual abasement before a mere image. I got a grip on you that nothing can shake now."

"Don't speak like this," she said. "It's too much for me. And there is a whole long night before us."

"You don't think that I dealt with you sentimentally enough perhaps? But the sentiment was there; as clear a flame as ever burned on earth from the most remote ages before that eternal thing which is in you, which is your heirloom. And is it my fault that what I had to give was real flame, and not a mystic's incense? It is neither your fault nor mine. And now whatever we say to each other at night or in daylight, that sentiment must be taken for granted. It will be there on the day I die—when you won't be there."

She continued to look fixedly at the red embers; and from her lips that hardly moved came the quietest possible whisper: "Nothing would be easier than to die for you."

"Really," I cried. "And you expect me perhaps after this to kiss your feet in a transport of gratitude while I hug the pride of your words to my breast. But as it happens there is nothing in me but contempt for this sublime declaration. How dare you offer me this charlatanism of passion? What has it got to do between you and me who are the only two beings in the world that may safely say that we have no need of shams between ourselves? Is it possible that you are a charlatan at heart? Not from egoism, I admit, but from some sort of fear. Yet, should you be sincere, then—listen well to me—I would never forgive you. I would visit your grave every day to curse you for an evil thing."

"Evil thing," she echoed softly.

"Would you prefer to be a sham—that one could forget?"

"You will never forget me," she said in the same tone at the glowing embers. "Evil or good. But, my dear, I feel neither an evil nor a sham. I have got to be what I am, and that, *amigo*, is not so easy; because I may be simple, but like all those on whom there is no peace I am not One. No, I am not One!"

"You are all the women in the world," I whispered

A A

bending over her. She didn't seem to be aware of anything and only spoke—always to the glow.

"If I were that I would say: God help them then. But that would be more appropriate for Therese. For me, I can only give them my infinite compassion. I have too much reverence in me to invoke the name of a God of whom clever men have robbed me a long time ago. How could I help it? For the talk was clever and—and I had a mind. And I am also, as Therese says, naturally sinful. Yes, my dear, I may be naturally wicked but I am not evil and I could die for you."

"You!" I said. "You are afraid to die."

"Yes. But not for you."

The whole structure of glowing logs fell down, raising a small turmoil of white ashes and sparks. The tiny crash seemed to wake her up thoroughly. She turned her head upon the cushion to look at me.

"It's a very extraordinary thing, we two coming together like this," she said with conviction. "You coming in without knowing I was here and then telling me that you can't very well go out of the room. That sounds funny. I wouldn't have been angry if you had said that you wouldn't. It would have hurt me. But nobody ever paid much attention to my feelings. Why do you smile like this?"

"At a thought. Without any charlatanism of passion I am able to tell you of something to match your devotion. I was not afraid for your sake to come within a hair's breadth of what to all the world would have been a squalid crime. Note that you and I are persons of honour. And there might have been a criminal trial at the end of it for me. Perhaps the scaffold."

"Do you say these horrors to make me tremble?"

"Oh, you needn't tremble. There shall be no crime. I need not risk the scaffold, since now you are safe. But I entered this room meditating resolutely on the ways of murder, calculating possibilities and chances without the slightest compunction. It's all over now. It was all over directly I saw you here, but it had been so near that I shudder yet."

She must have been very startled because for a time she couldn't speak. Then in a faint voice :

" For me ! For me ! " she faltered out twice.

" For you—or for myself ? Yet it couldn't have been selfish. What would it have been to me that you remained in the world ? I never expected to see you again. I even composed a most beautiful letter of farewell. Such a letter as no woman had ever received."

Instantly she shot out a hand towards me. The edges of the fur cloak fell apart. A wave of the faintest possible scent floated into my nostrils.

" Let me have it," she said imperiously.

" You can't have it. It's all in my head. No woman will read it. I suspect it was something that could never have been written. But what a farewell ! And now I suppose we shall say good-bye without even a handshake. But you are safe ! Only I must ask you not to come out of this room till I tell you you may."

I was extremely anxious that Señor Ortega should never even catch a glimpse of Doña Rita, never guess how near he had been to her. I was extremely anxious the fellow should depart for Tolosa and get shot in a ravine ; or go to the Devil in his own way, as long as he lost the track of Doña Rita completely. He then, probably, would get mad and get shut up, or else get cured, forget all about it, and devote himself to his vocation, whatever it was—keep a shop and grow fat. All this flashed through my mind in an instant and while I was still dazzled by those comforting images, the voice of Doña Rita pulled me up with a jerk.

" You mean not out of this house ? "

" No, I mean not out of this room," I said with some embarrassment.

" What do you mean ? Is there something in the house then ? This is most extraordinary ! Stay in this room ? And you, too, it seems ? Are you also afraid for yourself ? "

" I can't even give you an idea how afraid I was. I am

not so much now.  But you know very well, Doña Rita,
that I never carry any sort of weapon in my pocket."

" Why don't you, then ? " she asked in a flash of scorn
which bewitched me so completely for an instant that I
couldn't even smile at it.

" Because if I am unconventionalized I am an old European," I murmured gently.  " No, *Excellentissima*, I shall
go through life without as much as a switch in my hand.
It's no use your being angry.  Adapting to this great moment
some words you've heard before : I am like that.  Such is
my character ! "

Doña Rita frankly stared at me—a most unusual expression for her to have.  Suddenly she sat up.

" Don George," she said with lovely animation, " I insist
upon knowing who is in my house."

" You insist ! . . . But Therese says it is *her* house."

Had there been anything handy, such as a cigarette box,
for instance, it would have gone sailing through the air
spouting cigarettes as it went.  Rosy all over, cheeks, neck,
shoulders, she seemed lighted up softly from inside like a
beautiful transparency.  But she didn't raise her voice.

" You and Therese have sworn my ruin.  If you don't
tell me what you mean I will go outside and shout up the
stairs to make her come down.  I know there is no one but
the three of us in the house."

" Yes, three; but not counting my Jacobin.  There is a
Jacobin in the house."

" A Jac . . . !  Oh, George, is this the time to jest ? "
she began in persuasive tones when a faint but peculiar
noise stilled her lips as though they had been suddenly
frozen.  She became quiet all over instantly.  I, on the
contrary, made an involuntary movement before I, too,
became as still as death.  We strained our ears ; but that
peculiar metallic rattle had been so slight and the silence
now was so perfect that it was very difficult to believe one's
senses.  Doña Rita looked inquisitively at me.  I gave her
a slight nod.  We remained looking into each other's eyes
while we listened and listened till the silence became un-

bearable. Doña Rita whispered composedly : "Did you hear ? "

"I am asking myself . . . I almost think I didn't."

"Don't shuffle with me. It was a scraping noise."

"Something fell."

"Something ! What thing ? What are the things that fall by themselves ? Who is that man of whom you spoke ? Is there a man ? "

"No doubt about it whatever. I brought him here myself."

"What for ? "

"Why shouldn't I have a Jacobin of my own ? Haven't you one, too ? But mine is a different problem from that white-haired humbug of yours. He is a genuine article. There must be plenty like him about. He has scores to settle with half a dozen people, he says, and he clamours for revolutions to give him a chance."

"But why did you bring him here ? "

"I don't know—from sudden affection . . ."

All this passed in such low tones that we seemed to make out the words more by watching each other's lips than through our sense of hearing. Man is a strange animal. I didn't care what I said. All I wanted was to keep her in her pose, excited and still, sitting up with her hair loose, softly glowing, the dark brown fur making a wonderful contrast with the white lace on her breast. All I was thinking of was that she was adorable and too lovely for words ! I cared for nothing but that sublimely æsthetic impression. It summed up all life, all joy, all poetry ! It had a divine strain. I am certain that I was not in my right mind. I suppose I was not quite sane. I am convinced that at that moment of the four people in the house it was Doña Rita who upon the whole was the most sane. She observed my face and I am sure she read there something of my inward exaltation. She knew what to do. In the softest possible tone and hardly above her breath she commanded : " George, come to yourself."

Her gentleness had the effect of evening light. I was

soothed. Her confidence in her own power touched me profoundly. I suppose my love was too great for madness to get hold of me. I can't say that I passed to a complete calm, but I became slightly ashamed of myself. I whispered :

"No, it was not from affection, it was for the love of you that I brought him here. That imbecile H. was going to send him to Tolosa."

"That Jacobin !" Doña Rita was immensely surprised, as she might well have been. Then resigned to the incomprehensible : "Yes," she breathed out, "what did you do with him ? "

"I put him to bed in the studio."

How lovely she was with the effort of close attention depicted in the turn of her head and in her whole face honestly trying to approve. "And then ? " she inquired.

"Then I came in here to face calmly the necessity of doing away with a human life. I didn't shirk it for a moment. That's what a short twelvemonth has brought me to. Don't think I am reproaching you, O blind force ! You are justified because you *are*. Whatever had to happen you would not even have heard of it."

Horror darkened her marvellous radiance. Then her face became utterly blank with the tremendous effort to understand. Absolute silence reigned in the house. It seemed to me that everything had been said now that mattered in the world ; and that the world itself had reached its ultimate stage, had reached its appointed end of an eternal, phantomlike silence. Suddenly Doña Rita raised a warning finger. I had heard nothing and shook my head ; but she nodded hers and murmured excitedly, "Yes, yes, in the fencing-room, as before."

In the same way I answered her : "Impossible ! The door is locked and Therese has the key." She asked then in the most cautious manner,

"Have you seen Therese to-night ? "

"Yes," I confessed without misgiving. "I left her making up the fellow's bed when I came in here."

" The bed of the Jacobin ? " she said in a peculiar tone as if she were humouring a lunatic.

" I think I had better tell you he is a Spaniard—that he seems to know you from early days. . . ." I glanced at her face, it was extremely tense, apprehensive. For myself I had no longer any doubt as to the man and I hoped she would reach the correct conclusion herself. But I believe she was too distracted and worried to think consecutively. She only seemed to feel some terror in the air. In very pity I bent down and whispered carefully near her ear, " His name is Ortega."

I expected some effect from that name but I never expected what happened. With the sudden, free, spontaneous agility of a young animal she leaped off the sofa, leaving her slippers behind, and in one bound reached almost the middle of the room. The vigour, the instinctive precision of that spring, were something amazing. I just escaped being knocked over. She landed lightly on her bare feet with a perfect balance, without the slightest suspicion of swaying in her instant immobility. It lasted less than a second, then she spun round distractedly and darted at the first door she could see. My own agility was just enough to enable me to grip the back of the fur coat and then catch her round the body before she could wriggle herself out of the sleeves. She was muttering all the time, " No, no, no." She abandoned herself to me just for an instant during which I got her back to the middle of the room. There she attempted to free herself and I let her go at once. With her face very close to mine, but apparently not knowing what she was looking at she repeated again twice, " No—No," with an intonation which might well have brought dampness to my eyes but which only made me regret that I didn't kill the honest Ortega at sight. Suddenly Doña Rita swung round and seizing her loose hair with both hands started twisting it up before one of the sumptuous mirrors. The wide fur sleeves slipped down her white arms. In a brusque movement like a downward stab she transfixed the whole mass of tawny glints and sparks with the arrow of gold which she perceived lying there, before her, on the marble console. Then she sprang away from the glass muttering feverishly, "Out—out—out of this house," and trying with an awful, senseless stare to dodge past me who had put myself in her way with open arms. At last I managed to seize her by the shoulders and in the extremity of my distress I shook her roughly. If she hadn't quieted down then I believe my heart would have broken. I spluttered right into her face : "I won't let you. Here you stay." She seemed to recognize me at last, and suddenly still, perfectly firm on her white feet, she let her arms fall and, from an abyss of desolation, whispered, "Oh ! George ! No ! No ! Not Ortega."

There was a passion of mature grief in this tone of appeal. And yet she remained as touching and helpless as a distressed child. It had all the simplicity and depth of a child's emotion. It tugged at one's heart-strings in the same direct way. But what could one do ? How could one soothe her ? It was impossible to pat her on the head, take her on the knee, give her a chocolate or show her a picture-book. I found myself absolutely without resource. Completely at a loss.

"Yes, Ortega. Well, what of it ? " I whispered with immense assurance.

## VII

My brain was in a whirl. I am safe to say that at this precise moment there was nobody completely sane in the house. Setting apart Therese and Ortega, both in the grip of unspeakable passions, all the moral economy of Doña Rita had gone to pieces. Everything was gone except her strong sense of life with all its implied menaces. The woman was a mere chaos of sensations and vitality. I, too, suffered most from inability to get hold of some fundamental thought. The one on which I could best build some hopes was the thought that, of course, Ortega did not know anything. I whispered this into the ear of Doña Rita, into her precious, her beautifully shaped ear.

But she shook her head, very much like an inconsolable child and very much with a child's complete pessimism she murmured, " Therese has told him."

The words, " Oh, nonsense," never passed my lips, because I could not cheat myself into denying that there had been a noise; and that the noise was in the fencing-room. I knew that room. There was nothing there that by the wildest stretch of imagination could be conceived as falling with that particular sound. There was a table with a tall strip of looking-glass above it at one end; but since Blunt took away his campaigning kit there was no small object of any sort on the console or anywhere else that could have been jarred off in some mysterious manner. Along one of the walls there was the whole complicated apparatus of solid brass pipes, and quite close to it an enormous bath sunk into the floor. The greatest part of the room along its whole length was covered with matting and had nothing else but a long, narrow leather-upholstered bench fixed to the wall. And that was all. And the door leading to the studio was locked. And Therese had the key. And it flashed on my mind, independently of Doña Rita's pessimism, by the force of personal conviction, that, of course, Therese would tell him. I beheld the whole succession of events perfectly connected and tending to that particular conclusion. Therese would tell him ! I could see the contrasted heads of those two formidable lunatics close together in a dark mist of whispers compounded of greed, piety, and jealousy, plotting in a sense of perfect security as if under the very wing of Providence. So at least Therese would think. She could not be but under the impression that (providentially) I had been called out for the rest of the night.

And now there was one sane person in the house, for I had regained complete command of my thoughts. Working in a logical succession of images they showed me at last as clearly as a picture on a wall, Therese pressing with fervour the key into the fevered palm of the rich, prestigious, virtuous cousin, so that he should go and urge his self-sacrificing offer to Rita, and gain merit before Him whose Eye sees all the actions of men. And this image of those two with the key in the studio seemed to me a most monstrous conception of fanaticism, of a perfectly horrible aberration. For who could mistake the state that made José Ortega the figure he was, inspiring both pity and fear? I could not deny that I understood, not the full extent but the exact nature of his suffering. Young as I was I had solved for myself that grotesque and sombre personality. His contact with me, the personal contact with (as he thought) one of the actual lovers of that woman who brought to him as a boy the curse of the gods, had tipped over the trembling scales. No doubt I was very near death in the " grand salon " of the Maison Dorée, only that his torture had gone too far. It seemed to me that I ought to have heard his very soul scream while we were seated at supper. But in a moment he had ceased to care for me. I was nothing. To the crazy exaggeration of his jealousy I was but one amongst a hundred thousand. What was my death? Nothing. All mankind had possessed that woman. I knew what his wooing of her would be : Mine—or Dead.

All this ought to have had the clearness of noon-day, even to the veriest idiot that ever lived; and Therese was, properly speaking, exactly that. An idiot. A one-ideaed creature. Only the idea was complex; therefore it was impossible really to say what she wasn't capable of. This was what made her obscure processes so awful. She had at times the most amazing perceptions. Who could tell where her simplicity ended and her cunning began? She had also the faculty of never forgetting any fact bearing upon her one idea; and I remembered now that the conversation with me about the will had produced on her an indelible impression of the Law's surprising justness. Recalling her naïve admiration of the " just " law that required no " paper " from a sister, I saw her casting loose the raging fate with a sanctimonious air. And Therese would naturally give the key of the fencing-room to her dear, virtuous, grateful, disinterested cousin, to that damned soul with delicate whiskers, because she would think it just possible that Rita might have locked the door leading from her room into the hall; whereas there was no earthly reason, not the slightest likelihood, that she would bother about the other. Righteousness demanded that the erring sister should be taken unawares.

All the above is the analysis of one short moment. Images are to words like light to sound—incomparably swifter. And all this was really one flash of light through my mind. A comforting thought succeeded it: that both doors were locked and that really there was no danger.

However, there had been that noise—the why and the how of it? Of course in the dark he might have fallen into the bath, but that wouldn's have been a faint noise. It wouldn't have been a rattle. There was absolutely nothing he could knock over. He might have dropped a candle-stick if Therese had left him her own. That was possible, but then those thick mats—and then, anyway, why should he drop it? and, hang it all, why shouldn't he have gone straight on and tried the door? I had suddenly a sickening vision of the fellow crouching at the key-hole, listening, listening, listening, for some movement or sigh of the sleeper he was ready to tear away from the world, alive or dead. I had a conviction that he was still listening. Why? Goodness knows! He may have been only gloating over the assurance that the night was long and that he had all these hours to himself.

I was pretty certain that he could have heard nothing of our whispers, the room was too big for that and the door too solid. I hadn't the same confidence in the efficiency of the lock. Still! . . . Guarding my lips with my hand I urged Dona Rita to go back to the sofa. She wouldn't answer me, and when I got hold of her arm I discovered that she wouldn't move. She had taken root in that thick-pile Aubusson carpet; and she was so rigidly still all over that the brilliant stones in the shaft of the arrow of gold, with the six candles

at the head of the sofa blazing full on them, emitted no
sparkle.

I was extremely anxious that she shouldn't betray herself.
I reasoned, save the mark, as a psychologist. I had no doubt
that the man knew of her being there; but he only knew it
by hearsay. And that was bad enough. I could not help
feeling that if he obtained some evidence for his senses by
any sort of noise, voice, or movement, his madness would
gain strength enough to burst the lock. I was rather
ridiculously worried about the locks. A horrid mistrust of
the whole house possessed me. I saw it in the light of a deadly
trap. I had no weapon, I couldn't say whether he had one
or not. I wasn't afraid of a struggle as far as I, myself, was
concerned, but I was afraid of it for Doña Rita. To be
rolling at her feet, locked in a literally tooth-and-nail struggle
with Ortega would have been odious. I wanted to spare her
feelings, just as I would have been anxious to save from any
contact with mud the feet of that goatherd of the mountains
with a symbolic face. I looked at her face. For immobility
it might have been a carving. I wished I knew how to deal
with that embodied mystery, to influence it, to manage it.
Oh, how I longed for the gift of authority! In addition,
since I had become completely sane, all my scruples against
laying hold of her had returned. I felt shy and embarrassed.
My eyes were fixed on the bronze handle of the fencing-
room door as if it were something alive. I braced myself
up against the moment when it would move. This was what
was going to happen next. It would move very gently. My
heart began to thump. But I was prepared to keep myself
as still as death and I hoped Doña Rita would have sense
enough to do the same. I stole another glance at her face
and at that moment I heard the word: "Beloved!" form
itself in the still air of the room, weak, distinct, piteous, like
the last request of the dying.

With great presence of mind I whispered into Doña Rita's
ear: "Perfect silence!" and was overjoyed to discover that
she had heard me, understood me; that she even had command over her rigid lips. She answered me in a breath

(our cheeks were nearly touching) : " Take me out of this house."

I glanced at all her clothing scattered about the room and hissed forcibly the warning " Perfect immobility " ; noticing with relief that she didn't offer to move, though animation was returning to her and her lips had remained parted in an awful, unintended effect of a smile. And I don't know whether I was pleased when she, who was not to be touched, gripped my wrist suddenly. It had the air of being done on purpose because almost instantly another : " Beloved ! " louder, more agonized if possible, got into the room and, yes, went home to my heart. It was followed without any transition, preparation, or warning, by a positively bellowed : " Speak, perjured beast ! " which I felt pass in a thrill right through Doña Rita like an electric shock, leaving her as motionless as before.

Till he shook the door handle, which he did immediately afterwards, I wasn't certain through which door he had spoken. The two doors (in different walls) were rather near each other. It was as I expected. He was in the fencing-room, thoroughly aroused, his senses on the alert to catch the slightest sound. A situation not to be trifled with. Leaving the room was for us out of the question. It was quite possible for him to dash round into the hall before we could get clear of the front door. As to making a bolt of it upstairs there was the same objection ; and to allow ourselves to be chased all over the empty house by this maniac would have been mere folly. There was no advantage in locking ourselves up anywhere upstairs where the original doors and locks were much lighter. No, true safety was in absolute stillness and silence, so that even his rage should be brought to doubt at last and die expended, or choke him before it died ; I didn't care which.

For me to go out and meet him would have been stupid. Now I was certain that he was armed. I had remembered the wall in the fencing-room decorated with trophies of cold steel in all the civilized and savage forms ; sheaves of assegais, in the guise of columns and grouped between them stars and suns of choppers, swords, knives; from Italy, from Damascus, from Abyssinia, from the ends of the world. Ortega had only to make his barbarous choice. I suppose he had got up on the bench, and fumbling about amongst them must have brought one down, which, falling, had produced that rattling noise. But in any case to go to meet him would have been folly, because, after all, I might have been overpowered (even with bare hands) and then Doña Rita would have been left utterly defenceless.

"He will speak," came to me the ghostly, terrified murmur of her voice. "Take me out of the house before he begins to speak."

"Keep still," I whispered. "He will soon get tired of this."

"You don't know him."

"Oh, yes, I do. Been with him two hours."

At this she let go my wrist and covered her face with her hands passionately. When she dropped them she had the look of one morally crushed.

"What did he say to you?"

"He raved."

"Listen to me. It was all true!"

"I daresay, but what of that?"

These ghostly words passed between us hardly louder than thoughts; but after my last answer she ceased and gave me a searching stare, then drew in a long breath. The voice on the other side of the door burst out with an impassioned request for a little pity, just a little, and went on begging for a few words, for two words, for one word—one poor little word. Then it gave up, then repeated once more, "Say you are there, Rita. Say one word, just one word. Say 'yes.' Come! Just one little yes."

"You see," I said. She only lowered her eyelids over the anxious glance she had turned on me.

For a minute we could have had the illusion that he had stolen away, unheard, on the thick mats. But I don't think that either of us was deceived. The voice returned, stammering words without connection, pausing and faltering, till suddenly steadied it soared into impassioned entreaty, sank to low, harsh tones, voluble, lofty sometimes and sometimes abject. When it paused it left us looking profoundly at each other.

"It's almost comic," I whispered.

"Yes. One could laugh," she assented, with a sort of sinister conviction. Never had I seen her look exactly like that, for an instant another, an incredible Rita ! "Haven't I laughed at him innumerable times ? " she added in a sombre whisper.

He was muttering to himself out there, and unexpectedly shouted : "What ? " as though he had fancied he had heard something. He waited a while before he started up again with a loud : "Speak up, Queen of the goats, with your goat tricks. . . ." All was still for a time, then came a most awful bang on the door. He must have stepped back a pace to hurl himself bodily against the panels. The whole house seemed to shake. He repeated that performance once more, and then varied it by a prolonged drumming with his fists. It *was* comic. But I felt myself struggling mentally with an invading gloom, as though I were no longer sure of myself.

"Take me out," whispered Doña Rita feverishly, " take me out of this house before it is too late."

"You will have to stand it," I answered.

"So be it ; but then you must go away yourself. Go now, before it is too late."

I didn't condescend to answer this. The drumming on the panels stopped and the absurd thunder of it died out in the house. I don't know why precisely then I had the acute vision of the red mouth of José Ortega wriggling with rage between his funny whiskers. He began afresh but in a tired tone :

"Do you expect a fellow to forget your tricks, you wicked little devil ? Haven't you ever seen me dodging about to get a sight of you amongst those pretty gentlemen, on horseback, like a princess, with pure cheeks like a carved saint ? I wonder I didn't throw stones at you. I wonder I didn't run after you shouting the tale—curse my timidity ! But I daresay

they knew as much as I did. More. All the new tricks—if
that were possible."

While he was making this uproar, Doña Rita put her fingers
in her ears and then suddenly changed her mind and clapped
her hands over my ears. Instinctively I disengaged my head
but she persisted. We had a short tussle without moving
from the spot, and suddenly I had my head free, and there
was complete silence. He had screamed himself out of
breath, but Doña Rita muttering : " Too late, too late," got
her hands away from my grip and slipping altogether out of
her fur coat seized some garment lying on a chair near by (I
think it was her skirt), with the intention of dressing herself,
I imagine, and rushing out of the house. Determined to
prevent this, but indeed without thinking very much what I
was doing, I got hold of her arm. That struggle was silent,
too ; but I used the least force possible and she managed to
give me an unexpected push. Stepping back to save myself
from falling I overturned the little table, bearing the six-
branched candlestick. It hit the floor, rebounded with a
dull ring on the carpet, and by the time it came to a rest every
single candle was out. He on the other side of the door
naturally heard the noise and greeted it with a triumphant
screech : " Aha ! I've managed to wake you up," the very
savagery of which had a laughable effect. I felt the weight
of Doña Rita grow on my arm and thought it best to let her
sink on the floor, wishing to be free in my movements and
really afraid that now he had actually heard a noise he would
infallibly burst the door. But he didn't even thump it. He
seemed to have exhausted himself in that scream. There was
no other light in the room but the darkened glow of the
embers and I could hardly make out amongst the shadows
of furniture Doña Rita sunk on her knees in a penitential
and despairing attitude. Before this collapse I, who had
been wrestling desperately with her a moment before, felt
that I dare not touch her. This emotion, too, I could not
understand ; this abandonment of herself, this conscience-
stricken humility. A humbly imploring request to open the
door came from the other side. Ortega kept on repeating :

" Open the door, open the door," in such an amazing variety
of intonations, imperative, whining, persuasive, insinuating,
and even unexpectedly jocose, that I really stood there
smiling to myself, yet with a gloomy and uneasy heart. Then
he remarked, parenthetically as it were, " Oh, you know how
to torment a man, you brown-skinned, lean, grinning, dishevelled imp, you. And mark," he expounded further, in a
curiously doctoral tone—" you are in all your limbs hateful :
your eyes are hateful and your mouth is hateful, and your
hair is hateful, and your body is cold and vicious like a snake
—and altogether you are perdition."

This statement was astonishingly deliberate. He drew
a moaning breath after it and uttered in a heartrending
tone, " You know, Rita, that I cannot live without you. I
haven't lived. I am not living now. This isn't life. Come,
Rita, you can't take a boy's soul away and then let him grow
up and go about the world, poor devil, while you go amongst
the rich from one pair of arms to another, showing all your
best tricks. But I will forgive you if you only open the door,"
he ended in an inflated tone : " You remember how you
swore time after time to be my wife. You are more fit to
be Satan's wife but I don't mind. You shall be *my* wife ! "

A sound near the floor made me bend down hastily with
a stern : " Don't laugh," for in his grotesque, almost
burlesque discourses there seemed to me to be truth, passion,
and horror enough to move a mountain.

Suddenly suspicion seized him out there. With perfectly
farcical unexpectedness he yelled shrilly : " Oh, you deceitful
wretch ! You won't escape me ! I will have you. . . ."

And in a manner of speaking he vanished. Of course I
couldn't see him but somehow that was the impression. I
had hardly time to receive it when crash ! . . . he was
already at the other door. I suppose he thought that his
prey was escaping him. His swiftness was amazing, almost
inconceivable, more like the effect of a trick or of a mechanism.
The thump on the door was awful as if he had not been able
to stop himself in time. The shock seemed enough to stun
an elephant. It was really funny. And after the crash there

was a moment of silence as if he were recovering himself. The next thing was a low grunt, and at once he picked up the thread of his fixed idea.

"You will have to be my wife. I have no shame. You swore you would be and so you will have to be." Stifled low sounds made me bend down again to the kneeling form, white in the flush of the dark red glow. "For goodness' sake don't," I whispered down. She was struggling with an appalling fit of merriment, repeating to herself, "Yes, every day, for two months. Sixty times at least, sixty times at least." Her voice was rising high. She was struggling against laughter, but when I tried to put my hand over her lips I felt her face wet with tears. She turned it this way and that, eluding my hand with repressed low, little moans. I lost my caution and said, "Be quiet," so sharply as to startle myself (and her, too) into expectant stillness.

Ortega's voice in the hall asked distinctly : "Eh ? What's this ? " and then he kept still on his side listening, but he must have thought that his ears had deceived him. He was getting tired, too. He was keeping quiet out there—resting. Presently he sighed deeply ; then in a harsh melancholy tone he started again.

"My love, my soul, my life, do speak to me. What am I that you should take so much trouble to pretend that you aren't there ? Do speak to me," he repeated tremulously, following this mechanical appeal with a string of extravagantly endearing names, some of them quite childish, which all of a sudden stopped dead ; and then after a pause there came a distinct, unutterably weary : "What shall I do now ? " as though he were speaking to himself.

I shuddered to hear rising from the floor, by my side, a vibrating, scornful : "Do ! Why, slink off home looking over your shoulder as you used to years ago when I had done with you—all but the laughter."

"Rita," I murmured, appalled. He must have been struck dumb for a moment. Then, goodness only knows why, in his dismay or rage he was moved to speak in French with a most ridiculous accent.

"So you have found your tongue at last—*Catin!* You were that from the cradle. Don't you remember how . . ."

Doña Rita sprang to her feet at my side with a loud cry, "No, George, no," which bewildered me completely. The suddenness, the loudness of it made the ensuing silence on both sides of the door perfectly awful. It seemed to me that if I didn't resist with all my might something in me would die on the instant. In the straight, falling folds of the night-dress she looked cold like a block of marble; while I, too, was turned into stone by the terrific clamour in the hall.

"Therese, Therese," yelled Ortega. "She has got a man in there." He ran to the foot of the stairs and screamed again, "Therese, Therese! There is a man with her. A man! Come down, you miserable, starved peasant, come down and see."

I don't know where Therese was but I am sure that this voice reached her, terrible, as if clamouring to heaven, and with a shrill over-note which made me certain that if she was in bed the only thing she would think of doing would be to put her head under the bed-clothes. With a final yell: "Come down and see," he flew back at the door of the room and started shaking it violently.

It was a double door, very tall, and there must have been a lot of things loose about its fittings, bolts, latches, and all those brass applications with broken screws, because it rattled, it clattered, it jingled; and produced also the sound as of thunder rolling in the big, empty hall. It was deafening, distressing, and vaguely alarming as if it could bring the house down. At the same time the futility of it had, it cannot be denied, a comic effect. The very magnitude of the racket he raised was funny. But he couldn't keep up that violent exertion continuously, and when he stopped to rest we could hear him shouting to himself in vengeful tones. He saw it all! He had been decoyed there! (Rattle, rattle, rattle.) He had been decoyed into that town, he screamed, getting more and more excited by the noise he made himself, in order to be exposed to this! (Rattle, rattle.) By this shameless "*Catin! Catin! Catin!*"

He started at the door again with superhuman vigour.

Behind me I heard Doña Rita laughing softly, statuesque, turned all dark in the fading glow. I called out to her quite openly, "Do keep your self-control." And she called back to me in a clear voice : "Oh, my dear, will you ever consent to speak to me after all this ? But don't ask for the impossible. He was born to be laughed at."

"Yes," I cried. "But don't let yourself go."

I don't know whether Ortega heard us. He was exerting then his utmost strength of lung against the infamous plot to expose him to the derision of the fiendish associates of that obscene woman ! . . . Then he began another interlude upon the door, so sustained and strong that I had the thought that this was growing absurdly impossible, that either the plaster would begin to fall off the ceiling or he would drop dead next moment, out there.

He stopped, uttered a few curses at the door, and seemed calmer from sheer exhaustion.

"This story will be all over the world," we heard him begin. "Deceived, decoyed, inveighed, in order to be made a laughing-stock before the most debased of all mankind, that woman and her associates." This was really a meditation. And then he screamed : "I will kill you all." Once more he started worrying the door but it was a startlingly feeble effort which he abandoned almost at once. He must have been at the end of his strength. Doña Rita from the middle of the room asked me recklessly loud : "Tell me ! Wasn't he born to be laughed at ?" I didn't answer her. I was so near the door that I thought I ought to hear him panting there. He was terrifying, but he was not serious. He was at the end of his strength, of his breath, of every kind of endurance, but I did not know it. He was done up, finished ; but perhaps he did not know it himself. How still he was ! Just as I began to wonder at it, I heard him distinctly give a slap to his forehead. "I see it all !" he cried. "That miserable, canting peasant-woman upstairs has arranged it all. No doubt she consulted her priests. I must regain my self-respect. Let her die first." I heard him make a dash for the foot of the stairs. I was appalled; yet to think of Therese being hoisted with her own petard was like a turn of affairs in a farce. A very ferocious farce. Instinctively I unlocked the door. Doña Rita's contralto laugh rang out loud, bitter, and contemptuous; and I heard Ortega's distracted screaming as if under torture. "It hurts! It hurts! It hurts!" I hesitated just an instant, half a second, no more, but before I could open the door wide there was in the hall a short groan and the sound of a heavy fall.

The sight of Ortega lying on his back at the foot of the stairs arrested me in the doorway. One of his legs was drawn up, the other extended fully, his foot very near the pedestal of the silver statuette holding the feeble and tenacious gleam which made the shadows so heavy in that hall. One of his arms lay across his breast. The other arm was extended full length on the white-and-black pavement with the hand palm upwards and the fingers rigidly spread out. The shadow of the lowest step slanted across his face but one whisker and part of his chin could be made out. He appeared strangely flattened. He didn't move at all. He was in his shirt-sleeves. I felt an extreme distaste for that sight. The characteristic sound of a key worrying in the lock stole into my ears. I couldn't locate it but I didn't attend much to that at first. I was engaged in watching Señor Ortega. But for his raised leg he clung so flat to the floor and had taken on himself such a distorted shape that he might have been the mere shadow of Señor Ortega. It was rather fascinating to see him so quiet at the end of all that fury, clamour, passion, and uproar. Surely there was never anything so still in the world as this Ortega. I had a bizarre notion that he was not to be disturbed.

A noise like the rattling of chain links, a small grind and click exploded in the stillness of the hall and a voice began to swear in Italian. These surprising sounds were quite welcome, they recalled me to myself, and I perceived they came from the front door which seemed pushed a little ajar. Was somebody trying to get in? I had no objection, I went to the door and said: "Wait a moment, it's on the chain." The deep voice on the other side said : " What an extraordinary thing," and I assented mentally. It was extraordinary. The chain was never put up, but Therese was a thorough sort of person, and on this night she had put it up to keep no one out except myself. It was the old Italian and his daughters returning from the ball who were trying to get in.

Suddenly I became intensely alive to the whole situation. I bounded back, closed the door of Blunt's room, and the next moment was speaking to the Italian. " A little patience." My hands trembled but I managed to take down the chain and as I allowed the door to swing open a little more I put myself in his way. He was burly, venerable, a little indignant, and full of thanks. Behind him his two girls, in short-skirted costumes, white stockings, and low shoes, their heads powdered and earrings sparkling in their ears, huddled together behind their father, wrapped up in their light mantles. One had kept her little black mask on her face, the other held hers in her hand.

The Italian was surprised at my blocking the way and remarked pleasantly, " It's cold outside, Signor." I said, " Yes," and added in a hurried whisper : " There is a dead man in the hall." He didn't say a single word but put me aside a little, projected his body in for one searching glance. " Your daughters," I murmured. He said kindly, " *Va bene, va bene.*" And then to them, " Come in, girls."

There is nothing like dealing with a man who has had a long past of out-of-the-way experiences. The skill with which he rounded up and drove the girls across the hall, paternal and irresistible, venerable and reassuring, was a sight to see. They had no time for more than one scared look over the shoulder. He hustled them in and locked them up safely in their part of the house, then crossed the hall with a quick practical stride. When near Señor Ortega he trod short just in time and said : " In truth, blood " ; then selecting the place, knelt down by the body in his tall hat and respectable overcoat, his white beard giving him immense authority somehow. " But—this man is not dead," he exclaimed, looking up at me. With profound sagacity, inherent as it were in his great beard, he never took the trouble to put any questions to me and seemed certain that I had nothing to do with the ghastly sight. " He managed to give himself an enormous gash in his side," was his calm remark. " And what a weapon ! " he exclaimed, getting it out from under the body. It was an Abyssinian or Nubian production of a bizarre shape ; the clumsiest thing imaginable, partaking of a sickle and a chopper with a sharp edge and a pointed end. A mere cruel-looking curio of inconceivable clumsiness to European eyes.

The old man let it drop with amused disdain. " You had better take hold of his legs," he decided without appeal. I certainly had no inclination to argue. When we lifted him up the head of Señor Ortega fell back desolately, making an awful, defenceless display of his large, white throat.

We found the lamp burning in the studio and the bed made up on the couch on which we deposited our burden. My venerable friend jerked the upper sheet away at once and started tearing it into strips.

" You may leave him to me," said that efficient sage, " but the doctor is your affair. If you don't want this business to make a noise you will have to find a discreet man."

He was most benevolently interested in all the proceedings. He remarked with a patriarchal smile as he tore the sheet noisily : " You had better not lose any time." I didn't lose any time. I crammed into the next hour an astonishing amount of bodily activity. Without more words I flew out bare-headed into the last night of Carnival. Luckily I was certain of the right sort of doctor. He was an iron-grey man of forty and of a stout habit of body but who was able to put on a spurt. In the cold, dark, and deserted by-streets, he ran with earnest and ponderous footsteps, which echoed loudly in the cold night air, while I skimmed along the ground a pace or two in front of him. It was only on arriving at the house that I perceived that I had left the front door wide open. All the town, every evil in the world could have entered the black-and-white hall. But I had no time to meditate upon my imprudence. The doctor and I worked in silence for nearly an hour and it was only then while he was washing his hands in the fencing-room that he asked :

" What was he up to, that imbecile ? "

" Oh, he was examining this curiosity," I said.

" Oh, yes, and it accidentally went off," said the doctor, looking contemptuously at the Nubian knife I had thrown on the table. Then while wiping his hands : " I would bet there is a woman somewhere under this ; but that of course does not affect the nature of the wound. I hope this blood-letting will do him good."

" Nothing will do him any good," I said.

" Curious house this," went on the doctor. " It belongs to a curious sort of woman, too. I happened to see her once or twice. I shouldn't wonder if she were to raise considerable trouble in the track of her pretty feet as she goes along. I believe you know her well."

" Yes."

" Curious people in the house, too. There was a Carlist officer here, a lean, tall, dark man, who couldn't sleep. He consulted me once. Do you know what became of him ? "

" No."

The doctor had finished wiping his hands and flung the towel far away.

" Considerable nervous over-strain. Seemed to have a restless brain. Not a good thing, that. For the rest a perfect gentleman. And this Spaniard here, do you know him ? "

" Enough not to care what happens to him," I said, " except for the trouble he might cause to the Carlist sympathizers here, should the police get hold of this affair."

" Well, then, he must take his chance in the seclusion of that conservatory sort of place where you have put him. I'll try to find somebody we can trust to look after him. Meantime, I will leave the case to you."

## VIII

DIRECTLY I had shut the door after the doctor I started shouting for Therese. "Come down at once, you wretched hypocrite," I yelled at the foot of the stairs in a sort of frenzy as though I had been a second Ortega. Not even an echo answered me; but all of a sudden a small flame flickered descending from the upper darkness and Therese appeared on the first floor landing carrying a lighted candle in front of a livid, hard face, closed against remorse, compassion, or mercy by the meanness of her righteousness and of her rapacious instincts. She was fully dressed in that abominable brown stuff with motionless folds, and as I watched her coming down step by step she might have been made of wood. I stepped back and pointed my finger at the darkness of the passage leading to the studio. She passed within a foot of me, her pale eyes staring straight ahead, her face still with disappointment and fury. Yet it is only my surmise. She might have been made thus inhuman by the force of an invisible purpose. I waited a moment, then, stealthily, with extreme caution, I opened the door of the so-called Captain Blunt's room.

The glow of embers was all but out. It was cold and dark in there; but before I closed the door behind me the dim light from the hall showed me Doña Rita standing on the very same spot where I had left her, statuesque in her night-dress. Even after I shut the door she loomed up enormous, indistinctly rigid and inanimate. I picked up the candelabra, groped for a candle all over the carpet, found one, and lighted it. All that time Doña Rita didn't stir. When I turned towards her she seemed to be slowly awakening from a trance. She was deathly pale and by contrast the melted, sapphire-blue of her eyes looked black as coal. They moved a little in my direction, incurious, recognizing me slowly. But when they had recognized me completely she raised her hands and hid her face in them. A whole minute or more passed. Then I said in a low tone : " Look at me," and she let them fall slowly as if accepting the inevitable.

"Shall I make up the fire?" . . . I waited. "Do you hear me?" She made no sound and with the tip of my finger I touched her bare shoulder. But for its elasticity it might have been frozen. At once I looked round for the fur coat; it seemed to me that there was not a moment to lose if she was to be saved, as though we had been lost on an Arctic plain. I had to put her arms into the sleeves, myself, one after another. They were cold, lifeless, but flexible. Then I moved in front of her and buttoned the thing close round her throat. To do that I had actually to raise her chin with my finger, and it sank slowly down again. I buttoned all the other buttons right down to the ground. It was a very long and splendid fur. Before rising from my kneeling position I felt her feet. Mere ice. The intimacy of this sort of attendance helped the growth of my authority. "Lie down," I murmured, "I shall pile on you every blanket I can find here," but she only shook her head.

Not even in the days when she ran "shrill as a cicada and thin as a match" through the chill mists of her native mountains could she ever have felt so cold, so wretched, and so desolate. Her very soul, her grave, indignant, and fantastic soul, seemed to drowse like an exhausted traveller surrendering himself to the sleep of death. But when I asked her again to lie down she managed to answer me, "Not in this room." The dumb spell was broken. She turned her head from side to side, but oh! how cold she was! It seemed to come out of her, numbing me, too; and the very diamonds on the arrow of gold sparkled like hoar frost in the light of the one candle.

"Not in this room; not here," she protested, with that peculiar suavity of tone which made her voice unforgettable, irresistible, no matter what she said. "Not after all this! I couldn't close my eyes in this place. It's full of corruption and ugliness all round, in me, too, everywhere except in your heart, which has nothing to do where I breathe. And

here you may leave me.  But wherever you go remember
that I am not evil, I am not evil."

I said : " I don't intend to leave you here.  There is my
room upstairs.  You have been in it before."

" Oh, you have heard of that," she whispered.  The
beginning of a wan smile vanished from her lips.

" I also think you can't stay in this room ; and, surely,
you needn't hesitate . . ."

" No.  It doesn't matter now.  He has killed me.  Rita
is dead."

While we exchanged these words I had retrieved the
quilted, blue slippers and had put them on her feet.  She
was very tractable.  Then taking her by the arm I led her
towards the door.

" He has killed me," she repeated in a sigh.  " The little
joy that was in me."

" He has tried to kill himself out there in the hall," I
said.  She put back like a frightened child but she couldn't
be dragged on as a child can be.

I assured her that the man was no longer there but she
only repeated, " I can't get through the hall.  I can't walk.
I can't . . ."

" Well," I said, flinging the door open and seizing her
suddenly in my arms, " if you can't walk then you shall be
carried," and I lifted her from the ground so abruptly that
she could not help catching me round the neck as any child
almost will do instinctively when you pick it up.

I ought really to have put those blue slippers in my pocket.
One dropped off at the bottom of the stairs as I was stepping
over an unpleasant-looking mess on the marble pavement,
and the other was lost a little way up the flight when, for
some reason (perhaps from a sense of insecurity), she began
to struggle.  Though I had an odd sense of being engaged
in a sort of nursery adventure she was no child to carry.
I could just do it.  But not if she chose to struggle.  I set
her down hastily and only supported her round the waist for
the rest of the way.  My room, of course, was perfectly
dark but I led her straight to the sofa at once and let her

fall on it. Then as if I had in sober truth rescued her from an Alpine height or an Arctic floe, I busied myself with nothing but lighting the gas and starting the fire. I didn't even pause to lock my door. All the time I was aware of her presence behind me, nay, of something deeper and more my own—of her existence itself—of a small blue flame, blue like her eyes, flickering and clear within her frozen body. When I turned to her she was sitting very stiff and upright, with her feet posed hieratically on the carpet and her head emerging out of the ample fur collar, such as a gem-like flower above the rim of a dark vase. I tore the blankets and the pillows off my bed and piled them up in readiness in a great heap on the floor near the couch. My reason for this was that the room was large, too large for the fireplace, and the couch was nearest to the fire. She gave no sign but one of her wistful attempts at a smile. In a most business-like way I took the arrow out of her hair and laid it on the centre table. The tawny mass fell loose at once about her shoulders and made her look even more desolate than before. But there was an invincible need of gaiety in her heart. She said funnily, looking at the arrow sparkling in the gas light :

" Ah ! That poor philistinish ornament ! "

An echo of our early days, not more innocent but so much more youthful, was in her tone ; and we both, as if touched with poignant regret, looked at each other with enlightened eyes.

"Yes," I said, " how far away all this is. And you wouldn't leave even that object behind when you came last in here. Perhaps it is for that reason it haunted me—mostly at night. I dreamed of you sometimes as a huntress nymph gleaming white through the foliage and throwing this arrow like a dart straight at my heart. But it never reached it. It always fell at my feet as I woke up. The huntress never meant to strike down that particular quarry."

" The huntress was wild but she was not evil. And she was no nymph, but only a goatherd girl. Dream of her no more, my dear."

I had the strength of mind to make a sign of assent and busied myself arranging a couple of pillows at one end of the sofa. "Upon my soul, goatherd, you are not responsible," I said. "You are not! Lay down that uneasy head," I continued, forcing a half-playful note into my immense sadness, "that has even dreamed of a crown—but not for itself."

She lay down quietly. I covered her up, looked once into her eyes and felt the restlessness of fatigue overpower me so that I wanted to stagger out, walk straight before me, stagger on and on till I dropped. In the end I lost myself in thought. I woke with a start to her voice saying positively:

"No. Not even in this room. I can't close my eyes. Impossible. I have a horror of myself. That voice in my ears. All true. All true."

She was sitting up, two masses of tawny hair fell on each side of her tense face. I threw away the pillows from which she had risen and sat down behind her on the couch. "Perhaps like this," I suggested, drawing her head gently on my breast. She didn't resist, she didn't even sigh, she didn't look at me or attempt to settle herself in any way. It was I who settled her after taking up a position which I thought I should be able to keep for hours—for ages. After a time I grew composed enough to become aware of the ticking of the clock, even to take pleasure in it. The beat recorded the moments of her rest, while I sat, keeping as still as if my life depended upon it with my eyes fixed idly on the arrow of gold gleaming and glittering dimly on the table under the lowered gas-jet. And presently my breathing fell into the quiet rhythm of the sleep which descended on her at last. My thought was that now nothing mattered in the world because I had the world safe resting in my arms—or was it in my heart?

Suddenly my heart seemed torn in two within my breast and half of my breath knocked out of me. It was a tumultuous awakening. The day had come. Doña Rita had opened her eyes, found herself in my arms, and instantly had flung herself out of them with one sudden effort. I saw

her already standing in the filtered sunshine of the closed
shutters, with all the childlike horror and shame of that night
vibrating afresh in the awakened body of the woman.

"Daylight," she whispered in an appalled voice. "Don't
look at me, George. I can't face daylight. No—not with
you. Before we set eyes on each other all that past was like
nothing. I had crushed it all in my new pride. Nothing
could touch the Rita whose hand was kissed by you. But
now! Never in daylight."

I sat there stupid with surprise and grief. This was no
longer the adventure of venturesome children in a nursery-
book. A grown man's bitterness, informed, suspicious,
resembling hatred, welled out of my heart.

"All this means that you are going to desert me again?"
I said with contempt. "All right. I won't throw stones
after you . . . Are you going, then?"

She lowered her head slowly with a backward gesture of
her arm as if to keep me off, for I had sprung to my feet all
at once as if mad.

"Then go quickly," I said. "You are afraid of living
flesh and blood. What are you running after? Honesty,
as you say, or some distinguished carcass to feed your vanity
on? I know how cold you can be—and yet live. What
have I done to you? You go to sleep in my arms, wake up
and go away. Is it to impress me? Charlatanism of
character, my dear."

She stepped forward on her bare feet as firm on that floor
which seemed to heave up and down before my eyes as she
had ever been—goatherd child leaping on the rocks of her
native hills which she was never to see again. I snatched
the arrow of gold from the table and threw it after her.

"Don't forget this thing," I cried, "you would never
forgive yourself for leaving it behind."

It struck the back of the fur coat and fell on the floor
behind her. She never looked round. She walked to the
door, opened it without haste, and on the landing in the
diffused light from the ground-glass skylight there appeared,
rigid, like an implacable and obscure fate, the awful Therese—

waiting for her sister. The heavy ends of a big black shawl
thrown over her head hung massively in biblical folds. With
a faint cry of dismay Doña Rita stopped just within my
room.

The two women faced each other for a few moments
silently. Therese spoke first. There was no austerity in her
tone. Her voice was as usual, pertinacious, unfeeling, with
a slight plaint in it; terrible in its unchanged purpose.

"I have been standing here before this door all night,"
she said. "I don't know how I lived through it. I thought
I would die a hundred times for shame. So that's how you
are spending your time? You are worse than shameless.
But God may still forgive you. You have a soul. You are
my sister. I will never abandon you—till you die."

"What is it?" Doña Rita was heard wistfully, "my soul
or this house that you won't abandon."

"Come out and bow your head in humiliation. I am
your sister and I shall help you to pray to God and all the
Saints. Come away from that poor young gentleman who
like all the others can have nothing but contempt and disgust
for you in his heart. Come and hide your head where no
one will reproach you—but I, your sister. Come out and
beat your breast: come, poor Sinner, and let me kiss you,
for you are my sister!"

While Therese was speaking Doña Rita stepped back a
pace and as the other moved forward still extending the
hand of sisterly love, she slammed the door in Therese's
face. "You abominable girl!" she cried fiercely. Then
she turned about and walked towards me who had not
moved. I felt hardly alive but for the cruel pain that
possessed my whole being. On the way she stooped to pick
up the arrow of gold and then moved on quicker, holding it
out to me in her open palm.

"You thought I wouldn't give it to you. *Amigo*, I
wanted nothing so much as to give it to you. And now,
perhaps—you will take it."

"Not without the woman," I said sombrely.

"Take it," she said. "I haven't the courage to deliver

myself up to Therese.  No.  Not even for your sake.  Don't you think I have been miserable enough yet ? "

I snatched the arrow out of her hand then and ridiculously pressed it to my breast; but as I opened my lips she who knew what was struggling for utterance in my heart cried in a ringing tone :

"Speak no words of love, George !  Not yet.  Not in this house of ill-luck and falsehood.  Not within a hundred miles of this house, where they came clinging to me all profaned from the mouth of that man.  Haven't you heard them—the horrible things ?  And what can words have to do between you and me ? "

Her hands were stretched out imploringly.  I said, childishly disconcerted :

"But, Rita, how can I help using words of love to you ?  They come of themselves on my lips ! "

"They come !  Ah !  But I shall seal your lips with the thing itself," she said.  "Like this. . . ."

## SECOND NOTE

THE narrative of our man goes on for some six months more, from this, the last night of the Carnival season up to and beyond the season of roses. The tone of it is much less of exultation than might have been expected. Love as is well known having nothing to do with reason, being insensible to forebodings and even blind to evidence, the surrender of those two beings to a precarious bliss has nothing very astonishing in itself; and its portrayal, as he attempts it, lacks dramatic interest. The sentimental interest could only have a fascination for readers themselves actually in love. The response of a reader depends on the mood of the moment, so much so that a book may seem extremely interesting when read late at night, but might appear merely a lot of vapid verbiage in the morning. My conviction is that the mood in which the continuation of his story would appear sympathetic is very rare. This consideration has induced me to suppress it—all but the actual facts which round up the previous events and satisfy such curiosity as might have been aroused by the foregoing narrative.

It is to be remarked that this period is characterized more by a deep and joyous tenderness than by sheer passion. All fierceness of spirit seems to have burnt itself out in their preliminary hesitations and struggles against each other and themselves. Whether love in its entirety has, speaking generally, the same elementary meaning for women as for men, is very doubtful. Civilization has been at work there. But the fact is that those two display, in every phase of discovery and response, an exact accord. Both show themselves amazingly ingenuous in the practice of sentiment. I believe that those who know women won't be surprised to hear me say that she was as new to love as he was. During their retreat in the region of the Maritime Alps, in a small house built of dry stones and embowered with roses, they appear all through to be less like released lovers than as companions who had found out each other's fitness in a specially intense way. Upon the whole, I think that there must be some truth in his insistence of there having always been something childlike in their relation. In the unreserved and instant sharing of all thoughts, all impressions, all sensations, we see the naïveness of a children's foolhardy adventure. This unreserve expressed for him the whole truth of the situation. With her it may have been different. It might have been assumed; yet nobody is altogether a comedian; and even comedians themselves have got to believe in the part they play. Of the two she appears much the more assured and confident. But if in this she was a comedienne then it was but a great achievement of her ineradicable honesty. Having once renounced her honourable scruples she took good care that he should taste no flavour of misgivings in the cup. Being older it was she who imparted its character to the situation. As to the man if he had any superiority of his own it was simply the superiority of him who loves with the greater self-surrender.

This is what appears from the pages I have discreetly suppressed—partly out of regard for the pages themselves. In every, even terrestrial, mystery there is as it were a sacred core. A sustained commentary on love is not fit for every eye. A universal experience is exactly the sort of thing which is most difficult to appraise justly in a particular instance.

How this particular instance affected Rose, who was the only companion of the two hermits in their rose-embowered hut of stones, I regret not to be able to report; but I will venture to say that for reasons on which I need not enlarge, the girl could not have been very reassured by what she saw. It seems to me that her devotion could never be appeased; for the conviction must have been growing on her that, no matter what happened, Madame could never have any friends. It may be that Doña Rita had given her a glimpse of the unavoidable end, and that the girl's tarnished eyes masked a certain amount of apprehensive, helpless desolation.

What meantime was becoming of the fortune of Henry Allègre is another curious question. We have been told that it was too big to be tied up in a sack and thrown into the sea. That part of it represented by the fabulous collections was still being protected by the police. But for the rest, it may be assumed that its power and significance were lost to an interested world for something like six months. What is certain is that the late Henry Allègre's man of affairs found himself comparatively idle. The holiday must have done much good to his harassed brain. He had received a note from Doña Rita saying that she had gone into retreat and that she did not mean to send him her address, not being in the humour to be worried with letters on any subject whatever. "It's enough for you "—she wrote— "to know that I am alive." Later, at irregular intervals, he received scraps of paper bearing the stamps of various post offices and containing the simple statement : "I am still alive," signed with an enormous, flourished exuberant R. I imagine Rose had to travel some distances by rail to post those messages. A thick veil of secrecy had been lowered between the world and the lovers ; yet even this veil turned out not altogether impenetrable.

He—it would be convenient to call him Monsieur George to the end—shared with Doña Rita her perfect detachment from all mundane affairs ; but he had to make two short visits to Marseilles. The first was prompted by his loyal affection for Dominic. He wanted to discover what had happened or was happening to Dominic and to find out whether he could do something for that man. But Dominic was not the sort of person for whom one can do much. Monsieur George did not even see him. It looked uncommonly as if Dominic's heart were broken. Monsieur George remained concealed for twenty-four hours in the very house in which Madame Léonore had her café. He spent most of that time in conversing with Madame Léonore about Dominic. She was distressed, but her mind was made up. That bright-eyed, nonchalant, and passionate woman was making arrangements to dispose of her café before departing to join Dominic. She would not say where. Having ascertained that his assistance was not required Monsieur George, in his own words, " managed to sneak out of the town without being seen by a single soul that mattered."

The second occasion was very prosaic and shockingly incongruous with the super-mundane colouring of these days. He had neither the fortune of Henry Allègre nor a man of affairs of his own. But some rent had to be paid to somebody for the stone hut and Rose could not go marketing in the tiny hamlet at the foot of the hill without a little money. There came a time when Monsieur George had to descend from the heights of his love in order, in his own words, " to get a supply of cash." As he had disappeared very suddenly and completely for a time from the eyes of mankind it was necessary that he should show himself and sign some papers. That business was transacted in the office of the banker mentioned in the story. Monsieur George wished to avoid seeing the man himself but in this he did not succeed. The interview was short. The banker naturally asked no questions, made no allusions to persons and events, and didn't even mention the great Legitimist Principle which presented to him now no interest whatever. But for the moment all the world was talking of the Carlist enterprise. It had collapsed utterly, leaving behind, as usual, a large crop of recriminations, charges of incompetency and treachery, and a certain amount of scandalous gossip. The banker (his wife's salon had been very Carlist indeed) declared that he had never believed in the success of the cause. " You are well out of it," he remarked with a chilly smile to Monsieur George. The latter merely observed that he had been very little " in it " as a matter of fact, and that he was quite indifferent to the whole affair.

" You left a few of your feathers in it, nevertheless," the banker concluded with a wooden face and with the curtness of a man who knows.

Monsieur George ought to have taken the very next train out of the town but he yielded to the temptation to discover what had happened to the house in the street of the Consuls after he and Doña Rita had stolen out of it like two scared yet jubilant children. All he discovered was a strange, fat woman, a sort of virago, who had, apparently, been put in as a caretaker by the man of affairs. She made some difficulties to admit that she had been in charge for the last four months ; ever since the person who was there before had eloped with some Spaniard who had been lying in the house ill with fever for more than six weeks. No, she never saw the person. Neither had she seen the Spaniard. She had only heard the talk of the street. Of course she didn't know where these people had gone. She manifested some impatience to get rid of Monsieur George and even attempted to push him towards the door. It was, he says, a very funny experience. He noticed the feeble flame of the gas-jet in the hall still waiting for extinction in the general collapse of the world.

Then he decided to have a bit of dinner at the Restaurant de la Gare where he felt pretty certain he would not meet any of his friends. He could not have asked Madame Léonore for hospitality because Madame Léonore had gone away already. His acquaintances were not the sort of people likely to happen casually into a restaurant of that kind and moreover he took the precaution to seat himself at a small table so as to face the wall. Yet before long he felt a hand laid gently on his shoulder, and, looking up, saw one of his acquaintances, a member of the Royalist club, a young man of a very cheerful disposition but whose face looked down at him with a grave and anxious expression.

Monsieur George was far from delighted. His surprise was extreme when in the course of the first phrases exchanged with him he learned that this acquaintance had come to the station with the hope of finding him there.

"You haven't been seen for some time," he said. "You were perhaps somewhere where the news from the world couldn't reach you ? There have been many changes

amongst our friends and amongst people one used to hear of
so much. There is Madame de Lastaola, for instance, who
seems to have vanished from the world which was so much
interested in her. You have no idea where she may be
now?"

Monsieur George remarked grumpily that he couldn't
say.

The other tried to appear at ease. Tongues were wagging
about it in Paris. There was a sort of international financier,
a fellow with an Italian name, a shady personality, who had
been looking for her all over Europe and talked in clubs—
astonishing how such fellows get into the best clubs—oh!
Azzolati was his name. But perhaps what a fellow like that
said did not matter. The funniest thing was that there was
no man of any position in the world who had disappeared
at the same time. A friend in Paris wrote to him that a
certain well-known journalist had rushed South to investigate
the mystery but had returned no wiser than he went.

Monsieur George remarked more unamiably than before
that he really could not help all that.

"No," said the other with extreme gentleness, "only
of all the people more or less connected with the Carlist
affair you are the only one that had also disappeared before
the final collapse."

"What!" cried Monsieur George.

"Just so," said the other meaningly. "You know that
all my people like you very much, though they hold various
opinions as to your discretion. Only the other day Jane,
you know my married sister, and I were talking about you.
She was extremely distressed. I assured her that you must
be very far away or very deeply buried somewhere not to
have given a sign of life under this provocation."

Naturally Monsieur George wanted to know what it was
all about; and the other appeared greatly relieved.

"I was sure you couldn't have heard. I don't want to
be indiscreet, I don't want to ask you where you were. It
came to my ears that you had been seen at the bank to-day
and I made a special effort to lay hold of you before you

vanished again; for, after all, we have been always good friends and all our lot here liked you very much. Listen. You know a certain Captain Blunt, don't you?"

Monsieur George owned to knowing Captain Blunt but only very slightly. His friend then informed him that this Captain Blunt was apparently well acquainted with Madame de Lastaola, or, at any rate, pretended to be. He was an honourable man, a member of a good club, he was very Parisian in a way, and all this, he continued, made all the worse that of which he was under the painful necessity of warning Monsieur George. This Blunt on three distinct occasions when the name of Madame de Lastaola came up in conversation in a mixed company of men had expressed his regret that she should have become the prey of a young adventurer who was exploiting her shamelessly. He talked like a man certain of his facts and as he mentioned names . . .

"In fact," the young man burst out excitedly, "it is *your* name that he mentions. And in order to fix the exact personality he always takes care to add that you are that young fellow who was known as Monsieur George all over the South amongst the initiated Carlists."

How Blunt had got enough information to base that atrocious calumny upon, Monsieur George couldn't imagine. But there it was. He kept silent in his indignation till his friend murmured, "I expect you will want him to know that you are here."

"Yes," said Monsieur George, "and I hope you will consent to act for me altogether. First of all, pray, let him know by wire that I am waiting for him. This will be enough to fetch him down here, I can assure you. You may ask him also to bring two friends with him. I don't intend this to be an affair for Parisian journalists to write paragraphs about."

"Yes. That sort of thing must be stopped at once," the other admitted. He assented to Monsieur George's request that the meeting should be arranged for at his elder brother's country place where the family stayed very seldom. There was a most convenient walled garden there. And then

Monsieur George caught his train promising to be back on the fourth day and leaving all further arrangements to his friend. He prided himself on his impenetrability before Doña Rita; on the happiness without a shadow of those four days. However, Doña Rita must have had the intuition of there being something in the wind, because on the evening of the very same day on which he left her again on some pretence or other, she was already ensconced in the house in the street of the Consuls, with the trustworthy Rose scouting all over the town to gain information.

Of the proceedings in the walled garden there is no need to speak in detail. They were conventionally correct, but an earnestness of purpose which could be felt in the very air lifted the business above the common run of affairs of honour. One bit of byplay unnoticed by the seconds, very busy for the moment with their arrangements, must be mentioned. Disregarding the severe rules of conduct in such cases Monsieur George approached his adversary and addressed him directly.

" Captain Blunt," he said, " the result of this meeting may go against me. In that case you will recognize publicly that you were wrong. For you are wrong and you know it. May I trust your honour ? "

In answer to that appeal Captain Blunt, always correct, didn't open his lips but only made a little bow. For the rest he was perfectly ruthless. If he was utterly incapable of being carried away by love there was nothing equivocal about his jealousy. Such psychology is not very rare and really from the point of view of the combat itself one cannot very well blame him. What happened was this. Monsieur George fired on the word and, whether luck or skill, managed to hit Captain Blunt in the upper part of the arm which was holding the pistol. That gentleman's arm dropped power-less by his side. But he did not drop his weapon. There was nothing equivocal about his determination. With the greatest deliberation he reached with his left hand for his pistol and taking careful aim shot Monsieur George through the left side of his breast. One may imagine the consternation

of the four seconds and the activity of the two surgeons in
the confined, drowsy heat of that walled garden. It was
within an easy drive of the town and as Monsieur George
was being conveyed there at a walking pace a little brougham
coming from the opposite direction pulled up at the side of
the road. A thickly veiled woman's head looked out of the
window, took in the state of affairs at a glance, and called out
in a firm voice : " Follow my carriage." The brougham
turning round took the lead. Long before this convoy
reached the town another carriage containing four gentlemen (of whom one was leaning back languidly with his arm
in a sling) whisked past and vanished ahead in a cloud of white,
Provençal dust. And this is the last appearance of Captain
Blunt in Monsieur George's narrative. Of course he was
only told of it later. At the time he was not in a condition
to notice things. His interest in his surroundings remained
of a hazy and nightmarish kind for many days together.
From time to time he had the impression that he was in a
room strangely familiar to him, that he had unsatisfactory
visions of Doña Rita, to whom he tried to speak as if nothing
had happened, but that she always put her hand on his
mouth to prevent him and then spoke to him herself in a
very strange voice which sometimes resembled the voice of
Rose. The face, too, sometimes resembled the face of Rose.
There were also one or two men's faces which he seemed to
know well enough though he didn't recall their names. He
could have done so with a slight effort, but it would have
been too much trouble. Then came a time when the
hallucinations of Doña Rita and the faithful Rose left him
altogether. Next came a period, perhaps a year, or perhaps
an hour, during which he seemed to dream all through his
past life. He felt no apprehension, he didn't try to speculate
as to the future. He felt that all possible conclusions were
out of his power, and therefore he was indifferent to everything. He was like that dream's disinterested spectator who
doesn't know what is going to happen next. Suddenly for
the first time in his life he had the soul-satisfying consciousness of floating off into deep slumber.

BB2

When he woke up after an hour, or a day, or a month, there was dusk in the room; but he recognized it perfectly. It was his apartment in Doña Rita's house; those were the familiar surroundings in which he had so often told himself that he must either die or go mad. But now he felt perfectly clear-headed and the full sensation of being alive came all over him, languidly delicious. The greatest beauty of it was that there was no need to move. This gave him a sort of moral satisfaction. Then the first thought independent of personal sensations came into his head. He wondered when Therese would come in and begin talking. He saw vaguely a human figure in the room but that was a man. He was speaking in a deadened voice which had yet a preternatural distinctness.

"This is the second case I have had in this house, and I am sure that directly or indirectly it was connected with that woman. She will go on like this leaving a track behind her and then some day there will be really a corpse. This young fellow might have been it."

"In this case, Doctor," said another voice, "one can't blame the woman very much. I assure you she made a very determined fight."

"What do you mean? That she didn't want to . . ."

"Yes. A very good fight. I heard all about it. It is easy to blame her, but, as she asked me despairingly, could she go through life veiled from head to foot or go out of it altogether into a convent? No, she isn't guilty. She is simply—what she is."

"And what's that?"

"Very much of a woman. Perhaps a little more at the mercy of contradictory impulses than other women. But that's not her fault. I really think she has been very honest."

The voices sank suddenly to a still lower murmur and presently the shape of the man went out of the room. Monsieur George heard distinctly the door open and shut. Then he spoke for the first time, discovering, with a particular pleasure, that it was quite easy to speak. He was even under the impression that he had shouted:

" Who is here ? "

From the shadow of the room (he recognized at once the characteristic outlines of the bulky shape) Mills advanced to the side of the bed. Doña Rita had telegraphed to him on the day of the duel and the man of books, leaving his retreat, had come as fast as boats and trains could carry him South. For, as he said later to Monsieur George, he had become fully awake to his part of the responsibility. And he added : " It was not of you alone that I was thinking." But the very first question that Monsieur George put to him was :

" How long is it since I saw you last ? "

" Something like ten months," answered Mills' kindly voice.

" Ah ! Is Therese outside the door ? She stood there all night, you know."

" Yes, I heard of it. She is hundreds of miles away now."

" Well, then, ask Rita to come in."

" I can't do that, my dear boy," said Mills with affectionate gentleness. He hesitated a moment. " Doña Rita went away yesterday," he said softly.

" Went away ? Why ? " asked Monsieur George.

" Because, I am thankful to say, your life is no longer in danger. And I have told you that she is gone because, strange as it may seem, I believe you can stand this news better now than later when you get stronger."

It must be believed that Mills was right. Monsieur George fell asleep before he could feel any pang at that intelligence. A sort of confused surprise was in his mind but nothing else, and then his eyes closed. The awakening was another matter. But that, too, Mills had foreseen. For days he attended the bedside patiently letting the man in the bed talk to him of Doña Rita but saying little himself; till one day he was asked pointedly whether she had ever talked to him openly. And then he said that she had, on more than one occasion. " She told me amongst other things," Mills said, " if this is any satisfaction to you to know, that till she met you she knew nothing of love. That you were to her in more senses than one a complete revelation."

"And then she went away. Ran away from the revelation," said the man in the bed bitterly.

"What's the good of being angry?" remonstrated Mills, gently. "You know that this world is not a world for lovers, not even for such lovers as you two who have nothing to do with the world as it is. No, a world of lovers would be impossible. It would be a mere ruin of lives which seem to be meant for something else. What this something is, I don't know; and I am certain," he said with playful compassion, "that she and you will never find out."

A few days later they were again talking of Doña Rita. Mills said:

"Before she left the house she gave me that arrow she used to wear in her hair to hand over to you as a keepsake and also to prevent you, she said, from dreaming of her. This message sounds rather cryptic."

"Oh, I understand perfectly," said Monsieur George. "Don't give me the thing now. Leave it somewhere where I can find it some day when I am alone. But when you write to her you may tell her that now at last—surer than Mr. Blunt's bullet—the arrow has found its mark. There will be no more dreaming. Tell her. She will understand."

"I don't even know where she is," murmured Mills.

"No, but her man of affairs knows. . . . Tell me, Mills, what will become of her?"

"She will be wasted," said Mills sadly. "She is a most unfortunate creature. Not even poverty could save her now. She cannot go back to her goats. Yet who can tell? She may find something in life. She may! It won't be love. She has sacrificed that chance to the integrity of your life—heroically. Do you remember telling her once that you meant to live your life integrally—oh, you lawless young pedant! Well, she is gone; but you may be sure that whatever she finds now in life it will not be peace. You understand me? Not even in a convent."

"She was supremely lovable," said the wounded man, speaking of her as if she were lying dead already on his oppressed heart.

"And elusive," struck in Mills in a low voice. "Some of them are like that. She will never change. Amid all the shames and shadows of that life there will always lie the ray of her perfect honesty. I don't know about your honesty, but yours will be the easier lot. You will always have your . . . other love—you pig-headed enthusiast of the sea."

"Then let me go to it," cried the enthusiast. "Let me go to it."

He went to it as soon as he had strength enough to feel the crushing weight of his loss (or his gain) fully, and discovered that he could bear it without flinching. After this discovery he was fit to face anything. He tells his correspondent that if he had been more romantic he would never have looked at any other woman. But on the contrary. No face worthy of attention escaped him. He looked at them all; and each reminded him of Doña Rita, either by some profound resemblance or by the startling force of contrast.

The faithful austerity of the sea protected him from the rumours that fly on the tongues of men. He never heard of her. Even the echoes of the sale of the great Allègre collection failed to reach him. And that event must have made noise enough in the world. But he never heard. He does not know. Then, years later, he was deprived even of the arrow. It was lost to him in a stormy catastrophe; and he confesses that next day he stood on a rocky, wind-assaulted shore, looking at the seas raging over the very spot of his loss and thought that it was well. It was not a thing that one could leave behind one for strange hands—for the cold eyes of ignorance. Like the old King of Thule with the gold goblet of his mistress he would have had to cast it into the sea, before he died. He says he smiled at the romantic notion. But what else could he have done with it?

# THE ROVER

After entering at break of day the inner roadstead of the Port of Toulon, exchanging several loud hails with one of the guardboats of the Fleet, which directed him where he was to take up his berth, Master-Gunner Peyrol let go the anchor of the sea-worn and battered ship in his charge, between the arsenal and the town, in full view of the principal quay. The course of his life, which in the opinion of any ordinary person might have been regarded as full of marvellous incidents (only he himself had never marvelled at them) had rendered him undemonstrative to such a degree, that he did not even let out a sigh of relief at the rumble of the chain. And yet it ended a most anxious six months of knocking about at sea with valuable merchandize in a damaged hull, most of the time on short rations, always on the lookout for English cruisers, once or twice on the verge of shipwreck and more than once on the verge of capture. But as to that, old Peyrol had made up his mind from the first to blow up his valuable charge—unemotionally, for such was his character, formed under the sun of the Indian seas in lawless contests with his kind for a little loot that vanished as soon as grasped, but mainly for bare life almost as precarious to hold through its ups and downs, and which now had lasted for fifty-eight years.

While his crew of half-starved scarecrows, hard as nails and ravenous as so many wolves for the delights of the shore, swarmed aloft to furl the sails nearly as thin and as patched as the grimy shirts on their backs, Peyrol took a survey of the quay. Groups were forming along its whole stretch to gaze at the new arrival. Peyrol noted particularly a good many men in red caps and said to himself : " Here they are." Amongst the crews of ships that had brought the tricolour into the seas of the East, there were hundreds professing sansculotte principles ; boastful and declamatory beggars he had thought them. But now he was beholding the shore breed. Those who had made the Revolution safe. The real thing. Peyrol after taking a good long look, went below into his cabin to make himself ready to go ashore.

He shaved his big cheeks with a real English razor, looted years ago from an officer's cabin in an English East Indiaman, captured by a ship he was serving in then. He put on a white shirt, a short blue jacket with metal buttons and a high roll-collar, a pair of white trousers which he fastened with a red bandana handkerchief, by way of a belt. With a black, shiny low-crowned hat on his head he made a very creditable prize-master. He beckoned from the poop to a boatman and got himself rowed to the quay.

By that time the crowd had grown to a large size. Peyrol's eyes ranged over it with no great apparent interest, though it was a fact that he had never in all his man's life seen so many idle white people massed together to stare at a sailor. He had been a rover of the outer seas; he had grown into a stranger to his native country. During the few minutes it took the boatman to row him to the steps, he felt like a navigator about to land on a newly discovered shore.

On putting his foot on it he was mobbed. The arrival of a prize made by a squadron of the Republic in distant seas was not an everyday occurrence in Toulon. The wildest rumours had been already set flying. Peyrol elbowed himself through the crowd somehow, but it continued to move after him. A voice cried out, "Where do you come from, citoyen?" "From the other side of the world," Peyrol boomed out.

He did not get rid of his followers till the door of the Port Office. There he reported himself to the proper officials as master of a prize taken off the Cape by Citoyen Renaud, Commander-in-Chief of the Republican Squadron in the Indian Seas. He had been ordered to make for Dunkerque but, said he, having been chased by the sacrés Anglais three times in a fortnight between Cape Verde and Cape Spartel, he had made up his mind to run into the Mediterranean where, he had understood from a Danish brig he had met at sea, there were no English men-of-war just then. And here he was; and there were his ship's papers and his own papers and everything in order. He mentioned also that he was tired of rolling about the seas, and that he longed for a period of repose on shore. But till all the legal business was settled he remained in Toulon roaming about the streets at a deliberate gait, enjoying general consideration as Citizen Peyrol, and looking everybody coldly in the eye.

His reticence about his past was of that kind which starts a lot of mysterious stories about a man. No doubt the maritime authorities of Toulon had a less cloudy idea of Peyrol's past, though it need not necessarily have been more exact. In the various offices connected with the sea where his duties took him, the wretched scribes, and even some of the chiefs, looked very hard at him as he went in and out, dressed very neatly, and always with his cudgel, which he used to leave outside the door of private offices when called in for an interview with one or another of the " gold-laced lot." Having, however, cut off his queue and got in touch with some prominent patriots of the Jacobin type, Peyrol cared little for people's stares, and whispers. The person that came nearest to trying his composure was a certain naval captain with a patch over one eye and a very threadbare uniform coat, who was doing some administrative work at the Port Office. That officer, looking up from some papers, remarked brusquely, " As a matter of fact you have been the best part of your life skimming the seas, if the truth were known. You must have been a deserter from the Navy at one time, whatever you may call yourself now."

There was not a quiver on the large cheeks of the gunner Peyrol.

" If there was anything of the sort it was in the time of kings and aristocrats," he said steadily. " And now I have brought in a prize, and a service letter from Citizen Renaud, commanding in the Indian seas. I can also give you the names of good Republicans in this town who know my sentiments. Nobody can say I was ever anti-revolutionary in my life. I knocked about the Eastern seas for forty-five years—that's true. But let me observe that it was the

seamen who stayed at home that let the English into the
Port of Toulon." He paused for a moment and then added.
" When one thinks of that, Citoyen Commandant, any little
slips I and fellows of my kind may have made five thousand
leagues from here and twenty years ago cannot have much
importance in these times of equality and fraternity."

" As to fraternity," remarked the post-captain in the
shabby coat, " the only one you are familiar with is the
brotherhood of the coast, I should say."

" Everybody in the Indian Ocean except milksops and
youngsters had to be," said the untroubled Citizen Peyrol.
" And we practised republican principles long before a
republic was thought of; for the Brothers of the Coast were
all equal and elected their own chiefs."

" They were an abominable lot of lawless ruffians,"
remarked the officer venomously, leaning back in his chair.
" You will not dare to deny that."

Citizen Peyrol refused to take up a defensive attitude.
He merely mentioned in a neutral tone that he had delivered
his trust to the Port Office all right, and as to his character
he had a certificate of civism from his section. He was a
patriot and entitled to his discharge. After being dismissed
by a nod he took up his cudgel outside the door and walked
out of the building with the calmness of rectitude. His large
face of the Roman type betrayed nothing to the wretched
quill-drivers who whispered on his passage. As he went
along the streets, he looked as usual everybody in the eye;
but that very same evening he vanished from Toulon.
It wasn't that he was afraid of anything. His mind was as
calm as the natural set of his florid face. Nobody could
know what his forty years or more of sea life had been, unless
he told them himself. And of that he didn't mean to tell
more than what he had told the inquisitive captain with the
patch over one eye. But he didn't want any bother for
certain other reasons; and more than anything else he
didn't want to be sent perhaps to serve in the fleet now fitting
out in Toulon. So at dusk he passed through the gate on
the road to Fréjus in a high two-wheeled cart belonging to
a well-known farmer whose habitation lay that way. His

personal belongings were brought down and piled up on the tailboard of the cart by some ragamuffin patriots whom he engaged in the street for that purpose. The only indiscretion he committed was to pay them for their trouble with a large handful of assignats. From such a prosperous seaman, however, this generosity was not so very compromising. He himself got into the cart over the wheel, with such slow and ponderous movements, that the friendly farmer felt called upon to remark: "Ah, we are not so young as we used to be—you and I." "I have also an awkward wound," said Citizen Peyrol sitting down heavily.

And so from farmer's cart to farmer's cart, getting lifts all along, jogging in a cloud of dust between stone walls and through little villages well known to him from his boyhood's days, in a landscape of stony hills, pale rocks, and dusty green of olive trees, Citizen Peyrol went on unmolested till he got down clumsily in the yard of an inn on the outskirts of the town of Hyères. The sun was setting to his right. Near a clump of dark pines with blood-red trunks in the sunset Peyrol perceived a rutty track branching off in the direction of the sea.

At that spot Citizen Peyrol had made up his mind to leave the high road. Every feature of the country with the darkly wooded rises, the barren flat expanse of stones and sombre bushes to his left, appealed to him with a sort of strange familiarity, because they had remained unchanged since the days of his boyhood. The very cartwheel tracks scored deep into the stony ground had kept their physiognomy; and far away, like a blue thread, there was the sea of the Hyères roadstead with a lumpy indigo swelling still beyond—which was the island of Porquerolles. He had an idea that he had been born on Porquerolles, but he really did not know. The notion of a father was absent from his mentality. What he remembered of his parents was a tall, lean, brown woman in rags, who was his mother. But then they were working together at a farm which was on the mainland. He had fragmentary memories of her shaking down olives, picking stones out of a field, or handling a manure fork like a man, tireless and fierce, with wisps of greyish hair flying about her bony face; and of himself running bare-footed in connection with a flock of turkeys, with hardly any clothes on his back. At night, by the farmer's favour, they were permitted to sleep in a sort of ruinous byre built of stones and with only half a roof on it, lying side by side on some old straw on the ground. And it was on a bundle of straw that his mother had tossed ill for two days and had died in the night. In the darkness, her silence, her cold face had given him an awful scare. He supposed they had buried her but he didn't know, because he had rushed out terror-struck, and never stopped till he got as far as a little place by the sea called Almanarre, where he hid himself on board a tartane that was lying there with no one on board. He went into the hold because he was afraid of some dogs on shore. He found down there a heap of empty sacks, which made a luxurious couch, and being exhausted went to sleep like a stone. Some time during the night the crew came on board and the tartane sailed for Marseilles. That was another awful scare—being hauled out by the scruff of the neck on the deck and being asked who the devil he was and what he was doing there. Only from that one he could not run away. There was water all around him and the whole world, including the coast not very far away, wobbled in a most alarming manner. Three bearded men stood about him and he tried to explain to them that he had been working at Peyrol's. Peyrol was the farmer's name. The boy didn't know that he had one of his own. Moreover he didn't know very well how to talk to people, and they must have misunderstood him. Thus the name of Peyrol stuck to him for life.

There the memories of his native country stopped, over-laid by other memories, with a multitude of impressions of endless oceans, of the Mozambique Channel, of Arabs and negroes, of Madagascar, of the coast of India, of islands and channels and reefs; of fights at sea, rows on shore, desperate slaughter and desperate thirst, of all sorts of ships one after another: merchant ships and frigates and privateers; of reckless men and enormous sprees. In the course of years he had learned to speak intelligibly and think connectedly, and even to read and write after a fashion. The name of the farmer Peyrol attached to his person on account of his inability to give a clear account of himself acquired a sort of reputation, both openly, in the ports of the East and, secretly, amongst the Brothers of the Coast, that strange fraternity with something masonic and not a little piratical in its constitution. Round the Cape of Storms, which is also the Cape of Good Hope, the words Republic, Nation, Tyranny, Liberty, Equality, and Fraternity, and the cult of the Supreme Being came floating on board ships from home : new cries and new ideas which did not upset the slowly developed intelligence of the gunner Peyrol. They seemed the invention of landsmen, of whom the seaman Peyrol knew very little—nothing, so to speak. Now after nearly fifty years of lawful and lawless sea-life Citizen Peyrol, at the yard gate of the roadside inn, looked at the late scene of his childhood. He looked at it without any animosity but a little puzzled as to his bearings amongst the features of the land. "Yes, it must be somewhere in that direction," he thought vaguely. Decidedly he would go no further along the high road. . . . A few yards away the woman of the inn stood looking at him, impressed by the good clothes, the great shaven cheeks, the well-to-do air of that seaman ; and suddenly Peyrol noticed her. With her anxious brown face, her grey locks, and her rustic appearance she might have been his mother, as he remembered her, only she wasn't in rags.

"Hé ! la mère," hailed Peyrol. "Have you got a man to lend a hand with my chest into the house ? "

He looked so prosperous and so authoritative that she piped without hesitation in a thin voice, "Mais oui, citoyen. He will be here in a moment."

In the dusk the clump of pines across the road looked very black against the quiet clear sky ; and Citizen Peyrol gazed at the scene of his young misery with the greatest possible placidity. Here he was after nearly fifty years, and to look at things it seemed like yesterday. He felt for all this neither love nor resentment. He felt a little funny as it were, and the funniest thing was the thought which crossed his mind that he could indulge his fancy (if he had a mind to it) to buy up all this land to the furthermost field, away over there where the track lost itself sinking into the flats bordering the sea where the small rise at the end of the Giens peninsula had assumed the appearance of a black cloud.

"Tell me, my friend," he said in his magisterial way to the farmhand with a tousled head of hair who was awaiting his good pleasure, "doesn't this track lead to Almanarre?"

"Yes," said the labourer, and Peyrol nodded. The man continued mouthing his words slowly as if unused to speech. "To Almanarre and further too, beyond the great pond right out to the end of the land, to Cape Esterel."

Peyrol was lending his big flat hairy ear. "If I had stayed in this country," he thought, "I would be talking like this fellow." And aloud he asked:

"Are there any houses there, at the end of the land?"

"Why, a hamlet, a hole, just a few houses round a church, and a farm where at one time they would give you a glass of wine."

## II

CITIZEN PEYROL stayed at the inn-yard gate till the night had swallowed up all those features of the land to which his eyes had clung as long as the last gleams of daylight. And even after the last gleams had gone he had remained for some time staring into the darkness, in which all he could distinguish was the white road at his feet and the black heads of pines where the cart track dipped towards the coast. He did not go indoors till some carters who had been refreshing themselves had departed with their big two-wheeled carts, piled up high with empty wine-casks, in the direction of Fréjus. The fact that they did not remain for the night pleased Peyrol. He ate his bit of supper alone, in silence, and with a gravity which intimidated the old woman who had aroused in him the memory of his mother. Having finished his pipe and obtained a bit of candle in a tin candlestick, Citizen Peyrol went heavily upstairs to rejoin his luggage. The crazy staircase shook and groaned under his feet as though he had been carrying a burden. The first thing he did was to close the shutters most carefully as though he had been afraid of a breath of night air. Next he bolted the door of the room. Then sitting on the floor, with the candlestick standing before him between his widely straggled legs, he began to undress, flinging off his coat and dragging his shirt hastily over his head. The secret of his heavy movements was disclosed then in the fact that he had been wearing next his bare skin—like a pious penitent his hair-shirt—a sort of waistcoat made of two thicknesses of old sail-cloth and stitched all over in the manner of a quilt with tarred twine. Three horn buttons closed it in front. He undid them, and after he had slipped off the two shoulder-straps which prevented this strange garment from sagging down on his hips he started rolling it up. Notwithstanding all his care there were during this operation several faint chinks of some metal which could not have been lead.

His bare torso thrown backwards and sustained by his rigid big arms heavily tattooed on the white skin above the elbows, Peyrol drew a long breath into his broad chest with a pepper and salt pelt down the breastbone. And not only was the breast of Citizen Peyrol relieved to the fullest of its athletic capacity, but a change had also come over his large physiognomy on which the expression of severe stolidity had been simply the result of physical discomfort. It isn't a trifle to have to carry girt about your ribs and hung from your shoulders a mass of mixed foreign coins equal to sixty or seventy thousand francs in hard cash; while as to the paper money of the Republic, Peyrol had had already enough experience of it to estimate the equivalent in cartloads. A thousand of them. Perhaps two thousand. Enough in any case to justify his flight of fancy, while looking at the country-side in the light of the sunset, that what he had on him would buy all that soil from which he had sprung : houses, woods, vines, olives, vegetable gardens, rocks and salt lagoons—in fact, the whole landscape, including the animals in it. But Peyrol did not care for the land at all. He did not want to

own any part of the solid earth for which he had no love.
All he wanted from it was a quiet nook, an obscure corner
out of men's sight where he could dig a hole unobserved.

That would have to be done pretty soon, he thought.
One could not live for an indefinite number of days with a
treasure strapped round one's chest. Meantime, an utter
stranger in his native country the landing on which was
perhaps the biggest adventure in his adventurous life, he
threw his jacket over the rolled-up waistcoat and laid his
head down on it after extinguishing the candle. The night
was warm. The floor of the room happened to be of planks,
not of tiles. He was no stranger to that sort of couch.
With his cudgel laid ready at his hand Peyrol slept soundly
till the noises and the voices about the house and on the
road woke him up shortly after sunrise. He threw open
the shutter, welcoming the morning light and the morning
breeze in the full enjoyment of idleness which, to a seaman
of his kind, is inseparable from the fact of being on shore.
There was nothing to trouble his thoughts ; and though his
physiognomy was far from being vacant, it did not wear
the aspect of profound meditation.

It had been by the merest accident that he had discovered
during the passage, in a secret recess within one of the lockers
of his prize, two bags of mixed coins : gold mohurs, Dutch
ducats, Spanish pieces, English guineas. After making that
discovery he had suffered from no doubts whatever. Loot,
big or little, was a natural fact of his freebooter's life. And
now when by the force of things he had become a master-
gunner of the Navy he was not going to give up his find to
confounded landsmen, mere sharks, hungry quill-drivers,
who would put it in their own pockets. As to imparting
the intelligence to his crew (all bad characters), he was much
too wise to do anything of the kind. They would not have
been above cutting his throat. An old fighting sea-dog, a
Brother of the Coast, had more right to such plunder than
anybody on earth. So at odd times while at sea, he had
busied himself within the privacy of his cabin in constructing
the ingenious canvas waistcoat in which he could take his
treasure ashore secretly. It was bulky, but his garments

were of an ample cut, and no wretched customs-guard would dare to lay hands on a successful prize-master going to the Port Admiral's offices to make his report. The scheme had worked perfectly. He found, however, that this secret garment, which was worth precisely its weight in gold, tried his endurance more than he had expected. It wearied his body and even depressed his spirits somewhat. It made him less active and also less communicative. It reminded him all the time that he must not get into trouble of any sort—keep clear of rows, of intimacies, of promiscuous jollities. This was one of the reasons why he had been anxious to get away from the town. Once, however, his head was laid on his treasure he could sleep the sleep of the just.

Nevertheless in the morning he shrank from putting it on again. With a mixture of sailor's carelessness and of old-standing belief in his own luck he simply stuffed the precious waistcoat up the flue of the empty fireplace. Then he dressed and had his breakfast. An hour later, mounted on a hired mule, he started down the track as calmly as though setting out to explore the mysteries of a desert island.

His aim was the end of the peninsula which, advancing like a colossal jetty into the sea, divides the picturesque roadstead of Hyères from the headlands and curves of the coast forming the approaches of the Port of Toulon. The path along which the sure-footed mule took him (for Peyrol, once he had put its head the right way, made no attempt at steering) descended rapidly to a plain of arid aspect, with the white gleams of the Salins in the distance, bounded by bluish hills of no great elevation. Soon all traces of human habitations disappeared from before his roaming eyes. This part of his native country was more foreign to him than the shores of the Mozambique Channel, the coral strands of India, the forests of Madagascar. Before long he found himself on the neck of the Giens peninsula, impregnated with salt and containing a blue lagoon, particularly blue, darker and even more still than the expanses of the sea to the right and left of it, from which it was separated by narrow strips of land not a hundred yards wide in places. The track ran indistinct, presenting no wheel-ruts, and with patches of efflorescent salt as white as snow between the tufts of wiry grass and the particularly dead-looking bushes. The whole neck of land was so low that it seemed to have no more thickness than a sheet of paper laid on the sea. Citizen Peyrol saw on the level of his eye, as if from a mere raft, sails of various craft, some white and some brown, while before him his native island of Porquerolles rose dull and solid beyond a wide strip of water. The mule, which knew rather better than Citizen Peyrol where it was going to, took him presently amongst the gentle rises at the end of the peninsula. The slopes were covered with scanty grass; crooked boundary walls of dry stones ran across the fields, and above them, here and there, peeped a low roof of red tiles shaded by the heads of delicate acacias. At a turn of the ravine appeared a village with its few houses, mostly with their blind walls to the path, and, at first, no living soul in sight. Three tall platanes, very ragged as to their bark and very poor as to foliage, stood in a group in an open space; and Citizen Peyrol was cheered up by the sight of a dog sleeping in the shade. The mule swerved with great determination towards a massive stone trough under the village fountain. Peyrol, looking round from the saddle while the mule drank, could see no signs of an inn. Then, examining the ground nearer to him, he perceived a ragged man sitting on a stone. He had a broad leathern belt and his legs were bare to the knee. He was contemplating the stranger on the mule with stony surprise. His dark nut-brown face contrasted strongly with his grey shock of hair. At a sign from Peyrol he showed no reluctance and approached him readily without changing the stony character of his stare.

The thought that if he had remained at home he would have probably looked like that man crossed unbidden the mind of Peyrol. With that gravity from which he seldom departed he inquired if there were any inhabitants besides himself in the village. Then, to Peyrol's surprise, that destitute idler smiled pleasantly and said that the people were out looking after their bits of land.

There was enough of the peasant-born in Peyrol, still, to remark that he had seen no man, woman, or child, or four-footed beast for hours, and that he would hardly have thought that there was any land worth looking after anywhere around. But the other insisted. Well, they were working on it all the same, at least those that had any.

At the sound of the voices the dog got up with a strange air of being all backbone, and, approaching in dismal fidelity, stood with his nose close to his master's calves.

" And you," said Peyrol, " you have no land then ? " The man took his time to answer. " I have a boat."

Peyrol became interested when the man explained that his boat was on the salt pond, the large, deserted and opaque sheet of water lying dead between the two great bays of the living sea. Peyrol wondered aloud why anyone should want a boat on it.

" There is fish there," said the man.

" And is the boat all your worldly goods ? " asked Peyrol. The flies buzzed, the mule hung its head, moving its ears and flapping its thin tail languidly.

" I have a sort of hut down by the lagoon and a net or two," the man confessed, as it were. Peyrol, looking down, completed the list by saying: " And this dog."

The man again took his time to say :

" He is company."

Peyrol sat as serious as a judge. " You haven't much to make a living of," he delivered himself at last. " However ! . . . Is there no inn, café, or some place where one could put up for a day ? I have heard up inland that there was some such place."

" I will show it to you," said the man, who then went back to where he had been sitting and picked up a large empty basket before he led the way. His dog followed with his head and tail low, and then came Peyrol dangling his heels against the sides of the intelligent mule, which seemed to know beforehand all that was going to happen. At the corner where the houses ended there stood an old wooden cross stuck into a square block of stone. The lonely boatman of the Lagoon of Pesquiers pointed in the direction of a branching path where the rises terminating the peninsula sank into a shallow pass. There were leaning pines on the skyline, and in the pass itself dull silvery green patches of olive orchards below a long yellow wall backed by dark cypresses, and the red roofs of buildings which seemed to belong to a farm.

" Will they lodge me there ? " asked Peyrol.

" I don't know. They will have plenty of room, that's certain. There are no travellers here. But as for a place of refreshment, it used to be that. You have only got to walk in. If he isn't there, the mistress is sure to be there to serve you. She belongs to the place. She was born on it. We know all about her."

" What sort of woman is she ? " asked Citizen Peyrol, who was very favourably impressed by the aspect of the place.

" Well, you are going there. You shall soon see. She is young."

" And the husband ? " asked Peyrol, who, looking down into the other's steady upward stare, detected a flicker in the brown, slightly faded eyes. " Why are you staring at me like this ? I haven't got a black skin, have I ? "

The other smiled, showing in the thick pepper and salt growth on his face as sound a set of teeth as Citizen Peyrol himself. There was in his bearing something embarrassed, but not unfriendly, and he uttered a phrase from which Peyrol discovered that the man before him, the lonely hirsute, sunburnt and barelegged human being at his stirrup, nourished patriotic suspicions as to his character. And this seemed to him outrageous. He wanted to know in a severe voice whether he looked like a confounded landsman of any kind. He swore also without, however, losing any of the dignity of expression inherent in his type of features and in the very modelling of his flesh.

" For an aristocrat you don't look like one, but neither do you look like a farmer or a pedlar or a patriot. You don't look like anything that has been seen here for years and years and years. You look like one, I dare hardly say what. You might be a priest."

Astonishment kept Peyrol perfectly quiet on his mule. " Do I dream ? " he asked himself mentally. " You aren't mad ? " he asked aloud. " Do you know what you are talking about ? Aren't you ashamed of yourself ? "

" All the same," persisted the other innocently, " it is much less than ten years ago since I saw one of them of the sort they call Bishops, who had a face exactly like yours."

Instinctively Peyrol passed his hand over his face. What could there be in it ? Peyrol could not remember ever having seen a Bishop in his life. The fellow stuck to his point, for he puckered his brow and murmured :

" Others too. . . . I remember perfectly. . . . It isn't so many years ago. Some of them skulk amongst the villages yet, for all the chasing they got from the patriots."

The sun blazed on the boulders and stones and bushes in the perfect stillness of the air. The mule, disregarding with republican austerity the neighbourhood of a stable within less than a hundred and twenty yards, dropped its head, and even its ears, and dozed as if in the middle of a desert. The dog, apparently changed into stone at his master's heel, seemed to be dozing too with his nose near the ground. Peyrol had fallen into a deep meditation, and the boatman of the lagoon awaited the solution of his doubts without eagerness and with something like a grin within his thick beard. Peyrol's face cleared. He had solved the problem, but there was a shade of vexation in his tone.

" Well, it can't be helped," he said. " I learned to shave from the English. I suppose that's what's the matter."

At the name of the English the boatman pricked up his ears.

" One can't tell where they are all gone to," he murmured. " Only three years ago they swarmed about this coast in their big ships. You saw nothing but them, and they were fighting all round Toulon on land. Then in a week or two, crac !—nobody ! Cleared out devil knows where. But perhaps you would know."

" Oh, yes," said Peyrol, " I know all about the English, don't you worry your head."

" I am not troubling my head. It is for you to think about what's best to say when you speak with him up there. I mean the master of the farm."

"He can't be a better patriot than I am, for all my shaven face," said Peyrol. "That would only seem strange to a savage like you."

With an unexpected sigh the man sat down at the foot of the cross, and, immediately, his dog went off a little way and curled himself up amongst the tufts of grass.

"We are all savages here," said the forlorn fisherman from the lagoon. "But the master up there is a real patriot from the town. If you were ever to go to Toulon and ask people about him they would tell you. He first became busy purveying the guillotine when they were purifying the town from all aristocrats. That was even before the English came in. After the English got driven out there was more of that work than the guillotine could do. They had to kill traitors in the streets, in cellars, in their beds. The corpses of men and women were lying in heaps along the quays. There were a good many of his sort that got the name of drinkers of blood. Well, he was one of the best of them. I am only just telling you."

Peyrol nodded. "That will do me all right," he said. And before he could pick up the reins and hit it with his heels the mule, as though it had just waited for his words, started off along the path.

In less than five minutes Peyrol was dismounting in front of a low, long addition to a tall farmhouse with very few windows and flanked by walls of stones enclosing not only the yard but apparently a field or two also. A gateway stood open to the left, but Peyrol dismounted at the door, through which he entered a bare room, with rough white-washed walls and a few wooden chairs and tables, which might have been a rustic café. He tapped with his knuckles on the table. A young woman with a fichu round her neck and a striped white and red skirt, with black hair and a red mouth, appeared in an inner doorway.

"Bonjour, citoyenne," said Peyrol. She was so startled by the unusual aspect of this stranger that she answered him only by a murmured "Bonjour," but in a moment she came forward and waited expectantly. The perfect oval of her face, the colour of her smooth cheeks, and the whiteness of her throat forced from the Citizen Peyrol a slight hiss through his clenched teeth.

"I am thirsty, of course," he said, "but what I really want is to know whether I can stay here."

The sound of a mule's hoofs outside caused Peyrol to start, but the woman arrested him.

"She is only going to the shed. She knows the way. As to what you said, the master will be here directly. Nobody ever comes here. And how long would you want to stay?"

The old rover of the seas looked at her searchingly.

"To tell you the truth, citoyenne, it may be in a manner of speaking for ever."

She smiled in a bright flash of teeth, without gaiety or any change in her restless eyes that roamed about the empty room as though Peyrol had come in attended by a mob of shades.

"It's like me," she said. "I lived as a child here."

"You are but little more than that now," said Peyrol, examining her with a feeling that was no longer surprise or curiosity, but seemed to be lodged in his very breast.

"Are you a patriot?" she asked, still surveying the invisible company in the room.

Peyrol, who had thought that he had "done with all that damned nonsense," felt angry and also at a loss for an answer.

"I am a Frenchman," he said bluntly.

"Arlette!" called out an aged woman's voice through the open inner door.

"What do you want?" she answered readily.

"There's a saddled mule come into the yard."

"All right. The man is here." Her eyes, which had steadied, began to wander again all round and about the motionless Peyrol. She moved a step nearer to him and asked in a low confidential tone: "Have you ever carried a woman's head on a pike?"

Peyrol, who had seen fights, massacres on land and sea, towns taken by assault by savage warriors, who had killed men in attack and defence, found himself at first bereft of speech by this simple question, and next moved to speak bitterly.

c c

"No. I have heard men boast of having done so. They were mostly braggarts with craven hearts. But what is all this to you?"

She was not listening to him, the edge of her white even teeth pressing her lower lip, her eyes never at rest. Peyrol remembered suddenly the sans-culotte—the blood-drinker. Her husband. Was it possible? . . . Well, perhaps it was possible. He could not tell. He felt his utter incompetence. As to catching her glance, you might just as well have tried to catch a wild sea-bird with your hands. And altogether she was like a sea-bird—not to be grasped. But Peyrol knew how to be patient, with that patience that is so often a form of courage. He was known for it. It had served him well in dangerous situations. Once it had positively saved his life. Nothing but patience. He could well wait now. He waited. And suddenly as if tamed by his patience this strange creature dropped her eyelids, advanced quite close to him and began to finger the lapel of his coat—something that a child might have done. Peyrol all but gasped with surprise, but he remained perfectly still. He was disposed to hold his breath. He was touched by a soft indefinite emotion, and as her eyelids remained lowered till her black lashes seemed to lie like a shadow on her pale cheek, there was no need for him to force a smile. After the first moment he was not even surprised. It was merely the sudden movement, not the nature of the act itself, that had startled him.

"Yes. You may stay. I think we shall be friends. I'll tell you about the Revolution."

At these words Peyrol, the man of violent deeds, felt something like a chill breath at the back of his head.

"What's the good of that?" he said.

"It must be," she said and backed away from him swiftly, and without raising her eyes turned round and was gone in a moment, so lightly that one would have thought her feet had not touched the ground. Peyrol, staring at the open kitchen door, saw after a moment an elderly woman's head, with brown thin cheeks and tied up in a coloured handkerchief, peeping at him fearfully.

"A bottle of wine, please," he shouted at it.

## III

THE affectation common to seamen of never being surprised at anything that sea or land can produce had become in Peyrol a second nature. Having learned from childhood to suppress every sign of wonder before all extraordinary sights and events, all strange people, all strange customs, and the most alarming phenomena of nature (as manifested, for instance, in the violence of volcanoes or the fury of human beings), he had really become indifferent—or only perhaps utterly inexpressive. He had seen so much that was bizarre or atrocious, and had heard so many astounding tales, that his usual mental reaction before a new experience was generally formulated in the words " J'en ai vu bien d'autres." The last thing which had touched him with the panic of the supernatural had been the death under a heap of rags of that gaunt, fierce woman, his mother; and the last thing that had nearly overwhelmed him at the age of twelve with another kind of terror was the riot of sound and the multitude of mankind on the quays in Marseilles, something perfectly inconceivable from which he had instantly taken refuge behind a stack of wheat sacks after having been chased ashore from the tartane. He had remained there quaking till a man in a cocked hat and with a sabre at his side (the boy had never seen either such a hat or such a sabre in his life) had seized him by the arm close to the armpit and had hauled him out from there; a man who might have been an ogre (only Peyrol had never heard of an ogre), but at any rate in his own way was alarming and wonderful beyond anything he could have imagined—if the faculty of imagination had been developed in him then. No doubt all this was enough to make one die of fright, but that possibility never occurred to him. Neither did he go mad; but being only a child, he had simply adapted himself, by means of passive acquiescence, to the new and inexplicable conditions of life in something like twenty-four hours. After that initiation the rest of his existence, from flying fishes to whales and on to black men and coral reefs, to decks running

with blood, and thirst in open boats, was comparatively plain
sailing. By the time he had heard of a Revolution in France
and of certain Immortal Principles causing the death of
many people, from the mouths of seamen and travellers and
year-old gazettes coming out of Europe, he was ready to
appreciate contemporary history in his own particular way.
Mutiny and throwing officers overboard. He had seen that
twice and he was on a different side each time. As to this
upset, he took no side. It was too far—too big—also not
distinct enough. But he acquired the revolutionary jargon
quickly enough and used it on occasions, with secret contempt.
What he had gone through, from a spell of crazy love for a
yellow girl to the experience of treachery from a bosom friend
and shipmate (and both those things Peyrol confessed to
himself he could never hope to understand), with all the
graduations of varied experience of men and passions between,
had put a drop of universal scorn, a wonderful sedative, into
the strange mixture which might have been called the
soul of the returned Peyrol.

Therefore he not only showed no surprise but did not feel
any when he beheld the master, in the right of his wife, of
the Escampobar Farm. The homeless Peyrol, sitting in the
bare salle with a bottle of wine before him, was in the act of
raising the glass to his lips when the man entered, ex-orator
in the sections, leader of red-capped mobs, hunter of the
ci-devants and priests, purveyor of the guillotine, in short a
blood-drinker. And Citizen Peyrol, who had never been
nearer than six thousand miles as the crow flies to the realities
of the Revolution, put down his glass and in his deep unemotional voice said : " Salut."

The other returned a much fainter " Salut," staring at the
stranger of whom he had heard already. His almond-shaped,
soft eyes were noticeably shiny and so was to a certain extent
the skin on his high but rounded cheekbones, coloured red
like a mask of which all the rest was but a mass of clipped
chestnut hair growing so thick and close around the lips as to
hide altogether the design of the mouth which, for all Citizen
Peyrol knew, might have been of a quite ferocious character.
A careworn forehead and a perpendicular nose suggested a

certain austerity proper to an ardent patriot. He held in his hand a long bright knife which he laid down on one of the tables at once. He didn't seem more than thirty years old, a well-made man of medium height, with a lack of resolution in his bearing. Something like disillusion was suggested by the set of his shoulders. The effect was subtle, but Peyrol became aware of it while he explained his case and finished the tale by declaring that he was a seaman of the Republic and that he had always done his duty before the enemy.

The blood-drinker had listened profoundly. The high arches of his eyebrows gave him an astonished look. He came close up to the table and spoke in a trembling voice.

"You may have! But you may all the same be corrupt. The seamen of the Republic were eaten up with corruption paid for with the gold of the tyrants. Who would have guessed it? They all talked like patriots. And yet the English entered the harbour and landed in the town without opposition. The armies of the Republic drove them out, but treachery stalks in the land, it comes up out of the ground, it sits at our hearthstones, lurks in the bosom of the representatives of the people, of our fathers, of our brothers. There was a time when civic virtue flourished, but now it has got to hide its head. And I will tell you why: there has not been enough killing. It seems as if there could never be enough of it. It's discouraging. Look what we have come to."

His voice died in his throat as though he had suddenly lost confidence in himself.

"Bring another glass, citoyen," said Peyrol, after a short pause, "and let's drink together. We will drink to the confusion of traitors. I detest treachery as much as any man, but . . ."

He waited till the other had returned, then poured out the wine, and after they had touched glasses and half emptied them, he put down his own and continued:

"But you see I have nothing to do with your politics. I was at the other side of the world, therefore you can't suspect me of being a traitor. You showed no mercy, you other sans-culottes, to the enemies of the Republic at home, and

I killed her enemies abroad far away. You were cutting off heads without much compunction. . . . ."

The other most unexpectedly shut his eyes for a moment, then opened them very wide. "Yes, yes," he assented very low. "Pity may be a crime."

"Yes. And I knocked the enemies of the Republic on the head whenever I had them before me without inquiring about the number. It seems to me that you and I ought to get on together."

The master of Escampobar farmhouse murmured, however, that in times like these nothing could be taken as proof positive. It behoved every patriot to nurse suspicion in his breast. No sign of impatience escaped Peyrol. He was rewarded for his self-restraint and the unshaken good-humour with which he had conducted the discussion by carrying his point. Citizen Scevola Bron (for that appeared to be the name of the master of the farm), an object of fear and dislike to the other inhabitants of the Giens peninsula, might have been influenced by a wish to have someone with whom he could exchange a few words from time to time. No villagers ever came up to the farm, or were likely to, unless perhaps in a body and animated with hostile intentions. They resented his presence in their part of the world sullenly.

"Where do you come from?" was the last question he asked.

"I left Toulon two days ago."

Citizen Scevola struck the table with his fist, but this manifestation of energy was very momentary.

"And that was the town of which by a decree not a stone upon another was to be left," he complained, much depressed.

"Most of it is still standing," Peyrol assured him calmly. "I don't know whether it deserved the fate you say was decreed for it. I was there for the last month or so and I know it contains some good patriots. I know because I made friends with them all." Thereupon Peyrol mentioned a few names which the retired sans-culotte greeted with a bitter smile and an ominous silence, as though the bearers of them had been only good for the scaffold and the guillotine.

"Come along and I will show you the place where you will

sleep," he said with a sigh, and Peyrol was only too ready. They entered the kitchen together. Through the open back door a large square of sunshine fell on the floor of stone flags. Outside one could see quite a mob of expectant chickens, while a yellow hen postured on the very doorstep, darting her head right and left with affectation. An old woman holding a bowl full of broken food put it down suddenly on a table and stared. The vastness and cleanliness of the place impressed Peyrol favourably.

"You will eat with us here," said his guide, and passed without stopping into a narrow passage giving access to a steep flight of stairs. Above the first landing a narrow spiral staircase led to the upper part of the farmhouse; and when the sans-culotte flung open the solid plank door at which it ended he disclosed to Peyrol a large low room containing a four-poster bedstead piled up high with folded blankets and spare pillows. There were also two wooden chairs and a large oval table.

"We could arrange this place for you," said the master, "but I don't know what the mistress will have to say," he added.

Peyrol, struck by the peculiar expression of his face, turned his head and saw the girl standing in the doorway. It was as though she had floated up after them, for not the slightest sound of rustle or footfall had warned Peyrol of her presence. The pure complexion of her white cheeks was set off brilliantly by her coral lips and the bands of raven black hair only partly covered by a muslin cap trimmed with lace. She made no sign, uttered no sound, behaved exactly as if there had been nobody in the room; and Peyrol suddenly averted his eyes from that mute and unconscious face with its roaming eyes.

In some way or other, however, the sans-culotte seemed to have ascertained her mind, for he said in a final tone:

"That's all right then," and there was a short silence, during which the woman shot her dark glances all round the room again and again, while on her lips there was a half-smile, not so much absent-minded as totally unmotived, which Peyrol observed with a side glance, but could not make anything of. She did not seem to know him at all.

"You have a view of salt water on three sides of you," remarked Peyrol's future host.

The farmhouse was a tall building, and this large attic with its three windows commanded on one side the view of Hyères Roadstead on the first plan, with further blue undulations of the coast as far as Fréjus; and on the other the vast semicircle of barren high hills, broken by the entrance to Toulon harbour guarded by forts and batteries, and ending in Cape Cépet, a squat mountain, with sombre folds and a base of brown rocks, with a white spot gleaming on the very summit of it, a ci-devant shrine dedicated to Our Lady, and a ci-devant place of pilgrimage. The noonday glare seemed absorbed by the gemlike surface of the sea perfectly flawless in the invincible depth of its colour.

"It's like being in a lighthouse," said Peyrol. "Not a bad place for a seaman to live in." The sight of the sails dotted about cheered his heart. The people of landsmen with their houses and animals and activities did not count. What made for him the life of any strange shore were the craft that belonged to it : canoes, catamarans, ballahous, praus, lorchas, mere dug-outs, or even rafts of tied logs with a bit of mat for a sail from which naked brown men fished along stretches of white sand crushed under the tropical skyline, sinister in its glare and with a thunder-cloud crouching on the horizon. But here he beheld a perfect serenity, nothing sombre on the shore, nothing ominous in the sunshine. The sky rested lightly on the distant and vaporous outline of the hills; and the immobility of all things seemed poised in the air like a gay mirage. On this tideless sea several tartanes lay becalmed in the Petite Passe between Porquerolles and Cape Esterel, yet theirs was not the stillness of death but of light slumber, the immobility of a smiling enchantment, of a Mediterranean fair day, breathless sometimes but never without life. Whatever enchantment Peyrol had known in his wanderings it had never been so remote from all thoughts of strife and death, so full of smiling security, making all his past appear to him like a chain of lurid days and sultry nights. He thought he would never want to get away from it, as though he had obscurely felt that his old rover's soul had been always rooted there.

Yes, this was the place for him; not because expediency dictated, but simply because his instinct of rest had found its home at last.

He turned away from the window and found himself face to face with the sans-culotte, who had apparently come up to him from behind, perhaps with the intention of tapping him on the shoulder, but who now turned away his head. The young woman had disappeared.

"Tell me, patron," said Peyrol, "is there anywhere near this house a little dent in the shore with a bit of beach in it perhaps where I could keep a boat?"

"What do you want a boat for?"

"To go fishing when I have a fancy to," answered Peyrol curtly.

Citizen Bron, suddenly subdued, told him that what he wanted was to be found a couple of hundred yards down the hill from the house. The coast, of course, was full of indentations, but this was a perfect little pool. And the Toulon blood-drinker's almond-shaped eyes became strangely sombre as they gazed at the attentive Peyrol. A perfect little pool, he repeated, opening from a cove that the English knew well. He paused. Peyrol observed without much animosity but in a tone of conviction that it was very difficult to keep off the English whenever there was a bit of salt water anywhere; but what could have brought English seamen to a spot like this he couldn't imagine.

"It was when their fleet first came here," said the patriot in a gloomy voice, "and hung round the coast before the anti-revolutionary traitors let them into Toulon, sold the sacred soil of their country for a handful of gold. Yes, in the days before the crime was consummated English officers used to land in that cove at night and walk up to this very house."

"What audacity!" commented Peyrol, who was really surprised. "But that's just like what they are." Still, it was hard to believe. But wasn't it only a tale?

The patriot flung one arm up in a strained gesture. "I swore to its truth before the tribunal," he said. "It was a dark story," he cried shrilly, and paused. "It cost her father his life," he said in a low voice . . . " her mother too—but the country was in danger," he added still lower.

Peyrol walked away to the western window and looked towards Toulon. In the middle of the great sheet of water within Cape Cicié a tall two-decker lay becalmed and the little dark dots on the water were her boats trying to tow her head round the right way. Peyrol watched them for a moment, and then walked back to the middle of the room.

" Did you actually drag him from this house to the guillotine ? " he asked in his unemotional voice.

The patriot shook his head thoughtfully, with downcast eyes. " No, he came over to Toulon just before the evacuation, this friend of the English . . . sailed over in a tartane he owned that is still lying here at the Madrague. He had his wife with him. They came over to take home their daughter, who was living then with some skulking old nuns. The victorious Republicans were closing in and the slaves of tyranny had to fly."

" Came to fetch their daughter," mused Peyrol. " Strange that guilty people should . . ."

The patriot looked up fiercely. " It was justice," he said loudly. " They were anti-revolutionists, and if they had never spoken to an Englishman in their life the atrocious crime was on their heads."

" H'm, stayed too long for their daughter," muttered Peyrol. " And so it was you who brought her home."

" I did," said the patron. For a moment his eyes evaded Peyrol's investigating glance, but in a moment he looked straight into his face. " No lessons of base superstition could corrupt her soul," he declared with exaltation. " I brought home a patriot."

Peyrol, very calm, gave him a hardly perceptible nod. " Well," he said, " all this won't prevent me sleeping very well in this room. I always thought I would like to live in a lighthouse when I got tired of roving about the seas. This is as near a lighthouse lantern as can be. You will see me with all my little affairs to-morrow," he added, moving towards the stairs. " Salut, citoyen."

There was in Peyrol a fund of self-command amounting

to placidity. There were men living in the East who had no doubt whatever that Peyrol was a calmly terrible man. And they would quote illustrative instances which from their own point of view were simply admirable. But all Peyrol had ever done was to behave rationally, as it seemed to him, in all sorts of dangerous circumstances without ever being led astray by the nature, or the cruelty, or the danger of any given situation. He adapted himself to the character of the event and to the very spirit of it, with a profound responsive feeling of a particularly unsentimental kind. Sentiment in itself was an artificiality of which he had never heard and if he had seen it in action would have appeared to him too puzzling to make anything of. That sort of genuineness in acceptance made him a satisfactory inmate of the Escampobar Farm. He duly turned up with all his cargo, as he called it, and was met at the door of the farmhouse itself by the young woman with the pale face and wandering eyes. Nothing could hold her attention for long amongst her familiar surroundings. Right and left and far away beyond you, she seemed to be looking for something while you were talking to her, so that you doubted whether she could follow what you said. But as a matter of fact she had all her wits about her. In the midst of this strange search for something that was not there she had enough detachment to smile at Peyrol. Then, withdrawing into the kitchen, she watched, as much as her restless eyes could watch anything, Peyrol's cargo and Peyrol himself passing up the stairs.

The most valuable part of Peyrol's cargo being strapped to his person, the first thing he did after being left alone in that attic room which was like the lantern of a lighthouse was to relieve himself of the burden and lay it on the foot of the bed. Then he sat down, and leaning his elbow far on the table he contemplated it with a feeling of complete relief. That plunder had never burdened his conscience. It had merely on occasion oppressed his body; and if it had at all affected his spirits it was not by its secrecy but by its mere weight, which was inconvenient, irritating, and towards the end of a day altogether insupportable. It made a free-limbed, deep-breathing sailor-man feel like a mere over-

loaded animal, thus extending whatever there was of compassion in Peyrol's nature towards the four-footed beasts
that carry men's burdens on the earth. The necessities of
a lawless life had taught Peyrol to be ruthless, but he had never
been cruel.

Sprawling in the chair, stripped to the waist, robust and
grey-haired, his head with a Roman profile propped up on a
mighty and tattooed forearm, he remained at ease, with his
eyes fixed on his treasure with an air of meditation. Yet
Peyrol was not meditating (as a superficial observer might
have thought) on the best place of concealment. It was not
that he had not had a great experience of that sort of property
which had always melted so quickly through his fingers.
What made him meditative was its character, not of a share
of a hard-won booty in toil, in risk, in danger, in privation,
but of a piece of luck personally his own. He knew what
plunder was and how soon it went; but this lot had come to
stay. He had it with him, away from the haunts of his
lifetime, as if in another world altogether. It couldn't be
drunk away, gambled away, squandered away in any sort of
familiar circumstances, or even given away. In that room,
raised a good many feet above his revolutionized native land
where he was more of a stranger than anywhere else in the
world, in this roomy garret full of light and as it were surrounded by the sea, in a great sense of peace and security,
Peyrol didn't see why he should bother his head about it so
very much. It came to him that he had never really cared for
any plunder that fell into his hands. No, never for any.
And to take particular care of this for which no one would
seek vengeance or attempt recovery would have been absurd.
Peyrol got up and opened his big sandalwood chest secured
with an enormous padlock, part, too, of some old plunder
gathered in a Chinese town in the Gulf of Tonkin, in company of certain Brothers of the Coast, who having boarded at
night a Portuguese schooner and sent her crew adrift in a
boat, had taken a cruise on their own account, years and years
and years ago. He was young then, very young, and the
chest fell to his share because nobody else would have anything to do with the cumbersome thing, and also for the

reason that the metal of the curiously wrought thick hoops
that strengthened it was not gold but mere brass. He, in his
innocence, had been rather pleased with the article. He had
carried it about with him into all sorts of places, and also he
had left it behind him—once for a whole year in a dark and
noisome cavern on a certain part of the Madagascar coast.
He had left it with various native chiefs, with Arabs, with a
gambling-hell keeper in Pondicherry, with his various
friends in short, and even with his enemies. Once he had
lost it altogether.

That was on the occasion when he had received a wound
which laid him open and gushing like a slashed wine-skin.
A sudden quarrel broke out in a company of Brothers over
some matter of policy complicated by personal jealousies, as
to which he was as innocent as a babe unborn. He never
knew who gave him the slash. Another Brother, a chum of
his, an English boy, had rushed in and hauled him out of the
fray, and then he had remembered nothing for days. Even
now when he looked at the scar he could not understand why
he had not died. That occurrence, with the wound and the
painful convalescence, was the first thing that sobered his
character somewhat. Many years afterwards, when in consequence of his altered views of mere lawlessness he was
serving as quartermaster on board the *Hirondelle*, a comparatively respectable privateer, he caught sight of that chest
again in Port Louis, of all places in the world, in a dark little
den of a shop kept by a lone Hindoo. The hour was late,
the side street was empty, and so Peyrol went in there to
claim his property, all fair, a dollar in one hand and a pistol
in the other, and was entreated abjectly to take it away.
He carried off the empty chest on his shoulder, and that same
night the privateer went to sea ; then only he found time to
ascertain that he had made no mistake, because, soon after he
had got it first, he had, in grim wantonness, scratched inside
the lid, with the point of his knife, the rude outline of a skull
and cross-bones into which he had rubbed afterwards a little
Chinese vermilion. And there it was, the whole design, as
fresh as ever.

In the garret full of light of the Escampobar farmhouse the

grey-haired Peyrol opened the chest, took all the contents
out of it, laying them neatly on the floor, and spread his
treasure—pockets downwards—over the bottom, which it
filled exactly. Busy on his knees he repacked the chest. A
jumper or two, a fine cloth jacket, a remnant piece of Mada-
polam muslin, costly stuff for which he had no use in the
world—a quantity of fine white shirts. Nobody would
dare to rummage in his chest, he thought, with the assurance
of a man who had been feared in his time. Then he rose,
and looking round the room and stretching his powerful arms,
he ceased to think of the treasure, of the future and even of
to-morrow, in the sudden conviction that he could make
himself very comfortable there.

## IV

IN a tiny bit of a looking-glass hung on the frame of the
east window, Peyrol, handling the unwearable English blade,
was shaving himself—for the day was Sunday. The years of
political changes ending with the proclamation of Napoleon
as Consul for life had not touched Peyrol except as to his
strong thick head of hair, which was nearly all white now.
After putting the razor away carefully, Peyrol introduced his
stockinged feet into a pair of sabots of the very best quality
and clattered downstairs. His brown cloth breeches were
untied at the knee and the sleeves of his shirt rolled up to his
shoulders. That sea rover turned rustic was now perfectly
at home in that farm which, like a lighthouse, commanded
the view of two roadsteads and of the open sea. He passed
through the kitchen. It was exactly as he had seen it first—
sunlight on the floor, red copper utensils shining on the
walls, the table in the middle scrubbed snowy white; and
it was only the old woman, Aunt Catherine, who seemed to
have acquired a sharper profile. The very hen manœuvring
her neck pretentiously on the doorstep, might have been
standing there for the last eight years. Peyrol shooed her
away, and going into the yard washed himself lavishly at the

pump. When he returned from the yard he looked so fresh
and hale that old Catherine complimented him in a thin voice
on his " bonne mine." Manners were changing, and she
addressed him no longer as citoyen but as Monsieur Peyrol.
He answered readily that if her heart was free he was ready to
lead her to the altar that very day. This was such an old
joke that Catherine took no notice of it whatever, but followed
him with her eyes as he crossed the kitchen into the salle,
which was cool, with its tables and benches washed clean,
and no living soul in it. Peyrol passed through to the front
of the house, leaving the outer door open. At the clatter
of his clogs a young man sitting outside on a bench turned his
head and greeted him by a careless nod. His face was rather
long, sunburnt and smooth, with a slightly curved nose and
a very well-shaped chin. He wore a dark blue naval jacket
open on a white shirt and a black neckerchief tied in a slip-
knot with long ends. White breeches and stockings and
black shoes with steel buckles completed his costume. A
brass-hilted sword in a black scabbard worn on a cross-belt
was lying on the ground at his feet. Peyrol, silver-headed
and ruddy, sat down on the bench at some little distance.
The level piece of rocky ground in front of the house was
not very extensive, falling away to the sea in a declivity
framed between the rises of two barren hills. The old rover
and the young seaman with their arms folded across their
chests gazed into space, exchanging no words, like close
intimates or like distant strangers. Neither did they stir
when the master of the Escampobar Farm appeared out of
the yard gate with a manure fork on his shoulder and started
to cross the piece of level ground. His grimy hands, his
rolled-up shirt-sleeves, the fork over the shoulder, the whole
of his working-day aspect had somehow an air of being a
manifestation; but the patriot dragged his dirty clogs low-
spiritedly in the fresh light of the young morning, in a way
no real worker on the land would ever do at the end of a day
of toil. Yet there were no signs of debility about his person.
His oval face with rounded cheek-bones remained unwrinkled
except at the corners of his almond-shaped, shiny, visionary's
eyes, which had not changed since the day when old Peyrol's

gaze had met them for the first time. A few white hairs on his tousled head and in the thin beard alone had marked the passage of years, and you would have had to look for them closely. Amongst the unchangeable rocks at the extreme end of the peninsula, time seemed to have stood still and idle while the group of people poised at that southernmost point of France had gone about their ceaseless toil, winning bread and wine from a stony-hearted earth.

The master of the farm, staring straight before him, passed before the two men towards the door of the salle, which Peyrol had left open. He leaned his fork against the wall before going in. The sound of a distant bell, the bell of the village where years ago the returned rover had watered his mule and had listened to the talk of the man with the dog, came up faint and abrupt in the great stillness of the upper space. The violent slamming of the salle door broke the silence between the two gazers on the sea.

" Does that fellow never rest ? " asked the young man in a low indifferent voice which covered the delicate tinkling of the bell, and without moving his head.

" Not on Sunday anyhow," answered the rover in the same detached manner. " What can you expect ? The church bell is like poison to him. That fellow, I verily believe, has been born a sans-culotte. Every ' decadi ' he puts on his best clothes, sticks a red cap on his head and wanders between the buildings like a lost soul in the light of day. A Jacobin, if ever there was one."

" Yes. There is hardly a hamlet in France where there isn't a sans-culotte or two. But some of them have managed to change their skins if nothing else."

" This one won't change his skin, and as to his inside he never had anything in him that could be moved. Aren't there some people that remember him in Toulon ? It isn't such a long time ago. And yet . . ." Peyrol turned slightly towards the young man . . . " And yet to look at him . . ."

The officer nodded and for a moment his face wore a troubled expression which did not escape the notice of Peyrol, who went on speaking easily :

"Some time ago, when the priests began to come back to the parishes, he, that fellow"—Peyrol jerked his head in the direction of the salle door—"would you believe it?—started for the village with a sabre hanging to his side and his red cap on his head. He made for the church door. What he wanted to do there I don't know. It surely could not have been to say the proper kind of prayers. Well, the people were very much elated about their reopened church, and as he went along some woman spied him out of a window and started the alarm. 'Eh, there! look! The Jacobin, the sans-culotte, the blood-drinker! Look at him.' Out rushed some of them, and a man or two that were working in their home patches vaulted over the low walls. Pretty soon there was a crowd, mostly women, each with the first thing she could snatch up—stick, kitchen knife, anything. A few men with spades and cudgels joined them by the water-trough. He didn't quite like that. What could he do? He turned and bolted up the hill like a hare. It takes some pluck to face a mob of angry women. He ran along the cart track without looking behind him, and they after him, yelling: 'A mort! A mort le buveur de sang!' He had been a horror and an abomination to the people for years, what with one story and another, and now they thought it was their chance. The priest over in the presbytery hears the noise, comes to the door. One look was enough for him. He is a fellow of about forty but a wiry, long-legged beggar, and agile—what? He just tucked up his skirts and dashed out, taking short cuts over the walls and leaping from boulder to boulder like a blessed goat. I was up in my room when the noise reached me there. I went to the window and saw the chase in full cry after him. I was beginning to think the fool would fetch all those furies along with him up here and that they would carry the house by boarding and do for the lot of us, when the priest cut in just in the nick of time. He could have tripped Scevola as easy as anything, but he lets him pass and stands in front of his parishioners with his arms extended. That did it. He saved the patron all right. What he could say to quieten them I don't know, but these were early days and they were very fond of their new priest.

He could have turned them round his little finger. I had my head and shoulders out of the window—it was interesting enough. They would have massacred all the accursed lot, as they used to call us down there—and when I drew in, behold there was the patronne standing behind me looking on too. You have been here often enough to know how she roams about the grounds and about the house, without a sound. A leaf doesn't pose itself lighter on the ground than her feet do. Well, I suppose she didn't know that I was upstairs, and came into the room just in her way of always looking for something that isn't there, and noticing me with my head stuck out, naturally came up to see what I was looking at. Her face wasn't any paler than usual but she was clawing the dress over her chest with her ten fingers—like this. I was confounded. Before I could find my tongue she just turned round and went out with no more sound than a shadow."

When Peyrol ceased, the ringing of the church bell went on faintly and then stopped as abruptly as it had begun.

"Talking about her shadow," said the young officer indolently, "I know her shadow."

Old Peyrol made a really pronounced movement. "What do you mean?" he asked. "Where?"

"I have got only one window in the room where they put me to sleep last night and I stood at it looking out. That's what I am here for—to look out, am I not? I woke up suddenly, and being awake I went to the window and looked out."

"One doesn't see shadows in the air," growled old Peyrol.

"No, but you see them on the ground, pretty black too when the moon is full. It fell across this open space here from the corner of the house."

"The patronne," exclaimed Peyrol in a low voice, "impossible!"

"Does the old woman that lives in the kitchen roam, do the village women roam as far as this?" asked the officer composedly. "You ought to know the habits of the people. It was a woman's shadow. The moon being to the west, it glided slanting from that corner of the house and glided back again. I know her shadow when I see it."

"Did you hear anything?" asked Peyrol after a moment of visible hesitation.

"The window being open, I heard somebody snoring. It couldn't have been you, you are too high. Moreover, from the snoring," he added grimly, "it must have been somebody with a good conscience. Not like you, old skimmer of the seas, because, you know, that's what you are, for all your gunner's warrant." He glanced out of the corner of his eyes at old Peyrol. "What makes you look so worried?"

"She roams, that cannot be denied," murmured Peyrol, with an uneasiness which he did not attempt to conceal.

"Evidently. I know a shadow when I see it, and when I saw it, it did not frighten me, not a quarter as much as the mere tale of it seems to have frightened you. However, that sans-culotte friend of yours must be a hard sleeper. Those purveyors of the guillotine all have a first-class fireproof Republican conscience. I have seen them at work up north when I was a boy running bare-foot in the gutters. . . ."

"The fellow always sleeps in that room," said Peyrol earnestly.

"But that's neither here nor there," went on the officer, "except that it may be convenient for roaming shadows to hear his conscience taking its ease."

Peyrol, excited, lowered his voice forcibly. "Lieutenant," he said, "if I had not seen from the first what was in your heart I would have contrived to get rid of you a long time ago in some way or other."

The lieutenant glanced sideways again and Peyrol let his raised fist fall heavily on his thigh. "I am old Peyrol, and this place, as lonely as a ship at sea, is like a ship to me and all in it are like shipmates. Never mind the patron. What I want to know is whether you heard anything? Any sound at all? Murmur, footstep?" A bitterly mocking smile touched the lips of the young man.

"Not a fairy footstep. Could you hear the fall of a leaf—and with that terrorist cur trumpeting right above my head? . . ." Without unfolding his arms he turned towards Peyrol, who was looking at him anxiously. . . . "You want to know, do you? Well, I will tell you what I heard and

you can make the best of it. I heard the sound of a stumble.
It wasn't a fairy either that stubbed its toe. It was something
in a heavy shoe. Then a stone went rolling down the ravine
in front of us interminably, then a silence as of death. I
didn't see anything moving. The way the moon was then
the ravine was in black shadow. And I didn't try to see."

Peyrol, with his elbow on his knee, leaned his head in the
palm of his hand. The officer repeated through his clenched
teeth : " Make the best of it."

Peyrol shook his head slightly. After having spoken, the
young officer leaned back against the wall, but next moment
the report of a piece of ordnance reached them as it were
from below, travelling around the rising ground to the left
in the form of a dull thud followed by a sighing sound that
seemed to seek an issue amongst the stony ridges and rocks
near by.

" That's the English corvette which has been dodging in
and out of Hyères Roads for the last week," said the young
officer, picking up his sword hastily. He stood up and
buckled the belt on, while Peyrol rose more deliberately from
the bench, and said :

" She can't be where we saw her at anchor last night.
That gun was near. She must have crossed over. There
has been enough wind for that at various times during the
night. But what could she be firing at down there in the
Petite Passe ? We had better go and see."

He strode off, followed by Peyrol. There was not a human
being in sight about the farm and not a sound of life except
for the lowing of a cow coming faintly from behind a wall.
Peyrol kept close behind the quickly moving officer who
followed the footpath marked faintly on the stony slope of the
hill.

" That gun was not shotted," he observed suddenly in a
deep steady voice.

The officer glanced over his shoulder.

" You may be right. You haven't been a gunner for
nothing. Not shotted, eh ? Then a signal gun. But who
to ? We have been observing that corvette now for days and
we know she has no companion."

He moved on, Peyrol following him on the awkward path without losing his wind and arguing in a steady voice : " She has no companion but she may have seen a friend at daylight this morning."

" Bah ! " retorted the officer without checking his pace. " You talk now like a child or else you take me for one. How far could she have seen ? What view could she have had at daylight if she was making her way to the Petite Passe where she is now ? Why, the islands would have masked for her two-thirds of the sea and just in the direction too where the English inshore squadron is hovering below the horizon. Funny blockade that ! You can't see a single English sail for days and days together, and then when you least expect them they come down all in a crowd as if ready to eat us alive. No, no ! There was no wind to bring her up a companion. But tell me, gunner, you who boast of knowing the bark of every English piece, what sort of gun was it ? "

Peyrol growled in answer.

" Why, a twelve. The heaviest she carries. She is only a corvette."

" Well, then, it was fired as a recall for one of her boats somewhere out of sight along the shore. With a coast like this, all points and bights, there would be nothing very extraordinary in that, would there ? "

" No," said Peyrol, stepping out steadily. " What is extraordinary is that she should have had a boat away at all."

" You are right there." The officer stopped suddenly. " Yes, it is really remarkable that she should have sent a boat away. And there is no other way to explain that gun."

Peyrol's face expressed no emotion of any sort.

" There is something there worth investigating," continued the officer with animation.

" If it is a matter of a boat," Peyrol said without the slightest excitement, " there can be nothing very deep in it. What could there be ? As likely as not they sent her inshore early in the morning with lines to try to catch some fish for the captain's breakfast. Why do you open your eyes like this ? Don't you know the English ? They have enough cheek for anything."

After uttering those words with a deliberation made venerable by his white hair, Peyrol made the gesture of wiping his brow, which was barely moist.

"Let us push on," said the lieutenant abruptly.

"Why hurry like this?" argued Peyrol without moving. "Those heavy clogs of mine are not adapted for scrambling on loose stones."

"Aren't they?" burst out the officer. "Well then, if you are tired you can sit down and fan yourself with your hat. Good-bye." And he strode away before Peyrol could utter a word.

The path following the contour of the hill took a turn towards its sea-face and very soon the lieutenant passed out of sight with startling suddenness. Then his head reappeared for a moment, only his head, and that too vanished suddenly. Peyrol remained perplexed. After gazing in the direction in which the officer had disappeared, he looked down at the farm buildings, now below him but not at a very great distance. He could see distinctly the pigeons walking on the roof ridges. Somebody was drawing water from the well in the middle of the yard. The patron, no doubt; but that man, who at one time had the power to send so many luckless persons to their death, did not count for old Peyrol. He had even ceased to be an offence to his sight and a disturber of his feelings. By himself he was nothing. He had never been anything but a creature of the universal blood-lust of the time. The very doubts about him had died out by now in old Peyrol's breast. The fellow was so insignificant that had Peyrol in a moment of particular attention discovered that he cast no shadow, he would not have been surprised. Below there he was reduced to the shape of a dwarf lugging a bucket away from the well. But where was she? Peyrol asked himself, shading his eyes with his hand. He knew that the patronne could not be very far away, because he had a sight of her during the morning; but that was before he had learned she had taken to roaming at night. His growing uneasiness came suddenly to an end when, turning his eyes away from the farm-buildings, where obviously she was not, he saw her appear, with nothing but the sky full of light at her

back, coming down round the very turn of the path which
had taken the lieutenant out of sight.

Peyrol moved briskly towards her. He wasn't a man to
lose time in idle wonder, and his sabots did not seem to weigh
heavy on his feet. The fermière, whom the villagers down
there spoke of as Arlette as though she had been a little girl,
but in a strange tone of shocked awe, walked with her head
drooping and her feet (as Peyrol used to say) touching the
ground as lightly as falling leaves. The clatter of the clogs
made her raise her black, clear eyes that had been smitten on
the very verge of womanhood by such sights of bloodshed
and terror as to leave in her a fear of looking steadily in any
direction for long, lest she should see coming through the
empty air some mutilated vision of the dead. Peyrol called
it trying not to see something that was not there ; and this
evasive yet frank mobility was so much a part of her being
that the steadiness with which she met his inquisitive glance
surprised old Peyrol for a moment. He asked without
beating about the bush :

" Did he speak to you ? "

She answered with something airy and provoking in her
voice, which also struck Peyrol as a novelty : " He never
stopped. He passed by as though he had not seen me "—
and then they both looked away from each other.

" Now, what is it you took into your head to watch for at
night ? "

She did not expect that question. She hung her head and
took a pleat of her skirt between her fingers, embarrassed like
a child.

" Why should I not ? " she murmured in a low shy note, as
if she had two voices within her.

" What did Catherine say ? "

" She was asleep, or perhaps only lying on her back with her
eyes shut."

" Does she do that ? " asked Peyrol with incredulity.

" Yes." Arlette gave Peyrol a queer, meaningless smile
with which her eyes had nothing to do. " Yes, she often
does. I have noticed that before. She lies there trembling
under her blankets till I come back."

"What drove you out last night?" Peyrol tried to catch her eyes, but they eluded him in the usual way. And now her face looked as though it couldn't smile.

"My heart," she said. For a moment Peyrol lost his tongue and even all power of motion. The fermière having lowered her eyelids, all her life seemed to have gone into her coral lips, vivid and without a quiver in the perfection of their design, and Peyrol, giving up the conversation with an upward fling of his arm, hurried up the path without looking behind him. But once round the turn of the path, he approached the lookout at an easier gait. It was a piece of smooth ground below the summit of the hill. It had quite a pronounced slope, so that a short and robust pine growing true out of the soil yet leaned well over the edge of the sheer drop of some fifty feet or so. The first thing that Peyrol's eyes took in was the water of the Petite Passe with the enormous shadow of the Porquerolles Island darkening more than half of its width at this still early hour. He could not see the whole of it, but on the part his glance embraced there was no ship of any kind. The lieutenant, leaning with his chest along the inclined pine, addressed him irritably.

"Squat! Do you think there are no glasses on board the Englishman?"

Peyrol obeyed without a word and for the space of a minute or so presented the bizarre sight of a rather bulky peasant with venerable white locks crawling on his hands and knees on a hillside for no visible reason. When he got to the foot of the pine he raised himself on his knees. The lieutenant, flattened against the inclined trunk and with a pocket glass glued to his eye, growled angrily:

"You can see her now, can't you?"

Peyrol in his kneeling position could see the ship now. She was less than a quarter of a mile from him up the coast, almost within hailing effort of his powerful voice. His unaided eyes could follow the movements of the men on board like dark dots about her decks. She had drifted so far within Cape Esterel that the low projecting mass of it seemed to be in actual contact with her stern. Her unexpected nearness made Peyrol **draw a sharp breath through his teeth.**

The lieutenant murmured, still keeping the glass to his eye :

"I can see the very epaulettes of the officers on the quarter-deck."

## V

As Peyrol and the lieutenant had surmised from the report of the gun, the English ship which the evening before was lying in Hyères Roads had got under way after dark. The light airs had taken her as far as the Petite Passe in the early part of the night, and then had abandoned her to the breathless moonlight, in which, bereft of all motion, she looked more like a white monument of stone dwarfed by the darkling masses of land on either hand than a fabric famed for its swiftness in attack or in flight.

Her captain was a man of about forty, with clean-shaven, full cheeks and mobile thin lips which he had a trick of compressing mysteriously before he spoke and sometimes also at the end of his speeches. He was alert in his movements and nocturnal in his habits.

Directly he found that the calm had taken complete possession of the night and was going to last for hours, Captain Vincent assumed his favourite attitude of leaning over the rail. It was then some time after midnight and in the pervading stillness the moon, riding on a speckless sky, seemed to pour her enchantment on an uninhabited planet. Captain Vincent did not mind the moon very much. Of course it made his ship visible from both shores of the Petite Passe. But after nearly a year of constant service in command of the extreme lookout ship of Admiral Nelson's blocking fleet he knew the emplacement of almost every gun of the shore defences. Where the breeze had left him he was safe from the biggest gun of the few that were mounted on Porquerolles. On the Giens side of the pass he knew for certain there was not even a popgun mounted anywhere. His long familiarity with that part of the coast had imbued him with the belief that he knew the habits of its population thoroughly. The gleams of light in their houses went out very early, and Captain Vincent felt convinced that they were all in their beds, including the gunners of the batteries who belonged to the local militia. Their interest in the movements of H.M.'s twenty-two gun sloop *Amelia* had grown stale by custom. She never interfered with their private affairs, and allowed the small coasting craft to go to and fro unmolested. They would have wondered if she had been more than two days away. Captain Vincent used to say grimly that the Hyères Roadstead had become like a second home to him.

For an hour or so Captain Vincent mused a bit on his real home, on matters of service and other unrelated things, then getting into motion in a very wide-awake manner, he superintended himself the dispatch of that boat the existence of which had been acutely surmised by Lieutenant Réal and was a matter of no doubt whatever to old Peyrol. As to her mission, it had nothing to do with catching fish for the captain's breakfast. It was the captain's own gig, a very fast pulling boat. She was already alongside with her crew in her when the officer, who was going in charge, was beckoned to by the captain. He had a cutlass at his side and a brace of pistols in his belt, and there was a business-like air about him that showed he had been on such service before.

" This calm will last a good many hours," said the captain. " In this tideless sea you are certain to find the ship very much where she is now, but closer in shore. The attraction of the land—you know. "

" Yes, sir. The land does attract."

" Yes. Well, she may be allowed to put her side against any of these rocks. There would be no more danger than alongside a quay with a sea like this. Just look at the water in the pass, Mr. Bolt. Like the floor of a ballroom. Pull close along shore when you return. I'll expect you back at dawn."

Captain Vincent paused suddenly. A doubt crossed his mind as to the wisdom of this nocturnal expedition. The hammer-head of the peninsula with its sea-face invisible from both sides of the coast was an ideal spot for a secret landing.

Its lonely character appealed to his imagination, which in the first instance had been stimulated by a chance remark of Mr. Bolt himself.

The fact was that the week before, when the *Amelia* was cruising off the peninsula, Bolt, looking at the coast, mentioned that he knew that part of it well; he had actually been ashore there a good many years ago, while serving with Lord Howe's fleet. He described the nature of the path, the aspect of a little village on the reverse slope, and had much to say about a certain farmhouse where he had been more than once, and had even stayed for twenty-hour hours at a time on more than one occasion.

This had aroused Captain Vincent's curiosity. He sent for Bolt and had a long conversation with him. He listened with great interest to Bolt's story, how one day a man was seen from the deck of the ship in which Bolt was serving then, waving a white sheet or tablecloth amongst the rocks at the water's edge. It might have been a trap; but, as the man seemed alone and the shore was within range of the ship's guns, a boat was sent to take him off.

"And that, sir," Bolt pursued impressively, "was, I verily believe, the very first communication that Lord Howe had from the royalists in Toulon." Afterwards Bolt described to Captain Vincent the meetings of the Toulon royalists with the officers of the fleet. From the back of the farm he, Bolt himself, had often watched for hours the entrance of the Toulon harbour on the lookout for the boat bringing over the royalist emissaries. Then he would make an agreed signal to the advanced squadron and some English officers would land on their side and meet the Frenchmen at the farmhouse. It was as simple as that. The people of the farmhouse, husband and wife, were well-to-do, good class altogether, and staunch royalists. He had got to know them well.

Captain Vincent wondered whether the same people were still living there. Bolt could see no reason why they shouldn't be. It wasn't more than ten years ago, and they were by no means an old couple. As far as he could make out, the farm was their own property. He, Bolt, knew only very few French words at that time. It was much later, after he had been made a prisoner and kept inland in France till the Peace of Amiens, that he had picked up a smattering of the lingo. His captivity had done away with his feeble chance of promotion, he could not help remarking. Bolt was a master's mate still.

Captain Vincent, in common with a good many officers of all ranks in Lord Nelson's fleet, had his misgivings about the system of distant blockade from which the Admiral apparently would not depart. Yet one could not blame Lord Nelson. Everybody in the fleet understood that what was in his mind was the destruction of the enemy; and if the enemy was closely blockaded he would never come out to be destroyed. On the other hand it was clear that as things were conducted the French had too many chances left them to slip out unobserved and vanish from all human knowledge for months. Those possibilities were a constant worry to Captain Vincent, who had thrown himself with the ardour of passion into the special duty with which he was entrusted. Oh, for a pair of eyes fastened night and day on the entrance of the harbour of Toulon! Oh, for the power to look at the very state of French ships and into the very secrets of French minds!

But he said nothing of this to Bolt. He only observed that the character of the French Government was changed and that the minds of the royalist people in the farmhouse might have changed too, since they had got back the exercise of their religion. Bolt's answer was that he had had a lot to do with royalists, in his time, on board Lord Howe's fleet, both before and after Toulon was evacuated. All sorts, men and women, barbers and noblemen, sailors and tradesmen; almost every kind of royalist one could think of; and his opinion was that a royalist never changed. As to the place itself, he only wished the captain had seen it. It was the sort of spot that nothing could change. He made bold to say that it would be just the same a hundred years hence.

The earnestness of his officer caused Captain Vincent to look hard at him. He was a man of about his own age, but while Vincent was a comparatively young captain, Bolt was an old master's mate. Each understood the other perfectly.

Captain Vincent fidgeted for a while and then observed abstractedly that he was not a man to put a noose round a dog's neck, let alone a good seaman's.

This cryptic pronouncement caused no wonder to appear in Bolt's attentive gaze. He only became a little thoughtful before he said in the same abstracted tone that an officer in uniform was not likely to be hanged for a spy. The service was risky, of course. It was necessary, for its success, that, assuming the same people were there, it should be undertaken by a man well known to the inhabitants. Then he added that he was certain of being recognized. And while he enlarged on the extremely good terms he had been on with the owners of the farm, especially the farmer's wife, a comely motherly woman, who had been very kind to him, and had all her wits about her, Captain Vincent, looking at the master's mate's bushy whiskers, thought that these in themselves were enough to ensure recognition. This impression was so strong that he had asked point blank : " You haven't altered the growth of the hair on your face, Mr. Bolt, since then ? "

There was just a touch of indignation in Bolt's negative reply ; for he was proud of his whiskers. He declared he was ready to take the most desperate chances for the service of his king and his country.

Captain Vincent added : " For the sake of Lord Nelson, too." One understood well what his Lordship wished to bring about by that blockade at sixty leagues off. He was talking to a sailor, and there was no need to say any more. Did Bolt think that he could persuade those people to conceal him in their house on that lonely shore end of the peninsula for some considerable time ? Bolt thought it was the easiest thing in the world. He would simply go up there and renew the old acquaintance, but he did not mean to do that in a reckless manner. It would have to be done at night, when of course there would be no one about. He would land just where he used to before, wrapped up in a Mediterranean sailor's cloak—he had one of his own—over his uniform, and simply go straight to the door, at which he would knock. Ten to one the farmer himself would come down to open it. He knew enough French by now, he hoped, to persuade those people to conceal him in some room having a view in the right direction; and there he would stick day after day on the watch, taking a little exercise in the middle of the night, ready to live on mere bread and water if necessary, so as not to arouse suspicion amongst the farmhands. And who knows if, with the farmer's help, he could not get some news of what was going on actually within the port. Then from time to time he could go down in the dead of night, signal to the ship and make his report. Bolt expressed the hope that the *Amelia* would remain as much as possible in sight of the coast. It would cheer him up to see her about. Captain Vincent naturally assented. He pointed out to Bolt, however, that his post would become most important exactly when the ship had been chased away or driven by the weather off her station, as could very easily happen. "You would be then the eyes of Lord Nelson's fleet, Mr. Bolt—think of that. The actual eyes of Lord Nelson's fleet!"

After dispatching his officer, Captain Vincent spent the night on deck. The break of day came at last, much paler than the moonlight which it replaced. And still no boat. And again Captain Vincent asked himself if he had not acted indiscreetly. Impenetrable, and looking as fresh as if he had just come up on deck, he argued the point with himself till the rising sun clearing the ridge on Porquerolles Island flashed its level rays upon his ship with her dew-darkened sails and dripping rigging. He roused himself then to tell his first lieutenant to get the boats out to tow the ship away from the shore. The report of the gun he ordered to be fired expressed simply his irritation. The *Amelia*, pointing towards the middle of the Passe, was moving at a snail's pace behind her string of boats. Minutes passed. And then suddenly Captain Vincent perceived his boat pulling back in shore according to orders. When nearly abreast of the ship, she darted away, making for her side. Mr. Bolt clambered on board, alone, ordering the gig to go ahead and help with the towing. Captain Vincent, standing apart on the quarter-deck, received him with a grimly questioning look.

Mr. Bolt's first words were to the effect that he believed the confounded spot to be bewitched. Then he glanced at

the group of officers on the other side of the quarter-deck.
Captain Vincent led the way to his cabin. There he turned
and looked at his officer, who, with an air of distraction,
mumbled : " There are night-walkers there."

" Come, Bolt, what the devil have you seen ? Did you
get near the house at all ? "

" I got within twenty yards of the door, sir," said Bolt.
And encouraged by the captain's much less ferocious—
" Well ? " began his tale.   He did not pull up to the path
which he knew, but to a little bit of beach on which he told
his men to haul up the boat and wait for him.  The beach
was concealed by a thick growth of bushes on the landward
side and by some rocks from the sea.   Then he went to what
he called the ravine, still avoiding the path, so that as a matter
of fact he made his way up on his hands and knees mostly,
very carefully and slowly amongst the loose stones, till by
holding on to a bush he brought his eyes on a level with the
piece of flat ground in front of the farmhouse.

The familiar aspect of the buildings, totally unchanged
from the time when he had played his part in what appeared
as a most successful operation at the beginning of the war,
inspired Bolt with great confidence in the success of his
present enterprise, vague as it was, but the great charm of
which lay, no doubt, in mental associations with his younger
years.  Nothing seemed easier than to stride across the forty
yards of open ground and rouse the farmer whom he remembered so well, the well-to-do man, a grave, sagacious royalist
in his humble way ; certainly, in Bolt's view, no traitor to his
country, and preserving so well his dignity in ambiguous
circumstances.  To Bolt's simple vision neither that man nor
his wife could have changed.

In this view of Arlette's parents Bolt was influenced by
the consciousness of there having been no change in himself.
He was the same Jack Bolt, and everything around him was
the same as if he had left the spot only yesterday.  Already
he saw himself in the kitchen which he knew so well, seated
by the light of a single candle before a glass of wine and talking
his best French to that worthy farmer of sound principles.
The whole thing was as well as done.  He imagined himself

a secret inmate of that building, closely confined indeed, but sustained by the possible great results of his watchfulness, in many ways more comfortable than on board the *Amelia* and with the glorious consciousness that he was, in Captain Vincent's phrase, the actual physical eyes of the Fleet.

He didn't, of course, talk of his private feelings to Captain Vincent. All those thoughts and emotions were compressed in the space of not much more than a minute or two while, holding on with one hand to his bush and having got a good foothold for one of his feet, he indulged in that pleasant anticipatory sense of success. In the old days the farmer's wife used to be a light sleeper. The farmhands which, he remembered, lived in the village or were distributed in stables and outhouses, did not give him any concern. He wouldn't need to knock heavily. He pictured to himself the farmer's wife sitting up in bed, listening, then rousing her husband, who, as likely as not, would take the gun standing against the dresser downstairs and come to the door.

And then everything would be all right. . . . But perhaps . . . yes ! It was just as likely the farmer would simply open the window and hold a parley. That really was most likely. Naturally. In his place Bolt felt he would do that very thing. Yes, that was what a man in a lonely house, in the middle of the night, would do most naturally. And he imagined himself whispering mysteriously his answers up the wall to the obvious questions—" Ami "—" Bolt "—" Ouvrez-moi "—" vive le roi "—or things of that sort. And in sequence to those vivid images it occurred to Bolt that the best thing he could do would be to throw small stones against the window shutter, the sort of sound most likely to rouse a light sleeper. He wasn't quite sure which window on the floor above the ground floor was that of those people's bedroom, but there were anyhow only three of them. In a moment he would have sprung up from his foothold on to the level if, raising his eyes for another look at the front of the house, he had not perceived that one of the windows was already open. How he could have failed to notice that before, he couldn't explain.

He confessed to Captain Vincent in the course of his narrative that " this open window, sir, checked me dead.

In fact, sir, it shook my confidence, for you know, sir, that no native of these parts would dream of sleeping with his window open. It struck me that there was something wrong there; and I remained where I was."

That fascination of repose, of secretive friendliness, which houses present at night, was gone. By the power of an open window, a black square in the moon-lighted wall, the farmhouse took on the aspect of a man-trap. Bolt assured Captain Vincent that the window would not have stopped him; he would have gone on all the same, though with an uncertain mind. But while he was thinking it out there glided without a sound before his irresolute eyes from somewhere a white vision—a woman. He could see her black hair flowing down her back. A woman whom anybody would have been excused for taking for a ghost. "I won't say that she froze my blood, sir, but she made me cold all over for a moment. Lots of people have seen ghosts, at least they say so, and I have an open mind about that. She was a weird thing to look at in the moonlight. She did not act like a sleep-walker either. If she had not come out of a grave, then she had jumped out of bed. But when she stole back and hid herself round the corner of the house I knew she was not a ghost. She could not have seen me. There she stood in the black shadow watching for something—or waiting for somebody," added Bolt in a grim tone. "She looked crazy," he conceded charitably.

One thing was clear to him: there had been changes in that farmhouse since his time. Bolt resented them, as if that time had been only last week. The woman concealed round the corner remained in his full view, watchful, as if only waiting for him to show himself in the open, to run off screeching and rouse all the countryside. Bolt came quickly to the conclusion that he must withdraw from the slope. On lowering himself from his first position he had the misfortune to dislodge a stone. This circumstance precipitated his retreat. In a very few minutes he found himself by the shore. He paused to listen. Above him, up the ravine and all round amongst the rocks, everything was perfectly still. He walked along in the direction of his boat. There was nothing for it but to get away quietly and perhaps . . .

D D

"Yes, Mr. Bolt, I fear we shall have to give up our plan," interrupted Captain Vincent at that point. Bolt's assent came reluctantly, and then he braced himself to confess that this was not the worst. Before the astonished face of Captain Vincent he hastened to blurt it out. He was very sorry, he could in no way account for it, but—he had lost a man.

Captain Vincent seemed unable to believe his ears. "What do you say? Lost a man out of my boat's crew!" He was profoundly shocked. Bolt was correspondingly distressed. He narrated that, shortly after he had left them, the seamen had heard, or imagined they had heard, some faint and peculiar noises somewhere within the cove. The coxswain sent one of the men, the oldest of the boat's crew, along the shore to ascertain whether their boat hauled on the beach could be seen from the other side of the cove. The man—it was Symons—departed crawling on his hands and knees to make the circuit and, well—he had not returned. This was really the reason why the boat was so late in getting back to the ship. Of course Bolt did not like to give up the man. It was inconceivable that Symons should have deserted. He had left his cutlass behind and was completely unarmed, but had he been suddenly pounced upon he surely would have been able to let out a yell that could have been heard all over the cove. But till daybreak a profound stillness, in which it seemed a whisper could have been heard for miles, had reigned over the coast. It was as if Symons had been spirited away by some supernatural means, without a scuffle, without a cry. For it was inconceivable that he should have ventured inland and got captured there. It was equally inconceivable that there should have been on that particular night men ready to pounce upon Symons and knock him on the head so neatly as not to let him give a groan even.

Captain Vincent said: "All this is very fantastical, Mr. Bolt," and compressed his lips firmly for a moment before he continued: "But not much more than your woman. I suppose you did see something real. . . ."

"I tell you, sir, she stood there in full moonlight for ten minutes within a stone's throw of me," protested Bolt with a sort of desperation. "She seemed to have jumped out of bed only to look at the house. If she had a petticoat over her night-shift, that was all. Her back was to me. When she moved away I could not make out her face properly. Then she went to stand in the shadow of the house."

" On the watch," suggested Captain Vincent.

" Looked like it, sir," confessed Bolt.

" So there must have been somebody about," concluded Captain Vincent with assurance.

Bolt murmured a reluctant, " Must have been." He had expected to get into enormous trouble over this affair and was much relieved by the captain's quiet attitude. " I hope, sir, you approve of my conduct in not attempting to look for Symons at once ? "

" Yes. You acted prudently by not advancing inland," said the captain.

" I was afraid of spoiling our chances to carry out your plan, sir, by disclosing our presence on shore. And that could not have been avoided. Moreover, we were only five in all and not properly armed."

" The plan has gone down before your night-walker, Mr. Bolt," Captain Vincent declared dryly. " But we must try to find out what has become of our man if it can be done without risking too much."

" By landing a large party this very next night we could surround the house," Bolt suggested. " If we find friends there, well and good. If enemies, then we could carry off some of them on board for exchange perhaps. I am almost sorry I did not go back and kidnap that wench—whoever she was," he added recklessly. " Ah ! if it had only been a man ! "

" No doubt there was a man not very far off," said Captain Vincent equably. " That will do, Mr. Bolt. You had better go and get some rest now."

Bolt was glad to obey, for he was tired and hungry after his dismal failure. What vexed him most was its absurdity. Captain Vincent, though he too had passed a sleepless night, felt too restless to remain below. He followed his officer on deck.

## VI

By that time the *Amelia* had been towed half a mile or so away from Cape Esterel. This change had brought her nearer to the two watchers on the hill-side who would have been plainly visible to the people on her deck, but for the head of the pine which concealed their movements. Lieutenant Réal, bestriding the rugged trunk as high as he could get, had the whole of the English ship's deck open to the range of his pocket-glass which he used between the branches. He said to Peyrol suddenly :

" Her captain has just come on deck."

Peyrol, sitting at the foot of the tree, made no answer for a long while. A warm drowsiness lay over the land and seemed to press down his eyelids. But inwardly the old rover was intensely awake. Under the mask of his immobility, with half-shut eyes and idly clasped hands, he heard the lieutenant, perched up there near the head of the tree, mutter counting something : " One, two, three," and then a loud " Parbleu ! " after which the lieutenant in his trunk-bestriding attitude began to jerk himself backwards. Peyrol got up out of his way, but could not restrain himself from asking : " What's the matter now ? "

" I will tell you what's the matter," said the other, excitedly. As soon as he got his footing he walked up to old Peyrol and when quite close to him folded his arms across his chest.

" The first thing I did was to count the boats in the water. There was not a single one left on board. And now I just counted them again and found one more there. That ship had a boat out last night. How I missed seeing her pull out from under the land I don't know. I was watching the decks, I suppose, and she seems to have gone straight up to the tow-rope. But I was right. That Englishman had a boat out."

He seized Peyrol by both shoulders suddenly. " I believe you knew it all the time. You knew it, I tell you." Peyrol, shaken violently by the shoulders, raised his eyes to look at the angry face within a few inches of his own. In his worn gaze there was no fear or shame, but a troubled perplexity and obvious concern. He remained passive, merely remonstrating softly :

" Doucement. Doucement."

The lieutenant suddenly desisted with a final jerk which failed to stagger old Peyrol, who, directly he had been released, assumed an explanatory tone.

" For the ground is slippery here. If I had lost my footing I would not have been able to prevent myself from grabbing at you, and we would have gone down that cliff together ; which would have told those Englishmen more than twenty boats could have found out in as many nights."

Secretly Lieutenant Réal was daunted by Peyrol's mildness. It could not be shaken. Even physically he had an impression of the utter futility of his effort, as though he had tried to shake a rock. He threw himself on the ground, carelessly saying :

" As for instance."

Peyrol lowered himself with a deliberation appropriate to his grey hairs. " You don't suppose that out of a hundred and twenty or so pairs of eyes on board that ship there wouldn't be a dozen at least scanning the shore. Two men falling down a cliff would have been a startling sight. The English would have been interested enough to send a boat ashore to go through our pockets, and whether dead or only half dead we wouldn't have been in a state to prevent them. It wouldn't matter so much as to me, and I don't know what papers you may have in your pockets, but there are your shoulder straps, your uniform coat."

" I carry no papers in my pocket, and . . ." A sudden thought seemed to strike the lieutenant, a thought so intense and far-fetched as to give his mental effort a momentary aspect of vacancy. He shook it off and went on in a changed tone : " The shoulder straps would not have been much of a revelation by themselves."

" No. Not much. But enough to let her captain know that he had been watched. For what else could the dead body of a naval officer with a spyglass in his pocket mean ?

Hundreds of eyes may glance carelessly at that ship every
day from all parts of the coast, though I fancy those landsmen
hardly take the trouble to look at her now. But that's a
very different thing from being kept under observation.
However, I don't suppose all this matters much."

The lieutenant was recovering from the spell of that sudden
thought. "Papers in my pocket," he muttered to himself.
"That would be a perfect way." His parted lips came
together in a slightly sarcastic smile with which he met
Peyrol's puzzled, sidelong glance provoked by the inexplicable
character of these words.

"I bet," said the lieutenant, "that ever since I came here
first you have been more or less worrying your old head about
my motives and intentions."

Peyrol said simply: "You came here on service at first
and afterwards you came again because even in the Toulon
fleet an officer may get a few days' leave. As to your intentions, I won't say anything about them. Especially as
regards myself. About ten minutes ago anybody looking on
would have thought they were not friendly to me."

The lieutenant sat up suddenly. By that time the English
sloop, getting away from under the land, had become visible
even from the spot on which they sat.

"Look!" exclaimed Réal. "She seems to be forging
ahead in this calm."

Peyrol, startled, raised his eyes and saw the *Amelia* clear
of the edge of the cliff and heading across the Passe. All her
boats were already alongside, and yet, as a minute or two
of steady gazing was enough to convince Peyrol, she was not
stationary.

"She moves! There is no denying that. She moves.
Watch the white speck of that house on Porquerolles. There!
The end of her jibboom touches it now. In a moment her
head sails will mask it to us."

"I would never have believed it," muttered the lieutenant,
after a pause of intent gazing. "And look, Peyrol, look,
there is not a wrinkle on the water."

Peyrol, who had been shading his eyes from the sun, let
his hand fall. "Yes," he said, "she would answer to a

child's breath quicker than a feather, and the English very soon found it out when they got her. She was caught in Genoa only a few months after I came home and got my moorings here."

" I didn't know," murmured the young man.

" Aha, lieutenant," said Peyrol, pressing his finger to his breast, " it hurts here, doesn't it ? There is nobody but good Frenchmen here. Do you think it is a pleasure to me to watch that flag out there at her peak ? Look, you can see the whole of her now. Look at her ensign hanging down as if there were not a breath of wind under the heavens. . . ." He stamped his foot suddenly. " And yet she moves ! Those in Toulon that may be thinking of catching her dead or alive would have to think hard and make long plans and get good men to carry them out."

" There was some talk of it at the Toulon Admiralty," said Réal.

The rover shook his head. " They need not have sent you on the duty," he said. " I have been watching her now for a month, her and the man who has got her now. I know all his tricks and all his habits and all his dodges by this time. The man is a seaman, that must be said for him, but I can tell beforehand what he will do in any given case."

Lieutenant Réal lay down on his back again, his clasped hands under his head. He thought that this old man was not boasting. He knew a lot about the English ship, and if an attempt to capture her was to be made, his ideas would be worth having. Nevertheless, in his relations with old Peyrol Lieutenant Réal suffered from contradictory feelings. Réal was the son of a ci-devant couple—small provincial gentry—who both had lost their heads on the scaffold within the same week. As to their boy, he was apprenticed by order of the Delegate of the Revolutionary Committee of his town to a poor but pure-minded joiner, who could not provide him with shoes to run his errands in, but treated this aristocrat not unkindly. Nevertheless, at the end of the year the orphan ran away and volunteered as a boy on board one of the ships of the Republic about to sail on a distant expedition. At sea he found another standard of values.

In the course of some eight years, suppressing his faculties of
love and hatred, he arrived at the rank of an officer by sheer
merit, and had accustomed himself to look at men sceptically,
without much scorn or much respect.   His principles were
purely professional and he had never formed a friendship
in his life—more unfortunate in that respect than old Peyrol,
who at least had known the bonds of the lawless Brotherhood
of the Coast.   He was, of course, very self-contained.
Peyrol, whom he had found unexpectedly settled on the
peninsula, was the first human being to break through that
schooled reserve which the precariousness of all things had
forced on the orphan of the Revolution.   Peyrol's striking
personality had aroused Réal's interest, a mistrustful liking
mixed with some contempt of a purely doctrinaire kind.   It
was clear that the fellow had been next thing to a pirate at
one time or another—a sort of past which could not com-
mend itself to a naval officer.

Still, Peyrol had broken through : and, presently, the
peculiarities of all those people at the farm, each individual
one of them, had entered through the breach.

Lieutenant Réal, on his back, closing his eyes to the glare
of the sky, meditated on old Peyrol, while Peyrol himself,
with his white head bare in the sunshine, seemed to be sitting
by the side of a corpse.   What in that man impressed
Lieutenant Réal was the faculty of shrewd insight.   The facts
of Réal's connection with the farmhouse on the peninsula
were much as Peyrol had stated.   First on specific duty
about establishing a signal station, then, when that project
had been given up, voluntary visits.   Not belonging to any
ship of the fleet but doing shore duty at the Arsenal, Lieutenant Réal had spent several periods of short leave at the
farm, where indeed nobody could tell whether he had come
on duty or on leave.   He personally could not—or perhaps
would not—tell even to himself why it was that he came
there.   He had been growing sick of his work.   He had no
place in the world to go to, and no one either.   Was it
Peyrol he was coming to see ?   A mute, strangely suspicious,
defiant understanding had established itself imperceptibly
between him and that lawless old man who might have been

suspected to have come there only to die, if the whole robust personality of Peyrol with its quiet vitality had not been antagonistic to the notion of death. That rover behaved as though he had all the time in the world at his command.

Peyrol spoke suddenly, with his eyes fixed in front of him as if he were addressing the Island of Porquerolles, eight miles away.

"Yes—I know all her moves, though I must say that this trick of dodging close to our peninsula is something new."

"H'm! Fish for the captain's breakfast," mumbled Réal without opening his eyes. "Where is she now?"

"In the middle of the Passe, busy hoisting in her boats. And still moving! That ship will keep her way as long as the flame of a candle on her deck will not stand upright."

"That ship is a marvel."

"She has been built by French shipwrights," said old Peyrol bitterly.

This was the last sound for a long time. Then the lieutenant said in an indifferent tone: "You are very positive about that. How do you know?"

"I have been looking at her for a month, whatever name she might have had or whatever name the English call her by now. Did you ever see such a bow on an English-built ship?"

The lieutenant remained silent, as though he had lost all interest and there had been no such thing as an English man-of-war within a mile. But all the time he was thinking hard. He had been told confidentially of a certain piece of service to be performed on instructions received from Paris. Not an operation of war, but service of the greatest importance. The risk of it was not so much deadly as particularly odious. A brave man might well have shrunk from it; and there are risks (not death) from which a resolute man might shrink without shame.

"Have you ever tasted of prison, Peyrol?" he asked suddenly, in an affectedly sleepy voice.

It roused Peyrol nearly into a shout. "Heavens! No! Prison! What do you mean by prison? . . . I have been a captive to savages," he added, calming down, "but that's

D D 2

a very old story. I was young and foolish then. Later,
when a grown man, I was a slave to the famous Ali-Kassim.
I spent a fortnight with chains on my legs and arms in the
yard of a mud fort on the shores of the Persian Gulf. There
was nearly a score of us Brothers of the Coast in the same
predicament . . . in consequence of a shipwreck."

"Yes. . . ." The lieutenant was very languid indeed. . . .
"And I dare say you all took service with that bloodthirsty
old pirate."

"There was not a single one of his thousands of blackamoors that could lay a gun properly. But Ali-Kassim made
war like a prince. We sailed, a regular fleet, across the gulf,
took a town on the coast of Arabia somewhere, and looted it.
Then I and the others managed to get hold of an armed
dhow, and we fought our way right through the blackamoor's
fleet. Several of us died of thirst later. All the same, it was
a great affair. But don't you talk to me of prisons. A
proper man if given a chance to fight can always get himself
killed. You understand me?"

"Yes, I understand you," drawled the lieutenant. "I
think I know you pretty well. I suppose an English
prison . . ."

"That is a horrible subject of conversation," interrupted
Peyrol in a loud, emotional tone. "Naturally, any death
is better than a prison. Any death! What is it you have
in your mind, lieutenant?"

"Oh, it isn't that I want you to die," drawled Réal in an
uninterested manner.

Peyrol, his entwined fingers clasping his legs, gazed fixedly
at the English sloop floating idly in the Passe while he gave
up all his mind to the consideration of these words that had
floated out, idly too, into the peace and silence of the morning.
Then he asked in a low tone:

"Do you want to frighten me?"

The lieutenant laughed harshly. Neither by word,
gesture nor glance did Peyrol acknowledge the enigmatic
and unpleasant sound. But when it ceased the silence grew
so oppressive between the two men that they got up by a
common impulse. The lieutenant sprang to his feet lightly.

The uprising of Peyrol took more time and had more dignity. They stood side by side unable to detach their longing eyes from the enemy ship below their feet.

" I wonder why he put himself into this curious position," said the officer.

" I wonder ? " growled Peyrol curtly. " If there had been only a couple of eighteen-pounders placed on the rocky ledge to the left of us, we could have unrigged her in about ten minutes."

" Good old gunner," commented Réal ironically. " And what afterwards ? Swim off, you and I, with our cutlasses in our teeth and take her by boarding, what ? "

This sally provoked in Peyrol an austere smile. " No ! No ! " he protested soberly. " But why not let Toulon know ? Bring out a frigate or two and catch him alive. Many a time have I planned his capture just to ease my heart. Often I have stared at night out of my window upstairs across the bay to where I knew he was lying at anchor, and thinking of a little surprise I could arrange for him if I were not only old Peyrol, the gunner."

" Yes. And keeping out of the way at that, with a bad note against his name in the books of the Admiralty in Toulon."

" You can't say I have tried to hide myself from you who are a naval officer," struck in Peyrol quickly. " I fear no man. I did not run. I simply went away from Toulon. Nobody had given me an order to stay there. And you can't say I ran very far either."

" That was the cleverest move of all. You knew what you were doing."

" Here you go again, hinting at something crooked like that fellow with big epaulettes at the Port Office that seemed to be longing to put me under arrest just because I brought a prize from the Indian Ocean, eight thousand miles, dodging clear of every Englishman that came in my way, which was more perhaps than he could have done. I have my gunner's warrant signed by Citizen Renaud, a chef d'escadre. It wasn't given me for twirling my thumbs or hiding in the cable tier when the enemy was about. There were on board our ships some patriots that weren't above doing that sort of thing, I can tell you. But republic or no republic, that kind wasn't likely to get a gunner's warrant."

" That's all right," said Réal, with his eyes fixed on the English ship, the head of which was swung to the north-ward now. . . . " Look, she seems to have lost her way at last," he remarked parenthetically to Peyrol, who also glanced that way and nodded. . . . " That's all right. But it's on record that you managed in a very short time to get very thick with a lot of patriots ashore. Section leaders. Terrorists. . . ."

" Why, yes. I wanted to hear what they had to say. They talked like a drunken crew of scallywags that had stolen a ship. But at any rate it wasn't such as they that had sold the Port to the English. They were a lot of bloodthirsty landlubbers. I did get out of town as soon as I could. I remembered I was born around here. I knew no other bit of France, and I didn't care to go any further. Nobody came to look for me."

" No, not here. I suppose they thought it was too near. They did look for you, a little, but they gave it up. Perhaps if they had persevered and made an Admiral of you we would not have been beaten at Aboukir."

At the mention of that name Peyrol shook his fist at the serene Mediterranean sky. " And yet we were no worse men than the English," he cried, " and there are no such ships as ours in the world. You see, lieutenant, the repub-lican god of these talkers would never give us seamen a chance of fair play."

The lieutenant looked round in surprise. " What do you know about a republican god ? " he asked. ' What on earth do you mean ? "

" I have heard of and seen more gods than you could ever dream of in a long night's sleep, in every corner of the earth, in the very heart of forests, which is an inconceivable thing. Figures, stones, sticks. There must be something in the idea. . . . And what I meant," he continued in a resentful tone, " is that their republican god, which is neither stick nor stone, but seems to be some kind of lubber, has never given us seamen a chief like that one the soldiers have got ashore."

Lieutenant Réal looked at Peyrol with unsmiling attention, then remarked quietly, "Well, the god of the aristocrats is coming back again, and it looks as if he were bringing an emperor along with him. You've heard something of that, you people in the farmhouse? Haven't you?"

"No," said Peyrol. "I have heard no talk of an Emperor. But what does it matter? Under one name or another a chief can be no more than a chief, and that general whom they have been calling Consul is a good chief—nobody can deny that."

After saying those words in a dogmatic tone, Peyrol looked up at the sun and suggested that it was time to go down to the farmhouse "pour manger la soupe." With a suddenly gloomy face Réal moved off, followed by Peyrol. At the first turn of the path they got the view of the Escampobar buildings with the pigeons still walking on the ridges of the roofs, of the sunny orchards and yards without a living soul in them. Peyrol remarked that everybody, no doubt, was in the kitchen waiting for his and the lieutenant's return. He himself was properly hungry. "And you, lieutenant?"

The lieutenant was not hungry. Hearing this declaration made in a peevish tone, Peyrol gave a sagacious movement of his head behind the lieutenant's back. Well, whatever happened, a man had to eat. He, Peyrol, knew what it was to be altogether without food; but even half-rations was a poor show, very poor show for anybody who had to work or to fight. For himself he couldn't imagine any conjuncture that would prevent him having a meal as long as there was something to eat within reach.

His unwonted garrulity provoked no response, but Peyrol continued to talk in that strain as though his thoughts were concentrated on food, while his eyes roved here and there and his ears were open for the slightest sound. When they arrived in front of the house Peyrol stopped to glance anxiously down the path to the coast, letting the lieutenant enter the café. The Mediterranean, in that part which could be seen from the door of the café, was as empty of all sail as a yet undiscovered sea. The dull tinkle of a cracked bell on the neck of some wandering cow was the only sound that reached him, accentuating the Sunday peace of the farm. Two goats were lying down on the western slope of the hill. It all had a very reassuring effect and the anxious expression on Peyrol's face was passing away when suddenly one of the goats leaped to its feet. The rover gave a start and became rigid in a pose of tense apprehension. A man who is in such a frame of mind that a leaping goat makes him start cannot be happy. However, the other goat remained lying down. There was really no reason for alarm, and Peyrol, composing his features as near as possible to their usual placid expression, followed the lieutenant into the house.

## VII

A SINGLE cover having been laid at the end of a long table in the salle for the lieutenant, he had his meal there while the others sat down to theirs in the kitchen, the usual strangely assorted company served by the anxious and silent Catherine. Peyrol, thoughtful and hungry, faced Citizen Scevola in his working clothes and very much withdrawn within himself. Scevola's aspect was more feverish than usual, with the red patches on his cheek-bones very marked above the thick beard. From time to time the mistress of the farm would get up from her place by the side of old Peyrol and go out into the salle to attend to the lieutenant. The other three people seemed unconscious of her absences. Towards the end of the meal Peyrol leaned back in his wooden chair and let his gaze rest on the ex-terrorist who had not finished yet, and was still busy over his plate with the air of a man who had done a long morning's work. The door leading from the kitchen to the salle stood wide open, but no sound of voices ever came from there.

Till lately Peyrol had not concerned himself very much with the mental states of the people with whom he lived. Now, however, he wondered to himself what could be the thoughts of the ex-terrorist patriot, that sanguinary and extremely poor creature occupying the position of master of the Escampobar Farm. But when Citizen Scevola raised his head at last to take a long drink of wine there was nothing new on that face which in its high colour resembled so much a painted mask. Their eyes met.

"Sacrebleu!" exclaimed Peyrol at last. "If you never say anything to anybody like this you will forget how to speak at last."

The patriot smiled from the depths of his beard, a smile which Peyrol for some reason, mere prejudice perhaps, always thought resembled the defensive grin of some small wild animal afraid of being cornered.

"What is there to talk about?" he retorted. "You live with us; you haven't budged from here; I suppose you have counted the bunches of grapes in the enclosure and the figs on the fig-tree on the west wall many times over. . . ." He paused to lend an ear to the dead silence in the salle, and then said with a slight rise of tone, "You and I know everything that is going on here."

Peyrol wrinkled the corners of his eyes in a keen, searching glance. Catherine clearing the table bore herself as if she had been completely deaf. Her face, of a walnut colour, with sunken cheeks and lips, might have been a carving in the marvellous immobility of its fine wrinkles. Her carriage was upright and her hands swift in their movements. Peyrol said: "We don't want to talk about the farm. Haven't you heard any news lately?"

The patriot shook his head violently. Of public news he had a horror. Everything was lost. The country was ruled by perjurers and renegades. All the patriotic virtues were dead. He struck the table with his fist and then remained listening as though the blow could have roused an echo in the silent house. Not the faintest sound came from anywhere. Citizen Scevola sighed. It seemed to him that he was the only patriot left, and even in his retirement his life was not safe.

"I know," said Peyrol. "I saw the whole affair out of the window. You can run like a hare, citizen."

"Was I to allow myself to be sacrificed by those super-stitious brutes?" argued Citizen Scevola in a high-pitched voice and with genuine indignation, which Peyrol watched coldly. He could hardly catch the mutter of "Perhaps it would have been just as well if I had let those reactionary dogs kill me that time."

The old woman washing up at the sink glanced uneasily towards the door of the salle.

"No!" shouted the lonely sans-culotte. "It isn't possible! There must be plenty of patriots left in France. The sacred fire is not burnt out yet."

For a short time he presented the appearance of a man who is sitting with ashes on his head and desolation in his heart. His almond-shaped eyes looked dull, extinguished. But after a moment he gave a sidelong look at Peyrol as if to watch the effect and began declaiming in a low voice and apparently as if rehearsing a speech to himself: "No, it isn't possible. Some day tyranny will stumble and then it will be time to pull it down again. We will come out in our thousands and—ça ira!"

Those words, and even the passionate energy of the tone, left Peyrol unmoved. With his head sustained by his thick brown hand he was thinking of something else so obviously as to depress again the feebly struggling spirit of terrorism in the lonely breast of Citizen Scevola. The glow of reflected sunlight in the kitchen became darkened by the body of the fisherman of the lagoon, mumbling a shy greeting to the company from the frame of the doorway. Without altering his position Peyrol turned his eyes on him curiously. Catherine, wiping her hands on her apron, remarked: "You come late for your dinner, Michel." He stepped in then, took from the old woman's hand an earthenware pot and a large hunk of bread and carried it out at once into the yard. Peyrol and the sans-culotte got up from the table. The latter, after hesitating like somebody who has lost his way, went brusquely into the passage, while Peyrol, avoiding Catherine's anxious stare, made for the back-yard. Through the open door of the salle he obtained a glimpse of Arlette sitting upright with her hands in her lap gazing at somebody he could not see, but who could be no other than Lieutenant Réal.

In the blaze and heat of the yard the chickens, broken up into small groups, were having their siesta in patches of shade. But Peyrol cared nothing for the sun. Michel, who was eating his dinner under the pent roof of the cart-shed, put the earthenware pot down on the ground and joined his master at the well encircled by a low wall of stones and topped by an arch of wrought iron on which a wild fig-tree had twined a slender offshoot. After his dog's death the fisherman had abandoned the salt lagoon, leaving his rotting punt exposed on the dismal shore and his miserable nets shut up in the dark hut. He did not care for another dog, and besides, who was there to give him a dog? He was the last of men. Somebody must be last. There was no place for him in the life of the village. So one fine morning he had walked up to the farm in order to see Peyrol. More correctly perhaps, to let himself be seen by Peyrol. That was exactly Michel's only hope. He sat down on a stone outside the gate with a small bundle, consisting mainly of an old blanket, and a crooked stick lying on the ground near him, and looking the most lonely, mild and harmless creature on this earth. Peyrol had listened gravely to his confused tale of the dog's death. He, personally, would not have made a friend of a dog like Michel's dog, but he understood per-fectly the sudden breaking up of the establishment on the shore of the lagoon. So when Michel had concluded with the words, " I thought I would come up here," Peyrol, without waiting for a plain request, had said : " Très bien. You will be my crew," and had pointed down the path leading to the sea-shore. And as Michel, picking up his bundle and stick, started off, waiting for no further directions, he had shouted after him : " You will find a loaf of bread and a bottle of wine in a locker aft, to break your fast on."

These had been the only formalities of Michel's engagement to serve as " crew " on board Peyrol's boat. The rover, indeed, had tried without loss of time to carry out his pur-pose of getting something of his own that would float. It was not so easy to find anything worthy. The miserable population of Madrague, a tiny fishing hamlet facing towards Toulon, had nothing to sell. Moreover, Peyrol looked with contempt on all their possessions. He would have as soon bought a catamaran of three logs of wood tied together with rattans as one of their boats; but lonely and prominent on the beach, lying on her side in weatherbeaten melancholy, there was a two-masted tartane with her sun-whitened cordage hanging in festoons and her dry masts showing long cracks. No man was ever seen dozing under the shade of her hull, on which the Mediterranean gulls made themselves very much at home. She looked a wreck thrown high up on the land by a disdainful sea. Peyrol, having surveyed her from a distance, saw that the rudder still hung in its place. He ran his eye along her body and said to himself that a craft with such lines would sail well. She was much bigger than anything he had thought of, but in her size, too, there was a fascination. It seemed to bring all the shores of the Mediterranean within his reach, Baleares and Corsica, Barbary and Spain. Peyrol had sailed over hundreds of leagues of ocean in craft that were no bigger. At his back, in silent wonder, a knot of fishermen's wives, bareheaded and lean, with a swarm of ragged children clinging to their skirts, watched the first stranger they had seen for years.

Peyrol borrowed a short ladder in the hamlet (he knew better than to trust his weight to any of the ropes hanging over the side) and carried it down to the beach, followed at a respectful distance by the staring women and children: a phenomenon and a wonder to the natives, as it had happened to him before on more than one island in distant seas. He clambered on board the neglected tartane and stood on the decked fore-part, the centre of all eyes. A gull flew away with an angry scream. The bottom of the open hold contained nothing but a little sand, a few broken pieces of wood, a rusty hook, and some few stalks of straw which the wind must have carried for miles before they found their rest in there. The decked after-part had a small skylight and a companion, and Peyrol's eyes rested fascinated on an enormous padlock which secured its sliding door. It was as if there had been secrets or treasures inside—and yet most probably it was empty. Peyrol turned his head away and with the whole strength of his lungs shouted in the direction of the fishermen's wives, who had been joined by two very old men and a hunchbacked cripple swinging between two crutches.

"Is there anybody looking after this tartane, a care-taker?"

At first the only answer was a movement of recoil. Only the hunchback held his ground and shouted back in an unexpectedly strong voice:

"You are the first man that has been on board her for years."

The wives of the fishermen admired his boldness, for Peyrol indeed appeared to them a very formidable being.

"I might have guessed that," thought Peyrol. "She is in a dreadful mess." The disturbed gull had brought some friends as indignant as itself and they circled at different levels uttering wild cries over Peyrol's head. He shouted again:

"Who does she belong to?"

The being on crutches lifted a finger towards the circling birds and answered in a deep tone:

"They are the only ones I know." Then, as Peyrol gazed down at him over the side, he went on: "This craft used to belong to Escampobar. You know Escampobar? It's a house in the hollow between the hills there."

"Yes, I know Escampobar," yelled Peyrol, turning away and leaning against the mast in a pose which he did not change for a long time. His immobility tired out the crowd. They moved slowly in a body towards their hovels, the hunchback bringing up the rear with long swings between his crutches, and Peyrol remained alone with the angry gulls. He lingered on board the tragic craft which had taken Arlette's parents to their death in the vengeful massacre of Toulon and had brought the youthful Arlette and Citizen Scevola back to Escampobar, where old Catherine, left alone at that time, had waited for days for somebody's return. Days of anguish and prayer, while she listened to the booming of guns about Toulon and with an almost greater but different terror to the dead silence which ensued.

Peyrol, enjoying the sensation of some sort of craft under his feet, indulged in no images of horror connected with that desolate tartane. It was late in the evening before he returned to the farm, so that he had to have his supper alone. The women had retired, only the sans-culotte, smoking a short pipe out of doors, had followed him into the kitchen and asked where he had been and whether he had lost his way. This question gave Peyrol an opening. He had been to Madrague and had seen a very fine tartane lying perishing on the beach.

"They told me down there that she belonged to you, citoyen."

At this the terrorist only blinked.

"What's the matter? Isn't she the craft you came here in? Won't you sell her to me?" Peyrol waited a little. "What objection can you have?"

It appeared that the patriot had no positive objections. He mumbled something about the tartane being very dirty. This caused Peyrol to look at him with intense astonishment.

"I am ready to take her off your hands as she stands."

"I will be frank with you, citoyen. You see, when she lay at the quay in Toulon a lot of fugitive traitors, men and women, and children too, swarmed on board of her, and cut the ropes with a view of escaping, but the avengers were not far behind and made short work of them. When we discovered her behind the Arsenal I and another man, had to throw a lot of bodies overboard, out of the hold and the cabin. You will find her very dirty all over. We had no time to clear up." Peyrol felt inclined to laugh. He had seen decks swimming in blood and had himself helped to throw dead bodies overboard after a fight; but he eyed the citizen with an unfriendly eye. He thought to himself: "He had a hand in that massacre, no doubt," but he made no audible remark. He only thought of the enormous padlock securing that emptied charnel-house at the stern. The terrorist insisted. "We really had not a moment to clean her up. The circumstances were such that it was necessary for me to get away quickly lest some of the false patriots should do me some carmagnole or other. There had been bitter quarrelling in my section. I was not alone in getting away, you know."

Peyrol waved his arm to cut short the explanation. But before he and the terrorist had parted for the night Peyrol could regard himself as the owner of the tragic tartane.

Next day he returned to the hamlet and took up his quarters there for a time. The awe he had inspired wore off, though no one cared to come very near the tartane. Peyrol did not want any help. He wrenched off the enormous padlock himself with a bar of iron and let the light of day into the little cabin which did indeed bear the traces of the massacre in the stains of blood on its woodwork, but contained nothing else except a wisp of long hair and a woman's ear-ring, a cheap thing which Peyrol picked up and looked at for a long time. The associations of such finds were not foreign to his past. He could without very strong emotion figure to himself the little place choked with corpses. He sat down and looked about at the stains and splashes which had been untouched by sunlight for years. The cheap little ear-ring lay before him on the rough-hewn table between the lockers, and he shook his head at it weightily. He, at any rate, had never been a butcher.

Peyrol, unassisted, did all the cleaning. Then he turned *con amore* to the fitting out of the tartane. The habits of activity still clung to him. He welcomed something to do; this congenial task had all the air of preparation for a voyage, which was a pleasing dream, and it brought every evening the satisfaction of something achieved to that illusory end. He rove new gear, scraped the masts himself, did all the sweeping, scrubbing and painting single-handed, working steadily and hopefully as though he had been preparing his escape from a desert island; and directly he had cleaned and renovated the dark little hole of a cabin he took to sleeping on board. Once only he went up on a visit to the farm for a couple of days, as if to give himself a holiday. He passed them mostly in observing Arlette. She was perhaps the first problematic human being he had ever been in contact with. Peyrol had no contempt for women. He had seen them love, suffer, endure, riot, and even fight for their own hand, very much like men. Generally with men and women you had to be on your guard, but in some ways women were more to be trusted. As a matter of fact, his country-women were to him less known than any other kind. From his experience of many different races, however, he had a vague idea that women were very much alike everywhere. This one was a lovable creature. She produced on him the effect of a child, aroused a kind of intimate emotion which he had not known before to exist by itself in a man. He was startled by its detached character. "Is it that I am getting old?" he asked himself suddenly one evening, as he sat on the bench against the wall looking straight before him, after she had crossed his line of sight.

He felt himself an object of observation to Catherine, whom he used to detect peeping at him round the corners or through half-opened doors. On his part he would stare at her openly, aware of the impression he produced on her : mingled curiosity and awe. He had the idea she did not disapprove of his presence at the farm, where, it was plain to him, she had a far from easy life. This had no relation to the fact that she did all the household work. She was a woman of about his own age, straight as a dart but with a wrinkled face. One evening as they were sitting alone in the kitchen Peyrol said to her : "You must have been a handsome girl in your day, Catherine. It's strange you never got married."

She turned to him under the high mantel of the fireplace and seemed struck all of a heap, unbelieving, amazed, so that Peyrol was quite provoked. "What's the matter? If the old moke in the yard had spoken you could not look more surprised. You can't deny that you were a handsome girl."

She recovered from her scare to say : "I was born here, grew up here, and early in my life I made up my mind to die here."

"A strange notion," said Peyrol, "for a young girl to take into her head."

"It's not a thing to talk about," said the old woman, stooping to get a pot out of the warm ashes. "I did not think, then," she went on, with her back to Peyrol, " that

I would live long. When I was eighteen I fell in love with a priest."

"Ah, bah!" exclaimed Peyrol under his breath.

"That was the time when I prayed for death," she pursued in a quiet voice. "I spent nights on my knees upstairs in that room where you sleep now. I shunned everybody. People began to say I was crazy. We have always been hated by the rabble about here. They have poisonous tongues. I got the nickname of 'la fiancée du prêtre.' Yes, I was handsome, but who would have looked at me if I had wanted to be looked at? My only luck was to have a fine man for a brother. He understood. No word passed his lips, but sometimes when we were alone, and not even his wife was by, he would lay his hand on my shoulder gently. From that time to this I have not been to church, and I never will go. But I have no quarrel with God now."

There were no signs of watchfulness and care in her bearing now. She stood straight as an arrow before Peyrol and looked at him with a confident air. The rover was not yet ready to speak. He only nodded twice, and Catherine turned away to put the pot to cool in the sink. "Yes, I wished to die. But I did not, and now I have got something to do," she said, sitting down near the fireplace and taking her chin in her hand. "And I dare say you know what that is," she added.

Peyrol got up deliberately.

"Well! bonsoir," he said. "I am off to Madrague. I want to begin work again on the tartane at daylight."

"Don't talk to me about the tartane! She took my brother away for ever. I stood on the shore watching her sails growing smaller and smaller. Then I came up alone to this farmhouse."

Moving calmly her faded lips which no lover or child had ever kissed, old Catherine told Peyrol of the days and nights of waiting, with the distant growl of the big guns in her ears. She used to sit outside on the bench longing for news, watching the flickers in the sky and listening to heavy bursts of gunfire coming over the water. Then came a night as if the world were coming to an end. All the sky was lighted up, the earth shook to its foundations, and she felt the house rock, so that jumping up from the bench she screamed with fear. That night she never went to bed. Next morning she saw the sea covered with sails, while a black and yellow cloud of smoke hung over Toulon. A man coming up from Madrague told her that he believed that the whole town had been blown up. She gave him a bottle of wine and he helped her to feed the stock that evening. Before going home he expressed the opinion that there could not be a soul left alive in Toulon, because the few that survived would have gone away in the English ships. Nearly a week later she was dozing by the fire when voices outside woke her up, and she beheld standing in the middle of the salle, pale like a corpse out of a grave, with a blood-soaked blanket over her shoulders and a red cap on her head, a ghastly-looking young girl in whom she suddenly recognized her niece. She screamed in her terror : " François, François ! " This was her brother's name, and she thought he was outside. Her scream scared the girl, who ran out of the door. All was still outside. Once more she screamed " François ! " and, tottering as far as the door, she saw her niece clinging to a strange man in a red cap and with a sabre by his side, who yelled excitedly : " You won't see François again. Vive la République ! "

" I recognized the son Bron," went on Catherine. " I knew his parents. When the troubles began he left his home to follow the Revolution. I walked straight up to him and took the girl away from his side. She didn't want much coaxing. The child always loved me," she continued, getting up from the stool and moving a little closer to Peyrol. " She remembered her Aunt Catherine. I tore the horrid blanket off her shoulders. Her hair was clotted with blood and her clothes all stained with it. I took her upstairs. She was as helpless as a little child. I undressed her and examined her all over. She had no hurt anywhere. I was sure of that—but of what more could I be sure ? I couldn't make sense of the things she babbled at me. Her very voice distracted me. She fell asleep directly I had put her into my bed, and I stood there looking down at her, nearly going out of my mind with the thought of what that child may have been dragged through. When I went downstairs I found that good-for-nothing inside the house. He was ranting up and down the salle, vapouring and boasting till I thought all this must be an awful dream. My head was in a whirl. He laid claim to her, and God knows what. I seemed to understand things that made my hair stir on my head. I stood there clasping my hands with all the strength I had, for fear I should go out of my senses."

" He frightened you," said Peyrol, looking at her steadily. Catherine moved a step nearer to him.

" What ? The son Bron, frighten me ! He was the butt of all the girls, mooning about amongst the people outside the church on feast days in the time of the King. All the countryside knew about him. No. What I said to myself was that I mustn't let him kill me. There upstairs was the child I had just got away from him, and there was I, all alone with that man with the sabre and unable to get hold of a kitchen knife even."

" And so he remained," said Peyrol.

" What would you have had me to do ? " asked Catherine steadily. " He had brought the child back out of those shambles. It was a long time before I got an idea of what had happened. I don't know everything even yet, and I suppose I will never know. In a very few days my mind was more at ease about Arlette, but it was a long time before she would speak and then it was never anything to the purpose. And what could I have done single-handed ? There was nobody I would condescend to call to my help. We of the Escampobar have never been in favour with the peasants here," she said proudly. " And that is all I can tell you."

Her voice faltered, she sat down on the stool again and took her chin in the palm of her hand. As Peyrol left the house to go to the hamlet he saw Arlette and the patron come round the corner of the yard wall walking side by side but as if unconscious of each other.

That night he slept on board the renovated tartane and the rising sun found him at work about the hull. By that time he had ceased to be the object of awed contemplation to the inhabitants of the hamlet, who still, however, kept up a mistrustful attitude. His only intermediary for communicating with them was the miserable cripple. He was Peyrol's only company, in fact, during his period of work on the tartane. He had more activity, audacity, and intelligence, it seemed to Peyrol, than all the rest of the inhabitants put together. Early in the morning he could be seen making his way on his crutches with a pendulum motion towards the hull on which Peyrol would have been already an hour or or so at work. Peyrol then would throw him over a sound rope's end and the cripple, leaning his crutches against the side of the tartane, would pull his wretched little carcass, all withered below the waist, up the rope, hand over hand, with extreme ease. There, sitting on the small foredeck with his back against the mast and his thin, twisted legs folded in front of him, he would keep Peyrol company, talking to him along the whole length of the tartane in a strained voice and sharing his midday meal, as of right, since it was he generally who brought the provisions slung round his neck in a quaint flat basket. Thus were the hours of labour shortened for Peyrol by shrewd remarks and bits of local gossip. How the cripple got hold of it it was difficult to imagine, and the rover had not enough knowledge of European superstitions to suspect him of flying through the night on a broomstick like a sort of male witch—for there was a manliness in that twisted scrap of humanity which struck Peyrol from the first. His very voice was manly and the character of his gossip was not feminine. He did indeed mention to Peyrol that people used to take him about the neighbourhood in carts for the purpose of playing a fiddle at weddings and other festive occasions; but this seemed hardly adequate, and even he himself confessed that there was not much of that sort of thing going on during the Revolution, when people didn't like to attract attention and everything was done in a hole-and-corner manner. There were no priests to officiate at weddings, and if there were no ceremonies how could there be rejoicings? Of course children were born as before, but there were no christenings— and people got to look funny somehow or other. Their countenances got changed somehow; the very boys and girls seemed to have something on their minds.

Peyrol, busy about one thing and another, listened without appearing to pay much attention to the story of the Revolution, as if to the tale of an intelligent islander on the other side of the world talking of bloody rites and amazing hopes of some religion unknown to the rest of mankind. But there was something biting in the speech of that cripple which confused his thoughts a little. Sarcasm was a mystery which he could not understand. On one occasion he remarked to his friend the cripple as they sat together on the foredeck munching the bread and figs of their midday meal:

"There must have been something in it. But it doesn't seem to have done much for you people here."

"To be sure," retorted the scrap of man vivaciously, "it hasn't straightened my back or given me a pair of legs like yours."

Peyrol, whose trousers were rolled up above the knee because he had been washing the hold, looked at his calves complacently. "You could hardly have expected that," he remarked with simplicity.

"Ah, but you don't know what people with properly made bodies expected or pretended to," said the cripple. "Everything was going to be changed. Everybody was going to tie up his dog with a string of sausages for the sake of principles." His long face, which, in repose, had an expression of suffering peculiar to cripples, was lighted up by an enormous grin. "They must feel jolly well sold by this time," he added. "And of course that vexes them, but I am not vexed. I was never vexed with my father and mother. While the poor things were alive I never went hungry—not very hungry. They couldn't have been very proud of me." He paused and seemed to contemplate himself mentally. "I don't know what I would have done in their place. Something very different. But then, don't you see, I know what it means to be like I am. Of course they couldn't know, and I don't suppose the poor people had very much sense. A priest from Almanarre—Almanarre is a sort of village up there where there is a church. . . ."

Peyrol interrupted him by remarking that he knew all about Almanarre. This, on his part, was a simple delusion because in reality he knew much less of Almanarre than of Zanzibar or any pirate village from there up to Cape Guardafui. And the cripple contemplated him with his brown eyes, which had an upward cast naturally.

"You know . . . ! For me," he went on, in a tone of quiet decision, "you are a man fallen from the sky. Well, a priest from Almanarre came to bury them. A fine man with a stern face. The finest man I have seen from that time till you dropped on us here. There was a story of a girl having fallen in love with him some years before. I was old enough then to have heard something of it, but that's neither here nor there. Moreover, many people wouldn't believe the tale."

Peyrol, without looking at the cripple, tried to imagine what sort of child he might have been—what sort of youth? The rover had seen staggering deformities, dreadful mutilations which were the cruel work of man : but it was amongst people with dusky skins. And that made a great difference. But what he had heard and seen since he had come back to his native land, the tales, the facts, and also the faces, reached his sensibility with a particular force, because of that feeling that came to him so suddenly after a whole lifetime spent amongst Indians, Malagashes, Arabs, blackamoors of all sorts, that he belonged there, to this land, and had escaped all those things by a mere hair's breadth. His companion completed his significant silence, which seemed to have been occupied with thoughts very much like his own, by saying :

"All this was in the King's time. They didn't cut off his head till several years afterwards. It didn't make my life any easier for me, but since those Republicans had deposed God and flung Him out of all the churches I have forgiven Him all my troubles."

"Spoken like a man," said Peyrol. Only the misshapen character of the cripple's back prevented Peyrol from giving him a hearty slap. He got up to begin his afternoon's work. It was a bit of inside painting, and from the foredeck the cripple watched him at it with dreamy eyes and something ironic on his lips.

It was not till the sun had travelled over Cape Cicié, which could be seen across the water like dark mist in the glare, that he opened his lips to ask: "And what do you propose to do with this tartane, citoyen?"

Peyrol answered simply that the tartane was fit to go anywhere now, the very moment she took the water.

"You could go as far as Genoa and Naples and even further," suggested the cripple.

"Much further," said Peyrol.

"And you have been fitting her out like this for a voyage?"

"Certainly," said Peyrol, using his brush steadily.

"Somehow I fancy it will not be a long one."

Peyrol never checked the to-and-fro movement of his brush, but it was with an effort. The fact was that he had discovered in himself a distinct reluctance to go away from the Escampobar Farm. His desire to have something of his own that could float was no longer associated with any desire to wander. The cripple was right. The voyage of the renovated tartane would not take her very far. What was surprising was the fellow being so very positive about it. He seemed able to read people's thoughts.

The dragging of the renovated tartane into the water was a great affair. Everybody in the hamlet, including the women, did a full day's work and there was never so much coin passed from hand to hand in the hamlet in all the days of its obscure history. Swinging between his crutches on a low sand-ridge the cripple surveyed the whole of the beach. It was he that had persuaded the villagers to lend a hand and had arranged the terms for their assistance. It was he also who, through a very miserable-looking pedlar (the only one who frequented the peninsula), had got in touch with some rich persons in Fréjus who had changed for Peyrol a few of his gold pieces for current money. He had expedited the course of the most exciting and interesting experience of his life, and now planted on the sand on his two sticks in the manner of a beacon he watched the last operation. The rover, as if about to launch himself upon a track of a thousand miles, walked up to shake hands with him and look once more at the soft eyes and the ironic smile.

"There is no denying it—you are a man."

"Don't talk like this to me, citoyen," said the cripple in a trembling voice. Till then, suspended between his two sticks and with his shoulders as high as his ears, he had not looked towards the approaching Peyrol. "This is too much of a compliment!"

"I tell you," insisted the rover roughly, and as if the insignificance of mortal envelopes had presented itself to him for the first time at the end of his roving life, "I tell you that there is that in you which would make a chum one would like to have alongside one in a tight place."

As he went away from the cripple towards the tartane, while the whole population of the hamlet disposed around her waited for his word, some on land and some waist-deep in the water holding ropes in their hands, Peyrol had a slight shudder at the thought: "Suppose I had been born like that." Ever since he had put his foot on his native lany such thoughts had haunted him. They would have been impossible anywhere else. He could not have been like and blackamoor, good, bad or indifferent, hale or crippled, king or slave; but here, on this Southern shore that had called to him irresistibly as he had approached the Straits of Gibraltar on what he had felt to be his last voyage, any woman, lean and old enough, might have been his mother; he might have been any Frenchman of them all, even one of those he pitied, even one of those he despised. He felt the grip of his origins from the crown of his head to the soles of his feet while he clambered on board the tartane as if for a long and distant voyage. As a matter of fact he knew very well that with a bit of luck it would be over in about an hour. When the tartane took the water the feeling of being afloat plucked at his very heart. Some Madrague fishermen had been persuaded by the cripple to help old Peyrol to sail the tartane round to the cove below the Escampobar Farm. A glorious sun shone upon that short passage and the cove itself was full of sparkling light when they arrived. The few

Escampobar goats wandering on the hillside pretending to feed where no grass was visible to the naked eye never even raised their heads. A gentle breeze drove the tartane, as fresh as paint could make her, opposite a narrow crack in the cliff which gave admittance to a tiny basin, no bigger than a village pond, concealed at the foot of the southern hill. It was there that old Peyrol, aided by the Madrague men, who had their boat with them, towed his ship, the first really that he ever owned.

Once in, the tartane nearly filled the little basin, and the fishermen, getting into their boat, rowed away for home. Peyrol, by spending the afternoon in dragging ropes ashore and fastening them to various boulders and dwarf trees, moored her to his complete satisfaction. She was as safe from the tempests there as a house ashore.

After he had made everything fast on board and had furled the sails neatly, a matter of some time for one man, Peyrol contemplated his arrangements, which savoured of rest much more than of wandering, and found them good. Though he never meant to abandon his room at the farmhouse, he felt that his true home was in the tartane, and he rejoiced at the idea that it was concealed from all eyes except perhaps the eyes of the goats when their arduous feeding took them on the southern slope. He lingered on board, he even threw open the sliding door of the little cabin, which now smelt of fresh paint, not of stale blood. Before he started for the farm the sun had travelled far beyond Spain, and all the sky to the west was yellow, while on the side of Italy it presented a sombre canopy pierced here and there with the light of stars. Catherine put a plate on the table, but nobody asked him any questions.

He spent a lot of his time on board, going down early, coming up at midday " pour manger la soupe," and sleeping on board almost every night. He did not like to leave the tartane alone for so many hours. Often, having climbed a little way up to the house, he would turn round for a last look at her in the gathering dusk, and actually would go back again. After Michel had been enlisted for a crew and had taken his abode on board for good, Peyrol found it a much easier matter to spend his nights in the lantern-like room at the top of the farmhouse.

Often waking up at night he would get up to look at the starry sky out of all his three windows in succession, and think : " Now there is nothing in the world to prevent me getting out to sea in less than an hour." As a matter of fact it was possible for two men to manage the tartane. Thus Pyrol's thought was comfortingly true in every way, for he loved to feel himself free, and Michel of the lagoon, after the death of his depressed dog, had no tie on earth. It was a fine thought which somehow made it quite easy for Peyrol to go back to his four-poster and resume his slumbers.

## VIII

PERCHED sideways on the circular wall bordering the well, in the full blaze of the midday sun, the rover of the distant seas and the fisherman of the lagoon, sharing between them a most surprising secret, had the air of two men conferring in the dark. The first word that Peyrol said was, " Well ? "

" All quiet," said the other.

" Have you fastened the cabin door properly ? "

" You know what the fastenings are like."

Peyrol could not deny that. It was a sufficient answer. It shifted the responsibility on to his shoulders, and all his life he had been accustomed to trust to the work of his own hands, in peace and in war. Yet he looked doubtfully at Michel before he remarked :

" Yes, but I know the man too."

There could be no greater contrast than those two faces ; Peyrol's clean, like a carving of stone, and only very little softened by time, and that of the owner of the late dog, hirsute, with many silver threads, with something elusive in the features and the vagueness of expression of a baby in arms. " Yes, I know the man," repeated Peyrol. Michel's mouth fell open at this, a small oval set a little crookedly in the innocent face.

"He will never wake," he suggested timidly.

The possession of a common and momentous secret draws men together. Peyrol condescended to explain.

"You don't know the thickness of his skull. I do."

He spoke as though he had made it himself. Michel, who in the face of that positive statement had forgotten to shut his mouth, had nothing to say.

"He breathes all right?" asked Peyrol.

"Yes. After I got out and locked the door I listened for a bit and I thought I heard him snore."

Peyrol looked interested and also slightly anxious.

"I had to come up and show myself this morning as if nothing had happened," he said. "The officer has been here for two days, and he might have taken it into his head to go down to the tartane. I have been on the stretch all the morning. A goat jumping up was enough to give me a turn. Fancy him running up here with his broken head all bandaged up, with you after him."

This seemed to be too much for Michel. He said almost indignantly:

"The man's half killed."

"It takes a lot to even half kill a Brother of the Coast. There are men and men. You, for instance," Peyrol continued placidly, "you would have been altogether killed if it had been your head that got in the way. And there are animals, beasts twice your size, regular monsters, that may be killed with nothing more than just a tap on the nose. That's well known. I was really afraid he would overcome you in some way or other. . . ."

"Come, maître! One isn't a little child," protested Michel against this accumulation of improbabilities. He did it, however, only in a whisper and with childlike shyness. Peyrol folded his arms on his breast:

"Go, finish your soup," he commanded in a low voice, "and then go down to the tartane. You locked the cabin door properly, you said?"

"Yes, I have," protested Michel, staggered by this display of anxiety. "He could sooner burst the deck above his head, as you know."

E E

"All the same, take a small spar and shore up that door against the heel of the mast. And then watch outside. Don't you go in to him on any account. Stay on deck and keep a lookout for me. There is a tangle here that won't be easily cleared and I must be very careful. I will try to slip away and get down as soon as I get rid of that officer."

The conference in the sunshine being ended, Peyrol walked leisurely out of the yard gate, and protruding his head beyond the corner of the house, saw Lieutenant Réal sitting on the bench. This he had expected to see. But he had not expected to see him there alone. It was just like this : wherever Arlette happened to be, there were worrying possibilities. But she might have been helping her aunt in the kitchen with her sleeves rolled up on such white arms as Peyrol had never seen on any woman before. The way she had taken to dressing her hair in a plait with a broad black velvet ribbon and an Arlesian cap was very becoming. She was wearing now her mother's clothes of which there were chestfuls, altered for her of course. The late mistress of the Escampobar Farm had been an Arlesienne. Well-to-do, too. Yes, even for women's clothes the Escampobar natives could do without intercourse with the outer world. It was quite time that this confounded lieutenant went back to Toulon. This was the third day. His short leave must be up. Peyrol's attitude towards naval officers had been always guarded and suspicious. His relations with them had been very mixed. They had been his enemies and his superiors. He had been chased by them. He had been trusted by them. The Revolution had made a clean cut across the consistency of his wild life—Brother of the Coast and gunner in the national Navy—and yet he was always the same man. It was like that, too, with them. Officers of the King, officers of the Republic, it was only changing the skin. All alike looked askance at a free rover. Even this one could not forget his epaulettes when talking to him. Scorn and mistrust of epaulettes were rooted deeply in old Peyrol. Yet he did not absolutely hate Lieutenant Réal. Only the fellow's coming to the farm was generally a curse and his presence at that particular moment a confounded nuisance and to a certain extent even a danger. " I have no mind to be hauled to Toulon by the scruff of my neck," Peyrol said to himself. There was no trusting those epaulette-wearers. Any one of them was capable of jumping on his best friend on account of some officer-like notion or other.

Peyrol, stepping round the corner, sat down by the side of Lieutenant Réal with the feeling somehow of coming to grips with a slippery customer. The lieutenant, as he sat there, unaware of Peyrol's survey of his person, gave no notion of slipperiness. On the contrary, he looked rather immovably established. Very much at home. Too much at home. Even after Peyrol sat down by his side he continued to look immovable—or at least difficult to get rid of. In the still noonday heat the faint shrilling of cicadas was the only sound of life heard for quite a long time. Delicate, evanescent, cheerful, careless sort of life, yet not without passion. A sudden gloom seemed to be cast over the joy of the cicadas by the lieutenant's voice though the words were the most perfunctory possible.

" Tiens ! Vous voilà."

In the stress of the situation Peyrol at once asked himself : Now why does he say that ? Where did he expect me to be ? The lieutenant need not have spoken at all. He had known him now for about two years off and on, and it had happened many times that they had sat side by side on that bench in a sort of " at arm's length " equality without exchanging a single word. And why could he not have kept quiet now ? That naval officer never spoke without an object, but what could one make of words like that ? Peyrol achieved an insincere yawn and suggested mildly :

" A bit of siesta wouldn't be amiss. What do you think, lieutenant ? "

And to himself he thought : " No fear, he won't go to his room." He would stay there and thereby keep him, Peyrol, from going down to the cove. He turned his eyes on that naval officer, and if extreme and concentrated desire and mere force of will could have had any effect Lieutenant Réal would certainly have been removed suddenly from that bench. But he didn't move. And Peyrol was astonished to see that man smile, but what astonished him still more was to hear him say :

"The trouble is that you have never been frank with me, Peyrol."

"Frank with you," repeated the rover. "You want me to be frank with you? Well, I have wished you to the devil many times."

"That's better," said Lieutenant Réal. "But why? I never tried to do you any harm."

"Me harm," cried Peyrol, "to me?" . . . But he faltered in his indignation as if frightened at it and ended in a very quiet tone : "You have been nosing in a lot of dirty papers to find something against a man who was not doing *you* any harm and was a seaman before you were born."

"Quite a mistake. There was no nosing amongst papers. I came on them quite by accident. I won't deny I was *intrigué* finding a man of your sort living in this place. But don't be uneasy. Nobody would trouble his head about you. It's a long time since you have been forgotten. Have no fear."

"You! You talk to me of fear . . .? No," cried the rover, "it's enough to turn a fellow into a sans-culotte if it weren't for the sight of that specimen sneaking around here."

The lieutenant turned his head sharply, and for a moment the naval officer and the free sea rover looked at each other gloomily. When Peyrol spoke again he had changed his mood.

"Why should I fear anybody? I owe nothing to anybody. I have given them up the prize ship in order and everything else, except my luck; and for that I account to nobody," he added darkly.

"I don't know what you are driving at," the lieutenant said after a moment of thought. "All I know is that you seem to have given up your share of the prize money. There is no record of you ever claiming it."

Peyrol did not like the sarcastic tone. "You have a nasty tongue," he said, "with your damned trick of talking as if you were made of different clay."

"No offence," said the lieutenant, grave but a little

puzzled. "Nobody will drag out that against you. It has been paid years ago to the Invalides' fund. All this is buried and forgotten."

Peyrol was grumbling and swearing to himself with such concentration that the lieutenant stopped and waited till he had finished.

"And there is no record of desertion or anything like that," he continued then. "You stand there as *disparu*. I believe that after searching for you a little they came to the conclusion that you had come by your death somehow or other."

"Did they? Well, perhaps old Peyrol is dead. At any rate he has buried himself here." The rover suffered from great instability of feelings, for he passed in a flash from melancholy into fierceness. "And he was quiet enough till you came sniffing around this hole. More than once in my life I had occasion to wonder how soon the jackals would have a chance to dig up my carcass; but to have a naval officer come scratching round here was the last thing. . . ." Again a change came over him. "What can you want here?" he whispered, suddenly depressed.

The lieutenant fell into the humour of that discourse. "I don't want to disturb the dead," he said, turning full to the rover, who after his last words had fixed his eyes on the ground. "I want to talk to the gunner Peyrol."

Peyrol, without raising his eyes from the ground, growled: "He isn't there. He is *disparu*. Go and look at the papers again. Vanished. Nobody here."

"That," said Lieutenant Réal in a conversational tone, "that is a lie. He was talking to me this morning on the hill-side as we were looking at the English ship. He knows all about her. He told me he spent nights making plans for her capture. He seemed to be a fellow with his heart in the right place. Un homme de cœur. You know him."

Peyrol raised his big head slowly and looked at the lieutenant.

"Humph," he grunted. A heavy, non-committal grunt. His old heart was stirred, but the tangle was such that he had to be on his guard with any man who wore epaulettes. His profile preserved the immobility of a head struck on a medal while he listened to the lieutenant assuring him that this time he had come to Escampobar on purpose to speak with the gunner Peyrol. That he had not done so before was because it was a very confidential matter. At this point the lieutenant stopped and Peyrol made no sign. Inwardly he was asking himself what the lieutenant was driving at. But the lieutenant seemed to have shifted his ground. His tone, too, was slightly different. More practical.

"You say you have made a study of that English ship's movements. Well, for instance, suppose a breeze springs up, as it very likely will towards the evening, could you tell me where she will be to-night? I mean, what her captain is likely to do."

"No, I couldn't," said Peyrol.

"But you said you have been observing him minutely for weeks. There aren't so many alternatives, and taking the weather and everything into consideration, you can judge almost with certainty."

"No," said Peyrol again. "It so happens that I can't."

"Can't you? Then you are worse than any of the old admirals that you think so little of. Why can't you?"

"I will tell you why," said Peyrol after a pause and with a face more like a carving than ever. "It's because the fellow has never come so far this way before. Therefore I don't know what he has got in his mind, and in consequence I can't guess what he will do next. I may be able to tell you some other day but not to-day. Next time when you come . . . to see the old gunner."

"No, it must be this time."

"Do you mean you are going to stay here to-night?"

"Did you think I was here on leave? I tell you I am on service. Don't you believe me?"

Peyrol let out a heavy sigh. "Yes, I believe you. And so they are thinking of catching her alive. And you are sent on service. Well, that doesn't make it any easier for me to see you here."

"You are a strange man, Peyrol," said the lieutenant; "I believe you wish me dead."

"No. Only out of this. But you are right. Peyrol

is no friend either to your face or to your voice. They have done harm enough already."

They had never attained to such intimate terms before. There was no need for them to look at each other. The lieutenant thought: "Ah! he can't keep his jealousy in." There was no scorn or malice in that thought. It was much more like despair. He said mildly:

"You snarl like an old dog, Peyrol."

"I have felt sometimes as if I could fly at your throat," said Peyrol in a sort of calm whisper. "And it amuses you the more."

"Amuses me. Do I look light-hearted?"

Again Peyrol turned his head slowly for a long, steady stare. And again the naval officer and the rover gazed at each other with a searching and sombre frankness. This new-born intimacy could go no further.

"Listen to me, Peyrol. . . ."

"No," said the other. "If you want to talk, talk to the gunner."

Though he seemed to have adopted the notion of a double personality, the rover did not seem to be much easier in one character than in the other. Furrows of perplexity appeared on his brow, and as the lieutenant did not speak at once, Peyrol the gunner asked impatiently:

"So they are thinking of catching her alive." It did not please him to hear the lieutenant say that it was not exactly this that the chiefs in Toulon had in their minds. Peyrol at once expressed the opinion that of all the naval chiefs that ever were, Citizen Renaud was the only one that was worth anything. Lieutenant Réal, disregarding the challenging tone, kept to the point.

"What they want to know is whether that English corvette interferes much with the coast traffic."

"No, she doesn't," said Peyrol, "she leaves poor people alone unless, I suppose, some craft acts suspiciously. I have seen her give chase to one or two. But even those she did not detain. Michel—you know Michel?—has heard from the mainland people that she has captured several at various times. Of course, strictly speaking, nobody is safe."

"Well, no. I wonder now what that Englishman would call ' acting suspiciously.' "

"Ah, now you are asking something. Don't you know what an Englishman is ? One day easy and casual, next day ready to pounce on you like a tiger. Hard in the morning, careless in the afternoon, and only reliable in a fight, whether with or against you, but for the rest perfectly fantastic. You might think a little touched in the head, and there again it would not do to trust to that notion either."

The lieutenant lending an attentive ear, Peyrol smoothed his brow and discoursed with gusto of Englishmen as if they had been a strange, very little-known tribe. "In a manner of speaking," he concluded, "the oldest bird of them all can be caught with chaff, but not every day." He shook his head, smiling to himself faintly, as if remembering a quaint passage or two.

"You didn't get all that knowledge of the English while you were a gunner," observed the lieutenant dryly.

"There you go again," said Peyrol. "And what's that to you where I learned it all ? Suppose I learned it all from a man who is dead now. Put it down to that."

"I see. It amounts to this, that one can't get at the back of their minds very easily."

"No," said Peyrol, then added grumpily, "and some Frenchmen are not much better. I wish I could get at the back of your mind."

"You would find a service matter there, gunner, that's what you would find there, and a matter that seems nothing much at first sight, but when you look into it, is about as difficult to manage properly as anything you ever undertook in your life. It puzzled all the big-wigs. It must have, since I was called in. Of course I work on shore at the Admiralty, and I was in the way. They showed me the order from Paris and I could see at once the difficulty of it. I pointed it out and I was told . . ."

"To come here," struck in Peyrol.

"No. To make arrangements to carry it out."

"And you began by coming here. You are always coming here."

" I began by looking for a man," said the naval officer with emphasis.

Peyrol looked at him searchingly. " Do you mean to say that in the whole fleet you couldn't have found a man ? "

" I never attempted to look for one there. My chief agreed with me that it isn't a service for navy men."

" Well, it must be something nasty for a naval man to admit that much. What is the order ? I don't suppose you came over here without being ready to show it to me."

The lieutenant plunged his hand into the inside pocket of his naval jacket and then brought it out empty.

" Understand, Peyrol," he said earnestly, " this is not a service of fighting. Good men are plentiful for that. The object is to play the enemy a trick."

" Trick ? " said Peyrol in a judicial tone, " that's all right. I have seen in the Indian seas Monsieur Surcouf play tricks on the English . . . seen them with my own eyes, deceptions, disguises, and such-like. . . . That's quite sound in war."

" Certainly. The order for this one comes from the First Consul himself, for it is no small matter. It's to deceive the English Admiral."

" What—that Nelson ? Ah ! but he is a cunning one."

After expressing that opinion the old rover pulled out a red bandana handkerchief and after rubbing his face with it, repeated his opinion deliberately : " Celui-là est un malin."

This time the lieutenant really brought out a paper from his pocket and saying, "I have copied the order for you to see," handed it to the rover, who took it from him with a doubtful air.

Lieutenant Réal watched old Peyrol handling it at arm's length, then with his arm bent trying to adjust the distance to his eyesight, and wondered whether he had copied it in a hand big enough to be read easily by the gunner Peyrol. The order ran like this : " You will make up a packet of dispatches and pretended private letters as if from officers, containing a clear statement besides hints calculated to convince the enemy that the destination of the fleet now fitting in Toulon is for Egypt and generally for the East. That packet you will send by sea in some small craft to Naples,

taking care that the vessel should fall into the enemy's hands."
The Préfet Maritime had called Réal, had shown him the
paragraph of the letter from Paris, had turned the page over
and laid his finger on the signature, " Bonaparte." Then,
after giving him a meaning glance, the admiral locked up the
paper in a drawer and put the key in his pocket. Lieutenant
Réal had written the passage down from memory directly
the notion of consulting Peyrol had occurred to him.

The rover, screwing his eyes and pursing his lips, had come
to the end of it. The lieutenant extended his hand negligently and took the paper away : " Well, what do you think ? "
he asked. " You understand that there can be no question
of any ship of war being sacrificed to that dodge. What do
you think of it ? "

" Easier said than done," opined Peyrol curtly.

" That's what I told my admiral."

" Is he a lubber, so that you had to explain it to him ? "

" No, gunner, he is not. He listened to me, nodding his
head."

" And what did he say when you finished ? "

" He said : ' Parfaitement. Have you got any ideas
about it ? ' And I said—listen to me, gunner—I said :
' Oui, mon Amiral, I think I've got a man,' and the admiral
interrupted me at once : ' All right, you don't want to talk
to me about him, I put you in charge of that affair and give
you a week to arrange it. When it's done report to me.
Meantime you may just as well take this packet.' They were
already prepared, Peyrol, all those faked letters and dispatches.
I carried it out of the admiral's room, a parcel done up in
sail-cloth, properly corded and sealed. I have had it in my
possession for three days. It's upstairs in my valise."

" That doesn't advance you very much," growled old
Peyrol.

" No," admitted the lieutenant. " I can also dispose of a
few thousand francs."

" Francs," repeated Peyrol. " Well, you had better get
back to Toulon and try to bribe some man to put his head
into the jaws of the English lion."

Réal reflected, then said slowly, " I wouldn't tell any man

that. Of course a service of danger, that would be understood."

"It would be. And if you could get a fellow with some sense in his caboche, he would naturally try to slip past the English fleet and maybe do it, too. And then where's your trick?"

"We could give him a course to steer."

"Yes. And it may happen that your course would just take him clear of all Nelson's fleet, for you never can tell what the English are doing. They might be watering in Sardinia."

"Some cruisers are sure to be out and pick him up."

"Maybe. But that's not doing the job, that's taking a chance. Do you think you are talking to a toothless baby—or what?"

"No, my gunner. It will take a strong man's teeth to undo that knot." A moment of silence followed. Then Peyrol assumed a dogmatic tone.

"I will tell you what it is, lieutenant. This seems to me just the sort of order that a land-lubber would give to good seamen. You daren't deny that."

"I don't deny it," the lieutenant admitted. "And look at the whole difficulty. For supposing even that the tartane blunders right into the English fleet, as if it had been indeed arranged, they would just look into her hold or perhaps poke their noses here and there, but it would never occur to them to search for despatches, would it? Our man, of course, would have them well hidden, wouldn't he? He is not to know. And if he were ass enough to leave them lying about the decks, the English would at once smell a rat there. But what I think he would do would be to throw the despatches overboard."

"Yes—unless he is told the nature of the job," said Peyrol.

"Evidently. But where's the bribe big enough to induce a man to taste of the English pontoons?"

"The man will take the bribe all right and then will do his best not to be caught; and if he can't avoid that, he will take jolly good care that the English should find nothing on board his tartane. Oh no, lieutenant, any damn scallywag that owns a tartane will take a couple of thousand francs from your hand as tame as can be; but as to deceiving the English Admiral, it's the very devil of an affair. Didn't you think of all that before you spoke to the big epaulettes that gave you the job?"

"I did see it, and I put it all before him," the lieutenant said, lowering his voice still more, for their conversation had been carried on in undertones though the house behind them was silent and solitude reigned round the approaches of Escampobar Farm. It was the hour of siesta—for those that could sleep. The lieutenant, edging closer towards the old man, almost breathed the words in his ear.

"What I wanted was to hear you say all those things. Do you understand now what I meant this morning on the lookout? Don't you remember what I said?"

Peyrol, gazing into space, spoke in a level murmur.

"I remember a naval officer trying to shake old Peyrol off his feet and not managing to do it. I may be *disparu* but I am too solid yet for any blancbec that loses his temper, devil only knows why. And it's a good thing that you didn't manage it, else I would have taken you down with me, and we would have made our last somersault together for the amusement of an English ship's company. A pretty end that!"

"Don't you remember me saying, when you mentioned that the English would have sent a boat to go through our pockets, that this would have been the perfect way?" In his stony immobility, with the other man leaning towards his ear, Peyrol seemed a mere insensible receptacle for whispers, and the lieutenant went on forcibly: "Well, it was in allusion to this affair, for, look here, gunner, what could be more convincing, if they had found the packet of dispatches on me! What would have been their surprise, their wonder! Not the slightest doubt could enter their heads. Could it, gunner? Of course it couldn't. I can imagine the captain of that corvette crowding sail on her to get this packet into the admiral's hands. The secret of the Toulon fleet's destination found on the body of a dead officer. Wouldn't they have exulted at their enormous piece of luck! But they wouldn't have called it accidental. Oh no! They would have called it providential. I know the English a little too. They like to have God on their side—the only ally they never need pay a subsidy to. Come, gunner, would it not have been a perfect way?"

Lieutenant Réal threw himself back, and Peyrol, still like a carven image of grim dreaminess, growled softly:

"Time yet. The English ship is still in the Passe." He waited a little in his uncanny living-statue manner before he added viciously: "You don't seem in a hurry to go and take that leap."

"Upon my word, I am almost sick enough of life to do it," the lieutenant said in a conversational tone.

"Well, don't forget to run upstairs and take that packet with you before you go," said Peyrol as before. "But don't wait for me, I am not sick of life. I am *disparu*, and that's good enough. There's no need for me to die."

And at last he moved in his seat, swung his head from side to side as if to make sure that his neck had not been turned to stone, emitted a short laugh, and grumbled: "*Disparu!* Hein! Well, I am damned!" as if the word "vanished" had been a gross insult to enter against a man's name in a register. It seemed to rankle, as Lieutenant Réal observed with some surprise; or else it was something inarticulate that rankled, manifesting itself in that funny way. The lieutenant, too, had a moment of anger which flamed and went out at once in the deadly cold philosophic reflection: "We are victims of the destiny which has brought us together." Then again his resentment flamed. Why should he have stumbled against that girl or that woman, he didn't know how he must think of her, and suffer so horribly for it? He who had endeavoured almost from a boy to destroy all the softer feelings within himself. His changing moods of distaste, of wonder at himself and at the unexpected turns of life, wore the aspect of profound abstraction, from which he was recalled by an outburst of Peyrol's, not loud but fierce enough.

"No," cried Peyrol, "I am too old to break my bones for the sake of a lubberly soldier in Paris who fancies he has invented something clever."

"I don't ask you to," the lieutenant said, with extreme severity, in what Peyrol would call an epaulette-wearer's voice. "You old sea-bandit. And it wouldn't be for the sake of a soldier anyhow. You and I are Frenchmen after all."

"You have discovered that, have you?"

"Yes," said Réal. "This morning, listening to your talk on the hillside with that English corvette within one might say a stone's throw."

"Yes," groaned Peyrol. "A French-built ship!" He struck his breast a resounding blow. "It hurts one there to see her. It seemed to me I could jump down on her deck single-handed."

"Yes, there you and I understood each other," said the lieutenant. "But look here, this affair is a much bigger thing than getting back a captured corvette. In reality it is much more than merely playing a trick on an admiral. It's a part of a deep plan, Peyrol! It's another stroke to help us on the way towards a great victory at sea."

"Us!" said Peyrol. "I am a sea-bandit and you are a sea-officer. What do you mean by us?"

"I mean all Frenchmen," said the lieutenant. "Or, let us say simply France, which you too have served."

Peyrol, whose stone-effigy bearing had become humanized almost against his will, gave an appreciative nod and said: "You've got something in your mind. Now what is it? If you will trust a sea-bandit."

"No, I will trust a gunner of the Republic. It occurred to me that for this great affair we could make use of this corvette that you have been observing so long. For to count on the capture of any old tartane by the fleet in a way that would not arouse suspicion is no use."

"A lubberly notion," assented Peyrol, with more heartiness than he had ever displayed towards Lieutenant Réal.

"Yes, but there's that corvette. Couldn't something be arranged to make them swallow the whole thing, somehow, some way? You laugh . . . Why?"

"I laugh because it would be a great joke," said Peyrol, whose hilarity was very short-lived. "That fellow on board, he thinks himself very clever. I never set my eyes on him, but

I used to feel that I knew him as if he were my own brother; but now . . ."

He stopped short. Lieutenant Réal, after observing the sudden change on his countenance, said in an impressive manner :

" I think you have just had an idea."

" Not the slightest," said Peyrol, turning suddenly into stone, as if by enchantment. The lieutenant did not feel discouraged, and he was not surprised to hear the effigy of Peyrol pronounce : " All the same one could see." Then very abruptly : " You meant to stay here to-night ? "

" Yes. I will only go down to Madrague and leave word with the sailing barge which was to come to-day from Toulon to go back without me."

" No, lieutenant. You must return to Toulon to-day. When you get there you must turn out some of those damned quill-drivers at the Port Office if it were midnight and have papers made out for a tartane—oh, any name you like. Some sort of papers. And then you must come back as soon as you can. Why not go down to Madrague now and see whether the barge isn't already there ? If she is, then by starting at once you may get back here some time about midnight."

He got up impetuously, and the lieutenant stood up too. Hesitation was imprinted on his whole attitude. Peyrol's aspect was not animated, but his Roman face with its severe aspect gave him a great air of authority.

" Won't you tell me something more ? " asked the lieutenant.

" No," said the rover. " Not till we meet again. If you return during the night don't you try to get into the house. Wait outside. Don't rouse anybody. I will be about, and if there is anything to say I will say it to you then. What are you looking about you for ? You don't want to go up for your valise. Your pistols up in your room too ? What do you want with pistols, only to go to Toulon and back with a naval boat's crew ? " He actually laid his hand on the lieutenant's shoulder and impelled him gently towards the track leading to Madrague. Réal turned his head at the touch and their eyes met with the strained closeness of a wrestler's hug.

It was the lieutenant who gave way before the unflinchingly direct stare of the old Brother of the Coast. He gave way under the cover of a sarcastic smile and a very airy " I see you want me out of the way for some reason or other," which produced not the slightest effect upon Peyrol, who stood with his arm pointing towards Madrague. When the lieutenant turned his back on him Peyrol's pointing arm fell down by his side; but he watched the lieutenant out of sight before he turned too and moved in a contrary direction.

## IX

On losing sight of the perplexed lieutenant, Peyrol discovered that his own mind was a perfect blank. He started to get down to his tartane after one sidelong look at the face of the house which contained quite a different problem. Let that wait. His head feeling strangely empty, he felt the pressing necessity of furnishing it with some thought without loss of time. He scrambled down steep places, caught at bushes, stepped from stone to stone, with the assurance of long practice, with mechanical precision and without for a moment relaxing his efforts to capture some definite scheme which he could put into his head. To his right the cove lay full of pale light, while the rest of the Mediterranean extended beyond it in a dark, unruffled blue. Peyrol was making for the little basin where his tartane had been hidden for years, like a jewel in a casket meant only for the secret rejoicing of his eye, of no more practical use than a miser's hoard—and as precious ! Coming upon a hollow in the ground where grew a few bushes and even a few blades of grass, Peyrol sat down to rest. In that position his visible world was limited to a stony slope, a few boulders, the bush against which he leaned and the vista of a piece of empty sea-horizon. He perceived that he detested that lieutenant much more when he didn't see him. There was something in the fellow. Well, at any rate he had got rid of him for, say, eight or ten hours. An uneasiness came over the old rover, a sense of the endangered stability of things, which was anything but welcome. He wondered at it, and the thought " I am growing old " intruded on him again. And yet he was aware of his sturdy body. He could still creep stealthily like an Indian and with his trusty cudgel knock a man over with a certain aim at the back of his head, and with force enough to fell him like a bullock. He had done that thing no further back than two o'clock the night before, not twelve hours ago, as easy as easy and without an undue sense of exertion. This fact cheered him up. But still he could not find an idea for his head. Not what one could call a real idea. It wouldn't come. It was no use sitting there.

He got up and after a few strides came to a stony ridge from which he could see the two white blunt mastheads of his tartane. Her hull was hidden from him by the formation of the shore, in which the most prominent feature was a big flat piece of rock. That was the spot on which not twelve hours before Peyrol, unable to rest in his bed and coming to seek sleep in his tartane, had seen by moonlight a man standing above his vessel and looking down at her, a characteristic forked black shape that certainly had no business to be there. Peyrol, by a sudden and logical deduction, had said to himself : " Landed from an English boat." Why, how, wherefore, he did not stay to consider. He acted at once like a man accustomed for many years to meet emergencies of the most unexpected kind. The dark figure, lost in a sort of attentive amazement, heard nothing, suspected nothing. The impact of the thick end of the cudgel came down on its head like a thunder-bolt from the blue. The sides of the little basin echoed the crash. But he could not have heard it. The force of the blow flung the senseless body over the edge of the flat rock and down headlong into the open hold of the tartane, which received it with the sound of a muffled drum. Peyrol could not have done the job better at the age of twenty. No. Not so well. There was swiftness, mature judgment—and the sound of the muffled drum was followed by a perfect silence, without a sigh, without a moan. Peyrol ran round a little

promontory to where the shore shelved down to the level
of the tartane's rail and got on board. And still the silence
remained perfect in the cold moonlight and amongst the
deep shadows of the rocks. It remained perfect because
Michel, who always slept under the half-deck forward, being
wakened by the thump which had made the whole tartane
tremble, had lost the power of speech. With his head just
protruding from under the half-deck, arrested on all fours
and shivering violently like a dog that had been washed
with hot water, he was kept from advancing further by his
terror of this bewitched corpse that had come on board
flying through the air. He would not have touched it for
anything.

The " You there, Michel," pronounced in an undertone,
acted like a moral tonic. This then was not the doing of
the Evil One ; it was no sorcery ! And even if it had been,
now that Peyrol was there, Michel had lost all fear. He
ventured not a single question while he helped Peyrol to
turn over the limp body. Its face was covered with blood
from the cut on the forehead which it had got by striking
the sharp edge of the keelson. What accounted for the
head not being completely smashed and for no limbs being
broken was the fact that on its way through the air the
victim of undue curiosity had come in contact with and
had snapped like a carrot one of the foremast shrouds.
Raising his eyes casually, Peyrol noticed the broken rope,
and at once put his hand on the man's breast.

" His heart beats yet," he murmured. " Go and light
the cabin lamp, Michel."

" You going to take that thing into the cabin ? "

" Yes," said Peyrol. " The cabin is used to that kind of
thing," and suddenly he felt very bitter. " It has been a
death-trap for better people than this fellow, whoever
he is."

While Michel was away executing that order Peyrol's eyes
roamed all over the shores of the basin, for he could not
divest himself of the idea that there must be more Englishmen dodging about. That one of the corvette's boats was
still in the cove he had not the slightest doubt. As to the

motive of her coming, it was incomprehensible. Only that senseless form lying at his feet could perhaps have told him : but Peyrol had little hope that it would ever speak again. If his friends started to look for their shipmate there was just a bare chance that they would not discover the existence of the basin. Peyrol stooped and felt the body all over. He found no weapon of any kind on it. There was only a common clasp-knife on a lanyard round its neck.

That soul of obedience, Michel, returning from aft, was directed to throw a couple of bucketfuls of salt water upon the bloody head with its face upturned to the moon. The lowering of the body down into the cabin was a matter of some little difficulty. It was heavy. They laid it full length on a locker, and after Michel with a strange tidiness had arranged its arms along its sides it looked incredibly rigid. The dripping head with soaked hair was like the head of a drowned man with a gaping pink gash on the forehead.

" Go on deck to keep a lookout," said Peyrol. " We may have to fight yet before the night's out."

After Michel left him Peyrol began by flinging off his jacket and, without a pause, dragging his shirt off over his head. It was a very fine shirt. The Brothers of the Coast in their hours of ease were by no means a ragged crowd, and Peyrol the gunner had preserved a taste for fine linen. He tore the shirt into long strips, sat down on the locker and took the wet head on his knees. He bandaged it with some skill, working as calmly as though he had been practising on a dummy. Then the experienced Peyrol sought the lifeless hand and felt the pulse. The spirit had not fled yet. The rover, stripped to the waist, his powerful arms folded on the grizzled pelt of his bare breast, sat gazing down at the inert face in his lap with the eyes closed peacefully under the white band covering the forehead. He contemplated the heavy jaw combined oddly with a certain roundness of cheek, the noticeably broad nose with a sharp tip and a faint dent across the bridge, either natural or the result of some old injury. A face of brown clay, roughly modelled, with a lot of black eyelashes stuck on the closed lids and looking artificially youthful on that physiognomy forty years old or more. And Peyrol thought of his youth. Not his own youth; that he was never anxious to recapture. It was of that man's youth that he thought, of how that face had looked twenty years ago. Suddenly he shifted his position, and putting his lips to the ear of that inanimate head, yelled with all the force of his lungs:

"Hullo! Hullo! Wake up, shipmate."

It seemed enough to wake up the dead. A faint "Voilà! Voilà!" was the answer from a distance, and presently Michel put his head into the cabin with an anxious grin and a gleam in the round eyes.

"You called, maître?"

"Yes," said Peyrol. "Come along and help me to shift him."

"Overboard?" murmured Michel readily.

"No," said Peyrol, "into that bunk. Steady! Don't bang his head," he cried with unexpected tenderness. "Throw a blanket over him. Stay in the cabin and keep his bandages wetted with salt water. I don't think anybody will trouble you to-night. I am going to the house."

"The day is not very far off," remarked Michel.

This was one reason the more why Peyrol was in a hurry to get back to the house and steal up to his room unseen. He drew on his jacket over his bare skin, picked up his cudgel, recommended Michel not to let that strange bird get out of the cabin on any account. As Michel was convinced that the man would never walk again in his life, he received those instructions without particular emotion.

The dawn had broken some time before Peyrol, on his way up to Escampobar happened to look round and had the luck to actually see with his own eyes the English man-of-war's boat pulling out of the cove. This confirmed his surmises but did not enlighten him a bit as to the causes. Puzzled and uneasy, he approached the house through the farmyard. Catherine, always the first up, stood at the open kitchen door. She moved aside and would have let him pass without remark, if Peyrol himself had not asked in a whisper: "Anything new?" She answered him in the same tone: "She has taken to roaming at night." Peyrol stole silently up to his bedroom, from which he descended an hour later as though he had spent all the night in his bed up there.

It was this nocturnal adventure which had affected the character of Peyrol's forenoon talk with the lieutenant. What with one thing and another, he found it very trying. Now that he had got rid of Réal for several hours, the rover had to turn his attention to that other invader of the strained, questionable, and ominous in its origins, peace of the Escampobar Farm. As he sat on the flat rock with his eyes fixed idly on the few drops of blood betraying his last night's work to the high heaven, and trying to get hold of something definite that he could think about, Peyrol became aware of a faint thundering noise. Faint as it was, it filled the whole basin. He soon guessed its nature, and his face lost its perplexity. He picked up his cudgel, got on his feet briskly, muttering to himself, "He's anything but dead," and hurried on board the tartane.

On the after-deck Michel was keeping a lookout. He had carried out the orders he had received by the well. Besides being secured by the very obvious padlock, the cabin door was shored up by a spar which made it stand as firm as a rock. The thundering noise seemed to issue from its immovable substance magically. It ceased for a moment, and a sort of distracted continuous growling could be heard. Then the thundering began again. Michel reported:

"This is the third time he starts this game."

"Not much strength in this," remarked Peyrol gravely.

"That he can do it at all is a miracle," said Michel, showing a certain excitement. "He stands on the ladder and beats the door with his fists. He is getting better. He began about half an hour after I got back on board. He drummed for a bit and then fell off the ladder. I heard him. I had my ear against the scuttle. He lay there and talked to himself for a long time. Then he went at it again." Peyrol approached the scuttle while Michel added his opinion: "He will go on like that for ever. You can't stop him."

"Easy there," said Peyrol, in a deep authoritative voice. "Time you finish that noise."

These words brought instantly a deathlike silence. Michel ceased to grin. He wondered at the power of these few words of a foreign language.

Peyrol himself smiled faintly. It was ages since he had uttered a sentence of English. He waited complacently until Michel had unbarred and unlocked the door of the cabin. After it was thrown open he boomed out a warning: "Stand clear!" and, turning about, went down with great deliberation, ordering Michel to go forward and keep a lookout.

Down there the man with the bandaged head was hanging on to the table and swearing feebly without intermission. Peyrol, after listening for a time with an air of interested recognition, as one would to a tune heard many years ago, stopped it by a deep-voiced:

"That will do." After a short silence he added: "You look *bien malade, hein*? What you call sick," in a tone which if not tender was certainly not hostile. "We will remedy that."

"Who are you?" asked the prisoner, looking frightened and throwing his arm up quickly to guard his head against the coming blow. But Peyrol's uplifted hand fell only on his shoulder in a hearty slap which made him sit down suddenly on a locker in a partly collapsed attitude and unable to speak. But though very much dazed, he was able to watch Peyrol open a cupboard and produce from there a small demijohn and two tin cups. He took heart to say plaintively: "My throat's like tinder," and then suspiciously: "Was it you who broke my head?"

"It was me," admitted Peyrol, sitting down on the opposite side of the table and leaning back to look at his prisoner comfortably.

"What the devil did you do that for?" inquired the other with a sort of faint fierceness which left Peyrol unmoved.

"Because you put your nose where you no business. Understand? I see you there under the moon, *penché,* eating my tartane with your eyes. You never hear me, hein ? "

" I believe you walked on air. Did you mean to kill me ? "

" Yes, in preference to letting you go and make a story of it on board your cursed corvette."

" Well then, now's your chance to finish me. I am as weak as a kitten."

" How did you say that ? Kitten ? Ha, ha, ha," laughed Peyrol. " You make a nice petit chat." He seized the demijohn by the neck and filled the mugs. " There," he went on, pushing one towards the prisoner—" it's good drink—that."

Symons' state was as though the blow had robbed him of all power of resistance, of all faculty of surprise and generally of all the means by which a man may assert himself, except bitter resentment. His head was aching, it seemed to him enormous, too heavy for his neck and as if full of hot smoke. He took a drink under Peyrol's fixed gaze and with uncertain movements put down the mug. He looked drowsy for a moment. Presently a little colour deepened his bronze ; he hitched himself up on the locker and said in a strong voice :

" You played a damned dirty trick on me. Call yourself a man, walking on air behind a fellow's back and felling him like a bullock."

Peyrol nodded calmly and sipped from his mug.

" If I had met you anywhere else but looking at my tartane I would have done nothing to you. I would have permitted you to go back to your boat. Where was your damned boat ? "

" How can I tell you ? I can't tell where I am. I've never been here before. How long have I been here ? "

" Oh, about fourteen hours," said Peyrol.

" My head feels as if it would fall off if I moved," grumbled the other. . . . " You are a damned bungler, that's what you are."

" What for—bungler ? "

" For not finishing me off at once."

He seized the mug and emptied it down his throat. Peyrol drank too, observing him all the time. He put the mug down with extreme gentleness and said slowly :

"How could I know it was you? I hit hard enough to crack the skull of any other man."

"What do you mean? What do you know about my skull? What are you driving at? I don't know you, you white-headed villain, going about at night knocking people on the head from behind. Did you do for our officer, too?"

"Oh yes! Your officer. What was he up to? What trouble did you people come to make here, anyhow?"

"Do you think they tell a boat's crew? Go and ask our officer. He went up the gully and our coxswain got the jumps. He says to me : 'You are lightfooted, Sam,' says he; 'you just creep round the head of the cove and see if our boat can be seen across from the other side. Well, I couldn't see anything. That was all right. But I thought I would climb a little higher amongst the rocks. . . ."

He paused drowsily.

"That was a silly thing to do," remarked Peyrol in an encouraging voice.

"I would've sooner expected to see an elephant inland than a craft lying in a pool that seemed no bigger than my hand. Could not understand how she got there. Couldn't help going down to find out—and the next thing I knew I was lying on my back with my head tied up, in a bunk in this kennel of a cabin here. Why couldn't you have given me a hail and engaged me properly, yardarm to yardarm? You would have got me all the same, because all I had in the way of weapons was the clasp-knife which you have looted off me."

"Up on the shelf there," said Peyrol, looking round. "No, my friend, I wasn't going to take the risk of seeing you spread your wings and fly."

"You need not have been afraid for your tartane. Our boat was after no tartane. We wouldn't have taken your tartane for a gift. Why, we see them by dozens every day —those tartanes."

Peyrol filled the two mugs again. "Ah," he said, "I

dare say you see many tartanes, but this one is not like the others. You a sailor—and you couldn't see that she was something extraordinary."

"Hellfire and gunpowder!" cried the other. "How can you expect me to have seen anything? I just noticed that her sails were bent before your club hit me on the head." He raised his hands to his head and groaned. "Oh lord, I feel as though I had been drunk for a month."

Peyrol's prisoner did look somewhat as though he had got his head broken in a drunken brawl. But to Peyrol his appearance was not repulsive. The rover preserved a tender memory of his freebooter's life with its lawless spirit and its spacious scene of action, before the change in the state of affairs in the Indian Ocean, the astounding rumours from the outer world, made him reflect on its precarious character. It was true that he had deserted the French flag when quite a youngster; but at that time that flag was white; and now it was a flag of three colours. He had known the practice of liberty, equality and fraternity as understood in the haunts, open or secret, of the Brotherhood of the Coast. So the change, if one could believe what people talked about, could not be very great. The rover had also his own positive notions as to what these three words were worth. Liberty—to hold your own in the world if you could. Equality—yes! But no body of men ever accomplished anything without a chief. All this was worth what it was worth. He regarded fraternity somewhat differently. Of course brothers would quarrel amongst themselves; it was during a fierce quarrel that flamed up suddenly in a company of Brothers that he had received the most dangerous wound of his life. But for that Peyrol nursed no grudge against anybody. In his view the claim of the Brotherhood was a claim for help against the outside world. And here he was sitting opposite a Brother whose head he had broken on sufficient grounds. There he was across the table looking dishevelled and dazed, uncomprehending and aggrieved, and that head of his proved as hard as ages ago when the nickname of Testa Dura had been given to him by a Brother of Italian origin on some occasion or other, some butting match no doubt; just as he, Peyrol himself, was known for a time on both sides of the Mozambique Channel as Poigne-de-Fer, after an incident when in the presence of the Brothers he played at arm's length with the windpipe of an obstreperous negro sorcerer with an enormous girth of chest. The villagers brought out food with alacrity, and the sorcerer was never the same man again. It had been a great display.

Yes, no doubt it was Testa Dura; the young neophyte of the order (where and how picked up Peyrol never heard), strange to the camp, simple-minded and much impressed by the swaggering cosmopolitan company in which he found himself. He had attached himself to Peyrol in preference to some of his own countrymen, of whom there were several in that band, and used to run after him like a little dog and certainly had acted a good shipmate's part on the occasion of that wound, which had neither killed nor cowed Peyrol, but merely had given him an opportunity to reflect at leisure on the conduct of his own life.

The first suspicion of that amazing fact had intruded on Peyrol while he was bandaging that head by the light of the smoky lamp. Since the fellow still lived, it was not in Peyrol to finish him off or let him lie unattended like a dog. And then this was a sailor. His being English was no obstacle to the development of Peyrol's mixed feelings in which hatred certainly had no place. Amongst the members of the Brotherhood it was the Englishmen whom he preferred. He had also found amongst them that particular and loyal appreciation, which a Frenchman of character and ability will receive from Englishmen sooner than from any other nation. Peyrol had at times been a leader, without ever trying for it very much, for he was not ambitious. The lead used to fall to him mostly at a time of crisis of some sort; and when he had got the lead it was on the Englishmen that he used to depend most.

And so that youngster had turned into this English man-of-war's man! In the fact itself there was nothing impossible. You found Brothers of the Coast in all sorts of ships and in all sorts of places. Peyrol had found one once

in a very ancient and hopeless cripple practising the pro-
fession of a beggar on the steps of Manila cathedral, and
had left him the richer by two broad gold pieces to add to
his secret hoard. There was a tale of a Brother of the
Coast having become a mandarin in China, and Peyrol
believed it. One never knew where and in what position
one would find a Brother of the Coast. The wonderful
thing was that this one should have come to seek him out,
to put himself in the way of his cudgel. Peyrol's greatest
concern had been all through that Sunday morning to conceal the whole adventure from Lieutenant Réal. As against
a wearer of epaulettes, mutual protection was the first duty
between Brothers of the Coast. The unexpectedness of
that claim coming to him after twenty years invested it with
an extraordinary strength. What he would do with the
fellow he didn't know. But since that morning the situation
had changed. Peyrol had received the lieutenant's confidence and had got on terms with him in a special way.
He fell into profound thought.

"Sacrèe tête dure," he muttered without rousing himself. Peyrol was annoyed a little at not having been recognized. He could not conceive how difficult it would have
been for Symons to identify this portly deliberate person
with a white head of hair as the object of his youthful
admiration, the black-ringletted French Brother in the
prime of life of whom everybody thought so much. Peyrol
was roused by hearing the other declare suddenly :

"I am an Englishman, I am. I am not going to knuckle
under to anybody. What are you going to do with me ? "

"I will do what I please," said Peyrol, who had been
asking himself exactly the same question.

"Well, then, be quick about it, whatever it is. I don't
care a damn what you do, but—be—quick—about it."

He tried to be emphatic ; but as a matter of fact the last
words came out in a faltering tone. And old Peyrol was
touched. He thought that if he were to let him drink the
mugful standing there, it would make him dead drunk.
But he took the risk. So he said only :

"Allons—drink ! " The other did not wait for a second

invitation but could not control very well the movements
of his arm extended towards the mug. Peyrol raised his
on high.

"Trinquons, eh?" he proposed. But in his precarious
condition the Englishman remained unforgiving.

"I'm damned if I do," he said indignantly, but so low
that Peyrol had to turn his ear to catch the words. "You
will have to explain to me first what you meant by knocking
me on the head."

He drank, staring all the time at Peyrol in a manner which
was meant to give offence but which struck Peyrol as so
childlike that he burst into a laugh.

"Sacré imbécile, Va! Did I not tell you it was because
of the tartane? If it hadn't been for the tartane I would
have hidden from you. I would have crouched behind a
bush like a—what do you call them?—liévre."

The other, who was feeling the effect of the drink, stared
with frank incredulity.

"You are of no account," continued Peyrol. "Ah! if
you had been an officer I would have gone for you anywhere.
Did you say your officer went up the gully?"

Symons sighed deeply and easily. "That's the way he
went. We had heard on board of a house thereabouts."

"Oh, he went to the house!" said Peyrol. "Well, if
he did get there he must be very sorry for himself. There
is half a company of infantry billeted in the farm."

This inspired fib went down easily with the English sailor.
Soldiers were stationed in many parts of the coast as any
seaman of the blockading fleet knew very well. To the
many expressions which had passed over the face of that man
recovering from a long period of unconsciousness there was
added the shade of dismay.

"What the devil have they stuck soldiers on this piece
of rock for?" he asked.

"Oh, signalling post and things like that. I am not
likely to tell you everything. Why! you might escape."

That phrase reached the soberest spot in the whole of
Symons' individuality. Things were happening, then. Mr.
Bolt was a prisoner. But the main idea evoked in his con-

fused mind was that he would be given up to those soldiers before very long. The prospect of captivity made his heart sink, and he resolved to give as much trouble as he could.

"You will have to get some of these soldiers to carry me up. I won't walk. I won't. Not after having had my brains nearly knocked out from behind. I tell you straight! I won't walk. Not a step. They will have to carry me ashore."

Peyrol only shook his head deprecatingly.

"Now you go and get a corporal with a file of men," insisted Symons obstinately. "I want to be made a proper prisoner of. Who the devil are you? You had no right to interfere. I believe you are a civilian. A common marinero, whatever you may call yourself. You look to me a pretty fishy marinero at that. Where did you learn English? In prison—eh? You ain't going to keep me in this damned dog-hole, on board your rubbishy tartane. Go and get that corporal, I tell you."

He looked suddenly very tired and only murmured: "I am an Englishman, I am."

Peyrol's patience was positively angelic.

"Don't you talk about the tartane," he said impressively, making his words as distinct as possible. "I told you she was not like the other tartanes. That is because she is a courier boat. Every time she goes to sea she makes a pied-de-nez, what you call thumb to the nose, to all your English cruisers. I do not mind telling you because you are my prisoner. You will soon learn French now."

"Who are you? The caretaker of this thing or what?" asked the undaunted Symons. But Peyrol's mysterious silence seemed to intimidate him at last. He became dejected and began to curse in a languid tone all boat expeditions, the coxswain of the gig and his own infernal luck.

Peyrol sat alert and attentive like a man interested in an experiment, while after a moment Symons' face began to look as if he had been hit with a club again, but not as hard as before. A film came over his round eyes and the words "fishy marinero" made their way out of his lips in a sort of death-bed voice. Yet such was the hardness of his head that he actually rallied enough to address Peyrol in an ingratiating tone.

"Come, grandfather!" He tried to push the mug across the table, and upset it. "Come! Let us finish what's in that tiny bottle of yours."

"No," said Peyrol, drawing the demijohn to his side of the table and putting the cork in.

"No?" repeated Symons in an unbelieving voice and looking at the demijohn fixedly . . . "you must be a tinker." . . . He tried to say something more under Peyrol's watchful eyes, failed once or twice, and suddenly pronounced the word "cochon" so correctly as to make old Peyrol start. After that it was no use looking at him any more. Peyrol busied himself in locking up the demijohn and the mugs. When he turned round most of the prisoner's body was extended over the table and no sound came from it, not even a snore.

When Peyrol got outside, pulling to the door of the cuddy behind him, Michel hastened from forward to receive the master's orders. But Peyrol stood so long on the after-deck meditating profoundly with his hand over his mouth that Michel became fidgety and ventured a cheerful: "It looks as if he were not going to die."

"He is dead," said Peyrol with grim jocularity. "Dead drunk. And you very likely will not see me till to-morrow sometime."

"But what am I to do?" asked Michel timidly.

"Nothing," said Peyrol. "Of course you must not let him set fire to the tartane."

"But suppose," insisted Michel, "he should give signs of escaping."

"If you see him trying to escape," said Peyrol with mock solemnity, "then, Michel, it will be a sign for you to get out of his way as quickly as you can. A man who would try to escape with a head like this on him would just swallow you at one mouthful."

He picked up his cudgel and, stepping ashore, went off without as much as a look at his faithful henchman. Michel listened to him scrambling amongst the stones, and his habitual amiably vacant face acquired a sort of dignity from the utter and absolute blankness that came over it.


# X

It was only after reaching the level ground in front of the farmhouse that Peyrol took time to pause and resume his contact with the exterior world.

While he had been closeted with his prisoner the sky had got covered with a thin layer of cloud, in one of those swift changes of weather that are not unusual in the Mediterranean. This grey vapour, drifting high up, close against the disc of the sun, seemed to enlarge the space behind its veil, add to the vastness of a shadowless world no longer hard and brilliant but all softened in the contours of its masses and in the faint line of the horizon, as if ready to dissolve in the immensity of the infinite.

Familiar and indifferent to his eyes, material and shadowy, the extent of the changeable sea had gone pale under the pale sun in a mysterious and emotional response. Mysterious too was the great oval patch of dark water to the west; and also a broad blue lane traced on the dull silver of the waters in a parabolic curve described magistrally by an invisible finger for a symbol of endless wandering. The face of the farmhouse might have been the face of a house from which all the inhabitants had fled suddenly. In the high part of the building the window of the lieutenant's room remained open, both glass and shutter. By the door of the salle the stable fork leaning against the wall seemed to have been forgotten by the sans-culotte. This aspect of abandonment struck Peyrol with more force than usual. He had been thinking so hard of all these people, that to find no one about seemed unnatural and even depressing. He had seen many abandoned places in his life, grass huts, mud forts, kings' palaces—temples from which every white-robed soul had fled. Temples, however, never looked quite empty.

The gods clung to their own. Peyrol's eyes rested on the bench against the wall of the salle. In the usual course of things it should have been occupied by the lieutenant, who had the habit of sitting there with hardly a movement, for hours, like a spider watching for the coming of a fly. This paralysing comparison held Peyrol motionless with a twisted mouth and a frown on his brow, before the evoked vision, coloured and precise, of the man, more troubling than the reality had ever been.

He came to himself with a start. What sort of occupation was this, 'crè nom de nom, staring at a silly bench with no one on it? Was he going wrong in his head? Or was it that he was getting really old? He had noticed old men losing themselves like that. But he had something to do. First of all he had to go and see what the English sloop in the Passe was doing.

While he was making his way towards the lookout on the hill where the inclined pine hung peering over the cliff as if an insatiable curiosity were holding it in that precarious position, Peyrol had another view from above of the farmyard and of the buildings and was again affected by their deserted appearance. Not a soul, not even an animal seemed to have been left; only on the roofs the pigeons walked with a smart elegance. Peyrol hurried on and presently saw the English ship well over on the Porquerolles side with her yards braced up and her head to the southward. There was a little wind in the Passe, while the dull silver of the open had a darkling rim of rippled water far away to the east in that quarter where, far or near, but mostly out of sight, the British fleet kept its endless watch. Not a shadow of a spar or gleam of sail on the horizon betrayed its presence; but Peyrol would not have been surprised to see a crowd of ships surge up, people the horizon with hostile life, come in running, and dot the sea with their ordered groups all about Cape Cicié, parading their damned impudence. Then indeed that corvette, the big factor of everyday life on that stretch of coast, would become very small potatoes indeed; and the man in command of her (he had been Peyrol's personal adversary in many

imaginary encounters fought to a finish in the room upstairs)
—then indeed that Englishman would have to mind his
steps. He would be ordered to come within hail of the
admiral, be sent here and there, made to run like a little
dog and as likely as not get called on board the flagship and
get a dressing down for something or other.

Peyrol thought for a moment that the impudence of this
Englishman was going to take the form of running along
the peninsula and looking into the very cove; for the
corvette's head was falling off slowly. A fear for his tartane
clutched Peyrol's heart till he remembered that the Englishman did not know of her existence. Of course not. His
cudgel had been absolutely effective in stopping that bit of
information. The only Englishman who knew of the existence of the tartane was that fellow with the broken head.
Peyrol actually laughed at his momentary scare. Moreover, it was evident that the Englishman did not mean to
parade in front of the peninsula. He did not mean to be
impudent. The sloop's yards were swung right round and
she came again to the wind but now heading to the northward back from where she came. Peyrol saw at once that
the Englishman meant to pass to windward of Cape Esterel,
probably with the intention of anchoring for the night off
the long white beach which in a regular curve closes the
roadstead of Hyères on that side.

Peyrol pictured her to himself, on the clouded night, not
so very dark, since the full moon was but a day old, lying
at anchor within hail of the low shore, with her sails furled
and looking profoundly asleep, but with the watch on deck
lying by the guns. He gnashed his teeth. It had come to
this at last, that the captain of the *Amelia* could do nothing
with his ship without putting Peyrol into a rage. Oh, for
forty Brothers, or sixty, picked ones, he thought, to teach
the fellow what it might cost him taking liberties along the
French coast! Ships had been carried by surprise before,
on nights when there was just light enough to see the whites
of each other's eyes in a close tussle. And what would be
the crew of that Englishman? Something between ninety
and a hundred altogether, boys and landsmen included.

F F

. . . Peyrol shook his fist for a good-bye, just when Cape Esterel shut off the English sloop from his sight. But in his heart of hearts that seaman of cosmopolitan associations knew very well that no forty or sixty, not any given hundred Brothers of the Coast would have been enough to capture that corvette making herself at home within ten miles of where he had first opened his eyes to the world.

He shook his head dismally at the leaning pine, his only companion. The disinherited soul of that rover ranging for so many years a lawless ocean with the coasts of two continents for a raiding ground, had come back to its crag, circling like a seabird in the dusk and longing for a great sea victory for its people : that inland multitude of which Peyrol knew nothing except the few individuals on that peninsula cut off from the rest of the land by the dead water of a salt lagoon : and where only a strain of manliness in a miserable cripple and an unaccountable charm of a half-crazed woman had found response in his heart.

This scheme of false dispatches was but a detail in a plan for a great, a destructive victory. Just a detail, but not a trifle all the same. Nothing connected with the deception of an admiral could be called trifling. And such an admiral too. It was, Peyrol felt vaguely, a scheme that only a confounded landsman would invent. It behoved the sailors, however, to make a workable thing of it. It would have to be worked through that corvette.

And here Peyrol was brought up by the question that all his life had not been able to settle for him—and that was whether the English were really very stupid or very acute. That difficulty had presented itself with every fresh case. The old rover had enough genius in him to have arrived at a general conclusion that if they were to be deceived at all it could not be done very well by words but rather by deeds ; not by mere wriggling, but by deep craft concealed under some sort of straightforward action. That conviction, however, did not take him forward in this case, which was one in which much thinking would be necessary.

The *Amelia* had disappeared behind Cape Esterel, and Peyrol wondered with a certain anxiety whether this meant that the Englishman had given up his man for good. " If he has," said Peyrol to himself, " I am bound to see him pass out again from beyond Cape Esterel before it gets dark." If, however, he did not see the ship again within the next hour or two, then she would be anchored off the beach, to wait for the night before making some attempt to discover what had become of her man. This could be done only by sending out one or two boats to explore the coast, and no doubt to enter the cove—perhaps even to land a small search party.

After coming to this conclusion Peyrol began deliberately to charge his pipe. Had he spared a moment for a glance inland, he might have caught a whisk of a black skirt, the gleam of a white fichu—Arlette running down the faint track leading from Escampobar to the village in the hollow; the same track in fact up which Citizen Scevola, while indulging in the strange freak to visit the church, had been chased by the incensed faithful. But Peyrol, while charging and lighting his pipe, had kept his eyes fastened on Cape Esterel. Then, throwing his arm affectionately over the trunk of the pine, he had settled himself to watch. Far below him the roadstead, with its play of grey and bright gleams, looked like a plaque of mother-of-pearl in a frame of yellow rocks and dark green ravines set off inland by the masses of the hills displaying the tint of the finest purple; while above his head the sun behind a cloud-veil hung like a silver disc.

That afternoon, after waiting in vain for Lieutenant Réal to appear outside in the usual way, Arlette, the mistress of Escampobar, had gone unwillingly into the kitchen where Catherine sat upright in a heavy capacious wooden arm-chair, the back of which rose above the top of her white muslin cap. Even in her old age, even in her hours of ease, Catherine preserved the upright carriage of the family that had held Escampobar for so many generations. It would have been easy to believe that like some characters famous in the world Catherine would have wished to die standing up and with unbowed shoulders.

With her sense of hearing undecayed she detected the

light footsteps in the salle long before Arlette entered the
kitchen. That woman, who had faced alone and unaided
(except for her brother's comprehending silence) the anguish
of passion in a forbidden love, and of terrors comparable to
those of the Judgment Day, neither turned her face, quiet
without serenity, nor her eyes, fearless but without fire, in
the direction of her niece.

Arlette glanced on all sides, even at the walls, even at the
mound of ashes under the big overmantel, nursing in its
heart a spark of fire, before she sat down and leaned her
elbow on the table.

"You wander about like a soul in pain," said her aunt,
sitting by the hearth like an old queen on her throne.

"And you sit here eating your heart out."

"Formerly," remarked Catherine, "old women like me
could always go over their prayers, but now . . ."

"I believe you have not been to church for years. I
remember Scevola telling me that a long time ago. Was it
because you didn't like people's eyes? I have fancied sometimes that most people in the world must have been massacred
long ago."

Catherine turned her face away. Arlette rested her head
on her half-closed hand, and her eyes, losing their steadiness,
began to tremble amongst cruel visions. She got up suddenly
and caressed the thin, half-averted, withered cheek with the
tips of her fingers, and in a low voice, with that marvellous
cadence that plucked at one's heart-strings, she said coaxingly:

"Those were dreams, weren't they?"

In her immobility the old woman called with all the
might of her will for the presence of Peyrol. She had never
been able to shake off a superstitious fear of that niece
restored to her from the terrors of a Judgment Day in
which the world had been given over to the devils. She
was always afraid that this girl, wandering about with restless eyes and a dim smile on her silent lips, would suddenly
say something atrocious, unfit to be heard, calling for vengeance from heaven, unless Peyrol were by. That stranger
come from "par delà les mers" was out of it altogether,
cared probably for no one in the world but had struck her

imagination by his massive aspect, his deliberation suggesting a mighty force like the reposeful attitude of a lion. Arlette desisted from caressing the irresponsive cheek, exclaimed petulantly, " I am awake now ! " and went out of the kitchen without having asked her aunt the question she had meant to ask, which was whether she knew what had become of the lieutenant.

Her heart had failed her. She let herself drop on the bench outside the door of the salle. " What is the matter with them all ? " she thought. " I can't make them out. What wonder is it that I have not been able to sleep ? " Even Peyrol, so different from all mankind, who from the first moment when he stood before her had the power to soothe her aimless unrest, even Peyrol would now sit for hours with the lieutenant on the bench, gazing into the air and keeping him in talk about things without sense, as if on purpose to prevent him from thinking of her. Well, he could not do that. But the enormous change implied in the fact that every day had a to-morrow now, and that all the people around her had ceased to be mere phantoms for her wandering glances to glide over without concern, made her feel the need of support from somebody, from somewhere. She could have cried aloud for it.

She sprang up and walked along the whole front of the farm building. At the end of the wall enclosing the orchard she called out in a modulated undertone : " Eugène," not because she hoped that the lieutenant was anywhere within earshot, but for the pleasure of hearing the sound of the name uttered for once above a whisper. She turned about and at the end of the wall on the yard side she repeated her call, drinking in the sound that came from her lips, " Eugène, Eugène," with a sort of half-exulting despair. It was in such dizzy moments that she wanted a steadying support. But all was still. She heard no friendly murmur, not even a sigh. Above her head under the thin grey sky a big mulberry-tree stirred no leaf. Step by step, as if unconsciously, she began to move down the track. At the end of fifty yards she opened the inland view, the roofs of the village between the green tops of the platanes overshadowing the fountain, and just beyond the flat blue-grey level of the salt lagoon, smooth and dull like a slab of lead. But what drew her on was the church-tower, where, in a round arch, she could see the black speck of the bell which, escaping the requisitions of the Republican wars, and dwelling mute above the locked-up empty church, had only lately recovered its voice. She ran on, but when she had come near enough to make out the figures moving about the village fountain, she checked herself, hesitated a moment and then took the footpath leading to the presbytery.

She pushed open the little gate with the broken latch. The humble building of rough stones, from between which much mortar had crumbled out, looked as though it had been sinking slowly into the ground. The beds of the plot in front were choked with weeds, because the abbé had no taste for gardening. When the heiress of Escampobar opened the door, he was walking up and down the largest room which was his bedroom and sitting-room and where he also took his meals. He was a gaunt man with a long, as if convulsed, face. In his young days he had been tutor to the sons of a great noble, but he did not emigrate with his employer. Neither did he submit to the Republic. He had lived in his native land like a hunted wild beast, and there had been many tales of his activities, warlike and others. When the hierarchy was re-established he found no favour in the eyes of his superiors. He had remained too much of a royalist. He had accepted, without a word, the charge of this miserable parish, where he had acquired influence quickly enough. His sacerdotalism lay in him like a cold passion. Though accessible enough, he never walked abroad without his breviary, acknowledging the solemnly bared heads by a curt nod. He was not exactly feared, but some of the oldest inhabitants who remembered the previous incumbent, an old man who died in the garden after having been dragged out of bed by some patriots anxious to take him to prison in Hyères, jerked their heads sideways in a knowing manner when their curé was mentioned.

On seeing this apparition in an Arlesian cap and silk skirt, a white fichu, and otherwise as completely different as any princess could be from the rustics with whom he was in daily contact, his face expressed the blankest astonishment. Then—for he knew enough of the gossip of his community —his straight, thick eyebrows came together inimically. This was no doubt the woman of whom he had heard his parishioners talk with bated breath as having given herself and her property up to a Jacobin, a Toulon sans-culotte who had either delivered her parents to execution or had murdered them himself during the first three days of massacres. No one was very sure which it was, but the rest was current knowledge. The abbé, though persuaded that any amount of moral turpitude was possible in a godless country, had not accepted all that tale literally. No doubt those people were Republican and impious, and the state of affairs up there was scandalous and horrible. He struggled with his feelings of repulsion and managed to smooth his brow and waited. He could not imagine what that woman with mature form and a youthful face could want at the presbytery. Suddenly it occurred to him that perhaps she wanted to thank him—it was a very old occurrence—for interposing between the fury of the villagers and that man. He couldn't call him, even in his thoughts, her husband, for apart from all other circumstances, that connection could not imply any kind of marriage to a priest, had even there been a legal form observed. His visitor was apparently disconcerted by the expression of his face, the austere aloofness of his attitude, and only a low murmur escaped her lips. He bent his head and was not very certain what he had heard.

"You come to seek my aid?" he asked in a doubting tone.

She nodded slightly, and the abbé went to the door she had left half open and looked out. There was not a soul in sight between the presbytery and the village, or between the presbytery and the church. He went back to face her, saying:

"We are as alone as we can well be. The old woman in the kitchen is as deaf as a post."

Now that he had been looking at Arlette closer the abbé

felt a sort of dread. The carmine of those lips, the pellucid, unstained, unfathomable blackness of those eyes, the pallor of her cheeks, suggested to him something provokingly pagan, something distastefully different from the common sinners of this earth. And now she was ready to speak. He arrested her with a raised hand.

"Wait," he said. "I have never seen you before. I don't even know properly who you are. None of you belong to my flock—for you are from Escampobar, are you not?" Sombre under their bony arches, his eyes fastened on her face, noticed the delicacy of features, the naïve pertinacity of her stare. She said:

"I am the daughter."

"The daughter! . . . Oh! I see. . . . Much evil is spoken of you."

She said a little impatiently: "By that rabble?" and the priest remained mute for a moment. "What do they say? In my father's time they wouldn't have dared to say anything. The only thing I saw of them for years and years was when they were yelping like curs on the heels of Scevola."

The absence of scorn in her tone was perfectly annihilating. Gentle sounds flowed from her lips and a disturbing charm from her strange equanimity. The abbé frowned heavily at these fascinations, which seemed to have in them something diabolic.

"They are simple souls, neglected, fallen back into darkness. It isn't their fault. But they have natural feelings of humanity which were outraged. I saved him from their indignation. There are things that must be left to divine justice."

He was exasperated by the unconsciousness of that fair face.

"That man whose name you have just pronounced and which I have heard coupled with the epithet of blood-drinker is regarded as the master of Escampobar Farm. He has been living there for years. How is that?"

"Yes, it is a long time ago since he brought me back to the house. Years ago. Catherine let him stay."

"Who is Catherine?" the abbé asked harshly.

"She is my father's sister who was left at home to wait. She had given up all hope of seeing any of us again, when one morning Scevola came with me to the door. Then she let him stay. He is a poor creature. What else could Catherine have done? And what is it to us up there how the people in the village regard him?" She dropped her eyes and seemed to fall into deep thought, then added, "It was only later that I discovered that he was a poor creature, even quite lately. They call him blood-drinker, do they? What of that? All the time he was afraid of his own shadow."

She ceased but did not raise her eyes.

"You are no longer a child," began the abbé in a severe voice, frowning at her downcast eyes, and he heard a murmur: "Not very long." He disregarded it and continued: "I ask you, is this all that you have to tell me about that man? I hope that at least you are no hypocrite."

"Monsieur l'Abbé," she said, raising her eyes fearlessly, "what more am I to tell you about him? I can tell you things that will make your hair stand on end, but it wouldn't be about him."

For all answer the abbé made a weary gesture and turned away to walk up and down the room. His face expressed neither curiosity nor pity, but a sort of repugnance which he made an effort to overcome. He dropped into a deep and shabby old arm-chair, the only object of luxury in the room, and pointed to a wooden straight-backed stool. Arlette sat down on it and began to speak. The abbé listened, but looking far away; his big bony hands rested on the arms of the chair. After the first words he interrupted her: "This is your own story you are telling me?"

"Yes," said Arlette.

"Is it necessary that I should know?"

"Yes, Monsieur l'Abbé."

"But why?"

He bent his head a little, without, however, ceasing to look far away. Her voice now was very low. Suddenly the abbé threw himself back.

F F 2

"You want to tell me your story because you have fallen in love with a man?"

"No, because that has brought me back to myself. Nothing else could have done it."

He turned his head to look at her grimly, but he said nothing and looked away again. He listened. At the beginning he muttered once or twice, "Yes, I have heard that," and then kept silent, not looking at her at all. Once he interrupted her by a question: "You were confirmed before the convent was forcibly entered and the nuns dispersed?"

"Yes," she said, "a year before that or more."

"And then two of those ladies took you with them towards Toulon."

"Yes, the other girls had their relations near by. They took me with them thinking to communicate with my parents, but it was difficult. Then the English came and my parents sailed over to try and get some news of me. It was safe for my father to be in Toulon then. Perhaps you think that he was a traitor to his country?" she asked, and waited with parted lips. With an impassible face the abbé murmured: "He was a good royalist," in a tone of bitter fatalism, which seemed to absolve that man and all the other men of whose actions and errors he had ever heard.

For a long time, Arlette continued, her father could not discover the house where the nuns had taken refuge. He only obtained some information on the very day before the English evacuated Toulon. Late in the day he appeared before her and took her away. The town was full of retreating foreign troops. Her father left her with her mother and went out again to make preparations for sailing home that very night; but the tartane was no longer in the place where he had left her lying. The two Madrague men that he had for a crew had disappeared also. Thus the family was trapped in that town full of tumult and confusion. Ships and houses were bursting into flames. Appalling explosions of gunpowder shook the earth. She spent that night on her knees with her face hidden in her mother's

lap, while her father kept watch by the barricaded door
with a pistol in each hand.

In the morning the house was filled with savage yells.
People were heard rushing up the stairs, and the door was
burst in. She jumped up at the crash and flung herself
down on her knees in a corner with her face to the wall.
There was a murderous uproar, she heard two shots fired,
then somebody seized her by the arm and pulled her up to
her feet. It was Scevola. He dragged her to the door.
The bodies of her father and mother were lying across the
doorway. The room was full of gunpowder smoke. She
wanted to fling herself on the bodies and cling to them, but
Scevola took her under the arms and lifted her over them.
He seized her hand and made her run with him, or rather
dragged her downstairs. Outside on the pavement some
dreadful men and many fierce women with knives joined
them. They ran along the streets brandishing pikes and
sabres, pursuing other groups of unarmed people, who fled
round corners with loud shrieks.

"I ran in the midst of them, Monsieur l'Abbé," Arlette
went on in a breathless murmur. "Whenever I saw any
water I wanted to throw myself into it, but I was surrounded
on all sides, I was jostled and pushed and most of the time
Scevola held my hand very tight. When they stopped at
a wine shop they would offer me some wine. My tongue
stuck to the roof of my mouth and I drank. The wine,
the pavements, the arms and faces, everything was red. I
had red splashes all over me. I had to run with them all
day, and all the time I felt as if I were falling down, and
down, and down. The houses were nodding at me. The
sun would go out at times. And suddenly I heard myself
yelling exactly like the others. Do you understand, Monsieur
l'Abbé? The very same words!"

The eyes of the priest in their deep orbits glided towards
her and then resumed their far-away fixity. Between his
fatalism and his faith he was not very far from the belief of
Satan taking possession of rebellious mankind, exposing the
nakedness of hearts like flint and of the homicidal souls of
the Revolution.

"I have heard something of that," he whispered stealthily.
She affirmed with quiet earnestness: "Yet at that time
I resisted with all my might."

That night Scevola put her under the care of a woman
called Perose. She was young and pretty, and was a native
of Arles, her mother's country. She kept an inn. That
woman locked her up in her own room, which was next to
the room where the patriots kept on shouting, singing and
making speeches far into the night. Several times the
woman would look in for a moment, make a hopeless gesture
at her with both arms, and vanish again. Later, on many
other nights, when all the band lay asleep on benches and
on the floor, Perose would steal into the room, fall on her
knees by the bed on which Arlette sat upright, open-eyed
and raving silently to herself, embrace her feet and cry
herself to sleep. But in the morning she would jump up
briskly and say: "Come. The great affair is to keep our
life in our bodies. Come along to help in the work of
justice"; and they would join the band that was making
ready for another day of traitor-hunting. But after a time
the victims, of which the streets were full at first, had to be
sought for in back yards, ferreted out of their hiding-places,
dragged up out of the cellars or down from the garrets of
the houses, which would be entered by the band with howls
of death and vengeance.

"Then, Monsieur l'Abbé," said Arlette, "I let myself
go at last. I could resist no longer. I said to myself: 'If
it is so then it must be right.' But most of the time I was
like a person half asleep and dreaming things that it is
impossible to believe. About that time, I don't know why,
the woman Perose hinted to me that Scevola was a poor
creature. Next night, while all the band lay fast asleep in
the big room, Perose and Scevola helped me out of the
window into the street and led me to the quay behind the
arsenal. Scevola had found our tartane lying at the pontoon
and one of the Madrague men with her. The other had
disappeared. Perose fell on my neck and cried a little.
She gave me a kiss and said: 'My time will come soon.
You, Scevola, don't you show yourself in Toulon, because

nobody believes in you any more. Adieu, Arlette. Vive la Nation!' and she vanished in the night. I waited on the pontoon shivering in my torn clothes, listening to Scevola and the man throwing dead bodies overboard out of the tartane. Splash, splash, splash. And suddenly I felt I must run away, but they were after me in a moment, dragged me back and threw me down into that cabin which smelt of blood. But when I got back to the farm all feeling had left me. I did not feel myself exist. I saw things round me here and there, but I couldn't look at anything for long. Something was gone out of me. I know now that it was not my heart, but then I didn't mind what it was. I felt light and empty, and a little cold all the time, but I could smile at people. Nothing could matter. Nothing could mean anything. I cared for no one. I wanted nothing. I wasn't alive at all, Monsieur l'Abbé. People seemed to see me and would talk to me, and it seemed funny —till one day I felt my heart beat."

"Why precisely did you come to me with this tale?" asked the abbé in a low voice.

"Because you are a priest. Have you forgotten that I have been brought up in a convent? I have not forgotten how to pray. But I am afraid of the world now. What must I do?"

"Repent!" thundered the abbé, getting up. He saw her candid gaze uplifted, and lowered his voice forcibly. "You must look with fearless sincerity into the darkness of your soul. Remember whence the only true help can come. Those whom God has visited by a trial such as yours cannot be held guiltless of their enormities. Withdraw from the world. Descend within yourself and abandon the vain thoughts of what people call happiness. Be an example to yourself of the sinfulness of our nature and of the weakness of our humanity. You may have been possessed. What do I know? Perhaps it was permitted in order to lead your soul to saintliness through a life of seclusion and prayer. To that it would be my duty to help you. Meantime you must pray to be given strength for a complete renunciation."

Arlette, lowering her eyes slowly, appealed to the abbé as a symbolic figure of spiritual mystery. " What can be God's designs on this creature ? " he asked himself.

" Monsieur le Curé," she said quietly, " I felt the need to pray to-day for the first time in many years. When I left home it was only to go to your church."

" The church stands open to the worst of sinners," said the abbé.

" I know. But I would have had to pass before all those villagers : and you, Abbé, know well what they are capable of."

" Perhaps," murmured the abbé, " it would be better not to put their charity to the test."

" I must pray before I go back again. I thought you would let me come in through the sacristy."

" It would be inhuman to refuse your request," he said, rousing himself and taking down a key that hung on the wall. He put on his broad-brimmed hat and without a word led the way through the wicket-gate and along the path which he always used himself and which was out of sight of the village fountain. After they had entered the damp and dilapidated sacristy he locked the door behind them and only then opened another, a smaller one, leading into the church. When he stood aside, Arlette became aware of the chilly odour as of freshly turned-up earth mingled with a faint scent of incense. In the deep dusk of the nave a single little flame glimmered before an image of the Virgin. The abbé whispered as she passed on :

" There before the great altar abase yourself and pray for grace and strength and mercy in this world full of crimes against God and men."

She did not look at him. Through the thin soles of her shoes she could feel the chill of the flagstones. The abbé left the door ajar, sat down on a rush-bottomed chair, the only one in the sacristy, folded his arms and let his chin fall on his breast. He seemed to be sleeping profoundly, but at the end of half an hour he got up and, going to the door-way, stood looking at the kneeling figure sunk low on the altar steps. Arlette's face was buried in her hands in a passion of piety and prayer. The abbé waited patiently for a good many minutes more, before he raised his voice in a grave murmur which filled the whole dark place.

"It is time for you to leave. I am going to ring for vespers."

The view of her complete absorption before the Most High had touched him. He stepped back into the sacristy and after a time heard the faintest possible swish of the black silk skirt of the Escampobar daughter in her Arlesian costume. She entered the sacristy lightly with shining eyes, and the abbé looked at her with some emotion.

"You have prayed well, my daughter," he said. "No forgiveness will be refused to you, for you have suffered much. Put your trust in the grace of God."

She raised her head and stayed her footsteps for a moment. In the dark little place he could see the gleam of her eyes swimming in tears.

"Yes, Monsieur l'Abbé," she said in her clear seductive voice. "I have prayed and I feel answered. I entreated the merciful God to keep the heart of the man I love always true to me or else to let me die before I set my eyes on him again."

The abbé paled under his tan of a village priest and leaned his shoulders against the wall without a word.

## XI

AFTER leaving the church by the sacristy door Arlette never looked back. The abbé saw her flit past the presbytery, and the building hid her from his sight. He did not accuse her of duplicity. He had deceived himself. A heathen. White as her skin was, the blackness of her hair and of her eyes, the dusky red of her lips, suggested a strain of Saracen blood. He gave her up without a sigh.

Arlette walked rapidly towards Escampobar as if she could not get there soon enough; but as she neared the first enclosed field her steps became slower, and after hesitating

awhile she sat down between two olive trees, near a wall
bordered by a growth of thin grass at the foot. " And if I
have been possessed," she argued to herself, " as the abbé
said, what is it to me as I am now ? That evil spirit cast
my true self out of my body and then cast away the body
too. For years I have been living empty. There has been
no meaning in anything."

But now her true self had returned matured in its mysterious exile, hopeful and eager for love. She was certain
that it had never been far away from that outcast body
which Catherine had told her lately was fit for no man's
arms. That was all that old woman knew about it, thought
Arlette, not in scorn but rather in pity. She knew better,
she had gone to heaven for truth in that long prostration with
its ardent prayers and its moment of ecstasy, before an
unlighted altar.

She knew its meaning well, and also the meaning of
another—of a terrestrial revelation which had come to her
that day at noon while she waited on the lieutenant. Everybody else was in the kitchen ; she and Réal were as much
alone together as had ever happened to them in their lives.
That day she could not deny herself the delight to be near
him, to watch him covertly, to hear him perhaps utter a
few words, to experience that strange satisfying consciousness
of her own existence which nothing but Réal's presence could
give her ; a sort of unimpassioned but all-absorbing bliss,
warmth, courage, confidence ! . . . She backed away from
Réal's table, seated herself facing him and cast down her
eyes. There was a great stillness in the salle except for the
murmur of the voices in the kitchen. She had at first
stolen a glance or two, and then peeping again through her
eyelashes, as it were, she saw his eyes rest on her with a
peculiar meaning. This had never happened before. She
jumped up, thinking that he wanted something, and while
she stood in front of him with her hand resting on the table
he stooped suddenly, pressed it to the table with his lips and
began kissing it passionately without a sound, endlessly. . . .
More startled than surprised at first, then infinitely happy,
she was beginning to breathe quickly, when he left off and

threw himself back in the chair. She walked away from the
table and sat down again to gaze at him openly, steadily,
without a smile. But he was not looking at her. His
passionate lips were set hard now and his face had an expression of stern despair. No word passed between them.
Brusquely he got up with averted eyes and went outside,
leaving the food before him unfinished.

In the usual course of things, on any other day, she would
have got up and followed him, for she had always yielded to
the fascination that had first roused her faculties. She
would have gone out just to pass in front of him once or
twice. But this time she had not obeyed what was stronger
than fascination, something within herself, which at the
same time prompted and restrained her. She only raised
her arm and looked at her hand. It was true. It had
happened. He had kissed it. Formerly she cared not how
gloomy he was as long as he remained somewhere where she
could look at him—which she would do at every opportunity
with an open and unbridled innocence. But now she knew
better than to do that. She had got up, had passed through
the kitchen, meeting without embarrassment Catherine's
inquisitive glance, and had gone upstairs. When she came
down after a time, he was nowhere to be seen, and everybody
else too seemed to have gone into hiding; Michel, Peyrol,
Scevola. . . . But if she had met Scevola she would not
have spoken to him. It was now a very long time since she
had volunteered a conversation with Scevola. She guessed,
however, that Scevola had simply gone to lie down in his
lair, a narrow shabby room lighted by one glazed little
window high up in the end wall. Catherine had put him
in there on the very day he had brought her niece home,
and he had retained it for his own ever since. She could
even picture him to herself in there stretched on his pallet.
She was capable of that now. Formerly, for years after her
return, people that were out of her sight were out of her
mind also. Had they run away and left her she would not
have thought of them at all. She would have wandered in
and out of the empty house and round the empty fields
without giving anybody a thought. Peyrol was the first

human being she had noticed for years. Peyrol, since he had come, had always existed for her. And as a matter of fact the rover was generally very much in evidence about the farm. That afternoon, however, even Peyrol was not to be seen. Her uneasiness began to grow, but she felt a strange reluctance to go into the kitchen, where she knew her aunt would be sitting in the arm-chair like a presiding genius of the house taking its rest, and unreadable in her immobility. And yet she felt she must talk about Réal to somebody. This was how the idea of going down to the church had come to her. She would talk of him to the priest and to God. The force of old associations asserted itself. She had been taught to believe that one could tell everything to a priest, and that the omnipotent God who knew everything could be prayed to, asked for grace, for strength, for mercy, for protection, for pity. She had done it and felt she had been heard.

Her heart had quietened down while she rested under the wall. Pulling out a long stalk of grass, she twined it round her fingers absently. The veil of cloud had thickened over her head, early dusk had descended upon the earth, and she had not found out what had become of Réal. She jumped to her feet wildly. But directly she had done that she felt the need of self-control. It was with her usual light step that she approached the front of the house and for the first time in her life perceived how barren and sombre it looked when Réal was not about. She slipped in quietly through the door of the main building and ran upstairs. It was dark on the landing. She passed by the door leading into the room occupied by her aunt and herself. It had been her father and mother's bedroom. The other big room was the lieutenant's during his visits to Escampobar. Without even a rustle of her dress, like a shadow, she glided along the passage, turned the handle without noise and went in. After shutting the door behind her she listened. There was no sound in the house. Scevola was either already down in the yard or still lying open-eyed on his tumbled pallet in raging sulks about something. She had once accidentally caught him at it, down on his face, one eye and cheek of which were buried in the pillow, the other eye glaring savagely, and had been scared away by a thick mutter: " Keep off. Don't approach me." And all this had meant nothing to her then.

Having ascertained that the inside of the house was as still as the grave, Arlette walked across to the window, which, when the lieutenant was occupying the room, stood always open and with the shutter pushed right back against the wall. It was, of course, uncurtained, and as she came near to it Arlette caught sight of Peyrol coming down the hill on his return from the lookout. His white head gleamed like silver against the slope of the ground and by and by passed out of her sight, while her ear caught the sound of his footsteps below the window. They passed into the house, but she did not hear him come upstairs. He had gone into the kitchen. To Catherine. They would talk about her and Eugène. But what would they say ? She was so new to life that everything appeared dangerous : talk, attitudes, glances. She felt frightened at the mere idea of silence between those two. It was possible. Suppose they didn't say anything to each other. That would be awful.

Yet she remained calm like a sensible person, who knows that rushing about in excitement is not the way to meet unknown dangers. She swept her eyes over the room and saw the lieutenant's valise in a corner. That was really what she had wanted to see. He wasn't gone then. But it didn't tell her, though she opened it, what had become of him. As to his return, she had no doubt whatever about that. He had always returned. She noticed particularly a large packet sewn up in sail-cloth and with three large red seals on the seam. It didn't, however, arrest her thoughts. Those were still hovering about Catherine and Peyrol downstairs. How changed they were. Had they ever thought that she was mad ? She became indignant. " How could I have prevented that ? " she asked herself with despair. She sat down on the edge of the bed in her usual attitude, her feet crossed, her hands lying in her lap. She felt on one

of them the impress of Réal's lips, soothing, reassuring like
every certitude, but she was aware of a still remaining confusion in her mind, an indefinite weariness like the strain of
an imperfect vision trying to discern shifting outlines, floating
shapes, incomprehensible signs.   She could not resist the
temptation of resting her tired body, just for a little while.

She lay down on the very edge of the bed, the kissed
hand tucked under her cheek.   The faculty of thinking
abandoned her altogether, but she remained open-eyed,
wide awake.   In that position, without hearing the slightest
sound, she saw the door handle move down as far as it
would go, perfectly noiseless, as though the lock had been
oiled not long before.   Her impulse was to leap right out
into the middle of the room, but she restrained herself and
only swung herself into a sitting posture.   The bed had not
creaked.   She lowered her feet gently to the ground, and
by the time when holding her breath she put her ear against
the door, the handle had come back into position.   She had
detected no sound outside.   Not the faintest.   Nothing.
It never occurred to her to doubt her own eyes, but the
whole thing had been so noiseless that it could not have
disturbed the lightest sleeper.   She was sure that had she
been lying on her other side, that is with her back to the
door, she would have known nothing.   It was some time
before she walked away from the door and sat on a chair
which stood near a heavy and much-carved table, an heirloom,
more appropriate to a chateau than to a farmhouse.   The
dust of many months covered its smooth oval surface of
dark, finely grained wood.

" It must have been Scevola," thought Arlette.   It could
have been no one else.   What could he have wanted ?   She
gave herself up to the thought, but really she did not care.
The absent Réal occupied all her mind.   With an unconscious slowness her fingers traced in the dust on the table
the initials E. A. and achieved a circle round them.   Then
she jumped up, unlocked the door and went downstairs.
In the kitchen, as she fully expected, she found Scevola
with the others.   Directly she appeared he got up and ran
upstairs, but returned almost immediately, looking as if he

had seen a ghost, and when Peyrol asked him some insignificant question his lips and even his chin trembled before he could command his voice. He avoided looking anybody in the face. The others too seemed shy of meeting each other's eyes, and the evening meal of the Escampobar seemed haunted by the absent lieutenant. Peyrol, besides, had his prisoner to think of. His existence presented a most interesting problem, and the proceedings of the English ship was another, closely connected with it and full of dangerous possibilities, Catherine's black and ungleaming eyes seemed to have sunk deeper in their sockets, but her face wore its habitual severe aloofness of expression. Suddenly Scevola spoke as if in answer to some thought of his own.

"What has lost us was moderation."

Peyrol swallowed the piece of bread and butter which he had been masticating slowly, and asked :

"What are you alluding to, citoyen ? "

"I am alluding to the Republic," answered Scevola in a more assured tone than usual. "Moderation I say. We patriots held our hand too soon. All the children of the ci-devants and all the children of traitors should have been killed together with their fathers and mothers. Contempt for civic virtues and love of tyranny were inborn in them all. They grow up and trample on all the sacred principles. . . . The work of the Terror is undone ! "

"What do you propose to do about it ? " growled Peyrol. "No use declaiming here or anywhere for that matter. You wouldn't find anybody to listen to you—you cannibal," he added in a good-humoured tone. Arlette, leaning her head on her left hand, was tracing with the forefinger of her right invisible initials on the tablecloth. Catherine, stooping to light a four-beaked oil lamp mounted on a brass pedestal, turned her finely carved face over her shoulder. The sansculotte jumped up, flinging his arms about. His hair was tousled from his sleepless tumbling on his pallet. The unbuttoned sleeves of his shirt flapped against his thin hairy forearms. He no longer looked as though he had seen a ghost. He opened a wide black mouth, but Peyrol raised his finger at him calmly.

"No, no. The time when your own people up La Boyère way—don't they live up there?—trembled at the idea of you coming to visit them with a lot of patriot scallyways at your back is past. You have nobody at your back; and if you started spouting like this at large, people would rise up and hunt you down like a mad dog."

Scevola, who had shut his mouth, glanced over his shoulder, and as if impressed by his unsupported state went out of the kitchen, reeling, like a man who had been drinking. He had drunk nothing but water. Peyrol looked thoughtfully at the door which the indignant sans-culotte had slammed after him. During the colloquy between the two men, Arlette had disappeared into the salle. Catherine, straightening her long back, put the oil lamp with its four smoky flames on the table. It lighted her face from below. Peyrol moved it slightly aside before he spoke.

"It was lucky for you," he said, gazing upwards, "that Scevola hadn't even one other like himself when he came here."

"Yes," she admitted. "I had to face him alone, from first to last. But can you see me between him and Arlette? In those days he raved terribly, but he was dazed and tired out. Afterwards I recovered myself and I could argue with him firmly. I used to say to him, 'Look, she is so young, and she has no knowledge of herself.' Why, for months the only thing she would say that one could understand was 'Look how it spurts, look how it splashes!' He talked to me of his republican virtue. He was not a profligate. He could wait. She was, he said, sacred to him, and things like that. He would walk up and down for hours talking of her and I would sit there listening to him with the key of the room the child was locked in, in my pocket. I temporized, and, as you say yourself, it was perhaps because he had no one at his back that he did not try to kill me, which he might have done any day. I temporized. And after all, why should he want to kill me? He told me more than once he was sure to have Arlette for his own. Many a time he made me shiver explaining why it must be so. She owed her life to him. Oh! that dreadful crazy life. You know he is one of those men that can be patient as far as women are concerned."

Peyrol nodded understandingly. "Yes, some are like that. That kind is more impatient sometimes to spill blood. Still I think that your life was one long narrow escape, at least till I turned up here."

"Things had settled down, somehow," murmured Catherine. "But all the same I was glad when you appeared here, a grey-headed man, serious."

"Grey hairs will come to any sort of man," observed Peyrol acidly, "and you did not know me. You don't know anything of me even now."

"There have been Peyrols living less than half a day's journey from here," observed Catherine in a reminiscent tone.

"That's all right," said the rover in such a peculiar tone that she asked him sharply: "What's the matter? Aren't you one of them? Isn't Peyrol your name?"

"I have had many names and this was one of them. So this name and my grey hair pleased you, Catherine? They gave you confidence in me, hein?"

"I wasn't sorry to see you come. Scevola too, I believe. He heard that patriots were being hunted down, here and there, and he was growing quieter every day. You roused the child wonderfully."

"And did that please Scevola too?"

"Before you came she never spoke to anybody unless first spoken to. She didn't seem to care where she was. At the same time," added Catherine after a pause, "she didn't care what happened to her either. Oh, I have had some heavy hours thinking it all over, in the daytime doing my work, and at night while I lay awake, listening to her breathing. And I growing older all the time, and, who knows, with my last hour ready to strike. I often thought that when I felt it coming I would speak to you as I am speaking to you now."

"Oh, you did think," said Peyrol in an undertone. "Because of my grey hairs, I suppose."

"Yes. And because you came from beyond the seas,"

Catherine said with unbending mien and in an unflinching voice. " Don't you know that the first time Arlette saw you she spoke to you and that it was the first time I heard her speak of her own accord since she had been brought back by that man, and I had to wash her from head to foot before I put her into her mother's bed ? "

" The first time," repeated Peyrol.

" It was like a miracle happening," said Catherine, " and it was you that had done it."

" Then it must be that some Indian witch has given me the power," muttered Peyrol, so low that Catherine could not hear the words. But she did not seem to care, and presently went on again :

" And the child took to you wonderfully. Some sentiment was aroused in her at last."

" Yes," assented Peyrol grimly. " She did take to me. She learned to talk to—the old man."

" It's something in you that seems to have opened her mind and unloosed her tongue," said Catherine, speaking with a sort of regal composure down at Peyrol, like a chieftainess of a tribe. " I often used to look from afar at you two talking and wonder what she . . ."

" She talked like a child," struck in Peyrol abruptly. " And so you were going to speak to me before your last hour came. Why, you are not making ready to die yet ? "

" Listen, Peyrol. If anybody's last hour is near, it isn't mine. You just look about you a little. It was time I spoke to you."

" Why, I am not going to kill anybody," muttered Peyrol. " You are getting strange ideas into your head."

" It is as I said," insisted Catherine without animation. " Death seems to cling to her skirts. She has been running with it madly. Let us keep her feet out of more human blood."

Peyrol, who had let his head fall on his breast, jerked it up suddenly. " What on earth are you talking about ? " he cried angrily. " I don't understand you at all."

" You have not seen the state she was in when I got her back into my hands," remarked Catherine. . . . " I suppose you know where the lieutenant is. What made him go off like that? Where did he go to?"

"I know," said Peyrol. "And he may be back to-night."

"You know where he is! And of course you know why he has gone away and why he is coming back," pronounced Catherine in an ominous voice. "Well, you had better tell him that unless he has a pair of eyes at the back of his head he had better not return here—not return at all; for if he does, nothing can save him from a treacherous blow."

"No man was ever safe from treachery," opined Peyrol after a moment's silence. "I won't pretend not to understand what you mean."

"You heard as well as I what Scevola said just before he went out. The lieutenant is the child of some ci-devant and Arlette of a man they called a traitor to his country. You can see yourself what was in his mind."

"He is a chicken-hearted spouter," said Peyrol contemptuously, but it did not affect Catherine's attitude of an old sibyl risen from the tripod to prophesy calmly atrocious disasters. "It's all his republicanism," commented Peyrol with increased scorn. "He has got a fit of it on."

"No, that's jealousy," said Catherine. "Maybe he has ceased to care for her in all these years. It is a long time since he has left off worrying me. With a creature like that I thought that if I let him be master here . . . But no! I know that after the lieutenant started coming here his awful fancies have come back. He is not sleeping at night. His republicanism is always there. But don't you know, Peyrol, that there may be jealousy without love?"

"You think so," said the rover profoundly. He pondered full of his own experience. "And he has tasted blood too," he muttered after a pause. "You may be right."

"I may be right," repeated Catherine in a slightly indignant tone. "Every time I see Arlette near him I tremble lest it should come to words and to a bad blow. And when they are both out of my sight it is still worse. At this moment I am wondering where they are. They may be together and I daren't raise my voice to call her away for fear of rousing his fury."

"But it's the lieutenant he is after," observed Peyrol in a lowered voice. "Well, I can't stop the lieutenant coming back."

"Where is she? Where is he?" whispered Catherine in a tone betraying her secret anguish.

Peyrol rose quietly and went into the salle, leaving the door open. Catherine heard the latch of the outer door being lifted cautiously. In a few moments Peyrol returned as quietly as he had gone out.

"I stepped out to look at the weather. The moon is about to rise and the clouds have thinned down. One can see a star here and there." He lowered his voice considerably. "Arlette is sitting on the bench humming a little song to herself. I really wonder whether she knew I was standing within a few feet of her."

"She doesn't want to hear or see anybody except one man," affirmed Catherine, now in complete control of her voice. "And she was humming a song, did you say? She who would sit for hours without making a sound. And God knows what song it could have been!"

"Yes, there's a great change in her," admitted Peyrol, with a heavy sigh. "This lieutenant," he continued after a pause, "has always behaved coldly to her. I noticed him many times turn his face away when he saw her coming towards us. You know what these epaulette-wearers are, Catherine. And then this one has some worm of his own that is gnawing at him. I doubt whether he has ever forgotten that he was a ci-devant boy. Yet I do believe that she does not want to see and hear anybody but him. Is it because she has been deranged in her head for so long?"

"No, Peyrol," said the old woman. "It isn't that. You want to know how I can tell. For years nothing could make her either laugh or cry. You know that yourself. You have seen her every day. Would you believe that within the last month she has been both crying and laughing on my breast without knowing why?"

"This I don't understand," said Peyrol.

"But I do. That lieutenant has got only to whistle to make her run after him. Yes, Peyrol. That is so. She has no fear, no shame, no pride. I myself have been nearly like that." Her fine brown face seemed to grow more impassive before she went on much lower and as if arguing with herself: "Only I at least was never blood-mad. I was fit for any man's arms. . . . But then that man is not a priest."

The last words made Peyrol start. He had almost forgotten that story. He said to himself: "She knows, she has had the experience!"

"Look here, Catherine," he said decisively, "the lieutenant is coming back. He will be here probably about midnight. But one thing I can tell you: he is not coming back to whistle her away. Oh no! It is not for her sake that he will come back."

"Well, if it isn't for her that he is coming back then it must be because death has beckoned to him," she announced in a tone of solemn, unemotional conviction. "A man who has received a sign from death—nothing can stop him!"

Peyrol, who had seen death face to face many times, looked at Catherine's fine brown profile curiously.

"It is a fact," he murmured, "that men who rush out to seek death do not often find it. So one must have a sign? What sort of sign would it be?"

"How is anybody to know?" asked Catherine, staring across the kitchen at the wall. "Even those to whom it is made do not recognize it for what it is. But they obey all the same. I tell you, Peyrol, nothing can stop them. It may be a glance, or a smile, or a shadow on the water, or a thought that passes through the head. For my poor brother and sister-in-law it was the face of their child."

Peyrol folded his arms on his breast and dropped his head. Melancholy was a sentiment to which he was a stranger; for what has melancholy to do with the life of a sea-rover, a Brother of the Coast, a simple, venturesome, precarious life, full of risks and leaving no time for introspection or for that momentary self-forgetfulness which is called gaiety? Sombre fury, fierce merriment, he had known in passing gusts, coming from outside; but never this intimate inward sense of the vanity of all things, that doubt of the power within himself.

"I wonder what the sign for me will be," he thought: and concluded with self-contempt that for him there would be no sign, that he would have to die in his bed like an old yard dog in his kennel. Having reached that depth of despondency, there was nothing more before him but a black gulf into which his consciousness sank like a stone.

The silence which had lasted perhaps a minute after Catherine had finished speaking was traversed suddenly by a clear high voice saying:

"What are you two plotting here?"

Arlette stood in the doorway of the salle. The gleam of light in the whites of her eyes set off her black and pene-trating glance. The surprise was complete. The profile of Catherine, who was standing by the table, became, if possible, harder; a sharp carving of an old prophetess of some desert tribe. Arlette made three steps forward. In Peyrol even extreme astonishment was deliberate. He had been famous for never looking as though he had been caught unprepared. Age had accentuated that trait of a born leader. He only slipped off the edge of the table and said in his deep voice:

"Why, patronne! We haven't said a word to each other for ever so long."

Arlette moved nearer still. "I know," she cried. "It was horrible. I have been watching you two. Scevola came and dumped himself on the bench close to me. He began to talk to me, and so I went away. That man bores me. And here I find you people saying nothing. It's insupportable. What has come to you both? Say, you, Papa Peyrol—don't you like me any more?" Her voice filled the kitchen. Peyrol went to the salle door and shut it. While coming back he was staggered by the brilliance of life within her that seemed to pale the flames of the lamp. He said half in jest:

"I don't know whether I didn't like you better when you were quieter."

"And you would like best to see me still quieter in my grave."

She dazzled him. Vitality streamed out of her eyes, her lips, her whole person, enveloped her like a halo and . . . yes, truly, the faintest possible flush had appeared on her cheeks, played on them faintly rosy like the light of a distant flame on the snow. She raised her arms up in the air and let her hands fall from on high on Peyrol's shoulders, captured his desperately dodging eyes with her black and compelling glance, put out all her instinctive seduction—while he felt a growing fierceness in the grip of her fingers.

"No! I can't hold it in! Monsieur Peyrol, Papa Peyrol, old gunner, you horrid sea-wolf, be an angel and tell me where he is."

The rover, whom only that morning the powerful grasp of Lieutenant Réal found as unshakable as a rock, felt all his strength vanish under the hands of that woman. He said thickly:

"He has gone to Toulon. He had to go."

"What for? Speak the truth to me!"

"Truth is not for everybody to know," mumbled Peyrol, with a sinking sensation as though the very ground were going soft under his feet. "On service," he added in a growl. Her hands slipped suddenly from his big shoulders. "On service?" she repeated. "What service?" Her voice sank and the words "Oh, yes! His service" were hardly heard by Peyrol, who as soon as her hands had left his shoulders felt his strength returning to him and the yielding earth grow firm again under his feet. Right in front of him Arlette, silent, with her arms hanging down before her with entwined fingers, seemed stunned because Lieutenant Réal was not free from all earthly connections, like a visiting angel from heaven depending only on God to whom she had prayed. She had to share him with some service that could order him about. She felt in herself a strength, a power, greater than any service.

"Peyrol," she cried low, "don't break my heart, my new heart, that has just begun to beat. Feel how it beats. Who could bear it?" She seized the rover's thick hairy paw and pressed it hard against her breast. "Tell me when he will be back."

"Listen, patronne, you had better go upstairs," began

Peyrol with a great effort and snatching his captured hand away. He staggered backwards a little while Arlette shouted at him :

"You can't order me about as you used to do." In all the changes from entreaty to anger she never struck a false note, so that her emotional outburst had the heart-moving power of inspired art. She turned round with a tempestuous swish to Catherine, who had neither stirred nor emitted a sound : "Nothing you two can do will make any difference now." The next moment she was facing Peyrol again. "You frighten me with your white hairs. Come ! . . . am I to go on my knees to you ? . . . There !"

The rover caught her under the elbows, swung her up clear of the ground, and set her down on her feet, as if she had been a child. Directly he had let her go she stamped her foot at him.

"Are you stupid ?" she cried. "Don't you understand that something has happened to-day ?"

Through all this scene Peyrol had kept his head as creditably as could have been expected, in the manner of a seaman caught by a white squall in the tropics. But at those words a dozen thoughts tried to rush together through his mind, in chase of that startling declaration. Something had happened ! Where ? How ? Whom to ? What thing ? It couldn't be anything between her and the lieutenant. He had, it seemed to him, never lost sight of the lieutenant from the first hour when they met in the morning till he had sent him off to Toulon by an actual push on the shoulder ; except while he was having his dinner in the next room with the door open and for a few minutes spent in talking with Michel in the yard. But that was only a very few minutes, and directly afterwards the first sight of the lieutenant sitting gloomily on the bench like a lonely crow did not suggest either elation or excitement or any emotion connected with a woman. In the face of these difficulties Peyrol's mind became suddenly a blank.

"Voyons, patronne," he began, unable to think of anything else to say. "What's all this fuss about ? I expect him to be back here about midnight."

He was extremely relieved to notice that she believed him. It was the truth. For indeed he did not know what he could have invented on the spur of the moment that would get her out of the way and induce her to go to bed. She treated him to a sinister frown and a terribly menacing " If you had lied. . . . Oh ! "

He produced an indulgent smile. " Compose yourself. He will be here soon after midnight. You may go to sleep with an easy mind."

She turned her back on him contemptuously, and said curtly, " Come along, aunt," and went to the door leading to the passage. There she turned for a moment with her hand on the door handle.

" You are changed. I can't trust either of you. You are not the same people."

She went out. Only then did Catherine detach her gaze from the wall to meet Peyrol's eyes. " Did you hear what she said ? We ! Changed ! It is she herself. . . ."

Peyrol nodded twice, and there was a long pause during which even the flames of the lamp did not stir.

" Go after her, Mademoiselle Catherine," he said at last with a shade of sympathy in his tone. She did not move. " Allons—du courage," he urged her deferentially as it were. " Try to put her to sleep."


# XII

UPRIGHT and deliberate, Catherine left the kitchen, and in the passage outside found Arlette waiting for her with a lighted candle in her hand. Her heart was filled with sudden desolation by the beauty of that young face enhaloed in the patch of light, with the profound darkness as of a dungeon for a background. At once her niece led the way upstairs, muttering savagely through her pretty teeth : " He thinks I could go to sleep. Old imbecile ! "

Peyrol did not take his eyes off Catherine's straight back

till the door had closed after her. Only then he relieved himself by letting the air escape through his pursed lips and rolling his eyes freely about. He picked up the lamp by the ring on the top of the central rod and went into the salle, closing behind him the door of the dark kitchen. He stood the lamp on the very table on which Lieutenant Réal had had his midday meal. A small white cloth was still spread on it, and there was his chair askew as he had pushed it back when he got up. Another of the many chairs in the salle was turned round conspicuously to face the table. These things made Peyrol remark to himself bitterly : " She sat and stared at him as if he had been gilt all over, with three heads and seven arms on his body "—a comparison reminiscent of certain idols he had seen in an Indian temple. Though not an iconoclast, Peyrol felt positively sick at the recollection, and hastened to step outside. The great cloud had broken up and the mighty fragments were moving to the westward in stately flight before the rising moon. Scevola, who had been lying extended full length on the bench, swung himself up suddenly, very upright.

" Had a little nap in the open ? " asked Peyrol, letting his eyes roam through the luminous space under the departing rearguard of the clouds jostling each other up there.

" I did not sleep," said the sans-culotte. " I haven't closed my eyes—not for one moment."

" That must be because you weren't sleepy," suggested the deliberate Peyrol, whose thoughts were far away with the English ship. His mental eye contemplated her black image against the white beach of the Salins describing a sparkling curve under the moon ; and meantime he went on slowly, " for it could not have been noise that kept you awake." On the level of Escampobar the shadows lay long on the ground while the side of the lookout hill remained yet black but edged with an increasing brightness. And the amenity of the stillness was such that it softened for a moment Peyrol's hard inward attitude towards all mankind, including even the captain of the English ship. The old rover savoured a moment of serenity in the midst of his cares.

"This is an accursed spot," declared Scevola suddenly.

Peyrol, without turning his head, looked at him sideways. Though he had sprung up from his reclining posture smartly enough, the citizen had gone slack all over and was sitting all in a heap. His shoulders were hunched up, his hands reposed on his knees. With his staring eyes he resembled a sick child in the moonlight.

"It's the very spot for hatching treacheries. One feels steeped in them up to the neck."

He shuddered and yawned a long irresistible nervous yawn with the gleam of unexpected long canines in a retracted, gaping mouth giving away the restless panther lurking in the man.

"Oh yes, there's treachery about right enough. You couldn't conceive that, citoyen?"

"Of course I couldn't," assented Peyrol with serene contempt. "What is this treachery that you are concocting?" he added carelessly, in a social way, while enjoying the charm of a moonlit evening. Scevola, who did not expect that turn, managed, however, to produce a rattling sort of laugh almost at once.

"That's a good one, ha! ha! ha! . . . Me! . . . concocting! . . . Why me?"

"Well," said Peyrol carelessly, "there are not many of us to carry out treacheries about here. The women are gone upstairs; Michel is down at the tartane. There's me, and you would not dare suspect me of treachery. Well, there remains only you."

Scevola roused himself. "This is not much of a jest," he said. "I have been a treason-hunter. I . . ."

He checked that strain. He was full of purely emotional suspicions. Peyrol was talking like this only to annoy him and to get him out of the way; but in the particular state of his feelings Scevola was acutely aware of every syllable of these offensive remarks. "Aha," he thought to himself, "he doesn't mention the lieutenant." This omission seemed to the patriot of immense importance. If Peyrol had not mentioned the lieutenant it was because those two had been plotting some treachery together, all the afternoon on

G G

board that tartane. That's why nothing had been seen of
them for the best part of the day. As a matter of fact,
Scevola too had observed Peyrol returning to the farm in
the evening, only he had observed him from another window
than Arlette. This was a few minutes before his attempt
to open the lieutenant's door, in order to find out whether
Réal was in his room. He had tiptoed away, uncertain,
and going into the kitchen had found only Catherine and
Peyrol there. Directly Arlette joined them a sudden inspiration made him run upstairs and try the door again. It was
open now! A clear proof that it was Arlette who had
been locked up in there. The discovery that she made
herself at home like this in the lieutenant's room gave
Scevola such a sickening shock that he thought he would die
of it. It was beyond doubt now that the lieutenant had
been conspiring with Peyrol down on board that tartane;
for what else could they have been doing there? But why
had not Réal come up in the evening with Peyrol? Scevola
asked himself, sitting on the bench with his hands clasped
between his knees. . . . " It's their cunning," he concluded
suddenly. " Conspirators always avoid being seen together.
Ha ! "

It was as if somebody had let off a lot of fireworks in his
brain. He was illuminated, dazzled, confused, with a hissing
in his ears and showers of sparks before his eyes. When he
raised his head he saw he was alone. Peyrol had vanished.
Scevola seemed to remember that he had heard somebody
pronounce the word " Good-night " and the door of the
salle slam. And sure enough the door of the salle was shut
now. A dim light shone in the window that was next to
it. Peyrol had extinguished three of the lamp flames, and
was now reclining on one of the long tables with that faculty
of accommodating himself to a plank an old sea-dog never
loses. He had decided to remain below simply to be handy,
and he didn't lie down on one of the benches along the
wall because they were too narrow. He left one wick
burning, so that the lieutenant should know where to look
for him, and he was tired enough to think that he would
snatch a couple of hours' sleep before Réal could return

from Toulon. He settled himself with one arm under his head as if he were on the deck of a privateer, and it never occurred to him that Scevola was looking through the panes ; but they were so small and dusty that the patriot could see nothing. His movement had been purely instinctive. He wasn't even aware that he had looked in. He went away from there, walked to the end of the building, spun round and walked back again to the other end ; and it was as if he had been afraid of going beyond the wall against which he reeled sometimes. Conspiracy, conspiracy, he thought. He was now absolutely certain that the lieutenant was still hiding in that tartane, and was only waiting till all was quiet to sneak back to his room in which Scevola had proof positive that Arlette was in the habit of making herself at home. To rob him of his right to Arlette was part of the conspiracy, no doubt.

"Have I been a slave to those two women, have I waited all those years, only to see that corrupt creature go off infamously with a ci-devant, with a conspiring aristocrat ? "

He became giddy with virtuous fury. There was enough evidence there for any revolutionary tribunal to cut all their heads off. Tribunal ! There was no tribunal ! No revolutionary justice ! No patriots ! He hit his shoulder against the wall in his distress with such force that he rebounded. This world was no place for patriots.

"If I had betrayed myself in the kitchen they would have murdered me in there."

As it was he thought that he had said too much. Too much. "Prudence ! Caution ! " he repeated to himself, gesticulating with both arms. Suddenly he stumbled, and there was an amazing metallic clatter made by something that fell at his feet.

"They are trying to kill me now," he thought, shaking with fright. He gave himself up for dead. Profound silence reigned all round. Nothing more happened. He stooped fearfully to look and recognized his own stable fork lying on the ground. He remembered he had left it at noon leaning against the wall. His own foot had made it fall. He threw himself upon it greedily. "Here's what I need," he muttered feverishly. "I suppose that by now the lieutenant would think I am gone to bed."

He flattened himself upright against the wall with the fork held along his body like a grounded musket. The moon clearing the hill-top flooded suddenly the front of the house with its cold light, but he didn't know it; he imagined himself still to be ambushed in the shadow and remained motionless, glaring at the path leading towards the cove. His teeth chattered with savage impatience.

He was so plainly visible in his deathlike rigidity that Michel, coming up out of the ravine, stopped dead short, believing him an apparition not belonging to this earth. Scevola, on his side, noticed the moving shadow cast by a man—that man !—and charged forward without reflection, the prongs of the fork lowered like a bayonet. He didn't shout. He came straight on, growling like a dog, and lunged headlong with his weapon.

Michel, a primitive untroubled by anything so uncertain as intelligence, executed an instantaneous sideways leap with the precision of a wild animal; but he was enough of a man to become afterwards paralysed with astonishment. The impetus of the rush carried Scevola several yards down the hill, before he could turn round and assume an offensive attitude. Then the two adversaries recognized each other. The terrorist exclaimed : "Michel !" and Michel hastened to pick up a large stone from the ground.

"Hey, you, Scevola," he cried, not very loud but very threatening. "What are these tricks ? . . . Keep away, or I will heave that piece of rock at your head, and I am good at that."

Scevola grounded the fork with a thud. "I didn't recognize you," he said.

"That's a story. Who did you think I was ? Not the other ! I haven't got a bandaged head, have I ? "

Scevola began to scramble up. "What's this ? " he asked. "What head did you say ? "

"I say that if you come near I will knock you over with that stone," answered Michel. "You aren't to be trusted when the moon is full. Not recognize ! There's a silly excuse for flying at people like this. You haven't got anything against me, have you ? "

" No," said the ex-terrorist in a dubious tone and keeping a watchful eye on Michel, who was still holding the stone in his hand.

" People have been saying for years that you are a kind of lunatic," Michel criticized fearlessly, because the other's discomfiture was evident enough to put heart into the timid hare. " If a fellow cannot come up now to get a snooze in the shed without being run at with a fork, well . . ."

" I was only going to put this fork away," Scevola burst out volubly. " I had left it leaning against the wall, and as I was passing along I suddenly saw it, so I thought I would put it in the stable before I went to bed. That's all."

Michel's mouth fell open a bit.

" Now what do you think I would want with a stable fork at this time of night, if it wasn't to put it away ? " argued Scevola.

" What indeed ! " mumbled Michel, who began to doubt the evidence of his senses.

" You go about mooning like a fool and imagine a lot of silly things, you great stupid imbecile. All I wanted to do was to ask whether everything was all right down there, and you, idiot, bound to one side like a goat and pick up a stone. The moon has affected your head, not mine. Now drop it."

Michel, accustomed to do what he was told, opened his fingers slowly, not quite convinced but thinking there might be something in it. Scevola, perceiving his advantage, scolded on :

" You are dangerous. You ought to have your feet and hands tied every full moon. What did you say about a head just now ? What head ? "

" I said that I didn't have a broken head."

" Was that all ? " said Scevola. He was asking himself what on earth could have happened down there during the afternoon to cause a broken head. Clearly, it must have been either a fight or an accident, but in any case he considered that it was for him a favourable circumstance, for obviously a man with a bandaged head is at a disadvantage. He was inclined to think it must have been some silly accident, and he regretted profoundly that the lieutenant had not killed himself outright. He turned sourly to Michel.

" Now you may go into the shed. And don't try any of your tricks with me any more, because next time you pick up a stone I will shoot you like a dog.'"

He began to move towards the yard gate which stood always open, throwing over his shoulder an order to Michel : " Go into the salle. Somebody has left a light in there. They all seem to have gone crazy to-day. Take the lamp into the kitchen and put it out, and see that the door into the yard is shut. I am going to bed." He passed through the gateway, but he did not penetrate into the yard very far. He stopped to watch Michel obeying the order. Scevola, advancing his head cautiously beyond the pillar of the gate, waited till he had seen Michel open the door of the salle and then bounded out again across the level space, and down the ravine path. It was a matter of less than a minute. His fork was still on his shoulder. His only desire was not to be interfered with, and for the rest he did not care what they all did, what they would think and how they would behave. The fixed idea had taken complete possession of him. He had no plan, but he had a principle on which to act ; and that was to get at the lieutenant unawares, and if the fellow died without knowing what hand had struck him, so much the better. Scevola was going to act in the cause of virtue and justice. It was not to be a matter of personal contest at all. Meantime, Michel, having gone into the salle, had discovered Peyrol fast asleep on a table. Though his reverence for Peyrol was unbounded, his simplicity was such that he shook his master by the shoulder as he would have done any common mortal. The rover passed from a state of inertia into a sitting posture so quickly that Michel stepped back a pace and waited to be addressed. But as Peyrol only stared at him, Michel took the initiative in a concise phrase :

" He's at it ! "

Peyrol did not seem completely awake : " What is it you mean ? " he asked.

" He is making motions to escape."

Peyrol was wide awake now. He even swung his feet off the table.

" Is he ? Haven't you locked the cabin door ? "

Michel, very frightened, explained that he had never been told to do that.

" No ? " remarked Peyrol placidly. " I must have forgotten." But Michel remained agitated, and murmured : " He is escaping."

" That's all right," said Peyrol. " What are you fussing about ? How far can he escape, do you think ? "

A slow grin appeared on Michel's face. " If he tries to scramble over the top of the rocks, he will get a broken neck in no time," he said. " And he certainly won't get very far, that's a fact."

" Well—you see," said Peyrol.

" And he doesn't seem strong either. He crawled out of the cabin door and got as far as the little water cask and he dipped and dipped into it. It must be half empty by now. After that he got on to his legs. I cleared out ashore directly I heard him move," he went on in a tone of intense self-approval. " I hid myself behind a rock and watched him."

" Quite right," observed Peyrol. After that word of commendation, Michel's face wore a constant grin.

" He sat on the after-deck," he went on as if relating an immense joke, " with his feet dangling down the hold, and may the devil take me if I don't think he had a nap with his back against the cask. He was nodding and catching himself up, with that big white head of his. Well, I got tired of watching that, and as you told me to keep out of his way, I thought I would come up here and sleep in the shed. That was right, wasn't it ? "

" Quite right," repeated Peyrol. " Well, you go now into the shed. And so you left him sitting on the after-deck ? "

" Yes," said Michel. " But he was rousing himself. I

hadn't got away more than ten yards when I heard an awful thump on board. I think he tried to get up and fell down the hold."

"Fell down the hold?" repeated Peyrol sharply.

"Yes, notre maître. I thought at first I would go back and see, but you had warned me against him, hadn't you? And I really think that nothing can kill him."

Peyrol got down from the table with an air of concern which would have astonished Michel, if he had not been utterly incapable of observing things.

"This must be seen to," murmured the rover, buttoning the waistband of his trousers. "My cudgel there, in the corner. Now you go to the shed. What the devil are you doing at the door? Don't you know the way to the shed?" This last observation was caused by Michel remaining in the doorway of the salle with his head out and looking to right and left along the front of the house. "What's come to you? You don't suppose he has been able to follow you so quick as this up here?"

"Oh no, notre maître, quite impossible. I saw that sacré Scevola promenading up and down here. I don't want to meet him again."

"Was he promenading outside?" asked Peyrol, with annoyance. "Well, what do you think he can do to you? What notions have you got in your silly head? You are getting worse and worse. Out you go."

Peyrol extinguished the lamp and, going out, closed the door without the slighest noise. The intelligence about Scevola being on the move did not please him very much, but he reflected that probably the sans-culotte had fallen asleep again, and after waking up was on his way to bed when Michel caught sight of him. He had his own view of the patriot's psychology and did not think the women were in any danger. Nevertheless he went to the shed and heard the rustling of straw as Michel settled himself for the night.

"Debout," he cried low. "Sh, don't make any noise. I want you to go into the house and sleep at the bottom of the stairs. If you hear voices, go up, and if you see Scevola about, knock him down. You aren't afraid of him, are you ? "

" No, if you tell me not to be," said Michel, who, picking up his shoes, a present from Peyrol, walked barefoot towards the house. The rover watched him slipping noiselessly through the salle door. Having thus, so to speak, guarded his base, Peyrol proceeded down the ravine with a very deliberate caution. When he got as far as the little hollow in the ground from which the mastheads of the tartane could be seen, he squatted and waited. He didn't know what his prisoner had done or was doing, and he did not want to blunder into the way of his escape. The day-old moon was high enough to have shortened the shadows almost to nothing and all the rocks were inundated by a yellow sheen, while the bushes by contrast looked very black. Peyrol reflected that he was not very well concealed. The continued silence impressed him in the end. " He has got away," he thought. And yet he was not sure. Nobody could be sure. He reckoned it was about an hour since Michel had left the tartane ; time enough for a man, even on all fours, to crawl down to the shore of the cove. Peyrol wished he had not hit so hard. His object could have been attained with half the force. On the other hand all the proceedings of his prisoner, as reported by Michel, seemed quite rational. Naturally the fellow was badly shaken. Peyrol felt as though he wanted to go on board and give him some encouragement, and even active assistance.

The report of a gun from seaward cut his breath short as he lay there meditating. Within a minute there was a second report, sending another wave of deep sound among the crags and hills of the peninsula. The ensuing silence was so profound that it seemed to extend to the very inside of Peyrol's head, and lull all his thoughts for a moment. But he had understood. He said to himself that after this his prisoner, if he had life enough left in him to stir a limb, would rather die than not try to make his way to the seashore. The ship was calling to her man.

In fact those two guns had proceeded from the *Amelia*. After passing beyond Cape Esterel, Captain Vincent dropped

an anchor underfoot off the beach just as Peyrol had surmised
he would do.   From about six o'clock till nine the *Amelia*
lay there with her unfurled sails hanging in the gear.   Just
before the moon rose the captain came up on deck and after
a short conference with his first lieutenant, directed the
master to get the ship under way and put her head again
for the Petite Passe.   Then he went below, and presently
word was passed on deck that the captain wanted Mr. Bolt.
When the master's mate appeared in his cabin, Captain
Vincent motioned him to a chair.

" I don't think I ought to have listened to you," he said.
" Still, the idea was fascinating, but how it would strike
other people it is hard to say.   The losing of our man is the
worst feature.   I have an idea that we might recover him.
He may have been captured by the peasants or have met
with an accident.   It's unbearable to think of him lying at
the foot of some rock with a broken leg.   I have ordered the
first and second cutters to be manned, and I propose that
you should take command of them and enter the cove and,
if necessary, advance a little inland to investigate.   As far
as we know there have never been any troops on that peninsula.   The first thing you will do is to examine the coast."

He talked for some time, giving more minute instructions,
and then went on deck.   The *Amelia*, with the two cutters
towing alongside, reached about half-way down the Passe
and then the boats were ordered to proceed.   Just before
they shoved off two guns were fired in quick succession.

" Like this, Bolt," explained Captain Vincent, " Symons
will guess that we are looking for him ; and if he is hiding
anywhere near the shore he will be sure to come down
where he can be seen by you."


# XIII

THE motive force of a fixed idea is very great.   In the case
of Scevola it was great enough to launch him down the
slope and to rob him for the moment of all caution.   He

bounded amongst the boulders, using the handle of the stable fork for a staff. He paid no regard to the nature of the ground, till he got a fall and found himself sprawling on his face, while the stable fork went clattering down until it was stopped by a bush. It was this circumstance which saved Peyrol's prisoner from being caught unawares. Since he had got out of the little cabin, simply because after coming to himself he had perceived it was open, Symons had been greatly refreshed by long drinks of cold water and by his little nap in the fresh air. Every moment he was feeling in better command of his limbs. As to the command of his thoughts, that was coming to him too, rather quickly. The advantage of having a very thick skull became evident in the fact that as soon as he had dragged himself out of that cabin he knew where he was. The next thing he did was to look at the moon, to judge of the passage of time. Then he gave way to an immense surprise at the fact of being alone aboard the tartane. As he sat with his legs dangling into the open hold he tried to guess how it came about that the cabin had been left unlocked and unguarded.

He went on thinking about this unexpected situation. What could have become of that white-headed villain? Was he dodging about somewhere watching for a chance to give him another tap on the head? Symons felt suddenly very unsafe sitting there on the after-deck in the full light of the moon. Instinct rather than reason suggested to him that he ought to get down into the dark hold. It seemed a great undertaking at first, but once he started he accomplished it with the greatest ease, though he could not avoid knocking down a small spar which was leaning up against the deck. It preceded him into the hold with a loud crash which gave poor Symons an attack of palpitation of the heart. He sat on the keelson of the tartane and gasped, but after a while reflected that all this did not matter. His head felt very big, his neck was very painful and one shoulder was certainly very stiff. He could never stand up against that old ruffian. But what had become of him? Why! He had gone to fetch the soldiers! After that conclusion Symons became more composed. He began to try to remember things. When he had last seen that old fellow it was daylight, and now—Symons looked up at the moon again—it must be near six bells in the first watch. No doubt the old scoundrel was sitting in a wine shop drinking with the soldiers. They would be here soon enough! The idea of being a prisoner of war made his heart sink a little. His ship appeared to him invested with an extraordinary number of lovable features which included Captain Vincent and the first lieutenant. He would have been glad to shake hands even with the corporal, a surly and malicious marine acting as master-at-arms of the ship. " I wonder where she is now," he thought dismally, feeling his distaste for captivity grow with the increase of his strength.

It was at this moment that he heard the noise of Scevola's fall. It was pretty close; but afterwards he heard no voices and footsteps heralding the approach of a body of men. If this was the old ruffian coming back, then he was coming back alone. At once Symons started on all fours for the fore end of the tartane. He had an idea that ensconced under the foredeck he would be in a better position to parley with the enemy and that perhaps he could find there a handspike or some piece of iron to defend himself with. Just as he had settled himself in his hiding-place Scevola stepped from the shore on to the after-deck.

At the very first glance Symons perceived that this one was very unlike the man he expected to see. He felt rather disappointed. As Scevola stood still in full moonlight Symons congratulated himself on having taken up a position under the foredeck. That fellow, who had a beard, was like a sparrow in body compared with the other; but he was armed dangerously with something that looked to Symons either like a trident or fishgrains on a staff. " A devil of a weapon that," he thought, appalled. And what on earth did that beggar want on board? What could he be after?

The new-comer acted strangely at first. He stood stock still, craning his neck here and there, peering along the whole length of the tartane, then crossing the deck he repeated all those performances on the other side. "He has noticed that the cabin door is open. He's trying to see where I've got to. He will be coming forward to look for me," said Symons to himself. "If he corners me here with that beastly pronged affair I am done for." For a moment he debated within himself whether it wouldn't be better to make a dash for it and scramble ashore; but in the end he mistrusted his strength. "He would run me down for sure," he concluded. "And he means no good, that's certain. No man would go about at night with a confounded thing like that if he didn't mean to do for somebody."

Scevola, after keeping perfectly still, straining his ears for any sound from below where he supposed Lieutenant Réal to be, stooped down to the cabin scuttle and called in a low voice : "Are you there, lieutenant ? " Symons saw these motions and could not imagine their purport. That excellent able seaman of proved courage in many cutting-out expeditions broke into a slight perspiration. In the light of the moon the prongs of the fork, polished by much use, shone like silver, and the whole aspect of the stranger was weird and dangerous in the extreme. Who could that man be after, but him, himself ?

Scevola, receiving no answer, remained in a stooping position. He could not detect the slightest sound of breathing down there. He remained in this position so long that Symons became quite interested. "He must think I am still down there," he whispered to himself. The next proceeding was quite astonishing. The man, taking up a position on one side of the cuddy scuttle and holding his horrid weapon as one would a boarding pike, uttered a terrific whoop and went on yelling in French with such volubility that he quite frightened Symons. Suddenly he left off, moved away from the scuttle and looked at a loss what to do next. Anybody who could have then seen Symons' protruded head with his face turned aft would have seen on it an expression of horror. "The cunning beast," he thought. "If I had been down there, with the row he made, I would have surely rushed on deck and then he would have had me." Symons experienced the feeling of a very narrow escape; yet it brought not much relief. It was simply a matter of time. The fellow's homicidal purpose was evident. He was bound before long to come forward. Symons saw him move, and thought, "Now he's coming," and prepared himself for a dash. "If I can dodge past these blamed prongs I might be able to take him by the throat," he reflected, without, however, feeling much confidence in himself.

But to his great relief Scevola's purpose was simply to conceal the fork in the hold in such a manner that the handle of it just reached the edge of the afterdeck. In that position it was of course invisible to anybody coming from the shore. Scevola had made up his mind that the lieutenant was out of the tartane. He had wandered away along the shore and would probably be back in a moment. Meantime it had occurred to him to see if he could discover anything compromising in the cabin. He did not take the fork down with him because in that confined space it would have been useless and rather a source of embarrassment than otherwise should the returning lieutenant find him there. He cast a circular glance around the basin and then prepared to go down.

Every movement of his was watched by Symons. He guessed Scevola's purpose by his movements, and said to himself: "Here's my only chance, and not a second to be lost either." Directly Scevola turned his back on the forepart of the tartane in order to go down the little cabin ladder, Symons crawled out from his concealment. He ran along the hold on all fours for fear the other should turn his head round before disappearing below, but directly he judged that the man had touched bottom, he stood on his feet and catching hold of the main rigging swung himself on the after-deck and, as it were in the same movement, flung himself on the doors of the cabin, which came together with a crash. How he could secure them he had not thought, but as a matter of fact he saw the padlock hanging on a staple on one side; the key was in it, and it was a matter of a fraction of a second to secure the doors effectually.

Almost simultaneously with the crash of the cabin door there was a shrill exclamation of surprise down there, and just as Symons had turned the key the man he had trapped made an effort to break out. That, however, did not disturb Symons. He knew the strength of that door. His first action was to get possession of the stable fork. At once he felt himself a match for any single man, or even two men, unless they had fire-arms. He had no hope, however, of being able to resist the soldiers and really had no intention of doing so. He expected to see them appear at any moment led by that confounded marinero. As to what the farmer man had come for on board the tartane he had not the slightest doubt about it. Not being troubled by too much imagination, it seemed to him obvious that it was to kill an Englishman and for nothing else. " Well, I am jiggered," he exclaimed mentally. " The damned savage ! I haven't done anything to him. They must be a murderous lot hereabouts." He looked anxiously up the slope. He would have welcomed the arrival of soldiers. He wanted more than ever to be made a proper prisoner, but a profound stillness reigned on the shore and a most absolute silence down below in the cabin. Absolute. No word, no movement. The silence of the grave. " He's scared to death," thought Symons, hitting in his simplicity on the exact truth. " It would serve him jolly well right if I went down there and ran him through with that thing. I would do it for a shilling, too." He was getting angry. It occurred to him also that there was some wine down there too. He discovered he was very thirsty and he felt rather faint. He sat down on the little skylight to think the matter over while awaiting the soldiers. He even gave a friendly thought to Peyrol himself. He was quite aware that he could have gone ashore and hidden himself for a time, but that meant in the end being hunted among the rocks and, certainly, captured ; with the additional risk of getting a musket ball through his body.

The first gun of the *Amelia* lifted him to his feet as though he had been snatched up by the hair of his head. He intended to give a resounding cheer, but produced only a feeble gurgle in his throat. His ship was talking to him. They hadn't given him up. At the second report he scrambled ashore with the agility of a cat—in fact, with so much agility that he had a fit of giddiness. After it passed off he returned deliberately to the tartane to get hold of the stable fork. Then, trembling with emotion, he staggered off quietly and resolutely with the only purpose of getting down to the seashore. He knew that as long as he kept downhill he would be all right. The ground in this part being a smooth rocky surface and Symons being bare-footed, he passed at no great distance from Peyrol without being heard. When he got on rough ground he used the stable fork for a staff. Slowly as he moved, he was not really strong enough to be sure-footed. Ten minutes later or so Peyrol, lying ensconced behind a bush, heard the noise of a rolling stone far away in the direction of the cove. Instantly the patient Peyrol got on his feet and started towards the cove himself. Perhaps he would have smiled if the import-ance and gravity of the affair in which he was engaged had not given all his thoughts a serious cast. Pursuing a higher path than the one followed by Symons, he had presently the satisfaction of seeing the fugitive, made very noticeable by the white bandages about his head, engaged in the last part of the steep descent. No nurse could have watched with more anxiety the adventure of a little boy than Peyrol the progress of his former prisoner. He was very glad to perceive that he had had the sense to take what looked like the tartane's boathook to help himself with. As Symons' figure sank lower and lower in his descent Peyrol moved on, step by step, till at last he saw him from above sitting down on the seashore, looking very forlorn and lonely, with his bandaged head between his hands. Instantly Peyrol sat down too, protected by a projecting rock. And it is safe to say that with that there came a complete cessation of all sound and movement on the lonely head of the peninsula for a full half-hour.

Peyrol was not in doubt as to what was going to happen. He was as certain that the corvette's boat or boats were now on the way to the cove as though he had seen them leave the side of the *Amelia*. But he began to get a little impatient. He wanted to see the end of this episode. Most of the time he was watching Symons. "Sacré tête dure," he thought. "He has gone to sleep." Indeed Symons' immobility was so complete that he might have been dead from his exertions : only Peyrol had a conviction that his once youthful chum was not the sort of person that dies easily. The part of the cove he had reached was all right for Peyrol's purpose. But it would have been quite easy for a boat or boats to fail to notice Symons, and the consequence of that would be that the English would probably land in several parties for a search, discover the tartane. . . . Peyrol shuddered.

Suddenly he made out a boat just clear of the eastern point of the cove. Mr. Bolt had been hugging the coast and progressing very slowly, according to his instructions, till he had reached the edge of the point's shadow where it lay ragged and black on the moonlit water. Peyrol could see the oars rise and fall. Then another boat glided into view. Peyrol's alarm for his tartane grew intolerable. "Wake up, animal, wake up," he mumbled through his teeth. Slowly they glided on, and the first cutter was on the point of passing by the man on the shore when Peyrol was relieved by the hail of "Boat ahoy!" reaching him faintly where he knelt leaning forward, an absorbed spectator.

He saw the boat heading for Symons, who was standing up now and making desperate signs with both arms. Then he saw him dragged in over the bows, the boat back out, and then both of them tossed oars and floated side by side on the sparkling water of the cove.

Peyrol got up from his knees. They had their man now. But perhaps they would persist in landing, since there must have been some other purpose at first in the mind of the captain of the English corvette. This suspense did not last long. Peyrol saw the oars fall in the water, and in a very few minutes the boats, pulling round, disappeared one after another behind the eastern point of the cove.

"That's done," muttered Peyrol to himself. "I will never see the silly Hard-head again." He had a strange notion that those English boats had carried off something

belonging to him, not a man but a part of his own life, the
sensation of a regained touch with the far-off days in the
Indian Ocean. He walked down quickly as if to examine
the spot from which Testa Dura had left the soil of France.
He was in a hurry now to get back to the farmhouse and
meet Lieutenant Réal, who would be due back from Toulon.
The way by the cove was as short as any other. When he
got down he surveyed the empty shore and wondered at a
feeling of emptiness within himself. While walking up
towards the foot of the ravine he saw an object lying on the
ground. It was a stable fork. He stood over it asking himself, " How on earth did this thing come here ? " as though
he had been too surprised to pick it up. Even after he had
done so he remained motionless, meditating on it. He connected it with some activity of Scevola, since he was the
man to whom it belonged, but that was no sort of explanation
of its presence on that spot, unless . . .

" Could he have drowned himself ? " thought Peyrol,
looking at the smooth and luminous water of the cove. It
could give him no answer. Then at arm's length he contemplated his find. At last he shook his head, shouldered
the fork, and with slow steps continued on his way.


XIV

THE midnight meeting of Lieutenant Réal and Peyrol was
perfectly silent. Peyrol, sitting on the bench outside the
salle, had heard the footsteps coming up the Madrague
track long before the lieutenant became visible. But he did
not move. He did not even look at him. The lieutenant,
unbuckling his sword-belt, sat down without uttering a word.
The moon, the only witness of the meeting, seemed to shine
on two friends so identical in thought and feeling that they
could commune with each other without words. It was
Peyrol who spoke first.

" You are up to time."

" I had the deuce of a job to hunt up the people and

get the certificate stamped. Everything was shut up. The Port-Admiral was giving a dinner-party, but he came out to speak to me when I sent in my name. And all the time, do you know, gunner, I was wondering whether I would ever see you again in my life. Even after I had the certificate, such as it is, in my pocket, I wondered whether I would."

"What the devil did you think was going to happen to me?" growled Peyrol, perfunctorily. He had thrown the incomprehensible stable fork under the narrow bench, and with his feet drawn in he could feel it there, lying against the wall.

"No, the question with me was whether I would ever come here again."

Réal drew a folded paper from his pocket and dropped it on the bench. Peyrol picked it up carelessly. That thing was meant only to throw dust into Englishmen's eyes. The lieutenant, after a moment's silence, went on with the sincerity of a man who suffered too much to keep his trouble to himself.

"I had a hard struggle."

"That was too late," said Peyrol, very positively. "You had to come back here for very shame; and now you have come, you don't look very happy."

"Never mind my looks, gunner. I have made up my mind."

A ferocious, not unpleasing thought flashed through Peyrol's mind. It was that this intruder on the Escampobar sinister solitude in which he, Peyrol, kept order, was under a delusion. Mind! Pah! His mind had nothing to do with his return. He had returned because, in Catherine's words, "death had made a sign to him." Meantime, Lieutenant Réal raised his hat to wipe his moist brow.

"I made up my mind to play the part of dispatch-bearer. As you have said yourself, Peyrol, one could not bribe a man—I mean an honest man—so you will have to find the vessel and leave the rest to me. In two or three days . . . You are under a moral obligation to let me have your tartane."

Peyrol did not answer. He was thinking that Réal had

got his sign, but whether it meant death from starvation or disease on board an English prison hulk, or in some other way, it was impossible to say. This naval officer was not a man he could trust; to whom he could, for instance, tell the story of his prisoner and what he had done with him. Indeed, the story was altogether incredible. The Englishman commanding that corvette had no visible, conceivable or probable reason for sending a boat ashore to the cove of all places in the world. Peyrol himself could hardly believe that it had happened. And he thought: " If I were to tell that lieutenant he would only think that I was an old scoundrel who had been in treasonable communication with the English for God knows how long. No words of mine could persuade him that this was as unforeseen to me as the moon falling from the sky."

" I wonder," he burst out, but not very loud, " what made you keep on coming back here time after time ! " Réal leaned his back against the wall and folded his arms in the familiar attitude of their leisurely talks.

" Ennui, Peyrol," he said in a far-away tone. " Confounded boredom."

Peyrol also, as if unable to resist the force of example, assumed the same attitude, and said :

" You seem to be a man that makes no friends."

" True, Peyrol. I think I am that sort of man."

" What, no friends at all ? Not even a little friend of any sort ? "

Lieutenant Réal leaned the back of his head against the wall and made no answer. Peyrol got on his legs.

" Oh then, it wouldn't matter to anybody if you were to disappear for years in an English hulk. And so if I were to give you my tartane you would go ? "

" Yes, I would go this moment."

Peyrol laughed quite loud, tilting his head back. All at once the laugh stopped short and the lieutenant was amazed to see him reel as though he had been hit in the chest. While giving way to his bitter mirth, the rover had caught sight of Arlette's face at the open window of the lieutenant's room. He sat heavily on the bench and was unable to make a sound. The lieutenant was startled enough to detach the back of his head from the wall to look at him. Peyrol stooped low suddenly and began to drag the stable fork from its concealment. Then he got on his feet and stood leaning on it, glaring down at Réal, who gazed upwards with languid surprise. Peyrol was asking himself, " Shall I pick him up on that pair of prongs, carry him down and fling him in the sea ? " He felt suddenly overcome by a heaviness of arms and a heaviness of heart that made all movement impossible. His stiffened and powerless limbs refused all service. . . . Let Catherine look after her niece. He was sure that the old woman was not very far away. The lieutenant saw him absorbed in examining the points of the prongs carefully. There was something queer about all this.

" Hallo, Peyrol ! What's the matter ? " he couldn't help asking.

" I was just looking," said Peyrol. " One prong is chipped a little. I found this thing in a most unlikely place."

The lieutenant still gazed at him curiously.

" I know ! It was under the bench."

" H'm," said Peyrol, who had recovered some self-control. " It belongs to Scevola."

" Does it ? " said the lieutenant, falling back again.

His interest seemed exhausted, but Peyrol didn't move.

" You go about with a face fit for a funeral," he remarked suddenly in a deep voice. " Hang it all, lieutenant, I have heard you laugh once or twice, but the devil take me if I ever saw you smile. It is as if you had been bewitched in your cradle."

Lieutenant Réal got up as if moved by a spring. " Bewitched," he repeated, standing very stiff : " in my cradle, eh ? . . . No, I don't think it was so early as that."

He walked forward with a tense still face straight at Peyrol as though he had been blind. Startled, the rover stepped out of the way and, turning on his heels, followed him with his eyes. The lieutenant paced on, as if drawn by a magnet, in the direction of the door of the house. Peyrol, his eyes fastened on Réal's back, let him nearly reach it before he called out tentatively : " I say, lieutenant ! " To his extreme surprise, Réal swung round as if to a touch.

" Oh yes," he answered, also in an undertone. " We will have to discuss that matter to-morrow."

Peyrol, who had approached him close, said in a whisper which sounded quite fierce : " Discuss ? No ! We will have to carry it out to-morrow. I have been waiting half the night just to tell you that."

Lieutenant Réal nodded. The expression on his face was so stony that Peyrol doubted whether he had understood. He added :

" It isn't going to be child's play." The lieutenant was about to open the door when Peyrol said : " A moment," and again the lieutenant turned about silently.

" Michel is sleeping somewhere on the stairs. Will you just stir him up and tell him I am waiting outside ? We two will have to finish our night on board the tartane, and start work at break of day to get her ready for sea. Yes, lieutenant, by noon. In twelve hours' time you will be saying good-bye to la belle France."

Lieutenant Réal's eyes, staring over his shoulder, seemed glazed and motionless in the moonlight like the eyes of a dead man. But he went in. Peyrol heard presently sounds within of somebody staggering in the passage and Michel projected himself outside headlong, but after a stumble or two pulled up scratching his head and looking on every side in the moonlight without perceiving Peyrol, who was regarding him from a distance of five feet. At last Peyrol said :

" Come, wake up ! Michel ! Michel ! "

" Voilà, notre maître."

" Look at what I have picked up," said Peyrol. " Take it and put it away."

Michel didn't offer to touch the stable fork extended to him by Peyrol.

" What's the matter with you ? " asked Peyrol.

" Nothing, nothing ! Only last time I saw it, it was on Scevola's shoulder." He glanced up at the sky. " A little better than an hour ago."

" What was he doing ? "

" Going into the yard to put it away."

" Well, now *you* go into the yard to put it away," said Peyrol, " and don't be long about it." He waited with his hand over his chin till his henchman reappeared before him. But Michel had not got over his surprise.

" He was going to bed, you know," he said.

" Eh, what ? He was going. . . . He hasn't gone to sleep in the stable, perchance ? He does sometimes, you know."

" I know. I looked. He isn't there," said Michel, very awake and round-eyed.

Peyrol started towards the cove. After three or four steps he turned round and found Michel motionless where he had left him.

" Come on," he cried, " we will have to fit the tartane for sea directly the day breaks."

Standing in the lieutenant's room just clear of the open window, Arlette listened to their voices and to the sound of their footsteps diminishing down the slope. Before they had quite died out she became aware of a light tread approaching the door of the room.

Lieutenant Réal had spoken the truth. While in Toulon he had more than once said to himself that he could never go back to that fatal farmhouse. His mental state was quite pitiable. Honour, decency, every principle, forbade him to trifle with the feelings of a poor creature with her mind darkened by a very terrifying, atrocious and, as it were, guilty experience. And suddenly he had given way to a base impulse and had betrayed himself by kissing her hand ! He recognized with despair that this was no trifling, but that the impulse had come from the very depths of his being. It was an awful discovery for a man who on emerging from boyhood had laid for himself a rigidly straight line of conduct amongst the unbridled passions and the clamouring falsehoods of revolution which seemed to have destroyed in him all capacity for the softer emotions. Taciturn and guarded, he had formed no intimacies. Relations he had none. He had kept clear of social connections. It was in his character. At first he visited Escampobar because when he took his leave he had no place in the world to go to, and a few days there were a complete change from the odious town. He enjoyed the sense of remoteness from ordinary mankind. He had developed a liking for old Peyrol, the only man who had nothing to do with the Revolution—who had not even seen it at work. The sincere lawlessness of the ex-Brother of the Coast was refreshing. That one was neither a hypocrite nor a fool. When he robbed or killed, it was not in the name of the sacred revolutionary principles or for the love of humanity.

Of course Réal had remarked at once Arlette's black, profound and unquiet eyes and the persistent dim smile on her lips, her mysterious silences and the rare sound of her voice which made a caress of every word. He heard something of her story from the reluctant Peyrol, who did not care to talk about it. It awakened in Réal more bitter indignation than pity. But it stimulated his imagination, confirmed him in that scorn and angry loathing for the Revolution he had felt as a boy and had nursed secretly ever since. She attracted him by her unapproachable aspect. Later he tried not to notice that, in common parlance, she was inclined to hang about him. He used to catch her gazing at him stealthily. But he was free from masculine vanity. It was one day in Toulon that it suddenly dawned on him what her mute interest in his person might mean. He was then sitting outside a café sipping some drink or other with three or four officers, and not listening to their uninteresting conversation. He marvelled that this sort of illumination should come to him like this, under these circumstances; that he should have thought of her while seated in the street with these men round him, in the midst of more or less professional talk! And then it suddenly dawned on him that he had been thinking of nothing but that woman for days.

He got up brusquely, flung the money for his drink on the table, and without a word left his companions. But he had the reputation of an eccentric man and they did not even comment on his abrupt departure. It was a clear evening. He walked straight out of town, and that night

wandered beyond the fortifications, not noticing the direction
he took. All the countryside was asleep. There was not a
human being stirring, and his progress in that desolate part
of the country between the forts could have been traced
only by the barking of dogs in the rare hamlets and scattered
habitations.

"What has become of my rectitude, of my self-respect,
of the firmness of my mind ? " he asked himself pedantically.
"I have let myself be mastered by an unworthy passion for
a mere mortal envelope stained with crime and without a
mind ! "

His despair at this awful discovery was so profound that
if he had not been in uniform he would have tried to commit
suicide with the small pistol he had in his pocket. He shrank
from the act, and the thought of the sensation it would
produce, from the gossip and comments it would raise, the
dishonouring suspicions it would provoke. "No," he said
to himself, "what I will have to do is to unmark my linen,
put on civilian clothes and walk out much farther away,
miles beyond the forts, hide myself in some wood or in an
overgrown hollow and put an end to my life there. The
gendarmes or a garde-champêtre discovering my body after
a few days, a complete stranger without marks of identity,
and being unable to find out anything about me, will give
me an obscure burial in some village churchyard."

On that resolution he turned back abruptly and at daybreak found himself outside the gate of the town. He had
to wait till it was opened, and then the morning was so far
advanced that he had to go straight to work at his office at
the Toulon Admiralty. Nobody noticed anything peculiar
about him that day. He went through his routine tasks
with outward composure, but all the same he never ceased
arguing with himself. By the time he returned to his
quarters he had come to the conclusion that as an officer in
war-time he had no right to take his own life. His principles
would not permit him to do that. In this reasoning he was
perfectly sincere. During a deadly struggle against an
irreconcilable enemy his life belonged to his country. But
there were moments when his loneliness, haunted by the

forbidden vision of Escampobar with the figure of that distracted girl, mysterious, awful, pale, irresistible in her
strangeness, passing along the walls, appearing on the hill-
paths, looking out of the window, became unbearable. He
spent hours of solitary anguish shut up in his quarters, and
the opinion amongst his comrades was that Réal's misanthropy was getting beyond all bounds.

One day it dawned upon him clearly that he could not
stand this. It affected his power of thinking. " I shall
begin to talk nonsense to people," he said to himself.
" Hasn't there been once a poor devil who fell in love with
a picture or a statue ? He used to go and contemplate it.
His misfortune cannot be compared with mine ! Well, I
will go to look at her as at a picture too ; a picture as untouch-
able as if it had been under glass." And he went on a visit
to Escampobar at the very first opportunity. He made up
for himself a repellent face, he clung to Peyrol for society,
out there on the bench, both with their arms folded and
gazing into space. But whenever Arlette crossed his line of
sight it was as if something had moved in his breast. Yet
these visits made life just bearable ; they enabled him to
attend to his work without beginning to talk nonsense to
people. He said to himself that he was strong enough to
rise above temptation, that he would never overstep the
line ; but it had happened to him upstairs in his room at
the farm, to weep tears of sheer tenderness while thinking
of his fate. These tears would put out for a while the
gnawing fire of his passion. He assumed austerity like an
armour and in his prudence he, as a matter of fact, looked
very seldom at Arlette for fear of being caught in the
act.

The discovery that she had taken to wandering at night
had upset him all the same, because that sort of thing was
unaccountable. It gave him a shock which unsettled, not
his resolution, but his fortitude. That morning he had
allowed himself, while she was waiting on him, to be caught
looking at her, and then, losing his self-control, had given
her that kiss on the hand. Directly he had done it he was
appalled. He had overstepped the line. Under the cir-

cumstances this was an absolute moral disaster. The full consciousness of it came to him slowly. In fact, this moment of fatal weakness was one of the reasons why he had let himself be sent off so unceremoniously by Peyrol to Toulon. Even while crossing over he thought the only thing was not to come back any more. Yet while battling with himself he went on with the execution of the plan. A bitter irony presided over his dual state. Before leaving the Admiral, who had received him in full uniform in a room lighted by a single candle, he was suddenly moved to say : " I suppose if there is no other way I am authorized to go myself," and the Admiral had answered : " I didn't contemplate that, but if you are willing I don't see any objection. I would only advise you to go in uniform in the character of an officer entrusted with dispatches. No doubt in time the Government would arrange for your exchange. But bear in mind that it would be a long captivity, and you must understand it might affect your promotion."

At the foot of the grand staircase in the lighted hall of the official building Réal suddenly thought : " And now I must go back to Escampobar." Indeed he had to go to Escampobar because the false dispatches were there in the valise he had left behind. He couldn't go back to the Admiral and explain that he had lost them. They would look on him as an unutterable idiot or a man gone mad. While walking to the quay where the naval boat was waiting for him he said to himself : " This, in truth, is my last visit for years—perhaps for life."

Going back in the boat, notwithstanding that the breeze was very light, he would not let the men take to the oars. He didn't want to return before the women had gone to bed. He said to himself that the proper and honest thing to do was not to see Arlette again. He even managed to persuade himself that his uncontrolled impulse had had no meaning for that witless and unhappy creature. She had neither started, nor exclaimed ; she had made no sign. She had remained passive and then she had backed away and sat down quietly. He could not even remember that she had coloured at all. As to himself, he had enough self-control to rise from the table and go out without looking at her again. Neither did she make a sign. What could startle that body without mind? She had made nothing of it, he thought with self-contempt. "Body without mind! Body without mind!" he repeated with angry derision directed at himself. And all at once he thought: "No. It isn't that. All in her is mystery, seduction, enchantment. And then—what do I care for her mind!"

This thought wrung from him a faint groan, so that the coxswain asked respectfully: "Are you in pain, mon lieutenant?" "It's nothing," he muttered and set his teeth with the desperation of a man under torture.

While talking with Peyrol outside the house, the words "I won't see her again," and "body without mind," rang through his head. By the time he had left Peyrol and walked up the stairs his endurance was absolutely at an end. All he wanted was to be alone. Going along the dark passage he noticed that the door of Catherine's room was standing ajar. But that did not arrest his attention. He was approaching a state of insensibility. As he put his hand on the door-handle of his room he said to himself: "It will soon be over!"

He was so tired out that he was almost unable to hold up his head, and on going in he didn't see Arlette, who stood against the wall on one side of the window, out of the moonlight and in the darkest corner of the room. He only became aware of somebody's presence in the room as she flitted past him with the faintest possible rustle, when he staggered back two paces and heard behind him the key being turned in the lock. If the whole house had fallen into ruins, bringing him to the ground, he could not have been more overwhelmed and, in a manner, more utterly bereft of all his senses. The first that came back to him was the sense of touch when Arlette seized his hand. He regained his hearing next. She was whispering to him: "At last! At last! But you are careless. If it had been Scevola instead of me in this room you would have been dead now. I have seen him at work." He felt a significant pressure on his hand, but he couldn't see her properly yet, though he was aware of her nearness with every fibre of his body. " It wasn't yesterday though," she added in a low tone. Then suddenly : " Come to the window so that I may look at you."

A great square of moonlight lay on the floor. He obeyed the tug like a little child. She caught hold of his other hand as it hung by his side. He was rigid all over, without joints, and it did not seem to him that he was breathing. With her face a little below his, she stared at him closely, whispering gently : " Eugène, Eugène," and suddenly the livid immobility of his face frightened her. " You say nothing. You look ill. What is the matter ? Are you hurt ? " She let go his insensitive hands and began to feel him all over for evidence of some injury. She even snatched off his hat and flung it away in her haste to discover that his head was unharmed ; but finding no sign of bodily damage, she calmed down like a sensible, practical person. With her hands clasped round his neck she hung back a little. Her little even teeth gleamed, her black eyes, immensely profound, looked into his, not with a transport of passion or fear, but with a sort of reposeful satisfaction, with a searching and appropriating expression. He came back to life with a low and reckless exclamation, felt horribly insecure at once as if he were standing on a lofty pinnacle above a noise as of breaking waves in his ears, in fear lest her fingers should part and she would fall off and be lost to him for ever. He flung his arms round her waist and hugged her close to his breast. In the great silence, in the bright moonlight falling through the window, they stood like that for a long, long time. He looked at her head resting on his shoulder. Her eyes were closed, and the expression of her unsmiling face was that of a delightful dream, something infinitely ethereal, peaceful and, as it were, eternal. Its appeal pierced his heart with a pointed sweetness. " She is exquisite. It's a miracle," he thought with a sort of terror. " It's impossible."

She made a movement to disengage herself, and instinctively he resisted, pressing her closer to his breast. She yielded for a moment and then tried again. He let her go. She stood at arm's length, her hands on his shoulders, and her charm struck him suddenly as funny in the seriousness of expression as of a very capable, practical woman.

"All this is very well," she said in a businesslike undertone. "We will have to think how to get away from here. I don't mean now, this moment," she added, feeling his slight start. "Scévola is thirsting for your blood." She detached one hand to point a finger at the inner wall of the room, and lowered her voice. "He's there, you know. Don't trust Peyrol either. I was looking at you two out there. He has changed. I can trust him no longer." Her murmur vibrated. "He and Catherine behave strangely. I don't know what came to them. He doesn't talk to me. When I sit down near him he turns his shoulder to me. . . ."

She felt Réal sway under her hands, paused in concern and said: "You are tired." But as he didn't move, she actually led him to a chair, pushed him into it, and sat on the floor at his feet. She rested her head against his knees and kept possession of one of his hands. A sigh escaped her. "I knew this was going to be," she said very low. "But I was taken by surprise."

"Oh, you knew it was going to be," he repeated faintly.

"Yes! I had prayed for it. Have you ever been prayed for, Eugène?" she asked, lingering on his name with delight.

"Not since I was a child," answered Réal in a sombre tone.

"Oh yes! You have been prayed for to-day. I went down to the church. . . ." Réal could hardly believe his ears. . . . "The abbé let me in by the sacristy door. He told me to renounce the world. I was ready to renounce anything for you." Réal, turning his face to the darkest part of the room, seemed to see the spectre of fatality awaiting its time to move forward and crush that calm, confident joy. He shook off the dreadful illusion, raised her hand to his lips for a lingering kiss, and then asked:

"So you knew that it was going to be? Everything? Yes! And of me, what did you think?"

She pressed strongly the hand to which she had been clinging all the time. "I thought this."

"But what did you think of my conduct at times? You

see, I did not know what was going to be. I . . . I was afraid," he added under his breath.

"Conduct? What conduct? You came, you went. When you were not here I thought of you, and when you were here I could look my fill at you. I tell you I knew how it was going to be. I was not afraid then."

"You went about with a little smile," he whispered, as one would mention an inconceivable marvel.

"I was warm and quiet," murmured Arlette, as if on the borders of dreamland. Tender murmurs flowed from her lips describing a state of blissful tranquillity in phrases that sounded like the veriest nonsense, incredible, convincing and soothing to Réal's conscience.

"You were perfect," it went on. "Whenever you came near me everything seemed different."

"What do you mean? How different?"

"Altogether. The light, the very stones of the house, the hills, the little flowers amongst the rocks! Even Nanette was different."

Nanette was a white Angora with long silken hair, a pet that lived mostly in the yard.

"Oh, Nanette was different too," said Réal, whom delight in the modulations of that voice had cut off from all reality, and even from a consciousness of himself, while he sat stooping over that head resting against his knee, the soft grip of her hand being his only contact with the world.

"Yes. Prettier. It's only the people. . . ." She ceased on an uncertain note. The crested wave of enchantment seemed to have passed over his head, ebbing out faster than the sea, leaving the dreary expanses of the sand. He felt a chill at the roots of his hair.

"What people?" he asked.

"They are so changed. Listen, to-night while you were away—why did you go away?—I caught those two in the kitchen, saying nothing to each other. That Peyrol—he is terrible."

He was struck by the tone of awe, by its profound conviction. He could not know that Peyrol, unforeseen, unexpected, inexplicable, had given by his mere appearance at

Escampobar a moral and even a physical jolt to all her being, that he was to her an immense figure, like a messenger from the unknown entering the solitude of Escampobar; something immensely strong, with inexhaustible power, unaffected by familiarity and remaining invincible.

"He will say nothing, he will listen to nothing. He can do what he likes?"

"Can he?" muttered Réal.

She sat on the floor, moved her head up and down several times as if to say that there could be no doubt about that.

"Is he, too, thirsting for my blood?" asked Réal bitterly.

"No, no. It isn't that. You could defend yourself. I could watch over you. I have been watching over you. Only two nights ago I thought I heard noises outside and I went downstairs, fearing for you; your window was open but I could see nobody, and yet I felt . . . No, it isn't that! It's worse. I don't know what he wants to do. I can't help being fond of him, but I begin to fear him now. When he first came here and I saw him he was just the same—only his hair was not so white—big, quiet. It seemed to me that something moved in my head. He was gentle, you know. I had to smile at him. If was as if I had recognized him. I said to myself: 'That's he, the man himself.'"

"And when I came?" asked Réal with a feeling of dismay.

"You! You were expected," she said in a low tone, with a slight tinge of surprise at the question, but still evidently thinking of the Peyrol mystery. "Yes, I caught them at it last evening, he and Catherine, in the kitchen, looking at each other and as quiet as mice. I told him he couldn't order me about. Oh, mon chéri, mon chéri, don't you listen to Peyrol—don't let him . . ."

With only a slight touch on his knee she sprang to her feet. Réal stood up too.

"He can do nothing to me," he mumbled.

"Don't tell him anything. Nobody can guess what he thinks, and now even I cannot tell what he means when he speaks. It was as if he knew a secret." She put an accent into those words which made Réal feel moved almost to tears. He repeated that Peyrol could have no influence over him, and he felt that he was speaking the truth. He was in the power of his own word. Ever since he had left the Admiral in a gold-embroidered uniform, impatient to return to his guests, he was on a service for which he had volunteered. For a moment he had the sensation of an iron hoop very tight round his chest. She peered at his face closely, and it was more than he could bear.

"All right. I'll be careful," he said. "And Catherine, is she also dangerous?"

In the sheen of the moonlight Arlette, her neck and head above the gleams of the fichu, visible and elusive, smiled at him and moved a step closer.

"Poor Aunt Catherine," she said. . . . "Put your arm round me, Eugène. . . . She can do nothing. She used to follow me with her eyes always. She thought I didn't notice, but I did. And now she seems unable to look me in the face. Peyrol too, for that matter. He used to follow me with his eyes. Often I wondered what made them look at me like that. Can you tell, Eugène? But it's all changed now."

"Yes, it is all changed," said Réal in a tone which he tried to make as light as possible. "Does Catherine know you are here?"

"When we went upstairs this evening I lay down all dressed on my bed and she sat on hers. The candle was out, but in the moonlight I could see her quite plainly with her hands on her lap. When I could lie still no longer I simply got up and went out of the room. She was still sitting at the foot of her bed. All I did was to put my finger on my lips and then she dropped her head. I don't think I quite closed the door. . . . Hold me tighter, Eugène, I am tired. . . . Strange, you know! Formerly, a long time ago, before I ever saw you, I never rested and never felt tired." She stopped her murmur suddenly and lifted a finger recommending silence. She listened and Réal listened too, he did not know for what; and in this sudden concentration on a point, all that had happened since he

H H

had entered the room seemed to him a dream in its improbability and in the more than lifelike force dreams have in their inconsequence. Even the woman letting herself go on his arm seemed to have no weight, as it might have happened in a dream.

"She is there," breathed Arlette suddenly, rising on tiptoe to reach up to his ear. "She must have heard you go past."

"Where is she?" asked Réal with the same intense secrecy.

"Outside the door. She must have been listening to the murmur of our voices. . . ." Arlette breathed into his ear as if relating an enormity. "She told me one day that I was one of those who are fit for no man's arms."

At this he flung his other arm round her and looked into her enlarged as if frightened eyes, while she clasped him with all her strength and they stood like that a long time, lips pressed on lips without a kiss and breathless in the closeness of their contact. To him the stillness seemed to extend to the limits of the universe. The thought " Am I going to die?" flashed through that stillness and lost itself in it like a spark flying in an everlasting night. The only result of it was the tightening of his hold on Arlette.

An aged and uncertain voice was heard uttering the word "Arlette." Catherine, who had been listening to their murmurs, could not bear the long silence. They heard her trembling tones as distinctly as though she had been in the room. Réal felt as if it had saved his life. They separated silently.

"Go away," called out Arlette.

"Arl. . . ."

"Be quiet," she cried louder. "You can do nothing."

"Arlette," came through the door, tremulous and commanding.

"She will wake up Scevola," remarked Arlette to Réal in a conversational tone. And they both waited for sounds that did not come. Arlette pointed her finger at the wall. "He is there, you know."

"He is asleep," muttered Réal. But the thought " I am

lost " which he formulated in his mind had no reference to
Scevola.

" He is afraid," said Arlette contemptuously in an undertone. " But that means little. He would quake with fright
one moment and rush out to do murder the next."

Slowly, as if drawn by the irresistible authority of the old
woman, they had been moving towards the door. Réal
thought with the sudden enlightenment of passion : " If she
does not go now I won't have the strength to part from her
in the morning." He had no image of death before his eyes
but of a long and intolerable separation. A sigh verging
upon a moan reached them from the other side of the door
and made the air around them heavy with sorrow against
which locks and keys will not avail.

" You had better go to her," he whispered in a penetrating
tone.

" Of course I will," said Arlette with some feeling. " Poor
old thing. She and I have only each other in the world,
but I am the daughter here, she must do what I tell her."
With one of her hands on Réal's shoulder she put her mouth
close to the door and said distinctly :

" I am coming directly. Go back to your room and
wait for me," as if she had no doubt of being obeyed.

A profound silence ensued. Perhaps Catherine had gone
already. Réal and Arlette stood still for a whole minute as
if both had been changed into stone.

" Go now," said Réal in a hoarse, hardly audible
voice.

She gave him a quick kiss on the lips, and again they
stood like a pair of enchanted lovers, bewitched into
immobility.

" If she stays on," thought Réal, " I shall never have the
courage to tear myself away, and then I shall have to blow
my brains out." But when at last she moved he seized her
again and held her as if she had been his very life. When he
let her go he was appalled by hearing a very faint laugh of
her secret joy.

" Why do you laugh ? " he asked in a scared tone.

She stopped to answer him over her shoulder.

" I laughed because I thought of all the days to come. Days and days and days. Have you thought of them ? "

" Yes," Réal faltered, like a man stabbed to the heart, holding the door half open. And he was glad to have something to hold on to.

She slipped out with a soft rustle of her silk skirt, but before he had time to close the door behind her she put back her arm for an instant. He had just time to press the palm of her hand to his lips. It was cool. She snatched it away and he had the strength of mind to shut the door after her. He felt like a man chained to the wall and dying of thirst, from whom a cold drink is snatched away. The room became dark suddenly. He thought, " A cloud over the moon, a cloud over the moon, an enormous cloud," while he walked rigidly to the window, insecure and swaying as if on a tight rope. After a moment he perceived the moon in a sky on which there was no sign of the smallest cloud anywhere. He said to himself : " I suppose I nearly died just now. But no," he went on thinking with deliberate cruelty, " oh no, I shall not die. I shall only suffer, suffer, suffer. . . ."

" Suffer, suffer." Only by stumbling against the side of the bed did he discover that he had gone away from the window. At once he flung himself on it violently with his face buried in the pillow, which he bit to restrain the cry of distress about to burst through his lips. Natures schooled into insensibility, when once overcome by a mastering passion are, like vanquished giants, ready for despair. He, a man on service, felt himself shrinking from death and that doubt contained in itself all possible doubts of his own fortitude. The only thing he knew was that he would be gone to-morrow morning. He shuddered along his whole extended length, then lay still gripping a handful of bedclothes in each hand to prevent himself from leaping up in panicky restlessness. He was saying to himself pedantically, " I must lie down and rest, I must rest to have strength for to-morrow, I must rest," while the tremendous struggle to keep still broke out in waves of perspiration on his forehead. At last sudden oblivion must have descended on him because he turned over and sat up suddenly with the sound of the word " Ecoutez " in his ears.

A strange, dim, cold light filled the room; a light he did not recognize for anything he had known before, and at the foot of his bed stood a figure in dark garments with a dark shawl over its head, with a fleshless predatory face and dark hollows for its eyes, silent, expectant, implacable. . . . " Is this death ? " he asked himself, staring at it terrified. It resembled Catherine. It said again : " Ecoutez." He took away his eyes from it, and glancing down noticed that his clothes were torn open on his chest. He would not look up at that thing, whatever it was, spectre or old woman, and said :

" Yes, I hear you."

" You are an honest man." It was Catherine's unemotional voice. " The day has broken. You will go away."

" Yes," he said without raising his head.

" She is asleep," went on Catherine or whoever it was, " exhausted, and you would have to shake her hard before she would wake. You will go. You know," the voice continued inflexibly, " she is my niece, and you know that there is death in the folds of her skirt and blood about her feet. She is for no man."

Réal felt all the anguish of an unearthly experience. This thing that looked like Catherine and spoke like a cruel fate had to be faced. He raised his head in this light that seemed to him appalling and not of this world.

" Listen well to me, you too," he said. " If she had all the madness of the world and the sin of all the murders of the Revolution on her shoulders I would still hug her to my breast. Do you understand ? "

The apparition which resembled Catherine lowered and raised its hooded head slowly. " There was a time when I could have hugged l'enfer même to my breast. He went away. He had his vow. You have only your honesty. You will go."

" I have my duty," said Lieutenant Réal in measured tones, as if calmed by the excess of horror that old woman inspired him with.

" Go without disturbing her, without looking at her."

" I will carry my shoes in my hand," he said. He sighed

deeply and felt as if sleepy. " It is very early," he muttered.

" Peyrol is already down at the well," announced Catherine. " What can he be doing there all this time ? " she added in a troubled voice. Réal, with his feet now on the ground, gave her a side glance, but she was already gliding away, and when he looked again she had vanished from the room and the door was shut.


## XV

CATHERINE, going downstairs, found Peyrol still at the well. He seemed to be looking into it with extreme interest.

" Your coffee is ready, Peyrol," she shouted to him from the doorway.

He turned very sharply like a man surprised and came along smiling.

" That's pleasant news, Mademoiselle Catherine," he said. " You are down early."

" Yes," she admitted, " but you too, Peyrol. Is Michel about ? Let him come and have some coffee too."

" Michel's at the tartane. Perhaps you don't know that she is going to make a little voyage." He drank a mouthful of coffee and took a bite out of a slice of bread. He was hungry. He had been up all night and had even had a con- versation with Citizen Scevola. He had also done some work with Michel after daylight ; however, there had not been much to do because the tartane was always kept ready for sea. Then after having locked up again Citizen Scevola, who was extremely concerned as to what was going to happen to him but was left in a state of uncertainty, he had come up to the farm, had gone upstairs, where he was busy with various things for a time, and then had stolen down very cautiously to the well, where Catherine, whom he had not expected downstairs so early, had seen him before she went into Lieutenant Réal's room. While he enjoyed his coffee he listened without any signs of surprise to Catherine's comments upon the disappearance of Scevola. She had looked into his den. He had not slept on his pallet last night, of that she was certain, and he was nowhere to be seen, not even in the most distant field, from the points of vantage around the farm. It was inconceivable that he should have slipped away to Madrague, where he disliked to go, or to the village, where he was afraid to go. Peyrol remarked that whatever happened to him he was no great loss, but Catherine was not to be soothed.

"It frightens a body," she said. "He may be hiding somewhere to jump on one treacherously. You know what I mean, Peyrol."

"Well, the lieutenant will have nothing to fear, as he's going away. As to myself, Scevola and I are good friends. I had a long talk with him quite recently. You two women can manage him perfectly; and then, who knows, perhaps he has gone away for good."

Catherine stared at him, if such a word as stare can be applied to a profound contemplative gaze. "The lieutenant has nothing to fear from him," she repeated cautiously.

"No, he is going away. Didn't you know it?" The old woman continued to look at him profoundly. "Yes, he is on service."

For another minute or so Catherine continued silent in her contemplative attitude. Then her hesitation came to an end. She could not resist the desire to inform Peyrol of the events of the night. As she went on Peyrol forgot the half-full bowl of coffee and his half-eaten piece of bread. Catherine's voice flowed with austerity. She stood there, imposing and solemn like a peasant-priestess. The relation of what had been to her a soul-shaking experience did not take much time, and she finished with the words, "The lieutenant is an honest man." And after a pause she insisted further: "There is no denying it. He has acted like an honest man."

For a moment longer, Peyrol continued to look at the coffee in the bowl, then without warning got up with such violence that the chair behind him was thrown back upon the flagstones.

"Where is he, that honest man?" he shouted suddenly in stentorian tones which not only caused Catherine to raise her hands, but frightened himself, and he dropped at once to a mere forcible utterance. " Where is that man ? Let me see him."

Even Catherine's hieratic composure was disturbed.

" Why ? " she said, looking really disconcerted, " he will be down here directly. This bowl of coffee is for him."

Peyrol made as if to leave the kitchen, but Catherine stopped him. " For God's sake, Monsieur Peyrol," she said, half in entreaty and half in command, " don't wake up the child. Let her sleep. Oh, let her sleep ! Don't wake her up. God only knows how long it is since she has slept properly. I could not tell you. I daren't think of it." She was shocked by hearing Peyrol declare : " All this is confounded nonsense." But he sat down again, seemed to catch sight of the coffee bowl and emptied what was left in it down his throat.

" I don't want her on my hands more crazy than she has been before," said Catherine in a sort of exasperation but in a very low tone. This phrase in its selfish form expressed a real and profound compassion for her niece. She dreaded the moment when that fatal Arlette would wake up and the dreadful complications of life which her slumbers had suspended would have to be picked up again. Peyrol fidgeted on his seat.

" And so he told you he was going ? He actually did tell you that ? " he asked.

" He promised to go before the child wakes up. . . . At once."

" But, sacré nom d'un chien, there is never any wind before eleven o'clock," Peyrol exclaimed in a tone of profound annoyance, yet trying to moderate his voice, while Catherine, indulgent to his changing moods, only compressed her lips and nodded at him soothingly. " It is impossible to work with people like that," he mumbled.

" Do you know, Monsieur Peyrol, that she has been to see the priest ? " Catherine was heard suddenly towering above her end of the table. The two women had had a talk before Arlette had been induced by her aunt to lie down. Peyrol gave a start.

"What? Priest? . . . Now look here, Catherine," he went on with repressed ferocity, "do you imagine that all this interests me in the least?"

"I can think of nothing but that niece of mine. We two have nobody but each other in the world," she went on, reproducing the very phrase Arlette had used to Réal. She seemed to be thinking aloud, but noticed that Peyrol was listening with attention. "He wanted to shut her up from everybody," and the old woman clasped her meagre hands with a sudden gesture. "I suppose there are still some convents about the world."

"You and the patronne are mad together," declared Peyrol. "All this only shows what an ass the curé is. I don't know much about these things, though I have seen some nuns in my time, and some very queer ones too, but it seems to me that they don't take crazy people into convents. Don't you be afraid. I tell you that." He stopped, because the inner door of the kitchen came open and Lieutenant Réal stepped in. His sword hung on his forearm by the belt, his hat was on his head. He dropped his little valise on the floor and sat down in the nearest chair to put on his shoes, which he had brought down in his other hand. Then he came up to the table. Peyrol, who had kept his eyes on him, thought: "Here is one who looks like a moth scorched in the fire." Réal's eyes were sunk, his cheeks seemed hollowed, and the whole face had an arid and dry aspect.

"Well, you are in a fine state for the work of deceiving the enemy," Peyrol observed. "Why, to look at you, nobody would believe a word you said. You are not going to be ill, I hope. You are on service. You haven't got the right to be ill. I say, Mademoiselle Catherine, produce the bottle, you know, my private bottle. . . ." He snatched it from Catherine's hand, poured some brandy into the lieutenant's coffee, pushed the bowl towards him and waited. "Nom de nom!" he said forcibly, "don't you know what this is for? It's for you to drink." Réal obeyed with a strange, automatic docility. "And now," said Peyrol, getting up, "I will go to my room and shave. This is a great day—the day we are going to see the lieutenant off."

H H 2

Till then Réal had not uttered a word, but directly the door closed behind Peyrol he raised his head.

"Catherine!" His voice was like a rustle in his throat. She was looking at him steadily, and he continued: "Listen, when she finds I am gone you tell her I will return soon. To-morrow. Always to-morrow."

"Yes, my good Monsieur," said Catherine in an unmoved voice but clasping her hands convulsively. "There is nothing else I would dare tell her!"

"She will believe you," whispered Réal wildly.

"Yes! She will believe me," repeated Catherine in a mournful tone.

Réal got up, put the sword-belt over his head, picked up the valise. There was a little flush on his cheeks.

"Adieu," he said to the silent old woman. She made no answer, but as he turned away she raised her hand a little, hesitated, and let it fall again. It seemed to her that the women of Escampobar had been singled out for divine wrath. Her niece appeared to her like the scapegoat charged with all the murders and blasphemies of the Revolution. She herself, too, had been cast out from the grace of God. But that had been a long time ago. She had made her peace with Heaven since. Again she raised her hand and, this time, made in the air the sign of the cross at the back of Lieutenant Réal.

Meanwhile, upstairs Peyrol, scraping his big flat cheek with an English razor-blade at the window, saw Lieutenant Réal on the path to the shore; and high above there, commanding a vast view of sea and land, he shrugged his shoulders impatiently with no visible provocation. One could not trust those epaulette-wearers. They would cram a fellow's head with notions either for their own sake or for the sake of the service. Still, he was too old a bird to be caught with chaff; and besides, that long-legged stiff beggar going down the path, with all his officer airs, was honest enough. At any rate he knew a seaman when he saw one, though he was as cold-blooded as a fish. Peyrol had a smile which was a little awry.

Cleaning the razor-blade (one of a set of twelve in a case) he had a vision of a brilliantly hazy ocean and an English

Indiaman with her yards braced all ways, her canvas blowing loose above her blood-stained decks overrun by a lot of privateersmen, and with the island of Ceylon swelling like a thin blue cloud on the far horizon.  He had always wished to own a set of English blades and there he had got it, fell over it as it were, lying on the floor of a cabin which had been already ransacked.  " For good steel—it was good steel," he thought, looking at the blade fixedly.  And there it was, nearly worn out.  The others too.  That steel !  And here he was, holding the case in his hand as though he had just picked it up from the floor.  Same case.  Same man.  And the steel worn out.

He shut the case brusquely, flung it into his sea-chest, which was standing open, and slammed the lid down.  The feeling which was in his breast, and had been known to more articulate men than himself, was that life was a dream less substantial than the vision of Ceylon lying like a cloud on the sea.  Dream left astern.  Dream straight ahead.  This disenchanted philosophy took the shape of fierce swearing. " Sacré nom de nom de nom . . . Tonnerre de bon Dieu ! "

While tying his neckcloth he handled it with fury as though he meant to strangle himself with it.  He rammed a soft cap on to his venerable locks recklessly, seized his cudgel—but before leaving the room walked up to the window giving on the east.  He could not see the Petite Passe on account of the lookout hill, but to the left a great portion of the Hyères Roadstead lay spread out before him, pale grey in the morning light, with the land about Cape Blanc swelling in the distance with all its details blurred as yet and only one conspicuous object presenting to his sight something that might have been a lighthouse by its shape, but which Peyrol knew very well was the English corvette already under way and with all her canvas set.

This sight pleased Peyrol mainly because he had expected it.  The Englishman was doing exactly what he had expected he would do, and Peyrol looked towards the English cruiser with a smile of malicious triumph as if he were confronting her captain.  For some reason or other he imagined Captain

Vincent as long-faced, with yellow teeth and a wig, whereas that officer wore his own hair and had a set of teeth which would have done honour to a London belle, and was really the hidden cause of Captain Vincent appearing so often wreathed in smiles.

That ship at this great distance and steering in his direction held Peyrol at the window long enough for the increasing light of the morning to burst into sunshine, colouring and filling-in the flat outline of the land with tints of wood and rock and field, with clear dots of buildings enlivening the view. The sun threw a sort of halo around the ship. Recollecting himself, Peyrol left the room and shut the door quietly. Quietly too he descended the stairs from his garret. On the landing he underwent a short inward struggle, at the end of which he approached the door of Catherine's room and opening it a little, put his head in. Across the whole width of it he saw Arlette fast asleep. Her aunt had thrown a light coverlet over her. Her low shoes stood at the foot of the bed. Her black hair lay loose on the pillow; and Peyrol's gaze became arrested by the long eyelashes on her pale cheek. Suddenly he fancied she moved, and he withdrew his head sharply, pulling the door to. He listened for a moment as if tempted to open it again, but judging it too risky, continued on his way downstairs. At his reappearance in the kitchen Catherine turned sharply. She was dressed for the day, with a big white cap on her head, a black bodice and a brown skirt with ample folds. She had a pair of varnished sabots on her feet over her shoes.

"No signs of Scevola," she said, advancing towards Peyrol. "And Michel, too, has not been here yet."

Peyrol thought that if she had been only shorter, what with her black eyes and slightly curved nose she would have looked like a witch. But witches can read people's thoughts, and he looked openly at Catherine with the pleasant conviction that she could not read his thoughts. He said:

"I took good care not to make any noise upstairs, Mademoiselle Catherine. When I am gone the house will be empty and quiet enough."

She had a curious expression. She struck Peyrol suddenly

as if she were lost in that kitchen in which she had reigned for many years. He continued:

"You will be alone all the morning."

She seemed to be listening to some distant sound, and after Peyrol had added, "Everything is all right now," she nodded, and after a moment said in a manner that for her was unexpectedly impulsive:

"Monsieur Peyrol, I am tired of life."

He shrugged his shoulders and with somewhat sinister jocosity remarked:

"I will tell you what it is; you ought to have been married."

She turned her back on him abruptly.

"No offence," Peyrol excused himself in a tone of gloom rather than of apology. "It is no use to attach any importance to things. What is this life? Phew! Nobody can remember one-tenth of it. Here I am; and, you know, I would bet that if one of my old-time chums came along and saw me like this, here with you—I mean one of those chums that stand up for a fellow in a scrimmage and look after him should he be hurt—well, I bet," he repeated, "he wouldn't know me. He would say to himself, perhaps, 'Hullo! here's a comfortable married couple.'"

He paused. Catherine, with her back to him and calling him, not Monsieur, but Peyrol, *tout court*, remarked, not exactly with displeasure, but rather with an ominous accent, that this was no time for idle talk. Peyrol, however, continued, though his tone was very far from being that of idle talk:

"But you see, Mademoiselle Catherine, you were not like the others. You allowed yourself to be struck all of a heap, and at the same time you were too hard on yourself."

Her long thin frame bent low to work the bellows under the enormous overmantel; she assented: "Perhaps! We Escampobar women were always hard on ourselves."

"That's what I say. If you had had things happen to you which happened to me. . . ."

"But you men, you are different. It doesn't matter what you do. You have got your own strength. You need not be hard on yourselves. You go from one thing to another thoughtlessly."

He remained looking at her searchingly, with something like a hint of a smile on his shaven lips, but she turned away to the sink, where one of the women working about the farm had deposited a great pile of vegetables. She started on them with a broken-bladed knife, preserving her sibylline air, even in that homely occupation.

" It will be a good soup, I see, at noon to-day," said the rover suddenly. He turned on his heels and went out through the salle. The whole world lay open to him, or at any rate the whole of the Mediterranean, viewed down the ravine between the two hills. The bell of the farm's milch-cow, which had a talent for keeping herself invisible, reached him from the right, but he could not see as much as the tips of her horns, though he looked for them. He stepped out sturdily. He had not gone twenty yards down the ravine when another sound made him stand still as if changed into stone. It was a faint noise resembling very much the hollow rumble an empty farm-cart would make on a stony road, but Peyrol looked up at the sky, and though it was perfectly clear, he did not seem pleased with its aspect. He had a hill on each side of him and the placid cove below his feet. He muttered " H'm ! Thunder at sunrise. It must be in the west. It only wanted that ! " He feared it would first kill the little breeze that was and then knock the weather up altogether. For a moment all his faculties seemed paralysed by that faint sound. On that sea ruled by the gods of Olympus he might have been a pagan mariner subject to Jupiter's caprices ; but like a defiant pagan he shook his fist vaguely at space, which answered him by a short and threatening mutter. Then he swung on his way till he caught sight of the two mastheads of the tartane, when he stopped to listen. No sound of any sort reached him from there, and he went on his way thinking, " ' Go from one thing to another thought-lessly ' ! Indeed ! . . . That's all old Catherine knows about it." He had so many things to think of that he did not know which to lay hold of first. He just let them lie jumbled up in his head. His feelings too were in a state of confusion, and vaguely he felt that his conduct was at the mercy of an internal conflict. The consciousness of that fact accounted perhaps for his sardonic attitude towards himself and outwardly towards those whom he perceived on board the tartane, and especially towards the lieutenant, whom he saw sitting on the deck leaning against the head of the rudder, characteristically aloof from the two other persons on board. Michel, also, characteristically, was standing on the top of the little cabin scuttle, obviously looking out for his " maître." Citizen Scevola, sitting on deck, seemed at first sight to be at liberty, but as a matter of fact he was not. He was loosely tied up to a stanchion by three turns of the mainsheet with the knot in such a position that he could not get at it without attracting attention; and that situation seemed also somewhat characteristic of Citizen Scevola with its air of half liberty, half suspicion and, as it were, contemptuous restraint. The sans-culotte, whose late experiences had nearly unsettled his reason, first by their utter incomprehensibility and afterwards by the enigmatical attitude of Peyrol, had dropped his head and folded his arms on his breast. And that attitude was dubious, too. It might have been resignation or it might have been profound sleep. The rover addressed himself first to the lieutenant.

" Le moment approche," said Peyrol with a queer twitch at a corner of his lip, while under his soft woollen cap his venerable locks stirred in the breath of a suddenly warm air. " The great moment—eh ? "

He leaned over the big tiller, and seemed to be hovering above the lieutenant's shoulder.

" What's this infernal company ? " murmured the latter without even looking at Peyrol.

" All old friends—quoi ? " said Peyrol in a homely tone. " We will keep that little affair amongst ourselves. The fewer the men, the greater the glory. Catherine is getting the vegetables ready for the noonday soup and the Englishman is coming down towards the Passe, where he will arrive about noon, too ready to have his eye put out. You know, lieutenant, that will be your job. You may depend on me for sending you off when the moment comes. For what is it to you? You have no friends, you have not even a petite amie. As to expecting an old rover like me—oh no, lieutenant! Of course liberty is sweet, but what do you know of it, you epaulette-wearers? Moreover, I am no good for quarter-deck talks and all that politeness."

" I wish, Peyrol, you would not talk so much," said Lieutenant Réal, turning his head slightly. He was struck by the strange expression on the old rover's face. " And I don't see what the actual moment matters. I am going to look for the fleet. All you have to do is to hoist the sails for me and then scramble ashore."

" Very simple," observed Peyrol through his teeth, and then began to sing :

> " Quoique leurs chapeaux sont bien laids
> God-dam! Moi, j'aime les Anglais
> Ils ont un si bon caractere!"

but interrupted himself suddenly to hail Scevola :

" Hé! Citoyen!" and then remarked, confidentially to Réal : " He isn't asleep, you know, but he isn't like the English, he has a sacré mauvais caractère. He got into his head," continued Peyrol, in a loud and innocent tone, " that you locked him up in this cabin last night. Did you notice the venomous glance he gave you just now? "

Both Lieutenant Réal and the innocent Michel appeared surprised at his boisterousness ; but all the time Peyrol was thinking : " I wish to goodness I knew how that thunderstorm is getting on and what course it is shaping. I can't find that out unless I go up to the farm and get a view to the westward. It may be as far as the Rhone Valley ; no doubt it is and it will come out of it too, curses on it. One won't be able to reckon on half an hour of steady wind from any quarter." He directed a look of ironic gaiety at all the faces in turn. Michel met it with a faithful-dog gaze and innocently open mouth. Scevola kept his chin buried on his chest. Lieutenant Réal was insensible to outward impressions, and his absent stare made nothing of Peyrol. The rover himself presently fell into thought. The last stir of air died out in the little basin, and the sun clearing Porquerolles inundated it with a sudden light, in which Michel blinked like an owl.

"It's hot early," he announced aloud, but only because he had formed the habit of talking to himself. He would not have presumed to offer an opinion unless asked by Peyrol.

His voice having recalled Peyrol to himself, he proposed to masthead the yards, and even asked Lieutenant Réal to help in that operation, which was accomplished in silence, except for the faint squeaking of the blocks. The sails, however, were kept hauled up in the gear.

"Like this," said Peyrol, "you have only to let go the ropes and you will be under canvas at once."

Without answering Réal returned to his position by the rudder-head. He was saying to himself: "I am sneaking off. No, there is honour, duty. And of course I will return. But when? They will forget all about me and I shall never be exchanged. This war may last for years,—" and illogically he wished he could have had a God to whom he could pray for relief in his anguish. "She will be in despair," he thought, writhing inwardly at the mental picture of a distracted Arlette. Life, however, had embittered his spirit early, and he said to himself: "But in a month's time will she even give me a thought?" Instantly he felt remorseful with a remorse strong enough to lift him to his feet as if he were morally obliged to go up again and confess to Arlette this sacrilegious cynicism of thought. "I am mad," he muttered, perching himself on the low rail. His lapse from faith plunged him into such a depth of unhappiness that he felt all his strength of will go out of him. He sat there apathetic and suffering. He meditated dully: "Young men have been known to die suddenly; why should not I? I am, as a matter of fact, at the end of my endurance. I am half dead already. Yes! but what is left of that life does not belong to me now."

"Peyrol," he said, in such a piercing tone that even Scevola jerked his head up; but he made an effort to reduce his shrillness and went on speaking very carefully: "I have left a letter for the Secretary-General at the Majorité to pay twenty-five hundred francs to Jean—you are Jean, are you not ?—Peyrol, price of the tartane in which I sail. Is that right ? "

" What did you do that for ? " asked Peyrol with an extremely stony face. " To get me into trouble ? "

" Don't be a fool, gunner, nobody remembers your name. It is buried under a stack of blackened paper. I must ask you to go there and tell them that you have seen with your own eyes Lieutenant Réal sail away on his mission."

The stoniness of Peyrol persisted, but his eyes were full of fury. " Oh yes, I see myself going there. Twenty-five hundred francs ! Twenty-five hundred fiddlesticks." His tone changed suddenly. " I heard someone say that you were an honest man, and I suppose this is a proof of it. Well, to the devil with your honesty." He glared at the lieutenant, and then thought : " He doesn't even pretend to listen to what I say "—and another sort of anger, partly contemptuous and with something of dim sympathy in it, replaced his downright fury. " Pah ! " he said, spat over the side, and walking up to Réal with great deliberation, slapped him on the shoulder. The only effect of this proceeding was to make Réal look up at him without any expression whatever.

Peyrol then picked up the lieutenant's valise and carried it down into the cuddy. As he passed by, Citizen Scevola uttered the word " Citoyen," but it was only when he came back again that Peyrol condescended to say " Well ? "

" What are you going to do with me ? " asked Scevola.

" You would not give me an account of how you came on board this tartane," said Peyrol in a tone that sounded almost friendly, " therefore I need not tell you what I will do with you."

A low muttering of thunder followed so close upon his words that it might have come out of Peyrol's own lips. The rover gazed uneasily at the sky. It was still clear over-head, and at the bottom of that little basin surrounded by rocks there was no view in any other direction ; but even as he gazed there was a sort of flicker in the sunshine, succeeded by a mighty but distant clap of thunder. For the next half-hour Peyrol and Michel were busy ashore taking a long line from the tartane to the entrance of the little basin, where they fastened the end of it to a bush. This was for the purpose of hauling the tartane out into the cove. Then they came aboard again. The bit of sky above their heads was still clear, but while walking with the hauling line near the cove Peyrol had got a glimpse of the edge of the cloud. The sun grew scorching all of a sudden, and in the stagnating air a mysterious change seemed to come over the quality and the colour of the light. Peyrol flung his cap on the deck, baring his head to the subtle menace of the breathless stillness of the air.

"Phew! Ca chauffe," he muttered, rolling up the sleeves of his jacket. He wiped his forehead with his mighty forearm upon which a mermaid with an immensely long fishtail was tattooed. Perceiving the lieutenant's belted sword lying on the deck, he picked it up and without any ceremony threw it down the cabin stairs. As he was passing again near Scevola, the sans-culotte raised his voice.

"I believe you are one of those wretches corrupted by English gold," he cried like one inspired. His shining eyes, his red cheeks, testified to the fire of patriotism burning in his breast, and he used that conventional phrase of revolutionary time, a time when, intoxicated with oratory, he used to run about dealing death to traitors of both sexes and all ages. But his denunciation was received in such profound silence that his own belief in it wavered. His words had sunk into an abysmal stillness and the next sound was Peyrol speaking to Réal.

"I am afraid you will get very wet, lieutenant, before long," and then, looking at Réal, he thought with great conviction: "Wet! He wouldn't mind getting drowned." Standing stock still, he fretted and fumed inwardly, wondering where precisely the English ship was by this time and where the devil that thunderstorm had got to: for the sky had become as mute as the oppressed earth. Réal asked:

"Is it not time to haul out, gunner?"

And Peyrol said:

"There is not a breath of wind anywhere for miles." He was gratified by the fairly loud mutter rolling apparently along the inland hills. Over the pool a little ragged cloud torn from the purple robe of the storm floated, arrested and thin like a bit of dark gauze.

Above at the farm Catherine had heard, too, the ominous mutter and came to the door of the salle. From there she could see the purple cloud itself, convoluted and solid, and its sinister shadow lying over the hills. The oncoming of the storm added to her sense of uneasiness at finding herself all alone in the house. Michel had not come up. She would have welcomed Michel, to whom she hardly ever spoke, simply as a person belonging to the usual order of things. She was not talkative, but somehow she would have liked somebody to speak to just for a moment. This cessation of all sound, voices or footsteps, around the buildings was not welcome; but looking at the cloud, she thought that their would be noise enough presently. However, stepping back into the kitchen, she was met by a sound that made her regret the oppressive silence, by its piercing and terrifying character; it was a shriek in the upper part of the house, where, as far as she knew, there was only Arlette asleep. In her attempt to cross the kitchen to the foot of the stairs the weight of her accumulated years fell upon the old woman. She felt suddenly very feeble and hardly able to breathe. And all at once the thought " Scevola ! Was he murdering her up there ? " paralysed the last remnant of her physical powers. What else could it be ? She fell, as if shot, into a chair under the first shock and found herself unable to move. Only her brain remained active, and she raised her hands to her eyes as if to shut out the image of the horrors upstairs. She heard nothing more from above. Arlette was dead. She thought that now it was her turn. While her body quailed before the brutal violence, her weary spirit longed ardently for the end. Let him come ! Let all this be over at last, with a blow on the head or a stab in the breast. She had not the courage to uncover her eyes. She waited. But after about a minute—it seemed to her interminable— she heard rapid footsteps overhead. Arlette was running here and there. Catherine uncovered her eyes and was about to rise when she heard at the top of the stairs the name of Peyrol shouted with a desperate accent. Then again, after the shortest of pauses, the cry of "Peyrol, Peyrol!" and then the sound of feet running downstairs. There was another shriek, "Peyrol!" just outside the door before it flew open. Who was pursuing her? Catherine managed to stand up. Steadying herself with one hand on the table, she presented an undaunted front to her niece, who ran into the kitchen with loose hair flying and the appearance of wildest distraction in her eyes.

The staircase door had slammed to behind her. Nobody was pursuing her; and Catherine, putting forth her lean brown arm, arrested Arlette's flight with such a jerk that the two women swung against each other. She seized her niece by the shoulders.

"What is this, in Heaven's name? Where are you rushing to?" she cried, and the other, as if suddenly exhausted, whispered:

"I woke up from an awful dream."

The kitchen grew dark under the cloud that hung over the house now. There was a feeble flicker of lightning and a faint crash, far away.

The old woman gave her niece a little shake. "Dreams are nothing," she said. "You are awake now. . . ." And indeed Catherine thought that no dream could be so bad as the realities which kept hold of one through the long waking hours.

"They were killing him," moaned Arlette, beginning to tremble and struggle in her aunt's arms. "I tell you they were killing him."

"Be quiet. Were you dreaming of Peyrol?"

She became still in a moment and then whispered: "No, Eugène."

She had seen Réal set upon by a mob of men and women, all dripping with blood, in a livid cold light, in front of a stretch of mere shells of houses with cracked walls and broken windows, and going down in the midst of a forest of raised arms, brandishing sabres, clubs, knives, axes. There was also a man flourishing a red rag on a stick, while another was beating a drum which boomed above the sickening sound of broken glass falling like rain on the pavement. And away

round the corner of an empty street came Peyrol, whom she
recognized by his white head, walking without haste, swinging
his cudgel regularly. The terrible thing was that Peyrol
looked straight at her, not noticing anything, composed,
without a frown or a smile, unseeing and deaf, while she waved
her arms and shrieked desperately to him for help. She woke
up with the piercing sound of his name in her ears and with
the impression of the dream so powerful that even now, looking distractedly into her aunt's face, she could see the bare
arms of that murderous crowd raised above Réal's sinking
head. Yet the name that had sprung to her lips on waking
was the name of Peyrol. She pushed her aunt away with
such force that the old woman staggered backwards, and to
save herself had to catch hold of the overmantel above her
head. Arlette ran to the door of the salle, looked in, came
back to her aunt and shouted: " Where is he? "

Catherine really did not know which path the lieutenant
had taken. She understood very well that " he " meant
Réal.

She said : " He went away a long time ago "; grasped
her niece's arm and added with an effort to steady her voice :
" He is coming back, Arlette—for nothing will keep him
away from you."

Arlette, as if mechanically, was whispering to herself the
magic name, " Peyrol, Peyrol ! " then cried : " I want
Eugène now. This moment."

Catherine's face wore a look of unflinching patience.
" He has departed on service," she said. Her niece looked
at her with enormous eyes, coal-black, profound, and immovable, while in a forcible and distracted tone she said : " You
and Peyrol have been plotting to rob me of my reason. But
I will know how to make that old man give him up. He is
mine ! " She spun round wildly, like a person looking for a
way of escape from a deadly peril, and rushed out blindly.

About Escampobar the air was murky but calm and the
silence was so profound that it was possible to hear the first
heavy drops of rain striking the ground. In the intimidat-
ing shadow of the storm-cloud, Arlette stood irresolute for a
moment, but it was to Peyrol, the man of mystery and

power, that her thoughts turned. She was ready to embrace his knees, to entreat and to scold. " Peyrol, Peyrol ! " she cried twice, and lent her ear as if expecting an answer. Then she shouted : " I want him back."

Catherine, alone in the kitchen, moving with dignity, sat down in the arm-chair with the tall back, like a senator in his curule chair awaiting the blow of a barbarous fate.

Arlette flew down the slope. The first sign of her coming was a faint thin scream which really the rover alone heard and understood. He pressed his lips in a particular way, showing his appreciation of the coming difficulty. The next moment he saw, poised on a detached boulder and thinly veiled by the first perpendicular shower, Arlette, who, catching sight of the tartane with the men on board of her, let out a prolonged shriek of mingled triumph and despair : " Peyrol ! Help ! Pey—rol ! "

Réal jumped to his feet with an extremely scared face, but Peyrol extended an arresting arm. " She is calling to me," he said, gazing at the figure poised on the rock. " Well leaped ! Sacré nom ! . . . Well leaped ! " And he muttered to himself soberly : " She will break her legs or her neck."

" I see you, Peyrol," screamed Arlette, who seemed to be flying through the air. " Don't you dare."

" Yes, here I am," shouted the rover, striking his breast with his fist.

Lieutenant Réal put both his hands over his face. Michel looked on open-mouthed, very much as if watching a performance in a circus ; but Scevola cast his eyes down. Arlette came on board with such an impetus that Peyrol had to step forward and save her from a fall which would have stunned her. She struggled in his arms with extreme violence. The heiress of Escampobar, with her loose black hair, seemed the incarnation of pale fury. " Misérable ! Don't you dare ! " A roll of thunder covered her voice, but when it had passed away she was heard again in suppliant tones. " Peyrol, my friend, my dear old friend. Give him back to me," and all the time her body writhed in the arms of the old seaman. " You used to love me, Peyrol," she cried, without ceasing to struggle, and suddenly struck the rover twice in the face with

her clenched fist.   Peyrol's head received the two blows as
if it had been made of marble, but he felt with fear her body
become still, grow rigid in his arms.   A heavy squall enveloped
the group of people on board the tartane.   Peyrol laid
Arlette gently on the deck.   Her eyes were closed, her hands
remained clenched; every sign of life had left her white
face.   Peyrol stood up and looked at the tall rocks streaming
with water.   The rain swept over the tartane with an angry
swishing roar to which was added the sound of water rushing
violently down the folds and seams of the precipitous shore,
vanishing gradually from his sight, as if this had been the
beginning of a destroying and universal deluge—the end of
all things.

Lieutenant Réal, kneeling on one knee, contemplated the
pale face of Arlette.   Distinct, yet mingling with the faint
growl of distant thunder, Peyrol's voice was heard saying:

" We can't put her ashore and leave her lying in the rain.
She must be taken up to the house."   Arlette's soaked
clothes clung to her limbs while the lieutenant, his bare head
dripping with rainwater, looked as if he had just saved her
from drowning.   Peyrol gazed down inscrutably at the
woman stretched on the deck and at the kneeling man.
" She has fainted from rage at her old Peyrol," he went on
rather dreamily.   " Strange things do happen.   However,
lieutenant, you had better take her under the arms and step
ashore first.   I will help you.   Ready?   Lift."

The movements of the two men had to be careful and their
progress was slow on the lower, steep part of the slope.
After going up more than two-thirds of the way, they rested
their insensible burden on a flat stone.   Réal continued to
sustain the shoulders, but Peyrol lowered the feet gently.

" Ha!" he said.   " You will be able to carry her yourself
the rest of the way and give her up to old Catherine.   Get
a firm footing and I will lift her and place her in your arms.
You can walk the distance quite easily.   There. . . . Hold
her a little higher, or her feet will be catching on the
stones."

Arlette's hair was hanging far below the lieutenant's arm
in an inert and heavy mass.   The thunderstorm was passing

away, leaving a cloudy sky. And Peyrol thought with a profound sigh : " I am tired."

" She is light," said Réal.

" Parbleu, she is light. If she were dead you would find her heavy enough. Allons, mon lieutenant. No ! I am not coming. What's the good ? I'll stay down here. I have no mind to listen to Catherine's scolding."

The lieutenant, looking absorbed into the face resting in the hollow of his arm, never averted his gaze—not even when Peyrol, stooping over Arlette, kissed the white forehead near the roots of the hair, black as a raven's wing.

" What am I to do ? " muttered Réal.

" Do ? Why, give her up to old Catherine. And you may just as well tell her that I will be coming along directly. That will cheer her up. I used to count for something in that house. Allez ! For our time is very short."

With these words he turned away and walked slowly down to the tartane. A breeze had sprung up. He felt it on his wet neck and was grateful for the cool touch which recalled him to himself, to his old wandering self which had known no softness and no hesitation in the face of any risk offered by life.

As he stepped on board, the shower passed away, Michel, wet to the skin, was still in the very same attitude, gazing up the slope. Citizen Scevola had drawn his knees up and was holding his head in his hands ; whether because of rain or cold or for some other reason, his teeth were chattering audibly with a continuous and distressing rattle. Peyrol flung off his jacket, heavy with water, with a strange air as if it was of no more use to his mortal envelope, squared his broad shoulders, and directed Michel, in a deep, quiet voice, to let go the lines holding the tartane to the shore. The faithful henchman was taken aback and required one of Peyrol's authoritative " Allez ! " to put him in motion. Meantime the rover cast off the tiller lines and laid his hand with an air of mastery on the stout piece of wood projecting horizontally from the rudder-head about the level of his hip. The voices and the movements of his companions caused Citizen Scevola to master the desperate trembling of his jaw. He wriggled a little in his bonds, and the question that had been on his lips for a good many hours was uttered again.

"What are you going to do with me?"

"What do you think of a little promenade at sea?" Peyrol asked in a tone that was not unkindly.

Citizen Scevola, who had seemed totally and completely cast down and subdued, let out a most unexpected screech.

"Unbind me. Put me ashore."

Michel, busy forward, was moved to smile as though he had possessed a cultivated sense of incongruity. Peyrol remained serious.

"You shall be untied presently," he assured the blood-drinking patriot, who had been for so many years the reputed possessor not only of Escampobar but of the Escampobar heiress that, living on appearances, he had almost come to believe in that ownership himself. No wonder he screeched at this rude awakening. Peyrol raised his voice: "Haul on the line, Michel."

As, directly the ropes had been let go, the tartane had swung clear of the shore, the movements given her by Michel carried her towards the entrance by which the basin communicated with the cove. Peyrol attended to the helm, and in a moment, gliding through the narrow gap, the tartane carrying her way, shot out almost into the middle of the cove.

A little wind could be felt, running light wrinkles over the water, but outside the overshadowed sea was already speckled with white caps. Peyrol helped Michel to haul aft the sheets and then went back to the tiller. The pretty spick-and-span craft that had been lying idle for so long began to glide into the wide world. Michel gazed at the shore as if lost in admiration. Citizen Scevola's head had fallen on his knees while his nerveless hands clasped his legs loosely. He was the very image of dejection.

"Hé, Michel! Come here and cast loose the citizen. It is only fair that he should be untied for a little excursion at sea."

When his order had been executed, Peyrol addressed himself to the desolate figure on the deck.

"Like this, should the tartane get capsized in a squall, you will have an equal chance with us to swim for your life."

Scevola disdained to answer. He was engaged in biting his knee with rage in a stealthy fashion.

"You came on board for some murderous purpose. Who you were after, unless it was myself, God only knows. I feel quite justified in giving you a little outing at sea. I won't conceal from you, citizen, that it may not be without risk to life or limb. But you have only yourself to thank for being here."

As the tartane drew clear of the cove, she felt more the weight of the breeze and darted forward with a lively motion. A vaguely contented smile lighted up Michel's hairy countenance.

"She feels the sea," said Peyrol, who enjoyed the swift movement of his vessel. "This is different from your lagoon, Michel."

"To be sure," said Michel with becoming gravity.

"Doesn't it seem funny to you, as you look back at the shore, to think that you have left nothing and nobody behind?"

Michel assumed the aspect of a man confronted by an intellectual problem. Since he had become Peyrol's henchman he had lost the habit of thinking altogether. Directions and orders were easy things to apprehend; but a conversation with him whom he called "notre maître" was a serious matter demanding great and concentrated attention.

"Possibly," he murmured, looking strangely self-conscious.

"Well, you are lucky, take my word for it," said the rover, watching the course of his little vessel along the head of the peninsula. "You have not even a dog to miss you."

"I have only you, Maître Peyrol."

"That's what I was thinking," said Peyrol half to himself, while Michel, who had good sea-legs, kept his balance to the movements of the craft without taking his eyes from the rover's face.

"No," Peyrol exclaimed suddenly, after a moment of meditation, "I could not leave you behind." He extended his open palm towards Michel.

"Put your hand in there," he said.

Michel hesitated for a moment before this extraordinary proposal. At last he did so, and Peyrol, holding the bereaved fisherman's hand in a powerful grip, said:

"If I had gone away by myself, I would have left you marooned on this earth like a man thrown out to die on a desert island." Some dim perception of the solemnity of the occasion seemed to enter Michel's primitive brain. He connected Peyrol's words with the sense of his own insignificant position at the tail of all mankind, and, timidly, he murmured with his clear, innocent glance unclouded, the fundamental axiom of his philosophy:

"Somebody must be last in this world."

"Well, then, you will have to forgive me all that may happen between this and the hour of sunset."

The tartane, obeying the helm, fell off before the wind, with her head to the eastward.

Peyrol murmured: "She has not forgotten how to walk the seas." His unsubdued heart, heavy for so many days, had a moment of buoyancy—the illusion of immense freedom.

At that moment Réal, amazed at finding no tartane in the basin, was running madly towards the cove, where he was sure Peyrol must be waiting to give her up to him. He ran out on to the very rock on which Peyrol's late prisoner had sat after his escape, too tired to care, yet cheered by the hope of liberty. But Réal was in a worse plight. He could see no shadowy form through the thin veil of rain which pitted the sheltered piece of water framed in the rocks. The little craft had been spirited away. Impossible! There must be something wrong with his eyes! Again the barren hillsides echoed the name of "Peyrol," shouted with all the force of Réal's lungs. He shouted it only once, and about five minutes afterwards appeared at the kitchen-door, panting, streaming with water as if he had fought his way up from the bottom of the sea. In the tall-backed arm-chair Arlette lay, with her limbs relaxed, her head on Catherine's arm, her face white as death. He saw her open her black eyes, enormous and as if not of this world; he saw old Catherine turn her head, heard a cry of surprise, and saw a sort of struggle beginning between the two women. He screamed at them like a madman: "Peyrol has betrayed me!" and in an instant, with a bang of the door, he was gone.

The rain had ceased. Above his head the unbroken mass of clouds moved to the eastward, and he moved in the same direction, as if he too were driven by the wind up the hillside, towards the lookout. When he reached the spot and, gasping, flung one arm round the trunk of the leaning tree, the only thing he was aware of during the sombre pause in the unrest of the elements was the distracting turmoil of his thoughts. After a moment he perceived through the rain the English ship with her topsails lowered on the caps, forging ahead slowly across the northern entrance of the Petite Passe. His distress fastened insanely on the notion of there being a connection between that enemy ship and Peyrol's inexplicable conduct. That old man had always meant to go himself! And when a moment after, looking to the southward, he made out the shadow of the tartane coming round the land in the midst of another squall, he muttered to himself a bitter "Of course!" She had both her sails set. Peyrol was indeed pressing her to the utmost in his shameful haste to traffic with the enemy. The truth was that from the position in which Réal first saw him, Peyrol could not yet see the English ship, and held confidently on his course up the middle of the strait. The man-of-war and the little tartane saw each other quite unexpectedly at a distance that was very little over a mile. Peyrol's heart flew into his mouth at finding himself so close to the enemy. On board the *Amelia* at first no notice was taken. It was simply a tartane making for shelter on the north side of Porquerolles. But when Peyrol suddenly altered his course, the master of the man-of-war, noticing the manœuvre, took up the long glass for a look. Captain Vincent was on deck and agreed with the master's remark that "there was a craft acting suspiciously." Before the *Amelia* could come round in the heavy squall, Peyrol was already under the battery of Por-

queolles and, so far, safe from capture. Captain Vincent
had no mind to bring his ship within reach of the battery
and risk damage in his rigging or hull for the sake of a small
coaster. However, the tale brought on board by Symons
of his discovery of a hidden craft, of his capture, and his
wonderful escape, had made every tartane an object of
interest to the whole ship's company. The *Amelia* remained
hove to in the strait while her officers watched the lateen sails
gliding to and fro under the protecting muzzles of the guns.
Captain Vincent himself had been impressed by Peyrol's
manœuvre. Coasting craft, as a rule, were not afraid of the
*Amelia*. After taking a few turns on the quarter-deck he
ordered Symons to be called aft.

The hero of a unique and mysterious adventure, which
had been the only subject of talk on board the corvette for
the last twenty-four hours, came along rolling, hat in hand,
and enjoying a secret sense of his importance.

"Take the glass," said the captain, "and have a look at
that vessel under the land. Is she anything like the tartane
that you say you have been aboard of ? "

Symons was very positive. " I think I can swear to those
painted mastheads, your honour. It is the last thing I
remember before that murderous ruffian knocked me senseless. The moon shone on them. I can make them out now
with the glass." As to the fellow boasting to him that the
tartane was a dispatch-boat and had already made some trips,
well, Symons begged his honour to believe that the beggar
was not sober at the time. He did not care what he blurted
out. The best proof of his condition was that he went
away to fetch the soldiers and forgot to come back. The
murderous old ruffian ! "You see, your honour," continued
Symons, " he thought I was not likely to escape after getting
a blow that would have killed nine out of any ten men. So
he went away to boast of what he had done before the people
ashore ; because one of his chums, worse than himself, came
down thinking he would kill me with a dam' big manure fork,
saving your honour's presence. A regular savage he was."

Symons paused, staring, as if astonished at the marvels
of his own tale. The old master, standing at his captain's

elbow, observed in a dispassionate tone that, anyway, that peninsula was not a bad jumping-off place for a craft intending to slip through the blockade. Symons, not being dismissed, waited, hat in hand, while Captain Vincent directed the master to fill on the ship and stand a little nearer to the battery. It was done, and presently there was a flash of a gun low down on the water's edge and a shot came skipping in the direction of the *Amelia*. It fell very short, but Captain Vincent judged the ship was close enough, and ordered her to be hove to again. Then Symons was told to take a look through the glass once more. After a long interval he lowered it and spoke impressively to his captain :

" I can make out three heads aboard, your honour, and one is white. I would swear to that white head anywhere."

Captain Vincent made no answer. All this seemed very odd to him ; but after all it was possible. The craft had certainly acted suspiciously. He spoke to the first lieutenant in a half-vexed tone.

" He has done a rather smart thing. He will dodge here till dark and then get away. It is perfectly absurd. I don't want to send the boats too close to the battery. And if I do he may simply sail away from them and be round the land long before we are ready to give him chase. Darkness will be his best friend. However, we will keep a watch on him in case he is tempted to give us the slip late in the afternoon. In that case we will have a good try to catch him. If he has anything aboard, I should like to get hold of it. It may be of some importance, after all."

On board the tartane, Peyrol put his own interpretation on the ship's movements. His object had been attained. The corvette had marked him for her prey. Satisfied as to that, Peyrol watched his opportunity and taking advantage of a long squall, with rain thick enough to blur the form of the English ship, he left the shelter of the battery to lead the Englishman a dance and keep up his character of a man anxious to avoid capture.

Réal, from his position on the lookout, saw in the thinning downpour the pointed lateen sails glide round the north end of Porquerolles and vanish behind the land. Some time afterwards the *Amelia* made sail in a manner that put it beyond doubt that she meant to chase. Her lofty canvas was shut off too presently by the land of Porquerolles. When she had disappeared Réal turned to Arlette.

" Let us go," he said.

Arlette, stimulated by the short glimpse of Réal at the kitchen door, whom she had taken for a vision of a lost man calling her to follow him to the end of the world, had torn herself out of the old woman's thin, bony arms which could not cope with the struggles of her body and the fierceness of her spirit. She had run straight to the lookout, though there was nothing to guide her there except a blind impulse to seek Réal wherever he might be. He was not aware of her having found him until she seized hold of his arm with a suddenness, energy and determination of which no one with a clouded mind could have been capable. He felt himself being taken possession of in a way that tore all his scruples out of his breast. Holding on to the trunk of the tree, he threw his other arm round her waist, and when she confessed to him that she did not know why she had run up there, but that if she had not found him she would have thrown herself over the cliff, he tightened his clasp with sudden exultation, as though she had been a gift prayed for instead of a stumbling-block for his pedantic conscience. Together they walked back. In the failing light the buildings awaited them, lifeless, the walls darkened by rain and the big slopes of the roofs glistening and sinister under the flying desolation of the clouds. In the kitchen Catherine heard their mingled footsteps, and rigid in the tall arm-chair awaited their coming. Arlette threw her arms round the old woman's neck, while Réal stood on one side, looking on. Thought after thought flew through his mind and vanished in the strong feeling of the irrevocable nature of the event handing him to the woman whom, in the revulsion of his feelings, he was inclined to think more sane than himself. Arlette, with one arm over the old woman's shoulders, kissed the wrinkled forehead under the white band of linen that, on the erect head, had the effect of a rustic diadem.

"To-morrow you and I will have to walk down to the church."

The austere dignity of Catherine's pose seemed to be shaken by this proposal to lead before the God with whom she had made her peace long ago that unhappy girl chosen to share in the guilt of impious and unspeakable horrors which had darkened her mind.

Arlette, still stooping over her aunt's face, extended a hand towards Réal, who, making a step forward, took it silently into his grasp.

"Oh yes, you will, Aunt," insisted Arlette. "You will have to come with me to pray for Peyrol, whom you and I shall never see any more."

Catherine's head dropped, whether in assent or grief; and Réal felt an unexpected and profound emotion, for he, too, was convinced that none of the three persons in the farm would ever see Peyrol again. It was as though the rover of the wide seas had left them to themselves in a sudden impulse of scorn, of magnanimity, of a passion weary of itself. However come by, Réal was ready to clasp for ever to his breast that woman touched by the red hand of the Revolution; for she, whose little feet had run ankle-deep through the terrors of death, had brought to him the sense of triumphant life.


XVI

ASTERN of the tartane, the sun, about to set, kindled a streak of dull crimson glow between the darkening sea and the overcast sky. The peninsula of Giens and the islands of Hyères formed one mass of land detaching itself very black against the fiery girdle of the horizon; but to the north the long stretch of the Alpine coast continued beyond sight its endless sinuosities under the stooping clouds.

The tartane seemed to be rushing together with the run of the waves into the arms of the oncoming night. A little more than a mile away on her lee quarter, the *Amelia*, under all plain sail, pressed to the end of the chase. It had lasted now for a good many hours, for Peyrol, when slipping away, had managed to get the advantage of the *Amelia* from the very start. While still within the large sheet of smooth water which is called the Hyères Roadstead, the tartane, which was really a craft of extraordinary speed, managed to gain positively on the sloop. Afterwards, by suddenly darting down the eastern passage between the two last islands of the group, Peyrol actually got out of sight of the chasing ship, being hidden by the Ile du Levant for a time. The *Amelia*, having to tack twice in order to follow, lost ground once more. Emerging into the open sea, she had to tack again, and then the position became that of a stern chase, which proverbially is known as a long chase. Peyrol's skilful seamanship had twice extracted from Captain Vincent a low murmur accompanied by a significant compression of lips. At one time the *Amelia* had been near enough the tartane to send a shot ahead of her. That one was followed by another, which whizzed extraordinarily close to the mastheads, but then Captain Vincent ordered the gun to be secured again. He said to his first lieutenant, who, his speaking-trumpet in hand, kept at his elbow : " We must not sink that craft on any account. If we could get only an hour's calm, we would carry her with the boats."

The lieutenant remarked that there was no hope of a calm for the next twenty-four hours at least.

" No," said Captain Vincent, " and in about an hour it will be dark, and then he may very well give us the slip. The coast is not very far off, and there are batteries on both sides of Fréjus, under any of which he will be as safe from capture as though he were hove up on the beach. And look," he exclaimed after a moment's pause, " this is what the fellow means to do."

" Yes, sir," said the lieutenant, keeping his eyes on the white speck ahead, dancing lightly on the short Mediterranean waves, " he is keeping off the wind."

" We will have him in less than an hour," said Captain Vincent, and made as if he meant to rub his hands, but suddenly leaned his elbow on the rail. " After all," he went on, " properly speaking, it is a race between the *Amelia* and the night."

" And it will be dark early to-day," said the first lieutenant, swinging the speaking-trumpet by its lanyard. " Shall we take the yards off the backstays, sir ? "

" No," said Captain Vincent. " There is a clever seaman aboard that tartane. He is running off now, but at any time he may haul up again. We must not follow him too closely, or we shall lose the advantage which we have now. That man is determined on making his escape."

If those words by some miracle could have been carried to the ears of Peyrol, they would have brought to his lips a smile of malicious and triumphant exultation. Ever since he had laid his hand on the tiller of the tartane, every faculty of his resourcefulness and seamanship had been bent on deceiving the English captain, that enemy whom he had never seen, the man whose mind he had constructed for himself from the evolutions of his ship. Leaning against the heavy tiller he addressed Michel, breaking the silence of the strenuous afternoon.

" This is the moment," his deep voice uttered quietly. " Ease off the mainsheet, Michel. A little now, only."

When Michel returned to the place where he had been sitting to windward, the rover noticed his eyes fixed on his face wonderingly. Some vague thoughts had been forming themselves slowly, incompletely, in Michel's brain. Peyrol met the utter innocence of the unspoken inquiry with a smile that, beginning sardonically on his manly and sensitive mouth, ended in something resembling tenderness.

" That's so, camarade," he said with particular stress and intonation, as if those words contained a full and sufficient answer. Most unexpectedly Michel's round and generally staring eyes blinked, as if dazzled. He too produced from somewhere in the depths of his being a queer, misty smile from which Peyrol averted his gaze.

" Where is the citizen ? " he asked, bearing hard against the tiller and staring straight ahead. " He isn't gone overboard, is he ? I don't seem to have seen him since we rounded the land near Porquerolles Castle."

Michel, after craning his head forward to look over the edge of the deck, announced that Scevola was sitting on the keelson.

"Go forward," said Peyrol, "and ease off the foresheet now a little. This tartane has wings," he added to himself.

Alone on the after-deck Peyrol turned his head to look at the *Amelia*. That ship, in consequence of holding her wind, was now crossing obliquely the wake of the tartane. At the same time she had diminished the distance. Nevertheless, Peyrol considered that had he really meant to escape, his chances were as eight to ten—practically an assured success. For a long time he had been contemplating the lofty pyramid of canvas towering against the fading red belt on the sky, when a lamentable groan made him look round. It was Scevola. The citizen had adopted the mode of progression on all fours, and while Peyrol looked at him he rolled to leeward, saved himself rather cleverly from going overboard, and holding on desperately to a cleat, shouted in a hollow voice, pointing with the other hand as if he had made a tremendous discovery : "La terre ! La terre !"

"Certainly," said Peyrol, steering with extreme nicety. "What of that ?"

"I don't want to be drowned !" cried the citizen in his new hollow voice. Peyrol reflected a bit before he spoke in a serious tone :

"If you stay where you are, I assure you that you will . . ." he glanced rapidly over his shoulder at the *Amelia* . . . "not die by drowning." He jerked his head sideways. "I know that man's mind."

"What man ? Whose mind ?" yelled Scevola with intense eagerness and bewilderment. "We are only three on board."

But Peyrol's mind was contemplating maliciously the figure of a man with long teeth, in a wig and with large buckles to his shoes. Such was his ideal conception of what the captain of the *Amelia* ought to look like. That officer, whose naturally good-humoured face wore then a look of severe resolution, had beckoned his first lieutenant to his side again.

"We are gaining," he said quietly. "I intend to close with him to windward. We won't risk any of his tricks. It is very difficult to outmanœuvre a Frenchman, as you know. Send a few armed marines on the forecastle ahead. I am afraid the only way to get hold of this tartane is to disable the men on board of her. I wish to goodness I could think of some other. When we close with her, let the marines fire a well-aimed volley. You must get some marines to stand by aft as well. I hope we may shoot away his halliards; once his sails are down on his deck he is ours for the trouble of putting a boat over the side."

For more than half an hour Captain Vincent stood silent, elbow on rail, keeping his eye on the tartane, while on board the latter Peyrol steered silent and watchful but intensely conscious of the enemy ship holding on in her relentless pursuit. The narrow red band was dying out of the sky. The French coast, black against the fading light, merged into the shadows gathering in the eastern board. Citizen Scevola, somewhat soothed by the assurance that he would not die by drowning, had elected to remain quiet where he had fallen, not daring to trust himself to move on the lively deck. Michel, squatting to windward, gazed intently at Peyrol in expectation of some order at any minute. But Peyrol uttered no word and made no sign. From time to time a burst of foam flew over the tartane, or a splash of water would come aboard with a scurrying noise.

It was not till the corvette had got within a long gunshot from the tartane that Peyrol opened his mouth.

"No!" he burst out, loud in the wind, as if giving vent to long anxious thinking, "no! I could not have left you behind with not even a dog for company. Devil take me if I don't think you would not have thanked me for it either. What do you say to that, Michel?"

A half-puzzled smile dwelt persistently on the guileless countenance of the ex-fisherman. He stated what he had always thought in respect of Peyrol's every remark: "I think you are right, maître."

"Listen, then, Michel. That ship will be alongside of

us in less than half an hour.   As she comes up they will open
on us with musketry."

" They will open on us. . . ." repeated Michel, looking
quite interested.   " But how do you know they will do that,
maître ? "

" Because her captain has got to obey what is in my
mind," said Peyrol, in a tone of positive and solemn conviction.   " He will do it as sure as if I were at his ear telling
him what to do.   He will do it because he is a first-rate
seaman, but I, Michel, I am just a little bit cleverer than
he."   He glanced over his shoulder at the *Amelia* rushing
after the tartane with swelling sails, and raised his voice
suddenly.   " He will do it because no more than half a mile
ahead of us is the spot where Peyrol will die ! "

Michel did not start.   He only shut his eyes for a time, and
the rover continued in a lower tone :

" I may be shot through the heart at once," he said ;
" and in that case you have my permission to let go the
halliards if you are alive yourself.   But if I live I mean to
put the helm down.   When I do that you will let go the
foresheet to help the tartane to fly into the wind's eye.
This is my last order to you.   Now go forward and fear
nothing.   Adieu."   Michel obeyed without a word.

Half a dozen of the *Amelia's* marines stood ranged on the
forecastle-head ready with their muskets.   Captain Vincent
walked into the lee waist to watch his chase.   When he
thought that the jibboom of the *Amelia* had drawn level
with the stern of the tartane he waved his hat and the
marines discharged their muskets.   Apparently no gear was
cut.   Captain Vincent observed the white-headed man, who
was steering, clap his hand to his left side, while he hove the
tiller to leeward and brought the tartane sharply into the
wind.   The marines on the poop fired in their turn, all the
reports merging into one.   Voices were heard on the decks
crying that they " had hit the white-haired chap."   Captain
Vincent shouted to the master :

" Get the ship round on the other tack."

The elderly seaman who was the master of the *Amelia*
took a critical look before he gave the necessary orders ;

and the *Amelia* closed on her chase with her decks resounding to the piping of boatswain's mates and the hoarse shout: "Hands shorten sail. About ship."

Peyrol, lying on his back under the swinging tiller, heard the calls shrilling and dying away; he heard the ominous rush of the *Amelia's* bow wave as the sloop foamed within ten yards of the tartane's stern; he even saw her upper yards coming down, and then everything vanished out of the clouded sky. There was nothing in his ears but the sound of the wind, the wash of the waves buffeting the little craft left without guidance, and the continuous thrashing of its foresail, the sheet of which Michel had let go according to orders. The tartane began to roll heavily, but Peyrol's right arm was sound and he managed to put it round a bollard to prevent himself from being flung about. A feeling of peace sank into him, not unmingled with pride. Everything he had planned had come to pass. He had meant to play that man a trick, and now the trick had been played. Played by him better than by any other old man on whom age had stolen, unnoticed, till the veil of peace was torn down by the touch of a sentiment unexpected like an intruder and cruel like an enemy.

Peyrol rolled his head to the left. All he could see were the legs of Citizen Scevola sliding nervelessly to and fro to the rolling of the vessel as if his body had been jammed somewhere. Dead, or only scared to death? And Michel? Was he dead or dying, that man without friends whom his pity had refused to leave behind marooned on the earth without even a dog for company. As to that, Peyrol felt no compunction; but he thought he would have liked to see Michel once more. He tried to utter his name, but his throat refused him even a whisper. He felt himself removed far away from that world of human sounds in which Arlette had screamed at him: "Peyrol, don't you dare!" He would never hear anybody's voice again! Under that grey sky there was nothing for him but the swish of breaking seas, and the ceaseless furious beating of the tartane's foresail. His plaything was knocking about terribly under him, with her tiller flying madly to and fro just clear of his head, and solid lumps of water coming on board over his prostrate body. Suddenly, in a desperate lurch which brought the whole Mediterranean with a ferocious snarl level with the slope of the little deck, Peyrol saw the *Amelia* bearing right down upon the tartane. The fear, not of death, but of failure, gripped his slowing-down heart. Was this blind Englishman going to run him down and sink the dispatches together with the craft? With a mighty effort of his ebbing strength Peyrol sat up and flung his arm round the shroud of the mainmast.

The *Amelia*, whose way had carried her past the tartane for a quarter of a mile before sail could be shortened and her yards swung on the other tack, was coming back to take possession of her chase. In the deepening dusk and amongst the foaming seas it was a matter of difficulty to make out the little craft. At the very moment when the master of the man-of-war, looking out anxiously from the forecastle-head, thought that she might perhaps have filled and gone down, he caught sight of her rolling in the trough of the sea, and so close that she seemed to be at the end of the *Amelia's* jib-boom. His heart flew in his mouth. "Hard a starboard!" he yelled, his order being passed along the decks.

Peyrol, sinking back on the deck, in another heavy lurch of his craft, saw for an instant the whole of the English corvette swing up into the clouds as if she meant to fling herself upon his very breast. A blown seatop flicked his face noisily, followed by a smooth interval, a silence of the waters. He beheld in a flash the days of his manhood, of strength and adventure. Suddenly an enormous voice like the roar of an angry sea-lion seemed to fill the whole of the empty sky in a mighty and commanding shout: "Steady!" . . . And with the sound of that familiar English word ringing in his ears Peyrol smiled to his visions and died.

The *Amelia*, stripped down to her topsails and hove to rose and fell easily, while on her quarter about a cable's length away Peyrol's tartane tumbled like a lifeless corpse amongst the seas. Captain Vincent, in his favourite attitude of leaning over the rail, kept his eyes fastened on his prize. Mr.

Bolt, who had been sent for, waited patiently till his commander turned round.

"Oh, here you are, Mr. Bolt. I have sent for you to go and take possession. You speak French, and there may still be somebody alive in her. If so, of course you will send him on board at once. I am sure there can be nobody unwounded there. It will anyhow be too dark to see much, but just have a good look round and secure everything in the way of papers you can lay your hands on. Haul aft the foresheet and sail her up to receive a tow-line. I intend to take her along and ransack her thoroughly in the morning; tear down the cuddy linings and so on, should you not find at once what I expect. . . ." Captain Vincent, his white teeth gleaming in the dusk, gave some further orders in a lower tone, and Mr. Bolt departed in a hurry. Half an hour afterwards he was back on board, and the *Amelia*, with the tartane in tow, made sail to the eastward in search of the blockading fleet.

Mr. Bolt, introduced into a cabin strongly lighted by a swinging lamp, tendered to his captain across the table a sail-cloth package corded and sealed, and a piece of paper folded in four, which, he explained, seemed to be a certificate of registry, strangely enough mentioning no name. Captain Vincent seized the grey canvas package eagerly.

"This looks like the very thing, Bolt," he said, turning it over in his hands. "What else did you find on board?"

Bolt said that he had found three dead men, two on the after-deck and one lying at the bottom of the open hold with the bare end of the foresheet in his hand—"shot down, I suppose, just as he had let it go," he commented. He described the appearance of the bodies and reported that he had disposed of them according to orders. In the tartane's cabin there was half a demijohn of wine and a loaf of bread in a locker; also, on the floor, a leather valise containing an officer's uniform coat and a change of clothing. He had lighted the lamp and saw that the linen was marked "E. Réal." An officer's sword on a board shoulder-belt was also lying on the floor. These things could not have belonged to the old chap with the white hair, who was a big man.

" Looks as if somebody had tumbled overboard," commented Bolt. Two of the bodies looked nondescript, but there was no doubt about that fine old fellow being a seaman.

" By heavens ! " said Captain Vincent, " he was that ! Do you know, Bolt, that he nearly managed to escape us. Another twenty minutes would have done it. How many wounds had he ? "

" Three I think, sir. I did not look closely," said Bolt.

" I hated the necessity of shooting brave men like dogs," said Captain Vincent. " Still, it was the only way ; and there may be something here," he went on, slapping the package with his open palm, " that will justify me in my own eyes. You may go now."

Captain Vincent did not turn in, but only lay down fully dressed on the couch till the officer of the watch, appearing at the door, told him that a ship of the fleet was in sight away to windward. Captain Vincent ordered the private night signal to be made. When he came on deck the towering shadow of a line-of-battle ship that seemed to reach to the very clouds was well within hail and a voice bellowed from her through a speaking-trumpet :

" What ship is that ? "

" His Majesty's sloop *Amelia*," hailed back Captain Vincent. " What ship is that, pray ? "

Instead of the usual answer, there was a short pause, and another voice spoke boisterously through the trumpet :

" Is that you, Vincent ? Don't you know the *Superb* when you see her ? "

" Not in the dark, Keats. How are you ? I am in a hurry to speak the Admiral."

" The fleet is lying by," came the voice, now with painstaking distinctness, across the murmurs, whispers and splashes of the black lane of water dividing the two ships. " The Admiral bears S.S.E. If you stretch on till daylight as you are, you will fetch him on the other tack in time for breakfast on board the *Victory*. Is anything up ? "

At every slight roll the sails of the *Amelia*, becalmed by the bulk of the seventy-four, flapped gently against the masts.

"Not much," hailed Captain Vincent. "I made a prize."

"Have you been in action?" came the swift inquiry.

"No, no. Piece of luck."

"Where's your prize?" roared the speaking-trumpet with interest.

"In my desk," roared Captain Vincent in reply. . . . "Enemy dispatches. . . . I say, Keats, fill on your ship. Fill on her, I say, or you will be falling on board of me." He stamped his foot impatiently. "Clap some hands at once on the tow-line, and run that tartane close under our stern," he called to the officer of the watch, "or else the old *Superb* will walk over her without ever knowing anything about it."

When Captain Vincent presented himself on board the *Victory* it was too late for him to be invited to share the Admiral's breakfast. He was told that Lord Nelson had not been seen on deck yet that morning; and presently word came that he wished to see Captain Vincent at once in his cabin. Being introduced, the captain of the *Amelia*, in undress uniform, with a sword by his side and his hat under his arm, was received kindly, made his bow and with a few words of explanation laid the packet on the big round table at which sat a silent secretary in black clothes, who had been obviously writing a letter from his Lordship's dictation. The Admiral had been walking up and down, and after he had greeted Captain Vincent he resumed his pacing of a nervous man. His empty sleeve had not yet been pinned on his breast, and swung slightly every time he turned in his walk. His thin locks fell lank against the pale cheeks, and the whole face in repose had an expression of suffering with which the fire of his one eye presented a startling contrast. He stopped short, and exclaimed while Captain Vincent towered over him in a respectful attitude:

"A tartane! Captured on board a tartane! How on earth did you pitch upon that one out of the hundreds you must see every month?"

"I must confess that I got hold accidentally of some curious information," said Captain Vincent. "It was all a piece of luck."

While the secretary was ripping open with a penknife the cover of the dispatches Lord Nelson took Captain Vincent out into the stern gallery. The quiet and sunshiny morning had the added charm of a cool, light breeze; and the *Victory*, under her three topsails and lower staysails, was moving slowly to the southward in the midst of the scattered fleet carrying for the most part the same sail as the Admiral. Only far away two or three ships could be seen covered with canvas, trying to close with the flag. Captain Vincent noted with satisfaction that the first lieutenant of the *Amelia* had been obliged to brace by his afteryards in order not to overrun the Admiral's quarter.

"Why!" exclaimed Lord Nelson suddenly, after looking at the sloop for a moment, "you have that tartane in tow!"

"I thought that your Lordship would perhaps like to see a 40-ton lateen craft which has led such a chase to, I dare say, the fastest sloop in His Majesty's service."

"How did it all begin?" asked the Admiral, continuing to look at the *Amelia*.

"As I have already hinted to your Lordship, certain information came in my way," began Captain Vincent, who did not think it necessary to enlarge upon that part of the story. "This tartane, which is not very different to look at from the other tartanes along the coast between Cette and Genoa, had started from a cove on the Giens peninsula. An old man with a white head of hair was entrusted with the service, and really they could have found nobody better. He came round Cape Esterel intending to pass through the Hyères Roadstead. Apparently he did not expect to find the *Amelia* in his way. And it was there that he made his only mistake. If he had kept on his course, I would probably have taken no more notice of him than of two other craft that were in sight then. But he acted suspiciously by hauling up for the battery on Porquerolles. This manœuvre in connection with the information of which I spoke decided me to overhaul him and see what he had on board." Captain Vincent then related concisely the episodes of the chase. "I assure your Lordship that I never gave an order with greater reluctance than to open musketry fire on that craft; but the old man had given such proofs of his seamanship and determination that there was nothing else for it. Why! at the very moment he had the *Amelia* alongside of him he still made a most clever attempt to prolong the chase. There were only a few minutes of daylight left, and in the darkness we might very well have lost him. Considering that they all could have saved their lives simply by striking their sails on deck, I cannot refuse them my admiration, and especially to the white-haired man."

The admiral, who had been all the time looking absently at the *Amelia* keeping her station with the tartane in tow, said:

"You have a very smart little ship, Vincent. Very fit for the work I have given you to do. French built, isn't she?"

"Yes, my Lord. They are great shipbuilders."

"You don't seem to hate the French, Vincent," said the Admiral, smiling faintly.

"Not that kind, my Lord," said Captain Vincent, with a bow. "I detest their political principles and the characters of their public men, but your Lordship will admit that for courage and determination we could not have found worthier adversaries anywhere on this globe."

"I never said that they were to be despised," said Lord Nelson. "Resource, courage, yes. . . . If that Toulon fleet gives me the slip, all our squadrons from Gibraltar to Brest will be in jeopardy. Why don't they come out and be done with it? Don't I keep far enough out of their way?" he cried.

Vincent remarked the nervous agitation of the frail figure with a concern augmented by a fit of coughing which came on the Admiral. He was quite alarmed by its violence. He watched the Commander-in-Chief in the Mediterranean choking and gasping so helplessly that he felt compelled to turn his eyes away from the painful spectacle; but he noticed also how quickly Lord Nelson recovered from the subsequent exhaustion.

"This is anxious work, Vincent," he said. "It is killing me. I aspire to repose somewhere in the country, in the midst of fields, out of reach of the sea and the Admiralty and dispatches and orders, and responsibility too. I have been just finishing a letter to tell them at home I have hardly enough breath in my body to carry me on from day to day. . . . But I am like that white-headed man you admire so much, Vincent," he pursued, with a weary smile, "I will stick to my task till perhaps some shot from the enemy puts an end to everything. . . . Let us see what there may be in those papers you have brought on board."

The secretary in the cabin had arranged them in separate piles.

"What is it all about?" asked the Admiral, beginning again to pace restlessly up and down the cabin.

"At the first glance, the most important, my Lord, are the orders for marine authorities in Corsica and Naples to made certain dispositions in view of an expedition to Egypt."

"I always thought so," said the Admiral, his eye gleaming at the attentive countenance of Captain Vincent. "This is a smart piece of work on your part, Vincent. I can do no better than send you back to your station. Yes . . . Egypt . . . the East. . . . Everything points that way," he soliloquised under Vincent's eyes, while the secretary, picking up the papers with care, rose quietly and went out to have them translated and to make an abstract for the Admiral.

"And yet who knows!" exclaimed Lord Nelson, standing still for a moment. "But the blame or the glory must be mine alone. I will seek counsel from no man." Captain Vincent felt himself forgotten, invisible, less than a shadow in the presence of a nature capable of such vehement feelings. "How long can he last?" he asked himself with sincere concern.

The Admiral, however, soon remembered his presence, and at the end of another ten minutes Captain Vincent left the *Victory*, feeling, like all officers who approached Lord Nelson, that he had been speaking with a personal friend; and with a renewed devotion for the great sea-officer's soul dwelling in the frail body of the Commander-in-Chief of

His Majesty's ships in the Mediterranean. While he was being pulled back to his ship a general signal went up in the *Victory* for the fleet to form line, as convenient, ahead and astern of the Admiral; followed by another to the *Amelia* to part company. Vincent accordingly gave his orders to make sail, and, directing the master to shape a course for Cape Cicié, went down into his cabin. He had been up nearly the whole of the last three nights, and he wanted to get a little sleep. His slumbers, however, were short and disturbed. Early in the afternoon he found himself broad awake and reviewing in his mind the events of the day before. The order to shoot three brave men in cold blood, terribly distasteful at the time, was lying heavily on him. Perhaps he had been impressed by Peyrol's white head, his obstinacy to escape him, the determination shown to the very last minute; by something in the whole episode that suggested a more than common devotion to duty and a spirit of daring defiance. With his robust health, simple good nature, and sanguine temperament touched with a little irony, Captain Vincent was a man of generous feelings and of easily moved sympathies.

"Yes," he reflected, "they have been asking for it. There could be only one end to that affair. But the fact remains that they were defenceless and unarmed and particularly harmless-looking, and at the same time as brave as any. That old chap now. . . ." He wondered how much of exact truth there was in Symons' tale of adventure. He concluded that the facts must have been true but that Symons' interpretation of them made it extraordinarily difficult to discover what really there was under all that. That craft certainly was fit for blockade running. Lord Nelson had been pleased. Captain Vincent went on deck with the kindliest feelings towards all men, alive and dead.

The afternoon had turned out very fine. The British fleet was just out of sight with the exception of one or two stragglers, under a press of canvas. A light breeze, in which only the *Amelia* could travel at five knots, hardly ruffled the profundity of the blue waters basking in the warm tenderness of the cloudless sky. To south and west the horizon was empty except for two specks very far apart, of which one shone white like a bit of silver and the other appeared black like a drop of ink. Captain Vincent, with his purpose firm in his mind, felt at peace with himself. As he was easily accessible to his officers, his first lieutenant ventured a question to which Captain Vincent replied :

" He looks very thin and worn out, but I don't think he is as ill as he thinks he is. I am sure you all would like to know that his Lordship is pleased with our yesterday's work —those papers were of some importance, you know—and generally with the *Amelia*. It was a queer chase, wasn't it ? " he went on. " That tartane was clearly and unmistakably running away from us. But she never had a chance against the *Amelia*."

During the latter part of that speech the first lieutenant glanced astern as if asking himself how long Captain Vincent proposed to drag that tartane behind the *Amelia*. The two keepers in her wondered also as to when they would be permitted to get back on board their ship. Symons, who was one of them, declared that he was sick and tired of steering the blamed thing. Moreover, the company on board made him uncomfortable ; for Symons was aware that in pursuance of Captain Vincent's orders, Mr. Bolt had had the three dead Frenchmen carried into the cuddy, which he afterwards secured with an enormous padlock that, apparently, belonged to it, and had taken the key on board the *Amelia*. As to one of them, Symons' unforgiving verdict was that it would have served him right to be thrown ashore for crows to peck his eyes out. And anyhow, he could not understand why he should have been turned into the coxswain of a floating hearse, and be damned to it. . . . He grumbled interminably.

Just about sunset, which is the time of burials at sea, the *Amelia* was hove to and, the rope being manned, the tartane was brought alongside and her two keepers ordered on board their ship. Captain Vincent, leaning over with his elbows on the rail, seemed lost in thought. At last the first lieutenant spoke.

"What are we going to do with that tartane, sir? Our men are on board."

"We are going to sink her by gunfire," declared Captain Vincent suddenly. "His ship makes a very good coffin for a seaman, and those men deserve better than to be thrown overboard to roll on the waves. Let them rest quietly at the bottom of the sea in the craft to which they had stuck so well."

The lieutenant, making no reply, waited for some more positive order. Every eye on the ship was turned on the captain. But Captain Vincent said nothing and seemed unable or unwilling to give it yet. He was feeling vaguely that in all his good intentions there was something wanting.

"Ah! Mr. Bolt," he said, catching sight of the master's mate in the waist. "Did they have a flag on board that craft?"

"I think she had a tiny bit of ensign when the chase began, sir, but it must have blown away. It is not at the end of her mainyard now." He looked over the side. "The halliards are rove, though," he added.

"We must have a French ensign somewhere on board," said Captain Vincent.

"Certainly, sir," struck in the master, who was listening.

"Well, Mr. Bolt," said Captain Vincent, "you have had most to do with all this. Take a few men with you, bend the French ensign on the halliards and sway his mainyard to the masthead." He smiled at all the faces turned towards him. "After all, they never surrendered and, by heavens, gentlemen, we will let them go down with their colours flying."

A profound but not disapproving silence reigned over the decks of the ship while Mr. Bolt with three or four hands was busy executing the order. Then suddenly above the topgallant rail of the *Amelia* appeared the upper curve of a lateen yard with the tricolour drooping from the point. A subdued murmur from all hands greeted this apparition. At the same time Captain Vincent ordered the line holding the tartane alongside to be cast off and the mainyard of the *Amelia* to be swung round. The sloop, shooting ahead of her prize, left her stationary on the sea, then putting the helm up, ran back abreast of her on the other side. The port bow-gun was ordered to fire a round, aiming well forward. That shot, however, went just over, taking the foremast out of the tartane. The next was more successful, striking the little hull between wind and water, and going out well under water on the other side. A third was fired, as the men said, just for luck, and that too took effect, a splintered hole appearing at the bow. After that the guns were secured and the *Amelia*, with no brace being touched, was brought to her course towards Cape Cicié. All hands on board of her with their backs to the sunset sky, clear like a pale topaz above the hard blue gem of the sea, watched the tartane give a sudden dip, followed by a slow, unchecked dive. At last the tricolour flag alone remained visible for a tense and interminable moment, pathetic and lonely, in the centre of a brimful horizon. All at once it vanished, like a flame blown upon, bringing to the beholders the sense of having been left face to face with an immense, suddenly created solitude. On the decks of the *Amelia* a low murmur died out.

\*　　\*　　\*　　\*　　\*　　\*

When Lieutenant Réal sailed away with the Toulon fleet on the great strategical cruise which was to end in the Battle of Trafalgar, Madame Réal returned with her aunt to her hereditary house at Escampobar. She had only spent a few weeks in town, where she was not much seen in public. The lieutenant and his wife lived in a little house near the western gate, and the lieutenant's official position, though he was employed on the staff to the last, was not sufficiently prominent to make her absence from official ceremonies at all remarkable. But this marriage was an object of mild interest in naval circles. Those—mostly men—who had seen Madame Réal at home, told stories of her dazzling complexion, of her magnificent black eyes, of her personal and attractive strangeness, and of the Arlesian costume she insisted on wearing, even after her marriage to an officer of the navy, being herself sprung from farmer stock. It was also said that her father and mother had fallen victims in the massacres of Toulon after the evacuation of the town; but all those stories varied in detail and were on the whole very vague. Whenever she went abroad Mrs. Réal was attended by her aunt, who aroused almost as much curiosity as herself: a magnificent old woman with upright carriage and an austere, brown, wrinkled face showing signs of past beauty. Catherine was also seen alone in the streets, where, as a matter of fact, people turned round to look after the thin and dignified figure, remarkable amongst the passers-by, whom she herself did not seem to see. About her escape from the massacres most wonderful tales were told, and she acquired the reputation of a heroine. Arlette's aunt was known to frequent the churches, which were all open to the faithful now, carrying even into the house of God her sibylline aspect of a prophetess and her austere manner. It was not at the services that she was seen most. People would see her oftener in an empty nave, standing slim and as straight as an arrow in the shade of a mighty pillar as if making a call on the Creator of all things, with whom she had made her peace generously, and now would petition only for pardon and reconciliation with her niece Arlette. For Catherine for a long time remained uncertain of the future. She did not get rid of her involuntary awe of her niece as a selected object of God's wrath until towards the end of her life. There was also another soul for which she was concerned. The pursuit of the tartane by the *Amelia* had been observed from various points of the islands that close the roadstead of Hyères, and the English ship had been seen from the Fort de la Vigie opening fire on her chase. The result, though the two vessels soon ran out of sight, could not be a matter of doubt. There was also the story told by a coaster, that got into Fréjus, of a tartane being fired on by a square-rigged man-of-war; but that apparently was the next day. All these rumours pointed one way and were the foundation of the report made by Lieutenant Réal to the Toulon Admiralty. That Peyrol went out to sea in his tartane, and was never seen again was, of course, an incontrovertible fact.

The day before the two women were to go back to Escampobar Catherine approached a priest in the church of Ste. Marie Majeure, a little unshaven fat man with a watery eye, in order to arrange for some masses to be said for the dead.

"But for whose soul are we to pray?" mumbled the priest in a wheezy low tone.

"Pray for the soul of Jean," said Catherine. "Yes, Jean. There is no other name."

Lieutenant Réal, wounded at Trafalgar, but escaping capture, retired with the rank of Capitaine de Frégate and vanished from the eyes of the naval world in Toulon, and indeed from the world altogether. Whatever sign brought him back to Escampobar on that momentous night was not meant to call him to his death but to a quiet and retired life, obscure in a sense but not devoid of dignity. In the course of years he became the Mayor of the Commune in that very same little village which had looked on Escampobar as the abode of iniquity, the sojourn of blood-drinkers and of wicked women.

One of the earliest excitements breaking the monotony of the Escampobar life was the discovery at the bottom of the well, one dry year when the water got very low, of some considerable obstruction. After a lot of trouble in getting it up, this obstruction turned out to be a garment made of sail-cloth, which had armholes and three horn buttons in front, and looked like a waistcoat; but it was lined, positively quilted, with a surprising quantity of gold pieces of various ages, coinages and nationalities. Nobody but Peyrol could have put it there. Catherine was able to give the exact date; because she remembered seeing him doing something at the well on the very morning before he went out to sea with Michel, carrying off Scevola. Captain Réal could guess easily the origin of that treasure, and he decided with his wife's approval to give it up to the Government as the hoard of a man who had died intestate with no discoverable relations, and whose very name had been a matter of uncertainty, even to himself. After that event the uncertain name of Peyrol found itself oftener and oftener on Monsieur and Madame Réal's lips, on which before it was but seldom heard; though the recollection of his white-headed, quiet, irresistible personality haunted every corner of the Escampobar fields. From that time they talked of him openly, as though he had come back to live again amongst them.

Many years afterwards, one fine evening Monsieur and Madame Réal, sitting on the bench outside the salle (the house had not been altered at all outside except that it was now kept whitewashed), began to talk of that episode and of the man who, coming from the seas, had crossed their lives to disappear at sea again.

"How did he get all that lot of gold?" wondered Madame Réal innocently. "He could not possibly want it; and, Eugène, why should he have put it down there?"

"That, ma chère amie," said Réal, "is not an easy question to answer. Men and women are not so simple as they seem. Even you, fermière (he used to give his wife that name jocularly sometimes), are not so simple as some people would take you to be. I think that if Peyrol were here he could not perhaps answer your question himself."

And they went on, reminding each other in short phrases, separated by long silences, of his peculiarities of person and behaviour, when, above the slope leading down to Madrague, there appeared, first the pointed ears and then the whole body of a very diminutive donkey of a light grey colour with dark points. Two pieces of wood, strangely shaped, projected on each side of his body as far as his head, like very long shafts of a cart. But the donkey dragged no cart after him. He was carrying on his back on a small pack-saddle the torso of a man who did not seem to have any legs. The little animal, beautifully groomed and with an intelligent and even impudent physiognomy, stopped in front of Monsieur and Madame Réal. The man, balancing himself cleverly on the pack-saddle with his withered legs crossed in front of him, slipped off, disengaged his crutches from each side of the donkey smartly, propped himself on them, and with his open palm gave the animal a resounding thwack which sent it trotting into the yard. The cripple of the Madrague in his quality of Peyrol's friend (for the rover had often talked of him both to the women and to Lieutenant Réal with great appreciation—"C'est un homme ça") had become a member of the Escampobar community. His employment was to run about the country on errands, most unfit, one would think, for a man without legs. But the donkey did all the walking while the cripple supplied the sharp wits and an unfailing memory. The poor fellow, snatching off his hat and holding it with one hand alongside his right crutch, approached to render his account of the day in the simple words : " Everything has been done as you ordered, Madame " ; then lingered, a privileged servant, familiar but respectful, attractive with his soft eyes, long face, and his pained smile.

" We were just talking of Peyrol," remarked Captain Réal.

" Ah, one could talk a long time of him," said the cripple. " He told me once that if I had been complete—with legs like everybody else, I suppose he meant—I would have made a good comrade away there in the distant seas. He had a great heart."

" Yes," murmured Madame Réal thoughtfully. Then, turning to her husband, she asked : " What sort of man was he really, Eugène ? " Captain Réal remained silent. " Did you ever ask yourself that question ? " she insisted.

" Yes," said Réal. " But the only certain thing we can say of him is that he was not a bad Frenchman."

" Everything's in that," murmured the cripple, with fervent conviction, in the silence that fell upon Réal's words and Arlette's faint sigh of memory.

The blue level of the Mediterranean, the charmer and the deceiver of audacious men, kept the secret of its fascination— hugged to its calm breast the victims of all the wars, calamities and tempests of its history, under the marvellous purity of the sunset sky. A few rosy clouds floated high up over the Esterel range. The breath of the evening breeze came to cool the heated rocks of Escampobar ; and the mulberry-tree, the only big tree on the head of the peninsula, standing like a sentinel at the gate of the yard, sighed faintly in a shudder of all its leaves as if regretting the Brother of the Coast, the man of dark deeds, but of large heart, who often at noonday would lie down to sleep under its shade.

Printed in Great Britain by
Richard Clay & Sons, Limited,
Bungay, Suffolk.